The Traitors

a novel by JOHN BRILEY

FOUNDED 1838

GPPS

the Traitors

G. P. Putnam's Sons   New York

For all the Brileys and Dalys . . .
but for two of them especially

> *To everything there is a season, and a time*
> *to every purpose under the heaven:*
> *A time to be born, and a time to die . . .*
> *a time to kill, and a time to heal. . . .*

ECCLESIASTES 3:1–13

Part I

1

i

Sitting inside the chopper, Hill could see the mist already settling in the trees when the big Huey took off alone, its rotors fanning up red dust and making the god-awful racket he'd come to hate. It was the moment he always wondered if this was *the* mission, his. The sickening, exciting fear. Like before a fight. Instead of everything being cool, sane, it was all butterflies. And if he had known it *was* to be his—his in a way he never could have foreseen—he couldn't have done anything about it. Nothing. It was like a dive from the high board: Once you leaped out into the air . . .

And he knew it. Not that it was to be *his* mission, but that any mission could be his. It always flipped his heartbeat up, made his cheeks burn, but you couldn't heed it, it'd pass.

But even with all that, he still got the charge he always felt when they rose above their clearing in the tall, shadowed forest—their little encampment in the middle of the highlands, with its circles of sandbags, the scattered trucks, the stacks of shells, gray figures walking from emplacement to emplacement. It was like living an old dream. Cowboys and Indians.

Back inside the chopper old chickenshit Pershing was already coming down the aisle, checking equipment, seeing your dog tags were polished, nails clipped, condoms in place—screw him. Hill glanced back out the window.

Clearing the trees, you could see the sun hanging down on the horizon, orange and red—and the mist creeping over the forest like some gas attack from outer space. Three months ago in Saigon, watching that sun from a balcony in Khan Hoi Street with the damp rising from the waterfront and covering the sampans like a gauze veil, he figured the Indians really had it made. Big permanent wide-screen Technicolor travelogue. But now it was ulcers all the way. Just to see

9

the sun near the horizon started his heart beating. Charlie was down there somewhere in the dark and mist. And for all the Air Cavalry tricks, the forays and encirclements, that little brown and yellow bastard had made the night his—where you couldn't trust a sound, a tree, a leaf. And they were headed out into the night. Into Charlie's night and Charlie's territory, where in seconds the whole goddamned jungle could open up on you or just one footstep could trip a mine that made you a legless, ball-less wonder for life.

"Let's have it, Hill."

He turned and held out his M-16. Much as Pershing pissed him off with that earnest, handsome, milk-chocolate face, Specialist Fifth George Hill had to admit he liked his little ole supersergeant. John Andrew Pershing—sergeant major—defender of the fucking faith . . . and in a crunch, soul brother. Hill grinned up sardonically at him as Pershing did the whole sergeant major bit, checking bolt, clip, trigger, mechanism, even the tape on the muzzle—must keep the mud and guck out of your M-16, or that prize of American ingenuity and manufacturing skill will blow your red, white, and blue face into a cheap supper for the mosquitoes, rats, and geckos. Pershing flipped the rifle back to Hill and grabbed his pack straps—checking their grip, balance. His eyes flickered with a smile. That's what Hill liked about him. For all his chickenshit, he had a sense of humor. You could always reason with a man who had a sense of humor.

Pershing passed on down the line. The chopper was lifting fast now and moving forward—Hill knew he'd never forget the sway and smell of a Huey. Not if he lived to be a million. Shit, the darkening jungle seemed to stretch out forever below them. All the bombs, defoliants, napalm—you'd think the whole damned country would look like the pictures of Con Thien—but there it stretched, endlessly, in all directions. It was always that way in the air. He could remember the first training days in Alabama. They'd fly for hours and hours and never see a farm or a road—just forest and fields and swamps. They say the world's overcrowded. Not from the air it ain't.

Hill slouched back. He watched as the others started blackening their faces. Hill was tall, stringy, but with broad shoulders and big, strong hands, and he didn't have to bother about blackening his face. Nature had done that for him. He didn't figure it was an advantage. But he didn't cry in his beer over it either.

Forty droning, dull-eyed minutes later the alert light went on. It was pitch black out there now. Just them and the night and Charlie. You'd think Charlie could hear the sound of the Huey for a hundred miles. Pershing signaled Hill up front. Hill smirked and moved along toward the cabin partition. Insurance. If pilot and copilot got hit, he was equipped to keep that gangly, fat-assed bird going. Two hours a month he flew one to "keep up his skill level." They ever turn that great duck over to him in the middle of a fire fight and they'd soon know how "skilled" he was. He'd turn out to be Charlie's number one secret weapon. The black bomber. Christ, how he wished he were back in Saigon. Money, women, hot showers. The biggest danger was collision with a pedicab.

Kerchuuuung! The first flare sailed out. A yellow, weird incandescence. They all strained to see. Nothing but jungle. The chopper tipped and accelerated at the same time. Hill grabbed for the overhead. Jesus, now they were committed. It'd be tip, sway, zoom—like a damn ball on a string—zigzagging above the treetops till they found it —or didn't find it and had to give up. Stomach, brain, and pulse hated those swinging, lurching sallies through the air, but he'd gladly accept fifteen minutes of it, rather than go through with the fight. Live to fight another day—that's the motto etched on my ass. Damn. He's settling; they've spotted it. He crouched to peer through the window. More flares were going out now. It was like seeing everything through yellow-smoked glass. And there it was. Target for the night. A little clutch of huts, strung along on each side of a tiny stream. They were going in fast at an angle of about forty degrees. That goddamned Janowitz was flying. Cowboy. You needed to get in fast, but moderation, baby, moderation.

Janowitz brought it in like a rocket, then hovered just at the last moment and laid it down like a leaf falling on autumn grass. The big bastard was good. They were on the only bit of open field anywhere near the village, he'd seen that. It was a perfect place for an ambush, and now that the flares had faded there was no knowing. But gung ho Pershing was shoving open the hatch and darting across the field for the dark cover of the woods. Miller and Polnicki went after him. If they made it, they'd cover for the rest. If they didn't, their families would get pensions for the rest of their lives. Either way, you couldn't lose.

There was nothing to fill the night but the sound of the chopper.

The rest barreled out, fanning quickly, quietly, to all sides of the clearing, and George Hill was last, stretching those long legs in awkward-looking strides that didn't hide the fear behind them but ate up ground in huge, frantic bites.

He dived for the dark obscurity of the forest. He'd sacrifice his dignity for his ass any day. He did a tumble roll. The one useful thing they'd taught him in parachute school. And he came out of it ready to fight. Black as the inside of a tomb, but he heard no enemy other than the silence of the jungle. Then a hiss—

"Come on, Tarzan—over here."

Pershing. Hill moved in the direction of the sound. God, it was dark. They'd have to lie there, waiting until their eyes got used to it. And what might old Charlie be doing then? One good thing, they hadn't started on the chopper. That was their favorite. A chopper a day keeps Big Sammy away. So first move to star-spangled Sam. But Hill had a funny feeling, a private message in the gut. Usually by now . . .

"Stay here. I'm going to make a quick circuit."

Ole supersergeant Pershing on the ball, earning his stripes. Fuck me, how can one bastard be so conscientious? He hadn't swallowed the book—he'd chewed it, rolled it, sucked it, digested it, sent it through his bloodstream until he was a little beaming brown-skinned edition all on his own. And happy. Man, he loved himself; he loved the world. The little book had all the answers.

Hill got low, in firing position, slipped the tape loose from the muzzle. No need to shoot through nice new tape. He always felt it slowed the bullet a little, no matter what they said. He wanted *all* the odds on his side. He watched as Janowitz lifted the chopper into the star-flecked sky. Boy, this was the minute to be a chopper crew. Take 'em in, dump 'em out, and get the hell back in time for a shower and a cold beer. And look at him escalate that baby. There were moments he'd give his right gonad for the coordination Janowitz had: zoom down the floor, dribble past one big blue, fake left, backhanded dribble around another, twist, fake a shot, arch back, turn, over the head, one flip—off the backboard for two points and the fucking crowd goes mad! And the big Jewish get made it look so easy.

In seconds it was gone. No chopper, no sound. Just the jungle. He listened, tense. All the dark jungle sounds started coming in: the cicadas, a distant monkey scream, the buzz of a million bugs, the sluggish, oozing sound of battalions of night creatures—real and imaginary—slithering through the undergrowth, burrowing in the wet slime to eat or be eaten. It always shivered his spine—until he thought of *his* prey. Charlie slinking around somewhere, maybe closing in on him now, through the surrounding blackness of the jungle. There was no shiver then, just a dry queasiness. An itch on the finger he knew he had to control.

12

Pershing came back quietly through the underbrush, giving the little whistle that was the password. "One of these days . . . you're going to miss me, honey." Man, you can whistle that again. Funny about old hairless Charlie, he couldn't whistle an American tune to save his ass. Took him two weeks to master the first three notes of "Darktown Strutters Ball," and by that time there'd been fourteen other songs used.

"It looks like we got 'em," Pershing muttered.

Three cheers for our side. Pershing, the perpetual gold-star optimist.

"I sent Miller and Polnicki through to cover the village. I don't think anybody's had time to get out."

"What if they got a radio?" Hill said bluntly.

"That's a chance we take."

The stupid bastard loves it.

"We'll wait three minutes more, then clear that thatch by the river and move in," Pershing said. He sounded confident and cool, but Hill knew he wasn't as unafraid as he made out. It wasn't Charlie that shook him. Pershing could take six Charlies without working up a sweat—that Hill knew. But Pershing worried like the rest of them when it came to thoughts of a ragged shaft of bamboo springing up from a jungle trap and lancing through your legs or guts—maybe pinning leg *to* gut like they'd seen it do to Garbedian outside Bien Hoa. God, there was no forgetting that. Garbedian screaming, pinned right to the spot, oozing blood, intestine, writhing like a wounded caterpillar—and shrieking those god-awful screams. And all the time the fight just went on. Garbedian screaming, the Charlies grabbing for him, the rest of the patrol fighting hand to hand. And they left him. There was no getting him off that stake—not with VC pouring in everyplace—and it wasn't a spot they could defend. If Pershing had been in charge, they'd have stayed. Hill knew that. But that lieutenant ordered them out—crying like a baby. Thank God, Hill thought, that wasn't a decision he'd had to make. Thank the goddamned Lord. The lieutenant got it that very week. The short happy life of lieutenant—he couldn't even remember the guy's name now. Just another white lieutenant.

No, it wasn't that John Andrew Pershing wasn't afraid. Hill knew he was as afraid as any of them. But he was ready. One hundred and eighty-five pounds, five feet eight inches of tuned-up muscle—hard, flexible, taut, and resilient as steel. And he could take every fieldpiece in the outfit apart and put it back together blindfolded. And faster than the men who used them. He'd read Mao Tse-tung and Uncle Ho,

13

and he knew tactics, countertactics, psych war, the lot. Put him against any NCO on this side, or Charlie's side, and the bastard would know he was in a contest. It was only the impersonal, unexpected thrusts that worried Pershing. The booby traps, the doors that exploded in your hand, the sudden firmness in the squeezy mud that meant no foot if you put one more ounce of pressure on. That's what got to him —though Hill knew he did his best to keep it out of his mind. He went to his damn confession and communion before each mission. Prayed to God and kept busy.

"Come on, let's go!" Pershing whispered. He slipped off toward the dark hulk of thatch. Hill waited a few seconds before following. He was cautious and out to save his own skin first, last, and always, but he knew, too, that once the fight started, Pershing counted on him— and Miller—above all the rest. Him, Pershing, and Miller. That new little Southern kid, Russell, skinny as a fart in the wind—he was going to be good, too. He could drop a flea on a rat's back at a hundred yards. He never looked like he'd live through the day, with that sallow skin and the bags hanging under his eyes, but he never grumbled, and he sure could move when it counted.

The thatch was really a bamboo frame for drying grass and palm fronds. It looked like a trap, and Pershing approached it through the dark respectfully. Hill angled right, crouching low, giving him automatic cover, trying to penetrate the blackness for signs of anything. He noticed little hillbilly Russell doing the same, but the rest of the lard asses were moving up, half on the run, eyes on the jungle like the only danger was there. You didn't stay healthy too long out here if you only looked for trouble from where it *ought* to come.

Hill kept one eye on Pershing as Pershing circled the thatch, melding with the dark ground, testing the whole area cautiously. Finally, he signaled them in. It was clean. Hill shook his head—bang, bang —all of them but him and Russell'd be dead now if it wasn't. You gotta think, you gotta cover the angles—all the time.

"Hill, take your guys left," Pershing whispered when they all were assembled, crouched beside the thatch. "Miller should be on your side of the stream at the far end." Hill nodded. Pershing'd take the rest around the other side—the weak side. You couldn't count on Polnicki. Sergeant brownnoser. He was in for a soft job and retirement pay, but he had one great gift. Suck ass as much as he liked, he could make you hate him quicker than any man alive. And somewhere, some brass had hated him just enough to send him from a cushy desk out to the real live war. But not to worry. Old Instant Distaste figured if

14

he could just brown-nose the enemy not to shoot him, he'd soon be home and secure. A hero, and he naturally did not intend to risk his little toe in aid of anything. So Pershing always dumped Miller and Hill on one side and rode Polnicki's tail on the other.

Hill waded slowly across the black ribbon of water that separated the two sides of the village. And he didn't pretend he was any fucking Pershing. He sent young Martin out in front. Scout. He was not going to be the first man through that ink-black woods. If there was an ambush or a little plantation of booby traps, he didn't propose to be the lucky prizewinner to discover it. And Martin, he was so geedee stupid he hardly knew what to be afraid of. But he sure as hell was afraid of Big George Hill. A man who carried a razor and was prepared to use it was beyond the ken of poor little Peter Martin, and when Hill said move, he moved.

They made it through the woods. When they found Miller, he was sitting crouched, his hands curled around a cigarette, not letting the light escape but getting the relief of a smoke. Hill plopped next to him, and the others stood around just glancing uncomfortably over their shoulders at the acres of unexplored darkness around them. None of them had been together as long as Hill and Miller, and like any group, they'd soon sensed the pecking order and fallen into place. They mixed when mixing was offered and kept out of the way when it wasn't.

Miller gave Hill a smoke, but when Martin pulled one out at the same time, Miller glared at him so sharply Martin stuffed it back with only a look of guilt.

Hill drew deeply. Life was weird. Black, wet, clinging jungle, in the middle of Indian country, no odds on coming out in one piece, even a funny premonition that wouldn't go away that this junket was special—loaded, not even a dry piece of ground to put your butt on—and yet there it was. That feeling. Him and Miller. It was like that chick in Saigon was telling him about Buddha. In some queer primeval way him and Miller were One. It wasn't just that they knew what the other was thinking, or had gone through it all before, or thought the same things about the other guys in the outfit. For that instant it was far deeper than that, just crouching there together in the dark, smoking, not even looking at each other. He'd never felt it out of the Army—sure as hell not with a white guy. And an ofay like Miller least of all. But he could remember all the older guys talking about comradeship during the war—the "real" war with Hitler. He never thought it was pure shit because they *all* said it, but he never really knew what they meant until he was out in some godforsaken hole with a good chance for a bullet up his ass. Yeah, life was weird. Against all the odds, he knew he was happy squatting there in the damp—maybe as happy as he'd ever be.

Miller finally broke the silence. "I'll spread 'em out. You park here as anchor. I'll take the river at the other end, down by that thatch, did you see it?"

"Yeah, we checked it before we moved in."

Miller nodded. "I didn't see any paths on this side." It was a question really.

"Me either. They must go in and out of the village on the other side."

"Doesn't make sense. Not with houses on both sides of the stream."

It worried them both. Hill's heart beat faster with that premonition. They sat for a few moments in silence, both thinking about it, but they couldn't come up with an answer. Miller finally looked at him. Hill just shook his head.

"If Pershing calls, mention it to him." Hill nodded. Miller stood and stretched, still scowling doubtfully; then he signaled the others to follow him and started back around the huts. He'd place a man every few yards, making a half circle all around this side, the small side of the village. And Pershing would be doing the same on the other side. In minutes they'd have the place surrounded and be dug in well enough so that even if something were wrong, they could put up a helluva fight until help came.

ii

Hill dug a narrow, shallow trench, quietly, careful with each move of the shovel. He preferred not to think what he was crawling down with, but he knew the lower he got, the better off he was. He had a good position. Clear view of the village in front of him, almost unbroken field of fire. Behind him a solid pine, and he'd cut rattan stalks and put them all around the blind side of the tree. Anyone trying to get close to him from there would make as much noise as a combine harvester.

It was some time after he had settled in, and just truly got to hating the bugs, when he saw a dark figure, silhouetted against the surrounding blackness, crouching low, cross the stream and head in his direction.

"One of these days—"

"You're going to miss me, honey."

Pershing sagged into Hill's foxhole as if he meant to stop. He took a couple of deep breaths—not saying a word, while Hill peered out with special caution. Still no sign that they'd been detected in any way.

"Any sign of life over there?" Hill asked without looking.

"Nope."

"Miller said to tell you we didn't see any tracks on this side."

Pershing leaned over, looking out at the village now with Hill. Their eyes had gradually become accustomed to the dark, and they could make out bits of the huts through the damp mist. Pershing's voice was laced with concern.

"Not one dog bark, no geese honking, nothing."

"If it's an ambush, they were pretty stupid to let us get settled."

Pershing grunted, but he had that constipated look around his eyes that always came when things didn't quite fit the book. He didn't want some sonuvabitching Indian outsmarting him, but he couldn't figure this one. And the idea that Charlie might just be sitting there, watching them, waiting for his moment, made his temples pound, Hill could tell.

"How long we got to wait?" Hill asked.

Pershing checked his watch. "Too long. The chopper with the loudspeaker doesn't come in until dawn."

"Did Polnicki spot anything?"

"No." The disgust in his voice was so thick Hill knew Pershing was unsure if Polnicki did anything but hide behind a tree—and, as the moments wore on, was more and more unsure. "Someday I'm going to catch that bastard with just one shoelace untied and I'm going to hang him by his only living member."

Hill smiled. The one man in the whole goddamned Army who knew the book as well as John Andrew Pershing was Polnicki. He knew the regulations backward, forward, upside down—and he used them never to commit himself, never to make a decision, never to lift a goddamned finger, but to catch him out was like trying to catch a fly pissin'.

"You goin' over to keep an eye on him?"

"No, I'm not," Pershing said with biting finality. "I've got the pimp parked right across the biggest path out of there. And Guery is backing him up with the M-6o. I've told 'im, if he moves, I'll shoot him personally."

Hill smiled. And in a second Pershing began to chuckle himself. "The paper-pushing Saigon commando. Much as I hate the bastard, I'm so glad he's here and not down there living it up in sin city!" And then they both chuckled.

"*Ohh,* baby." Hill sighed. "How I wish I was back there with my little dollies and all that gorgeous loot."

"Listen, son, I got you outa there just in time."

"You're a worrier, daddy, a worrier. I had that fucking thing greased."

"Yeah. And one flat tire and you'd be in old LBJ for the rest of your ignorant days."

"Better there than here," Hill lied. The Long Binh Jail got dubbed LBJ as a joke, but there was no joke about being in it. Like most GI jails, it was a camp for authorized sadism—and you didn't have to be long in any man's army to know that if you went out looking for sadists, you were going to find 'em. And when you started promoting 'em for efficiency—so long as they didn't actually mangle the flesh so much it'd show up poor when the chaplain made his weekly rounds—then you were going to get some very eager, ingenious boys. Hill knew guys who'd gone into LBJ tough from the streets of Philly, Cleveland, Detroit—guys who could eat razor blades for breakfast, who'd beaten and been beaten with real skill—and man, when they came out, they were afraid. And it wasn't the whiteys who took care of you, no, sirree, it was the big black brotherhood. Those black bastards who were sergeants first class bucking to be master, staffs bucking to be firsts. Cunts who'd found a home in the Army—not like Pershing—but scum, who looked forward to that pension at forty just like Polnicki did, looked big in the PX, and in the meantime loved every minute of gut hammering and spine cracking they got in in the name of dear old Uncle Sam and patriotism. It was the one thing that chilled him about his operation in Saigon. If he ever got caught . . . The thing was, watch the angles, *all* the angles—and don't get caught.

"It'd take a lot more than a flat to sew me up, Pershing baby, I got it figured better than that."

"No, you haven't."

Hill smirked derisively. But it was funny. Even out here, slouched down in the goddamned mud wondering if you had Charlie or he had you, wondering if you'd even live to see the fucking sun again, when the very thought of one of his little brown dolls lying on a pink PX nylon sheet—twisting with the itch for it, smoky-eyed, lifting her little boobies with her hands to make it more appealing—when just the thought of it was enough to give him a hard-on, still and all Pershing could chill him with the threat of getting caught, the threat of LBJ. And he could remember the Saigon nights he'd awakened in a cold sweat, worrying—worrying more than worrywart Pershing ever dreamed of worrying. But it was in a good cause. Money. And he knew damn well he'd never get another chance like it, and if he didn't take it now, he'd be a busboy or elevator operator the rest of his mother-fucking life. It was worth a little risk. But he had to be careful. Had to figure the angles.

"Don't sweat it, daddy. You always figure the MP's and them Indian police got eyes everyplace, like Sunset Strip or something, coming on like gang busters. Once you figure that, you're lost. You might as well live by the book, like you. But it ain't true. The MP's are the stupid ones. They pick 'em that way. Thick heads and the football team. And the Indian police? Baby, with money you can buy police chief, mayor, *prime minister!* Hell, if I wanted, I could have the hooch delivered by police car—but why should I cut 'em in?"

He made it sound certain, like he did when he said it to himself on those nights when the worries came on. It was all true, of course. That's what made it sound so good. The catch was life. Fucking life. It always came up with surprises. Some idiot saying the wrong thing to the wrong guy. Somebody panicking. Some girl falling in love and having the nerve to go to somebody who mattered and spilling it all —a base commander maybe, even the U.S. embassy. And there was always the possibility of some other spade with the brains, guts, and drive of George Hill, trying to take over from him. He knew that he, George Hill, would be crafty enough to put the finger on some stud *he* wanted to get rid of, so that meant when another one came along, he'd figure a quiet word dropped in the right ear was the way to get Big George out of the way. It hadn't happened yet. None of it had, but it was what kept him smoking on worry nights.

But he'd played it cool, never tried to grab too much. And he didn't intend to hang around so long he'd be playing the narrow side of the odds. Worrying one night in fifty was good for you. It kept you on your toes. And the other forty-nine nights were like cloud nine. No Uncle Tom like Pershing nor the thoughts of LBJ were going to keep him away from it. And once he'd pulled the combat stint, he was going back into business.

"Tell you what, big daddy. As soon as we're back in Soulsville, I'm going to find three brand-new ones for you—and tie 'em all in a row, so there'll be enough for you."

Pershing laughed softly. He was still watching the village and scanning the woods distrustfully, but his eyes danced. He was all sergeant, and he never let women get in the way of duty, but, boy, when duty was done, he heard the call loud and clear. And what an instrument. It was the seventh wonder of the Air Cavalry. And Pershing was proud of it. It delighted ole supersergeant, his not-so-secret weapon, and yet it was more than that. He was proud, too. But it wasn't in the instrument, as George Hill had learned long ago. The sarge was married to the Army, and a girl was exercise—and they all seemed to know it. Never once—in Saigon, in the Philippines—had a girl got hung up on him, got so he was more important to her than food, air, life itself, like Hill had to admit they did over him. He never understood why, and he knew inside he never trusted it, never trusted love, or believed it would last. But it kept coming his way. While the sarge just had his exercise. Happy, robust exercise.

"You don't want me to ruin three young virgins for you, do you?" Pershing grinned.

"Ruin? Hell, after you've had at 'em, I'll be able to rent 'em out to two guys at a time. You'll be doing me a favor, Sarge."

Pershing laughed—almost too loud. They both scanned the field in front of them uneasily. The mist had become thicker. It must be getting near dawn, Hill thought. Pershing clutched his rifle. He was the supersergeant again—no nonsense.

"It's almost time." He was frowning, his mind still troubled by the unnatural silence, the pieces in the puzzle that didn't fit. "I'm going to check the other posts." He stood up straight—slowly, cautiously. A second; then he looked down at Hill. "If they make a break on the other side, I'm only leaving you, Miller and Russell on this side. I'll tell the others to circle around in back, so don't start pickin' 'em off if they go around behind you."

Hill nodded.

"And keep your right hand on that gunstock," Pershing said. "Save the organ practice for camp. I want your mind on those Indians out there."

He moved off stealthily. Hill knew those last words were as much threat as joke, but the great thing about Pershing was that he was straight all the way through. He never ducked a man's urge for ass, or to steal the government blind, or to screw off on every piece of work he could—or to be scared shitless. He never ignored big hunks of your nature by pretending they didn't exist. Others played the whole big team spirit game—give your balls for the Grand Old Flag and the heroic Air Cavalry. But John A. would square right off and say, "I know you bastards are here to get out of as much as you can and stay as far from the enemy as possible while you collect as much danger pay and promotion and Vietnamese ass as you can get your hands on without undue risk to life or limb. Well, I'm here to tell you the same thing is going through my mind, but I'm not letting *me* get away with it—and that goes for you *double*." Sometimes he seemed like a fucking minister with his righteousness, but Hill knew he was a lucky man to have wound up taking orders from that shining, handsome, round-faced mule.

iii

Fifteen minutes went by. And another fifteen minutes. Hill had the usual cramps, twitches, imaginary assaults by battalions of bugs, real attacks by dozens. Twice he thought he heard the chopper with the loudspeakers, "His Master's Voice," but nothing came. The mist was getting thicker and thicker. It penetrated until he was so damned cold he could almost wish for the soggy, humid, torrid heat of the day. Almost, but not quite. By experience he knew that when it started to get this cold, dawn was very near. The chopper should be close, but strain as he might, he couldn't pick up its hum.

The village still lay absolutely silent. Not a groan from a sleeping farmer having nightmares. No sound of someone making love. No cat meowing contentedly after a dinner of fat jungle rat. It was eerie. Once or twice before they'd surrounded villages that had seemed deserted. It was never so, of course, but it was always twice as unnerving as when the night was broken by little natural night sounds. A kid pissing from the thatch doorway onto a stone path. Anything.

Suddenly he heard a rustle of rattan behind him. Fear coursed through him. Silently he twisted in his foxhole, safety catch off, heart thumping like a bongo drum. The mist was thick as hell on the ground, but he could just make out a figure crouched low—to the left of the pine tree. He mustn't give himself away yet. Was there one of them—or a thousand? He drew a bead on the mist as though he could penetrate it by sheer willpower. The figure moved again, close. Something was wrong about it. Hill couldn't put his finger on it, but something was queer about that Indian. He lifted his rifle to firing position—all the time scanning the rest of the area for the others. He'd shoot only when he had to. The figure moved again. These gooks would sacrifice a man to reveal fire positions any day. The figure moved again. God. It *was* a trap. No dogs. They should've been wise. Now it was going to be a fight. Jesus, he hated a fire fight. Let me live, God. Let me fucking well live. The figure crouched lower. Had he spotted him?

"One of these days—"

The whistle. Hill sagged. Stupid sonuvabitch. No wonder the Indian looked wrong. It was one of their own guys, and Indians didn't move like Yanks and never would. He whistled back.

"You're going to miss me, honey."

Why had the gink waited so long? He might have shot a hole in his head. He should have given the signal twenty yards out, but maybe he didn't know where Hill was and couldn't spot him. He could see him crawling closer now. Looked like Martin. Figured. That idiot.

"He wants us on the other side."

"All of us?" Hill whispered softly.

"Yeah." The guy—it must have been Martin, though why the hell was Pershing using Martin for a job like this?—was already crawling away. Basic training crawl. The stupid shit. What was he going to do, crawl all the way to the other side of the village?

Hill looked around carefully. His heart was returning to normal. What the hell was going on? The choppers'd be here any minute, so why was Pershing changing everything now? Jesus, what a war.

He got himself in order. He could only see the top of a couple of huts above the thickening mist. Even the dark path of the river was no longer visible. One of the guys was slinking across his field of fire. Why did the sarge want them over there? That was the trouble—no matter how small the operation, you never knew what was going on.

Hill had just crossed the river—wet through as always!—when the first sound of the choppers clearly cut through the air. No time to locate anyone. He got down into firing position, waiting for action. When that noise penetrated the village, something would happen. It had to happen! He couldn't see anyone else, but he heard a safety click on his left. One of the guys.

The first chopper was closing fast, and he could already pick out the sound of the support chopper. He was tense with the promise of action, but he felt the wave of relief even as he got the preaction butterflies. If it was a trap, the Indians had waited too long. That support copter was an armor-plated gunship. It could blow the piss out of the whole village, and there were forty more troops inside, ready to come down and join in the chase if one developed. And if that weren't

22

enough, now that it was light they could get a squadron of jets in to bomb, napalm, and strafe the bastards right into oblivion. And the cowboys win again.

The first copter came in, hovering over the village. Pershing would be in contact with them. He couldn't hear the static of the radio. Pershing must be some distance from him. And no sign of life from the village. No, there it was. Chickens fluttering all over the place. And a dog. Why hadn't it barked before? Feet running. Poor Indians. There were times he felt sorry for them. Then it came—the great white chief's voice. The loudspeakers blaring from the chopper. He couldn't make out a word, but he knew what it was saying:

"Your village is surrounded by the forces of the Republic of South Vietnam. No one can escape. A respresentative of the South Vietnamese government will soon be among you. He will speak with you, and all authentic villagers will be left in peace. We intend no harm to anyone. Please remain calm, and remain in your houses. Free rice and medicine will be distributed to all." His Master's Voice.

What he didn't mention, of course, was that if they thought any of the men were Vietcong, there might be a little free show thrown in too. If they fought, a real live Western right on your doorstep. If they didn't fight, a little straightforward persuasion to talk. How's hanging from a tree by your wrists—back ass to—for starters? Then we got bayonet-at-the-throat drill. If that doesn't work, one of the Arvin, our fighting allies of South Vietnam, takes a villager into the jungle—a few screams, an accidental death. Then the others tend to become more talkative.

Hill hated this side of it really. Afterward he always half wished there'd *been* a fight. Of course, *they* never did any of the dirty work. That was always left to the South Vietnamese contingent—the bloody heroes of the Arvin. Our great little allies who'd run at the sight of unarmed kids of twelve if they were on their own, but would pound a man's brains out with delight if there were a pocketful of GI's around to back them up. There were GI outfits that got a kick out of knocking around Charlie when they caught one or thought they caught one. But not in John Andrew Pershing's outfit, they didn't. Old Charlie never knew how lucky he was when he got in the supersarge's clutches. By the book it was. Tough, but not brutal. Let one man give a VC an unnecessary cuff, and Pershing would have his ass for a month. Hill was grateful for that. Charlie was no nice Indian, but sometimes they were so young, and so fiercely defiant—he hated to see them pushed around just for the fun of it. Like World War I flyers it should be. Respect for

23

the enemy. Gentlemen, I present the Red Baron. He's to be our guest at dinner tonight. Champagne, Baron?

The copter was hovering, waiting for the sun to begin to pierce the haze—they'd learned that. Hill still couldn't see any farther right on the ground, but the tops of the Indian huts were clearing as the sun rose. He could see baskets, bamboo poles, a well. The stakes of a pigpen. No sound of pigs. No sense hiding your pigs, neighbors, we'll get them, too. It was a big mistake being born in South Vietnam, but you're going to have to live with it. Besides, if we leave you your pigs, the VC get them from you, so you lose either way. Tough shit for the Indians. On the other hand, you'd probably stab me in the back at the first goddamned chance. Everybody's got his problems, Jack, so just play it cool. You'll get hurt less, and I'll get the hell out of here quicker.

There was just a low, milky-white cloud now, swirling around the huts, rolling out over the center area and pathways—not three feet high. The loudspeaker was still working away at them, but there wasn't a sign of human life. He could see a skinny damned dog, slinking around, looking at the copter, whining. There was a nanny goat tethered near the pigpen. Some smart Indian probably figured he could get the Yanks to leave them their goat—milk for the kids. And he figured right. Pershing wouldn't touch that, and if the army military assistance officer "advising" the Arvin wanted otherwise, ole supersergeant would snow him and subtly threaten him so the brass would end up pretending he thought it was a good idea—yeah, leave them the goat, you're right, that's sound thinking. The sarge had a genius for twisting brass around his finger.

He could spot the reserve copter swaying, hovering over the field where they'd landed earlier. It was all set. And down came His Master's Voice. The wash clearing away a little circle of the milky mist. The Arvin commander came out first, ahead of his Vietnamese contingent. One of the flashy bastards. A captain. With a white silk scarf at the neck like Ky. Shit, he hated those pricks. Strutting around like heroes, uniforms pressed, neat, paid for like everything else by Uncle Sam. There was just a squad with him. Twelve men maybe. Shining new boots, medals. Christ, they gave 'em a medal for taking their daily shit. And the U.S. military assistance officer. Jesus, a lieutenant colonel. What the hell was a MAAG light colonel doing on a little operation like this? Had it got to the point where an Arvin captain wouldn't take orders from anything less than a U.S. light colonel? He could believe it.

The copter had just started to rise slowly—going to hover over the village as cover, when the machine gun opened up. Jesus, not a machine gun, a whole goddamned battery. Hill saw the Arvin captain stagger forward. Screwy expression, like wait, there must be some mistake. The U.S. light colonel was on the ground, but it didn't look as if he were hit; he'd just dived in as an experienced baby would. The Arvin squad was staggering around panicked. It was a split-second view, but planted in his mind like a big still photograph. He had whipped around immediately to let fly at the hut the machine-gun fire seemed to be coming from. But the minute he started firing he could see it wasn't one hut. It was three. One near the center and one at each corner.

Hill's heart was racing. What the hell'd it mean? They'd waited until it was almost hopeless and then opened up. They must have some plan. His goddamned premonition. He stopped firing for a second. You couldn't tell what the hell the shots were doing anyway. His eyes darted around the village. One Arvin was staggering around with blood spurting out of him. He must have got hit five times in the fraction of a second Hill was looking, but he didn't go down, just kept lurching wildly. Another seemed alive behind a grotesque barrier of fallen bodies, but for the rest it was quits. He didn't notice the U.S. colonel. What did catch his eye was the chopper. It was hanging about fifteen feet off the ground and floundering like a wounded duck. The windscreen was crazed from one end to the other, and the whole bird was snapping and sparking where bullets were ricocheting off—and going in. They were throwing everything at it, the tail getting the worst of it. Those bastards knew where it was soft, and the chopper was shuddering and squealing like a live animal. It wouldn't go down, and it couldn't get up.

Where the hell was the reserve copter? He tried to peer over the huts, but no sign of anything. Jesus, they were in for it. Then the worst thought: they were surrounded. Christ, yes, that explains what's happened to the reserve chopper. He squirmed around, his back to the village, gun aimed at the woods behind him. It was all lightening up, but there was still about a foot of mist on the ground. Hiding what? He could see someone moving on his right, and some of the guys firing. It was little Arnie Russell moving. The stupid bastard. You'd think he was on a coon hunt. He even held his gun like a hillbilly out for dinner.

Hill turned. The three VC machine guns were still lacing away at the copter, and it was beginning to flop like a fish out of water. There had to be some kind of defense rigged up inside those huts, because

25

they just kept firing, ignoring the attack from the ground altogether. Then Russell suddenly stood up and let go a blast. Ten shots from the M-16, Hill would have guessed. And he sank down again. So help me God, it was a fucking Georgia cracker out hunting coons. But goddamn, the center machine gun stopped firing. The bastard had hit something, Or somebody had hit something. It was too goddamned insane for Hill. His eyes concentrated on the woods again. He couldn't see a thing. And nothing across the stream. The woods were getting too light to hide much, and the underbrush had been cleared for maybe a hundred yards out from the village.

Then *wham!*—the ground shook under him. Metal flew everywhere. He knew instantly it wasn't mortar. Whatever it was, the one antidote was to *get down!* He kissed that mother earth with face, gut, groin, and thigh. He heard metal hit wood, the hiss of fire—napalm?—and for a couple of seconds the VC machine guns stopped. He waited a second longer, then twisted to take a fleeting look. It was the main chopper. It had crashed down and flipped. Landing gear spinning in the sky, tail smashed down in the trees, squashed like a huge bug. Parts of the sides had blown out, and fire was erupting in erratic black and yellow balloons from all sides of it. He could see a body hanging upside down from the pilot's seat. One cowboy down for sure.

And as suddenly as the instant of quiet had descended it was shattered again. The VC machine guns switched their fire to the field in front of them. Hill took a quick look at the woods behind him. Not a sign of anyone. Goddamn, by the book there should be a thousand Charlies running at them, bugles blowing, screaming bloody murder. But nothing. Then, out of the corner of his eye, he saw Pershing dart from one tree to another. Okay, ole supersergeant, get things organized. They could take care of three machine gun crews, they'd show them that.

Then, climbing up over the huts, he saw it. The reserve chopper! Finally. When the firing started, they'd probably gone in on the field, dumped the support troops, and now they were coming in to blast the shit out of the Indians. Well, better late than never! The support troops would be spreading, to snare stragglers—*and* they'd provide a first line against an ambush from the woods. Man, those Indians were going to regret this. They'd blow the bastards to Buddha and back! He fired a long, rewarding, angry round into the corner hut nearest him. The tracers showed him it was going right in where the machine gun was, but the machine-gun fire just kept coming.

Then the gunship opened up, all the way. Machine guns, recoilless rifles with 106-mm shells, 40-mm grenades from M-79's. The whole VC village fluttered. Dust, straw dust, matting bounced and flew into the air. There were cries of pain and a secondary explosion from the center hut.

On the instant Pershing rose and signaled them back. They'd retreat fifty yards or so until the gunship pulverized that thatched burg into a ghost town. Hill spotted a tree arching near the river and, crouching low, dashed to it. He hit it behind the tree, slithering into the mud, his feet sliding right into the stream. Fair enough. He left them there and pivoted around, tree between him and the village. He could tell by the pitch of the fire that the VC machine guns were firing again. Jesus, they must have concrete bunkers in there! Another salvo from the gunship—grenade launchers, 106's. He edged around the tree to take a look—and halfway around stopped dead.

The three huts on the other side of the stream from the main village were now standing clear in the light of the rising sun, and as Hill looked, the side of the center one was kicked out and toppled to the ground, just the usual straw matting held together on a bamboo frame. But behind it was no native hut, but a 20-mm antiaircraft gun mounted on solid pine logs and a full uniformed North Vietnamese crew wheeling its sight on to the gunship—and, baby, they knew what they were doing! That gun whipped down on target like a pistol!

Hill's first reaction was to scream at the copter—stupid, instinctive. But the pilot had seen the gun, too. The gunship swayed, pivoted backward, trying to get distance and move. The first shell exploded about twenty yards from it, and the chopper shook like a rattle. Some poor sonuvabitch toppled right out of the open gunport.

Hill slithered around the base of the tree, firing at the AA gun even as he moved. Another pumping shot from the antiaircraft gun. That goddamned gunship didn't have a chance, but he didn't hear any explosion. Hill's own tracers had fallen short. In a split second he lowered the elevation on his sight, but before he could trigger off a second burst, something opened up on him from the hut beside the antiaircraft gun. He slammed his head against the tree, and as he did, he heard the *poom, poom, poom* of a whole volley from the antiaircraft gun—and, echoing right on it, the gunship explode. It rattled, banged, boomed. He could even hear the cascading parts crashing into the forest, ripping and whining.

Hill elbowed around the tree angrily, but before he could even lift his head, mortars let loose from someplace, and the machine-gun fire was still waffling the tree trunk. Jesus Christ, there must be a battalion of them. He hoped Pershing and Miller were signaling for help, double time. Face flat on the ground, he tried to get a sense of the mortar fire. He heard a couple of screams, more machine-gun fire. This is when you thanked God for the mud of Vietnam. He burrowed in. And thank God, too, that Pershing was chickenshit and made them wear their flak suits. Hill didn't want any hot piece of mortar racing through his guts. He inched his face up, screwing his M-16 around so he could fire. He'd got the rhythm of the mortars, and now he was getting the feel of battle. Half anger, half fear, strong doses of cunning, malice, resolve. They'd show those little bastards they were in for a fight no matter how many of them there were.

He had a flat view across the stream. The goddamn antiaircraft crew were unbolting the gun, dismantling the base as if they were on some field exercise. There were machine guns in the huts on each side, and the mortars seemed to be firing from the woods just behind. Some bastard was calmly standing on the hut floor next to the AA gun, scanning the area with binoculars. Probably sighting for the mortars. Impudent prick. Hill inched his shoulder carefully over the stock of the M-16. He wanted accuracy on this shot—not just the usual flurry of lead. That was another pain about the damned M-16. It could toss the lead all right, but aiming farther than fifty yards with it was like trying to aim over fifty yards with a slingshot. He waited for another mortar round. He didn't dare turn to look; any movement might bring the machine-gun fire right in on him. Now, breath steady, he aimed, squeezed. One, two, three, four. Then he slammed his face down in the mud.

The machine gun raked all around him. One shot creased his helmet, jerking his neck. Man, they were covered. What the fuck was Charlie doing? Hill couldn't believe they'd stage a major attack in daylight. Not for one little unit. He wormed back and over a couple of feet. He had no idea what his burst of fire had done. But you almost never knew unless you were two feet from the guy. One thing he'd bet his balls on, that spotter for Uncle Ho wasn't standing there like a medic at short-order inspection anymore. If he hadn't got him, he'd sure as hell made him move ass!

Suddenly there was a helluvan explosion off on the other side of the village. What the hell was that? And where were the support troops? He could tell by the sound of the guns that most of the fire was VC. Once in a while a burst from our side, but, man, it was all Indians. All they could do was cool it, lie low, and do as much damage as they could

28

until the jets came in. A little low-level napalm would change the odds soon enough.

He inched his hand over his shoulder for his shovel. He'd hardly got it loosened from his pack when he picked up the change in the fire pattern. It'd become a sixth sense. He didn't even have to be thinking about it; but let the music of the guns change, and it threw his whole system on the alert. When the real trap had broken loose, there were five VC machine guns going. He couldn't figure how many mortars. The mortars were still blasting, but now only two of the VC machine guns were at it. He hunched up carefully.

Just in time to see three Charlies lugging a machine gun across the stream away from the village. He ducked down quick. But nothing came at him. He timed the mortars, then lifted his head again, aimed, and let fly at the machine-gun crew. One seemed to stumble, but there was no knowing. He ducked down again, but again no salvo. Just a second as another mortar round squashed in, and he was firing again, looking as he shot. No sign of the AA crew. The two VC machine guns that were still firing came from the huts on the other side of the river. Charlie was clearing out.

All right, baby, here's where you're a hero or a no-goodnik. Hill didn't even think it out beyond that. Thinking was as good as saying no. He waited, the mortar shelling nearest him went in. A second, and he sprang up and, crouching as low as he could, sprinted across the stream and raced for the woods. He lunged into them, going flat on his stomach. Count, pant, pray. The blessed trinity. No machine-gun fire. They hadn't seen him, or they weren't going to worry about him— one or the other. He waited until his breathing was a little steadier, then up on his elbows and crawling. Through the underbrush he could see the three huts on this side of the river and the fire coming from them. He could hear movement behind them, too, and shouts in Vietnamese, but he couldn't make anything out. He kept moving. Mustn't get too far from the river, or the jets'll give me a parboil when they start working these boys over.

He was almost at the spot where he'd dug in during the night. That was it. Scramble for that foxhole. They'd need a toothpick to get him out of there. He elbowed forward until he was certain he'd spotted the pine tree he'd used as cover from the rear. One glance out. The mortars still pounding in. He got a glimpse of Pershing and two others— couldn't identify them—racing for one of the village huts. Now things were moving. They'd get a little of their own back.

He was up in one move and highballing it to that foxhole. He hadn't got to the pine tree before he heard the shots screaming through the air. Somebody had spotted him. Panic in the stomach. Stop? Go on? Not a hundredth of a second to think about it. He dived for the foxhole, rolled, slithered, and crawled along the ground till he tumbled into it, bullets whining and snapping all around him. He'd liked to have taken time to be sick, but he knew he couldn't afford it. Not if those Indians figured he was a threat to their flank. He squirmed over, the breath rasping against his throat. He pulled a grenade from his hip, pulled the pin—one, two, God, he was winded, got to stop smoking. He let fly. Waiting. It went off. A scream, they *had* come for him. He wheeled into firing position. Three of them. The grenade had got one outright. Another was writhing on the ground; the third was crouching to fire, but coming forward. He let fly with the M-16. The guy went down. The odds were he got him, but he'd have to keep watching. He'd seen that kind get up and rush.

But the immediate danger was from another gang bang. He swiveled to check the woods behind. No sign of anything. Over the machine guns and mortars he could still hear the Indian talk from deep behind the huts. Nothing else. Then he saw a string of them dash for the woods from the center hut. Reflexively, he let off a burst at them.

Goddamn. One of them looked like a Yank!

He didn't have time to think about it. A section of the hut nearest him suddenly slammed out, revealing one of the machine-gun crews. They had swung around and were aiming right at him. There was nothing he could do but burrow. The bullets slammed in all around him, but it didn't bother him. They couldn't touch him there. What he had to do was wait until Pershing drew their fire from the other direction, then he'd have his turn—and *they* weren't in any foxholes!

And then, abruptly again, the tune changed. The machine guns stopped altogether, and without a break, the goddamnedest mortar barrage hammered in. He wasn't going to lift his head to get it sawed off by a hunk of white-hot mortar. But it was so heavy he couldn't get any set rhythm to it. It sounded as if they were raking the riverbank. What was going on? Goddamned war!

It seemed to go on forever. Two minutes was probably the truth of it. But you live through two minutes of a mortar barrage. It's long enough. And then, like flicking a light switch, it stopped. He hesitated a second, then inched up. No sign of anything. The Indian machine-gun crew was gone. And nothing seemed to be moving in the woods.

He saw Pershing dart across the stream, near the first hut. Little

Arnie Russell ghosted after him, still holding his rifle like a hillbilly after revenuers. They took to the dirt quick. And right, too. In a party organized like this shindig, you didn't take anything at face value. Those cunts were probably waiting for everyone to stand up and then they'd have another go. The mist had cleared from the woods, but there were still long shadows from the low angle of the sun, and even where there wasn't underbrush, you couldn't be sure if things were moving or not.

After all the shooting the silence sort of echoed around in your head. Some kid was crying, and there were groans from the village, but it seemed faint and distant. He kept scanning the woods and waiting. He saw Pershing and Russell cover a few more yards and farther down the stream another group move. Might be Miller, might be some support troops, he couldn't tell. But mostly it was silence.

Again maybe it was only a minute or two, but it stretched a couple of summers. Then it came, the sound of the jets. He saw Pershing roll over on his back nursing the squawk box. The babies came in low and swept past the village, then stood on their tails and circled around. Goddamned beautiful. He remembered when he used to envy them, whizzing in to the rescue, rat-a-tat-tat, *wham!* Sizzle! Zap! Plaster Charlie with lead, fire, and big orgasms of TNT—*Wham! Wham! Wham!*—and then he had got a good look at them. Tiny damned cockpit, gadgets, knobs and levers poking at you, can't move your butt for lack of space, and worst of all, it was all so ugly and massive. Not slick and sleek like it looked from down below, but just a big hunk of machinery, like driving a bulldozer. Not for him. Still, watching them flash through the blue sky, they looked sweet.

They zoomed out over the jungle. Pershing had told them the score, and now they'd beat the shit out of the woods. They'd knock down a lot of trees, but he didn't figure there was much chance they'd hurt Charlie. That cat had flown the coop. But it was safe now. Charlie wasn't going to hang around to knock off a few of them just to get blasted by big brother from the sky. A few more bodies weren't worth it. Not to an outfit that hauled around AA guns for kicks.

He pulled himself up, standing in the foxhole. Pershing was playing it by the book as usual. He raced to the woods, with Russell covering him. He signaled Miller to the other side, and Miller moseyed into the woods, too. He wouldn't disobey Pershing, but like Hill, he knew the action was over.

Hill took out a butt and lit up as Pershing scrambled about checking the perimeter. He wasn't halfway around when they heard the first bombs shudder the woods. Light up another thousand dollars of tax-payers' loot. Fifty bombs, fifty thousand dollars. Man, it's easy, we're big spenders from the West.

He stepped out of the foxhole and walked over to Russell who was still lying on the ground, covering Pershing.

"Why don't you put one between his legs, scare the bejesus out of him?" He grinned down, and Russell glanced up with that funny tooth-less grin. He had three false teeth on one side and always took them out before they went into action. Gave him the funniest goddamn look. Hill had half forgotten, and the sudden confrontation with that unexpected black space in the sallow face made him laugh. For a sec-ond Russell's huge, lugubrious eyes lit up, but they soon chilled, as though glum at the burden of hauling around the huge dark bags be-neath them. The sudden change reminded Hill that Russell'd never been in a battle where the Indians made the running. He was new, and he'd probably been scared right down to his little cracker toenails. But he'd done all right. He was going to be a good man, little Arnie Russell.

"Anybody hurt over there?" Hill asked, nodding back across the stream. He could hear cries and that kid yelling, but he meant were any of our guys hurt—and Russell'd know what he meant.

Russell nodded. His eyes were still anxiously following Pershing. Yeah, this little Southern boy had been shaken. Hill remembered the aftermaths of *his* first days of real fright. The shakes, the wanting to cry, the feeling like why does it have to be me. It'd pass. You got hard-ened to it. You didn't get over being scared; you just got over feeling sorry for yourself about it.

"You did all right over there," Hill said, watching Pershing and Miller come together and talk over by the edge of the woods. "I saw you get that center machine gunner. You're going to have to watch yourself; you'll end up a fucking hero." The black, toothless, almost shy grin. And Hill started back to the village. He couldn't stand the sound of that kid yelling.

iv

The village was alive. Where, before the fighting, there had been nothing but silence, there were now old men, old women, kids, and one or two young women. Chattering, crying, cowering. There were

32

no young men, of course. Those that were VC were gone, and those that weren't were probably hiding in the woods, waiting until the military pulled out. The young girls usually disappeared, too, especially when the Arvin were around. Nothing like a little rape to liven your day. Hill figured the fact that a couple of rapable ones had hung around proved the villagers knew about the ambush all right. Somebody must have convinced those dollies all the Arvin were going to be dead.

It was amazing how good the place looked for all the shooting. One thing about a Vietnamese village, if you didn't burn it down, you could bomb it and shoot it up for days, and it just looked the same. All that straw and bamboo—the stuff just went sailing through. And there were so damn many mudholes and ruts in the paths in, out and around the village a few hundred shell craters one way or the other didn't make much difference.

The guys were gathered in a little open area in front of the village. The chopper was still hanging nose to the ground, tail in the tree, burning quietly. And off to the right, Hill could see big hunks of the gunship, some of them knifed right through the trees like fancy metal wedges. Besides the Arvin bodies, he could see a couple of GI's lying with that rubbery sprawl that meant death. And there must have been fifteen, twenty wounded. Support troops, as well as their own unit. Polnicki was running around supervising the first aid or at least acting as if his shouting were doing some good. He never laid a hand on anybody, of course. Just, "You there! Get over here and see to this man!" The fucker could bleed to death before Polnicki'd perform. Hill turned into the main path of the village. And Polnicki spotted him.

"Hill! Get over here! We've got men injured."

Hill just walked on. He'd say he didn't hear him, and Pershing would always back him up. Polnicki sure as hell wouldn't follow him into the village. Somebody might want to hurt him.

The people backed away from him and chattered. A couple of old gals yelled bloody murder at him. And some cried. You could sure tell these people hadn't been in it much. Down in the delta, they just looked at you. They'd seen you before, in one form or another. He was moving toward where he could hear the kid yelling. He heard some groaning and a couple of cries from one of the huts, they must have got a hit from one of the gunship salvos. But most of 'em looked untouched. The VC must have had them dig trenches in the huts. It was common in the delta, common up here in the highlands, too, in places where there was a lot of fighting, but when you took a place that hadn't been hit before, it was sometimes murder what it did to the stupid fucking natives. People running around while the shooting was going on. Hill'd seen panicked kids doubled right over by machine-gun fire—and some woman racing out after them and getting it, too. And a little mortar fire was great for tearing into odd parts of the carcass. But a trench was protection against most of it. Only danger then was really from a direct hit or napalm. And most of these people were untouched, so when Charlie lined up the trap, they must have dug trenches in all the huts, and the unlucky ones just happened to get something direct. Since the gunship hadn't fired all that much, it couldn't have been too bad.

With his rifle, he shoved open the door where the crying was coming from. And his finger was on the trigger. This was the kind of range the M-16 *was* good for. Inside, the hut was still cool from the night, and he felt the cool air rush by him as he peered into the dark shadows of the place. There was no booby trap on the door, and a kid scrambled away from in front of it to someone out of sight, so there was no booby trap on the floor either. He could see the kid who was yelling on a mat across the room. A lined old woman was with him, squatting, trying to pacify him. The kid stopped bawling at the sight of Hill. The kid's right side and arm were streaked with blood, and in bawling he'd washed his face and chest with it, too. It looked shiny and gruesome, but Hill could tell that once the bleeding was stopped, it wouldn't be serious. And it wasn't hurting all that much, or he wouldn't have stopped crying. Ninety percent panic, ten percent pain, Hill figured. Gun still ready, he stepped in the open side, covering the area behind the door.

He backed away from the doorway—no sense exposing your back to some enthusiast with a knife. His eyes adjusted to the darkened interior. In the corner a woman maybe twenty-five or so was sitting on the floor holding a baby at her breast. The kid who'd scrambled out of the door was leaning against her on the other side. He could see now it was a girl, maybe four. Nobody else. His eyes went from the little girl back to the woman. A flash of sexual desire—urgent, involuntary—burned through him. God, a woman's breast. Always so unexpected white—no matter black, yellow, white woman, no matter how many you'd seen, it always threw you. And these goddamned Indians. Their eyes, their mouths, their fragile bones in that gentle, smooth flesh.

The baby was sucking hard at the nipple. Fast, desperate little gulps

34

at security in a mad, chaotic world. Suck up, kid, you're in for a hard ride. Hill moved to the boy with the old woman. She cowered, and the kid pulled away, but he glared at Hill with a cheeky insolence. Hill grinned. The kid had fat cheeks. You didn't see many kids in the country with fat cheeks. Some rich Saigon kids—yeah. But not in the country. These people had really been having it easy. The young woman—mama, Hill figured—started to rise, but Hill signaled her down. He bent and unsnapped his aid pack. The kid watched Hill unwrap a gauze bandage. Hill looked up—and the kid's belligerence forced another smile from him. He jerked his head at the kid, ordering him closer. The old woman, skeptical, but not so afraid now, gave him a little push. The kid moved closer. And Hill couldn't resist it. "Boo!" he said. The kid didn't blink, nothing. Lost joke. And Hill laughed at the futility of it.

He found the rip in the kid's arm. Something had creased him in the muscle fat and then pinked out a little hunk of flesh in his chest. By some damn miracle it looked as if it hadn't touched a bone, but the arm was pouring blood. Dark red. A vein. He sprayed the wounds with disinfectant and plastic seal. The kid flinched a couple of times but was more fascinated by the sprays than pained by the mechanics of it. Hill had bandaged the arm and was wrapping the gauze around the kid's chest when he heard a commotion outside.

He dropped the gauze and grabbed his gun—moving quickly to one side, away from the Indians and away, too, from the door. Bandaging the kid, he'd heard other sounds from outside, crying, some groans, people chattering and whispering. But this was different. Then he heard an American voice, "Get away!" and a push against the door.

It was Martin. A couple of Indians were hanging on him, begging or complaining—it was hard to tell.

"Okay, okay!" he said, and gave them a final shove. He turned and looked into the hut.

"What the hell are you doing?" Hill asked, going back to the kid. He could see that it wasn't trouble, whatever it was.

"I'm after you. And these geeks want me to give 'em some green stamps or something for showing me where you were. Go on, get away!" he yelled at the clingers again. Martin always had a half-assed grin on his face. Life, the war, everything was some kind of joke to him. He seemed never to have adjusted to how insane people are and always got a kick out of it. Hill wondered what the hell kind of family he was raised in. But yelling at the Indians with a grin on your face didn't scare 'em away, so Hill stood erect and glared out the

35

door. The two old babes pushing hardest at Martin shut up and started to back away.

"Close the door," Hill said. And Martin did.

"Polnicki sent me. He said you're to get your ass out there to help the wounded."

"Tell Polnicki he can kiss my little purple pimple."

"He might take you up on that—but I'm not about to make him the offer."

Hill looked at him, and Martin grinned. The stupid bastard was all right in his way.

"Okay," Hill said, "tell him you couldn't find me."

"We really got some wounded," Martin said with unexpected seriousness. "The support group was booby-trapped. They had dynamite buried under the trail from the clearing to the village, and when the support unit started out, they got it. The ones that lived are pretty messy."

That was the explosion he'd heard. Man, these bastards were ready for us. Anger seethed in him.

"Okay," Hill said, "I'm coming." He tied the chest bandage abruptly —and roughly. The kid flinched in pain but didn't cry out. Hill felt a second of pique. Shit, it's not the kid's fault. He rubbed the kid's head gruffly—it was meant to be friendly, but Hill couldn't make it friendly.

He picked up his rifle and started for the door. The young woman stirred and he looked at her. Goddamn, he'd like to fuck her. It'd be a good way to get even with the whole damn village. When his eyes went from her breast to her eyes, she was staring at him intently—and they began to fill with water. Hill hesitated for a second.

"Come on, man." Martin grabbed his arm. Hill pulled loose.

"Go on! I'll be right there."

Martin sighed and went out the door. The woman never took her eyes off Hill. He had a bone a yard long, and he still wanted to stab her, but there was something in her expression, as if she wanted to tell him something. A second went by. He was ready to give up and go out when she shifted slightly, lifting the baby a bit, exposing her ribs and stomach. Her tunic was black, but he could see that it was soaked in blood, and bits of her were oozing through rips in it. It looked like rotted meat wiggling with worms, and for a second it almost made him sick.

She still kept her eyes on him, and the baby sucked harder and harder, disturbed by the shift of position. Hill moved to her side and

36

knelt on one knee. He put his hand on her back and started to push her slowly down with the other hand. But she stopped him and shifted the baby to the other breast. Hill watched—and marveled at the mind of man. Half a minute ago he could have raped her without a by-your-leave, but that ugly gaping stomach had driven sex so far from his mind he could look at those two lovely boobies and feel so shriveled he felt he'd never screw a woman again. When the baby was firmly at it once more, she covered herself as best she could and stretched back on the mat.

Hill looked at the wound. Christ, she must be in terrible pain under that stoic gaze. He pulled a morphine capsule from the aid pack, snapped the case, and bent over her. He had to put the thing down while he ripped her sleeve. Then he plunged the needle into her arm. She winced a little but took it all with complete trust. The little girl had scampered back to the grandmother as soon as Hill had come close to her mother, but now he could sense her and the boy just behind him, watching.

Reluctantly he looked down at the stomach wound. He hated that kind worst of all. Bones, muscle, flesh—at least you felt you knew what you were doing. But guts were a different matter. He could see that the bleeding was not bad, and the tunic had been helpful in stemming it. But the whole thing was ripe for infection, and somewhere in there, there was obviously a hunk of metal. Lodged against a rib, maybe all the way through to her spine in the back. And it scared him.

"Hill!"

Martin had stuck his head back in the door. When he saw Hill wasn't moving, he came all the way in, standing over the woman and looking down at her and Hill. After he had a good look, he spoke. "We got guys in worse shape than that."

"Yeah, and we got someone looking after them, too. Don't give me that shit. And they'll get to a hospital and get taken care of."

"Well, what're you going to do?"

"I don't know." And he didn't. He didn't have a clue what to do about that wound, and he knew damned well that with a big batch of GI wounded any doctor coming out in the aid choppers wasn't going to take time to look at any Indians. And he knew, too, that after this trap the Military Assistance and Arvin boys would be in taking this village apart by the seams trying to find out everything they could—any *way* they could. That was the way the game was played. You slap my boys, we slap yours.

He looked in the woman's face. She looked drowsy—the morphine —but her dried lips parted in a little smile. He smiled back—vacantly. Baby, you got problems.

Then he did what he had to do. He sprayed the wound with disinfectant powder—and dumped the rest of the aid kit on the floor. Let them do with it what they could. He followed Martin out of the hut.

As they walked back through the village, he figured he'd get Pershing to try to con some medic into taking a look at her. It was all he could goddamned well do.

v

Of the forty support troops, eighteen had been killed outright, and two more died before the first medic chopper arrived. Eight more of them were badly wounded, along with two of Pershing's men. And there were another fifteen or so with wounds of some degree.

There were finally three medic teams working, with their choppers ferrying wounded and dead back and forth to Corps Area Command, before Hill cornered Pershing and tried to get him to pull a medic loose to look at the woman. He knew it was no use before that. Pershing came through with his usual "can do" optimism. But it wasn't justified. The medics were frantically trying to stem every drop of GI blood. They said the Indians would have to wait.

And then it was too late. Two choppers came in with a U.S. MAAG team and a company of Arvin. The U.S. team was full of brass. A couple of bird colonels, three or four light colonels, and a couple of majors. And the Arvin—now the enemy was gone—were spoiling for a fight. The ranking MAAG colonel talked to the ranking medic colonel, and they both shook their heads at the wounded still stacked around—and at the two copters strung out in the jungle. It was boiling hot now, and the sweat ran down their faces as they talked. Then the MAAG colonel turned away and signaled the Arvin into the village. Poor fucking Indians, Hill thought.

2

i

Once they'd figured it out, figured that maybe a traitor had been behind the whole trap, Pershing had reported it to the CO, and the Intelligence boys wouldn't let it drop. About every second day some new piece of brass would fly up from Regiment or even Corps. And Pershing would tell it all over again. They didn't pull any missions the whole time. Just grew fat lazing in the sun. Nobody pushed them, and if it hadn't been for old Pershing practicing the commandments as laid down by the Chief of Staff and his college of cardinals, they'd have got right out of condition.

But Pershing made them train maybe an hour every morning and play soccer or basketball for a couple of hours every afternoon—in that muggy goddamned heat. It kept you from eating too heavy. But Hill enjoyed it. It was all counting toward his combat stretch, and playing basketball against Janowitz every day, he was getting so he could just about make the cunt work up a sweat. The big Yid'd still score twenty-five points for every five of Hill's and laugh his balls off most of the time doing it, but Hill knew he was getting better and learning, and next to screwing he felt maybe he liked basketball best of all.

Then they got the word. A ranker was flying in from Saigon. Jesus, Hill laughed, if they played their cards right, maybe they could draw somebody from Washington. It was an ordinary chopper that brought him in, but the minute he stepped from the deck Hill knew there wasn't much ordinary about him. He was a bird colonel—and black. He had the usual chestful of medals—colonels are always giving each other medals—para's wings, and he wore a green beret.

They all were lined up at attention with Pershing just behind the CO so Hill couldn't see his reaction, but he couldn't help smiling. Hill was black, Pershing was black—so somebody Up There said, "Look, these spades aren't to be trusted. They're pulling our leg. The only way we'll get the truth is send one of their own down." He almost laughed out loud.

They met in the CO's hut—just the three of them. Even Miller wasn't there. So Hill figured he was right—it takes a spade to catch a spade—and he was grinning from ear to ear even as the colonel turned around, all starchy and man to man to take their salute.

"Something funny, soldier?"

"No, *sir!*" Hill half laughed saying it. He knew that in the circumstances he could get away with a lot, but he'd better not push it. He lifted his eyes to the wall beyond. He'd never have kept a straight face staring this guy in the eyes.

The colonel returned the salute and gestured that they sit down on the CO's cot. He plunked himself in the chair and held out a pack of smokes. Hill shook his head, the grin breaking out irrepressibly again. He knew the guy was trying to get the measure of them—and play the role himself. And the more he tried, the more it made Hill want to laugh.

The colonel was right shaken by it. So he tried to play it tough. Straight from the hip. No nonsense. Cowboys and Indians.

"All right. Suppose you tell me exactly what happened."

Pershing told him how they had circled the village. How he'd placed the men and then someone—a GI—had come along just before dawn and told all the troops on the one side of the stream that he, Pershing, wanted them all on the other side. So all our men there had moved off, and the VC had had that side of the stream all to themselves. When they whipped out the AA gun, there was no one to bother them— and the same applied when they set up the mortar barrage. And double when it came to making their getaway. We didn't have anybody near them.

The colonel had obviously heard all this before, but the telling of it again had sobered Hill, and when the colonel turned to him, he was thinking as seriously about it as they were.

"And *you* saw the GI?"

"No, sir. I *think* I saw a GI. I had just crossed the river and was holed up in the foxhole I'd dug during the night. It was after the AA gun had knocked out the gunship, and I was in a bit of a fire fight. When I let go this time, a stream of VC were coming out of the center hut on that side of the river, running to the woods. And one of them *looked* like a GI."

"How do you mean? Was he in uniform?"

"Yeah. I mean, yes, sir. He was in camouflaged fatigues. But lots of

40

Charlies wear them now. The thing is he was taller, and he was tanned, but I think he was white. And, you know, he sort of moved like a GI."

"*Hmm.*" The colonel was looking at Hill, close. His whole attitude reflected his suspicion that the story might be nothing more than a gigantic con by a couple of darktown cowards. And it pissed Hill off. Where it was funny before, he was now getting irritated. He wondered where this prick had come from. Harvard? Put a few black boys in on scholarships. Cleans up the image. "Course if he was *colored,* I'd have known right off he was a GI—or a black power boy who'd sold out to the yellows."

The colonel looked at him sharply. And Hill stared right back. Don't push me, baby. I'd take a razor to you as quick as to anyone else.

"But you also saw him when he told you Sergeant Pershing wanted you to move across the river."

"That's right. But so did all the other guys on that side. Why don't you have those cats in here for questioning?"

"I'm not questioning anyone. We just want to find out what happened."

"I see, sir. And you figure two colored guys are the only ones who'll tell the truth, is that it?"

"No, that isn't it!" The colonel had fire in his eyes. He was used to being sucked up to, Hill could tell that. He looked tough but sort of upper-class elegant. A good white man's nigger. Not as handsome as Pershing, but whiter—and not quite so potent-looking.

"You're here because you saw him. And Sergeant Pershing is here because he was in charge. Does that sound like a conspiracy to you?"

"Yes, sir." Hill stared at him flat, not reacting at all to the colonel's evident surprise. He was damned if he was going to pretend just to please the bastard.

The colonel sighed—and studied Hill again. Hill could see the wheels turning. His next line would be, now look, men, I'm going to be frank with you. Instead, he smiled.

"Yeah. There has been just the suspicion that maybe you boys didn't want to get in the way of any retreating VC." He looked at them closely, still smiling. "But don't get hung up about it. Most of them believe you. It's just such a frightening idea that if there's any chance at all that it might *not* be true, they want to chase it up. That's why I'm here."

"We've been in the way of VC going both ways—plenty of times," Pershing said stiffly. He was a proud man, and Hill realized by his tone of voice that this was the first time he had really understood what was behind headquarters' sending a spade colonel down to them.

"I know," the colonel said, "and believe me no one has knocked you or your record. Please take that from me straight."

"Even if Hill saw a white soldier, and he spoke English with an American accent *and* could whistle 'One of these days,' that doesn't mean he was a GI," Pershing said quietly. "There are a lot of French colons here who can pull off an American accent, and they whistle American songs as much as we do."

The colonel looked at him intently. Hill smiled. The old Harvard graduate didn't know what he had on his hands when he started crossing wits with his li'l ole sergeant major. It was amazing how bars, leaves, or eagles on a guy's shoulder convinced him he was a breed apart from those without them.

"That had occurred to us, of course," the colonel said. Hill could tell he was lying. All that fucking brass down there in Corps and Saigon. He could see it now. The report came through that a GI was spotted in a VC outfit, and they just took it at face value. Press the panic button and pray to God it wasn't true. He laughed out loud. The colonel stared at him irritatedly.

"But you did report you thought you'd seen a GI," he said. "It's stated that in all the reports."

"That's what I said, Colonel. But I'm just a dumb enlisted man. I leave the thinking to the officers."

"And why do you think you said it looked like a GI if it might have been a Frenchman?" the colonel retorted.

"Well, I thought it *did* look like a GI; it was only your insulting Sergeant Pershing here that threw up the possibility it might be a Frenchman."

The colonel held his temper—with effort—and went on. "When he told you to go to the other side of the river, did he use Sergeant Pershing's name?"

"No, sir. At least I don't think so. As I remember it, he just said, 'He wants us on the other side.' "

"And that was enough for you to go?" the colonel asked sarcastically.

"Yes, sir," Hill admitted. "You see, sir, unlike all you officers in Saigon, I wasn't expecting a GI in a VC outfit."

Pershing smiled. The colonel glared.

"Hill also reported that the man did the basic training crawl"—

42

Pershing offered this as a peace token—"and that contributed to the feeling he was a GI. But of course, the basic training crawl is common to most armies, and a Frenchman with military training is just as liable to use it as anyone."

The colonel was getting another lesson. But Pershing did it with great respect, as if he were only saying something the colonel knew all along. And the colonel liked it.

"And no one saw him in daylight besides Hill?"

"No, sir. At night, when he went from position to position, he stayed low and the ground was thick with mist. Hill and one of the other men reported they thought he was Martin—one of our men who's of average build, about five feet ten. But in the predawn fog, no one could really tell."

The colonel grinned thoughtfully at Pershing—grateful the sarge had taken him off the hook and impressed at the same time. Hill knew Pershing had made another conquest. Another hunk of brass he could call his own if the occasion ever demanded.

"Well I'm very grateful to you, Sergeant," and then with real effort, "and you, too, Hill. It sounds like a clever Frenchman tied up with that North Vietnamese AA team. We'll have to keep an eye out for them."

"Yes, sir," Pershing said, saluting neatly. He recognized the signs of the interview being over. Hill saluted perfunctorily.

"Nice of you to talk to us, Colonel." He could have bitten his fucking tongue off even as he said it, but he couldn't resist it.

"Not at all, Hill. I hope we meet again." Oh, threats yet! Hill thought. He didn't make colonel *just* on the basis of his color.

"Pleasure," Hill answered, and got out of there quick before he hung himself anymore.

ii

It took about ten days for the whole story to filter down to them. It developed that what had really unnerved the brass was not just the fact that there might be a GI working with the VC, but that the MAAG light colonel who had come in as an adviser with the Arvin was a hot-shot just arrived from the Defense Department with the latest win-the-hearts-and-minds operation flaming brightly in his little head. They had another plan to teach the Arvin how to beat the VC at their own

43

game. And what burned them was that the VC apparently knew he was coming to this village, and since his body had not been found, old Charlie probably had him alive someplace, getting all the latest psych war strategy before it had even begun to go in operation.

As a great red, white, and blue—and brown—patriot, Hill didn't figure they'd lost much, because he didn't think there was one cotton-pickin' chance in a million to teach the Arvin how to beat the VC at anything, unless it was running backward. And since the brass had decided that it *was* a Frenchman operating with that North Vietnamese AA outfit and that together they made a pretty lethal team, night encirclements were cut out altogether for a month, and they had fighter cover on every day mission. So he felt real looked after.

In fact, since he didn't know any of the guys who'd got killed, the only honest regret he could feel about the mission was the thought of that woman in the hut. He wondered what the hell had happened to her and whether she was alive or dead. He knew from the grapevine that after the Arvin had finished with the village, Army Intelligence had gone in to get as much info as they could about that VC group. And the kind of guy who gravitated to that job was not likely to be overflowing with the milk of human kindness. Justifying a little honest brutality with a pious I'm-doing-it-to-save-our-guys was just the incentive they needed for service above and beyond the call of duty.

But fuck it, it ain't my problem, Hill would tell himself. But now that there were no night missions, nor even the threat of night missions, the hours from sunset to sunrise stretched drearily. And once darkness fell, the sounds of the jungle and the muted evening rituals of the camp made the warm nights restless.

iii

It was a milk run and came after six days of nothing. Even Hill's common sense had been warped by the boredom of their tiny camp to the point where he had to admit he welcomed the prospect of *some* action—as long as it wasn't *too* ambitious.

They were out to clean up a little village on a tributary of the Yong Sai. Someone in the CIA or the Arvin network had reported that sampans from the village were carting VC supplies downriver at night. The plan was to land in a clearing north of the river, take a few prisoners, burn a few sampans, and get the hell out. Since it was daytime and they

44

were going to be supported by a gunship and a flight of jets, it was about as dangerous as walking down Thirty-eighth Street in Philly on a broad sunlit day—maybe not so dangerous. If he played it right, he might get to pat the bottoms of a few juicy squaws—and get his mind right back where it belonged. He'd had his fill of basketball; it was time he zeroed in on number one sport.

Janowitz was flying them. And Hill was riding in the forward cabin with him and Adnapoz. Playing ball together all the time, he and Janowitz had become fairly buddy-buddy. They were usually the two tallest, so he always guarded Janowitz. Not that he bothered the big stud much, but he worked hard and fouled him often, and Janowitz seemed to admire the effort. He never tired of laughing at Hill's awkward, ground-eating leaps about the flat red clay they called their court, and when Big George actually sank one—even if he had put an elbow in Janowitz's gut to do it—Janowitz always seemed as pleased as Hill himself. Course, he'd promptly flick in a couple of his own to show that things weren't getting out of hand, but still, Hill felt the mutual pleasure in their combat and enjoyed the casual camaraderie that had grown up between them.

Janowitz had taken him up on his last proficiency run—and scared the bejesus out of him playing Yo-Yo among some mangrove trees along a river bank. But then they'd spotted a small herd of deer and climbed a bit, chasing them through the forest—watching them leap and separate and come back together again for what must have been three or four miles. Hill liked the fact that Janowitz hadn't gone in low and panicked them, just rode high behind them, keeping them running like some aerial shepherd herding his flock to pasture. When they started to go up in the hills, they had turned back "in case they turn out to be VC deer leading us into a trap," Janowitz had said. Hill liked that, too. The big Yid was all right.

And going back across the rolling light-green, dark-green, blue and yellow-green, misty, shimmering all-green forest, they had not spoken at all. Until at the very end, when Janowitz had let him take the controls to bring it in. Hill had practically bounced them into their graves. He came in faster than he intended, with the back end too low—he always thought the nose was going to touch and overcompensated. They'd smacked down on the shocks and caromed back into the sky at an angle that had paralyzed him with the fear they were going to stall and crash in tail first. And Janowitz didn't exactly cool it either. He'd grabbed the controls and started functioning like a rooster in a henhouse full of foxes. He'd somehow got it level and then brought it slowly down himself. "Man," he'd said, "when you go back to civilian life, may I recommend you take up Ping-pong or even pro basketball before you turn to flying."

"I plan to pimp," Hill had said, "but I promise not to do it from no helicopter."

"I'm relieved," Janowitz had come back without a blink.

And that had been that. Hill was curious about what made Janowitz tick and envied his easy self-assurance almost as much as he envied his skill on the basketball court, but Janowitz was an officer and he was a specialist fifth, and he knew their "friendship" had grown as close as it ever would. They liked each other, and if they'd both been born Yids, or spades, or even officers, they'd have been like brothers, but even this much Hill valued. There was a kind of patronage in Janowitz's attitude to him—and he knew he was smarter than Janowitz ever guessed—but he didn't mind. Part of being smart was realizing it didn't matter. Janowitz saw him as a good-natured, amusing, colored rube. Fine. It didn't make any demands on him, and it didn't deprive him of anything—not out there in the highlands.

They followed the river most of the way, shortcutting across its bends and twists, but staying in the broad sweep of valley it and time had cut through the low hills. In the sunlight it glistened like some blue watery ribbon in a Technicolor travelogue of Florida—with thick cumulus clouds, white and puffy, standing in the wings for special effects. Up front, where you could see it all happening, Hill didn't mind the swaying and gut-dropping lurches so much. And if Janowitz hadn't got such pleasure out of flirting with treetops and hillsides, it would have been all sugar.

Adnapoz was map reading, and at last he signaled they were near and gave Janowitz a heading. They cut out across the forest and hills, and it was only two or three minutes before they were coming at the river again.

They all strained to spot the village. Adnapoz saw it first, off to the left, and Janowitz tipped the chopper sickeningly and glided in toward it as if he enjoyed functioning at a forty-five-degree angle. Hill had to catch himself from lurching right into the window and, as it felt, the forest below. He got his balance in time to see the houses spread in line along the river. One-storied, settled among the trees, with sailboats and sampans moored around bamboo pilings, a couple of fishermen midstream, kids and some women just off shore, man, it looked like a resort. Honeymooners and bosses screwing secretaries specially welcomed. Reduced rates Tuesday to Friday.

46

Janowitz had spotted the clearing in the woods a couple of hundred yards from the village and was actually bringing it in gently. They were drying coconuts in the field, making copra, and there were maybe twenty villagers staring up at them. Mostly women, but several men. They didn't run, just backed away toward the edge of the clearing.

The chopper rocked, like a boat washed by waves, and immediately Hill heard a crack. It was the jet squadron. They'd been riding way above them, though he hadn't seen them, and now they came roaring down to buzz the village. It was timed perfectly. The villagers would know they didn't have a chance in hell if they kicked up any trouble. He smiled as the jets rose and turned.

"Bastards!" Janowitz muttered. He hadn't liked their wash—spoiled his landing—so he lifted the chopper a bit and went in again. He turned it in a complete circle, about six feet off the ground, so they got a good look at the whole scene.

About half the Indians around the clearing carried those machete knives they use for splitting coconuts. Funny how sexy a woman looks carrying a machete knife, Hill thought. Must ask a psychiatrist about that someday. No doubt about it, it gave a nice little charge. The men were light brown, not as yellow as in the delta. It must be one of the subtribes. He'd learned some of them—Khmer, Meo, Nunc—not that he could tell the difference, just that they were tribes and different from the delta people. They all looked young, men and women, and handsome. God, there were times he hated his own skin. Black is beautiful—yeah. Black-spotted hide leather. Well, maybe not that bad, but when he saw one of these honey-skinned bastards with their soft, smooth skins, it made his blood simmer. The big genetic numbers racket—and your lucky draw. Fuck. When he was down in Saigon, it didn't seem to bother the dollies—but it bothered *him*.

Now that they had stopped moving forward and no air was coming in the vents, the glass cabin was getting hot as hell. When Janowitz inched it all the way in, they got a glimpse of the gunship cruising above the treetops down along the river. These cats were covered. Man, the sweat running down him, those little dollies out there with their machetes—too bad they weren't Arvin and could have a little rape session. It sounded good, awful good. If the Army knew what it was doing, it'd send him back to Saigon soon before little willie got out of control.

Then the first man broke from the back end. Hill grimaced. It was the lieutenant they'd put in charge. Richard Morris. Fresh from college, officer training, and Philippine staging area. An ignorant, ignorant bastard, and not long for this world, Hill judged. Pershing followed him out, dutiful even to a pimply-faced prick like that if he wore bars. The rest followed and fanned to an arrowhead, moving to the side of the clearing closest to the village and river. The Indians just stood there staring.

Hill tapped Janowitz adios on the shoulder and pushed through to the main cabin. He knew if he delayed too long, Pershing would have his ass. Martin was on the M-60 mounted in the chopper's barn doors. Hill scoffed. He knew Martin was as eager to get in that village as he was. Martin shrugged blithely, accepting being stuck instead in a hot-oven helicopter as another of life's absurd little jokes. The bastard'll die laughing, Hill thought.

Hill looked out at the clearing. The idling rotors were stirring some dust, but he could see the guys were already in the little stretch of woods between the clearing and the village. Miller had three guys, and they were rounding up the Indians around the clearing. That's for me, Hill thought. Pick out a ripe one to move along into the village. Miller already had them migrating in that direction.

"You'd better get moving; he's going to lift this thing," Martin said. The chopper was going to hover during the operation, but Hill knew Janowitz wasn't going to lift while he was still aboard. And like any honest civilian GI, he was savoring every second of freedom. Once he joined Miller or Pershing, he was one of the detail, under orders. It was subtle, but always there. You couldn't disagree with the sarge and say, "Piss off, I don't want to search that house, I want to search this one, or I just want to stand here and look at the river." If there was anything that convinced him he never wanted to be a Communist, it was that one little feeling in the Army. Man, no matter how you worked it, to *have* to take orders even from the sweetest, coolest cat in the world and not be free to quit or walk out or move someplace else was the end. And for the moment he enjoyed the freedom of standing there, cut off from the others, watching them, just feeling the breeze from the river and the whirling rotors—as an outsider. A free man.

Miller got the bunch around the clearing in one group and had them toss their machetes in a pile. Then he separated the men and the women. He and someone, looked like little Arnie Russell, took the men and started moseying them through the trees toward the village, and the other two guys took the women. That's for me, Hill leered, and was about to jump down when one of the guys started double-timing toward the chopper from the other side of the clearing. He was coming

48

hard, as if there were trouble. Oh, shit, Hill thought. Come on now, this is supposed to be a picnic; let's not hit the panic button. Must be that silly-ass lieutenant. He's seen a shadow and wants to make this a real live military operation.

The guy didn't lift his head from the run until he was right at the chopper. And when he did, it wasn't a face Hill recognized. The guy had his M-16 at port, and as he stood there in the little whirl of dust, he raised the gun right at Martin.

"Move away from that machine gun." Hill's heart flipped—and started bouncing like an engine out of sync. The guy looked scared and trigger-happy. Recognition swept Hill instantly. It was the guy at the village—the guy working with the VC. Martin was in firing position at the machine gun, but the guy had come in on the side of him, so Martin would have to swing the barrel to get him, and Hill had put his own M-16 over his shoulder to jump down. So he had them both. Martin just smiled—as usual.

"Don't get excited, Mac, I'm *supposed* to be on the machine gun," he said. Jesus, Hill thought, idiots are made, not born!

"Get back. I haven't got time to argue." It was weird. The guy was a GI, and a frightened one. He sounded normal, but what he was saying was not normal. Martin shrugged and leaned back. The guy raised his gun, and Hill saw a thick, heavyset get with a big paunch run toward them from the same place the first guy had come from. He was not one of their guys, Hill knew, but he was wearing GI fatigues and helmet and kept his head down as he moved.

Hill wondered if Janowitz would spot that it wasn't one of their outfit. Probably not. He'd ferried the whole camp at one time or another, and personnel were always changing. The first guy had motioned them back in the chopper. When the big one came, the first one signaled him for a boost, and the big one shoved him up. Hill saw that the big one was a VC. First really fat one he'd ever seen. He was built more like a Japanese judo wrestler than a VC, but he didn't look Japanese. He had Charlie's eyes and golden, honey skin, broad nose, and full mouth. But he looked fierce—two hundred and twenty pounds of trouble.

The GI one covered Hill and Martin while the big one scrambled up. He wasn't more than halfway there when Adnapoz shoved his nose into the cabin.

"Hill, get the hell out of—"

"Move! In here, quick!" It was the GI. He had his gun on Adnapoz. Adnapoz just stared at him for a second, then at the fat VC, and started to slam the door. The VC let go at him right from the floor, and the burst shattered the door, ricocheted off it, pierced it—and clobbered Adnapoz. The round seemed to go on forever. Hill jumped at the VC, but the guy moved like a panther. His foot caught Hill in the chest, tripped him, and when Hill thudded down on the floor, the VC was on his feet with his gun looking right down Hill's throat. I'm dead! Dead! Why the fuck did I have to be a hero? Hill waited four lifetimes. The shot never came. The fat VC backed away, keeping him covered—and Martin. Hill could see that the GI had run up toward the cockpit and had his gun on Janowitz. What the hell did they want. The chopper?

"Get up! Come on!" the GI was signaling Janowitz out. Janowitz just looked at him. "Come on!" The GI was getting more nervous, but Janowitz just stared at him. Then the radio crackled. When they'd landed, Janowitz had shoved his earphones down around his neck and turned up the volume. Hill could hear it even over the noise of the slowly turning rotor.

"Red Three, Red Three, this is Victor One. What the hell's going on down there, Hank?"

Janowitz just kept staring at the GI, and Hill could see the GI was shaken. He signaled hard with his rifle. "Come on, *out!*" Janowitz only leaned back, his eyes flat, cold, angry. The VC moved up across from the GI and said something in French. The GI nodded, and the VC pivoted and slammed the butt of his rifle across the side of Janowitz's head.

"Red Three, Red Three. This is Victor One. Hank, can you read me? Hank, report in. Over."

The GI shoved open the door, pushing Janowitz's crumpled frame against the window. Hill could see Adnapoz's body knifed awkwardly between his seat and the window. The bullets had ripped hell out of him. The GI fumbled with getting the bar mike loose from Janowitz and then slapped it over his own head. He wheeled, searching for the radio control, finally spotted it, and flicked the switch.

"Victor One, Victor One. This is, ah, Red Three. Hank here. We're having a little trouble with our compressor. Over."

He flicked the control switch again and waited tensely. The fat VC had turned to cover Hill and Martin, but he was listening, too.

"Red Three, this is Victor One. All right, Hank, but don't fart around with a goddamned compressor down there. Lift that thing to your position and let Adnapoz handle it."

The fat VC was listening to the radio, and the GI was facing the

50

wrong end. Martin lunged at the M-6o. It was a good chance, and Hill rolled out of the firing line. Later, when he thought about it, he knew that was what killed Martin. Because the VC turned the instant he moved, and he was firing while he swung. Martin's hand never reached the trigger. The VC moved three steps down the cabin firing the whole time, and Martin's forward movement was stopped; then he twisted and finally toppled sideways.

"I don't trust these damn VC, and I don't believe in taking unnecessary chances. If you can't fix it, just cut it out. Losing a compressor isn't the end of the goddamned world. Over."

The firing had stopped. Martin lay limp. The GI looked as shaken as Hill. He slowly flicked the radio control. "Roger. Wilco. Over and out." He took a long breath, then signaled toward Janowitz, and the fat VC threw his rifle over his shoulder and reached in the cabin and dragged Janowitz out. The GI pointed his gun at Hill and gestured him out of the chopper. Hill didn't need a second invitation.

They waited at the door, the GI nervously watching Hill and the woods in the direction of the village. But they couldn't see any of the unit. They were obviously all the way into the village by now. Hill glanced at Martin. Hill had been wrong: Martin hadn't died laughing. His face was frozen in that look of pain and surprise Hill had seen so often on the dead. The VC dragged Janowitz by his feet to the door, then jumped down and wrapped the big John across his shoulders. Janowitz was six four, and this guy wasn't more than five ten on his tiptoes. It looked ridiculous, but he was a bull and moved across the clearing without staggering, with Hill right behind him and the GI covering him from the rear.

When they got to the woods, about twenty VC appeared from nowhere. Half of them looked about fourteen, and the one who was obviously the leader couldn't have been more than twenty-one. They bound Hill's hands and arms with leather thongs and did the same to Janowitz, who was stirring a bit but still out. The fat VC had dumped him on the ground and gone into a huddle with the leader and the GI. Hill thought of trying to make a run for it, but a VC doll in a thick black tunic and those funny-looking pants came through the underbrush, put her rifle down, and knelt over Janowitz, washing his head with a gauze cloth. Hill didn't even see where she'd come from, but he figured it meant they were being watched. He wasn't running against those odds.

The GI and the young leader seemed confused about something. They kept looking from the chopper to the village and then to the woods behind them. The porky VC said something and laughed. Neither of the other two appreciated the joke. Finally, the leader signaled toward the woods away from the village, and a VC grabbed Hill's arm and shoved him along in that direction. They moved him so fast he didn't get a chance to see what they were doing with Janowitz, but he hadn't gone twenty yards into the undergrowth when he heard the gunship coming in. It scared the piss out of him. And the VC, too.

The whole line stopped moving. Hill looked back and saw three of them were carrying Janowitz, and he saw the GI run to the leader and start yakking excitedly. Through the treetops he could see the gunship coming down over the clearing—almost as though it were going to land on Janowitz's chopper. He could imagine the reaction when they spotted Adnapoz sprawled in the cabin.

The leader nodded to the GI and quickly motioned the group back toward the village. They moved double time with the little fart assigned to Hill jabbing him with his rifle all the way. Hill found it disturbingly hard to run with his hands tied behind his back, and the shoves from behind didn't help. He didn't know what these bastards had in mind, but he didn't see anything they had that could touch that armored gunship, and with the jets still in reserve and Pershing up front, he knew they had one chance in hell in getting out of there without being fried—and him, too, unless he made a break. But how? If he waited until the firing started, it might be too late. If he broke before, he'd be dead as a nigger on a tree. One fucking trouble with war—mistime by three seconds and, daddy, you'll never mistime again.

The underbrush started to thin near the village. He could see people moving around, and near the river some were running. He heard Miller's voice bellowing. The guy could be heard over five counties when he let go. Hill guessed the gunship had radioed down that something was up; Miller'd got the message and was moving. The VC fanned out but were still going fast toward the downstream side of the village. Hill couldn't figure it but guessed maybe they were going to try to lose themselves among the villagers. Crazy. No man from fourteen to sixty-four in this village was going anyplace but a prison camp.

Then the firing started. Hill never saw where it came from or what was hit, but he heard the shots and some screams, and then his little VC knocked him between the shoulder blades and tripped him. He went flat on his face. He turned his head as he went in but still smacked it on a root, and his ear felt as if it had been ripped off. In seconds

52

he could feel the blood streaming down. He swore if he lived he'd cut that little fucker's balls off.

It wasn't a heavy fire fight. Just bursts and shouts—the usual goddamned confusion. What terrified him was the thought that Pershing could be calling those jets in any second and they'd lay napalm along the line of the woods—and there he was flat on his ass, waiting for it.

He heard the gunship let go with a salvo, but it seemed far on the other side of the village, upstream. Then he heard the jets coming down. He was going to run for it. Goddamned if he was going to be burned alive! He hunched up and swiveled, but his little VC slammed him down. The planes came in, louder than all the firing, shouting, anything. He closed his eyes, heard them lift, and then the explosions. A second. He was still alive. He pivoted to look.

It wasn't napalm, and it was on the river. John Andrew Pershing was thinking, man! He didn't know what was going on in the woods, but he knew he could cut off any threat from the river by having the jets take out the sampans. Bastard should have been a general! And the jets had really nailed the stuff. Wood, bamboo, and water flying all over the place.

The little VC poked him and motioned him to run forward toward the river. Hill shook his head no. The VC jabbed him hard with the nozzle of his gun, but Hill still wouldn't move. The little bastard reached for a knife—fast, and like for real. And Hill wiggled up and, crouching as low as he could, ran. He could see others moving with him and he heard a big burst of gunfire, but nothing came near him. He was almost at one of the huts on the edge of the village when the little VC shoved him hard from behind again, and he nosed in. Sonuvabitch, he'd like to get his hands on that cunt.

The planes were coming in again. Only they were behind him—over the woods. He saw a couple of rockets go in and then the red and yellow balls of napalm flash through the jungle. Again old Pershing was thinking. He'd got one flank settled; now he was covering the other. But the VC had outsmarted him. If they'd stayed in the woods, some of that stuff might have got them. But he could see now what they were doing—getting in tight to the GI's in the village to nullify the advantage of the jets and the gunship. He wondered if they'd use him and Janowitz as shields.

He turned just in time to see a whole line of GI's run from a wooden shed by the river to a long house near the center of the village that

53

looked as if it were made of concrete bricks. Somebody was giving it to them all the way in, and one of the guys got hit just before he made it, but two others turned back and hauled him in. They'd be hard to move from there. What the hell did these VC think they were going to do?

Two of the jets were coming in again, this time perpendicular to the river. They seemed to be right on top of him, and without thinking, he pushed himself up to run. The little VC thudded him down with his rifle butt—and the jets swept over. More napalm. He was so close he could feel the rush of heat. It was just on his left—farther downstream. And this time it wasn't wasted. When the flash cleared, he saw it'd run right over two VC, who were just lying there burning along with the bushes and grass. Another thin one was running for the river, his whole back and head roaring with orange and white flame. He staggered and fell, got up again, ran a couple of steps and just sort of folded, leaning to the river—it wasn't three yards from him—then crumbled. Hill had never seen it that close. He closed his eyes, not even aware of the fighting for a second. Man, there must be an easier way to make a living.

Finally, Hill rolled over. The two jets came back, a little farther out this time. They were sealing off the village. Pershing really had this thing cooled. He knew that shittin' lieutenant wasn't smart enough or experienced enough to handle it like that, and if Pershing could concentrate a defense in that concrete house, the VC would rue the day they ever gave up fishing. What worried Hill was their reluctance to surrender. He wanted no part of a battle to the death—not when he was with the Indians.

He wormed up to glance at the concrete house. And it happened. He couldn't count them, but it must have been five mortar blasts—all zeroed right in on it. The bamboo roof went, a hunk of one wall blew, the whole place exploded. And before the dust settled, VC came from everywhere—like rats from a sewer. Some of them were obviously villagers, some the bunch that took him, but they swarmed all over the place. He knew the guys inside wouldn't have time to look up from the debris before they had them.

He heard another mortar barrage. Christ, they were in it. To the shoulder blades. A VC suddenly darted at them and shouted a bunch of bullshit to his little bastard, and the guy jabbed Hill again and nodded his head back toward the woods.

Hill didn't know what the hell to do. There was gunfire and more mortar explosions all around, but he couldn't tell where anybody

54

was. He hunched up to stand and, when he had his balance, pivoted and kicked. It was meant for business, but the guard twisted and caught it on the hipbone. It still sent him sprawling. But it also toppled Hill, and he landed on his back, on his bound arms. Pain lanced through him. The little guard scrambled up in a second and was all over Hill, jabbing him again and again with the muzzle of his gun. Hill thought every jab was going to break a rib and prayed to God someone would shoot the bastard while he was standing. But the prick finally got it out of his system and stopped long enough to signal Hill to his feet.

Hill moved along as fast and low as he could—and kept getting repeated jabs with the little VC's rifle for encouragement. This guy really bears a grudge, Hill thought. Much as it infuriated him, his real concern was with the jets and all that loose fire.

As they ran past the clearing where they'd landed, Hill saw two of the jets dive in toward the village again. Safe this round, he figured, and the deeper he got in the woods, the safer he knew he was. But all the time one corner of his mind was nagging at him: The farther you get from the village, the farther you get from release, baby. But watching that VC fry had more or less convinced him he should take one problem at a time.

The land started to rise about three hundred yards from the river, and he had begun to get really winded by the time they were a little way up the first hill. The VC jabbed him again. And he forced himself on, though slower now. He saw movement on his right, and he was suddenly looking at a line of about eight VC right in front of him. He stopped, and his VC panted up behind him. He said something to the others, and they all looked down at the village.

Some of the huts were burning; debris was floating down the river; the gunship was going right along the shore, laying into the whole place. Hill wondered where the hell all the villagers were. The jets were circling and peeling off, bombing along a line that ran diagonally out the other corner of the village. The forest lit up from the explosions, but Hill couldn't spot any gunfire except from the planes and the gunship.

The VC just stood there watching and talking for a couple of minutes. It really grabbed Hill. He'd been in a lot of battles, big ones, small ones, day and night ones, but never once had he stood and just watched one—never even been in a position where he could see the whole thing. In fact, he didn't think he'd ever been in an action where he knew what had happened until it was all over. Course, he didn't know what was going on in this one either, but he had a helluva view. He wondered about papa Pershing. Jesus, even that first mortar blast must have cut somebody down.

Finally, one of the VC said something loud and motioned Hill on. The guy actually smiled doing it, and Hill wondered what the hell he was so happy about. But it was a friendly smile, and he was in no position to be choosy. He nodded and started to move.

The VC walked aimlessly along with him, no one in particular watching him. They all were so damned small, Hill figured if he had his hands free, he could take them all at one go. He knew they were deceptive that way—wiry bastards and good at fighting with their feet in a way no American ever mastered—but he still figured he could lick the lot in a rumble.

They walked up to the crest of the first hill and down into the next little valley. Once they were below the hilltop, it was almost impossible to hear the sounds of the fighting in the village. The underbrush was thin—just tall grass with an occasional bush—but the cover up top was so thick it was almost cool in there. Christ, Hill thought, we could be a million miles from fighting.

They were climbing the next hill, the bombing audible again—but sounding remote, and no one saying anything, Hill thinking about Pershing, about breaking loose, when the VC who had smiled at him touched his arm and indicated off to their right. Hill went as directed. He knew the time to break was now, while the battle was still on and things were confused, but with his arms bound he couldn't run fast, and the VC kept bunched so that a clear break wasn't possible.

There was a big cluster of bush just ahead, and when Hill started to move around it, his little VC took his arm and moved him right up to it. He was almost in the stuff before he saw the cave mouth. It had looked like a shadow, but it was about four feet across and almost as high. A couple of the VC crawled in before him; then he got a shove and crouched to get in himself. The grinning VC pulled him back and cut the thong around his arms. Hill rubbed the bindings and felt the prickling as his circulation returned. He thought fleetingly of breaking for it then, but he got another shove from his VC, and the three men behind him were five or six feet too far away to be bowled over. He went with the shove and crawled into the cave.

3

The cave wasn't very big, and when Hill had cleared the entrance, he knocked his head on the ceiling, trying to stand erect. At first he couldn't get used to the darkness, and the only thing he could make out were two kerosene lamps burning in the distance and the shadows passing before them. He was led farther in and pulled down to a sitting position. Someone grabbed his arms and started binding them again. By the time they'd finished, Hill's eyes were adjusted enough to make out that it was his smiling VC friend. Some friend.

"Hi, Joe," the joker said brightly.

"Hi, Sam," Hill said back. Couldn't resist it. Just killed a few of your boys back there. Did ya now? I just killed a few of yours. Oh, yeah, that's a coincidence. Say, what'dya think of the White Sox? They've really fallen off, haven't they? Yeah, they sure have. See ya. Yeah, see ya. If Martin were alive, he'd have been smirking like the back end of a jackass—only trouble was Martin wasn't alive.

The grinning wonder left Hill without trying to figure out what "Hi, Sam" meant, and Hill could tell he really didn't understand what "Hi, Joe" meant either. Hill squinted to try to see what was in the cave, and his mind suddenly flooded with thoughts of the POW indoctrination they got in Oklahoma. The grinner had started it, he realized. They always said in camp that one of the Commies' standard psychological ploys was to greet you with the big brotherly-love bit. "Welcome, soldier, to the Democratic Republic of North Korea and freedom from the Wall Street warmongers" had been one of the favorite pitches in the Korean War—at least that's what they had told them. And they kept glad-handing you, until you refused to make a propaganda broadcast or something; then you could change overnight from a comrade-soldier to a Wall Street warmonger yourself, with all the delights that held in store.

He'd hated the fucking POW indoctrination and the sadistic bastards who did it. They'd smiled and simpered, and pounded the shit out of

57

him, hung him upside down by his ankles, doused him in ice water, imprisoned him in a slatwood box until he and the box were covered with shit and piss and puke. He'd gone three days without sleep, and they'd given him his own Pop art light show with psychedelic side effects provided by a few well-placed clouts on the head and a screaming stereo loudspeaker that goosed his nerve ends every time exhaustion seemed likely to make him a dropout before the show was over.

To him it had proved nothing. If that's what the Commies were going to do, he didn't need it done twice. And some moron screaming at him that he was going to kill him if he didn't tell him more than name, rank, and serial number, when he knew goddamned well he was in Oklahoma and the monkey in yellow paint was a master sergeant on permanent detail, didn't send him either.

The idea of being brainwashed scared him. He'd seen this one show at a camp in New Jersey, how they made everyone rat on one another—group criticism they called it—until everyone was playing you-tell-on-me, Jack, and-I'll-tell-on-you. Starts out simple, making you say things like Harris didn't clean his canteen cup this morning. Just to go along, just to say something. Then the other guy says something back about you, and it keeps getting more and more serious, until in a few weeks everyone is hating everyone, you can't trust your best buddy not to rat on even the smallest things. And they top it off by holding back your mail and giving you U.S. newspapers that only show you how bad things are at home and make you think everyone has forgotten the war, until pretty soon you're feeling the only ones you can trust or believe in are the Commies themselves. It sounded asinine, but he remembered how real it had come across.

So the rule was: Don't talk; don't take part in classes; give only your name, rank, and serial number. Your country was degraded by what happened to prisoners in Korea; don't let it happen to you. Well, screw that. Fight he would, resist he would, but he had no intention of being a martyr for the little white churches of New England or the glories of American democratic suburbia. This was *one* time when he felt it was an advantage to be black. These guys figured he was one of the oppressed. Well, let 'em. He'd drink their tea, eat their cookies, screw their women all they wanted him to. He'd resist the damned group criticisms, and he wasn't signing any documents—mostly because he knew they didn't kill you for not signing, and he wanted to go home with a clean record. But he felt he was on his own, and those bastards in Oklahoma had no more idea what was going to happen

58

to him than he did. The best thing he could do was to break for it when there was the first glimmer of a chance.

But there was no chance in the cave. As his eyes got used to the dark, he could see it had two small entrances. One was made by a small underground stream. From the cut it had made in the floor he figured it flooded pretty heavily during the monsoons. Its outlet was a long, thin crack from which the light outside was plainly visible. It opened at the bottom into a V big enough for a man to slip through. The entrance he had come in was to one side of that and he guessed had been blasted out of the rock. From the uneven height and contour of the ceiling he figured they'd done a lot of blasting to make the original cave bigger. Even so, the whole thing was only about the size of a Quonset hut.

Against one wall near one of the kerosene lamps he could see three dollies in black tunics with funny black hats—Garbo types with narrower brims—setting out medicine and bandages. They had half a dozen or so straw mats stretched out on the floor by them, and as his eyes got more and more used to the light, he could see the medicines and gauze were all GI stuff. He could even read the big stamp on one wooden box: CAUTION MEDICAL SUPPLIES FOR VIETNAM. HANDLE WITH CARE. UPJOHN BROTHERS, INC., KALAMAZOO, MICHIGAN. Sonuvabitch.

There were at least twenty VC in the cave. Bunched in three groups. One near the entrance he came in, they were the lot that brought him. Another leaning against the wall across from him. There might have been twelve or so in that bunch, and they didn't speak among themselves at all. Some stared at him, some at the nurses. He figured if anybody looked brainwashed, they did. Then by the other kerosene lamp two guys were squatting on the floor. They had a map in front of them, and they seemed to be talking about that, but they kept glancing at Hill and seemed to be talking about him, too. From Hill's point of view it looked as if they weren't too pleased. One was little, and the ugliest Vietnamese Hill had ever seen, with pitted skin and carbuncles.

With his breath back, his eyes functioning in the dark, and the tension of the battle gone, Hill's mind began to fill with questions. Will they torture me? Will they kill me if I don't play along, where do I go from here—and for how long? Christ, they keep saying it might be a ten-, twenty-year war. I'll be a damned old man before I get out. Ten years in a moldy prison camp. Rain and rice and swamp rats.

And malaria and dysentery and TB, too—without doctors or nice clean sheets or even a warm bed. Jesus. Think of all the back pay, baby, and don't get down. That came from the POW indoctrination, too. You'll get depressed, they said. You've got to fight being depressed and feeling sorry for yourself. Yeah, that was it, he'd send up a cheer and sing a chorus of "Hail, hail, the gang's all here." The screwballs! But they were right on one score: He was feeling depressed all right. If he felt like this after five minutes, how depressed would he be if they just took him along, no one talking to him for days and days on end? No mail, no medicine, no nothing. He could see if it got bad enough, he'd kiss Ho's ass at high noon on Hanoi's Main Street to get the hell out.

And then another thought pierced him—all his dollies in Saigon. God, all his plans and scheming. All the work he'd done. All gone to pot. He was ruined, and some bastards were down there living it up right this moment. Jesus, why hadn't he gone in with Pershing; why in hell didn't he break for it back there at the beginning?

He was just getting swamped by it when noises outside the cave distracted him. A couple of VC crawled through the same entrance he had. One was wounded, the other helping. Others followed, tugging through the narrow opening the wounded, carried on hammocks strung on thick bamboo poles. The VC by the entrance helped them over to where the nurses were. There were five wounded altogether, and then—crawling through that goddamned hole—came John Andrew Pershing.

Hill had never felt anything like it. It was as though he'd been trying to breathe underwater and suddenly he'd hit the surface. His whole being revived. He *wasn't* alone. It wasn't him and the Indians. Pershing was alive. Him and the supersarge. They'd do something!

And then it was a string of them. The damned pimply Lieutenant, Morris, and Miller, Arnie Russell, Matthews, Neubacher, Eposito, Czarnecke, York, Merrill. They all had their hands tied behind their backs and had to struggle to get through the entrance, and somehow every awkward move filled Hill's heart with more delight. The stupid, clumsy bastards. He loved them.

And then the GI who had waylaid the chopper climbed in. And after him, Janowitz. Then more VC, with the tough fat one and the leader last.

"Welcome to the cave dwellers' Hilton," Hill whispered to Pershing. He could tell the supersarge's eyes hadn't adjusted to the dark yet, but he knew his voice was enough.

"Well, at least you're not dead." Pershing didn't exactly sound over-joyed. "How many are with you?"

"Just me and the Indians, Sarge."

The VC who was sitting over the map—not the ugly one, the lean one—got up and started herding all the rest of the Americans over by Hill.

"This way! Get over there!" He had a French accent like a lot of Vietnamese who could speak English. Weird. They'd say "been" like an Englishman, *bee-n*. "This" like a Frenchman, *thees*. And "okay" like an American. This guy must have been an officer of some kind because when he started shoving, the others started shoving, too, until all the GI's were huddled in a tight circle. Hill had to stand to keep from getting trampled.

"Can you see Morris?" Pershing asked in a whisper. "He's wounded. So is Neubacher, but I don't think it's as bad."

"Yeah. He's over on our left. He's standing. He looks all right—"

"He's got a hunk of mortar in his shoulder." Pershing started worming his way left, and the guys folded and unfolded to let him. Hill was already pissed off at him. Worrying about the fucking lieutenant when they all were in it up to their elbows. If there was anything really wrong with the bastard, he'd be lying on the ground. Hill looked around heads for Neubacher. There he was, towheaded as a five-year-old, bent over like he really was in trouble. Eposito kept whispering to him, like a pep talk. The two of them were buddies. Both short and stocky, and they played catch by the goddamned hour—even in Saigon, when free time should have been spent humping the natives or recovering therefrom.

York was squashed against Hill. He was a good-looking guy, sort of a loner. Big shoulders, used to sing with a GI dance band in Saigon. Hill had booked them in one of his places once, but it didn't work out too good. They took themselves too seriously.

"How'd they get you guys?"

"Hill?" York had half twisted, but his eyes still weren't used to the dark.

"Yeah."

"I don't know about the others. Merrill and me were with Pershing. We holed up by a big hunk of concrete at the river and figured we had it made. While we were zapping at them in the woods, some Indians came out of the water and took us from behind. Didn't even see the bastards."

The leader of the VC was in a huddle around the kerosene lamp

61

with the two who had been reading the map and the fat one. The four of them seemed to be the wheels. The GI who started it all was against the other wall of the cave, near them, but not with them. He looked really shaken. Hill wondered whether he really was a GI or a Frenchman. Either way, Hill was pretty sure he was the one he'd seen with the North Vietnamese AA team. That made him look around. None of the Indians was in a North Vietnamese outfit. What the hell did that mean? Maybe he was wrong; maybe it wasn't the same guy. That'd be great if they had about a hundred of these guys. Jesus, Charlie was tricky enough without that. Then he realized he probably wouldn't be fighting Charlie for a long time. All he had to worry about was what Charlie was going to do to him now.

The fat one had laughed at one of his own jokes again, and this time the leader was laughing with him. It was a reserved laugh—like the boss laughing, but not really losing himself in it. And the two who had been at the map laughed, too—as if they enjoyed the joke, but were trying even harder to prove they enjoyed it to the boss. Brownnosers in every army, Hill thought. The leader said something, and immediately six or seven of the VC started crawling out through the hole.

While they were going out, Hill stiffened as he saw Pershing push right through a couple of them and head toward the leader. One of the ones he shoved reached out quick, got hold of the thong binding the sarge's arms, and yanked. The sarge seemed to falter a second, but then he jerked his hands down and pulled the VC right off-balance—and dragged him along to where the leader stood.

Some of the guys snickered. The VC pulled himself loose and scrambled to his feet like a shot. Pershing wheeled to face him. If the VC had any intent of getting even, he lost it. Maybe less from the threat in Pershing's face than from a soft word from the leader. The VC glared at the supersarge, then turned and followed the others out. Pershing turned back around to face the leader.

"We have two wounded. I request they be looked to."

The leader just stared at him for a second. The sarge had done it right. He didn't sound belligerent; he wasn't begging. Hill flooded with gratitude again. If he had to be captured, he was damned glad Pershing had been captured with him.

The leader didn't answer but walked over to the renegade GI. They talked together quietly. Finally, the leader said something to one of the VC, and they went in and grabbed Janowitz by the arm.

The leader motioned Janowitz down to where the wounded were being looked after and went along with him.

"He's not the—" Pershing tried to get the leader's attention, but the guy ignored him, and Pershing had enough sense not to push it.

Two more women had come in with the big group of VC, so there were five women, working on the wounded, and two VC men. One of the men was taller than most VC and had a big shock of black hair that made him look even bigger. Hill guessed he was a doctor and the other guy an aide. When the leader approached, the doctor rose from beside one of the wounded. The leader said something, and the doctor looked at Janowitz's head where he'd been hit by the rifle butt. The bruise was swollen badly and had gone green, but it didn't look serious. Even so, the doctor examined it carefully. Finally, he said something to the leader. For a second the leader looked at Janowitz as if he were debating whether he should have him for breakfast. Then he shrugged, said something to the VC guarding Janowitz, and the guy led Janowitz to a place by the stream. He made him sit down, and then one of the nurses brought him a cloth, and he dipped it in the stream and applied it to Janowitz's head.

That settled, the leader came slowly back to Pershing and nodded at the renegade GI.

"Where are the other wounded?" the GI said. He still hadn't moved from his position against the other wall. He sure had an American accent. If he wasn't a GI, he'd certainly gone to school in America or lived there or something.

Pershing went back to Neubacher.

"Come on, Bobby," he said gently. If anything, Neubacher was looking worse, bent right over, and Hill could see he'd taken something just below the neck. There was a big bandage on the wound, but it was so dark from blood Hill hadn't noticed it at first. As he moved forward, Hill could tell he was crying. Funny how it shook you up to see a guy like Neubacher cry.

Pershing shuffled along beside Neubacher, glaring at the renegade GI, showing his disgust that no one would help or free his hands so he could help. Hill was glad that his concern now seemed to be Neubacher rather than the lieutenant. Maybe he hadn't realized how badly Bobby was hurt. Lieutenant Morris had moved out behind them and was walking with his head right down on his chest. He was winged all right. A huge hunk of flesh had been torn right off his right shoulder blade. It looked gruesome enough, but unless the bone had been splintered, it wouldn't be fatal or crippling or anything.

VC and GI's were all watching as they moved to the wounded, but the doctor and his aide didn't pay attention to them at all. Pershing mumbled something to Neubacher, and he sat down on one of the straw mats. Then Pershing knelt and said something to the lieutenant. Morris knelt on another mat, and Pershing held out his arms to him, holding them up until the lieutenant was leaning on them. Then the sarge went down slow, twisting so his own head touched the ground, but keeping his arms as a break for Morris, so that the lieutenant went down, face first, but slow and easy. When he was on the mat, the sarge rolled his arms out from under him and stood up. The lieutenant was now on the mat, on his stomach, with the wound up.

The doctor still wasn't paying any attention. Pershing was staring at him, and Hill wondered if he'd explode. A long time seemed to go by, but the doctor deliberately avoided Pershing's eyes, though he must have been aware of his stare. Finally, the sarge turned and looked at the leader. Hill knew Pershing. He was almost impossible to drive to anger; it was one of his most infuriating qualities. Always cool reason. But when he did get mad—man, a natural disaster. Wild, intemperate, relentless. And Hill could see the fucking storm clouds crackling in his eyes.

The leader stared at him calmly a minute, then spoke in that same calm voice. What he was saying or who he was talking to, you couldn't tell, because he just kept staring at Pershing, like he was taking the measure of him and was rather amused.

The doctor said something to one of the nurses, and she came over to the lieutenant and looked at his wound. Then she cut the thong, freeing his arms. He must have been in real pain because when he dropped them to his side, he passed right out. The nurse turned unconcernedly and cut Neubacher free. She helped him down on his back and examined his neck carefully. While she was doing it, Hill looked at *their* wounded. One was bandaged for a head injury, but you couldn't tell how serious it was. One looked as if he'd got his arm mangled a bit. The worst one had had a big hunk of his jaw taken off, and you could see teeth and bone and flesh all jagged and looking so painful Hill shuddered involuntarily. The guy wasn't feeling any pain, though. He was out. Whether they'd put him out or nature had, either way he'd passed the point of feeling. The doctor was working on him, his hands moving fast as hell. But for all his speed he seemed calm and deliberate.

The one Hill wished they would put out of his misery was a kid who was burned. He looked about twelve, and his skin was that splotchy, blue, black, pink, and red mess that napalm made . . . and he was moaning and half crying. It had been just background noise before, but now that Hill's mind had zeroed in on it, he couldn't shake it. It was like a radio in somebody else's apartment, coming through the walls, nagging and inescapable. One of the nurses was working on him, but Hill kept hoping they'd just knock him out and wondering why the hell they didn't.

Distraction finally came when the string of VC the leader had sent out started piling back in the cave, carrying captured gear. Others went out and came back in with more stuff. It was as if they were unloading a warehouse out there. Not only had they taken rifles, machine guns, flamethrowers and mortars, but they'd stripped the helicopter, too. Aid kits, radio, ammunition, chutes. Hill wouldn't have been surprised to see them bring in the goddamned rotor blades!

"What the hell happened to the jets?" he whispered to York. "And the gunship? How did these bastards get all this shit?"

"That fucking traitor over there with the long hair." He nodded to the other side of the cave, where the GI with the VC was still flaked out against the wall. He'd taken his helmet off, and his hair *was* long. Hill figured he was about twenty-five, twenty-six. There were moments when he looked twenty-one, but he looked older sometimes, too—maybe twenty-nine.

"When they took us," York went on, "the first thing they did was grab Pershing's squawk box, and that bastard started panting and putting on an act—could have been anyone's voice—and he sent the fucking jets all over the place. They bombed the piss out of a lot of trees, but they sure didn't worry the VC."

Hill stared at the GI again. Man, that bastard had a lot to answer for. "Miller almost got away, but that fucker had them plant a wall of napalm behind him, and there was nothing he could do but toss in his cards."

Hill leaned back against the cave wall, his eyes still fixed on the GI. His hair was blond, dishwater, streaked with brown. He had smallish eyes, but thick eyebrows and lashes, so they looked like frightened eyes, timid rather than mean. And he looked as if he were on the verge of tears all the time. It wasn't just his eyes; it was the way he held his mouth, too, as if somebody'd just hurt his feelings and he was trying to act as if it didn't matter, but you knew he was already crying inside.

He seemed to sense Hill staring at him and looked up at him. His whole face was like his eyes. Small, sort of wounded-looking, as if he

65

were a mommy's boy out in the cold schoolyard with all these rough boys for the first time and wishing he was back home getting cocoa and hot toast and being told what a wonderful boy he was. There were girls who'd go for that fragile, hurt look, even though he wasn't anything particular to look at.

But he stared at Hill evenly, as though he sensed the estimate being made of him, and his eyes hardened and flashed in challenge. Don't splash my new shoes or I'll fight. Only maybe it was more than that. It was as if maybe he'd fought before and was willing to fight again. Hill had met that kind, too, the kind you beat the shit out of and they still won't say quits. Hopeless bastards who couldn't fight their way through a roomful of balloons, but you get tired of clobbering them because their refusal to knuckle under has no relationship whatsoever to their strength. Who the hell are you? Hill thought. What's your scene?

4

i

Neubacher died. So did the kid with the burns. The trouble was the VC apparently figured the area would be swarming with Air Cavalry and Arvin the next day, so they were forced to move that night. They split into two groups. It looked to Hill as if they split the prisoners carefully. He didn't give a shit because he was with Pershing, but Eposito, Matthews, Czarnecke, York, and Merrill were picked with the first group. All the really fit VC went with them, and Hill figured they were going to make a false trail because the leader, the wounded, the captured equipment, and Janowitz, to whom they were paying special attention, all went later with the rest.

The kid with the burns died first. Hill was so tired from walking up and down hills that he had his head down and was just forcing himself to put one foot in front of the other when the line stopped. All the GI's were tied together in one string, a leather loop running from neck to neck. And everyone had something on his back. Hill had an ammunition case strapped to him. When he stopped, he just panted for a time, not caring what the reason for the break was, only wishing he could lie down and sleep. Even on the wet ground. Then he heard the shoveling and looked around.

Three VC were digging, and the leader was bent over the hammock that the burned kid was being carried in. He stood back finally and said something to one of the VC in the line. The guy handed his rifle to another one and went over by the grave. They didn't dig it very deep. Hardly enough to cover him. When they'd put him in, the VC from the line made the sign of the cross and mumbled something. The leader stood to one side. He didn't take part in the prayer, but when it was over, he signaled to the guys shoveling to cover the body. The line was re-formed before they even finished. The whole thing hadn't taken more than three or four minutes. And they were on their way again.

Hill figured he was asleep on his feet when Neubacher died. He was jerked to consciousness by the line stopping, but he couldn't remember anything happening before that for hours. The mist was so thick he couldn't see more than a couple of guys in front of him. He remembered thinking thickly that it would be a good time to escape, but he was so tired it would have taken an exercise of will far beyond him to move even a few feet.

The ugly little VC who'd been in the cave came up behind him and grabbed his arm. Hill turned numbly, and the guy undid his neck and shoved him to one side. The lean one was there in the mist. He took Hill a little farther toward the back of the line. Miller was off to one side with little Arnie Russell. And Hill gradually made out Pershing and the VC leader and, behind them, the GI or Frenchman or whatever he was. They untied Hill's arms and handed him a shovel. And he was told to dig.

They hadn't dug much—Miller and Russell digging with him—when they brought up Neubacher in a hammock and put him next to the grave. The VC doctor stood beside him a minute. He looked angry, as though Neubacher had let him down. The leader said something to him in Vietnamese, but the doctor chose to ignore it and turned away, disappearing into the black night fog.

The grave wasn't half a foot deep when they signaled them out and two VC lowered Neubacher into it. Hill stood looking down at him. The blond hair seemed even whiter against the ashen skin than it had when he was alive. Like all deaths, it seemed unreal. You had to make an effort to realize he wouldn't just get up and start playing catch again. Hill wished he hadn't heard him crying. He'd always thought of him as a kid who'd never got beyond baseball to women. Without thinking about it it had been the whole whitey bit—sunlight, freckles, blond hair in the sun—Kellogg's Corn Flakes. And then seeing him bent over, sobbing, hurt—it was like the ad going wrong right in the middle and the kid suddenly dripping blood and crumbling into the dirt.

"Robert Dillan Neubacher. May the Lord have mercy on your soul." It was Pershing. He was at the foot of the grave, his hands still tied behind his back, his head bowed. He went on saying the Lord's Prayer, ending it the Catholic way, without the "For thine is the Kingdom, and the power, and the glory forever." Neubacher wasn't a Catholic, but the sarge probably figured that's the way God wanted to hear it, since that's the way *he* thought it was right. Hill knew it wasn't an insult to Neubacher; that wasn't in the sarge. "Rest

68

in peace." Pershing didn't move for a second, then looked up and nodded at them.

Miller shoveled in the first shovel. It splashed on Neubacher's chest and half covered his face. Hill was frozen. It was grotesque beyond anything he had ever experienced. Neubacher lying there, looking gray and wasted, like they should help him, pick him up, give him artificial respiration, anything—but not throw dirt on him, not smother him with mud. Another shovel went on. He had to fight the urge to shovel it all off. He stood there, not moving. No one said anything to him, but he didn't put on one shovelful. Just watched as the wet clods of earth splattered and then covered the pale mouth, the blond hair, and the sunny freckles of Robert Dillan Neubacher.

ii

They were still walking at dawn, though Hill didn't know how. He was conscious of being cold and wet from the damp, but so exhausted from lack of sleep he didn't care. In the night the mist had grown so thick he could hardly see beyond Miller, who had been put back in line in front of him. He had given up hating the unvarying, unavoidable landscape of Miller's thick shoulders going up and down, up and down. But not the sudden jerks at his neck. Even in his state of semi-sleep, with his eyes closed half the time, the pull of the tether on his neck when he got too far behind sent murderous thoughts flashing through his brain. He got so mad a couple of times he deliberately pulled back, jerking Miller—but also hurting his own neck. He always regretted it. He was too tired to sustain hatred, and two jerks in a row were two more than his body wanted. It dimly occurred to him that it probably would have been more painful if they hadn't put Pershing behind him. With someone slacking in the back and jerking him that way, too, he might have been goaded enough to lash out at someone, and even half-conscious, he knew that wouldn't do any good.

When dawn came and lit first the sky and then the treetops, he lost some of the terrible sleepiness. He was just as tired, but he could keep his eyes open, and he welcomed the sense of warmth that came as the mist slowly turned from a drenching gray miasma to glimmering crystal that splashed light from the leaves and the long, thin blades of grass. The whole line seemed to move faster. The leader moved up and down it, talking to the VC, apparently encouraging them to go even faster. Hill saw him glance at the sky warily from time to time.

It didn't seem long after daybreak when they heard the first sounds of planes over the early-morning chattering of the birds. The line stopped as if on command. The leader and the fat one ran up and down, placing VC and the wounded under the cover of foliage. Then the fat VC cut little Arnie Russell loose from the end of the line and hauled him against a tree opposite to where the rest of them had been forced to squat. He tied Russell's arms around the tree so he was hugging it. Hill couldn't help thinking the Georgia cracker'd probably get a hard-on. Then the fat one pulled a knife and leaned against the tree with the blade poised.

"One GI move, and I put this knife right in her back." Like many Vietnamese who had struggled to learn the mysteries of masculine and feminine in French, he found it beyond him to accommodate again to the simpler mysteries of masculine and feminine in English.

Hill spotted the renegade GI off by himself. He always seemed on his own, only talking occasionally to the leader. He still seemed in a funk about the raid, and Hill figured maybe something more had gone wrong than they knew about. Anyway the VC apparently trusted him completely because no one paid any attention to his movements. But as usual, the minute they stopped, the VC put two extra guards on Janowitz. They had something in store for *him* all right.

The planes were close now. No one moved. Hill felt the only one who might try to attract the attention of the planes was Pershing, and he hoped to God he would restrain his sense of duty in the face of the threat to Russell. Not that Hill gave that much of a shit for Russell. It was just that he knew that was probably the only thing that *would* restrain Pershing.

As it was, the planes didn't pass right overhead, and Hill never got a glimpse of one. When their roar died in the distance, the line was quickly reassembled, the fat one laughing at Russell and pounding him on the back. Russell gave him a gaunt, toothless grin, and the fat one laughed even harder.

For a time they marched at a fair speed, everyone awakened by the sun and the scare. But as the heat began to grow and the benefit of the slight rest faded, the exhaustion returned. Hill's eyes kept closing again and again. He had to piss something awful, and his mind kept wandering—dreaming he *was* pissing, getting up from his sack in the camp and walking to the latrine or pissing on a train with the wheels rumbling, rumbling underneath, echoing up the john; he even dreamed he was back home, walking down the hall past his mother's room, but each time he'd come out of it, thinking he had pissed and then aware of how bad he had to go. They had stopped two or three times during the night. He had no idea of the intervals and each time they'd untied them one at a time and let them piss, but it seemed hours since the last break. Hill wished he'd made a stink back when they were hiding from the planes. Yeah, that's what I should have done, and it almost relieved his leaden brain to think there had been a way out of the discomfort. It seemed to him he *had* to do something, fall in his tracks, piss, or just die of exhaustion, when they suddenly cleared the trees. They were in a small valley and before them were terraces of small rice paddies, and off to one side five or six huts. The line turned toward them.

iii

They put them in a hut. It was already hot enough so that its cool shade was a welcome relief from the muggy heat outside. Hill was convinced that nothing could keep him from falling asleep, but a wizened old man came in lugging an earthen pot that smelled like heaven, and he acceded willingly to the realization that he was even more hungry than he was tired. It was some kind of fish soup with rice, and they untied them to let them slurp it from little wooden bowls. It was hot and thin, but to Hill it tasted better than all the frozen turkey dinners and steaming rolls with butter that he got back at camp put together. Man, he thought, they say starvation is horrible, but it ain't *all* bad, not when only twelve hours or so of it can make a little slop taste like this.

The VC didn't tie their hands again. When they had first been untied, two VC had come in with automatics and squatted across from them. When the old man went out, they just sat there and nothing happened.

"Maybe we'd better sleep," Pershing said, shrugging. But before they could sprawl out, the leader came in. He was trailed by the two Hill had first seen in the cave studying the map, with the big fat one in between them. Hill muttered, "Tick, Tack, Toe." The others smirked, but Pershing glared at him. Nevertheless, the names stuck. It wasn't just that they found they usually ran in pack that way, behind the leader—the shifty one first, the fat comedian next, and the ugly little bastard last, Tick, Tack, Toe. But later, much later, they learned that the crafty thin one was named Tran Van Tho, and the big fat one Duong Tu Trach. Hill never remembered the little ugly one's full name, but his last name (like an American first name, the one you used with someone you knew) was Thao. So if it wasn't Tick, Tack, Toe, it was Tho, Trach, Thao, and as far as their bunch was concerned, Tick, Tack, Toe it was.

It was the lean one, Tick, who faced them. Pershing must have been as sleepy as the rest of them, because the guy had to stand there a moment before Pershing dug what the silence was about; then he stood up and called the whole lot to attention. Janowitz sort of scoffed, but he stood up like the rest. That seemed to satisfy Tick's sense of decorum. He turned to the door and shouted something, and two of the VC carried Lieutenant Morris in on a stretcher. The upper half of his body was bandaged, and while it looked like a good job, the night of travel had taken a lot out of him. He had big hollows under his eyes, and his face seemed all pimples and no face. Hill didn't think he could ever like the sonuvabitch, but he couldn't help feeling sorry for him.

Tick waited until they set the stretcher down; then he started reading to them. His voice was high-pitched and aggressive.

"The United States of America was one of the prosecuting parties at the Nuremberg Trials following World War Two where Fascist war criminals were tried, punished, and in some cases *executed* for war crimes. According to the Charter of the International Military Tribunal which was the basis for these trials, the following acts were listed as crimes for which there shall be *individual* responsibility, and any soldier committing them may be punished accordingly—whether he was acting under orders or not. They are—I quote—'ill-treatment of civilian populations. Murder or ill-treatment of prisoners of war. Wanton destruction of cities, towns or villages. Inhumane acts committed against any civilian population.' " He looked up and glared at them as though they had already been tried and found guilty. Then, before they had any chance to react at all, he reached forward and cut the stitched first looey's bars from Janowitz's uniform.

"War criminals have no rank."

He turned and walked out. The two VC who had brought Morris in picked up his stretcher and followed him. Then the leader, and his other two stooges, Big Tack and Toe, the little pock-marked one, marched out, too.

Hill wanted to laugh, but he was tired, so tired that if they wanted to execute him, he decided he'd worry about it when he'd had some sleep; then maybe the whole game of cowboys and Indians would make sense.

Throughout the day Hill woke frequently, but even so, it was not a light, useless sleep. The times he awakened to turn on the hard floor or move away from someone who had sprawled against him, he could feel the loss of fatigue, the passing of his numbing headache, the sense of normal strength returning to him. It seemed to him he dreamed all the time. It was all one dream, confused and ass-backward but always the same. It was a girl. He wasn't sure, but it seemed she was married or had been married, but he was in her house and she was in a kimono with nothing on underneath. She was white or sometimes maybe just passing for white, with lovely, shining legs, but almost no breasts at all. They kept talking and eating something or other, and sometimes her mother would come in and talk to her as though she always sat around with nothing on when men were around. And sometimes Hill would be running his hands up and down her legs and around her ass, and the mother would just go on talking about the curtains being dirty or something and then go out. Several times they went into a little bedroom off the living room. It was a wooden bungalow and sometimes an old-fashioned apartment. But there was always a double bed with brass railings. And it was all rumpled, sheets and blanket tumbled in piles and magazines scattered around. They'd lie down, and Hill would spread her kimono and run his hands all over her and lie on her and lick her, and always he was on the verge of fucking her. And she never resisted or got excited; she just went along. And sometimes when Hill woke up, he'd think he *had* fucked her, and then he'd realize he hadn't. And he'd doze off again, and the dream would start in the living room again, with her standing by a shelf with a radio on it, and him rubbing up against her and feeling her all over, and her just turning the dial, never getting any music, just commercials and weather and news. But he never got into her, never had an orgasm.

When Big Tack came in shouting to wake them up, he was in bed with her again, but he still hadn't got her.

iv

They marched all through the night again. Their hands were bound, and loaded like packhorses, they were strung in the same leather chain. But everything was more relaxed. The knots binding them were left loose, and the added freedom of movement made the whole exercise seem more reasonable. They even took a break about every hour, the VC talking among themselves, smoking, and even playing cards once or twice. Tack, the fat tough one, was the life of the party, always goosing one of the women or lying on his back and making cracks about the GI's. It all was in Vietnamese, and Hill couldn't understand it, but there was no doubt what was going on, because he'd say something and laugh like hell and then the others would sneak a look at them and they'd all laugh or grin stupidly.

Halfway through the night, they heard explosions. It sounded to Hill like shelling from artillery, but it was so distant he couldn't really be sure. Maybe it was aircraft. He was hauling Lieutenant Morris at the time, along with Janowitz. The first night the VC had done all that, but the second night they made the GI's each take a turn at it. Hill guessed they chose them in teams by height. When Tick had told Janowitz he was to be next on the pole, Pershing had squawked.

"That man's an officer. He doesn't do work details." He'd said it as though he were the commanding officer and making the rules. For a minute it stopped Tick; then he got a little hysterical and went up to the supersarge and started screaming that he was a war criminal and he'd talk when they gave him permission to talk, and as for Janowitz, as an officer he was more guilty than any, and he had his choice—take his turn at the pole or be shot on the spot. Hill had almost cracked up because in his anger Tick lost command of his English and he'd go to say something and stutter over a word about forty times before he got it out. He was so damned mad that it never got really funny, and Hill could tell the guy was a vicious bastard by nature, but it did take the punch out of his threat. Pershing had just looked at him steadily, as if he had been listening to George Wallace describing voting rights in Alabama. When he'd finished, Pershing turned his head calmly to Janowitz.

"They won't shoot you, sir. They obviously want you for something. And if they weaken our military discipline—" That's as far as he got. Tick brought his rifle butt up into Pershing's gut. He expected it to be enough, but Pershing was ready for it, and it doubled him a little, and that was all. The big fat one laughed.

"He's strong, okay?" he said in English. And he walked over as if he were going to have a go. Janowitz had been watching, but he didn't seem shaken at all.

"It's all right, Sergeant Pershing," he said, his voice dwelling on the "Sergeant," making it sound like a title of honor that he wasn't going

74

to drop just because the VC said he should. "I don't think it will endanger our military structure if I help with our own wounded."

Pershing looked at him. Hill could tell he was thinking about it, mulling over whether he should fight at the first challenge or let it drop, considering that Janowitz seemed to recognize what was at stake. Hill often admired the subtlety John Andrew was capable of, but it always pissed him that Pershing took so long to react. He was a good thinker, but a slow, slow one.

"Get in line, GI, or I fix you so we need a stretcher for you, okay?" It was Big Tack. He was in front of Pershing, his rifle at port, his feet spread. Oh, man, Hill thought. What a fight it'd be, these two. When the sarge wasn't tied, of course. They were both stocky without being short. Pershing weighed a hundred and eighty-five, Hill knew. It looked like Tack must weigh twenty to twenty-five pounds more, but ten of it was gut.

"Pershing!" It was Janowitz.

"Yes, sir."

"I'll help carry Lieutenant Morris, but I assure you I will resist any meaningful attempt to violate the articles of the Geneva Convention." It was a good bit. As much for the VC as Pershing. They all had been taught that the first step the Commies took was to try to break down ranks, so there was no discipline in the group. And they had all been taught the articles of the Geneva Convention concerning treatment of prisoners of war, about what an enemy could make you do and what he couldn't. Naturally the officers got the best of it. No work, separate quarters, they were in charge. But NCO's had some rights, too. The only catch was you couldn't take your ball and go home if the other side didn't want to play by the rules. He had thought it was a fucking joke back in Oklahoma when they taught it to them, but once he got out in the field, he *knew* it was a joke. All you had to do was see how the Arvin treated VC prisoners to get some idea of how the VC were going to treat *you*. Hill didn't know whether Janowitz was gung ho enough to believe it or whether he was smart enough to know that spelling out the book was just the thing to cool Pershing. Anyway it worked.

"Yes, sir," Pershing said quietly, and with a last taunting look at Tick, he stepped back in line.

They had strung Morris in a hammock on a long bamboo pole. When the VC carried him, there were two men on each end of the pole. But when Hill and Janowitz were put on, it was just the two of them. In five minutes Hill was aching from one end to the other. His shoulders and legs were the worst, but he found if he didn't stand erect, the base of his spine felt as if it had turned to solid rock, and if he didn't keep squeezing his hands around the pole, his arms lost their circulation and he thought they'd fall off. They were winding along a trail in a shallow valley that ran through a whole succession of hills. He'd see one silhouetted against the sky and it would seem to be the last one, then they'd get even with it and the silhouette of another would appear, and so it went on, endlessly.

After the first five minutes he and Janowitz had struck up a kind of rhythm, moving up and down over the little humps in the trail, managing the turns without pulling each other off-balance, even taking the climbs and descents up and down the bigger hills without unpredictable lurching. Morris slept off and on. Once he looked up and said, "Hello, Hill. It is Hill, isn't it?" He hadn't been with the outfit long enough to get them all straight, and he was from some burg in North Dakota and probably thought all niggers looked alike anyway.

"Yes, sir. It's Hill," he'd answered. The bastard looked so sick and weak Hill found himself hoping he wouldn't die, though he couldn't think of any rational reason why it made any difference to him. In fact, when he thought about it, it might even be better for Morris to konk out now, rather than go through what might be in store for him.

It was after their bodies had seemed to adjust to the load that they'd heard the distant shells. The leader had stopped the column, maybe a minute. Number one stooge, Tick, had run up to him, and they'd conferred over a map, lighting a match, with Big Tack putting his hat over it to shield it from the sky.

"Where do you think they're taking us?" Hill whispered. He was at the back. Janowitz up front.

"Laos," Janowitz whispered back. "See the Big Dipper—up on your right." Hill looked. They hadn't given him navigation training in his short course on the chopper, and he didn't know much about the stars, but he could recognize the Big Dipper.

"The two front stars on the lip point to the North Star, see it?"

Hill could see *lots* of stars, and which one was the North Star he had no clue, but he got the idea that north was off on their right, so they must be going almost due west, and that meant Janowitz was right—they were heading for Laos and the Ho Chi Minh Trail.

"Yeah, I see it," he lied.

Jesus, they were going to take them to North Vietnam. There was no chance of rescue or escape once they got them up there. He *would* be a prisoner for years. Maybe brainwashed. His whole life was at stake—now. He thought of dropping the pole and making a run for it. Maybe it was luck, maybe not, that he glanced back quickly to see what his chances were. Just off to one side, a VC was holding a burp gun on him and Janowitz. The renegade GI was next to him, leaning against a tree, and he was looking right at Hill as though he had a wire-tap to Hill's brain and knew exactly what he was thinking. Hill looked away and glanced in the other direction. Ugly little Toe was ready with his gun, too. There wasn't a chance in hell. He was going to North Vietnam . . . and there was nothing he could do to stop it.

5

i

They marched for a fair time after dawn came. Hill wondered if they were already in Laos and if that was what made the VC feel so secure, but just as he was convinced that was the case, the leader held up his hand and stopped the line. They pitched a camp right where they were but took elaborate precautions to hide it from the air. He guessed they might be near the border, and that, he knew, was pretty heavily patrolled.

He, Miller, and Arnie Russell were given machete knives and put to work chopping bamboo stalks. Four VC were guarding them. He was amused at the little game they were playing with Janowitz. They didn't put him on a work detail, but he and Pershing had to move Lieutenant Morris to a stream, where two of the VC women applied wet cloths to the lieutenant, evidently trying to break his fever. Then Janowitz and Pershing had to haul him back to where the doctor had set up, but before he could look at Morris, some chow was ready for him, so they had to carry him to where they were cooking and then back again to the doctor. By the time they'd finished moving him back and forth, Janowitz had done as much work as the rest. Big Tack laughed every time Janowitz shouldered the bamboo pole. He knew it was needling Pershing, but it wasn't actually breaking the previous arrangement, so there was nothing for Pershing to protest about.

They made a sort of corral from the bamboo stalks, driving them into the ground in a rough circle about fifteen feet in diameter. It averaged around four feet high with the splintered bamboo edges at the top, and it was a pretty effective prison. Two guards on the outside could keep an eye on the whole thing, and in daylight there was no chance of breaking out or climbing over. They had put it up under a thick cover of trees, but one of the VC had climbed up and cut down the branches that hung directly over it, so they'd have had to have been twelve feet tall to jump to the nearest branch.

All the GI's were herded in, and since the arrangement killed any idea of escape, Hill figured the best thing to do was to lie down and have a good rest. His shoulders were still sore from the hour of lugging Morris, and he had a perverse urge to brood over the prospect of being a prisoner for years and years and years. They brought food in to them. A tough shelled rice, with pieces of some kind of meat in it— eaten with dirty fingers from dirty wooden bowls. He didn't mind. He was starved, and the stuff was hot, and he could have eaten ten times what they gave him.

As he ate, he watched the others. They all seemed to have come to the realization they were now in it in a way they never expected to be. It was funny. You never really believed you'd personally get killed, but you somehow accepted the possibility. And the same with being wounded. He knew that in fire fights, when he didn't know what was going on and all hell was breaking loose, he used to panic at the thought of a piece of shell ripping into the back of his skull. In his imagination it never killed him, just maimed and hurt him terribly. The feeling was so strong sometimes that he'd put his hand behind his head for a few seconds—as though that would protect it from a hunk of mortar! It was frightening to the point of sickness sometimes, but he'd learned to live with it.

But being a prisoner of war had just never been one of the real possibilities. For pilots, yes. But no one in their outfit had ever been forced to surrender, and no one, as far as he knew, had thought about it the way you were forced almost daily to think of death or being wounded. But looking around at the faces, he could see they all were thinking about it now. Pershing, glum as *he* was; little Arnie Russell, the dark bags under his eyes looking purple and washed out, his eyes themselves dead, as if he were lost in some kind of psychosis; Miller, morose, sunk in himself without any sign of his usual "don't panic, Mac" competence and self-assurance; Janowitz, long legs sprawled out, his huge hands making the tiny bowl of rice look even more inadequate than it was, his face more solemn than he'd ever seen it. In fact, it was the first time Hill ever saw him when he really looked Jewish. His face was dark, and his big brown eyes, which usually flashed with some hint of humor, were as solemn as pictures of Moses. In fact, he looked like a slender Moses, Hill decided. Maybe it was all his early religious training, the veneration of Moses and Abraham and all the Biblical characters that explained it, but he suddenly felt very glad Janowitz was with them. Not the sudden flash of gratitude he'd got on seeing Pershing, but a slow feeling of warmth.

It was funny, he felt, how at home they all hated the Jews so. All the damned stores were owned by Jews. Any time you wanted money, you had to go to a Jew or work for a Jew or beg from a Jew. It was as though the Jews were the only ones who'd deal with black niggers, and then they did it only if there was enough profit in it. They'd do you a favor—they'd hire you for fifteen cents below the minimum wage, and you wouldn't report the income, and they wouldn't report they were hiring you. And you had to smile and say, "Thanks, man," and try to act friendly and steal as much as you could.

But they always came out on top, even if you robbed them blind. He had hated them as much as everyone else had in his neighborhood, but when he came in the Army and met Jews, it all seemed different. He remembered the first one was a guy named Diamond. Brownnoser, kept sucking around everyone, trying to make friends; then one day a big hunky kid called him a grabbin' Jewboy and tried to goad him into a fight. Diamond had tried to ease out of it, said we all had prejudices, he'd heard people say nasty things about Hungarians, too. It had come out without sounding chicken—or belligerent—and Hill had been impressed. But the hunky kid wouldn't give up, and finally he started slugging. It wasn't till he'd hit him in the face that Diamond actually fought back. And then it was the goddamnedest fight. The hunky was bigger and a better fighter, but he couldn't beat Diamond down. Diamond had big bones, and you could tell when he did land one, it hurt, and he just kept coming. The hunky beat the shit out of him for about fifteen minutes solid, but then he got tired, and Diamond began to cut him up. In the end he had the guy on the ground, not out, but too damned weak to want to go on.

Hill thought he'd brag about it and make it a big deal, but he never said anything, except once that it was stupid to fight. Hill didn't know why, but it changed his feeling about Jews somehow. There were so many other kinds of guys he met in the Army for the first time—redneck farmers, college guys, people he'd never heard of, Armenians and Czechs, they'd even had a couple of Japanese at basic—that after Diamond had fought like that, Jews just slipped into the pile of whiteys like the rest of them. He sort of took them as they came. He wondered what his mother would think of that! She hated Jews like they were twentieth-century slave traders. She never pulled a cash register slip from a bag of groceries without cursing the Jews as automatically as she praised God over Sunday dinner.

But as he looked at Janowitz, he remembered it was his mother, too, who used to cry over the stories in the Old Testament—though it never occurred to her to relate them to the sons of Moses, Abraham, and David who owned the local supermarket. Hill smiled at the idea, a thought, yeah, it's going to be a long trip, a long, long trip, but I'm lucky in one thing. Pershing and Janowitz, old Miller and even Arnie Russell. It ain't a bad crew.

ii

After they'd eaten, Tick, Tack, Toe came hopping into the corral, Tick in the lead, followed by Big Tack, with little Toe bringing up the rear as usual. Tick had always been the mouthpiece, but this time Big Tack came front and center, grinning at them all as if he were going to have them for dessert. For a second they just looked at him, one as glum as the other. Then Pershing called them to attention. Tack laughed, as if he didn't expect the honor and was very pleased. Then, as suddenly, the laugh was gone.

"Out!" he ordered, signaling toward the slit they'd left for an entrance. Pershing looked at Janowitz, and Janowitz just nodded as if to say, "What the hell, let's not make a big deal out of something we can't do anything about." And for once Pershing was subdued enough not to make every minute of his day a bright challenge to be overcome.

Toe led them toward the river. It was really two little streams pouring down from the hills. They joined about twenty-five yards below where they had pitched camp, at a little waterfall that dropped into a pool about ten yards long. Toe was leading them right to the waterfall.

Hill had seen the Arvin do the water torture. He'd seen guys do it at the YMCA at home for that matter. You just held a guy underwater until he had to breathe; then when his lungs were full of water, you dragged his head up, let him get a waterlogged breath, and then ducked him again. By the third time the guy was so sick and panicked he'd kill his own mother to be left off. The Arvin did it all the time to VC, men and women alike. At home Hill had always been too big or too fast for anyone to give him the treatment at the Y. But it had always scared him, even when he saw it done in fun. When the Arvin did it, it was sickening. The damned VC never wanted to talk, and so they'd dunk 'em and dunk 'em and dunk 'em until they were spewing water and puke and blood and finally would pass out. He'd seen guys left on riverbanks he thought would never come around.

He guessed Janowitz knew something the VC wanted to know, and they were probably going to let him see a little demonstration on the others before they gave him the chance to answer or not to answer. And obviously the better the demonstration, the quicker the answers were liable to come.

As they got closer and closer to the pool, he wondered how much he could take. He was going to fake as much as he could, but he knew once his head was underwater and his lungs were bursting, he was bound to panic like everyone else. They hadn't bound their arms, and he was so terrified by the idea he thought of running for it. There were guards on each side and behind, but the jungle was thick, and he'd seen guys miss at closer distances. He was just steeling himself when Miller beat him to it. It happened in seconds. Miller broke right, toward the streams. He had almost got to the first one with two VC after him when Hill wheeled to hit for the woods, figuring this was the time, but Miller's move had alerted the guards, and Hill found himself staring right into an automatic and a captured M-16. Pershing and Janowitz had had the same idea, and they all had their backs turned to the action when they heard the thump of Miller going down and a yelp of pain.

Hill turned back to see Big Tack sitting squarely on Miller's back. One of the VC had a rifle muzzle pointed at Miller's temple. Big Tack was grinning as he bounced up and down on Miller a couple of times as if he were a new kind of cushion or something. When they let him up, they manhandled the rest of them down to the pool.

Tack faced them and said, "Off with her clothes." They all just stared for a minute. It was Hill who first realized what he meant. His girls in Saigon were always doing the same, expecting adjectives to work the way they did in their fractured French.

"He wants us to strip," Hill said. It was hot as hell already, and the thought flashed through Hill's mind that they might be going to let them swim. It seemed crazy, and he remained wary of something more ingenious and unpleasant. But when they had their stuff off, Tack just signaled toward the water, and after a second Janowitz took him at his word and plunged in. They all followed. The water was cold at first, but after the sticky filth of their fatigues it felt like heaven. They moved around uneasily, but then it seemed that this was all that was going to happen. They were letting them swim. Not that it was deep enough to really swim, but in the deepest spot the water was almost up to Hill's waist.

As they finally relaxed, it became fun. They splashed one another and lay on their backs and kicked. There was always the lurking thought that it was a black joke and the guards, who were sitting around the sides watching them, would open up on them. Hill kept trying to push the thought aside on the ground that since they seemed to want something from Janowitz, they wouldn't go to all the trouble they'd gone to just to machine-gun him down in a remote swimming hole. But he still couldn't relax completely.

Then Big Tack and a couple of the guards stripped and came in with them. Tack started splashing at Pershing as if he had recognized his natural rival. Pershing, who almost always looked competent at anything physical, had never really learned to feel at home in the water. One of the minor drags of living in a ghetto, Hill thought wryly, you never have room for your own swimming pool. Pershing had learned to keep afloat since he had come in the Army, but Hill could tell he was ill at ease in any body of water more unpredictable than a bathtub. And Hill could see it was the other way around with Tack. The guy looked a bit too heavy on land, but when he hit that water, he was half fish.

It seemed the sarge might not take up the challenge, even though Tack was goading him with a big smile, but Janowitz broke the ice. As Tack floated by him, away from Pershing, Janowitz put his hand on the big VC's forehead and pushed down. Tack's head went under, and he did a neat flip underwater, coming back and grabbing Janowitz's legs, dumping him over on his back and rising out of the water like Hercules. Janowitz, who looked as if he might be as good in water as he was on the basketball court, came up in an easy glide splashing sheets of water at Tack. Hill joined in on the other side, and Tack had at them both, laughing as though this were what he lived for. One of the other VC in the pool started going at Hill, and that brought Pershing into it. In seconds they all were splashing—in two teams, VC and GI. All except Miller. He was down in the water, with just his head out, and he just watched, turning his head if they splashed at him, but never indicating he would or wanted to take part.

The whole thing lasted only a couple of minutes, when little Toe started jumping up and down on the side of the river shouting at Tack in Vietnamese. Tack stopped, and they all stopped with him. Toe didn't need to repeat, because once they'd stopped the splashing and shouting, they could hear the aircraft. The guards were standing and had their guns leveled at the GI's. Tack pointed toward the woods. "Go! Fast! No trick!"

The guards prodded them with their guns into the cover of the woods. The forest was so thick that even part of the pool was covered, and in the woods there was no chance they could be spotted. The planes came over low and not far from them. Hill wondered if they had heat sensors. If they did, they might pick up the heat from the fire they'd cooked the rice on. He was torn about what he wished. Splashing around in the water had driven the worst thoughts of years in a North Vietnamese prison camp from his mind, and he didn't want to get napalmed by his own planes, but if they were to escape at all, a raid now, before they were in Laos, was their only real chance.

But it didn't come. In ten minutes they were back in their corral. Tack had let them wash out their fatigues in the pool, and they'd gone back to camp dripping wet. It was so hot it felt good.

They had hardly got back when the young leader and his vice-president, Tick, came into the corral and joined the others. The renegade GI was with them. Pershing called the GI's to attention; then Big Tack ordered them to sit down in the middle of the corral. Two VC carried Lieutenant Morris in on a bamboo stretcher and put him on the ground next to them.

The young leader walked over to them, looking down at the whole group as if he were a kindergarten teacher and they were his new class. And he spoke condescendingly as if he were telling them how to cross a street: Look left, look right, look left again—quick march.

"You are all criminals fighting a war of aggression in a country many miles from your own homeland." Great start. Hill figured the guy couldn't be more than twenty-one or twenty-two at the outside, but he acted with this air of command as if he were a king's son or something. It was disconcerting because it worked. It made you feel like he *was* the king's son. He was trim and well built and obviously educated. Hill had heard him speaking French several times to the doctor, and it didn't surprise Hill that he spoke English, too, even though he'd been acting as if he didn't. He had a kind of English accent with the French honks from the nose every once in a while, but he didn't hesitate and didn't make mistakes.

"But the National Front of Liberation does not regard you as enemies."

Well, hoorah for the National Front of Liberation, Hill thought. Just stop shooting at me then, and I'll go home.

"We believe all peace-loving peoples of the world have the same interests at heart. You have been victimized by the capitalist press of the United States into believing you are fighting to preserve democracy in Vietnam. We are going to give you the opportunity to learn the

84

truth. Cooperation and sincere signs of repentance will not go unrewarded." He paused and looked at them, as though the juicy part were yet to come. "On the other hand, failure to cooperate will not go unnoticed either."

Hill wondered where the hell the speech had come from. It sounded formal, as if he had written what he was saying, but he said it like he was making it up as he went along. At POW indoctrination they had prepared them for this class bit. It wasn't any surprise. They'd even told them the VC sometimes began the treatment right in the field or while on the march. And they claimed that even when they were fighting, the VC's own troops got political indoctrination two or three hours a day. This was obviously *their* first class. The rule was: Listen if you have to, but don't say a word.

"Normally you will be expected to participate in your instruction, but in this first lesson you are only required to pay close attention." Then he squatted on the ground, folding his legs under him the way Asians do.

The renegade GI sprawled on the grass to one side of them, watching them all. And the three musketeers, Tick, Tack, and Toe, had stationed themselves so they were looking down at them from different angles. It put a peculiar kind of pressure on you. Hill stared at the young leader to keep from looking at the others, but he found that he was more aware of them standing over him than he was of his own guys sitting by his side.

"In America and in Europe you are not very familiar with the peoples of Vietnam, even the peoples of Asia. We, on the other hand, are rather more familiar with the peoples of America and Europe. Or should I say the *armies* of America and Europe.

"Soldiers of the West first came to Asia during what you call the Opium War. Your allies, the imperialist British, had begun a trade in opium in the only city of China where they were allowed to trade, Canton. The emperor, seeing the effects opium was having on his people, banned the trade and closed China to British merchants.

"The British naturally resented this resistance by mere Asians and promptly went to war. Their weapons then were as advanced as *your* weapons were to *ours* when you first came to Vietnam. But the British were rather more successful. They defeated the Chinese." He was staring at them coldly, seeing if they were reacting. None of them moved.

"China had to cede Britain's right to deal in opium," he continued, "and was forced to open other cities besides Canton to their merchant capitalists. In addition, the British secured a number of other concessions so that in their own country the Chinese found themselves being governed, tried, and sentenced by foreigners. Not just the British, but Germans, Frenchmen, and Americans, too. Eventually a group of Chinese religious—you called them fanatics—rose against this foreign intervention in Chinese affairs. The West was outraged, and British armies were joined by German, French, and *Americans* to put down these outrageous Orientals who dared to be so rebellious on their own soil. The American Marines were particularly proud of their kill ratio even then. And it was found that two Marines at one machine gun could kill very great numbers of crudely armed Orientals at very little cost to the American taxpayer.

"You will be pleased to hear that again the armies of the West were ultimately successful. The cost in Chinese dead was rather high, but then, we have not yet found a way to make Oriental deaths seem very significant in Western eyes. Perhaps it is our fault; there may be too many of us." He smiled again, but again it was obviously a thin veil for really burning anger.

"The West then divided China into territories controlled by various warlords, who were in turn supplied by various Western governments. It was all very orderly and profitable for the West, and as the benefits of your civilization spread, several advantages besides the spread of opium came to the Chinese, too. Each morning, for instance, in Shanghai, those who had starved to death in the streets on the previous night were picked up, first by horse-drawn carts and later by mechanized trucks manufactured in America and Germany. All Asia was deeply grateful for this sign of civilizing progress."

Hill found himself wondering how much of what the guy was saying was true. It sounded like the black power boys going after whitey. *That* he *knew* was true. He suspected what this guy was saying was probably as true as anything they were telling them in the States. It didn't change his mind about anything, but he had to admit he enjoyed the sheer nastiness of it, the pulling down of the pants of all the great and glorious legends and showing them to be the hairy-legged monsters they were. He wondered how they'd react if he started clapping his hands and saying, "Yeah, yeah!" and "Listen, brothers. Tell it to us like it is!" He had to fight a smile at the thought. No sense in getting your teeth kicked in over a little joke.

"Since your Marines had been so successful in demonstrating the virtues of democracy to China," the leader continued ironically, "the United States Navy generously decided to make a similar demonstration to Japan. The Japanese had wanted to be left to their own crude Oriental resources, but your Navy presented them with the more exciting choice of welcoming capitalist merchants or facing a broadside from their steel-lined ships. The Japanese, being a very quick and imitative people, not only supplied the correct answer to this example of liberty and freedom at work, but have imitated them religiously ever since. We have even had some experience of their battleships offering us the same kind of choices.

"In China a revolution against the warlords was begun by a young revolutionary called Sun Yat-sen. He wanted the same rights for the Chinese that Americans are said to have in America. He was very successful at first but needed help when the warlords joined together to defeat him. He had read of the American Revolution, and he appealed to America for help. No help was forthcoming. He had read of English parliamentary democracy and appealed to them for help. No help was forthcoming. Lastly, he appealed to Russia. Help was forthcoming."

He looked right at them. "It is strange how history tends to repeat itself." He said it as if they should know what the hell he meant, but Hill was lost. Had Ho Chi Minh appealed to the United States? If he had, they hadn't heard about it in Philly.

"With Russia's help the revolution succeeded, though it took many years and many, many lives," the leader continued. "When Sun Yat-sen died an old but respected man, he had many young followers who wished the revolution to continue. One was Chiang Kai-shek, another Mao Tse-tung. One night when they were meeting to decide how the government would be run without their leader, a monstrous series of murders was committed. Was it the Communists who committed this atrocity so many years ago? No. It was that great 'democrat' Chiang Kai-shek—who murdered all the Communists or suspected Communist members of Sun Yat-sen's ruling committee. All—except one." And now the smile was real. "Mao Tse-tung. In a life of mistakes, Chiang must regret this mistake most of all."

He held them all in his gaze, and the smile had turned to ice. Hill liked it—liked the skill, even liked the story, true or not.

"Chiang was a reactionary," the leader went on coldly, "and became a puppet of the landowners and merchants. His whole government was so corrupt it even angered your American General Stilwell, who was in China and demanded his government withdraw its support. But the capitalists of Wall Street had more power even than the American general, and it was finally Mao Tse-tung and the People's Army

87

that drove Chiang from the mainland of China as they will drive him from the American fortress of Formosa.

"For the first time," he said, singling out Pershing and staring directly at him, "for the first time in many generations there is no starvation in China. For the first time the peasants of China are free from the brutality of serfdom, of the landowners and the warlords; for the first time the children of the poor and the weak are being taught to read and write; for the first time the parents of the poor and weak know they will not have to sell their children in order to eat. The landowners, the capitalist merchants, and the mercenary soldiers of Chiang Kai-shek have suffered because of this, and one can understand how the landowners and capitalist merchants of America would attack the men who have brought this about, but"—his eyes narrowed, and the anger in his voice seemed strong enough to touch—"but one would think that the poor colored masses of America who know what serfdom is, who know what it is not to be educated and what it is to be hungry, one would think these people would at least be sympathetic to those who have struggled so hard to escape oppression in their own country."

He held Pershing's gaze in silence. Hill turned; he could see the sarge wanted to make a retort—badly. But he could also see that the leader had made some kind of impact.

"But it was not America who first brought the benefits of Western civilization to Vietnam," he continued. "It was the French. Very near the time *you* were so energetically doing the same for Japan. I am sure you will find the incident that began it very amusing." He laughed. "As a matter of fact, it *is* amusing.

"A French merchant was dealing in Hanoi. Noticing how weak and backward the Vietnamese emperor's army was, he gathered together seventy-five men in his own pay and one hundred and twenty-five mercenaries in the pay of someone else and, with that mighty force, seized control of all Hanoi." He laughed again. "You Americans must be somewhat chagrined that it was once so simple." He looked as though he expected them to enjoy the sarcasm, but no one was reacting at all.

"But of course, the emperor was not without some weapons to use against the industrious Monsieur Dupuis. He appealed immediately to the admiral of the French fleet himself, asking that he remove the offending Monsieur Dupuis from Hanoi. The French admiral answered that nothing would please him more and set sail at once for Haiphong. When his forces ultimately arrived, he was astounded to find

88

the city so weak. And it tempted him as only a Westerner *can* be tempted by weakness. In the end he felt there was nothing he could do but arrest Monsieur Dupuis and conquer the city and the country himself—in the name of France, of course. And this he did. It *is* amusing, *n'est-ce pas?*"

He looked from one to the other, but that edge of nastiness had crept back into his voice. When his eyes came to Hill, Hill started studying his own knees. The instant he did it, he could have kicked his ass. *He* wasn't a goddamned Frenchman.

"That was in *1883,* twenty years after the slaves were freed in America. So it will not surprise you that we had people who wanted to be free, too! A leader named Lui Yun-fu rose in the countryside. His followers wore what you call black pajamas, and they carried a black flag.

"And the Black Flag Army of the people of Vietnam reconquered Hanoi from the French. That Army of the Black Flag was fighting for the freedom of Vietnam against the West before the Russians had heard of Karl Marx! Before Sun Yat-sen was eighteen years old! Before Mao Tse-tung was born!

"But of course, for an Asian to reconquer his own land is considered an affront to Western civilization, and the French were very disturbed that their peace-loving soldiers and missionaries should be so insulted, so they prepared to conquer Vietnam with much larger forces. And to save the greater destruction of his people the Vietnamese emperor was forced to cede all effective control of his country to benefits of rule from Paris.

"And we did benefit. We grew large crops of rice, cotton, tea, coffee, sugar, and rubber. We mined tin and coal and salt. Of course, we did not waste these goods on ourselves. Instead, under the wise guidance of the French we became one of the biggest exporters of natural products in the world. The money that was thus earned by the wealth of our country and the work from our backs went quite properly to the French and the landlord class of merchant capitalists who were willing to lick the spittle of French plates—which is as it should be in any well-run country outside the West."

He seemed to realize how much he was getting under their skins because his pace quickened, his voice matching the sarcasm of his words.

"There were, I am afraid, ungrateful Vietnamese who continued to resist the gifts of French domination, and here one must credit the French. Though they lacked napalm and flamethrowers, pellet bombs, and claymore mines, they were masters at executions and torture. And hundreds *were* executed and tortured. People just will not learn what is good for them!

"When the Japanese conquered Southeast Asia in World War Two, the French Army surrendered, of course, and the Navy ran. But the French administration was stuck. However, it had proved so efficient at getting the Vietnamese to produce for others that the Japanese left them in control and only redirected the end product. The high principles of the French administration were such that it did not object to this arrangement since Japan was obviously becoming almost as moral and law-abiding and democratic as the *real* West.

"Another Vietnamese leader rose to lead the struggle for independence," he went on, "the struggle that had never really ceased among the backward and ungrateful natives. Like the other leaders in that struggle, he revered the tradition of the Black Flag, as I am told Americans revere the tradition of George Washington. He had even read of George Washington, and as his forces began to harass the armies of the Japanese in the hills and in the delta of the Mekong River, he appealed to America for arms and assistance. And he received some arms, a little assistance, and many words of encouragement. He read of the Four Freedoms for which the war against Japan and Germany were fought, and this man—Ho Chi Minh—was determined his people would share in the new world that would come with peace."

Hill had looked up again. He listened half-incredulously.

"When the atom bomb fell and Japan surrendered, there were still Japanese forces in Vietnam, held tight in the main cities by the black pajamaed army of Ho Chi Minh. His forces took Hanoi and Saigon, and he was proclaimed a national hero and the emperor, Bao Dai, the puppet of the French, the millionaire and playboy, the leader who served his people in Paris nightclubs and whorehouses, abdicated. A Republic of Vietnam was proclaimed. Ho Chi Minh was its president.

"This new republic was accompanied by no killings, no murders, no demands for blood revenge against the rich landlords or against the French. It was proclaimed with a quotation from the American Declaration of Independence that 'all men are created equal, that they are endowed by their Creator with certain unalienable Rights, that among these are Life, Liberty, and the pursuit of Happiness.' There were Buddhists and Catholics and other religious sects in the government, as well as Communists. Why not? They all were Vietnamese, and they be-

90

lieved, in their peasant ignorance, that the Republic of Vietnam in all its variety had as much right to existence as the Republic of France or Spain or South Africa or Japan or the USSR or Brazil or the United States.

"One day you may forgive us for our ignorance. At that time you did not. The British fleet, or part of it, soon arrived in Saigon with rocket ships, destroyers, heavily armed sailors and marines. The British admiral in charge took over the city, dismissed the government and cabled that he 'had thrown those scoundrels out!' Vietnam was given back to the French."

His voice suddenly sounded tired, as if he were tired of the struggle himself, as though he'd gone through it all, the whole lot from 1883 on, Hill thought.

"When the French returned, landlords—French, Chinese and Vietnamese—demanded back rents—sometimes for the whole period of the war. The peasants couldn't pay, of course, but having a peasant locked in an unpayable debt with interest mounting beyond any possibility of even his ancestors' paying, is one of the forms of Western civilization we are most familiar with. Certain retributions of a more physical kind were also taken. Ho Chi Minh remained ungrateful even in the face of all this and continued to fight. And by what must have been a mistake, the French were ultimately defeated and driven from Vietnam."

He smiled at them—acidly. "It is then we got to know you Americans more intimately. Of all the major powers, yours alone dissented from the Geneva Agreement which called for a nationwide election. An election only Ho Chi Minh could have won. For like Washington or Bolívar or Tito or Lenin, he was considered, by the poor illiterate revolutionaries he led, the father of his country. A hero and a savior. But America declared Bao Dai, the cheerful, fun-loving, Paris-bound Emperor of 'French' Vietnam, the leader of the 'State of Vietnam.' You had not yet invented South Vietnam.

"Since the whole of the world—even 'peace-loving democratic nations' like the United States—tended to regard Bao Dai as a male Marie Antoinette, the American government urged him to appoint a 'prime minister' for his new state. As he was used to listening to Western voices without question, he did.

"The appointment of Ngo Dinh Diem was done, of course, in the typical Western democratic way. That is, the people of Vietnam were not even told of it until it had happened. Since Diem was not an illiterate rebellious peasant, but one who had served the French and was rich enough to have been living for many years in America, the wisdom of this Western method can hardly be questioned."

He was no longer looking at them. His eyes were on the ground, and his voice had trailed off so that Hill had to strain to hear.

"Through all these years we had been one nation. Like most nations we were a mixture—different tribes, different religions—but not more so than China or Russia or the Philippines. To us there was no such thing as a South Vietnam or a North Vietnam. If you doubt my peasant knowledge of this, ask General Ky, who is a Northerner, born, raised, and educated in the North, as were *most* of the generals you have bought for your army of 'South' Vietnam. But America is a powerful nation with a powerful desire to bring Western democracy to Asia, and so there was never a national election for a national leader, and 'South' Vietnam became as real as South Africa or Alabama.

"Since those days the United States has brought the people of the territory they call South Vietnam the benefits of many different governments. They all have been essentially the same in that they have lived only because of the money and arms of the United States. They have been essentially the same in that they all have been corrupt; they all have protected the merchant capitalists, the landlords, the money-lenders—those who lived on the people like leeches and vermin under the French, those who continue to this day to live on the people like leeches and vermin."

He had stopped, his voice running down like a record player with the battery gone dead. Nobody moved. Nothing happened. Hill had been caught completely. It was hot and still within the bamboo confine, and sweat had long been running down his forehead, under his arms, along his back and between his legs. Finally, the young leader raised his head. He looked at them, and then he spoke—clearly, quietly.

"This is the heritage you bring with you—American soldiers."

iii

No one stirred for a long time. Finally, the leader stood and walked quietly from the confine. Again nobody moved. Then Tick led the other two musketeers out. Without saying anything, the two guards who had brought Lieutenant Morris in picked up his stretcher and took him out. Another guard moved in and parked right near the entrance with an automatic rifle spread across his lap. There were a few more seconds of silence, then—

"Shit!" Miller spat on the ground to show his disgust. Pershing looked at him quickly and nodded warningly toward the renegade GI, who was still lying on the ground about six feet from them.

"I don't give a good goddamn!" Miller said, glaring at the gate. "That little prick making it sound like they're all angels and we're monsters or some damned thing. They were running around in loincloths shooting bows and arrows at each other before we came, and they still would be if we hadn't!"

Janowitz laughed. "Maybe they'd rather shoot bows and arrows at each other than have us supplying them bullets to do it with." Hill could tell he wasn't mocking Miller, but Miller couldn't. Miller glared at Janowitz as if he were about to knock him on his ass.

"Maybe so, *sir,*" he said belligerently, "but I can introduce you to a lot of people in Saigon who don't want Ho Chi Minh or any other Communist telling them how to run their lives. And they don't think he's any national hero either!"

They all were standing now, and Pershing got in between Miller and Janowitz.

"Come on, we're all tired; let's get some sleep. There's nothing they'd like better than have us start arguing among ourselves." And again he nodded toward the GI character, who was still lying there on the ground watching them.

"How do you know that bastard isn't here to keep us from arguing?" Miller said, still angry. "Maybe that's just what he's here for, to keep us from talking, from deciding what we're going to do."

"We aren't going to do anything," Pershing answered. "They can talk till their tongues fall out, and we'll just listen and say nothing. And if he wants to spend his day watching us, let him. He won't hear anything but snoring because all we're going to do is sack out. That speech made me awful sleepy."

He laughed, and all the others, but Miller, forced a smile with him.

Good ole Pershing, Hill said to himself. He'll pull us through this yet. He grinned at Janowitz. Janowitz shrugged. He hadn't meant to needle Miller, and he seemed a little upset that he had.

"Don't sweat it, sir," Hill said. "Once they get organized, I'm sure they'll build a special corral for the officers. Meantime, you go ahead and curl up by my feet, and you'll find it smells just like the BOQ."

"Mighty kind of you, GI." Janowitz grinned. "I've met many an enlisted man whose feet stood up to the hot sun better than the other end of his anatomy, but I'm going to be democratic and breathe the same pungent air you do." He sprawled out on the ground beside Hill, staring up at the dappled leaves and the sky beyond.

Hill closed his eyes; then after a second he spoke. "What do you think of all that stuff?"

"I suppose that's the way it looks to a lot of them," Janowitz said very quietly. "He sort of left out that Ho was trained in Moscow and that Russia hasn't been chipping in to help in this little mess just because they have a scholarly interest in the au-dai."

Hill grinned. Too bad they couldn't lecture back. With Janowitz and Pershing they'd probably have half that VC outfit buying mutual funds and taking 'em all back to Saigon singing "Land of Hope and Glory." He twisted so he was looking right at Janowitz.

"Looks like they've gone to a lot of trouble to get hold of you," he said, glancing over to where the renegade was, to make sure he couldn't hear. "You don't figure they're planning to build a basketball team for the next Olympics, do you?"

"Hell, if that was the case," Janowitz said with a mockery to match Hill's, "they'd be as hot for you as they are for me."

"True," Hill replied, "but of course, the national press coverage on the Thirty-eighth Street Boys Club isn't quite up to what you cats at Michigan get."

"Yeah, the world's full of injustice," Janowitz sympathized. Then his voice grew serious. "I don't know what they've got in mind for me, Hill, but it doesn't worry me, because just between the two of us, I don't know anything you or any of the other guys at the camp don't know. I don't know how long it's going to take them to find that out or how disappointed they're going to be when they do—but I hope it's not going to be too painful for either of us."

Hill lay there for a time, thinking it over. If Janowitz was telling him the truth, the poor ape was in it up to his eyebrows. They obviously thought he knew something, and if he didn't, they'd assume he was holding out. And what did they do when guys held out? He didn't know for sure, but he'd seen those newsreels of brainwashed guys in Hanoi calling themselves criminals and asking to be forgiven by the North Vietnamese people. They looked like zombies. And some cat had told him once that the Russians had cut the balls of the Hungarian prime minister or president or something when he didn't see eye to eye with them about a five-year plan or some other earthshaking matter. If they did that to a prime minister, what wouldn't they do to a first lieutenant?

Well, he'd always envied Janowitz. Maybe now they were quits.

6

i

Janowitz had a hard time getting off. By nature he was an optimist, and he knew he had a way of getting on with people. It wasn't something he had to work at; it just happened. It always had. It made him smile even to think about it, but he felt he could even get on with this group of VC, too. That young leader, walking around like the student prince in an Oriental musical—and talking like an undergraduate at a meeting of the SDS. If he *were* playing basketball for Hanoi University, he'd needle a guy like that—but he'd get on with him.

And the big fat one, Tack. He struck him as a muscular version of his own Uncle Marv. Always pinching the women and laughing at his own jokes and loving a good roughhouse. A guy who loved the world as it came and made you feel the same way—in small doses anyway.

The only one he felt was a natural enemy was Tick, the skinny, violent one who'd lost his temper at Pershing and who seemed to be second-in-command. That one he could fear, but the others he felt he could live with—even as enemies—if it weren't for the fact that they had obviously picked him out specially—just as they had that MAAG lieutenant colonel.

And that's what he couldn't figure. What did they think he knew? And how far would they go before they realized he didn't know anything of value? The only thing he could imagine they might not already know were the frequencies of the VHF's at a few of the remote landing strips. But hell, he didn't know ten all told, and they could get the lot from one secret file at a dozen different bases and ten different offices in Saigon. And one thing he had grown very sure of since he had come to Vietnam was that there wasn't much in any file in Saigon that the VC didn't have as quickly as any outfit in the field.

So somebody had goofed someplace. He wondered if their bureaucracy was as fucked up as the American Army's. He could imagine hordes of VC NCO's and secretaries in some jungle tunnel passing papers back and forth and someone accidentally throwing his in the wrong file while they were having a tea break. Big joke—provided they didn't fracture his back before they discovered the mistake.

And what about the guy with them who seemed to be a GI? It made him restless thinking of him in the compound with them. He had been aware during most of the leader's little lesson on Western imperialism that the guy was studying him like some kind of botanical wonder. And he smiled again. I could get along with him, too. He looked like a lit major. The guy was frightened and nervous, Janowitz could tell that. Thinking about it, he was all the more certain he was a GI. A Frenchman would have done it with the fire and assurance of justified hate.

If he was a GI, what the hell was he doing working with the VC? Janowitz knew lots of people back at Michigan who despised the idea of America bombing the piss out of a lot of poor Asians. But he couldn't imagine any of them actually going over to the VC. That was carrying dissent a little too far!

Mind you, the traitor looked like the peace-protest type. He could see him with his arms linked with a couple of long-haired dolls trying to keep the Dow Chemical rep from sullying the halls of the Student Union.

All right, what was he doing? Brainwashed? Janowitz wasn't all that convinced about brainwashing. He thought the POW indoctrination they got at the staging area revealed the military mind at its most limited. The idea might have been right, but they made the Communists sound like omniscient visitors from another planet. If they had been as efficient, dedicated, and ruthless as those guys made out, the world would have been Communist long ago. People—even Communist people—were more complicated than that. When the NCAA squad had toured Europe, he had seen a lot of Communists for himself. They had looked a little drab and certainly didn't strike him as having the savvy or the money or even the will to be as fanatic and devious as the psych war boys in the Philippines envisioned. He'd heard about Stalin and the purges, but he'd also played basketball against the Russians, and he suspected the truth was somewhere in between the happy-go-lucky blonds who were turning into one hell of a problem on the basketball court and the abject specimens you saw in the old newsreels swearing listlessly to wild lies that would condemn themselves to disgrace and even death.

He'd read, too, about what people could do to you by depriving you of sleep and giving you alternating doses of cruelty and sympathetic understanding. And he didn't doubt that they could induce a mental breakdown in the healthiest of specimens, but what the hell good was a gibbering neurotic to them?

He doubted that the VC had the personnel or the time to induce so precise a breakdown on each prisoner that they could get exactly what they wanted. They might get him raving, but to get him raving to their tune, that was a different matter—unless he was so important that they were willing to provide some highly skilled psychologist to analyze him and figure exactly what measures to employ and for how long. But even if they had the people and skill to do that, he knew he wasn't worth it. He was just a chopper pilot who happened to have been a damn good college basketball player. And he doubted that the renegade GI with the VC was important enough for that kind of treatment either.

It all was racing around in his mind, the images of brainwashing, the mental picture of the guy sitting there watching him, the thoughts of the Russians he'd played ball against and the ones he'd seen in the movies—and through it all, the heat and his exhaustion were dragging him nearer and nearer to sleep—until the voices of the women laughing came through to him and he forced himself awake. He didn't quite know where he was for an instant; then he placed the laughter distantly, down by the water. He could hear the splashing.

They must be down there, swimming, playing, washing, dipping themselves in that cool blue water. God, he'd love to make love to them. All five. Not one was without a kind of sexiness. Even the relatively ugly one, too thin and with her nose all bent up, pugged. She had that full mouth they all had and solemn dark eyes. He could imagine her in passion, the solemn eyes burning, the wide mouth open and wet, her hands clutching at his back.

But the one who really turned him on was the very long-haired one. They all had long hair, pulled back in a bun down the neck, but little clutches of this one's hair kept falling loose and straggling in front on her face. It was black, coal black, and she had straight black eyebrows to match. Like the others, she wore her pants rolled up to about her knees, but even that way her legs were graceful enough to make him ache with desire. And she had good boobs and a tiny waist—glories that didn't go automatically with Vietnamese women for all their beauty.

But the thing that got him was her face. He'd watched her help the doctor while he was carting Morris around, and she'd blow that straggly

97

hair away and you'd see those huge hazel eyes, flecked with green, so intent and serious, like a kid solemnly playing nurse. It made him want to smile and take her in his arms at the same time. He must have fallen in love a thousand times in Saigon—maybe ten thousand times! —twice a minute sometimes, and he knew there were Vietnamese girls more beautiful than she, but watching her walk around that camp had convinced him he'd give a month's salary just to hold her for one night. And the screwing was secondary. He meant to *hold* her. To watch her, to make her laugh, to make her listen to him and be touched by what he said and how he said it—after he'd screwed her, of course. God, he hoped she spoke English.

He could imagine her now, standing down there in the pool, the water dripping down her bare flesh, her hair flowing over her breasts and, in back, just touching the curve of her smooth little bottom—man, if they really wanted those VHF frequencies, all they had to do was let him have a day with her at the pool. One day, one frequency. Ten days in all. Maybe he could rack his brain and remember a couple more. He was sure it wouldn't do anyone any harm, and it would do him a lot of good. And her, too. He could see her now, wet, glistening, smiling up at him, putting her arms around his waist, and pulling him close. God, from the hard-on he had now, he thought maybe he'd give them one frequency every *two* days. That was more like it. More patriotic. He smiled. And with the picture of her face smiling up at him, he finally went off to sleep.

ii

When he awakened, it was pitch-dark. He rolled over and found the renegade GI bending over him, staring at him.

"I'm Evans. Heyward Lee Evans from Bluefield, Virginia . . . It's a name you'd expect from Virginia." Janowitz sat up. He was the only one in the compound. Just this guy, and the guard by the entrance.

"We met once in Manila," Evans went on, "a University of Maryland course in political science. There were eight of us. The one you'd probably remember best was the officer's wife with the big eyes."

It was the right thing to say because now Janowitz did remember. It must have been eighteen months ago. He'd just come overseas and was amazed to learn that the Army had rigged up extension courses from the University of Maryland all over the world. You could take them even in Saigon. They gave only undergraduate credit, but a regular GI could earn a BA over the years and the Army would pay for his last six months on the campus at Maryland. There wasn't anything he could take toward a master's, but he had been interested in lots of things he never had time to take at Michigan, so he enrolled for poli sci and a course in Shakespeare. He'd dropped it after a couple of weeks because the sessions were at night, two hours apiece three times a week, and by the time you did your homework it shot the hell out of your free time. And after a few nights in town he felt Manila had more to teach him than the instructors they had at the base. He could vaguely remember the bright-eyed, all sweetness and American virginity officer's wife, but there was nothing in this guy's face that seemed even remotely familiar.

Tick, the leader's adjutant, the one Janowitz really distrusted, came into the compound and stared at them. Janowitz got up. He wondered where the others were and what was really going on.

"We'll talk about it again. I'm sure you'll remember—if you try," Evans said. And with that he walked out, not saying anything to the adjutant, hardly looking at him.

Janowitz started the night lugging Morris with Hill. They had got the knack of it the night before, but it was still hard work, and he was glad when the first break came. They had already turned north by that time, and he figured they were in Laos. He knew they'd still have to travel by night because the Air Force and the Royal Laotian Air Force—or at least CIA men in Royal Laotian Air Force planes—bombed the trail almost as thoroughly as they took care of the main runs up through North Vietnam.

No one had talked at all during the first hour out. Even the big one, Tack, seemed subdued. Janowitz had nothing to do but think about Evans and how he got from Manila to the VC. And what did it have to do with *him?* He kept trying to remember the classes and if there was any clue. All he could remember was they had talked about political theory, and it seemed to him it was just a lot of elaborate jargon to say something obvious, like the guy who gets the most votes wins—in fifteen easy pages of sesquipedalian verbiage. But all the thinking and recalling did no good. In the end he still couldn't remember Evans' face as being among that anonymous body of students, and he couldn't think of any reason why Evans might remember *him,* much less seek him out in the middle of the central highlands at the expense of one village shot up and several dead and wounded on both sides.

Tick, the adjutant, came to tie his hands after the first break, and

Janowitz turned his back to make it simpler. As he turned, he was almost face to face with his long-haired beauty. She had come to check Morris, whose hammock they'd strung between the branches of a tree just behind Janowitz. The sight of her was somehow so unexpected that it stopped everything in him—breath, heart, mind. One of his three Vietnamese words flashed through his brain: *mỹ*. It meant American, but it also meant beauty. Mỹ. Man, if he was mỹ, American, to her, she sure as hell was mỹ, beauty, to him. She looked up at him, and he thought she would smile. But she just tossed a clutch of hair aside and frowned as if he were a tree that had inconveniently got in her way. The image of her face glowing up at him, adoring and blissful, had been so firmly glued in his brain that her annoyed disregard came as a stunning douse of reality. She didn't love him, after all. The paradox of his warm imaginary world's being at least as vivid as the harsh real world struck him suddenly as wild. He grinned irrepressibly. The girl frowned up at him, looking puzzled and even more annoyed. And that made him laugh. The adjutant jerked tight on his knot, and the girl, his beauty, Mỹ, turned away, scowling and derisive. In a crazy world he found this sequence even funnier.

He was still grinning when they pulled him in line. But Sergeant Miller was in front of him, and his look of frozen contempt wiped the smile away. It would be impossible to explain what had amused him, and anyway he found something very disconcerting in Miller's attitude. He wasn't "military" in the pejorative sense. He just seemed proper— like a stern cantor in temple rebuking an unruly choirboy. From the beginning Miller had carried himself as though aware he was among those who had killed his friends and comrades. If there had been a tinge of American Legion patriotism about it, Janowitz would have told him to fuck off and paid no more attention than if Morris started pulling his serial number on him. But it was more than that—primal loyalty to the tribe, Janowitz thought flippantly—but that didn't cover it either. It had to do with Adnapoz and the other dead, with the things about America that weren't dirty and commercial and phony. And it made Janowitz feel a little like a betrayer for being so "broadminded." Hell, not two days before, that fat, jolly VC had shot Adnapoz, ended his life forever. And yesterday he was frolicking in the water with the bastard. War had grown impersonal, but it hadn't gone that far, not yet.

He smiled sheepishly at Miller and mentally thanked him. The line started to move off, and he fell into step, as the night mist began to settle in the forest.

They marched a long time into the next day. Janowitz wasn't too tired when dawn came, just cold, and he felt maybe he was getting used to the long route marches already. But as the heat came, fatigue came with it. All the VC talk stopped, and they just slogged on. The sweat poured off him, and he cursed all the cheap beer they got at camp and his habit of taking three or four long cool ones every night before he went to sleep. But at the same time there was nothing in this world that he'd have given more for than a cold beer.

When dawn came, the breaks had stopped, and after a while he felt as if they were going on forever. The way was easy now, a wide, clear trail, thickly covered on top and no indication of bombing at all. A couple of times they crossed streams, and he sloshed through, trying to get his feet as wet as he could, but the leader wouldn't stop, and he began to think the fucking VC were camels, as well as moles and mules and fox.

He was the only American not carrying something. That was one victory Pershing had won, because, except for making him help with Morris, they had never tried to give him any work to do after that first flare-up. Pershing could be a soap salesman with officers, but he worked miracles sometimes. If he hadn't seemed so rock solid, his smoothness might have been an irritant, but he was a real performer, and the few times Janowitz had seen him off duty he felt he was probably as likable as he looked. He knew that Miller had a blind, doglike loyalty to him. And though the combat zone tended to wipe out color, he didn't think a man with Miller's attitudes would have such unquestioning faith in a Negro if the guy didn't really have it on the ball.

He was feeling sorry for Miller most of the night. He was carting boxes of something wrapped in plastic—medicines, Janowitz guessed—and they'd tied the stuff high so as not to ride on his arms where they were looped together behind him. He could see it forced Miller's head forward, and he imagined it made his neck stiff as hell. During the night he could hear him breathing hard and struggling with every step. And when the breaks had come, he had flopped down exhausted. For this kind of life, you really needed to be as lean as the VC. A thick, muscular guy like Miller paid for every pound of muscle he was carting around.

The line finally stopped. Janowitz couldn't see up to the vanguard, but he figured they'd found a spot to camp. But nothing happened. Then he decided it must be aircraft. He listened. A hyena, maybe it was a monkey, was squawking distantly. Birds cawing and protesting their presence, but no sounds of the twentieth century at all.

Then the line moved forward a few feet and stopped again. The front was still obscured around a bend, but the next time it happened he saw that they had come to another stream. The leader and Big Tack were standing by it, letting each man in the line stop and drink—not too much—and then sending them on. Some break! They were really in a hurry about something.

The wounded were off to one side, and the five women were taking them water. As the line moved forward, Janowitz tried to get a good look at the beauty, Mŷ. He could pick her out, bent over one of the hammocks, the doctor right beside her. He guessed they were attending the one whose jaw had been blown off. There weren't many wounds that appealed to Janowitz—he had a heightened regard for the body beautiful and intact—but that was one of the worst wounds he'd ever seen. He thought of Miller and Adnapoz. It was a vicious circle all right. We blow someone's jaw off and they hate us, and they shoot up a guy who wouldn't purposely harm a fly and we hate *them*. But it's been going on since time began, and it didn't look like it was about to stop.

When Janowitz got to the water, the leader said something to Big Tack, and Tack turned to him as if he couldn't believe his ears. The leader spoke again—very calm and unruffled, but looking the fat one right in the eye. Tack stared for a second, then came over to Toe, the little tailender, who was just helping Janowitz down to the water so he could drink. Tack muttered something angrily, and they signaled Janowitz up before he had even touched the water. They untied him from the chain, and then Tack undid his hands, directing him with a jerk toward the wounded.

As they went by the leader, Janowitz could see the adjutant, Tick, leaning against a tree, smiling. Big Tack was muttering under his breath, and the leader kept his eyes on him as he passed, but Janowitz felt he was suppressing a smile himself.

A guard fell in behind Janowitz, and he realized what was going to happen. They were going to have him cart Morris again. But not with Hill. Tack was going to be taking the other end—and he didn't like it. Apparently that was the joke. Well, *funny,* Janowitz thought, but I don't like it either. And I want my drink. He stopped dead in his tracks. The guard behind him almost ran into him. Tack walked on for several steps before he realized Janowitz had stopped.

"I want to drink," Janowitz said, enunciating each word clearly.

Tack just stared at him a second, then cursed and said something angrily to the guard. The guard poked Janowitz in the back with his gun. Janowitz didn't move. Tack had already gone on. The guard poked again—hard. Janowitz turned and backed a step away. He was used to elbows in his ribs, but he had never mastered the primitive instinct to strike back—and he felt it now. The guard signaled him on. He was a kid of about fifteen, but he looked tough and cocksure. Janowitz shook his head no and, when the guard moved forward, circled slowly. He didn't want to do anything quick enough to force the kid to use his gun, but he wasn't moving on until he got his drink. He had been thirsty before they stopped, but the sight of the water and the feel of it on his feet had raised his thirst to an issue as powerful with him as anything short of his mother's honor. And for a drink at a moment like this, he felt his mother would probably say, "Son, there are times when we can compromise."

He heard Tack approaching—muttering. He half wheeled—not too fast. "I want a drink." The kid jabbed with the gun again. Janowitz jumped away. Tack reached out and grabbed him, hurling him to the ground with a force that was as powerful as it was unexpected. Oh, baby, Janowitz thought, I'm not going to like this prisoner of war game. Don't flare, son. Don't flare. He lay there a second.

"I want to drink," he said again. Tack came at him with his foot cocked. Janowitz twisted quickly, rolling so Tack was between him and the kid with the gun. The move beat Tack by a foot or two, and Tack threw up his hands exasperatedly—as though this were not his day; even prisoners objected to getting beatings. He turned to the guard and started yelling at him and then walked on to where the doctor was working. The guard signaled Janowitz to get up and nodded toward the river.

The kid was smart. He walked ahead of Janowitz, with his back to the river, so Janowitz had no chance to break for the woods. And when they got to the water, he crossed to the other side, so that while Janowitz drank, he was on one side of him, and Big Tack, the doctor, the wounded and their porters, as well as the nurses, were on the other.

Three of the wounded had already moved off when they got back to them. The nurses were hoisting their packs. They were small packs, but each nurse carried something, along with a rifle. Like the rest of them, they were perspiring, but Janowitz marveled at how fresh they looked. Mỹ hadn't seen him approach, and when she stood erect, she seemed to take no notice at all. She just blew the hair from her eyes and went off toward the line as though her mind were already on the dull necessity of trudging on for endless more miles. As she went by him, he realized she was even smaller than he had thought. Five feet, probably, when she stood absolutely erect. And she wasn't as pretty as he'd imagined. Everything was a little blunter, the nose, the cheekbones. The waist got him as she walked away, and the big clinging sweat spot. But that was pure sex, unadulterated by any differentiation of size, beauty, personality, or appeal.

The guard poked him with the gun, vindictively. He turned. Okay, Mac, I'll leave your women alone.

The support pole of Morris' hammock was hung between two trees. Morris was white and pale as birch bark, but he tried to greet Janowitz with a show of warmth.

"How goes it, Dick?"

"Better than walking," Morris croaked. Janowitz was surprised. He didn't think this guy was capable of a joke even when he was well.

"Listen, if you're goofing off, *I'm* going to ride this next stretch, and *you* can carry the pole."

Morris grinned again, but that was plainly the limit of his strength. Tack was already at the other end, and Janowitz hoisted. The four bearers who'd been carrying during the last hike became guards, ambling behind Janowitz as they moved to join the line, Big Tack leading the way and cursing under his breath the whole time.

When they got to where the leader and Tick were, the rest of the line had passed, but the leader still stood in midstream watching them, and Tick was still supporting a tree. When they got closer, Big Tack exploded at Tick. It sounded like "Up yours, you sonuvabitch" in Vietnamese, and then he turned to the leader and in a tone of voice only a little milder said something that Janowitz would have translated from intonation as meaning, "You and your idea of humor, someday someone's going to drop you in a shit house and close the lid!" Whatever it was, it was pretty good because both the leader and Tick burst out laughing. Tack just struggled on, muttering blackly.

They trekked on for what seemed hours to Janowitz. He had been hot and tired before, but now he was hotter, more tired—and hungry. He felt they would have to stop soon, and at every turn he looked for a site that seemed right for a camp—even checking the cover from above, because he knew that was their first consideration. They passed five or six places he thought would do fine, and each time he had to restrain himself from calling out.

Morris slept fitfully. He looked awful in daylight. Hauling him at night, you didn't see the red pimply swellings on his chalky skin. But in daylight you could tell that he was getting weaker and weaker. Janowitz figured the only way they could keep him in a hammock was to fill him full of morphine, so he wasn't surprised that his eyes looked dull and remote even when he was awake. But he was unprepared for the gaunt, ashen face and the thin arms that flopped about from time to time looking like ads for some Indian charity.

He had just about given up believing that they would ever stop or that he'd eat until they hit North Vietnam when they started down into a shallow valley that looked like a giant soup bowl. Tack was cursing more than ever, and he was dripping with sweat; even his pants looked as if they'd just been plunged into a bathtub. They got below the level of the surrounding trees on the rim—and suddenly the whole valley was alive.

It was a full-scale encampment. There were people everywhere. At least half of them were North Vietnamese troops, and parked under the trees and camouflage netting there were trucks, jeeps, and stacks and stacks of those camel bikes, the ones they rigged for hauling supplies.

The ground had a loose covering of twigs and branches that made walking difficult, and Janowitz saw groups of twenty to thirty women going along pulling up dead branches and tossing down fresh ones with green leaves. It was obviously a regular routine, and from the air it must have looked like any ordinary hunk of forest, but it was bigger than their own forward Air Cavalry camp, and from the number of people moving around, it must have had considerably more traffic going in and out.

No one paid much attention to them as they went down into the floor of the valley. Their column grew tighter, and the young leader walked up and down close to them. Like most leaders, he lost some of his stature and assurance in the presence of other, bigger leaders. Big Tack shouted at a group of women working in a large circle assembling or repairing mortars, Janowitz couldn't tell which. The camp had obviously revived Tack's spirits, and when one of the women yelled something back to him that sounded about as ribald as his yell to them, he opened with a spiel that was full of spitting and laughing and leering *oohs* and *aaahs* that sounded like a detailed history of his credits as a lover and satisfier of women. One or two of his remarks brought jeers from the women, but that seemed to spur him on even more, and he went on shouting to them until they finally were lost from sight between the trees and piles of equipment.

The column finally stopped a short way up one of the valley walls.

Caves had been dug in the sides of the hills, and they apparently served as headquarters because runners were coming and going all the time. Janowitz figured they probably served as air-raid shelters, too, when the bombers came. He noticed that for all the signs of mobility, the trucks and jeeps and bikes, the mobile artillery, even antiaircraft guns, nothing was actually moving. People were walking around, but nothing on wheels was rolling. That was for the night, he guessed, and he wondered if all this was to be shipped out to the South and how, if they had been heading right into it, they hadn't run into even one supply unit on their whole trek.

It didn't bother him long because the doctor suddenly came up to them with two uniformed carriers and they took Morris off. When they lifted the stretcher from him, it was like losing a piece of his own body, so deeply had the pole cut into his shoulder. They were moved immediately into a little copse—and there, to his amazement, were split-board tables and benches and huge caldrons of soup and pots of steaming rice. The VC untied the other GI's and let them sit at a table all to themselves. Everyone was so exhausted and hungry that no words passed. There was no need for talk; they all were thinking the same thing, feeling the same thing. All they wanted to do now was eat—and, with luck, get some sleep.

While they were eating, Tack came over carrying a giant earthen jug. He slapped it on the table and rested his arm on Janowitz's shoulder.

"You make a good water buffalo, GI; maybe your father was the peasant, okay, like me." When Janowitz didn't respond, Tack turned a little sour.

"Maybe tomorrow you *eat* like the peasant, okay? All of you. We don't need Yankee to go home. Dead Yankee better, right here from Vietnam." Nobody looked up. Finally, Tack removed his hand and walked away.

When they finished, their nemesis, Tick, took them farther up the hill. They passed a couple of groups being lectured. They didn't fool around about indoctrination, that was sure. Then, near the top, they saw a row of small caves. There were guards outside each one and another row with machine guns below that. The adjutant sent them into one. It was pitch black as they worked their way back. But it wasn't deep, and once they were inside, the light from the cave mouth made it easy to see the limits of the cave. About the size of a good living room. The ground was cold and hard, but they all stretched out and

106

went to sleep easily. Janowitz could only remember wondering who was in the other caves. How many prisoners did they have? And what did they intend to do with them?

iv

He had been dreaming and his head was pounding when they woke him up. It was night. He was aware groggily of feeling stiff, sore, and still haggard with the need of rest. Toe, the ugly little one, was nudging him with his rifle butt. For a second he hung between pounding dreams and an awareness of the noise of engines reverberating through the cave. When he finally shook off the dreams, he realized engines were revving up, moving, straining outside. After the days of jungle noises it grated like being on the helipad at Bien Hoa with fifty choppers taking off at the same time.

The young leader and Tick were standing behind Toe. Tick carried a green-tinted battery light that made everything seem even more disconnected. He motioned Janowitz to his feet, and then they woke Pershing. The Negro sergeant major reacted to the prod from the rifle butt like a shot. He rolled over, alert, ready. Then, when he saw the group of them, he rose slowly to his feet.

The leader and Tick led them out of the cave without waking the others. Two guards fell in behind. Janowitz glanced at Pershing, and Pershing nodded back, like don't worry, it's going to be all right. Janowitz grimaced wryly. He should be the one reassuring Pershing, not the other way around. He wondered how old Pershing was. He had a way of making you feel he was as old as war itself.

The whole valley was alive with action. Here and there there were other green-tinted lights, but only a few. Trucks, people, cycles—all seemed to be moving without lights. Janowitz was amazed at the rate of activity. It was like an anthill, people scurrying every which way, everyone seemingly oblivious of the others, but keeping in strict lines of passage. Most of the movement appeared to be on foot, but he could hear the roar of several large engines, and occasionally he caught a glimpse of the yellow and blue flare of a backfire among the foliage.

He guessed that it was still early evening. They'd had a quarter moon in the early hours of the night since they started the march, and he suspected it was that early moon that was giving the milky translucence to the clouds now.

They'd cut across the side of the valley wall, and the leader and Tick had already turned into a cave entrance when they heard a crash of metal and wood—followed by a huge crunch and the sound of cascading crates and violent Vietnamese voices, masculine and feminine. He and Pershing exchanged an amused glance. The ant heap wasn't all that well organized, after all. One of the guards shoved them on.

The cave mouth opened to what might be called an entrance hall. About six feet in, it turned sharply, and they were in a much larger room. There were three or four standing lights in here—all tinted green. And the floor was lined with stretchers. They were in neat rows, a VC on each. Janowitz saw one who'd lost his leg below the knee, but it must have been sometime ago, because now he was looking around calmly, smoking a thin, dirty cigarette. Some of the others were asleep, one or two moaning uncomfortably, but they all seemed bandaged and clean. At the far end of the room there was a long cloth divider. The young leader signaled him and Pershing up to it; then he led them through.

They were in a small operating room. There were battery lights all around the sides, but there was a huge moon-shaped light and reflector over the operating table. It looked like a Western hospital. White uniforms, gloves, operating equipment, nurses, respirator—everything he'd ever noticed in *Dr. Kildare*. Two doctors were working on someone. You could see a section of the body—it was the chest—but what they were doing he had no idea.

As soon as they'd finished sewing up the operating wound, with those quick, deft movements, the guy they were working on was carted off, and another was brought in from the room they'd come through. The nurses changed off, three that were busying themselves at the side relieving those helping the doctors, but the doctors just went right on. The few words that were spoken were all in French.

They watched two operations in quick succession. No one paid any attention to them, as if the three of them were part of the white sheets covering the walls.

Then they brought in Morris. He was unconscious and receiving blood plasma. Pershing glanced at Janowitz, but no one else made any sign of awareness of their special interest.

They started on his shoulder—it looked to Janowitz as if they were scraping the bone with a thin, sharp, spoonlike thing—when the young leader touched Janowitz's arm and signaled them out of the room.

They marched them back to their cave without any word of explanation, and when they got there, the leader turned away and disappeared in the darkness. Tick pushed them into the cave without giving them the benefit of the light, and then he walked off, too.

Janowitz and Pershing felt their way around the bodies on the floor and squatted down next to each other against the back of the cave. They waited for a few seconds, both suspicious that the little one, Toe, had lingered to hear what they might say.

"You think he's still out there?" Janowitz finally whispered.

"Probably," Pershing replied. "But if we keep it down, I don't think he can hear us over all that ruckus." The valley was still alive with the sounds of motors, clanking metal and shuffling feet.

"What do you think that was in aid of?" Janowitz said quietly.

"I don't know. But they don't seem very worried about letting us know what's here or how it's laid out. They must be pretty convinced we aren't going to escape."

"I don't see much chance that they're wrong."

"One air raid could change all that."

Janowitz didn't answer for a time. He hadn't been thinking about escape—although he knew that was what he was supposed to be thinking about. When they hit the camp, there were so many VC and North Vietnamese around, some mental stopcock had twisted, and thoughts of escape had been dried up at the source. Pershing was obviously not only thinking about it, but planning on how much he could tell Intelligence once he got back to camp.

"What I was wondering," Janowitz finally said, "was why they took us to see Morris. You think they're trying to convince us they're really goodies at heart?"

"That's how I'd call it. Morris took a beating on that march. I think they're trying to show us they weren't killing him deliberately."

"Why?"

"According to Mao Tse-tung, Communist armies must always demonstrate that they are disciplined and humane. No pillaging, no raping, concern for the wounded. 'Wherever our armies go, they must build good relations with the masses—and the more masses the better.'" Pershing chuckled. "That's not exactly it, but something like that."

And Janowitz was floored again. Pershing a student of Mao Tse-tung. Was it just the *Little Red Book* or more than that? Either way, it was becoming clearer and clearer why Miller and the others regarded him as God's Chief of Staff. "And you think they're that eager to convince *us*?" he said.

"Probably. At least it wouldn't surprise me. In the Korean War they spent hours on all our POW's. Part of it was to get control; part of it was to get selected personnel to participate in propaganda. But even with the hardened groups that wouldn't cooperate in any way, they were willing to spend hours trying to convince them life in China was moving toward paradise while our troops were exploited slaves of the capitalists. It's like a religion with them. Any convert matters, and they apparently feel that if they don't convert immediately, the lessons may sink in and work the miracle at some unforeseen moment in the future."

"You seem to know quite a lot about it." Janowitz didn't hide his surprise.

"I'm a soldier . . . a professional soldier. Knowing the enemy is part of my job. And since the Russians first tried to take over Berlin, Communism has been our enemy."

He sounded so competent and so certain Janowitz could feel the tension drain right out of him. It explained Miller's attitude toward Pershing, everything. He was not a blowhard, as Janowitz had suspected might be the case, but someone who really did perform.

Without facing it consciously, Janowitz had been wrestling with the knowledge that he was the only functioning officer in the group, the man with the ultimate responsibility for all of them. Doubt about what the VC wanted him for personally had been preoccupying him, but back in the furthest reaches of his brain the other responsibility had been gnawing at him, too. And now he knew he could share it. He had found someone he could count on.

He didn't feel the need to say anything more. After a few seconds he hunched down on the floor of the cave and went to sleep.

v

They were awakened by Big Tack. He was clanging the tube of a burned-out mortar with a flat piece of metal, and in the cave it echoed like an explosion in a boiler factory. Everyone was on his feet in seconds. Tack laughed and hit his clanger a couple of more times just for fun.

"My name is called Trach, Duong Tu Trach," he bellowed. "You are these Yankee comrades. With me, okay? Today we do some little work—then we have the breakfast." He hit the clanger a couple of more times and ushered them out into the daylight.

The sun was still high in the sky, and Janowitz guessed it might be about two or two thirty. The adjutant Tick—looking calculating as always—was standing outside with little Toe and four guards. They fell in behind, with Big Tack leading the band on as though he were out on a company outing.

As they moved along under the trees, they saw the same pattern as the day before. Little bands of women working here and there, troops —VC and North Vietnamese—in small groups getting instruction, eating, resting; stacks of equipment, bicycles, supplies. They went by the place they had eaten the night before, and there at one of the tables at the far end they saw some of the other guys from the camp. He didn't know all their names, but he recognized Merrill and York.

"Mer-rill!" Hill shouted, and in a split second Tack and one of the guards had hurled him to the ground, Tack's knee in his chest and the guard's gun point-blank in his face.

"That way! Go!" It was Tick shoving them, with the guards and Toe helping, pushing them along brusquely so their backs were to Merrill, York, and the others. Janowitz didn't see the point, but he wondered what Pershing was thinking now of "building good relations with the masses."

They were quick-marched about a hundred yards farther down one of the valley walls and then stopped. Hill had been bounced, pushed, and manhandled along until he was up with them. Then, as suddenly as the roughness started, it stopped. Big Tack moved to one side with Tick, and they talked quietly. Janowitz hazarded a look up the hill and could see Merrill and the others at the table. They seemed to be in a study session. He saw one of them raise his hand and then stand up and say something and then sit down.

The instructor was a woman—young—and Janowitz could see she was the kind of instructor every deserving GI dreamed of. Goddamn, he thought knowingly, these bastards *are* clever! He could imagine some bright-eyed idealist from Hanoi lecturing about Wall Street warmongers and capitalist aggressors and a bunch of GI's going along for the ride, some out of native courtesy, some for the sheer fun of it, some to avoid trouble, and some in the hopes that the full course of instruction led to remedial sessions in the sack with teacher. That, he imagined, was Merrill. Merrill was a supply sergeant, and Janowitz had got to know him well. He was a hard-nosed con man from Miami, and he could sell salt water to the Polynesians. A chick with the party line had about as much chance with him as a Salvation Army chorister with the devil.

Janowitz knew the ironclad rule was: Do not partake in classes—but he couldn't honestly see much harm in it. Nothing he'd ever seen or heard of their propaganda was likely to get much but a laugh from any of the GI's he'd ever met, and a guy like Merrill wouldn't believe his own mother that it was raining outside without sticking his head out the window to check first.

Finally, it dawned on him that Tick and Big Tack were now *deliberately* letting them see the others—because all the GI's, even Hill, were staring at them. Janowitz didn't have time to give that twist much thought because they started to move them on again. Big Tack went up to Hill and slapped him on the shoulder like a long-lost buddy.

"You talk when Trach say to talk, okay? Yes?"

Hill looked at him wryly. "Sure, dad. I got your message."

Janowitz grinned with the others. Big George was going to be an asset.

In a couple of minutes they stopped at a little clutch of bushes and were told to sit. Tick introduced himself formally for the first time, "I am Tran Van Tho." This was the day they learned all their proper names, though they remained Tick, Tack, Toe as far as the GI's were concerned. Tick, too, suggested they all now were a band of brothers. Janowitz didn't like him, and the more he saw, the less he liked. They sat in silence for a short time, and then the leader and the traitor, Evans, came along toward them. An older man—he might have been forty—in a North Vietnamese uniform was with them. He was an officer, but Janowitz wasn't sure of the rank. He was talking quietly with the young leader, and they stopped about ten yards from the group; then he went off to one side with Evans. The leader approached the group, nodding some message to Tick and Big Tack.

"From now on we all will be working together," he began. "I am Tan Trong Thai." He moved to Janowitz and tipped his dog tags. "You are Henry D. Janowitz." He said it solemnly, looking into Janowitz's eyes. Then he moved slowly to Pershing and, with the same quiet, almost scriptural voice, said, "John A. Pershing." And the same with Miller and Russell. Janowitz hadn't known Russell's name himself. And despite the leader's unexpected solemnity, Janowitz could hardly repress his amusement as Thai read out Russell's name and Russell's huge eyes stared gravely up at him from his skinny, sallow face.

Hill swung his dog tags out at Thai when he approached with a cool flippancy that undercut the leader's sedate ritual with a note of irreverent mockery. Thai stopped and stared at Hill for a couple of seconds.

"You are George S. Hill. I hope we will be friends." Thai's determined solemnity prevailed, made them all uncomfortable—even Hill, who finally lowered his eyes and made a close study of the brown and red dust between his legs.

"We are going to be together for many months," Thai continued, addressing them all now. Janowitz felt a chill twinge—"months." "I have told you of the struggle of the Vietnamese people against the imperialism of the West. And I remind you that by the laws of international justice which your own country has proclaimed, you are all condemned as war criminals for what you and other soldiers of the West have done to the peoples of Vietnam. But we do not seek revenge—or punishment. We accept you as unknowing tools of a corrupt government and only demand that you make an effort to understand your bourgeois philosophy and why the revolutionary peoples will always resist the American flag and the running dogs who hide beneath it.

"Today," he went on, "we begin. I want you to tell me a little about your homes. Your fathers' work. The taxes you must pay. Whether any in your families took part in the riots and demonstrations against American aggression in Vietnam." Janowitz stiffened. He hadn't expected it to come this way. He had thought the first test would come at night—a dark office, lights on him, and maybe Thai. A couple of rough guards. Pleasantries at first, then maybe a cuff or two, an electric shock. He'd seen too many movies maybe, because here it was, out in broad daylight, with all of them together, so any kind of brutality seemed impossible.

"Russell," the leader said unexpectedly, looking at the little Southerner. "Russell. Where is your home?"

The answer came very slowly. "My name is Arnold J. Russell. My rank is private first class. My serial number is sixteen one eighty-nine one fifty-four."

Thai was hardly more surprised than Janowitz. He had obviously expected at least a handle for argument. Like "I'm not talking." Then he could say, "Why?" and either get an answer or launch into a speech, but Russell had moved it onto a different plane. Janowitz felt a surge of what he recognized as red, white, and blue patriotism. One for our side.

Thai looked at Russell for a long time before he turned to Hill. "You are a man with an interesting background, I'm sure, Comrade Hill." Very pleasant. Then fiercely: "Where were you born?"

Hill looked up. There was a little grin on his face as though he were trying to suppress a laugh. God, Janowitz thought, he would have to see the absurdity of it. What's he going to do? He saw Hill glance over at Pershing—and Hill's eyes were bright with the thought of some mischief, and Pershing could see it as plainly as everyone else. His look to Hill might have killed a more sensitive man. It was threat military, personal, lethal. Big George shrugged resignedly. Pershing had subdued him. He turned back, contemplated his shoes a second, then looked up at Thai.

"You know my name," he said quietly. "My rank is specialist fifth class. Five bowls of rice to two says you know my serial number, too. Thirteen seventeen fifty-eight double six."

Big Tack took a step toward him with his rifle butt raised, but Thai raised his hand, and Tack stopped in his tracks. Thai walked over to Hill. He wasn't an inch away. He smiled, but when his words came, they grated with emotion.

"I did not know your serial number, Comrade Hill, but I have seen children scraping in charred woodland for nuts or insects to eat because your soldiers had burned their rice and your airplanes had scorched their land with fire and poisoned their crops with chemicals. Even if you do not cooperate, I will be able to teach you how much *five bowls of rice* means to them!"

He turned and walked away. They sat in silence for a time. Finally, Tick called them to attention, and they were marched back across the hillside, past the tables where the North Vietnamese troops were now eating, to their own cave. It was obvious *they* were not going to be fed.

When they settled in the cave, Pershing remained standing. All the time he spoke, he never once looked at Hill.

"The rule is to give your name, your rank, your serial number. No more. Nothing! Not please, thank you, yes, sir, no, sir, or fuck you! And we have just been given a first-class lesson in why. Nobody in this outfit has starved children. Nobody in this outfit *wants* to starve children! What happens to kids in VC villages is the same that's happened to kids in villages, towns, cities, on any goddamned farm—wherever and whenever they've been in the way of war. The people to blame are the people who *start* wars. But because one of you opened your goddamn mouth, we will go without food, and we were made to feel like the criminals they keep telling us we are!

"And that's bad for two reasons. They get us feeling guilty enough and we'll start talking, start trying to 'make up' for our 'crimes.' And the other reason is that when one guy puts us in the stew, it makes all the others angry—and the hungrier you get, the *angrier* you're going to get. And then they've got another tool to use against us. So what's the rule, Russell?"

Russell looked up, surprised. He glanced over at Hill, then very slowly again, "My name is Arnold J. Russell. My rank is private first class. My serial number is sixteen one eighty-nine one fifty-four." Janowitz grinned. It even reduced Pershing's anger. He turned to Hill.

"Is that right, Hill?"

"George S. Hill. Specialist fifth class. Thirteen seventeen fifty-eight double six." It came deadpan and like a shot. They all relaxed. Janowitz was doubly relieved. Pershing had obviously made a study of this POW bit and knew the ground rules, the methods—and the subtleties. And Russell and Hill had managed to salvage this first encounter without any real loss. Deep down in his heart he had wondered how Hill would react. After all, he was a Negro, and definitely not the type to run around singing "The Star-Spangled Banner." But it was obvious that, for all his horsing around, he was basically as loyal as the rest of them. And Pershing probably had a greater hold on him than he even had on Miller. The only real worry was how long the VC really meant to starve them and what new games they might introduce.

He was more than a little uncomfortable about his own position. He was the officer and technically should be in command. But it was a ridiculous technicality. He was an officer by virtue of his flying—he sure as hell wasn't a combat officer. Morris was the CO of this outfit, but more important than all that was the plain fact that Pershing was their real leader.

Janowitz felt that if he didn't open his mouth when he thought a leader should, he appeared weak and wishy-washy. But he also knew he was an outsider with only a legalistic right to intervene at all, and if he did, not only was he going to create antagonism, but he might also undermine Pershing. And that would obviously do more damage than any good he might momentarily achieve.

So the best he could do was to try to remain apart, like the outsider he was, and use his rank to support Pershing when it looked like it might help. It was against his nature because he was inclined to be a hubba-hubba leader, if not a disciplinarian, but he'd just have to cool it.

About an hour after they'd returned to the cave they heard a heavy bombing attack and, shortly after, the drone of planes flying at great height. B-52's. Janowitz guessed the bombing had been five or six miles away. He wondered how this camp would look on an air-reconnaissance photo and mentally challenged himself to think of revealing details he might spot. It was only fifteen minutes or so later when the first casualties began coming in. They could see a number of wounded and plenty of evidence of damage—from mangled bikes to a huge howitzer that had been smashed like a kid's toy.

It was almost sunset when they took them out again, and they were all savagely hungry. The lesson was simple and crude. Toe came into the cave and, imitating Thai, introduced himself formally—Than Chi Thao—then he ordered them out. They were led along the side of the hill, self-consciously past large groups of North Vietnamese who were sitting in circles, and finally parked almost at the crest of the hill looking down on the area with the tables. Then they watched as the other group with Merrill and York were brought in and fed.

Merrill and the others moved around freely—Janowitz could see only two guards with them, but he assumed that this was staged for their benefit and that there were probably six or seven more hidden in the bushes and trees. But he could see Merrill laughing and enjoying his meal. Janowitz was hungry, and it pissed him off. And the crudity of it pissed him off. And its effectiveness! It worked. He envied those bastards down there—pure and simple. He could turn it to hate and anger—but he couldn't turn it off.

They got the full treatment—watching the group with Merrill finish, lounge about the tables talking and laughing, some smoking. A VC came finally, and the whole group came to attention. The VC spoke to York, and York answered. Something was funny because the resulting laughter rolled all the way up the hillside to them. Then it was Merrill's turn to say something funny, and they all laughed at that, too. Janowitz had never been chickenshit—not even very military at all— but at that moment he could have reamed that crew until he made Captain Bligh sound like a psalm singer. Finally, the VC released the others, and they wandered away, out of formation. Janowitz's stomach was in knots—and he could tell he wasn't alone.

Twice during the night they were taken to watch other groups eating. The first time it was just an ordinary group of young VC. The second time he was so hungry his head was aching. It was a bunch of women, a strange mixture of old and very young, and a few kids that didn't look a day over twelve. They were chattering over their bowls, smiling, laughing . . . as though there were no such thing as a war. A big curved aluminum strip was strung like a floating mobile in the tree branches over the place where they had built a fire—evidently to shield it from night observation. It not only reflected the glow of the

116

fire but suffused the whole area around with a rosy tint. Janowitz and the others stood, first on one foot, then another, clutching themselves for warmth, watching the women, listening to their own stomachs growl, feeling their resistance was stupid and childish, knowing that was exactly what they were supposed to be thinking.

As Janowitz huddled there, feeling even colder because the area around the fire looked so warm, he remembered the mornings coming down to the ovens, his dad starting the fires, and that same red glow warming first the worktables, then the whole bakery. He could even smell the dough. And as he watched one half-toothless old crone, spitting with mirth, one of his pet theories recurred to him.

It had come to him long ago. His first year in high school. He had made the basketball team, the first freshman to hack it in the history of Highland Park. All season long he was number six, the first substitute. He had played in every game and sometimes *most* of the game. Once he was even high scorer—with twelve points. And they went to the finals, and he had gone in when Jerry Kregoski was injured in the first five minutes of the game. He was not only top scorer, but he scored the winning basket in the last seconds of the game.

The next day at school he was Mr. Big. Everybody from the principal on down was all grins and handshakes and congratulations and great, man . . . and it was going to be clear sailing, a certain scholarship to college, pro offers eventually, a golden horizon. And he was miserable. Oh, he smiled and grinned and took it all like cake, but inside he was dead. It wasn't anything he could put his finger on, just that he was lonely. He was the youngest on the team and didn't have a girl—didn't then really want a girl. But all the rest of the team went to parties after the final, and there had been people hanging around waiting for them when they came out, yelling and clapping them on the backs. He got several pats, but there was no one there he knew. His mother had been going to come, but she had to get up as usual at three to go to the bakery, and he had convinced her he was going to spend most of the night on the bench and it wasn't worth her losing sleep for. He'd ended up going home on the bus alone, trudging through the snow to the bus stop, standing under the yellow cadmium glow with a bunch of kids he didn't know, getting off at the stop before his own—by the billboards—so he could walk past Walgreen's and maybe see somebody he knew. But the place was empty, and he'd gone on, up the echoing, deserted stairs, to the dark, deserted apartment. His mother had left sandwiches and cake—and a note. "Your father would have been very proud of you." It had almost made him cry.

He'd gone in the living room and got the picture of his dad and put it across from him while he ate. And when he went to bed, he felt even worse.

The next day none of the celebrations touched him. He had every reason to be happy and he remained miserable. And at the moment when he was feeling lowest he'd come out of the john and almost bumped into Fred Dillard. Fred was about five feet four and wiggled along on two aluminum crutches strapped to his upper arm. He couldn't move his hips and had to swing and lurch along like a demonic parody of human grace. Watching him labor up and down stairs, especially when it was snowy or wet, was about as much as Janowitz could take. He wanted to reach out and carry him—but he knew that was wrong—and at the same time, watching the misshapen legs twist and dangle, he knew he could never be a doctor like Uncle Marv wanted him to be. He couldn't stand the sight of it—and the thought of handling and manipulating legs like that was enough to make him shudder visibly.

But when he had caromed off the wall to keep from hitting Fred, Fred's face had been alight with joy.

"Save that shoulder"—he had laughed—"we're going to need you next year!" Hank had grinned back, but in that instant the paradox floored him. There *he* was—already six feet, good-looking he knew, a basketball hero as a freshman, with a shining future, a glorious today . . . and he was Mr. Glum. And there was Fred—five four of twisted, malformed flesh, with a face like a wrinkled apple, a poor student with little future worth talking about, and even the simplest routines of life a major trial . . . and he glowed with happiness.

Hank had long known the easily mislaid truth that happiness isn't dolloped out with things or attributes or even fortune, that it obeys its own rules. But right then it occurred to him that maybe happiness came to people more or less evenly whatever their circumstances. He wondered if Fred didn't know as much happiness as he did despite the apparent difference in their advantages. Fred probably got as much of it from walking up a steep hill as *he* did from scoring twenty-five points against Central.

And as he got older, he found confirmation of the theory in many things. Pictures of the happiness of refugees landing on a Israeli desert shore in nothing but rags, people who had lived through hell but whose faces now wore more happiness than he'd ever seen on the faces of the rich and comfortable at home. The sheer gaiety he'd seen among the Negroes in Alabama, people who suffered as much material privation as anyone he had personally met, but who also seemed to know levels of happiness Southern whites could never achieve . . . and so incident after incident led him to the idea that maybe it was balanced. Maybe Somehow Someone Somewhere kept the scales even. He never exposed the thought to close analysis, but he frequently saw reason to think it might be true.

And now, watching those women eating with their fingers from wooden bowls: women whose lives were in instant danger of being ended by the brutality of hot lead, or mortar shards, or searing napalm; women who had probably already experienced the senseless death of children or husband or family; women whose wildest fantasies couldn't contemplate *ordinary* life in any decent American suburb with central heating, air conditioning, automatic dishwasher, refrigerator, television, record players, closets full of clothes, cars in the garage—hell, even inside toilets and hot and cold running water—women who didn't know dentists or schools or Simmons mattresses or a set of china. Yet there they were as happy as the women at his mother's bakery on their annual picnic. And he wondered wryly what happiness being a prisoner of war might bring him. One thing he felt certain of: It wouldn't come tonight. He was getting sharp pains in his stomach, and he felt bloated, though he knew there was nothing in there but air.

By the time they took them back to the cave he was cold and convinced he was too hungry to sleep. But when he curled up on the floor, he slept, though his stomach pained him and his head throbbed. It was a disturbed sleep, full of fragmented images of his mother and the bakery and his dad. Even his dad's coffin—only somehow also his own—with the golden menorah above it, for it was Hanukkah, and the candles shimmering, as though they were going to consume the whole room. And with the feelings of sickness and the dreams he felt weak and dependent and uncertain like a child again.

vi

When morning came, it took him a long time to shake it off. They were all awake before anyone came for them. And everyone moaned sleepily about being hungry. It wasn't long before Toe came and looked in the cave. Not ten minutes later, food was brought to the guards. Janowitz watched the guards eat, trying to pull himself out of the mood of his dreams. He knew he'd have to protest this starvation

119

bit, using the Geneva Convention on POW's and everything else he could to get the men food. He didn't believe for a minute they'd really starve them. It was a test of strength, and he had to fight. He kept reminding himself that people always said the second day of starvation was the worst, that if they held out, it'd be easier tomorrow.

But it was not until they took him out of the cave that he really functioned again. In the sunlight he gradually revived. He and Pershing were being led by Thai, the young leader, his adjutant Tick, and the renegade Evans across the valley toward the spot where they'd had the session yesterday. It was a good walk, and Janowitz was grateful, because it cleared his mind, and when they finally got there, he realized he needed a clear mind.

Morris was hanging in a hammock between the branches of a tree not far from the bushes where they'd had their study session. Two women nurses were with him, and he was getting plasma. He looked as bad as he ever had. Janowitz had ferried a lot of wounded, and experience had taught him enough to know that if Morris lived, it would be luck. His color was almost all gone, his breathing was shallow, and his lips were a watery blue. Tick started to speak, but Thai stopped him.

"This man," Thai said, quietly addressing himself right to Janowitz, "needs blood transfusions, a further operation to graft skin on his shoulder, medicines to fight infection. If he does not have them, he will die.

"You have seen that we have many wounded. We have few doctors. Little medicine. Less blood. We must ask ourselves if we can afford to use our resources to keep alive a war criminal—especially when those with him show no willingness to cooperate in the smallest degree."

God, Janowitz thought. That's the game. They're going to blackmail us with Morris, and he wondered if that was why they had dragged Morris all this way. A knife to use against them if they needed it.

"This is not the way I would choose," Thai went on. "But we must make our decision this morning." It didn't sound like a threat, more like an apology. But threat it was because he nodded up the hill. They could see the rest of the group coming down with Big Tack in the lead and Toe and a group of guards bringing up the rear.

Thai turned away and, with Tick, moved Morris so that he was hidden by some undergrowth. Evans directed Janowitz and Pershing over to the spot where they'd had the session the day before. Janowitz kept hoping Evans would leave them so he could talk to Pershing, but that was precisely what Evans was *not* going to do. Janowitz felt enor-

120

mous pressure to make their decision quickly. They couldn't argue it in front of the others.

"I think we'll have to go along—a little," he said softly to Pershing.

"No, sir. I'm sure that'd be a mistake. As long as Lieutenant Morris is alive, they can use him against us. But if they let him die, they will only harden our resistance. They know that. The more we hate them, the less they'll ever get from us. It's something they understand. They won't let the lieutenant die if they can help it."

It made a kind of sense, and Janowitz might have bought it, but Evans cut in—very calm, very convincing. "You're wrong. They will let him die. They *are* short of medicine and very short of blood. We could offer to donate it, if we have the right blood type in the group, but even so, he needs lots of attention. Unless it's 'worth' it, people much more powerful than Thai have decided it will not be given."

The fact that Evans was suddenly counting himself in among them was not lost on either Pershing or Janowitz, but even more important was the impression he gave that he was telling the truth. It even seemed to convince Pershing. But he faced Janowitz with the same stubborn resolve.

"For the lieutenant's sake, I'm sorry. But it doesn't make any difference. Name, rank, serial number—nothing else."

"We can't just let him die," Janowitz said quietly.

"The chance that you will die resisting the enemy goes with the uniform, sir." Pershing spoke as though he were only reasserting an accepted truth. "Lieutenant Morris might have died back at the village. He may die now. We can do everything we can to prevent it—short of aiding and abetting the enemy. If we fail, Lieutenant Morris has died in action—like many lieutenants before him."

It was mad. Janowitz felt Pershing was right, death went with the job, but thoughts of *Catch 22* went flashing through his brain: "But death means dead—they're going to let him die—like they're going to *kill* him. The guy has one life and they're going to take it away from him!" And yet it wasn't like *Catch 22*. They were in the hands of the enemy, and the enemy was asking for a kind of betrayal. That's when it crystallized. When he knew there was something wrong with Pershing's reasoning.

"Look, John—" He felt like an awkward ass using his first name, but he didn't want to say sarge, and he didn't want to say Pershing. He did want to put it as an equal—not as officer to enlisted man. "I agree with you that Morris might have been killed anytime. But he wasn't. He's alive and we can keep him alive."

"No, sir, it's—"

"Please, just hear me out. We *can* keep him alive, because all they want is for us to take part in their damn classes. All right! Shit, let's take part. We can't let Morris die because we're afraid to *talk* to them!" He eyed Evans belligerently. "If they want *military* information— okay, Morris will have to die. But if they just want to talk about American imperialism and a lot of shit like that, what the hell difference does it make? It's not going to get to *you*. It's not going to get to *me*. They sure as hell aren't going to faze Miller. I don't imagine Hill or that Southern kid give a good goddamn about politics one way or the other, but if they do weaken, I *know* that you and I together can handle them."

He could see Big Tack coming through the trees just behind them. They had seconds.

"You don't understand, sir," Pershing said challengingly. "They'll split us. Have us hating each other—*and* the people at home. Give them the wedge and they'll tear us apart. That's why we've *got* to—"

"Bullshit! They aren't that smart! And we aren't that dumb! You can't kiss off a man's life because you're afraid you can't hold your own against *this* lot." He jerked his head toward Evans.

"They weren't smart enough to invent the system, sir. But they're smart enough to use it. And one thing we learned from Korea was that the only real defense is silence."

"This isn't Korea. We know what they're doing." He tried to keep a drag sheet on his temper. "John, if it looks as if they're winning, we'll revert to silence. But we can't just let Morris die because we're afraid of words."

"You aren't making sense. Believe me, sir, once it starts, nothing can stop it." There was a finality about the statement. The last word. And it had to be. The whole group was there now. Thai ordered them to sit. Janowitz could see that Tick had placed himself just by the edge of the undergrowth that was hiding Morris—so that he served as a reminder to him and Pershing, but the others had no way of knowing Morris was there, much less why.

Thai seemed uncertain how to start. Then he barked at Hill, "Yesterday you did me the discourtesy of not answering a simple question! Perhaps today you will be a little more courteous, Comrade Hill. Where were you born?" It was an officer's parade ground voice— arrogant, overweening, goading with all the confidence of one who knows his victim can't retaliate.

"George S. Hill. Specialist fifth class. Thirteen seventeen fifty-eight double six."

Thai glared. Then he turned quickly to Miller. "Perhaps you will tell us where *you* were born, Comrade Miller."

"Patrick D. Miller. Staff sergeant. Twenty-four six six nine one six six."

Thai sneered. He turned to Pershing. "Perhaps you will tell us where *you* were born, Comrade Pershing."

Janowitz held his breath. Thai was trying to humiliate the wrong man. If anything, his demonstration would have convinced Pershing there was real danger in conceding anything to them.

"Yes, sir. I was born in Shreveport, Louisiana."

Thai couldn't conceal the surprise in his voice.

"Is that still your home, Shreeport, Louisiana?" He had missed the *ve,* but it didn't matter. It didn't faze the almost breathless expectation.

"No, sir. My family moved to Los Angeles when I was two. I call that home."

It had begun.

Nothing much came out of the next twenty minutes they remained there. Thai became very civilized. Tick moved off pointedly, and Janowitz assumed Morris and the nurses did, too. Strangely, it didn't make Janowitz feel good. They'd saved Morris temporarily, but it was a hollow victory if he ever had one. Thai continued to question Pershing; they learned that he had a little daughter, that Pershing's wife had an apartment in Hawaii, where Pershing had gone on his last R and R leave. That Pershing's father had been a farm laborer in Louisiana but had become a bricklayer in Los Angeles and that he worked for a man who specialized in constructing patios. That Pershing had gone to Inglewood High. That his family had not taken part in anti-Vietnam riots.

Pershing answered each question thoughtfully, obviously giving only what was asked, nothing more. And each time he scrupulously called Thai sir—as Thai just as scrupulously called him Comrade. Not once did Pershing look at the other men, but they stared at him with an incredulity that didn't wane throughout the whole period. Janowitz had to grin at the thought of it. They could listen to him answer questions for twenty minutes and *still* remain astounded. That was the kind of faith they had in him. It was going to be a lot more difficult to break this group up than any VC ever dreamed.

When Thai called a halt to it, they were marched up to the tables and given a bowl of thick rice soup. Tick, Big Tack, and Toe hovered over them, grinning—and Evans sat down and ate with them, as though

123

he were one of them. At first no one in the group said a word. Pershing didn't look at anyone, but he ate just as eagerly as the rest. Janowitz smiled reassuringly at the questions that came at him with every glance, but the others were plainly concerned that something had been done to Pershing.

Janowitz remembered what had happened to Hill when he had spoken out of turn the day before, so he timed his words carefully—when the three musketeers were all concentrating elsewhere.

"Pershing took part today because they refused to give Morris medical attention unless we agreed to cooperate," he said quickly. "As long as they don't ask for military information—*and* as long as they continue to treat Morris—we'll go along just the way Pershing did this morning." It took them by surprise. From the way Big Tack turned, Janowitz decided he would have got a clout—if he hadn't made sure he could get it out before anyone could stop him. But it was too late, and Janowitz's mood began to communicate. Now that the others realized why Pershing had spoken, they could savor the feel of food in their stomachs. Hill even held his empty bowl out to Tack with a big smile and said, "Tell the chef it's fine. I'll take another."

Tack was confused, but he shook his head no.

"Will he hit us if we talk?" Russell asked Evans.

"No. You can talk all you like," Evans said.

"Ask him when's mail call," Hill said to Evans. Evans smiled, but before he could answer, Pershing spoke.

"This isn't a picnic. These bastards would starve you and kill Morris if they thought it'd do them any good—just remember that."

Hill looked at him and, after a second, nodded. He turned back to Evans. "Forget the mail, son." Russell laughed. But the point was made, and there was no more talk while they sat at the table. But they sat for a long time, sipping water, enjoying the sun.

The afternoon was peaceful—even amiable. Thai started with Hill. What Hill didn't say was apparently more important than what he did say, because after finding he had been born in Philadelphia, almost every question Thai put to him resulted in a twinkle, if not a downright laugh, from Hill. The answers always came out straight, but Janowitz suspected a lot of color was being left out. When Thai asked what his father did, not only did Hill burst into laughter, but Pershing did too. Finally, Hill said, "He's a retail salesman." And Pershing laughed until the water poured from his eyes.

Then it was Miller. He had been born in Nebraska—on a small farm outside Lincoln. His mother and father still lived on the farm,

124

and he owned a lease on a gas station in Sioux Falls, where he lived with his wife and two kids. When Thai asked if anyone in his family had participated in anti-Vietnam demonstrations—"riots" was the word Thai used—Miller spoke very quietly. "My younger brother is a conscientious objector." He said it as though it hurt, and kept his face down, but after a second he looked up, staring at Thai. "That's why I transferred from the Reserves and asked to be called up."

It was the only harsh moment of the afternoon. Thai had reacted with an understanding nod as though he were the commander of the induction center and knew exactly how Miller felt.

After that it was Russell's turn. He said he was born in Red Hill, Georgia. Thai asked what large American city it was near, and Russell answered Valdosta. It made everyone snicker except Russell and Thai. Russell because he was serious, Thai because he seemed intent on proving he knew a lot about America. Janowitz was willing to bet a thousand to one Thai had no more idea where Valdosta was than he did.

Russell described his father as a farmer and electrician. Thai seemed fascinated, and what kind of mental picture he drew was hard to guess, but for the rest of them Russell described exactly what they had expected—a farm three miles from a one-horse town, a county school with five teachers, a family of eight that didn't worry too much about Vietnam.

Russell was an appealing mixture. In an instant his sad eyes could light with an awareness of how comic his sadness could appear, of how comic the whole human condition could appear. He seemed only to need a reminder to see that it was all an ironic—sometimes macabre—joke. And some of his answers to Thai indicated a gift for timing and self-mockery that would have done him credit on the nightclub circuit. Watching him give his sober but dryly humorous answers, Janowitz could even imagine him in a spotlight, banjo on his knee, telling stories of the folks back home.

Thai had saved Janowitz for last. Janowitz realized he had to keep it strictly serious and as uninformative as possible. He had to set an example—he owed that, at least, to Pershing. It all worked fine—Detroit, father dead, mother nonpolitical—until he was asked where he had gone to school.

"University of Michigan."

"Ah. Then you are an intellectual?" Thai said.

"No." Janowitz grinned. "I'm not an intellectual."

"But you went to university." QED.

"Everyone in America goes to college—or almost everyone."

Thai looked bemusedly at the others. "None of your comrades have gone to university. Are they the exception—or you?"

"I went to the university because I could play basketball. I'm not an intellectual." It was useless trying to explain. Answer the questions directly, and keep it short.

"I am led to believe the intellectuals in America do not support the war against Vietnam." Thai made it a question, and Janowitz could see that nothing he said was going to convince this guy he was not an intellectual.

"I can't answer for the others. *I* support the war." He said it forcefully, and he could tell it had an impact. Thai stared at him for a moment, then thanked them all and left. After he was gone, Big Tack stood up and grinned at them.

"You have hungry? Eh, GI? Okay, we are eating." And eat they did. They were taken back to the tables and served a thin soup. As much as they wanted. And then a heaping bowl of rice with slivers of fish and pieces of vegetable and mushroom spiced through it. Janowitz had never tasted anything like it. They were given chopsticks, but only Hill could manage them, and the rest ate with their fingers. Janowitz had played with chopsticks in the Philippines and Saigon, but he was too hungry to fumble with them now. By the time they'd finished the sun was a huge orange balloon near the edge of the valley's rim. It was still warm, but not sweltering. Tack brought out a big jug, and Toe an armful of little wooden cups. They passed them around to everyone, including Evans, Tack, and Toe. Then Tack poured out a light-yellow drink. It was cool—the sides of the jug were moist, and the chill of the drink even made the wooden cups cool to the touch. A rice wine, Janowitz figured. It all was done very ritualistically. When Tack had filled his own glass, he placed the jug in the center of the table.

"You drink—a little at a time." Only it came out "ah leetle at a time." Then he raised his cup. "To your health—*à votre santé.*

Only Evans returned the toast. But they all drank, and Tack sauntered about as if this were the best of all possible worlds.

"Good, okay?" he said to Hill, slapping him on the back.

"Okay, good!" Hill came back and slapped *him* on the back—hard. Tack juggled his cup to keep from spilling it, then roared with laughter and clapped Hill on the back again.

Janowitz glanced at Pershing. Pershing shrugged. He didn't approve even of this, but he didn't seem really angry. And Janowitz remembered how less than twenty-four hours ago they had watched a similar

scene with Merrill and the others and it had seemed inconceivable—
a collapse of military discipline, of personal integrity. Yet here they
were, only superficially resisting the blandishments of Tack and his
feast. It was so elemental it was frightening. They had been starved,
and then they had been fed—carefully, so it would stick to their ribs.
And sipping the cool wine in the growing dusk, listening to the wind
rustle the leaves, seeing the broad, undeniably friendly grin on Tack's
face—the master of the feast who enjoyed it as much or more than
they did—it was impossible not to succumb to the simple euphoria
of physical well-being.

They sat around the tables for a long time. Evans tried to start a
couple of conversations, but they died against a wall of monosyllables
and grunts. For all the pervasive sense of comfort it was still possible
to dislike *him*. The others were VC—enemies—understandable, possibly even honorable, but Evans was at the very best a traitor, at worst
a suck-ass and murderer. The only good thing that could be said for
him was he didn't push it. When he decided no one would talk to him,
he shut up.

Gradually, as the darkness settled, the valley came to life. Motors
turned; people started moving all around them; voices, even song,
were heard. In a strange way it added to their euphoric ease—to be
sitting there, sipping wine, while all around them others were working.

Tick, the adjutant, finally returned and they were taken to their
prison cave. Janowitz felt he could sleep forever. They were hardly inside when the three stooges called to them and, standing at the cave
mouth, passed them each a sleeping bag. Janowitz took his from Toe,
and he couldn't help grinning. The idea, he realized, was that he would
feel grateful to that little Vietnamese excrescence for giving him a hunk
of quilt. And fight it as he tried, that's exactly what he felt—gratitude.

Evans didn't come into the cave with them, and he was grateful for
that, too. He bedded down next to Pershing. The quilted bag felt
marvelous, he felt marvelous, but he knew he had to get things square
with Pershing.

"I'm glad you changed your mind about Morris, John," he whispered. "I know it must have been hard, but I think it was the right decision, and I promise you we'll stick together and keep things in control."

"I didn't change my mind, sir. And I'd prefer that you call me Sergeant or Pershing." His voice wasn't angry, but it was chilly—and it
stunned Janowitz. He twisted so he could see Pershing, but his eyes

weren't adjusted to the dark enough to make out more than the silhouette next to him. Before he could frame an answer, Pershing spoke again.

"They've already tried to break down our military discipline, and they'll try harder. If we can't give orders that are obeyed, there'll be no holding us together and no control. If I'm John to you, and you're Hank to me, we'll be no more than that to the others. We've lost a lot already. It'd be a disaster to lose that, too—sir." Again there was no anger in his voice, but it bore a distinct burden of bitterness.

"You're right," Janowitz finally murmured. "I won't use John again —until we both agree we have the discipline situation solid." He paused a second. "You're a first-stringer . . . Sergeant Pershing . . . and if I had to be a fucking POW, I want you to know there's no one I'd rather be a POW with."

"By the time this is all over, I hope you still think so."

Janowitz chuckled. "By the time it's over I'll probably be as tame as you've made all the other officers in camp."

He could see Pershing's grin. At least he wasn't immune to flattery. Anyway it was probably true.

"Why did you say you hadn't changed your mind about Morris?" Janowitz asked more seriously.

"I hadn't."

"Why did you answer then?" Janowitz was bewildered.

"I knew that if I didn't answer, you would," Pershing replied. "And I knew if you were the first one to talk, you'd never keep your authority, bars or no bars—no matter what your reasons for talking or what you did to make up for it."

The regret in his voice, Janowitz knew, was a measure of his belief that they had made a mistake—maybe a fatal mistake.

He knew no answer for it, no way to reassure him. After all the VC had had it all their own way so far. Knowing what they were doing didn't alter the fact that it would be climbing a big mental mountain now to give up their chow, their warm comfortable sleeping bags, their sense of ease. Twelve hours ago it would have been easy—they hadn't had any of it. But now that they had, he knew how quickly they would seek rationalizations for keeping it. He resolved doggedly to resist that kind of self-indulgence with all the skill he had—even as he snuggled into the soothing warmth of his sleeping bag and gave in to the languor that had been calling him since the first sip of wine had settled in his full and grateful stomach.

7

i

The next three days were all peace and brotherhood. They went to a new spot outside the valley for their sessions—a stand of pine near a little river. It was quiet, and they felt very isolated. It was always the same group: four guards, Tick, Tack, Toe, plus Evans and Thai. It rained the first day. A soft, steady drizzle from a sky that looked as if it had never seen the sun. The VC walked around as though nothing were happening at all. They ate in it, talked in it, worked in it—like they were fish, Hill said bleakly as they were eating their midday meal, huddling over their bowls of rice to keep them dry.

That morning had been spent in a further—apparently aimless—exploration of their backgrounds. Janowitz tried to follow the course of it but decided that there wasn't any, that its real purpose was to loosen them up, make them feel free to talk. Thai prodded only when faced with silence; otherwise he let whoever was talking ramble as much as they liked. He never asked military questions, just "sociological" ones—how much their fathers made, whether they had refrigerators and cars, how much education their parents had, who owned the places where they worked.

Janowitz was surprised how eager they all were to talk on these subjects. Even Miller willingly went into a long description of how he managed his own gas station and garage. How free he was to determine his own policy, the rewards he got, the kind of service he gave his customers and how his success depended on its being superior to his rivals' on two of the other corners at the junction where his station was located. Part of his willingness was obviously an attempt to prove to the VC the merits of the free enterprise system, but to Janowitz it also seemed obvious that the method tapped a real human proclivity—talking about oneself to a captive audience.

In the next two days he was to see that none of them could resist it. It only required the mildest proddings from Thai, and all of them—Pershing and himself included—were willing to gas on about how they had got where they were, what their home life had been like, what their towns and cities were like. Russell talked of hunting and fishing—in the hot summer and the crisp, polychrome fall—and it made them all homesick, even though Janowitz had never been hunting in his life. Pershing told a tale of a huge family led by a stern, devoted, religious mother . . . and an obedient father. How cleanliness, hard work, and honesty had pulled them all up from poverty until now they stood firm—homeowners, car owners, parents of educated children, mother and father proudly ensconced in a sunny bungalow in Riverside—secure even from the grasping motorized undergrowth of Los Angeles proper.

Hill, who had always seemed to Janowitz a bubbling diamond of optimism, was the only one whose picture of home was tinged with darkness. That the others had sentimentalized a bit was as obvious as it was understandable. No one mentioned sickness, or despair, or failure—or any of the bleaker experiences that skip no one. Hill seemed not to want to either, but as he talked, it was as though he were ambling through a woods and kept bumping into old logs overturning an underworld of worms and rot, black leeches and scurrying centipedes that shivered the psyche.

He'd lived in a dozen places, all within six blocks of one another. An obscure father flitted around the edges of the story, sometimes a source of laughter, sometimes etching Hill's face with shadows of hate that made Janowitz feel his own life had been lived in a sheltered garden. But primarily there was a mother and two younger sisters—scrambling desperately for cover in a world of grasping landlords, unpaid grocery bills, repossessed furniture, welfare payments, and drunken, unpredictable "uncles" and miscellaneous visitors. Hill acted cynically amused by his mother's entertaining, but as he talked, it was clear that he, like the others, found that his words took him down unexpected byways, that there was no controlling the direction the memories flowed, and he would make some aside that made it easy—even for those who had never come near such a thing—to picture a dark, littered, unkempt apartment, a little boy faced with a vicious, rampaging adult male who only a few minutes before had been nuzzling and wrestling amorously with his mother—and now was ready to beat her, her kids, and anyone else who got in his way.

In an academic way Janowitz understood the kinds of psychological lacerations a boy could suffer from seeing his mother lushed up—and then mauled. The former probably being worse than the latter. But his understanding of a boy trying to protect his mother and sisters in an adult world too big for him was something he grasped with more than just intellectual comprehension. His own father had died when he was only thirteen. Technically Janowitz had been an adult—it was two months to the day after his bar mitzvah. And he was already taller than anyone in the family—Uncle Marv, his cousins, Davey and Jules. But along with the ache for his father went the terrible fear of his own inadequacy. He could remember the arguments when they first moved to the apartment building. Old man Allen in his undershirt yelling at his mother because Janowitz had left his bike in the hall. Janowitz had told him to get out and leave his mother alone, but he could still remember his fear—how powerful old Allen looked to him, with his thick arms and shoulders, and a violence of manner he'd never before seen in a man. It seemed the whole world knew by some sixth sense that his father was dead and harried and probed them in a way they never would have dared had he still been alive. It affected everyone—even Julie.

Julie was only two years Hank's senior, but she had always seemed one of the adults to him—before his dad died. And then suddenly even she looked to him as the man in the family. He remembered the nights he'd awakened thinking he'd heard burglars and wondering if his mother had gone to the bakery yet, and if he'd have to protect Julie from rape, and the cold fear that would come over him, knowing he would *have* to fight and feeling certain he would lose. It was nothing compared to what Hill must have gone through, but Janowitz knew enough to know how Hill must have felt.

How the guy had survived to smile at all was the wonder. Hill had apparently lived with it since long before he was thirteen, and with the mother he unwittingly described—flighty, tender, religious, vulnerable —with the arguments with landlords and creditors, it seemed a miracle he wasn't in a mental home. But it came out slowly that like Janowitz, he had grown big and fast and cunning. And unlike Janowitz, he had something other Negroes Janowitz had known had. He had been willing to kill. He was willing to stick a knife in someone or hit him on the head with a brick. It was terrifying—and probably necessary in the kind of environment Hill adumbrated. It gave them a peculiar advantage, that lack of restraint. The willingness to go too far. And as Hill told of his growing up, it almost seemed that it was this that finally brought some order into his life, into his mother's and his sisters'. Mess with them—and die. Or kill Hill. Take your choice. And with that choice, most of the men and the nagging landlords and the hounding creditors—even his father—had backed off.

Hill ended up saying he worked for a wholesale television outfit, but they all got the impression he either robbed the place blind or used it as a cover for something more rewarding. When Thai had asked his last question and Hill's voice had finally trailed to a close, Janowitz felt a respect for him he had never thought possible. He had always liked the guy, but now as he studied him, with his head bent, his fingers slowly kneading the laces on his boots, he felt he had found a brother.

After the first night Evans had moved into the cave with them. Janowitz thought at the time it was a device to keep them from plotting an escape now that they were being taken out of the confines of the valley proper. Later he thought there were other reasons, too. Evans' presence put an enormous restraint on their freedom to talk among themselves, and that, Janowitz figured, was probably one of the reasons they talked so much in the sessions. Then, too, in a strange way it drew them closer to Thai and the three stooges. As prisoners they resented Evans' thrusting himself on them so much they were actually glad to see Thai and his band every morning. Janowitz still had no idea what the VC were working toward, but he knew he and the others were being manipulated—manipulated very skillfully.

On the third day Thai took Janowitz and Pershing to see Morris. It was just after their evening meal, and they all were feeling pretty good. The long sessions of talk had brought them all closer, and since no one had really said anything damaging and all of them—even Hill—had managed to get in a few pertinent remarks about freedom and private enterprise, they all were feeling less guilty.

Morris was much improved. He was sleeping, but he had some color, and it seemed to Janowitz that he was past his crisis. Thai seemed very pleased—and proud. He smiled at Janowitz, and such had been the progress during the days that Janowitz smiled back.

When they left the cave where Morris was being tended, Thai turned to Pershing.

"It is Sunday. I thought you would like to go to mass." He might as well have said, "I'm going to introduce you to the Pope," for the shock it gave Pershing. He just stared, speechless, incredulous.

Thai took them to an area of the camp they'd never seen. Under the higher cover of the trees there were groups of thatched platforms supported by thick bamboo poles. Most of them were about seven feet high and being used as shelters for some of the supplies that would be damaged by rain. But under one of them an altar had been set up. It was already dusk, and the two candles on either side of the altar stood out like beacons calling the faithful.

They approached to within about ten yards—off to one side of the altar. Pershing watched for a long time, very distrustfully. When he was talking about his home, Pershing had said he was a Catholic, and of course, it was on his dog tags, so there was no mystery about Thai's knowing he was. The mystery, Janowitz knew, was what a priest—if that's what he really was—was doing out here. It seemed a big act to be putting on just for him and Pershing.

Janowitz watched the priest for a time with great fascination himself. He'd been to a mass once in Michigan. A gorgeous, sunlit, Coca-Cola girl. He'd met her at a sorority party—stole her from some slob on the hockey team—and they had had a spell of intense sessions holding hands in the library and dry-fucking against the back wall of her sorority. He'd gone to mass because she'd wanted him to—and because he was curious. It never came to much because he couldn't get into her, and he wasn't so hung up on her that he stopped falling madly in love with other girls, and anyway there was a limit to how much fun he got out of sterility games against a brick wall in subzero Michigan weather. But the mass had been pretty interesting. It was a sung mass, and it amazed him how much Judaism was left in Christianity. To hear most Catholics talk, it all started with Christ, but if they had ever gone to a synagogue, they'd have discovered that about fifty percent of the "Christianity" existed long before there ever was a Christ.

But what fascinated him about *this* mass was the incongruity of seeing a little Vietnamese, garbed in a black tunic and looking more like a Buddhist monk than a Catholic priest, doing all the rituals with the same sense of habit and essentially thoughtless routine—however solemn—that *real* priests—and even real rabbis—used. And it had the same hypnotic quality, too. A memory flashed through his brain of a film he'd seen at the Arts Cinema Club—about World War I. Two scenes were matched, face to face. A priest saying mass and giving communion to French soldiers, and then a priest saying mass and giving communion to German soldiers . . . and then the two groups roared into battle, yelling insanely, plowing through mud and barbed wire to stab and shoot and die.

What, he wondered, were these VC praying for? And his eyes went from the priest to the congregation. They all were kneeling when he looked. Probably twenty-five or thirty of them. A few—six or seven— were in North Vietnamese uniforms . . . and then he saw Mỹ.

At least half the group were women. Most of them old. But Mỹ was with two as young as she. The solemn intensity of her expression hit him as though he had been poleaxed by Big Tack. He wanted to laugh at her, and hold her, and love her all at the same time. There in the semidarkness she looked more beautiful than any memory he carried in his brain.

The priest had turned and raised the host, and Janowitz was aware that Pershing had gone on his knees beside him. *He* had obviously accepted that the priest was genuine. For a moment Janowitz didn't know what to do. He thought maybe he ought to kneel. He didn't hold with ignoring other people's rituals. You'd bow and curtsy for the Queen of England, and take your shoes off at a Shinto shrine, so he saw no reason for not kneeling in courtesy at a Catholic mass if that's what the Catholics expected you to do. But he became aware of Thai standing two or three paces behind him, and he decided it would be best to step back and stand with him.

Thai was watching stoically. He nodded when Janowitz joined him, but he kept his eyes on the ceremony. Janowitz watched Mỹ come forward to take communion. She wasn't wearing the fatigue uniform she had worn on the march, but a long white tunic that flowed over her like running water. Her front was cantilevered like some gentle invitation to pillow your head forever on its softness, and then the gown flowed on down, only curving gently for her bottom. She looked as if she couldn't have weighed more than ninety pounds all in. Fragile, delicate, but woman, whole and unstinting.

Janowitz was aware that his weakness for falling in love was a failing he really ought to do something about. He would have liked to have been the type who could just screw women and then forget about them. But even when he had gone to the whorehouses in Manila or Saigon, he was always distracted by some quality in a girl that made him insane for her as a particular woman—rather than as just a specimen of delicious flesh. A face that was tender, or witty, or vulnerable—and from that moment on the physical was always secondary. It was a great quality for a husband, Janowitz thought, but it happened all the time, so he figured—half-ruefully, half-blissfully—that the only possible solution for him was a harem.

But Mỹ really stoned him. She was good for three weeks of single-minded love at least, he figured—even in Saigon. And the way he felt at the moment out here in the jungle, it was like forever.

Then he saw Evans.

He was in line for communion. About three people behind Mỹ. The

134

sight snapped Janowitz right out of his reverie. He could see that Pershing had stiffened, too. He remained kneeling, but his eyes were fixed on Evans as Evans moved along, waiting his turn, then finally stood before the priest, holding out his tongue and taking the thin, round host.

In the time since they'd been held in the camp, Janowitz had built up a positive distaste for Evans, a mysterious, withdrawn, obvious traitor. But there in the light of the candles, with that same reflective, wounded look on his face that had molded Janowitz's first impression of him, Evans was only the oversolemn lit major again, the believer in Good Causes and the Universal Brotherhood of Man, the Campus Conscience who screwed women only as a Meeting of the Souls.

It crossed Janowitz's mind again that maybe it all was an act. The mass, Mỹ, Evans. He felt sure Thai had not brought them there so that Pershing could go to mass, but so that he and Pershing would see Evans. Perhaps that was even why they had got to see Morris—to give Evans time to get here before them.

Evans lowered his head and then circled back to the rear of the people praying. He knelt and then looked directly at Janowitz. For a second there was nothing in his face, then a small smile, and he lowered his head again—apparently in prayer. Janowitz knew he had to accept the possibility that it all was a fake. After all, they'd staged an elaborate raid just to get hold of him. And if they could do that, they sure as hell could put on a little performance like this. But despite the recognition of that possibility, he couldn't feel it was a fake. Mỹ, the priest, Evans—they gave not the least indication that what they were doing was false to them.

But it was even more than that. It was something in the way this registered as their accepted routine—in the faces of the people praying, in their chanting together, and making the sign of the cross together, some forgetting it, some doing it sloppily, some abstractedly muttering their prayers, some just staring, some watching the priest. The whole carried a conviction about it that was more powerful than his doubts.

The mass ended. Pershing hadn't taken communion, but after his first surprise at seeing Evans he seemed to concentrate on the mass. When he made the sign of the cross and turned back to them, Janowitz could see that he was disturbed. Janowitz smiled reassuringly. He tried to spot Evans, but Evans had lost himself in the darkness. So he looked for Mỹ, but by that time she too had disappeared.

When they got to the cave, Thai asked the others to come join them. Evans was already back. Pershing stood and watched him for a second, but Thai took the sergeant's arm and said, "Come along," and he moved off with the others.

Thai led them along the top of the valley wall until they came to another cave entrance. They could hear a lot of noise and laughter from inside. Thai signaled them in.

It was a large cave—five or six times the size of theirs—and as they pushed in, they realized it was being used as a theater. A 16-mm projector was running, and a white sheet on one wall provided the screen. Janowitz almost collapsed. It was a Laurel and Hardy picture . . . and the VC were dying over it. They stared at the screen as though they didn't want to miss the movement of one muscle on the face of even the most distant actor. And they rocked and rolled about in glee.

It was peculiar, but watching them react to this antique product of twentieth-century America made them seem more like savages than anything Janowitz had ever seen them do. Planting rice or harvesting it, walking down a street in Saigon, washing their fat, filthy water buffalo, even haggling at the street markets—in any of these things there was a sort of dignity about them that he always felt went with the peasant and the land. A quality you always credited to farmers in Maine and New Hampshire. People who knew the value of things in terms of soil and labor and the seasons. But sitting there grinning toothily at Laurel and Hardy, rocking and giggling like autistic children on an emotional binge, they reminded him of anthropological shorts on the natives of New Guinea. Thai had made a mistake. In the last three days Janowitz had come to feel very much at home in the life they were leading. The sessions on the pine needles, the PT breaks, the warm meals, the long nights of rest in the cool caves. And Thai and the three stooges were becoming more and more human all the time. Thai's questions—and evident understanding—had made him think there was little basic difference between any of them. But seeing them all—even Thai—gawking with intense, half-frenzied merriment at the silent buffooneries of Laurel and Hardy made him realize there was—a big difference—and he even *liked* Laurel and Hardy.

ii

The next day marked the beginning of the real battle. They all sensed it when they arrived at their private area. Thai was there ahead of them, as he usually was, but he seemed tense. Beside him there was a crate about the size of a whiskey box. Tick ordered them to sit, but nothing happened for some time; then something caught Thai's eyes, and they all turned to see. Four men were bringing Morris on a stretcher. Three women—evidently nurses—were strung out behind them. Janowitz's heart did an involuntary one and a half off the three-meter board because Mỹ was one of them. In fact, all three had made the trek with them. Besides Mỹ, there was the thin, pug-nosed one and the one who was Vietnam's answer to Janet Leigh—a tallish, slender one with knockers that wouldn't quit. She had big eyes and the sexiest face of them all, and Janowitz knew that if he had any sense he'd be thinking of nothing but fucking her—but Mỹ had got to him, and he watched her every move as they came nearer, glorying in her grace, responding like a lovesick colt when she blew a wisp of hair from before her eyes. She was smiling—something he wasn't used to—and it made him feel he had to get to her. If they were going to be going through this for a long time, as Thai had threatened, then he was going to get close to her—somehow.

Morris was awake. His smile of greeting to them was weak, but he looked as if he were going to make it. He was facedown on the stretcher, and he was left that way, but they made a little platform out of logs and he was settled about three feet off the ground, so that by tipping his head, he could see them all. It was pathetic in a way—his expression presumed they were all his lifelong buddies, but in fact, none of them really liked him—but they all made the effort and waved and smiled a little to indicate they were glad he was back.

Once he was settled, the men who carried him left, but the three nurses squatted behind Morris with their backs to the group. When he glanced at them later, it seemed to Janowitz that they were playing cards.

Thai began with an air of friendliness. He had done so the last two days—and succeeded. But today was different. He was straining, and they knew something was up.

"Comrades," he began, "we have come to know each other better. But there is still one area we have not spoken of. None of you has told us of your experiences in the Army. And this is wise," he added quickly, forcing a smile. "For, of course, there is no real need for you to tell us about your life in the Army. We know what you do to the women of Vietnam in the bars and houses of Tu Do Street and the waterfront in Saigon." He was looking with cold significance at Hill; then he turned to the others. Janowitz wondered what the hell that meant. "We know what you do to our villages and crops. We know the bribes you give to those Vietnamese who serve you."

His voice had grown bitter, and he stopped. When he began again, the strained friendliness was there once more. "But we know those are not the reasons that brought you to Vietnam. We do not believe you destroy us simply to destroy us. We do not believe you came from America to make whores of our women. We even know that you do not have to *force* your bribes into the hands of our merchants and our French-trained officers.

"And we know," he continued, "that you are taught that you are here to 'punish aggression'!" His face became taut, and he stared at Janowitz with unconcealed challenge. "Today we are going to see if what you have been taught is true."

He bent down to the little crate and lifted a stack of magazines. He turned to them and carefully let them see the covers. They were copies of *Time*. Janowitz couldn't help smiling. It was as though he were showing them the Tablets. Here, brothers, is the truth. What the hell did he expect from *Time?*

"We are not," he began, "going to ask you to believe what is written in *our* newspapers and magazines. We are going to look at your own capitalist press—a press you believe is honest. Is that not right, Comrade Pershing?"

A pause. "Reasonably honest," Pershing said cautiously.

"You do not think they would lie in *our* favor?"

"No."

"Comrade Janowitz. Do you think they would lie in our favor?"

"Not *Time*," Janowitz conceded with an irrepressible smile.

"No, indeed. Not *Time*," Thai repeated.

He looked through the pile he had in his hand and carefully distributed them to different members of the group. Janowitz took his and checked the cover and the first pages. December 23, 1966. It was well worn, but the real thing. A colored Christmas card on the publisher's page and a picture of Jackie Kennedy on the first page—it was about the row over Manchester's book. It seemed a million years ago. There were pictures taken after Kennedy's death, Johnson taking the oath on the plane, the casket being unloaded in Washington with Jackie and Bobby Kennedy watching. And by some weird mental twist, all that didn't seem as distant as Manchester's book about it. Julie Andrews' picture was on the cover, and as he flipped through the pages, he saw Richard Burton's face and Walt Disney's, a big Hertz ad, and, on the last page, Jack Kerouac. A different world.

There was a marker in each magazine and his was on a page that had pictures of General Ky and Madame Ky—a dish if ever there was one. Four sentences were heavily underlined, but before he got to read them, Thai spoke.

"You will all have a chance to read," he said, "but now I ask you to pay attention." He took out a sheet of paper. "Now. Comrade Hill will begin. Comrade, read what is underlined."

It all seemed childish, but Hill shrugged and flipped the pages to the marker and looked for the underlined bits. "Please pay attention," Thai demanded.

The VC had done a pretty skillful job, and Janowitz wondered how much of a part Evans had played in preparing it. They had issues dating back as far as 1958. And as recent as the last month's. The first quotes were recent ones, and all implied that America had gone to Vietnam to stop aggression from North Vietnam, that the war had started when "Giap gave the signal for invasion," and that two distinct countries were involved, North Vietnam and South Vietnam.

Then Thai asked for quotes from older issues. And *they* stated flatly that Vietnam had been "carved in half" at the Geneva Conference; that North and South Vietnam were one country—one even stated that Hanoi had no right even to the northern half, that the whole country belonged to the government the United States supported in the South—others reported that Diem's appointment as prime minister of the South had been approved and secured by the U.S. State Department; that he had then refused to hold the UN plebiscite that was supposed to pick a leader for the whole country—again with U.S. "approval"—and had thus broken the Geneva Agreement; that the Vietcong had fought in the South "for four years or more before the North Vietnamese arrived in force"; that Diem was corrupt and hated, but that no one would dare move against him "without American incitement or backing"; that before the big U.S. buildup in 1965 the VC had been winning and the government in the South was facing imminent collapse, and that at that time there had been only "one North Vietnamese unit in the South"—and *it* was up near the seventeenth parallel.

One of the guys would read his quote, and then Thai would say something or read from another magazine and show it to Pershing to confirm that he had read accurately. It all had a pace to it, and Thai wouldn't allow any wandering or horsing around. And when Miller read that when the South had faced collapse in 1965, there was only one North Vietnamese unit in the country, Thai jumped hard.

"So you did not come to Vietnam to drive out invading North Vietnamese troops—as your American generals claim, as your *Time* magazine claims. Their own words prove what liars they are. Read what they wrote four years ago, five years ago, ten years ago—and then read what they say now. Your generals have said there is no popular revolt in South Vietnam, that this is a war of aggression by the North against the South. They are liars."

He stopped. Then, more calmly, he began again. "Did America come to punish aggression from the North? No. You came to bolster the corrupt government you appointed in the South. And because your numbers and power were great, it was then that our brothers in the North came to help us. *You brought them here! Not the other way around.* Now, Comrade Russell! Read your quotation again."

Russell stumbled, and Thai wouldn't wait. "He read from the issue of June seventeenth, 1966, that the Vietcong were fighting for four years or more *before* the North Vietnamese arrived in force. That is the statement of your own right-wing magazine. So, you see, comrades, your capitalist press does tell the truth—but not all of the truth all of the time. If they could reverse history—or ignore it—they would convince you you are 'fighting aggression from the North.' But even today read your own estimates of North Vietnamese Army units in the South." He held up another issue. "Forty-five thousand North Vietnamese troops in the South—this year. That is your *Pentagon's* estimate. But on the same page I read, *you* have more than five hundred thousand troops! And the so-called South Vietnamese Army, your puppets, have more than six hundred thousand! All of you to fight forty-five thousand North Vietnamese invaders? No popular revolution? No, comrades, you are not here to punish aggression from the North. You are here, like the French, to support a regime that can live only with your dollars, can survive only because of your guns, a regime that would fall tomorrow if you left—because it commands no respect, no affection, no loyalty. It has not even the strength to incite fear!"

He paused defiantly; then he turned to Janowitz. "Please read the underlined section. The rest of the 'facts' you have. I am trying to help you find the truth between the lines."

Janowitz read. "Ky's Cabinet had nearly collapsed in a dispute between the Northern-born generals around Ky . . . and the native Southerners."

"Thank you," Thai said ironically. Then he read a quote from another issue about Ky's being a Northerner, and another about the head of the Buddhist party in the South being a Northerner . . . and each time he emphasized the word "Northerner." Then he read from another issue—King Hussein was on the cover—that the commander of the *North* Vietnamese troops in 1967 had died of a heart attack and that he was a man reared and educated in Hue. "And Hue is in 'South' Vietnam, as all of *you* have good reason to know." He held up another —General Giap was on the cover—and he smiled. "Even Giap went to the university in Hue . . . as did *Ho Chi Minh!*

"So you see there are generals from the North in the South, generals from the South in the North! And the same applies to Buddhists, and Catholics, and Caodaists—and Communists! There *are* Southerners and there *are* Northerners, as there are in the United States— but Vietnam is *one* country. In the words of your own *Time* magazine, it was 'carved in half' at Geneva. And your country has tried to keep it that way. Most Vietnamese have no idea where Geneva is, but they know their country cannot be cut into two by the words of the capitalist press or even by the armies of the nation that calls itself the most powerful in the world!"

He sat down, folding his legs under him. Hill flipped through the magazine he was holding; Russell shooed at a fly. It remained quiet for some time. Then, very calmly, Pershing spoke up.

"The United States realizes it is fighting the Vietcong, as well as the North Vietnamese. And we do not believe that cutting a country in half is the best way to solve its problems. But your country was already divided when we came to Vietnam—divided between Communists and non-Communists. The aggression we are here to fight is the aggression of the Communists who want to take over the other half of the country—whether it is above the seventeenth parallel or below it."

Thai stared at him.

"You've given us only selected readings from these magazines," Janowitz added in support. "I wish you'd let us read them all. Among other things, I think you'd find that thousands of people fled from the North to the safety of the South when the country was divided. That there are Northern generals—who are *not* Communist—in the South, and Southern generals—who *are* Communist—in the North proves not so much that Vietnam is one country as that it's one part Communist and one part non-Communist. And we're here to see that the non-Communist part doesn't collapse in face of violence from the Communist part."

And Thai stared at *him*. Miller touched Janowitz reassuringly on the shoulder. Hill was grinning broadly.

"The National Liberation Front is not Communist." It was Evans. "There are people in it who are Buddhists and Catholics and Cao-daists and some who are nothing at all."

So that's why we saw the mass last night, Janowitz thought. They're trying to show us the VC aren't really VC at all, just Rinso White angels with a bad reputation. But before he or Pershing could retort, Miller opened up.

"If you're on their side, why don't you sit over with them? You won't get anything by sucking up to us—unless it's a broken neck one night."

"One broken neck," Tick cut in severely, "will lead to a firing squad for all of you."

"I'm on their side," Evans said quietly, his face flushing. "But that doesn't alter what I said. The National Liberation Front is not Communist. It is a government that contains Communists, but all these people around you aren't Commies."

Unexpectedly he reached forward and took the magazine Miller held in his hand. He flipped the pages, and then he stopped. "Here's a nice one. 'Some 16,000 U.S. troops traded blows with an elusive *Communist* enemy . . . so far most of the blood was *Red*. In a week of fighting more than 900 Viet Cong'—that means Communist—'died. . . . Six times the *Red* soldiers launched human wave charges . . . eleven companies accounted for 200 *Red* dead' . . . and so on." He tossed the magazine back at Miller. "Everything in that magazine, everything you've heard and read since we got involved in this war, has stated or implied that every one of those 'Red dead' were Communists. Well, I can tell you that when the National Liberation Front counts its dead, there are Buddhists among them, and Catholics, and many others who've got even less idea of what Marxism is than you."

His voice remained low, but it was angry. Miller seemed stopped for a minute. He stared at Evans like a boxer who's taken a blow that momentarily befuddles his senses, and Janowitz wondered if he was thinking of his younger brother, if there had been arguments like this in his home; he was looking at Evans, but was he really seeing that younger brother?

"They're Communists or they wouldn't be fighting," he said finally.

Evans stood up and walked to the crate. He fumbled in the magazines, then pulled one out. On it there was a picture of the South African doctor who did the first heart transplant. Evans opened it up to the first page.

"Would you read that?" He held the magazine out. Miller hesitated, then in an abrupt, violent move, sent it sailing. It whacked into a tree branch and fell several yards from them.

There was a moment of silence; then Evans walked over to the magazine and picked it up. He started back, but Thai's voice stopped him.

"Let Comrade Morris read it."

Evans looked at him, as though questioning the decision, but Thai did not raise his eyes from the ground. Evans walked slowly over to Morris' stretcher.

Morris had been lying there, half dozing, half listening. Now he tried to hunch himself up on his stretcher, but a grimace of pain flashed across his face. Evans crouched next to the stretcher and held the magazine down below it so that Morris could tilt his head over the side and see it. Morris moved his good arm and took the magazine. Evans let him have it and stepped back a little. When he was clear, Morris jerked his arm and sent the magazine flying again. His face flopped onto the stretcher, but it was turned so he was looking right at the rest of them. He was grim-lipped. Janowitz had to smile. There was plenty of heroic posturing behind the gesture—and that was funny—but there was unexpected defiance behind it, too—and that was rewarding.

None of the VC knew what to do. Evans finally walked over and picked up the magazine again.

"The date," he said, "was December fifteenth, 1967. It's a report of a speech by the *Vice President* of the United States. These are his words. Quote: 'It may be that at some future date some of the *non-communist* members of the N.L.F. may very well want to be brought into a government and may very well be the very ones we have to negotiate with.' "

He walked back to the group and placed the magazine right in front of Miller—the article faceup. "We have always been told we were fighting Communists. This very magazine uses that word exclusively to describe the National Liberation Front in every other story in it. I went through the same indoctrination programs you did. We are told they're Communists, we constantly refer to them as Communists —well, many of them *are* Communists. I am only making the point to you now that the Vice President of the United States belatedly referred to back there in December, 1967. They are not *all* Communists. They never have been all Communists."

He couldn't keep the patronage out of his voice—an intellectual making the obvious clear to the neighborhood beer drinkers—but he returned to his place next to Miller like a buddy. Miller never looked at the magazine, and for a time no one spoke. Janowitz's mind raced. He knew the Army indoctrination sheets and lectures had been simplistic crap, put out by so-called information officers on the assumption that everyone was a thirteen-year-old idiot. And Saigon brass were always shooting their mouths off about its not being a civil war, but a war of aggression by the North, when any ass who'd looked at television for a week knew damn well the ones we couldn't beat were the VC, not the North Vietnamese troops who were constantly getting walloped in the big engagements. Janowitz just assumed everyone over ten took the generals and the indoctrination shit with the same healthy grain of salt he did, but he could see he was going to have to say something or Evans would have succeeded in leaving the impression that the United States was fighting in Vietnam for no good reason at all. Before the moment came, Miller turned to Evans.

"Are you telling me the Communists aren't running this show?"

"No," Evans answered, "I'm only trying to tell you that most of those we call VC are not Communist."

"If they do what the Communists tell them, what difference does it make?"

Evans hesitated. "I don't know," he said solemnly. All of a sudden he sounded like a campus philosopher uncertain even that the sun was coming up tomorrow. "I only know that thousands of people we kill for being Communist aren't Communist"—he looked across at Pershing— "and that to say this is a fight between Communists on one side and non-Communists on the other is an oversimplification."

His voice had fallen so that it was almost inaudible. Janowitz could tell why. For the first time the guys weren't ignoring him. They all were staring at him the way Miller was—because Evans was suddenly talking like a peacenik. And while it separated him from them on one level, on another it made him a part of their own lives, a part of America, recognized and known.

And he wasn't like Thai, whose mind was obviously made up and who had all the answers. Evans sounded like many people back home about Vietnam, as if he weren't really sure what the hell was going on —and that made him seem less strange, too. But more than anything, Janowitz felt, it was Miller's attitude. He suddenly seemed to be trying to figure Evans out, to having turned from blankly despising him to trying to see why he could be so stupid or perverse. And Janowitz wondered if Evans bore any physical resemblance to Miller's brother. He couldn't imagine it—the one slight, sensitive-looking; the other thick, husky, and forthright of face and manner. Nevertheless, it was

144

Miller's speaking to Evans as one of them, as another American, that had broken the barrier more than anything else.

Now they all were looking at Evans—not as a traitor, but with the sort of tolerant contempt most Americans feel for the intellectual, especially the baffled intellectual.

Again Pershing came up with the right answer. His words came almost as quietly as Evans' but as though he were explaining something that was very obvious.

"There may be lots of VC who aren't Communists, but the Communists give the orders, and at the top their policy is determined by North Vietnamese who *are* Communist. If the VC win, it won't be the Catholics or Buddhists among them who will run Vietnam—it'll be the Communists. We're fighting to see if this country will be run by the Communists or whether all the other people will get a say in how it's going to be run, too."

Evans smiled cynically. "You think the people in this country have ever had a say in how the country is run?"

"Not before," Janowitz admitted, "but they have had an election. A real one with secret ballots and real choices. Not the kinds of elections you get in Moscow or East Berlin."

Evans looked discomfited. As if he hadn't expected to be attacked and were both embarrassed and off-balance. Janowitz wondered if he had set himself up as an expert with Thai and the VC and was in a jam because he'd run across two people who could argue as well as he could.

"It's a funny election," Evans said, "that bans the biggest party in the country, is run by the Army, and where the vote is taken only in villages and towns the Army controls by the power of American troops."

"Yeah, funny"—Janowitz smiled—"but somehow it doesn't crack me up as much as a Russian election, where ninety-nine point eight percent of the people vote for the top dog." Hill broke into laughter, and the others followed him like children after the Pied Piper.

Thai stood up. It was a signal for Tick, Tack, Toe, and the guards as well. Evans seemed to accept that the session was finished—not that he looked as if he had anything else to say. Thai faced Pershing.

"Comrade Pershing, you will conduct physical training," he said.

"Yes, sir," Pershing said absently. His mind seemed to be on something else. Big Tack and ugly Toe had started gathering the magazines and putting them back in the crate when what was brewing in Pershing's brain finally came to boil. "Sir!" he shouted.

Thai had already started to walk off, listening pensively while Tick buzzed intently in his ear. At Pershing's call, Thai turned slowly.

"Could we have a minute more of your time?" Pershing asked. Thai hunched his shoulders. Pershing moved quickly to the magazine Evans had placed in front of Miller. He flipped through the pages, found what he was seeking, turned back the page, and looked down at Evans.

"This magazine that carries the story about the Vice President saying there are non-Communists among the VC also carries another story," he said. "I thought I remembered because I knew it happened just before Christmas." He looked down at the magazine. "It's about the massacre at Dak Son. You may remember it yourself. The village of Montagnards who were attacked by VC with flamethrowers, machine guns, and rockets.

"It says here that two hundred and fifty-two unarmed villagers were killed and another one hundred were taken prisoner into the hills. You're right, though, the article calls the people who did it Vietcong and Reds and Communists. If it makes you feel better to know that some of them were Catholics or Buddhists or any other damned thing, it doesn't change my mind one fucking bit. I don't like any of them. And that's what I'm here to fight."

He dropped the magazine at Evans' feet. It flopped open—they all could see the pictures of the ransacked village and the wounded villagers. Evans seemed about to say something back, but he didn't. After a few seconds Thai turned and walked off, with Tick running along to catch up with him. Little Toe reached over and took the magazine from in front of Evans and threw it in the crate.

Finally, Pershing turned to the rest of them. He was smiling. "Now," he said, "I think we'll have us a little exercise."

iii

The rest of the day had gone all their way. After PT they'd been taken back for lunch, and even Big Tack was subdued—not the genial, laughing host he usually was at mealtimes. In the afternoon they didn't go back for a session for the first time in three days. Tack brought them a deck of cards—made in Cleveland, Ohio—and they played poker most of the afternoon. Pershing requested they be let out of the cave for PT twice—and each time the request was granted. When they were heading back to the cave the second time, they heard distant bombing and saw a whole pattern of contrails off to the north.

They felt exultant and wanted to talk, but Evans stayed with them and had the usual braking effect on their willingness to open up. Dinner was a feast—hot rice, vegetables, and strips of meat—and they lingered over it. Hill asked Big Tack if they could have some more of that joy juice, and sure enough, once he understood what was meant, Tack produced a mug of rice wine. They went back to the cave only when they grew tired of sitting.

Janowitz was especially pleased by Pershing's buoyancy. Pershing obviously hated the fact they were taking part in the sessions, but it looked as though he no longer feared any real damage from them. They had saved Morris, or at least got him on the road to recovery, and if anything, they were more united than ever. And the bombing had made them feel less cut off, less securely in the hands of Victor Charlie. When he stretched out in the sleeping bag, Janowitz was feeling good —as good, he noted to himself, as he had on many a night back in their own camp.

He had hardly settled in when Evans brought his sleeping bag over next to him. Evans didn't speak at first, just lit up a cigarette and smoked silently. Janowitz was sleepy, but Evans' presence made him restless. He sure was a funny guy. How in hell had he ever got tied up with the VC? Probably a prisoner who'd fallen for the indoctrination bit, and now he wanted to relieve his guilt by taking as many with him as he could.

Evans smoked the whole cigarette without saying a word. When he took out another, Janowitz felt he couldn't stick it out any longer. Pershing was already snoring on one side of him, and from the breathing and snorting around the cave it seemed everyone else was, too. He propped himself up on one elbow.

"Do you want to say something to me?" he said brusquely.

Evans lit his cigarette and took a couple of puffs before he spoke. The light from the cigarette end lit his face when he drew, and Janowitz could see his thoughtful, worried expression. It mitigated his annoyance. The poor sonuvabitch has really got himself in it.

"I was just wondering," Evans finally said, "if you really believe all that stuff you said today." He sounded hurt.

"What stuff?" Janowitz asked, finding it hard not to laugh.

"About elections and giving the Vietnamese a vote, all that."

"Well, it isn't exactly news that the Russians don't have much of a ballot, is it?"

"No. I just thought you realized it was more complicated than that."

He didn't say anything more for a long time. Janowitz knew it was more complicated than that, but essentially that was the truth. He remembered that Evans claimed he first saw him in a poli sci class in Manila. What did they plan? An in-depth defense of the Communist system? He wasn't sure he could argue on that level—not with someone who was really knowledgeable. He felt he was quicker mentally than Evans, but he suddenly had doubts that all the days would be as easy as this one had been.

Evans kept on smoking. Finally, he spoke—still very quietly.

"I wonder how much freedom there is in a choice, say, between a Johnson and a Nixon?" He paused, taking a long, thoughtful puff on his cigarette.

"In some second-rate hotel some second-rate men decide the people of America will be given a choice between their mediocrity and the mediocrity the second-rate men on the other side pick. Then for four years—whether he keeps his promises or not, whether he's honest or not, whether we like him or not—the winning mediocrity is President of us all, master of Army, Navy, Air Force, of hydrogen bombs and Polaris submarines, of the CIA and the NSA, and all manner of things none of us really knows anything about."

He said it all speculatively, as though he were trying to figure it out as he spoke it. Again he stopped for a long time. Then:

"I guess the popular phrase is that it may not be a good system, but it's better than anyone else has got." He stood up and picked up his sleeping bag. "I thought maybe you weren't so sure—or at least not so sure that you felt it was worth killing people over."

He walked off and went back to the place where he usually slept. Across from Hill and Russell.

For a long time Janowitz couldn't get off. He kept trying to remember what the hell he'd said back in that class in Manila. He watched Evans from where he lay—not that he could see him, just the tip of his cigarette, dull crimson, bright crimson, on and off like a circuit light. He realized that in a really sophisticated argument about the merits of American "democracy" one had to concede a lot of points. And he certainly didn't see his tour in Vietnam as an exercise in "killing" people to preserve the sanctity of the Democratic and Republican Party conventions! He guessed what he really believed was that Vietnam had the chance of *becoming* a democracy, and that's what he was fighting for, and maybe, deep down, because he was afraid that if the Communists took over more and more of the globe, they'd be fighting one day in the States. But he faced the fact that he hadn't really thought it out, not thought it out so he could argue it or defend it. But even so, what was it all in aid of? Surely they didn't think they could make another Evans

148

of him? He pondered it all, but he hadn't found an answer by the time sleep finally caught him.

iv

It was hard to remember what happened before the bombing. Even when they woke up, there was the smell of trouble in the air, but none of them could have guessed it would be as severe as it turned out. The first thing they noticed was that Evans was gone. Strangely, it made them all nervous, and no one burst out in talk as they thought they would once they had shaken him.

Outside, the camp was alive with activity. Engines were still working, people were scurrying about—the whole atmosphere was tense and anxious. They watched from the cave mouth for a long time before little Toe came to take them to breakfast. They had already seen more trucks than they'd noticed before, and when they wound their way across the side of the hill, they saw a whole string more of them being industriously camouflaged by squads of North Vietnamese soldiers.

Usually by morning all the work had stopped and their indoctrination groups were spread out under the trees all along the side of the valley. But this morning everyone was working, and they could hear shouts—arbitrary, sometimes angry—from all sides of the valley. When they sat, Hill nodded to the sky off to the northeast, and there was a huge pattern of contrails—and it wasn't yet an hour past dawn. They couldn't hear any bombing, but the tension around them was strong enough to touch.

When they had finished, Toe and the guards led them out to their usual spot outside the valley. They could see lines of North Vietnamese troops coming along toward the camp, each carrying his wiggling branches from camouflage so that when you didn't concentrate it looked as if the whole jungle were moving—you didn't see the men at all. And Birnam wood is come to Dunsinane, Janowitz thought. As usual it was Pershing who zeroed in on the relevance of all the activity. Janowitz heard it in whispered fragments from Hill, who was walking just behind him.

"The supersarge says . . . we're to break . . . if there's . . . any action. Stay away . . . from villages. If you get caught . . . say you got lost . . . South . . . three day's march . . . then east . . . two days' march."

Evans was already at their usual meeting place with Thai, Tick, and Tack. Toe ordered them to sit in front of Evans, but after they did, nothing happened for quite a time. They heard the distant sound of planes a couple of times, but it was very faint, and the VC acted as though nothing had happened at all. Finally, the bearers came with Morris.

The women were there, too. Mỹ helped as they settled Morris in place and, as she turned to go, glanced over at Janowitz. He felt as if an ice cube were stuck right in the base of his throat. He had decided she regarded prisoners as he regarded sweat. In Vietnam it was there, you brushed it aside occasionally, but you didn't waste time paying any attention to it. But suddenly her eyes had sought him out purposely. He couldn't swallow; he couldn't react. She held him in her gaze. Maybe it wasn't for the minute it seemed to him, maybe it was for only a couple of seconds, but it was deliberate and measured. Then she blew away a wisp of hair and walked around Morris to the other women.

He died. He hadn't even smiled. Just a blank, dumb stare. And he hadn't shaved since he was captured; he must look like a skid row bum! But he didn't feel like one—the food and sleep and exercise had started the sexual juices flowing like the spring floods. And Mỹ sent his whole blood supply right to his groin. And then she looked at him, and what did he do? Gawk at her like a demented idiot.

Now that Morris was there, Evans faced them all. Thai and the three stooges walked down by the stream, close, but not taking part. It seemed that one layer of pretense was being lifted anyway. Evans was running this session, not pretending he was one of the prisoners. He pulled a notebook from his back pocket.

"Yesterday," Evans began, "we spent some time reading from what the National Liberation Front calls the capitalist press. Today I want to read to you from a Communist writer. You've heard of him. Ho Chi Minh." He smiled—a shit-eating grin about as phony as plastic toast.

He opened the book and read: "To serve the masses, one must live with the masses, see their needs, discover their wishes, and act according to them, not according to your own wishes, however well-intentioned."

He flipped a few pages and read again: "We must act with respect for the human dignity of all people, even enemies of the revolution. Changing people's ideology cannot be done by threats or intimidation. Nor can it be done by a few lectures. Persuasion must be long-term. As long as we serve the people wholeheartedly and are modest and prudent, we will win them to socialism and democracy."

150

It went on for some time. Janowitz was not surprised by the content. During his last year at Michigan, Mao's *Little Red Book* had been the latest "in" reading.

It hadn't exactly been fascinating material and the jargon of "people's socialism" and "capitalist imperialism" and "bourgeois ideology" and all that shit had made it read like a parody. But as he had got into it, he could see that it wasn't any *Mein Kampf*. It was more boring than fanatic. There was an assumption that there was such a thing as "the masses" and that they wanted to be "served" by a bunch of dedicated eager beavers, but no word of bloodletting or vengeance. Even when he wrote about the "enemy" and "war," it was: "Do not damage crops"; "Take nothing from the masses"; "Do not ill-treat captives." Compared to Stokely Carmichael or Eddie Rickenbacker, it was practically saintly.

Evans finally stopped reading. He hesitated, looking down at the ground. "I've been in Vietnam almost eighteen months—seven of them with the National Liberation Front," he said. "I won't say I'm unbiased. Basically I was against the United States' being in Vietnam before I came here.

"I didn't believe then that we came to fight invading conquerors, and I still don't believe it," he continued. "The people we came to fight aren't oppressors, and they don't owe allegiance to Moscow or Peking. I don't pretend to know what their leaders think or feel, but I know that these soldiers are taught each day not only that it is their duty to support the welfare of the people—in the way Ho teaches, in the way Mao teaches—but that they cannot exist *without* the cooperation of the people."

Janowitz was watching him as intently as the others. He was no bumbling intellectual, this one. Once he started talking, he spoke fluently; all the modesty and hesitation evaporated. It was clear he was an experienced speaker, and you could see he planned the thing for the level of the group; it was almost like Army indoctrination in reverse. And he did it so well Janowitz wondered if he'd been a teacher. It sort of fit the image.

"You know the kind of indoctrination the VC get—day in and day out." He grinned at them. "You're going to get some of it yourselves. But I can tell you that they aren't told victory is around the corner. On the contrary, they're told many times that the war may go on for twenty years, even forty years. They've been told that America is the richest and most powerful nation in the world and that in Vietnam the U.S. will win again and again and again. But they are also told that the National Front can fail again and again and again—and still win in the end. Because they are armed with the hearts of the people and with the cause of the people." He turned to Hill. It wasn't exactly fire in his eyes, but there was a no-nonsense firmness.

"Hill, you know quite a bit about the Vietnamese, from personal experience." There was that bit about Hill again; Janowitz wondered what the hell was behind it. "Have you ever *seen* any evidence of cruelty to civilians by the National Liberation Front?"

"Ooooooooeee!" said Hill with a big grin on his face.

"Have you?" Evans demanded. Hill didn't answer.

"Come on, Hill. I just want you to tell me if you have ever seen with your own eyes *one* example of deliberate cruelty."

Hill hesitated. "Well, I must confess the VC haven't made a big thing of hangin' around to meet me personally," he said. "And they haven't arranged any little demonstrations for my benefit. But if you promise you won't get real offended like, I'd prefer to believe all I read about the teachers and headmen and stuff they kill than I would to rely on the whole eighteen months of your personal inspection of the problem."

It forced a smile from all of them. The atmosphere was a little dicey, but Hill had a talent for irreverent humor that must have driven the stoutest teachers up the wall.

"You haven't *personally seen* any evidence, though?"

"No," Hill said after a thoughtful pause. "Course, I don't have any *personal* evidence that Johnson is President of the United States either. Now you may tell me it's all a big hoax and you've personally seen Ho Chi Minh running things over there in the White House, and as long as you got your thumb on the food supplies, I'm gonna have to come right out and admit you're probably right."

Miller laughed so hard Janowitz thought he was going to break a rib. Evans finally smirked at Hill.

"Since your eyes have not provided you with any direct evidence," he said, "perhaps you could use your head—if that isn't asking too much. By the Pentagon's estimates—and by their own admission the Pentagon has *overestimated* the forces operating against them for the past two years running—the so-called allies outnumber the National Front and the North Vietnamese by four to one. And if you count only uniformed regulars, it's *ten* to one. And you know the kind of casualty rate the National Front has. Now, tell me, Hill, in your wisdom, do you honestly think the National Front could survive at all at those odds if the local villagers turned against them, if the people in the countryside didn't think they were fighting their cause?"

"Did it ever occur to you in *your* wisdom—" Pershing cut in.

"After me, please, Pershing!" It came fast and hard. They all were taken by surprise; none of them expected toughness from Evans. He kept his eyes fixed on Hill.

"And the Arvin troops. What do you think they're fighting for, Hill? The troops you find yourself with now are told the Arvin are fighting for the landlords, for the Americans who pay off the wealthy and bomb the peasants, herding them into camps without water or work or proper food. Do you personally think they're wrong? Have you personally *seen* with your own eyes the refugee camps with shit running in the street, with fat rats and skinny children. Have you, Hill?"

He stared at Hill. No one said anything. He was experienced all right, Janowitz thought.

"What exactly happened at Dak Son, I do not know," he said with a note of hesitation. So that was it, Janowitz thought! All this because yesterday Pershing tripped him up on Dak Son.

"I can't quote to you from *Time*," he went on, "though I would like to. But I can show you a release that appeared in another journal some of you may have heard of—it is not so anti-Communist as *Time,* but it *is* known for its honesty." He picked up a newspaper out of the box.

"It begins, 'Weeping survivors of an alleged North Vietnamese reprisal massacre today buried their dead in shallow graves among the blackened ruins of their village.'" He looked down at Hill again. "'Alleged,' Hill, because some people are as skeptical as you, and no one has *proved* these were North Vietnamese troops . . . and because our own sweet CIA has admitted to hiring bandit groups to pose as members of the National Front and raid villages in their name. But let us believers stand together and say they *were* North Vietnamese. The article goes on, 'On Monday about five hundred North Vietnamese troops swept into the village . . . to wreak revenge on tribesmen *who had betrayed their positions to South Vietnamese forces.'* Now that little bit was left out of *Time*'s report. Reuters carried it, and others, but not most U.S. press reports. It goes on to say that *South* Vietnamese officials 'said that acting on information given by the villagers, South Vietnamese forces killed hundreds of North Vietnamese in air strikes.' *Time* left that out, too."

He handed the newspaper to Pershing. It was the Manchester *Guardian.*

"There are always atrocities in war, and perhaps as soldiers you may understand how other soldiers would react when their positions had been betrayed, when they'd lost many of their own dead. That doesn't justify it . . . but I ask you, Pershing, if you think it happened regularly, if that were policy or even *permitted* by the National Front or the North Vietnamese, do you think we wouldn't hear about it week in and week out—not only in *Time*, but on every television station and in every newspaper in America?"

"We hear a lot about assassinations and terror—" Pershing said.

"I'm talking about Dak Son!" Evans cut in.

"No," Pershing came back sharply. "We don't hear about a lot of Dak Sons. The VC wants to control villagers, not kill them. And they gain control by killing a few—not by wiping out most of the village, like they did at Dak Son. That doesn't pay."

Evans smiled. "You'd make quite a Communist, Pershing," he said slowly.

"Well, you got a long wait, sonny boy, if you think you're ever going to live to see the day," Pershing snapped.

"I don't want to make you a Communist," Evans said. "I just think you have a lot in common with them."

Janowitz had to smile. Pershing's dedication *was* a little like a Communist's.

"Dak Son was one event," Evans continued, "not a pattern. It happened to a village of Montagnards. Strange that it should be so." He bent to the box and pulled out a *Time*. "March tenth, 1967," he said. "It says a group of American jets 'grievously erred last week,' by bombing a friendly Montagnard village, 'killing ninety-five civilians'— they don't mention if they were men, women, or children—and 'wounding two hundred.' And how did they manage that total? Well, according to *Time*, it only took two delta-wing fighter-bombers, and *according to Time*, they first dropped 'anti-personnel fragmentation bombs and delayed-fuse bombs' and when that was over, they 'strafed the survivors with cannon fire.' There you are, Pershing, read it!" He slammed the magazine at Pershing. Pershing only glanced at it; he obviously didn't doubt it.

"And you know what an antipersonnel bomb—a CBU—is, of that I'm sure. Steel pellets flung at almost bullet speed in all directions. They drop them in first. And they hit the slow—the ones who can't run fast enough at the first sound of aircraft—the young and the very old. Then when the rescuers go in to help them, the delayed-action bombs go off and get them, too. That's good military strategy. That's the product of a big Pentagon think tank. That isn't atrocity! That's just tactical warfare against a dirty and stubborn enemy—whatever his age or sex! Even if you're not sure he *is* the enemy.

"And *Time,* which was so sensitive about the massacre at Dak Son, what do they say about this? They say, 'unfortunately American jets grievously erred.' Erred in bombing and strafing a village that way? Hell, no! Erred because it was a *friendly village!* You've seen and *I've* seen dozens of villages in South Vietnam that have been bombed by our planes. Not two planes, but ten, twelve planes. It's not hard, we've dropped more bombs on *South* Vietnam than we did on Japan in all of World War II! Never mind what we've done to North Vietnam. And our bombing and strafing of men, women, and children isn't a *onetime* incident. It goes on every goddamned day! It is the *policy* of our country! You know it, and I know it, and every bastard from here to Saigon knows it! Because we do it from an airplane instead of on the ground doesn't give us any fucking right to point at Dak Son and say look at those murdering pigs!"

His fluency and rage took them all by surprise. A peacenik all right! Janowitz thought. And he remembered that it was that mood of defiant rage that took the laugh out of the demonstrations on campus; guys who used to make cracks stopped making cracks—and either raged back or stuck up for them—and it had the same impact here. There was no temptation to be flippant.

"How many hundreds, how many *thousands,* do you think have been slaughtered by our pellet bombs, our napalm, and our strafing?" Evans went on, more quietly but still tense with emotion. "Just count the children, Pershing! Never mind the men; never mind the fathers, the mothers, the old, or the sick. Just count the children!"

"If the Vietcong have so much regard for children—" Pershing started.

"Let them stop fighting! Is that it?" Evans rasped back. "Let them turn over their country, first to the French and now to us . . . or to the government we approve of, whichever government that happens to be at the moment!

"Yes, I've heard pinheaded patriots make that remark, Pershing. Guys who would die by fire themselves rather than let someone conquer the United States, guys who'd think their wives and children well spent to keep America free of foreign invaders.

"And when the National Front raided the cities—Saigon, Da Nang, Hue, Dalat—the screams went up about terrorists and how the Vietcong had no regard for human life. All those lard asses back in the States watching television from their upholstered armchairs, seeing civilians being chased and mauled and terrified. Only Communists could be so damned cruel to their own kind! By fighting in places where we aren't prepared for them to fight, don't they realize they risk human life? Why, hell, our gallant boys have to bomb buildings full of civilians to get rid of them, and we have to send gunships in and batter the piss out of several square blocks—whether there are civilians in them or not. I tell you those Communists just don't have any decency."

"Funny, Mac, but—"

"Shut up, Hill! Our dear fellow citizens back home see the civilians suffering when the Front raids Saigon or Da Nang, Pershing. They've got a right to their ignorance. But not you. Not any of *us!* There may not be television cameras around when our 'terrorists' in airplanes come flying in and pulverize a whole village because one gunshot is fired from it; they don't see the civilians we strafe and bomb on the off-chance one of them might be a Charlie. Or because the poor bastards happen to have been born in territory Charlie controls. About *half* the country, Pershing! At least VC 'terrorists' fire at enemies—our 'terrorists' have a fine airborne impartiality!"

Pershing held his head up for a moment as though he were going to retort; then he lowered it. He wasn't angry himself. Janowitz had seen that same look many times in the States. When reasonable people were faced with the kind of anger about Vietnam that Evans was now displaying. It was a kind of hopelessness. Like I know we're killing kids and civilians, and I don't like it any more than you do, and I understand why you're mad, but what the hell do you do?

But Evans wasn't through.

"You talk about *freedom,* Pershing! Well, let me tell you a kid who is burned or maimed or has seen his parents ripped apart before his eyes has life-long limitations on his freedom you wouldn't understand! And a dead child has no freedom at all!"

He glared at Pershing. And for the first time Pershing was looking at him without contempt. Evans a traitor was one thing, but Evans a misguided peacenik acting on these kinds of emotions was something rather different.

"I didn't want this war, man," Pershing finally said softly. "I don't know anybody in America who did. I'm not here to conquer Vietnam or to colonize it . . . and I don't know anyone else who is either. I'm not fighting for the landlords or the rich. And I care as much about the people of Vietnam as I do about the people at home . . . and I think you know it."

It got to Evans. He swallowed a couple of times nervously, then turned to the crate of *Times.* Janowitz was really impressed. God, he liked Pershing.

156

"You talk about terror killings," Evans said. "Why don't we see if *Time* was saying a few years ago what it and the Pentagon are saying now about terror killings." He fumbled through some magazines and pulled one out. He was still trying to debate, but Pershing had taken all the sting out of him. His voice had lost its authority.

As Evans flipped through the magazine's pages, Janowitz became aware of movement off to their left. Big Tack was coming up from the river, and the three nurses had stood up.

"August fourth, 1961," Evans read, and stopped—suddenly aware of the movement all around him. A whistle was blown from somewhere close, and immediately Thai and the three stooges ran to the group. The guards had already come to their feet and were looking around nervously. There were more whistles now, and distantly they could hear bugles blowing.

"There!" Russell was pointing to their left. It was a tight formation, three squadrons of B-52's, high. It was funny, they'd seen the contrails earlier and had heard aircraft, but these seemed almost right above them, and there was no sound yet. There must be a high-speed wind up there, Janowitz thought automatically.

"Up! Up!" Tack was shouting at them.

"Watch your chances," Pershing whispered as he rose. Thai was saying something to Evans, and Evans turned quickly.

"Janowitz! Hill! Over there! Get Morris!" He started moving toward Morris' stretcher, and little Toe darted through the group, his pistol drawn—the first time anyone but a guard had had a gun on them since they had come to the camp.

When they picked up the stretcher, Hill in front, Janowitz behind, the three nurses were tying Morris down by running gauze over and around the stretcher. Toe shoved his pistol into Janowitz's ribs.

"You go!" he shouted. The guards had split up Miller, Pershing, and Russell and they were already double-timing up the trail toward the camp. As Janowitz and Hill started to jog after them, the pug-nosed little nurse darted to Thai and started chattering a blue streak at him. They could hear the planes now, and she kept looking over her shoulder at them as they ran along.

She was distracting Thai and Tick. Tack was running on ahead of the whole group. Evans wasn't armed. That left only Toe and the two nurses to worry about him, Janowitz thought. Toe was running along beside the stretcher, between him and Hill. He still had his gun out, but he had to duck from branches, and he was watching the planes, too. Janowitz was sure he could drop the stretcher, knock Toe on his ass, get his gun, and get the hell out before anyone could do anything about it. And the way they all were staring at those planes they'd never chase him.

The only catch was what it might do to Morris. He was carrying his feet, so it wouldn't be like dropping him on his head, but there would sure as hell be a jolt. Painful, but he'd probably live through it. The question was: Would they pick him up and carry him on into the valley? Morris was looking at him, half-grinning, but obviously in pain from the bouncing. The planes sounded closer, louder.

He decided to do it. The odds were Toe and the nurses would take care of Morris. Then he heard them coming in. The whine of bombs. VC whistles, shouts. Evans yelling, "Get down!"

Hill and Janowitz went down together, guiding the stretcher down reasonably softly. The bombs sounded right on them. Janowitz covered up, but even as he buried his head he saw the two nurses fall across Morris, covering their heads with their hands but shielding him with their bodies.

The first string of bombs exploded around them like a timpani climax—wham, wham-wham-wham-wham-*wham!* Janowitz's face was slammed into the ground. His teeth bit on his tongue and cut it badly. Each bomb hammered him into the ground, gashing his face, knocking the wind right out of him. He'd been under mortar attack, but nothing like this. It was as though the ground were living, thudding into him relentlessly. The sound reverberated in his ears—it was bomb, flash, falling trees, flying dust; it was whirlwind, cyclone, and TNT explosion all at once.

And then the trail of bombs thundered off—toward the valley. He had just got his wind when he heard a huge explosion ahead. They'd hit munitions, he guessed. And that'd tip them off, if they didn't already know. There'd be more bombs. Lots more bombs.

He tried to struggle to his feet to run for it. But Thai was there, yelling, pointing toward the river. The pug-nosed nurse was pulling the other two off Morris. The bombing was still loud, and they could actually feel the earth trembling, but this run had passed them. Away from the river he could see a huge ball of black and orange fire climbing hundreds of feet into the air. It looked a half mile across. Toe jabbed him hard with his pistol and pointed to the stretcher.

Janowitz grabbed his end, and Hill lifted with him. The side of Hill's face had been scraped raw. Mỹ and big tits seemed unharmed, but they'd had Morris to cushion them from the ground. Maybe they weren't so dumb, he thought as they scrambled through the underbrush. Thai and the pug-nosed one were leading the way. Through the greenery he could see the others paralleling them—running along toward the river.

Again it flashed through Janowitz's mind—now, run for it. Toe was on his right, not paying any attention to him. Mỹ was running alongside Morris, wiping his brow over and over with her hand. Janowitz could see that Morris was crying. His eyes went back to Mỹ. The branches were slapping her in the face, and she was panting for breath, but she just kept moving her hand again and again over Morris' forehead. God, Janowitz thought, women will be the death of me yet. He didn't drop the stretcher.

The riverbank was muddy underfoot. They could still hear explosions and the drone of the planes and the crackle of burning timber behind them, but there was nothing close. Thai waded halfway out in the stream, looking up and down frantically, but uncertain which way to head. The pug-nosed nurse was yelling at him, pointing downriver toward the valley. Finally, he shrugged, and they started trotting as fast as they could along the river's edge in that direction.

The mud was impossible, and Hill moved out a little way into the river. It was broad and shallow, hardly a foot deep at its deepest. Running in it was harder on the legs, and twice they almost fell on stones, but they could move steadily. Mỹ went down three or four times. She was soaked and covered with mud, but each time she struggled up and tried to keep reassuring Morris. It killed Janowitz to even look at him. He wasn't crying out loud, but his lips were quivering like a kid's, and tears were pouring down his face. And he was praying. Janowitz could see his lips forming the words, frantically, as though the number of prayers per minute might save him.

Toe was bringing up the rear now, cursing and spitting as he ran. They hadn't gone far when they heard the other bunch reach the river behind them. Then all of a sudden there were shouts and a shot. Janowitz turned, and Hill must have, too, because they went off-balance and Janowitz was on his knees in the water. The stretcher was submerged, and Morris was coughing and gagging with water before they got it up.

When Janowitz looked back again, Toe and the nurse with big tits were running toward the other group, where Big Tack was floundering in midstream. Pershing, Miller, and Russell were racing out of the water on the other side of the river. Miller and Pershing went flat the minute they hit the bank and started crawling like lizards for the undergrowth. But Russell kept running; another shot rang out, and he wheeled as if someone had spun him with coiled spring. Big Tack stood in the middle of the river, aiming his pistol with both hands. Two of the guards were running across the river after Pershing and Miller. Another was lying in a heap on the bank.

Thai suddenly shouted something angrily in Vietnamese. He was in the river only a couple of yards from Janowitz, and his unexpected presence took Janowitz by surprise. Thai had his gun pointed right at Janowitz, but he was shouting back at Toe and Evans.

"Go on, forward!" Thai finally called to Hill. Hill struggled ahead. Janowitz moved with him, glancing over across the river. It looked as if Pershing and Miller might have made it. He couldn't see the guards who'd gone in after them, but from the shouting it didn't sound as if they'd caught them. He got a glimpse of Toe tossing Evans the rifle of the guard who was stretched out on the riverside before they came to a little bend that cut off the view behind them.

About fifty yards ahead the pug-nosed nurse was perched up the side of the bank where it rose as the river started to knife toward the valley.

"Hurry!" Thai shouted. He had stayed only a couple of feet from Janowitz, his gun always pointed right at him. Hill stumbled but, by taking a dunking himself, managed not to drop the stretcher. Morris was tilted dangerously, and he let out a scream, but Mỹ grabbed him by his shoulders and kept him from sliding into the water. When they got upright again, they all could hear the planes coming back.

"Hurry, hurry!" It was Evans who had rounded the corner, carrying the dead guard's rifle. Janowitz could see the planes coming at them across the valley.

They scrambled on as fast as they could toward the pug-nosed nurse. As they got closer, Janowitz could see timber beams across a small opening in the bank behind her. He knew he was pushing Hill. Couldn't push him too hard or he'd fall again, but, God, he wanted to make that cave!

The first cluster of bombs came sweeping gently down, as if they were on a long, invisible slide. They went in; then one second, two—and the ground trembled, a rumble and a god-awful explosion. It was ahead of them, in the valley, but more bombs were sliding down the sky from other planes. They plunged on.

The pug-nosed nurse was half in the cave, and she took the end of the stretcher from Hill. Then they heard the whistle of bombs.

"Shove!" Thai shouted, and they thrust the stretcher on into the cave. The whistle was on top of them. Janowitz spun for the water.

160

What happened he didn't know. He remembered the surface of the water was right at his face when his ears seemed to burst. There was no sound he could remember, just the shock of pain in his ears.

When he came to, he was spitting water, puking it out, and was being dragged by his shoulders just above the surface. He could hear explosions all around him, and the water was black and being splashed by pellets of mud and stone. It was Hill who flopped him against the bank. Hill's nose was pouring blood, and he was soaking wet. Janowitz shook his head and nodded that he was all right, but he almost went down again when Hill let go. Then he *was* all right. He could taste blood in his mouth and realized his nose was bleeding, too. He rubbed the blood away. Fire was ballooning up across the river from them, and he could see trees collapsing lazily as if they were just leaning over on a cushion of air.

Hill was struggling toward the cave entrance. Janowitz could see now that the top of the little hillock above it had been hit and caved right in like a crater. The pug-nosed nurse and Mỹ were digging away with their hands at the mud and dirt that clogged the entrance. The pug-nosed one was standing hip-deep in dirt. Morris was trapped in there someplace.

Janowitz struggled across to them, his head throbbing from the bursting pom-poms of antiaircraft fire and the pounding of the bombs. When he got next to Hill, he could only see Morris' hips and chest. His feet and his face were buried, but they could tell he was still breathing from the movement of his chest. They all dug frantically with their hands, but as quickly as they dug, more mud oozed down on him from the sides of the cave. Janowitz looked around for Thai. He was back along the river, not more than fifteen yards away, helping Evans, who seemed to be just coming back to consciousness.

Janowitz could hear aircraft approaching again. They were coming in, across the valley ninety degrees from their last run. His head was clearing, and he could make out the antiaircraft guns more clearly, but he thanked God he hadn't been in the valley. Then he remembered the caves. Maybe they were all safe in there; maybe it was just the equipment that was getting pounded to hell.

Hill had wormed his hands into the mud and made a bridge over Morris' face. Janowitz dug hard under it, clearing a passage. He could feel Morris' nose and his eyebrow. Mỹ saw what they were doing and scrambled around by Hill's side, pulling away dirt from above to keep it from falling on them.

With all the other noise, they didn't even hear the next run of bombs coming in. The first series crashed in, shivering the mudbank and the fractured timber where the cave mouth had been. It slammed Janowitz's hand down hard on Morris' face, and his own face went into the mud, but the bombs weren't close enough to cause real damage, and when he pulled his face clear, he smiled at Hill, glad they had taken the shock without losing what progress they had made. They scratched on, and more and more of Morris' face came free of the packed mud. Janowitz forced his finger right down into Morris' mouth and got it clear. Morris was jerking spasmodically, but he didn't seem to be conscious.

They heard a sudden whistle louder than the crackling fire, louder than the echoing thunder of the other explosions, louder than the pompoms of the AA guns. Janowitz slammed his hand over Morris' face and went down as the bombs shattered around them. An ocean of mud lifted, catapulting Janowitz into the air. He came down on one arm, and immediately the ground whacked him again, knocking him over on his back. He landed absolutely flat and the whole riverbank quaked under him, shuddering as if the whole earth were collapsing.

There were a dozen more explosions, and mountains of flames were rising all around them. Janowitz scrambled to his feet on the shaking earth and pushed toward the cave. Hill was on his haunches, staring. The whole hillock that had held the cave was just folding in on itself, mud, stones, little trees being swallowed as though tumbling into some bottomless well. He and Hill scrambled frantically toward the collapsing center where Morris had been. But there was no hope. Hill started pulling at something—and then Janowitz saw the pug-nosed nurse. Her face was tipped back so that her mouth was up, but she was covered with mud, and a hunk of the broken timber from the cave entrance was wedged with its jagged edges right against her neck. It was this Hill was trying to free, and as Janowitz crawled to help him, he could see dark blood oozing out in the thick mud.

He didn't see where she had come from, but suddenly Mỹ was next to them, fighting the subsiding mud, clawing to free the girl, but the little pug-nosed face was sinking, and it was beyond their power to stop it. And then there was another shuddering explosion, the whole hillside rumbled and sagged again, and she started slithering farther down, her mouth working with hysterical, silent convulsions to clear the mud. Janowitz struggled to get to her, but his weight speeded her fall, and she slid away, her frantic eyes, clotted with mud, staring unbelievingly at the sky.

They all dug on insanely, trying to grab some part of her. Hill got

162

an arm, and he and Janowitz tugged at it, but their hands were slippery and her arm was slippery, and Janowitz kept thinking of that splintered log, lodged at her neck, and wondering if they were pulling it into her—and he quit. Hill looked at him and slowly released his grip. Mỹ was bent over on her knees in the mud, rocking back and forth, crying or praying or hysterical—Janowitz couldn't tell. He felt half-hysterical himself.

Hill nudged him. He was pointing to the river. Thai was lying there on the bank, pinned by a sapling, either dead or unconscious, it was hard to tell. Janowitz was surprised he was so stung by the sight. When it came right down to it, he had kind of liked Thai.

Hill tugged at him again, nodding to the fire sweeping all around them. The whole jungle seemed to be ablaze. Only on the far side of the river in the direction away from the valley was it clear. North, Janowitz thought immediately, shit. But it was the only way they could go. He looked at Mỹ. Should they try to take her—or leave her?

"Come on," Hill said and started sliding down into the river. Janowitz hesitated again. If she ran downriver toward the valley she could still probably make those caves before the fire got her. But he couldn't just leave her. He grabbed her arm. She didn't respond at all, just kept rocking. He pulled her up. My God, she was a feather.

"Fire!" he said loudly, pointing around at the blaze. There wasn't really any need. The flames were as high as young hills all around the back of them, and clouds of black and orange gases were billowing hundreds of feet into the air. "Fire!" he repeated, not even knowing if she understood the language. He pointed downriver toward the valley. "Go! Go quickly!"

He gave her a little shove, and she slid numbly down toward the river, her feet sinking deep into the mud. Holy God, Janowitz thought, you've got to fight instinct. She was so tiny, so helpless-looking, and she'd weighed nothing, nothing at all. He wanted to grab her arm and shepherd her to safety.

"Janowitz!" It was Hill. He was plunging down the middle of the river. Janowitz turned and scrambled down the pile of still-moving mud. Poor fucking Morris. Rest in peace. Shalom . . . May God so greet you.

He lunged through the water, and when he reached the bend, Hill was peering around carefully.

"Looks clear," Hill yelled. He had to yell because the roar of the fire was like a gale. The nearest flames still seemed to be a quarter to a half mile away, but the sound was a winter blizzard. And all around the sky behind them, huge shoots of smoke and gas gushed and billowed like erupting crowns on midsummer thunderheads.

"Let's go!" Janowitz shouted, and headed across river to the only place where the sky was clear ahead. There was no sign of anyone, and Janowitz wondered if they ought to stick to the river or cut through the edge of the forest that wasn't aflame. He twisted for a quick look behind. Smoke and flame everywhere. Those B-52's must have carried magnesium incendiaries, as well as the big bombs. The way the fire was raging he knew they didn't dare go through the forest. They had no choice but to go north—upriver.

Hill was gulping air behind him in big gasps. Janowitz glanced at his big awkward leaps through the ankle-deep water, and even then it made him want to smile.

"Look!" Hill wheezed. A veritable cloud of birds swarmed toward them. There were birds he knew and hundreds he'd never seen before. And as they swept past them, they could hear the frantic chirping of monkeys coming behind, and soon they caught glimpses of deer, jackals, monkeys, rats, even snakes leaping, scurrying through the forest around them. Once a deer came leaping right out in the river, took one look at them with its wild, dilated eyes, wheeled, and leaped back toward the fire.

Janowitz was gasping for air, and the river had started to climb, so it took twice the energy to keep going. They had to pause every time they came to a bend to see if it was clear ahead, but each time getting going again was harder and harder. Hill's mouth was open, and the air rasped through as he strained for breath. Janowitz checked the flames behind them. Despite the panic in the jungle, the fire itself hadn't closed on them. The whole sky behind was a cloud of black, but the smoke seemed to be going straight up, so he concluded there wasn't much wind. What they were feeling was air being sucked into the fire. He decided at the next bend they could afford to take a breather.

"Let's cool it for a second," he puffed when they got to it. Hill didn't need a second invitation. He flopped into the water, just holding his head above it and heaving for air.

They heard something lunging through the underbrush and turned unconcernedly to see, thinking it must be another deer or a monkey or something—but as it pushed toward them, they knew it was human. In an instant Hill had flopped over and pulled a rock from the riverbed. Janowitz started to break for cover in the forest.

"Hey, wait!" It was Miller. Janowitz turned back just in time to see him flop down in the water next to Hill. If anything, he was panting harder than they were.

164

"I been chasing . . . you guys . . . for five . . . minutes!" he gasped in angry snatches between breaths. "I been yelling . . . you fuckers . . . must be deaf." He was sitting in the shallow water, his head bent between his knees as his lungs pumped and pumped in brief, heavy swallows.

"Where's Pershing?" Janowitz asked. Miller kept gasping for air, shaking his head. Finally, he got enough wind to speak again.

"I don't know . . . I lost them all . . . I was heading east . . . when I heard Tack between me and the fire." He paused, but they knew more was coming. "I figured . . . the best chance . . . was to get back to the river. . . . Then I saw you guys . . . but I . . . I couldn't catch you."

Janowitz looked at the fire again. The black and gray clouds seemed to be advancing on them, and he could see pinnacles of flame among them. They'd have to move, but it looked as if they could keep ahead of it.

"We'd better get moving," he said. "We don't have to run so fast, but we can't sit here." Hill and Miller dragged themselves up with the automatic obedience of the enlisted soldier. Janowitz dunked his head in the water and when he brushed at the mud in his hair, he had a second's recollection of Mŷ. He wondered if she had made it to the valley. God, she was light; he couldn't get over that.

They jogged on, and when they came to the next bend, the river curved sharply to the left. It meant they'd be moving parallel to the fire front for what looked to be a long stretch.

"We'd better step it up," Janowitz shouted, and started running faster. The shot went right by his ear. He felt the wind; then he heard the retort. He stopped dead. Hill pushed into him, and Miller stumbled toward the middle of the stream. A VC moved out of the bushes not twenty yards in front of them. Like all goddamned VC, get two feet from them and they look like the jungle!

The VC came at them crouching, his finger on the trigger, and his eyes challenging them to move. He was spotted with soot and sweat, and his face was splotched with burn where it wasn't black. He was breathing hard, too, and his eyes were almost as wild as the animals' they'd seen. As he got closer, he kept signaling with his rifle—down, down. He looked so frenzied they all went down on their knees in the water. He motioned Janowitz away from Hill, and Janowitz crawled a couple of paces off. The VC was almost on Hill by then. He pointed his rifle at Hill's head, and Janowitz thought, my God, he's going to shoot. Then he suddenly struck out with the butt of the gun and caught Hill on the side of the head. Hill fell sideways. Janowitz started to rise, but the gun was brought back to firing position as fast as it had been made into a club. Hill didn't try to pull himself up, but the VC went after him, keeping the gun pointed right at his head until the last second, then wheeling it in a lightning move and catching him across his eye and cheekbone. Janowitz felt the crunch himself. The VC danced back a little, watching them all with the same frenzied caution. There was no doubt he'd shoot at the slightest provocation, but he seemed to want to beat them to a pulp first.

He moved toward Janowitz. Janowitz concentrated. Don't tense, relax, baby, one, two and in the bucket. He leaned a little left. Give the guy a target, then dodge, and with any luck he'd have one of his legs. The VC closed. His move came faster than Janowitz anticipated, but he was riding with the blow when it hit him. It hurt, but he twisted and lunged for a leg. Then it felt as if the side of his face had caved in. The second clout had come too fast, and Janowitz went headfirst into the water. He gulped groggily, pulled himself out, and took another smash on the forehead that snapped his head back with a crack even he could hear through his dulled senses. He folded again toward the water and, as he went in, caught another whack on the side of the temple. Again the water gagged him and half revived him. He pulled his head up.

It was to a different scene. The VC had moved back a couple of paces, and Evans and Toe were splashing toward them from around the bend. Toe was shouting, and the VC was spitting something back. Janowitz was too groggy to care. He only knew enough to dunk his head again. He held it as long as he could, then pulled it up again. It was clearer now. He shook himself—and cared a little more about whether he was going to live or not.

The VC had stepped back even farther. He was still covering them, and Toe was still shouting at him, but suddenly the VC pivoted his gun on to Toe and Evans and shouted fiercely. Toe stopped. Then the VC turned his gun on Miller. He was going to shoot. It was step one, step two—and a shot.

But it was Evans. He had hit the VC. Blood gushed from the side of his neck. He turned wildly and fired at Evans—and Evans, in perfect firing line position, pumped two more shots into him. The second one caught the side of his head—bone cracked, flesh flew, and the guy started sideways and then collapsed into the water. It was like a tableau. Nobody moved. Evans turned his gun on Toe.

Toe was terrified. He started backing away. "No—you friend. *Je vous en prie . . . avoir pitie!*"

"Ce pistolet-là! Vite!" Evans shouted at him. Toe passed him his gun and shot a terrified glance toward Janowitz and the others. *"Allons!"* Evans yelled, nodding toward them, and he pushed Toe along in front of him.

"Just keep running," Evans yelled at Janowitz. "We ought to be able to keep ahead of the fire." He expected them to move, but Janowitz was almost as stunned as Toe.

"Why don't you toss me that pistol?" Miller said. Toe was among them now. Evans only three or four paces away. But he had stopped when they didn't move as he directed.

Evans looked down at the body of the VC in the river. Light-pink blood was rippling downstream from his head.

"All right. You keep the pistol, and I'll take *his* gun," Miller said calmly, and he moved toward the dead VC.

"I'll shoot you, Miller! Just as I shot him!" Evans barked, his voice high and strained. He had pulled his rifle down to cover Miller, and Miller froze. It was insane, but there was no doubt that he meant what he said. He stared angrily at Miller for a minute; then he took Toe's pistol from his belt and very deliberately threw it over his head into the river.

"Now if you don't want to be burned to death, I suggest you start moving." He nodded ahead, upriver. Miller shrugged and started off. Hill picked himself up and with a wry glance at Janowitz started jogging after him.

They trotted along blankly for a time, but then they began to feel the heat of the fire, and they needed no urging to speed up. When they finally reached the bend where the river turned north again, Evans shouted at them to halt.

"Into the middle, Miller," he directed. Miller glared at him but pushed out into midstream. "Get next to him, Hill." Hill made it in two leaps.

Evans stepped ahead then, keeping his rifle on them, skirting clear of Janowitz and Toe. He checked the river ahead, then turned to Miller. "There are . . . more bends ahead as it climbs," he panted. "Every time . . . we come to one . . . you and Hill get out in the middle . . . where I can keep an eye on you. If you try to break . . . I'll shoot." He was puffing as hard as the rest of them, but he kept staring at Miller. When he'd got enough wind for more, it came quietly, almost modestly. "I was infantry, Miller. I'm a good shot." Then he signaled them on.

The river climbed more and more steeply into the hills, and after about ten minutes they had to take a break. All of them were heaving their guts up for air. Only little Toe, who looked as if he weren't in condition to carry a cigarette ration back from the PX, wasn't truly winded.

When they finally got their wind back, Evans moved them on more slowly. They couldn't feel the heat any more. The sky was still gray, and every time they turned, they could see clouds of smoke still climbing. It was way up there now—alto-cumulus, Janowitz thought to himself.

A few minutes later there was another shot. They all stopped. Evans was taking his gun from his shoulder.

"Hill," he said, "there's a bird in there. Red, green, yellow—I don't know what all, but you can't miss it. It fell by that silver tree, the thing without the leaves. Go get it, but if I say stop, stop."

Janowitz watched Hill go. This was Hill's chance. Did Evans realize it? Once in that woods, even a couple of feet, and Hill could dive for cover quicker than the fastest shot could get one off at him. And then Evans would have to choose between going after him and letting the others escape or just forgetting about him. He must be gambling that Hill wasn't that eager to make the trek back through VC territory on his own.

It was a good bet. Hill hadn't gone five paces in when he moved quickly and held up a huge multicolored bird. Evans had proved to them again he could use that rifle. Hill came back to the river, and Evans signaled them all on.

They camped high up. The forest was so thick Janowitz never got a full view, but they seemed to be on a ridge that ran north and south. He caught glimpses of ridges left and right at about the same altitude, and they went on as far as the eye could see. It reminded him a little of the Appalachians.

They could see the fire stretching out below them. Huge clouds of smoke were still rising, and the sun remained veiled and weak behind it the whole day. But the fire itself was burning out. There was a long, thin tongue reaching off to the west where the flame was still red and yellow, but below them they saw only occasional sparks and glowing embers through the rising smoke.

Evans had pulled them into a little clearing along the side of the narrowing stream. He made Toe cut some scrub to provide cover for them. When he was done, they had a view up- and downstream, but they were pretty effectively screened from anyone who didn't come right into the clearing itself. The VC had taught Evans a lot.

When Toe had finished, Evans took him to one side and talked to him quietly. It was all in French and all very earnest, though at first Toe seemed not so much convinced by Evans as fearful of the gun he held. But finally, Toe nodded agreement, got up, and went to Hill. He took Hill's dog tags off, then pulled his hands behind him and twisted the dog tags so that they made a loose bind. Then he cut a piece off the bottom of one of the legs of Hill's fatigues and bound it around the dog tags. The operation was repeated on Miller and Janowitz. The binding and tags made an effective handcuff. When he finished, Toe separated the three of them, so they were about six feet apart. Then he squatted beside Evans as if they were going to sit out the war.

"Who the hell's side are you on?" Miller finally asked after they had sat staring at each other for several minutes. Evans made a kind of weary grimace, but he didn't answer.

It seemed that they watched the smoke clouds rising for hours. There was a lot of chatter in the forest all around them, as though the animals were still nervously discussing the fire, but the human silence was total. Evans withdrew into himself, his face getting that wounded, nervous look. Janowitz was surprised for the hundred millionth time in his life at how complex people really were. There was no one Evans —there were obviously dozens of Evanses. And he probably hadn't seen them all yet.

It was hot, and the day had been long in more ways than one. Janowitz dozed off and on, aware of half dreams, half reminiscences of Morris, of Mỹ, and Thai. And once he woke up thinking the pug-nosed nurse was clawing to free him and *he* was sinking into the mud. When he finally woke for good, Toe was roasting the bird over a little fire. The smell filled him with hunger. The sun was low—almost clear of the smoke clouds to the west.

Evans had Toe untie them to eat, and he marched them down to the river to drink. Janowitz still felt sluggish and sleepy, and when they were rebound and Miller and Hill promptly sacked out again, Janowitz flopped down and went off himself.

He didn't sleep long. When he awoke, it was dark, but the wood was still glowing in their fire. Toe was asleep, and Evans was leaning against a tree, keeping guard on them.

Janowitz pulled himself up to a sitting position. Evans looked across at him with one of those funny, tentative grins of his. Janowitz studied him with matching uncertainty.

"Will you be in trouble for shooting that VC?" he asked quietly.

"I don't know," Evans shrugged.

169

"How the hell did you get yourself into this mess? Were you a POW?" It wasn't a cross-examination. He was curious about Evans, even felt sorry for him, and he *had* saved their lives. Evans took the question as it came.

"No, I wasn't. I just took a walk one day—and hoped they'd capture me before they shot me."

"Jesus!"

Evans grinned again, sick, as though he understood what he was saying.

"You carry a big conscience," Janowitz said finally. "You really think these guys are all that much better than we are?"

"No—just not all that much worse."

"Where'd you learn all the French?"

"At school first—but I lived in Europe for a while."

"France?"

"Belgium." He grinned. "Louvain. At the university there's a training college for priests—a very old and famous one."

Janowitz couldn't hide the unexpectedness of it. So that explained the speech technique. Of course. A sermon, that's what they'd got.

"Yes . . . I'm a failed priest too," Evans said. "No, not even that," he added more reflectively. "I never actually took orders. I just came close—and then left."

"You took a walk one day?" Janowitz offered. Evans smiled—but he didn't answer. "But you're still a Catholic?"

"I don't know," Evans said thoughtfully, then grimaced, as though confused by his own indecision.

Janowitz didn't speak for a moment, but his mind was running fast.

"If you're not that sure about the VC either," he said, trying to sound as sympathetic as he could, "this is the time to take off. We don't have to kill Toe. Just tie him up and leave him. They'll find him. And when we get back—you saved us. I'm sure you won't have anything to worry about."

Evans looked across at him. It was as though he suddenly saw something unexpected and unpleasant.

"I'm not trying to trick you," Janowitz said.

"I know," Evans answered bleakly. "I wonder why you think I'm so insincere."

"Uncertain isn't the same as insincere—and if you *are* uncertain, I figure it's best to be uncertain on the side of your own country."

Evans snorted cynically. He stood up and looked out toward the

170

river. He didn't move for a while; then he just leaned into the tree next to him, resting his head and his shoulders against it. His back was still to Janowitz.

" 'My own country,' " he repeated as if to himself. "You know the first time I remember being aware of countries and how my country was different from everyone else's was during Budapest. The uprising against the Communists in Hungary. Do you remember that?" He was speaking quietly and hadn't turned around, but Janowitz grunted that he did. Not that he actually did, but he had read about it.

"It was the first time I was aware of politics, too," Evans went on. "I can remember asking my father where Hungary was and what a Communist was and why they were so cruel. And I can remember the last night of the uprising and the voice of Imre Nagy, their leader, saying that Russian tanks were in the streets, begging the West to help—and finally giving up. I forget what his last words were. 'Long live freedom' or 'Long live Hungary'—I don't really recall."

He turned around to Janowitz. "I remember my father was crying, and he took me by the shoulders and said, 'Don't ever forget that. Don't ever forget what you just heard.' "

He smiled wistfully and slithered down the tree to a sitting position again. "I've just about been the death of my old man," he said wryly, "but it'd turn him to stone if he realized how well I remembered that night." He laughed again. Janowitz didn't see the joke, but Evans was amused.

Finally, Evans looked up at him, his face sober. "What the Russians did there—well . . . it was ruthless, brutal . . . nothing will ever convince me the people of Hungary wanted the government the Russians foisted on them with their tanks and machine guns. I don't think they wanted the Hapsburgs back and twelve-hour days for the workers while the rich danced all night and slept all day. But they didn't want Kadar. I could hardly believe people could commit such injustice. I thought the 'heroes' of the world would do something about it—bomb the Russians or beat them up or something. Just think of it, the Russians ruthlessly killed hundreds of people just to keep Hungary on their side of the political fence.

"Then I came here," he said mordantly. "I learned how much the people of South Vietnam hated Diem and Bao Dai. They'd never heard of Ky or Thieu then—and they're about as devoted to them now as the Hungarians are to Kadar. And I saw the kind of people who were fighting beside us, and the kind of people who had the guts to fight against us. . . . And don't tell me any damned peasant charging an American flamethrower is doing it to conquer the world—any more than the Hungarians in Budapest were charging Russian tanks to 'destroy Communism.' They just want us to get out.

"And the more I looked, the more I realized we were doing in Vietnam exactly what the Russians had done in Hungary. Except for the rich and the military who profit from us, *no* one wants us in Vietnam. Except for the rich and the military, the only important heroes in Vietnam are Buddha and Ho Chi Minh. It's not the will of the Vietnamese that keeps us here; it's our refusal to let South Vietnam fall on the other side of the fence. And to prevent that, we're willing to raze a people and their country right to the ground. . . . 'My country' is making what Russia did to Budapest a triviality. That was an incident. This is a slaughter. More brutal, more selfish than anything that's happened in the world in the twenty-five years of my life. That's what *my* country is doing. . . . And Vietnam is not even on our border, as Hungary is on Russia's. . . . Vietnam is twelve thousand miles from the United States—and so goddamned small it couldn't be a threat to Luxembourg."

He stopped. And Janowitz knew that it would take more than words to change his mind.

Evans turned and looked at him. "You think I'm wrong?" he inquired challengingly.

It made Janowitz ponder what he'd said, not from the point of view of what it meant to Evans, but whether it was objectively true.

"Well?" Evans said pointedly, staring at him, waiting.

"I don't know," Janowitz answered. Evans grinned broadly. For an instant Janowitz didn't get it; then he realized he had sounded as baffled and confused by his own thoughts as Evans had previously sounded about his.

"Guess we were born at the wrong time," Janowitz said. "Back in World War II everyone knew the good guys from the bad guys."

Evans nodded. "I wonder if it wasn't better for the Germans, too. There wasn't any hypocrisy—we're killing you for your own good—they just claimed they were a superrace and went out to conquer the world. It was arrogant and repulsive—but at least it was straightforward." He chuckled. And suddenly it seemed bizarre and preposterous and a little funny to Janowitz, too.

Hill rolled over and looked up at both of them. His bewilderment at seeing the two of them chortling together made Janowitz laugh even harder.

"So what'd you guys do—find a bottle of booze?" Hill asked.

"No," Janowitz said, "we've been talking about—about Evans' father."

"Oh, yeah?" Hill said, frowning at Evans. "And what's he, a Baptist minister or something?"

"No." Evans laughed. "He's a capitalist. A full-fledged Goldwater, John Birch Society capitalist." And he convulsed himself.

"Well," Hill said dryly, "he must be right proud of you." And Evans almost doubled up. It was funny, but not *that* funny, Janowitz thought.

When Evans got some control of himself, he looked across at Hill. "I understand you're something of a capitalist, too, Hill."

Hill's eyes danced. He measured Evans impishly for a minute, then said, "Yeah—a bit. But I'm no Bircher like your father. I can't get rid of this tan."

Janowitz looked at Hill closely. What the hell were they on about? "What'd you do," he asked, "strike oil in the back streets of Philly?"

"Not Philly," Evans cut in. "Saigon."

Hill shrugged, and glanced coolly at Janowitz. "I got me a couple of cathouses down in Soulsville."

"*Three* cathouses," Evans corrected. Hill coldly nodded acknowledgment, but he suddenly looked a little wary.

"What'dya mean, you've got cathouses? You *own* them?" Janowitz said incredulously.

"That's it," Hill said blandly. "Just a little free enterprise at work."

"But how the hell—" Janowitz was still too astonished to understand.

"Well, you start out with a little investment; then you build on it. It's like selling soap or anything else. Only maybe it's easier."

"But you're in the goddamned Army!"

"That's inconvenient all right"—Hill grinned —"especially at times like this. But there are compensations."

Janowitz knew there were plenty of whorehouses in Saigon, he could even believe that some experienced NCO might run a couple, but nothing in his image of the awkward, gangling Big George of the basketball court at camp prepared him to accept Hill as a part-time entrepreneur in joy down in Soulsville.

"You see, if he weren't in the military," Evans said, still looking at Hill, but talking to Janowitz, "he'd really have to pay through the nose for PX booze. And he might have to pay black-market prices for steaks and things like refrigerators and air-conditioning units, beds, nylon sheets—but they all come cheap at the PX. So it's not all disadvantage being a GI *and* a capitalist."

"What the hell have you got?" Janowitz said to Hill in open won-

173

der. Hill was studying Evans with a look that promised trouble. He obviously didn't like the idea of everyone's knowing quite so much about his business.

"I got some nice places, that's all. A guy can come for a meal, drinks, a little music—have a few laughs and get laid." He turned to Evans. "If I went through the black market for everything, I'd be paying right into the hands of all those bastards you claim you're against."

Evans smiled. "Don't worry about me, Hill. You can stay as long as the troops stay. But when the Liberation Front takes over, you better get on the first boat."

"I'll be long gone, dad—provided you're going to let me out of this little excursion first." His tone of voice left no doubt the joking was over.

"The time may come when if you want to go back, you'll be allowed to go back."

"Oh, I'll want to go back. You can count on that, dad."

Evans propped himself against the tree, withdrawing into his shell again under the pressure of Hill's belligerence. Hill started to roll over to go back to sleep. He grinned slyly at Janowitz.

"You live right, I'll take you around one day, Lieutenant. Indoctrinate you into the ways of the flesh. Put you right off officers clubs for life." He rolled over, apparently fully aware of just how stunned Janowitz was.

Goddamn, Janowitz thought. He looked at Evans and acknowledged his bafflement with a wry arching of the eyebrows. Evans forced a smile, but he shifted his eyes away. Janowitz rolled over and with a sigh at his own innocence and the world's cockeyed confusion went to sleep.

v

They hid out for three days. There were more air strikes the first and second days. When Miller wondered out loud how long they were going to be forced to lie there in the goddamned woods, Evans asked him testily what he'd think if he were back in Nebraska and the North Vietnamese were bombing the piss out of them and suddenly three North Vietnamese came wandering along the road. They'd get strung up. And that was probably what would happen to them if they walked back into that camp. People had slaved their guts out to get that equip-

174

ment down from the North—men, women, boys, girls—and now most of it, and their camp, had been blown to pieces—and God knew how many people with it.

Evans traded guard duty with Toe, but by the third day Evans was looking haggard from fatigue, and Janowitz decided that this, as much as anything else, finally led him to start them down toward the camp.

They'd had one more talk—the night before they moved off. They were all awake, and Hill had guyingly asked Evans what kind of capitalist his father was. It was desperation really. For two days there had hardly been a word spoken. They'd heard fighter-bombers strafing and bombing the valley, some antiaircraft, and some other bombing far to the north, but it only served to clam them up all the more. On the third day the raids stopped. The sky was overcast, and Janowitz guessed the cover might be lower at the bases the planes were using in Thailand. Evans had killed a huge jungle rat, and they'd been hungry enough to eat some of it. He told them to pretend it was frog's legs! It hadn't helped much. They just watched Toe munching away greedily. Finally, Hill had asked him how he stood it. Evans translated, and Toe answered *he* pretended it was frog's legs. It had been their first laugh since that first night. And it loosened them up a little.

Evans had let Toe keep the fire going because, as dark settled in, the damp was cold. It was then, with the fire crackling and their stomachs pretending they were satisfied with hunks of rat, that Hill had put the question to Evans about his father.

"He's part of a family of capitalists, really," Evans answered, toying deliberately with the word "capitalist." "His grandfather owned a coal mine. It started the family fortune. My dad's father used some of the money to open a department store and a chemical plant—and he married the daughter of the second richest man in town: timber and property. My father inherited the department store and shares in all the rest. The coal mines aren't worth anything now—but we struggle along on what's left."

Hill laughed. "How come you aren't an officer?" he asked.

"I'm a black sheep," Evans said. "In a family of gray sheep," he added slowly. "I've got three older brothers. One helps Dad with the store and screws as many women as Dad can keep on the payroll. He's married, of course, and has three kids—but he doesn't let that interfere with his real calling. My other brother is like my dad. He'll take it over one day. He believes the world was meant to provide him with a profit—and he intends to see that it does. The brother nearest me is almost as bad as I am. He's always wanted to be a musician, and Dad has tried to tame him by letting him run the music and record department in the store, but I think he may lose."

"And that leaves you," Miller said unexpectedly. He sounded a bit bitter, as though he didn't feel all that sorry about the problems of the rich.

"Yeah—and that leaves me," Evans said with, if anything, more bitterness. "As long as I can remember I've hated the store, hated the way my uncles and aunts and cousins ran everything—and everybody —in town.

"Summers my mother used to take us all to Europe. One summer she became a convert to Catholicism. My dad despised it, but he couldn't shout her out of it. I . . . I suppose because he hated it so much, I became even more devout than my mother." He looked up at Miller. "I decided I wanted to be a priest." He kicked at the ground with the butt of the rifle, watching it mark the earth. "But I didn't finish. I went back home, and when the draft came, I let it come. I didn't want to go back to college, and I didn't want my dad to get me out any other way. . . . So I became a private—and my father remained a capitalist."

"So that's what you got against America—your dad." It was Miller who said it.

"Yes," Evans said calmly. "My dad *is* one of the things I've got against America."

And that was the end of the conversation. They all watched the fire for a long time; then one by one they went off to sleep.

Toe held the rifle when Janowitz awoke. Evans was sleeping beside him—but was restless and kept muttering things in his sleep. Finally, Hill and Miller woke. They all were stiff and sore, and their heads ached from lack of food. When Evans came to, he still looked as if he hadn't slept in a week. His eyes all bloodshot with big dark circles under them.

They heard voices and some shouting, and Toe grew restless. Finally, Evans let them take a stretch and a piss, and then he decided to start down. Janowitz assumed he'd untie them, but no such luck.

They hit the first burned patches about halfway down. It was amazing how many trees were still standing in the plain around the camp. They were black and charred—topless except for an occasional stray climber that for some reason hadn't burned—but it was still a jungle. A brown, black, and gray charcoal jungle. Farther down, the ground was still hot. They started to take a shortcut from the river, but it was so painful underfoot they had to go back. Logs were still smoking, and every once in a while they'd be startled by a sudden hissing when a bunch of vines or a crumpled bush would break into flame again.

They had almost reached the place where Morris had been trapped when they ran into a patrol of North Vietnamese troops moving upstream. The North Vietnamese didn't react at all at first—but when they realized it wasn't another patrol coming downstream, but a group of Americans, there was much shouting between Toe and the leader of the patrol. Toe finally won, but they took Evans' rifle away from him and shoved, punched, kicked, and knocked them all on downriver toward the camp. Miller made the mistake of kicking back at one when he had been knocked flat, and in a second about six of them started kicking him in the head and back until Janowitz thought they'd kill him. When he tried to interfere, one of them turned and jabbed the muzzle of his rifle in Janowitz's gut and pulled him head first into the water and started working *him* over. When the leader finally stopped it, Janowitz was bruised but in one piece, but Miller's nose and mouth were bleeding badly. They doused him several times in the river, and he finally seemed all right. He walked the rest of the way with his head up, but he didn't respond again to the pokes and maulings the troops gave him.

When they passed Morris' grave, Janowitz bowed his head for a second. Stupid rituals about the dead, but you felt worse if you didn't. He saw no sign of Thai's body or of Mỹ's. He kept looking all the rest of the way in, wondering if she'd made it or been trapped someplace by the fire. But he didn't see any bodies at all until they got right into the camp area, and then there was just one pile. Maybe fifteen in all, lined up along a ditch where women were digging to make a mass grave. There's a soul-shuddering gruesomeness about burned bodies. The scorched twisted flesh, the awkward wrenching of the bones. Lined up like that by the open grave, they looked like those old newsreels of the concentration camps. He turned away without trying to see if he could identify one of them as Mỹ.

The ground was as hot in the camp area as it was in the woods, but people were moving all over the place. The planes had really beat the shit out of it. There were smashed pieces of trucks and artillery all over. If they'd been building up for an offensive, as it looked, they could forget it. Nevertheless, a lot of the lighter stuff had evidently been saved in the caves. Strings of mortars were being carried out, and they passed one cave that was piled high with bicycles. Teams were already at work hauling charred saplings to cover the cave entrances, trying to make the camp look like nothing more than another piece of the burned-out waste.

They were taken to a big cave. There were three foot-pedaled

Singer sewing machines near the entrance and behind them stacks of camouflaged fatigue material. No one was at the machines, but at the other side of the cave four women were sorting mail from heavy blue sacks. It shook Janowitz up a little. He'd never seen a VC or a North Vietnamese reading mail, and somehow it had just never occurred to him that they got letters from home like everyone else. Not only that, but the women were working at a big cloth sorting rack, sorting with the same speed and gestures "real" mailmen sorted with. The women glanced over their shoulders at them when they came in, but otherwise they might never have existed.

Toe argued with the North Vietnamese leader about taking Evans along with them, but the guy wouldn't have it. He left two guards on them and, with Toe tailing along behind him, headed off for some higher authority. In a little while Higher Authority came back with them. Another North Vietnamese. Toe talked his arm off again, but Higher Authority just stared at them coldly, muttered something to Toe, and walked off. It was obvious no one knew what the hell was going on, and Janowitz figured the time had come to try to get some food. He made a pitch to Toe, and Toe disappeared again. Half an hour later he came back, not with food, but with another mouth: Russell.

Everyone reached out to grab him. It was strange, Janowitz thought. He hardly knew the little Southern hillbilly, but he couldn't have been happier if one of the Michigan basketball team had walked in. They all thumped him and hugged him—even taciturn Miller. It was a kind of crowd hysteria. He was one of them. He was alive. And they were reunited.

Russell's shoulder was bandaged and his arm in a sling, but other than that, he looked all right. He told them that after they'd winged him, he'd made it into the woods, but they'd had him in five minutes. They had hauled him along while they searched for Miller and Pershing, but when the fire got worse and worse, they gave up and headed back for camp. They had followed the river and partway down came on Thai and one of the nurses.

"Dead?" Janowitz asked.

"Well, Thai, he was out, but he wasn't dead. The nurse was trying to revive him, but there was something wrong with her. She'd gone loco or something. They finally had to force her to come on down. She kept trying to run into the woods. They had to tie her in the end."

Janowitz's heart did that flip. Just the mental image of her sent everything flying in him. He half wished he'd never touched her. He

178

could almost feel the lightness of her. Man, he needed to get back to Saigon, where there were women to spare. But in the meantime, he was stuck—and he longed to know if she was okay.

"How the hell'd you get through the bombing?" Hill asked, thumping Russell on his good arm.

"I prayed—when I wasn't cussing."

They all laughed. More than they needed to.

"You seen Pershing?" Miller asked more soberly.

"Nope." Russell looked around the group. "And I ain't seen Lieutenant Morris either."

"Morris is dead," Janowitz said.

"Oh. Well, that explains it then," Russell said quietly, not really knowing what to say.

That put the damper on their spirits. When it came right down to it, Morris wasn't very important to any of them either, but they all felt his loss as strongly as they had responded to their reunion with Russell.

They didn't get to eat until late that night. Russell had told them that he'd seen Thai the first day in the hospital, but not since. Tick and Tack were around camp someplace, but everything was so fucked up it might be some time before they could come claim them. Most of the VC and North Vietnamese had holed up in caves and hadn't been touched by the bombs, but that first day of the fire it had got so hot and the oxygen had got so low that people fainted all over the place and quite a few died. Russell said he'd never been so scared of death. There was soot and smoke everywhere, and he had been sweating so much he didn't think there was any more water left in him, and he couldn't get a breath to save his ass. He'd stood on his tiptoes, thinking the higher he could get, the better off he'd be, but he couldn't keep it up. He passed out a couple of times and kept fighting for air. He didn't mind dying, he thought for sure he was going to die anyway, but he couldn't stop fighting for air. It was frantic. The guards, everybody, were just staggering around clawing at their throats—coughing and gasping. It was raw and hot right down into your stomach.

The next day fighter-bombers had come in. They plastered the place with rockets and even scored a couple of direct hits into the caves, but after that fire it didn't seem like anything. Russell was no artist at description, but there wasn't one of them who hadn't been affected by his story when he finished.

"I wonder if the old supersarge made it," Hill said solemnly.

"If we lived through it, he would," Miller asserted grimly.

Janowitz's first reaction was to feel the same as Miller. But it suddenly hit him that if Pershing had escaped—or worse—fallen to the fire—*he* was now the leader of this group—not technically, but actually. It would mean a change in his relationships—especially with Hill. He would have to limit the buddy-buddy bit and prove that he could be as resolute as Pershing. Otherwise he knew Hill would replace the rules with the every-man-for-himself law of the Philadelphia jungle. And he'd do it quick. Janowitz almost smiled to himself. It could be quite a game—him and Hill—but he felt he could win comfortably at the odds. He had to take it slow, though; it would be wrong to try to take charge in some overt way when they were still uncertain about what had happened to Pershing. If it was to come, it had to be accepted as right by them all—not pushed by him. They'd go on as they were, but he'd have to be a little more careful.

It was Tick who finally brought them their food. It wasn't much, just a half bowl of rice with nothing else in it. And Tick didn't seem any too glad to see them. When they'd finished, he ordered two guards in, and they took Evans away like a prisoner. Russell was puzzled by it, and when they explained about Evans killing the VC, he was even more puzzled.

"He's going to end up gettin' shot by both sides if he don't watch hisself."

"He's a priest," Hill said, enjoying the paradox of it *and* Russell's bewilderment. Russell looked at him incredulously for a minute; then his eyes twinkled.

"Well, my old man always said you could trust a Catholic for two things: He's pious-mouthed as a preacher and deceitful as a rattlesnake."

"Your old man's quite a philosopher." Hill smiled.

"Yeah. You oughta hear what he says about colored." Russell grinned slyly. Hill all but burst a gut.

8

i

They didn't see Evans for two days. There was another bombing raid the second morning, but no new equipment had been moved in from the North, and the pilots were evidently uncertain they had the right target. They made two passes at the valley, ripping it with rockets, but that was it. The VC kept under cover and gave no returning fire. Later there were explosions in the distance, but whether the Air Force had found something or was just guessing was hard to say. Janowitz knew how much one bit of forest looked like every other bit once you got a couple of hundred feet in the air, and he imagined it was even worse over the charcoal uniformity of a burned-out wildfire like this one.

The planes had hardly gone when Thai came in with all three of his galloping knights. Thai's head was still bandaged, and the bandage covered one eye completely. He looked weak and under strain. Big Tack had a huge blue bruise across his face, but his spirits hadn't been damaged in the least. Janowitz, Miller, and Hill all still had bruises themselves from the beating they'd taken from the North Vietnamese patrol, and Tack grinned at them, pointing first to his bruise and then to theirs.

"Yankee planes no good, okay! We big comrades, see!"

Some comrades! Janowitz felt like telling him that for his money it was North Vietnamese rifle butts that were "no good." But he had to admit he was glad to see Tack again. If they had to be with VC, he preferred that big slob to any of the others he'd seen.

Thai gave them a lecture about trying to escape, reminding them they were criminals and could be shot for seeking to avoid their due punishment. All his earlier threats had sounded like ninety-nine percent propaganda, but this one came through like the real thing. He sounded tired, tired of them, tired of the burden they seemed to represent to him.

It was almost sunset when Tick came back with Evans. They spoke quietly for a time in front of the cave, speaking French very rapidly. Janowitz with his year of Michigan French couldn't get any of it. When Tick left, Evans came into the cave and squatted down against one of the sewing machines without speaking to any of them. Janowitz's first impulse was to ask him what happened, but he stopped himself. When Toe brought them food, Evans didn't eat.

They had enjoyed the last two nights. They had slept on the material that was gathered for uniforms, and they had been left strictly to themselves. Even without enough food it was recuperative. And they were just getting settled for another night's rest when Thai and the three stooges appeared again—packed for travel. They had a string of guards with them, and they carried sleeping bags, rain capes, and sacks of rice for each of the Americans. Outside, the guards had more load for them. Janowitz recognized the one they presented to him—a blue mailbag. The whole process had been organized like an assembly line and took them off-balance. Even as the mailbag was being strapped on his back, Janowitz thought he should protest. He was an officer; he didn't have to work. But it seemed so asinine. Without Pershing there to make a big deal about it, he'd have felt like an ass even bringing it up.

In the end the only one who didn't carry anything was Thai himself. When they started through the valley, Janowitz noticed more troops falling in line behind them, but he was near the front between Tack and Hill and couldn't tell how many of them there were.

When they took their first break, they were still in the burned-out area. Janowitz's eyes had become fully accustomed to the dark by then, and he slid down next to Hill. Without Pershing there, he felt even closer to Big George. He'd have to watch the officer bit, but he saw no reason for burying his feelings altogether.

"Well, she's alive," Hill said as Janowitz flopped down. Janowitz propped himself up on an elbow and looked where Hill nodded. The VC had broken into two groups. About eight of them he'd never seen before—three women, five or six men—had settled in a big circle about fifteen yards from the rest of them. But three of the others were moving toward Thai. It was Mỹ and big tits and the kid who had taken him to the river for a drink before he and Tack had carried Morris.

Janowitz studied Mỹ as well as he could in the dark. The sight of her just melted his insides. How could a woman do that to you? He didn't know whether he was reading things into it or not, but her face did look blank. He wondered if she really had gone psycho or if it had just been a temporary shock. She was in fatigues again and carried a pack, but she looked so graceful, as if she were gliding over the ground. He remembered once when they'd been grounded after a game in St. Louis, they'd had to come back by train and he'd met this girl who had the same kind of effect on him. It was nothing really, just the way she sort of chewed the lipstick off her lower lip and the way she'd smile quickly and brightly, but kind of modestly. She'd hung in his mind for weeks.

And his beauty was like that. He didn't know what it was, the way she moved, the way she blew away her hair, the solemn earnestness with which she approached everything. But whatever it was, it set him in motion.

She shifted her pack and sat down on the ground off to one side of Toe. Then she lifted her eyes to Janowitz and just stared. She looked as if she might cry, maybe she was crying—in the dark Janowitz couldn't really tell—but she kept looking at him, and he wanted to get up and go over and talk to her. Tell her he was sorry about pug nose, sorry about the war. She looked so numb and tiny. And the black, charred waste around them recalled the desperation of the fire and made her seem even more helpless. For the first time he wondered how old she was, how long had she been a "soldier" in the jungle, running from planes, marching all night, going without food, tending the wounded. Goddamn, why didn't she quit? A girl needn't do it; a girl like her couldn't be so hopped up on Communism—or even patriotism—that she had to go through this. She was too serene, too feminine. Long-suffering maybe, but not an aggressive patriot or student activist or aggressive anything.

"I think she's got the hots for you," Hill said dryly.

"You think you could arrange something," Janowitz cracked back. He still hadn't taken his eyes from Mỹ because she was still looking at him.

"You think she knows you're a big basketball star?"

"Probably not. But she might be able to guess that I'd give her a hundred dollars for the night if I found her in one of your places."

"Man, officers! I'd give you three like that for a hundred dollars."

"Not like that."

"You know what they say about the dark."

"Yeah, but I don't believe it. And neither do you." As good-natured as it was, he didn't really like joking about her this way.

"I'll tell you a secret about Vietnamese women," Hill said. "Don't smile at her. Just keep staring at her nice and sober. You smile and she'll flirt like hell with you, but the only way you'll get near her then is paying for it. But play it masterful, like you're some god who just might give her a break, and she'll crawl for you. Then once she's committed," he went on lightly, "you can do what you like. You can even smile at her once in a while."

Janowitz almost broke into a smile at that. But finally Mỹ had lowered her eyes, and she stayed like that, with her eyes downcast the rest of the break. When she got up, she didn't look at him at all. He didn't know what impact *his* technique had had on her, but he knew for sure that hers had been devastating.

By dawn they had passed out of the fire area altogether, and they camped in lush forest about three hundred yards from a large river. It wasn't long before they knew why they stayed so far from it. The first jets arrived as they were settling in. They heard rockets firing and a couple of bombs going in. Janowitz figured they must be in the area of a bridge or crossing of some kind. Half an hour later it was confirmed when a long string of camel bikes went by them. There was no acknowledgment between the groups, no signals or conversation, even though the convoy passed within feet of the camp.

When the sun was higher, Big Tack took them off to a tributary of the main river and let them douse themselves in the water. It felt great, and when they'd finished, they lay on the bank for a long time. But Tick finally appeared, and they were ordered back. As they passed through the forest, Janowitz saw movement on his right, and then there, half-obscured by the foliage, just standing still, staring at him, was Mỹ. She stood frozen, like a deer, her eyes solemnly examining him as if wondering if he were a dangerous enemy going to attack or just another harmless forest animal. He tried to work up a smile, and something happened to his face, but it wasn't really a smile. With her face still expressionless, she finally turned and disappeared, lost in the leafy undergrowth.

Tack pushed him.

"You move, okay? You are disappearing in this same forest, the tigers and the snakes make you quick, okay? They like Yankee meat." He laughed at his own humor, but as he moved off, he saw what had made Janowitz stop. All the women were moving through the forest to the river. For a second he clucked thoughtfully; then he slammed Janowitz on the back.

"Vietnamese girls okay! Okay?"

"Yeah"—Janowitz smiled weakly—"okay." He could see Tick

watching him up ahead, and it made him feel awkward and guilty—like a kid caught in masturbation.

Tack shrugged lugubriously. "Now women in Vietnam all equal like men. Comrades. Much better before. You trade one good ox, you get one good young girl. Now, revolutionary women all think they are better than the ox, better than *beaucoup* ox. But Trach"—he leered—"has more women than the ox, I tell you that!" And he thumped Janowitz on the back again.

During that day's encampment they were more loosely guarded. Their legs were tied with short rope halters so they couldn't run fast, but their hands were left free, and if they could have slipped the guards, they could easily have unbound their legs, but the VC were all around them, and two or three guards were on duty all the time.

Right after they had been tied, Thai came to them. The night's march hadn't done him any good, and he still seemed short-tempered, as though he questioned if they were worth the effort.

"Comrade Pershing was captured less than twenty-four hours after he escaped." He paused, letting it sink in. Janowitz could feel the clutch on his own throat, his heart beating faster. "He had made a signal indicating the direction of our camp. It is believed that signal was responsible for a rocket attack which killed a number of troops, both of the National Front and the People's Army of North Vietnam."

Janowitz caught Miller's tight smile, but the tone of Thai's voice made him fear for Pershing. He glanced at Evans. Evans' head was down; he knew something unpleasant was coming all right.

"It was not until another signal was made by our own soldiers that the attack was diverted," Thai continued. "Comrade Pershing has been tried by a people's court and found guilty of an act against the people of Vietnam punishable by death."

They all were staring at him—their faces blank with disbelief.

"However, Comrade Evans made an appeal to the court to suspend sentence, at least until the outcome of our mission with you."

Janowitz looked over at Evans again. He hadn't moved.

"If the mission succeeds, he asked that the case be reconsidered. . . . I concurred with this request." Thai looked from one to the other, his expression suggesting that he had concurred very reluctantly. "Comrade Pershing will rejoin us tomorrow or the following day at the latest." And with that he turned and walked slowly away.

Miller turned on Evans. "Is all that true?"

"Yes. I think so," Evans answered. "I hadn't been told what the

185

court decided, but if Thai says they voted to let him go, I imagine they have."

Evans didn't speak for a minute; then it came very quietly.

"He's been beaten up. I think one of his eyes has been badly damaged. Otherwise he'll probably be okay." The solemnity of Evans' voice gave them all an idea of the condition Pershing was in. "It wasn't Thai's doing, and I don't think it was the court's," he continued slowly. "You must remember the whole thing took place at a time of very great anger and frustration."

"You're quite an apologist for *their* anger, aren't you?" Miller said sharply.

Evans shrugged. "I've seen GI's who were pretty angry after being on the receiving end of a mortar attack."

"They didn't try any VC for murder!" Miller came back angrily.

Evans turned on him. "I don't like to see anyone hurt," he said. "But you're going to have to get used to the idea that I think Pershing would be better off—and so would a lot of other people—if we'd never come to Vietnam, if we were all back in the United States, where we belong."

Miller was stopped for a second, but not much longer. "I'll tell you one thing," he said with quiet venom, "it'd have been a helluva lot better if *you'd* never come to Vietnam."

Evans lowered his head. "I won't argue with you about that," he said quietly. He fiddled with the rope halter around his leg for a minute— he'd been tied, too, this time. "I'm sorry about what happened to Pershing," he said at last.

They all just looked at him. Janowitz grimaced at Hill, then asked the question bluntly. "What's all this in aid of, Evans? What the hell do you think you're going to get us to do?"

Evans looked up at him. He seemed to consider for a long time whether he should say anything or not, but in the end he spoke.

"I can't tell you. But I promise you that none of you will be forced. When the time comes you'll agree—or you'll drop out. And if you choose the latter, you'll simply be treated like any other prisoner of war—no better, no worse."

"You better drop me out right now," Miller said. "I'm not agreeing to do anything for the Vietcong, not if you offer me the moon for it or if you tear my balls off if I don't."

"We'll have to see," Evans replied.

"No, we won't," Miller said firmly. "I'm telling you now, you can lecture at me till the cows come home, but you won't get me to lift a finger." He smiled. "You're a little bit crazy if you think you can."

"I don't doubt I'm a little bit crazy." Evans grinned. "And you'll be glad to know I'm not betting on you, Miller. I just think you're sure enough of what you believe to listen to the other side without fear."

"That's right. That's exactly right."

"That's what I mean," Evans said. "You just stay unafraid." He held Miller's eyes for a minute and then stretched out as though he were going to sleep.

The rest of them exchanged glances, and then Janowitz flopped down beside Hill.

"You think he's crazy?" Janowitz whispered wryly.

"Like a fox." Hill grinned.

"Can you see yourself doing anything for the VC?"

Hill's grin grew very broad. "Well, now, Lieutenant," he said, "I guess the best I can say is, it depends . . . yeah, it just sorta depends."

Janowitz had to grin, too. Hill was a real pirate.

"You wouldn't shoot one of your own countrymen or anything like that, would you?" Janowitz murmured.

"Well, now, Lieutenant, what was this fellow countryman of mine doing, lynching a black man?"

Janowitz laughed out loud. The others rolled over, looking at him with a frown. "Assuming he *wasn't* lynching a black man," Janowitz finally muttered, "would you shoot him *then?*"

"Well, if he was lynching a white guy, I'd probably think about it for a while, but I don't guess I'd actually shoot him."

Janowitz almost burst out laughing again. Hill rolled over, half-smiling.

"No. I'll tell you true, Lieutenant. That Evans just made a big mistake with me. If he'd told us they were going to hang us up by the gonads if we didn't go along with this mission, well, I might have thought it over. I got a very high regard for my gonads.

"But the minute he said nothing was going to happen to them that didn't go along, why, he lost a prospect. Hell, I don't volunteer in *our* Army. I sure as hell ain't going to volunteer in theirs."

Janowitz smiled again. "Well, Hill," he said, "it sure is nice to know I can count on your patriotism."

Now it was Hill's turn to grin. "Don't mention it, Lieutenant. If we ever get our asses out of here, I just hope you'll make a note of it in my citation."

187

"Agreed," Janowitz replied. "You want me to mention the cathouses, too?"

Hill smirked. "No," he murmured expansively. "I know how much the boys appreciate it, but I'd just as soon my contributions to the health and welfare of our troops remained anonymous. Thanks to you just the same."

ii

Janowitz awoke at the sound of the planes. They seemed to be right over them, and he sat up sharply. Evans and Miller were awake, too, but Russell and Hill slept right on.

The planes were coming in low over the river, lambasting something with rockets and machine-gun fire. They made three passes. When they'd gone, he tried to settle back, but the sun was directly overhead and he couldn't get a place where it was cool. It was damp and close; the sweat hung on him. He twisted around and watched the light dancing in the leaves. Screwy war. Screwy world. One thing, with Pershing due back, he could forget taking over direct command—and revert to his role as supporting brass. There were catches to that, but it was best.

Someone moved. He glanced around. A VC hauling a container of water to the other group. God, he'd like to be lying in the river. He looked at the three guards. A young kid. A thick-armed one with a yellow kerchief around his hair. And Mỹ.

She was just beyond him on the other side of Russell, a rifle across her lap. And she was watching him steadfastly. His pulse stopped. She seemed tense and remote. Something *had* happened to her. You sensed the coiled spring inside—not ready to unwind in orderly progression, but to fly out in chaos . . . or collapse utterly. He longed to touch her, just to put his lips to hers.

He turned away slowly, and twice he turned back. Never did she take her eyes from him, and his heartbeat got faster and faster. He remembered all the times when an ounce of audacity lay between him and her, in one form or another.

He watched the sun in the trees, frightened. Could he touch her? Would she let him touch her? What was he frightened of? What did he have to lose? He didn't know, but his mouth was dry, his temples throbbing. He looked at Miller and Evans. Both had gone back to sleep. He counted. It was the only way to force himself. One. Two. Three. He sat up.

The other two guards glanced up. The VC who had been hauling water looked across at him. Janowitz stretched and wiggled around so that he was facing her. He had to force himself to meet her eyes. She was watching him still—her mouth open.

He steeled himself again. One. Two. Three. He stood up. He could sense a guard rising behind him. Restrained by the halter, he moved in short steps toward her. She raised her gun but didn't stand.

Looking down on her, he thought his heart would beat right out of his chest. The dark hair was so close. Her skin and mouth looked too soft for belief.

"Drink," he said. "I want to go to the river." He mimed as he spoke, pointing behind her toward the tributary Tack had taken them to. For the first time she took her eyes from him and glanced over at the other guards. He thought he saw Tick moving at the edge of the clearing, but he wouldn't look. He wanted it between him and her.

Finally, she turned back, wiggled a little away from him, and then rose, nodding for him to go ahead of her. He was wringing wet with sweat now, and as he moved awkwardly through the forest underbrush, he licked the salt from his lips. Twice he held branches for her, to keep them from swinging back into her face, but each time she simply paused, waiting for him to release the branch. Each time he had looked into her eyes, and she had simply stared back as though prepared to stand there looking at him forever. Only when the branch had finally swung clear did she advance—always keeping three or four yards behind him.

At the river he went down on his knees, dousing his face in the water. His head was throbbing from the excitement. He turned to her. She was watching him with that same expression, but he could see the movement of her chest. She was breathing almost as fast as he was.

He wanted to smile, but he couldn't. He indicated the river—did she want to drink? She waited, then moved to the river's edge, closer to him than she had to, too far away to touch. He didn't move. She bent and wiped her face with water. She stood erect again, and at last he could force a smile. Her eyes went from his eyes to his mouth. He felt dizzy from the intensity of it. One. Two. Three. He slowly held his hand out to her.

She had cried when he first clutched her to him. Silent tears pouring down her face as he kissed her forehead, cheeks, her mouth, her neck. And then she had held onto him, and his hands were inside her uniform, clutching, stroking the skin that felt softer than all the fantasies of the last weeks had imagined. She made no effort to stop him. Nothing. Just clinging to him as though as eager to receive him as he was to have her. And it had been so quick and so intense. He'd never had an orgasm so fast. And with her too, it was wild and burning. She came as fast as he, responding to the outburst of his emotion as he did to hers. And it wasn't over on orgasm. They lay twined together, clutching each other, feeling the sense of release, oneness, feeling the rightness of it.

As the ferocity of it began to fade, he held his head back to look at her. Her face was limpid, wide-eyed, with that note of feminine questioning. Now that it's over, now, what do you think? He leaned down and kissed her on the mouth, trying to show what he did think. So often before, he had felt dead after it was over. Ashes in his throat, once the sexual flood was expended. But not now. If anything, she was more beautiful to him, more desirable. He clung to her, enveloping her tiny, full body in his long arms.

It was then he felt the object in her hand. He held himself tense, then pulled back slowly, looking at her questioningly. A knot of pain came to her eyes. Then she pulled her hand from around his shoulder. The short knife in it had a thin blade that glistened in the sunlight. When she had come to him, she had left her gun by the riverbank where she stood. He had thought that was his last test. He knew that when they were making love, there had been nothing in her hand. She must have drawn the knife when he first held her and left it in the grass when they both were seized at the touching.

She held the knife at the crook of her shoulder, its point toward him. Of course, he thought, she'd know how to fight with a knife. She could probably slice him into little wedges before he knew what happened.

She studied him for seconds, then lowered her eyes. Slowly she turned the blade of the knife down, clutching it against her forearm, along the side of her breast, shielding it from his flesh and hers. He waited, but she didn't look up. Finally, he bent down and kissed each of her eyelids. Her other arm, still around his neck, pulled him close, and he held her again while she rocked with tears.

When they came back through the forest, he stopped while they were still hidden from the others and kissed her. Just the feel of her against his body and he was rampant, ready to put her down and make love to her for another year at least. But she pulled away. Not that once was enough for her either, he thought, but she had a duty—and a position.

190

When they entered the area, three new guards were on duty. He didn't see Tick. He hoped he'd been wrong, that it was someone else who'd been moving around when they left. He lay down and tried not to watch Mỹ walk back to where the other VC were sleeping, but at last he rolled over and caught a glimpse of her. She wasn't looking at him anymore.

iii

Janowitz thought he'd never wake up. When they tried to stir him, every muscle in his body was "delaxed." He just wanted to sleep peacefully on forever.

Food was being prepared over a fire by the women, and the GI's were put in line with the VC. Mỹ was sitting by the fire, eating but keeping the fire stoked from a stack of dead thick vines. She didn't look up at all until he was almost over her—and then it was just a glance. But he could see that some of her tension had gone, too, and a smile came to his face without his calling it. The mere sight of her was no longer heart-stopping, but it suffused him with warmth.

After they'd eaten, they broke up in session groups. The VC divided themselves into their three-man teams, one lecturing to the others, and the three musketeers marshaled the GI's to a clear spot in the forest. Tick took over as master of ceremonies. It was a couple of hours to sunset, and Thai had gone back to sleep as soon as he'd eaten. He looked even worse than he had the night before.

Tick was like most guys who know they're disliked. He carried himself with a contradictory air of defiance and sycophancy that only made matters worse. Janowitz had met many an American in Vietnam who considered himself naturally superior to the Indians—any of them, VC, merchants, women, any of them. Americans who figured the fuckers were too dumb or too lazy to open a Coca-Cola bottle if someone didn't show them how first and bribe them for the effort second. You couldn't trust them, they were dirty, and dirt poor—and too goddamned lazy to do anything about it.

With Tick it was the other way around. It was obvious from every move he made that he felt himself naturally superior to Americans. They were stupid, uncultured, unsophisticated purblind rubes who had the tastes of bauble-happy monkeys and a wanton gift for cruelty. Thai was different. He always seemed like an aristocrat with everyone. But

Tick saved a special hauteur for the Americans; with them his disdain was total.

But it was a measure of his insecurity that when he finally had a chance to put them through the hoops, it was Arnie Russell he chose as target.

"Tell me, Comrade Russell," he began, looking down on them as though it were about all he could do to bring himself to talk to them, "why are you here?"

Russell hesitated, genuinely confused. "Why, I reckon because you brought me," he said politely.

Hill smirked, and as usual, once Russell saw where the joke was, his eyes lit up with humor, but he kept looking at Tick, very respectfully.

"The question I am asking, Comrade Russell, is why you are in Vietnam?"

"Well, I was drafted." It was hard to tell if he had said it in complete innocence. But if not, the act was genuine enough to make Tick hold his temper, even though the rest of them were having difficulty to control their laughter.

"Is that why you're fighting? Because you were drafted?"

"Well, more or less, and 'cause they told me to."

"Weren't you told you were here to fight aggression from the North Vietnamese?"

"Yes, sir, I guess I was."

"Do you still think you are fighting aggression from the North?"

"Well, it don't rightly sound like it."

"But that's what your leaders told you you were doing?"

"Yes, sir."

"And they lied!"

"Well, they said we were fighting Communism."

"And are you fighting Communism?"

"Well, not right this minute, but I imagine I will directly I get out of here."

Miller spluttered, trying to hold the laugh in. The others started to crack, but Tick's glare of hostility kept them in rein.

"Do you know what Communism is, Comrade Russell?" he continued.

"Well, I reckon it's a dictatorship. Everybody telling a body what to do all the time."

"Are you against dictatorships?"

"Yes, sir."

"Is your country against dictatorships?"

"Yes, sir."

"Then I wonder," Tick said harshly, "why you aren't fighting the dictatorships in Spain and Portugal, in Greece and South America, in Formosa and the Middle East?"

"Well, I reckon if they sent me, I would," Russell replied quietly. Miller put his face in his hands. His whole body was quivering. Russell's eyes got that light again, but he kept a straight face for Tick.

"Most of those countries are *allies* of the United States, and yet they are *all* dictatorships! How do you explain that, Comrade Russell?"

"Well, I—I never was much of a one for politics. I know America ain't a dictatorship."

"Could you tell me what a dictatorship of the proletariat means?"

"Not right off."

"Can't you figure it out?" Tick asked severely.

"Well— Would you say it again, please?" Miller rocked. Janowitz was biting his lip to keep from bursting out.

"A dictatorship of the proletariat!"

"Well, I'd guess it'd mean a workers' dictatorship or something."

"Quite right! And do you think life in a workers' dictatorship would be the same as in a military dictatorship?"

"Well— If you were being dictated to, I reckon it would." It was too much for Miller. He rolled over on the ground clutching his sides, laughter pouring out of him until the tears streamed down his face. It set all of them off. And in the way it sometimes happens, once they had started, there was no stopping. The innocent sound of Russell's voice, the blank, stunned stare in Tick's eyes kept playing back in their heads and inducing more gusts of laughter. Only Russell remained sober—and that, of course, only made matters worse. Even Evans was convulsed, trying to dry the tears from his eyes, trying to sit upright and dutiful, but it was just too much.

All the other VC had stopped to look at them, and Big Tack finally stood and walked to where Thai slept, waking him to take control. And all of that made the laughter even harder to suppress.

When Thai walked back, the drawn severity of his face dampened the hysterics but couldn't immediately subdue them. He said a word or two to Tick, and Tick sat down.

"It is good your morale is so high," Thai said quietly. "You have many days' march ahead, and when you have finished, you will only be at the beginning."

193

He looked up then, and his tone, along with his pallor, brought them back down to earth.

"Education in democracy is part of the daily lives of our soldiers. It is now part of *your* daily lives. And as long as you remain with us, it will be so. It is in your interest that you take part with seriousness. Ridicule is a crude device," he said with sudden malice, "and it will be met with devices equally crude."

Miller sighed—threats again, it implied—but Thai had managed it. He'd taken the joy right out of them.

"I am going to ask Comrade Evans to help in broadening your political consciousness," he continued, still speaking softly. "It may be that you will make some effort to assist *him*."

He turned and started walking away. Evans shifted uncomfortably, looking as if he really didn't want to get involved in this. Thai stopped and turned back, looking directly at Evans.

"You should know," he said, "that Comrade Evans also faced a people's court for the murder of a soldier of the Army of the National Front." His eyes went from Evans to Miller. "A soldier killed to save your life, Comrade Miller. The crime has been confessed and recorded. But sentence will not be passed"—he paused—"for some time." He turned and walked on back to where he had been sleeping.

Janowitz looked at Evans. So that's what had happened. Miller was looking at Evans, too—with a particularly sick expression.

"I chose to do what I've done," Evans said almost apologetically. "I knew what the risks were, long ago."

Janowitz tried to shut his mind to it. Hell, they all faced risks every day, but why was murder on a battlefield so much easier to accept than a judicial murder? Evans had killed that guy to save them, there was no doubt of that, and now the VC would hold it over Evans, over all of them. If he didn't succeed in dragging them on the goddamned mission, whatever it was, they could fry him—legally, probably even justifiably from their point of view. What in God's name was the mission? What the hell did they expect them to do?

"My trouble," Evans said with a wry grin, "is that I had the wrong parents." He shrugged his shoulders resignedly. "And the reason I think you're going to help me eventually is that I think you had the wrong parents, too." It was the priest at work. Janowitz could almost see the starched collar, switching the idle chatter at the Youth League to God or the morality of sex before marriage or something. The self-effacing smile, the subtle approach—too calculated to be spontaneous, too clever to be fully honest.

194

"My father was a great believer in America," Evans went on, "and he made very sure all of us believed in it, too. My mother was worse. A member of the Daughters of the American Revolution and the Daughters of the Confederacy and Daughters of several other things." He smiled. "Over the desk in my bedroom there's a framed, embroidered cloth with a replica of the first flag and its thirteen stars, and below it Nathan Hale's words 'I only regret that I have but one life to lose for my country.' It was done by my great-grandmother. It was my father's, my grandfather's." His whimsical little smile faded altogether, and his face became dark and determined. "To tell you the truth, the fact that it was spoken by a revolutionary fighting the established government, a terrorist who was resisting the law, never really came home to me until I saw a revolutionary executed with a pistol in the streets of Saigon."

He had got to them all. Even Miller seemed shaken with self-doubt.

"He stood, proud and defiant, and said that he was dying to free his country. And then he was shot. I looked at those who shot him. I looked at him. In my years in Europe I had lost most of my American hysteria about a world Communist conspiracy, but even if I hadn't, I don't think I could have seen in him a man who wanted to imprison the world in a dictatorship of any kind—proletariat or otherwise." He smiled at Russell. Russell fidgeted uncomfortably.

"He was only a kid, a peasant—ignorant of life outside his village, never mind the world—fighting, at least he felt, for the freedom of his country.

"If his words had been 'I only regret that I have but one life to lose for my country,' it wouldn't have hit me harder.

"I didn't like the war to begin with, but that was the moment I realized it was against everything I had ever thought good about America. That was the moment I realized we are fighting here for the same reasons the Russians fought in Budapest—to suppress a revolutionary war of independence not unlike our own and to do it because we don't like the form of government the people will choose."

"That's the catch, isn't it?" Janowitz interrupted quietly. "Is it a government the people will choose or the Communists will impose?"

Evans shrugged. "Say we decide the *Russians* don't want the Communist government imposed on them by Russian Communists, do you think we ought to go in and shoot up their country like we're shooting up Vietnam?"

"Come off it," Janowitz retorted. He had been treating Evans squarely; he didn't think a debating point was the sort of answer he should get.

Evans blinked uncomfortably. "There may be several Communist countries that would vote to be non-Communist if they got the chance, but we don't attack *them*. Why pick on Vietnam?"

"We were asked to come here," Miller interjected.

"Yes, and we put the people in who asked us. And don't say we're here in defense of a SEATO nation," he added before Miller could reply. "South Vietnam isn't in SEATO—in fact, it wasn't even a nation until we made it one." He looked steadily at Miller. "So why *are* we here?" It was a rhetorical question, and he answered it quietly himself. "Because we don't want—we won't allow—South Vietnam to fall into the Communist world."

It hung in the air for a minute; then Miller answered him. "All right —I don't see anything wrong with that. What are we supposed to do, sit back and let them take over one country after another? If we do, I promise you one day it'll be our country that looks like this."

"Okay," Evans said. "In *your* mind we're tearing this country apart to keep another country from going Communist. In my mind we're tearing it apart to keep it from making the choice we know it would make if we got our tanks and planes and troops the hell out of here—and that's exactly what Russia did in Hungary."

"Shit!" Miller sneered.

"I'm not arguing about it, Miller," Evans came back. "Are you telling me, if we got our guns and planes and tanks out, the people *wouldn't* choose the Liberation Front?"

"What chance would they have to do otherwise? The Liberation Front or a knife in the back. Is that what you mean by life, liberty, and the pursuit of happiness?"

"No, that's not what I mean!" Evans replied, his face on fire. "You seem to forget the Arvin have more than *six hundred* thousand troops, Miller. They outnumber the Liberation Front five or six to one —and they always have. If they had the will to resist, they could. But that's *not my point!* For whatever reasons, votes or knives in the back, the fact is if we get our asses out of here, we know the country will belong to the Liberation Front—just as Hungary would have belonged to the Hungarians if the Russians had got out. Maybe some Hungarian Communists would have suffered—with knives in *their* backs—but *you* didn't think the Russians were justified in doing what they did to Hungary just to save some Hungarian Communists or their beliefs, did you?"

Miller didn't answer.

"Well, did you?"

"I don't have to answer you anything." Miller was angrily looking him straight in the eye.

"No, you don't have to answer," Evans said quietly. "I know you don't think the Russians were justified, though I imagine there were a lot of gung ho Russians who were only too eager to do what they did in Hungary to keep the country safe for them—just as there are a lot of gung ho Americans who are enthusiastically supporting what we're doing to Vietnam to keep it safe for us. My problem is that I can't see the virtue in one if the other is evil."

"It's simple," Miller said. "One country is yours."

"And my country right or—"

"No!" Miller snapped. "Just your country has as much right to be wrong as any other country. The Commies can bully and intimidate and conquer, and we're supposed to recite the Lord's Prayer at them, is that it?"

"The people of Vietnam haven't tried to bully or intimidate or conquer you. The bullying and intimidating came *after* we prevented Ho Chi Minh from taking the leadership of the country. He happens to be a Communist like Tito, but he's also a man—like Tito—who has led his country in a war of independence, and the country did not have to be bullied into accepting him."

"That's your story," Miller muttered blackly.

"That's right"—Evans smiled—"that's my story. I can't force you to believe it, Miller. But since you're a big believer in democracy, I know you won't hold it against me for believing what I do just as strongly as you believe what you do."

He was looking at Miller, and Miller snapped his head around, glaring at him defiantly. Evans was cute all right. It figured, Janowitz thought, priests *would* learn how to debate, and Evans had. He was playing on Miller like a Yo-Yo. Janowitz had to intercede, but he couldn't afford to get trapped the way Miller was, and he didn't think this was an argument he could win. But he sure as hell could switch the field of fire.

"You think we don't want Vietnam to be independent? You think we're out to colonize it, like Hungary? Is that what you believe?" he asked sardonically.

"No. I told you what I think," Evans replied with irritating indulgence. "We're willing to let Vietnam be independent—*if* it will be independent on *our* side. When it was clear that it was going to be independent and Communist, someone in our government decided it would be better to prevent that—at any cost. That's what I think."

"You're a fucking traitor," Miller cut in evenly. "That's what *I* think."

Evans' face got even redder than it had been before. He took a step forward and went down on his knees right in front of Miller, their faces only inches apart.

"There are a lot of things you can call me," he said, his voice a virulent whisper, "but . . . don't . . . you . . . call . . . me . . . that! *My* country is the country of Jefferson and Lincoln, of John Quincy Adams and Robert E. Lee—men who would despise what is being done here in the name of the country they loved. America is not that fucking uniform you wear, Miller! If our flag doesn't stand for decency and liberty, then it doesn't stand for anything. *I'm* not the traitor to that—and I won't be called a traitor by those who are!"

His eyes were burning, and his whole body was taut. Miller studied him in open bewilderment.

"You're a peculiar sonuvabitch," he finally said softly.

"I'm a Southerner," Evans replied coldly. His voice cracked. It was emotional and defiant. "That may make me peculiar, because twice my ancestors *have* been rebels—once against the British, once against what they considered the illegal and intolerable acts of the government of their time. Well, *I* have rebelled against what I consider the illegal and intolerable acts of the government of *my* time! But I am not a traitor!"

iv

Just after sunset they crossed the river. They could see why it was a target. The river was wide and fast as it wound through the hills, but at this stretch it flowed straight for almost half a mile. Near the middle, stone girders supported an old metal frame bridge. The center section had been destroyed, but the supports were really part of an outgrowth of rock, and though they'd been hit, you could see how easy it would be to repair the damage, throw a few planks over the river itself, and get the bridge working again.

But they had crossed well above the bridge, at a point where the river narrowed a bit. There were trees near the edge, and great poles of mahogany and teak had been put up among them with large tree

198

branches tied to them. The branches stuck out over the river on both sides so that it would look from the air as though there were natural cover at that spot. By the time they got to it some of the VC were tugging at thick hemp ropes—and rising out of the water was a wide woodplank bridge. There were big rocks in the middle to weight it down, and when it was just a few inches from the surface, some of the VC hustled out and rolled the rocks off to the shore. Then the bridge was secured by tying its support ropes to trees on either side. The whole operation hadn't taken five minutes.

Janowitz had to shake his head. When it came right down to it, it *was* a bit like the Revolutionary Army fighting the British—all the improvisation, even the forest, reminded him of the pictures in schoolbooks of the Revolutionaries slithering through the woods to attack the Redcoats. He had to be careful, or he'd be thinking like Evans.

While they were crossing, a VC had jostled Janowitz, whacking him with his pack in a way that almost sent him flying. It wasn't an accident, though the guy tried to act as if it were. And when they got to the other side and were waiting for Thai, who was last across, he got an elbow in his ribs so sharp and hard he almost yelled out. When he turned on the guy, he was face to face with two of them. They both were more than a head shorter than he was, but they were older, wiry and tough, and they looked ready to kill him.

He had caught a glimpse of Mỹ crossing the river. She hadn't looked at him, but he guessed that these boys had heard the story from one of the guards that they'd gone off to the river and suspected the worst. He almost smiled. If they only knew.

When they took their first break, he got a couple of more elbows and enough murderous looks to last him a lifetime. There was a lot of chatter among the VC group they didn't know, and finally, one of them came over to where Thai was stretched out and started gassing at him. Right in the middle of it, Big Tack, who was standing by Thai, let out a lecherous roar, and Janowitz knew they must be passing the news along.

"What the hell you grinning at?" Hill asked.

"You wouldn't believe me if I told you," Janowitz muttered.

Hill hunched up and looked at him suspiciously. He glanced across at the confab around Thai.

"You been pissing in their rice or something?" he said.

Janowitz laughed. "In a manner of speaking, I suppose you could say that," he answered. His laugh had brought hard stares from both VC groups, the one around Thai and the big group of newcomers.

He looked down; this wasn't the time to make a show of himself. He didn't want Mỹ to get in trouble, and he sure as hell didn't want her to think he was ridiculing her.

"Come on, what's up?" Hill whispered, taking it all in.

"Well—" Janowitz hesitated. "I—I made love to one of their dolls." He'd tried to say it seriously, but the stunned incredulity on Hill's face brought an irrepressible grin to his. Shit, why did he have to brag about it? Women were right: Men couldn't keep their mouths shut to save their souls.

"Which one," demanded Hill, "the one with the big boobs?"

Janowitz shook his head.

"The pretty one that's been eyeing ya!" Hill whispered it as though he'd solved the crime of the century. Janowitz nodded; he couldn't keep the damn grin off his face.

"Fuck *me!*" Hill moaned. "I'll be beatin' my meat for a month just thinking about it. I'll give you a hundred bucks to describe it move by move!"

"Don't look at her!" Janowitz whispered sharply. Hill had turned to her with the lech practically dripping down his face. He looked back at Janowitz knowingly.

"You're reserving it, are you?"

"I don't want to get her in trouble. And I don't want to make her sorry."

"Oh, boy, thinking, thinking all the time. Why wasn't I born an officer?" Hill stretched back good-naturedly on the ground. "Man, oh, man," he groaned; then he looked up suddenly. "When the hell did you do it?"

"While you were sleeping. She took me to the river for a drink."

Hill's grin grew as broad as his face. "Oh, baby," he said, "I'm going to be drinking so much my kidneys'll be screaming for relief."

Janowitz turned around and flopped out with his head to the ground. He didn't want Mỹ to see him grinning like a tomcat, but he just couldn't stop it.

"Jesus," Hill said, "I'd turned fuckin' right out of my mind. I haven't thought of it more than ten times a day for a week now. Now I gotta get me one of them if it costs me everything the Pentagon's got. Oh, man, I can just see you rolling on that warm grass. I'm going to die, that's all there is to it. I'm going to die right here."

"Shut up," Janowitz pleaded.

Shortly after the break was over, it began to rain, a drenching night rain, steamy and hot at first, and then gradually getting colder until all their bones ached and they longed for warmth. A couple of times Janowitz noticed Thai looking at him with somber interest. Janowitz knew that what had happened with Mỹ wasn't going to be all pleasure. The complications were just beginning.

They had been marching for perhaps two hours when they came to a crude dirt road. It was nothing but a narrow ribbon of ruts and puddles, but it was wide enough for a truck, and they began to meet groups of North Vietnamese soldiers moving south, camel bikes, crude oxcarts—some with fat car wheels, a few with stone wheels—and, after a time, a convoy of six trucks. Every once in a while they would pass a little siding where a truck could pull in and let another pass. They all were hidden under heavy foliage. They finally stopped at one, and three or four of the VC went into the jungle and came back with stacks of dead vines. They had a devil of a time starting them, but once they got them going, they made a good fire, and they all got around it for warmth.

Mỹ had found a place right across from him, and as she huddled close to the fire, she looked up at him. With the rain pouring down, and everyone looking at the sputtering flames, it was a curiously private moment. She was exquisite—more than that. It wasn't just him "falling in love" again; she had got inside him. He ached for her.

v

Near dawn they reached a plain of thick rain forest. They were held up for a long time while Thai and the three stooges went ahead for some reason. Standing still was far worse than marching in the rain, and they all moved about restlessly. Finally, Tick returned and signaled them forward. They turned off the road and headed into the forest. At first it seemed impenetrable, but a path had been hewn out, and once you were on it, you could move single file with comparative ease.

It led ultimately to a clearing about ten feet square. The sun was already up when they got to it. Tick had removed a broad covering of wood and grass matting—and revealed wooden steps leading down into the ground. They were wide enough for two men to walk down side by side. And when they were down, they were in a veritable underground city. They could hear the whine of ventilators and the deeper throbbing of what Janowitz supposed were diesel generators.

There was light from a few electric bulbs and dozens of candles, and little narrow tunnels went off in all directions. It reminded Janowitz of pictures he'd seen of the trenches in World War I. Big wooden beams supporting the roof, flat boards for walking, water dripping from the earthen walls, and two or three inches of mud oozing up around the footway, mosquitoes and gnats everyplace.

People kept passing them as they moved along, not paying any attention to them. They saw room after room with crude wooden bunks loaded with wounded and a long room with three or four tables where people were eating. There were sewing rooms and rooms stacked with equipment, a radio room and a room with three mimeograph machines whirring away. There were many men, but probably a third of the total were women. A lot of them looked as if they belonged in junior high, ten, eleven, twelve.

They finally came to a large room containing only a desk and one North Vietnamese officer and his aide. The officer checked each of their packs against some kind of master list and sent them off, one by one in different directions. Tick, Tack, and Toe had already dumped theirs and returned when the North Vietnamese officer checked Janowitz's mailbag. He said something to little Toe, and Toe motioned to Janowitz to follow him.

They went down another corridor—past more rooms, more wounded, a room with maps and a podium that looked like a briefing room. Janowitz was too tall for the tunnels and had to crouch all the time. Three very young girls coming up one of the tunnels giggled at him when they passed. He smiled back, and they giggled even more. Finally, Toe turned into an entrance, and they were in a mail-sorting room. There were two rows of cloth sorting racks in the middle of the room, and the walls were lined with others. Janowitz was invited to dump his sack and, after some checking, was presented with another, heavier one. All the sorters were women. They all were reacting to his presence, little sly smiles at one another and surreptitious glances at him. Some of them were pretty little dolls, and it was pleasantly titillating, but he was gone. For the time being anyway, he wanted only Mỹ.

When they went out, Toe consulted a penciled map and led him down another string of corridors. They came to a door that was closed, and Toe knocked on it doubtfully. There was an exchange in Vietnamese. Janowitz thought he recognized Thai's voice. Toe opened the door and motioned Janowitz in. Toe closed the door behind him and remained outside.

Inside, it *was* World War I. Wooden table, candle in a bottle, sandbags, wooden beams. Thai was lying on a wooden bunk. Tick was leaning against the wall in the corner opposite the door. It was a very small room, and to stand erect, Janowitz had to put himself between two of the ceiling beams.

Thai sat up slowly. He was looking badly bushed. Janowitz could see he'd been rebandaged. He crossed to the table and sat down. Then he looked at Janowitz for what seemed hours. He didn't say a word. He didn't look as if he were going to say a word. Finally, he pushed something across the table and nodded for Janowitz to pick it up. In the dim light it looked like a paperback book. Janowitz leaned forward and took it. It was a cardboard box, French printing on the outside. He couldn't read any of it. Thai indicated he open it. He slid it open. Smaller boxes. For Christ's sake—rubbers. It must have been a gross of rubbers. He looked up at Thai, unable to mask his half-amused bewilderment.

Thai was staring at him. It wasn't a friendly stare. Janowitz's mind suddenly started to fly. French contraceptives. Is it part of the plan? Are they using Mỹ to get me to do whatever the hell it is they want me to do? Emotionally he couldn't believe all that by the river had been put on, but he knew enough to realize that his vanity could blind him totally on that score. Maybe she hadn't wanted to make love to him; maybe that's what the tears were about. Perhaps the whole routine was a big act? Thai's look, the shoving around he'd got from the VC. All to convince him she was doing it on her own—and then. . . . Then what? Did they think he was nuts enough to do something because a broad asked him to? They were crazy. But he felt sick thinking about it. Had she been faking all that?

Thai kept looking at him. Janowitz glanced across to Tick. Tick seemed to be sneering even more than usually. Had that sonuvabitch deliberately sent Mỹ along with him; had he been awake after all?

"Is that all?" Janowitz asked, turning back angrily to Thai.

Thai nodded. Janowitz turned and opened the door. Toe grinned at him. The ugly little bastard, Janowitz thought. "Come on, where to?" he said sharply.

The meal was memorable chiefly because they had bread with it. Not stale black bread either, but warm French bread. And after, they got liberal mugs of rice and wine. It tasted good, but Janowitz's mood remained black. He couldn't drive Mỹ from his mind. He couldn't keep his anxiety about the damn mission from gnawing at his self-confidence. The more the VC invested in them, the harder he knew it would be for them to give up when he said no, and when he got back with the others, he knew from their expressions that Hill had told them about his scoring with Mỹ. Now everyone knew. When was he going to learn to keep his mouth shut? He tried to get their minds on other things by asking Evans if he had heard anything more about Pershing, but Evans said he hadn't. He only knew that if Pershing hadn't caught up with them by the time they were due to push off, Big Tack was to stay behind and wait for him. So the glances, the little leering smiles, that told Janowitz that everyone, even Evans, was thinking about him and Mỹ, continued. The only pleasure he got out of it was the thought of how they'd react if he pulled out his box of rubbers and told them Thai had given them to him with his paternal blessings.

After their meal they were taken to a small room with six wooden bunks. Two on each wall, except the wall with the door. On their way they'd been taken by what must have been the operating room. A string of patients were stacked in rooms on each side of it, there was a hum of machinery, and nurses were scurrying back and forth. Evans had taken a stenciled sheet of Vietnamese from a table near the entrance. When they'd flopped out in their bunks—only Russell fit them; the rest had to drape their feet over the end—Evans started reading pieces of it.

He couldn't read Vietnamese well enough to make sense of it, just picked out phrases like "the U.S. aggressor," "imperialist running dogs," "the People's Army," "U.S. monopoly capitalist aggressors"— they'd all laughed at that one, even Evans. Finally, Evans threw the sheet down.

"It's frightening to believe," he said, "but to at least a third of the world, all that makes real sense. And to another third, it's at least understandable. That's two-thirds of the entire world. Before I came here, I reacted to it like most Americans—it's so far from reality it hasn't any meaning at all. So, like most Americans, I just ignored it. Propaganda."

"And now you think it isn't, is that it?" Miller said waspishly. Their mood was too relaxed for argument, and he wasn't really arguing, just getting his two cents in, in case Evans was trying to make a point.

Evans laughed. "No, Miller," he said. "I still don't believe in 'the U.S. aggressor' or even 'U.S. monopoly capitalist aggressors.' But I have come to understand why *they* believe in it. And that may make me a sinner in your eyes, but to me it's better than shouting to the rooftops that we're right and everybody else is wrong . . . and when peo-

204

ple don't agree with us complain that they're anti-American—or Communists."

Miller farted. They all laughed. But Evans went right on.

"If you asked most of those guys in that hospital what they're fighting, almost to the man they'd answer, 'American imperialism.' And you won't blow it away with a fart."

"Is that why you took us by the hospital?" Janowitz said cynically. "To make a point?"

"I took you by the hospital because I thought it might strike you that this hospital is a long march from the battlefields. Their men go into battle knowing not only that they may die at a ratio of about ten to one against their American benefactors, but that, unlike the Americans, if they're wounded, they won't get picked up by a helicopter in a few minutes or a few hours and be flown to a fancy hospital. And believe it or not, these little yellow men can be afraid, too. And they have mothers and fathers and brothers and sisters who know that it may be days before their men get more than the crudest first aid and that they may have to be carried many miles before they can even *see* a doctor. That takes courage, too."

"Well, if they're fighting 'American imperialism' "—Miller sniggered—"it's misplaced courage. They've been snowed."

"Shit, stop waving the flag, Miller," Hill interjected. "You're gettin' as bad as he is. You can't knock Charlie's guts. You've said that a thousand times yourself."

"I'm not saying they haven't got guts," Miller answered. "They're fighting the wrong thing, that's all."

"Well, it sounds to me like we are, too," Hill said. And he looked at Evans. "And don't think that means I'm going to do anything for you! I don't do anything for anybody, but I think the way I want to." He turned back to Miller. "And I never did trust Johnson as far as I could spit, and you know goddamned right the Arvin and the rest of those shits down in Saigon are just Oriental gangsters."

"Does that make *us* wrong?" Miller snapped.

"It doesn't make us right."

Nobody said anything for a moment. Miller pulled out one of the skinny gray cigarettes Tack had given them. He lit up and puffed at the ceiling.

"Listen," he said, "nobody fights in this war any braver than the GI's." His voice was tight and strained. "If the VC are fighting for what they believe in, so are we." It was obvious the fact that Hill was black made it difficult for him, but he believed what he said—even for Negroes—only he wasn't sure they did. "And I don't think we're the ones who are wrong," he added defiantly.

"Most GI's think they're fighting for America," Evans said without antagonism, "for their homes. And man for man, they've been as courageous as most soldiers are, fighting for their homes. But they're not the only ones in the world who've ever been brave, and it's grotesque to see them fighting heroically in such an unworthy cause."

"If they're fighting for their homes, there's nothing unworthy about it," Janowitz commented.

"The VC are fighting for their homes, too," Evans answered, tilting his head to look at Janowitz. "And they can see only one reason why American troops fight so hard to dominate them in their own land. And that reason is imperialism, American imperialism. They *believe* in it." He turned back to Miller. "And I believe the reason the Arvin couldn't lick a Boy Scout troop from the Bronx is that they believe in American imperialism, *too*. They aren't fighting like men defending their homes; they're fighting like hired hands, helping to defend our presence here. Hell, seventy-five thousand of them *deserted* last year. Last year! The year we were *winning* the war! And the year before, it was more than one hundred thousand.

"And a lot of them joined the VC. Just tell me, Miller"—he grinned wryly—"if you were a native, how you'd fancy leaving your thirty or forty or one hundred American dollars a month, with all the planes and guns and tanks that go with it just to turn 'traitor' and take twenty-one cents a month as a member of the Liberation Front! Because that's what all these guys around you are getting for the risks they take, for fighting at the odds they do. Twenty-one cents a month. Now you tell me they think they're fighting in the *wrong* cause!"

"I don't give a shit what they believe!" Miller barked. "If they believe that crap about American imperialism, it's because they got their heads up their asses!"

Evans laughed with the rest of them. "Maybe," he said, "I'm just pointing out that it's possible we have our heads up our asses, too!"

"Thank you, Uncle Ho," Miller said curtly.

"Come the fuck off it, Miller," Hill said, grinning and shaking his head. "You're trying to outargue the sonuvabitch before he's even said what he's going to say. Cool it, man."

Miller flipped his cigarette butt at Hill. It was only half-humorous, but Hill made a big, gawky effort to duck and laughed. And the rest of them laughed at him. At that precise moment there was a thud and

206

a muffled explosion. And then a string of explosions—more distant. The light flickered. They all waited tensely. Being underground, they knew the impression of distance was false and the explosions were in fact quite close.

"American imperialists!" Russell said at last in a hushed voice. It cracked them up.

"That's what you get for throwing cigarettes at the natives, Miller," Hill said.

"Some native," Miller retorted. They all were speaking quietly, as though they might be overheard by the planes above.

"You're damned right I'm a native," Hill drawled back, mocking Evans' slight accent. "I want you to know, white boy, that my grand-mother was a slave and my great-grandmother was a slave, and over the can in my tenement my mammy has hung up a little embroidered corncob, a family treasure on which my great-granny had scribbled them famous words 'Watch your ass, son!' "

Miller collapsed on the floor. He shuddered with laughter. Hill was laughing with the rest of them, though he glanced a little sheepishly at Evans. Evans was smiling, but he had been nipped all right.

When the laughter finally subsided, they listened for more explosions, but the attack was evidently over. Hill suddenly clapped his hands and glanced over at Evans. "All right, daddy," he said, "come on, you tell us why these cats think that just because we bomb the piss out of them, fuck their women, and shoot up their men, we're imperialists."

It cracked them up all over again.

"Well," Evans finally drawled, "bombing, fucking, and shooting have been what foreign soldiers have done in Asia for as long as these peo-ple can remember. We don't look all that different."

"Listen, *all* soldiers—"

"For fuck's sake, shut up, Miller!" Hill bawled. "I'm going to cut your gonads off and stick 'em in your mouth. This isn't the Baptist Women's Bridge Club; we can all figure it out for ourselves." It was good-humored, and Miller raised a finger in the appropriate gesture, but he shut up.

Evans watched it all with amusement. Janowitz thought of how much the bastard had gained. They had despised him, and not one of them could have imagined that they'd ever accept him as one of them, but they had. He no longer seemed one of "them others"; he was on the squad now. And he felt it, too; there were fewer moments of the blinking, shy hesitancy and many more of confidence and even light-heartedness.

"When the French were in Vietnam—or Indochina as they called it—do you think they were imperialists?" he asked Miller good-naturedly.

"Can I talk now?" Miller yelled at Hill.

"No, you fucker, you can say yes or no and not a goddamned word more!" Hill bounced back.

Miller turned to Evans. "Yes," he answered, quite soberly.

"Me, too." Evans smiled. "But did you know that in the last two years they were here, when they were fighting a native army—an army headed by Ho Chi Minh, the same army he had led in the fight against the Japanese—the United States was supplying most of the French arms and ammunition? Because Ho was a Communist, John Foster Dulles decided the revolution was not to succeed. So the French were supplied with our helicopters, our guns, our tanks."

He put his hand up, stopping Miller before he could interrupt. "Wait! Let's just say you're a peasant in a rice paddy. You may have been fighting under a Communist, but you were fighting to get rid of the French. And you saw us helping the French. Now let me just remind you that all of Asia became 'colonial' in the same way. First, the white merchants moved in. Then Western armies came to protect them and their trade. And how did they do it? Remember Gunga Din and all that shit? They hired some of the natives to put on their uniforms, to fight under their advisers, and they paid off other natives to run a patsy local government that could survive only with their approval. It happened from Africa right across the world to the Philippines. Always the same pattern.

"And doesn't it sound just a little familiar to you? Shit, walk down any street in Saigon—Coca-Cola, Pepsi-Cola, General Electric, Kelvinator, as many American cars as there are French cars, American gas stations, U.S. tires, sun vizors, Gillette razor blades, you name it, they've got it. You can't take a shit in Saigon unless it's on American porcelain! Our salesmen have moved in in a way that makes the French look lazy and unorganized.

"And are our soldiers here to protect them? Well, if you're sitting in a paddy field, it looks like it. Have we hired natives to put on uniforms to fight for them—with our guns and advisers? Take one look at the Arvin, and it sure as hell looks like it. Have we had one puppet government right after another—not one of which could survive without us? Do our troops lord their money and power over the natives just like the French troops used to, have the same whorehouses and gin bins? And when the natives fight us, don't we call them terrorists and

208

murderers just like the French did? You see a bunch of Americans fighting Vietnamese in *their* country—and when we win, what the hell's the first thing we do? We run up the Stars and Strips! *Our* flag! That belongs to a country as far away as France. Does that sell them we're out here for *their* good? Why, these poor bastards have been fighting the English and the French and the Dutch and the Germans for so many generations—and it's always the same thing. A big charge, hundreds of natives mowed down, and then up goes a Western flag. Now *you* may be able to tell the difference between us and the rest of them, but I defy you to explain to me how the hell you expect the poor bastard in the rice paddy to tell the difference!"

There was a blank silence.

"Well, Miller, baby," Hill said at last, "I think he's got a case."

It brought them back to earth after Evans' rhetorical flight.

Evans was pleased, and he climbed off the pulpit. "And that's just the beginning—really. Look at our fleet cruising up and down off all these countries. Man, remember the British and gunboats." He laughed. "And you know those *Time* magazines, *they* use them on their own troops, in the indoctrination sessions. Not just *Time* but other Western publications. French ones especially. They don't usually let them read the whole things, mind you, but they take pieces from them—and boy, believe me, reading them from their point of view you get a different picture of the world."

"Don't you believe in freedom of the press?" Janowitz said wryly. "Or just pieces of it?"

"You know my answer to that," Evans replied confidently, "but I don't think you're going to argue with me that we've got a free press in America. Freer than Russia's, sure—but really free? Is that what they taught you at Michigan?" He scowled provocatively at Janowitz. "What newspaper is free to criticize the advertisers or so-called free enterprise itself? No, those sacred cows are as holy as the Politburo and dialectical materialism are to *Pravda* anyday—right?" Janowitz didn't answer.

"But don't get me wrong," Evans went on with a grin, "these people don't twist the news. They just pick particular items. Like our Sixth Fleet steaming around the Mediterranean and our Air Force operating from bases in Spain—a Fascist leftover from the thirties—and from Saudi Arabia—a feudal dinosaur. From Greece—a military dictatorship—and they get a picture of a vast, rich country with ships, planes, and troops all over the world, setting up a government here, trying to knock one down there—always ready to protect property interests or oil supplies or to keep a left-wing government out . . . but sure as hell *never* to right the wrongs of the ordinary people. And believe me, when they're done and they talk of American imperialists and American aggressors, they aren't spouting propaganda. They *mean* it! Even the educated ones like Thai."

"And with all *your* education and knowledge," Janowitz said coldly, "I suppose you do your best to straighten them out."

"I make a point where I can," Evans said evenly. "But the chance doesn't come up very often. I can see how we *do* look like imperialists and aggressors—can't you?"

"Maybe superficially," Janowitz said with irritation. "But you could read until you were blind and never find any evidence that we own a country! Or have ever sought to own one. You make it sound as if we're putting in governments and taking them out all around the world. We may have *backed* some governments in South Vietnam that didn't exactly smell like roses, but where do we go around the world setting up a government here and trying to knock one down there?"

"Well, Vietnam *is* the prime example to the Vietnamese, of course," Evans said. "It may have been a back-page item in some of *our* papers, but *they* didn't miss the President's sending in the Marines to get the government we wanted in the Dominican Republic—and, of course, they used it as a launching pad for a whole history of our sending the Marines into various Central and South American countries. It has been a bad habit, at the very least, in our history." He grinned.

"And Cuba, of course, is regarded as a classic case. A people's revolution against a corrupt—" He stopped, searching for the word. "Thug —who didn't really have the right to be dignified even with the name dictator, though a murdering, torturing, venal dictator he was. And the minute the revolution succeeds, we mount an invasion against it."

"They filled the place with Russian missiles; what did you want us to do, sit there and wait for them to shoot them off?" Miller sneered.

"You've got events turned around, Miller," Evans corrected. "We backed the invasion first—just after Kennedy was inaugurated, remember? *Then* Castro made the deal with the Russians for the missiles— that was after we'd tried to knock him out of the government. What did you expect *him* to do? Sit there and wait until we succeeded?"

"He's a Communist," Miller answered stiffly.

"That's right," Evans said. "Nobody's sure if he was at the time, but if he wasn't, sure we made him one. But even in horrible Communist Cuba, education is becoming universal for the first time; it's unusual for children under five to die—*not* the other way around—hospitals, schools, and houses are being built instead of swimming pools, country mansions, and nightclubs . . . and of course, the rich Cubans of yesterday who *were* educated, who *could* afford doctors, who lived in the mansions and frequented the nightclubs sit in Miami and howl for 'freedom.'

"Hell, when I listen to the discussions of Cuba around the night fires here in Vietnam, it provides such a classic case against us I sometimes wonder if the CIA men who were evidently behind it all weren't Communists themselves. They couldn't have done a better job." He turned to Janowitz, speaking lightly, but not letting a point drop. "Not only did we try to knock that government out, but we continue to blockade it and try to bring it down. And"—he smiled—"if I had my file here, I could cite *American* press reports that the right-wing military takeover in Greece could not have stood up for a week if the United States had withdrawn its support. There are even U.S. reports that the CIA engineered the whole thing. And I could show you American reports of torture in Greek prisons, of political blackmail and thuggery—as bad as anything we attribute to Castro—but one government we support, one we try to take down. Now we may think it's something else, but to these people it sounds just a little like imperialism!"

"A big gas, eh?" Janowitz said. He was mad. Not because he disagreed. He had to agree with a lot of it, and he could even see that Evans was essentially right about the point he was trying to make. "American imperialism" obviously *could* mean something real to these people. But though he was no fanatic patriot, he hated to see the States knocked that way, hated to see the truth being screwed around to give a false impression. Evans might only be trying to show them how that false impression was given, but he did it with a relish that raised Janowitz's ire.

"While you were sitting around those fires," Janowitz said, "I suppose you let them all know that the reason we reacted the way we did to Castro, the reason we've got a fleet that patrols all over the world, even the reason we're here in Vietnam, is that we're reacting to a real imperialism—an imperialism that *does* control countries, that makes a business of subverting the governments of other countries!"

"Thank you, Lieutenant," Miller muttered with quiet pleasure.

"Don't misunderstand me," Evans said calmly. "I'm not trying to defend what the Russians have done in Europe since the war . . . and in my mind if the world ever missed a chance at genuine peace, it happened when Stalin thumbed his nose at the peace we offered the whole world at the end of World War II. And I know we began all this in reaction to Russia's expansion during Stalin's time and their continued control of Eastern Europe. I'm simply trying to show you why 'American imperialism' means something to the Vietnamese—something they too react against. Maybe stupidly at times, but it's not garbage or bullshit, as we always claim when they call us imperialists and aggressors."

"You haven't answered me," Janowitz insisted. "Our fear of Communist expansion isn't garbage or bullshit either? That somehow doesn't bother them, huh?"

"Not at all," Evans answered sternly. "What the hell do you think one of these guys feels if he's called an agent of the *Russians?* Are you crazy? A peasant in the delta! It's a sick joke. And saying that they're Chinese agents is even sicker. They fought for their freedom from China as hard as they're fighting us—and they did it for a *thousand* years! If you think they're agents of the Chinese, why don't they invite Chinese 'volunteers' in? It's costing them blood to stay free of China right now

"And as for Russian imperialism, I'm afraid most of them haven't heard much about it. Hell, how much do you know about Asia in the nineteen forties? Could you have told me where Da Nang or even Saigon was before there was a war here? And you're a university graduate! Most of these people haven't seen the inside of a school!"

"But why do you find their ignorance so much more excusable than ours?" Janowitz persisted.

"I don't," Evans replied calmly. "But frankly I don't think it would affect them much if they *did* know about 'horrendous' Russia. They don't see why Russia can't be Communist if it wants—or China. And even though they don't know any more about the countries of Eastern Europe now than they do about Nebraska or Arkansas, they know that in those countries people eat, and go to school, and get medicine, and see doctors—things people in Asia have never got from *us!* Hell, to them a Hungarian or Pole or Czech is a rich man, and however 'enslaved' *we* think he is, he has more control over his life than an ordinary peasant here has ever had.

"Jesus," he went on reflectively, without anger, "if there were *one* Communist labor camp like the so-called refugee camps in Saigon, we'd fight the world because of the injustice of it. For two years now, they've been racked by diseases the world has forgotten about—people dying of cholera and plague, of typhus and dysentery, right in Saigon, most of them kids. While the rich just get richer, land is bought and sold for wild prices; expensive apartment buildings are built, fancy shops. And inflation rages so the poor can't even buy rice! And we tell them we're selling them freedom . . . and Communism is bad for them—so bad we'd rather kill them than let them taste it.

"Well, the wonder is not that they call us imperialists. It's that we're so blind we wonder why."

There was a long silence. At last Miller muttered quietly, "I wish Pershing was here."

Janowitz knew it wasn't meant as a slur against him, but he recognized Miller's feeling that Pershing could rebut all this was evidence, conscious or not, that Miller felt leadership was missing. And Janowitz knew it was his job to supply it. But what the hell did he say? Evans might be slanting it all, but for his money, there was too much truth in it to argue against. No, it was Evans' day. Maybe Pershing could change it, but *he* couldn't. . . . As a matter of fact, he was beginning to wonder if he wanted to.

vi

They all slept restlessly. Several times during the day Janowitz rolled over and met the eyes of Hill or Miller or Russell. He didn't know what was bugging them, but he knew what his own problem was all right. For the first time since his capture, the thought of being a prisoner for years and years had become a reality for him. He knew he wasn't going to participate in any VC mission—ever. But one by-product of all that chatter by Evans was the realization that the VC were not going to give up easily—on him or the war. And it suddenly haunted him that maybe several of the fat years of his life were going to go dwindling down a North Vietnamese drain. If not in torture or brainwashing, perhaps in emptiness. The three or four years of pro ball he was counting on, out the window, and the chance to finance a business or some independence, out with it. Even his goddamned hair. If the war lasted ten years, he might be as bald as Uncle Marv when he got out. Nobody'd even know him when he got back. He tried to think about Mỹ, but even that had gone sour. And once he said no to their plans for him, he knew that would be the end of her anyway. Somehow his capture had seemed a temporary piece of his life—even an adventure. And now, like a specter made flesh, it loomed out at him that captivity might *be* his life—the meat of it. The time he should be trying to live up to the ads in *Playboy*—dolls, beach parties, fast cars, skiing in the winter, touring Europe in the summer. And now it all might be squandered in sweat and red dust, a prisoner in some hot anonymous hole a million miles from nowhere, a prisoner to somebody else's mistake, to a cause he couldn't really hold in his heart, that was at best dubious, at worst wrong.

vii

When they took off that night, Pershing had still not caught up with them. Three trucks had been hit in a shelter just off the road, and they had to thread their way through a mass of VC carting stray parts and debris back to the headquarters. Janowitz felt a sense of relief when they'd seen the last of them, and it made him marvel at how completely a unit their own group had become. He was going to miss Thai and Tack—even little Toe—once they found he wasn't going to do what they wanted him to do. He'd be perfectly happy never seeing Tick again, but there'd be a wrench at leaving the rest, and if they took him to a separate camp without Hill or Russell, or Miller or Pershing, it'd be the end.

Mỹ had glanced at him a couple of times when they first gathered in the trench before the exit hatch, but he'd given her the frost treatment. He wished he had no doubts about that. But the more he'd thought about it, the more unlikely it was that she'd have thrown herself flat for an "enemy." It must have been part of the treatment. But even so, he couldn't shake the memory of her holding him, responding to him as if she needed him and wanted him.

When the first break came, the women went off into the woods as usual to water the flowers. The Vietnamese were like the French and Italians about things like that. The men pulled it out and held their hands half cocked over it and looked around nonchalantly. They never bothered to do more than turn sideways to the path. The women were almost as bad. They'd step into the woods, but never more than a couple of paces, and you could always see them pulling their pants down and squatting. They came out giggling and glancing at him. It made him feel foolish, and he was more than ever convinced that Mỹ was simply another device in a complicated plan to win him over. He glanced over at her angrily.

"From those giggles, man, I'd say you either struck out or pleased her mightily," Hill muttered in his ear. "Which was it?"

Janowitz had already been poleaxed. Mỹ was smiling—radiantly—and looking right at him. The other women were behind her, still fluttering among themselves and glancing sideways at him, but she was still and immobile. And the look of peace on her face drove everything else from his mind. She had been shaken by the fire, that he knew. And she'd stayed shaken until they'd made love by that river. And the way she was looking at him now made him feel *he* had pulled her out of that. Under orders, or not, she *had* loved it. And the message simmered through him until he wanted to take her right there on the dirt road, in front of them all. Let them think it was going to be of use to them—it wasn't. He'd have her as long as he could—and when it was over, it was over. He beamed back at her, blowing a little kiss.

"Oh, cute!" Hill said. "She likes that. Did you kiss it for her, or is that just a promise?"

"Listen, son"—Janowitz smiled—"I know what you'd kiss to get it. But it won't do you any good. I'm reserving that for officers."

"Figures," Hill replied. "White officers at that, I suppose."

"White Jewish officers," Janowitz snapped back.

Hill laughed. "Hell, you can circumcise me with a rusty canteen cup if you'll get your friend to talk me into the pants of big tits over there. Now she's strictly enlisted men's material."

"That's my reserve," Janowitz said. "If I don't actually get around to using it myself, I'll see what I can do about making the amenity available to the lower ranks."

"Goddamn, you got a future ahead of you." Hill grinned. "You're talking like a general already."

Russell slithered over next to them. "Hey, what's going on?" he whispered, anticipating that he'd enjoy the joke.

"Nothing," Hill said. "The lieutenant here was just telling me how he aimed to provide us all with a little Vietnamese tail here as part of our Rest and Recreation as POW's."

Russell grinned lasciviously. "I reckon I'd better put my name down right promptly for the one with the big tits then," he said.

Janowitz and Hill both chortled. "I told you she was enlisted men's material," Hill said.

"Well, in a pinch I'd be satisfied with seconds on yours, Lieutenant, if you're planning on giving her up." Russell leered.

"No, no," Hill mocked, "the lieutenant's a real officer. He's not going to give anything up. He wants his *and* big tits."

"I see," Russell said with the same bogus admiration for vested authority, "he's setting us an example!"

"That's it," Hill said. "They got five girls altogether. He gets four, and we get to split what's left."

"Provided you keep in line," Janowitz added with mock severity.

Miller wandered over, looking at all of them disapprovingly.

"What's the gas? You thinking about all those poor SOB's fighting for us down South?"

"Yeah! That's what we're thinking about all right," Hill shot back sharply. "What's your trouble, mother—was there a pea under your mattress?" Janowitz was struck again by how quickly Hill could turn from clown to street fighter, unwilling to take shit from anyone.

"I slept all right," Miller snapped back.

"Well, stop bleeding for the slobs down South, then," Hill retorted. "They can come up here, and I'll go down and fight for them any time they want."

Miller snorted and sat down next to Russell. Hill stretched flat, his head near Miller. "Come on, dad, take it easy," he said. "Nobody likes this, but we aren't going to make any points walking around like its glumsville all the time." Miller didn't answer. Thai was already walking up and down the line; the break would be over soon. "Look at those fucking stars," Hill said. "Until I came to this asshole of the East, I never knew there were so many stars."

Miller smirked, pulled out the pack of cigarettes he had gotten from Tack, and offered one to Hill. Hill took it, put it in his mouth, and lay there waiting for Miller to light it. Miller bent over, and when he'd got it lit, Hill blew the smoke casually in his face.

"Thanks, dad," he said with a grin.

Miller raised his arm in sham threat, and they all relaxed.

"What'd you think about all that crap he gave us yesterday?" Miller said softly, nodding toward Evans, who had been cornered by Tick the minute they'd stopped for the break.

"I don't think it was crap," Janowitz said. "I think what he said makes a lot of sense. They *are* always calling us imperialists and aggressors, and maybe if we were on their side of the fence, that's what it would look like to us."

"You're some officer," Miller said sarcastically.

"I didn't say we *were* imperialists or aggressors, Miller," Janowitz rejoined sharply. "I said I think I can see how *they* think we are, and I don't see any goddamned advantage in burying our heads in the sand about it. It doesn't alter our duty, but there's no obligation to think everything the enemy thinks is bullshit. And it doesn't *make* us imperialists or aggressors, but it sure as hell makes me wish we'd clean up our image a little. It might help all around."

"Yeah, well, they could clean up their image a lot, too," Miller replied, only half managing to keep the anger out of his voice.

"I agree." Janowitz grinned. "And I don't think any of us should get too shaken up by what Evans or any of the rest of them tell us. It's a dirty war—we all know it; we all knew it when we came. We don't have to like it. . . . So we've made mistakes. We aren't out to deliberately damage Vietnam, and on any reasonable terms they can have peace. They can't shake our faith in that, because that's the truth. And when it comes to their 'mission,' all the talk in the world isn't going to get one of us to do anything for them. But as long as they're talking, we're eating. So let's just let 'em talk." He was glad he got it out that way—offhand and temperate. Miller needed the reassurance; maybe Russell did, too. He tousled Russell's hair. Russell was so skinny the job of carrying a load all these miles must be tiring him— not that you could tell; he looked tired all the time anyway.

"You okay, Russell?" he asked with a broad smile. "Any of that stuff gettin' to you?"

Russell's face slowly broke into a sly, sardonic smile. "Hell, I don't rightly know what to think, Lieutenant," he said glumly. "My old man was a local dragon in the Ku Klux Klan—that's about all the politics I ever knowed. It was the only politics that mattered where I come from. And then I came into the Army, and most of the NCO's are niggers, and most of the officers are Jews or Catholics . . . and I'm taking orders from all of them. It's got me confused all right."

Hill started the laughter, and it spread like rushing water. They all bubbled with it—and Russell just kept staring from one to the other with that sly grin on his face. All the VC were staring at them. Thai had got the others loaded up, and they were ready to move now. He moved to them.

"Will you load up now?" he said with his commander's imperative.

"Yes, sir, boss," Russell muttered. "See." He shrugged at Janowitz, and they bubbled over again.

Much later in the night during the long break for chow it happened —whether by some miracle of divine accident or by the contrivance of human organization, he didn't know. But he was just about to plunk down with his bowl of rice when not ten feet away he saw Mỹ being relieved of a load of dead vines by one of the VC women. He was the first one back from the chow line, which was around a twist in the path, and when Mỹ saw him, she moved a half step back. Another foot and she'd vanish in the jungle. He smiled, partly in amusement at the providence of it, partly at the sight of her, and walked directly toward her. She backed farther into the undergrowth, and his smile was transformed by a flood of sexual passion. He was going to have her, and the blood suddenly pounded in his ears.

As always, they had camped near water, a wide, slow stream meandering through the low hills they had now entered. It was the best time of night. The muggy heat had passed, and the damp cold had not yet set in. There was no breeze at all. He took Mỹ's hand and led her to a distant spot on the riverbank, not just to get away from the others, but because he knew it was only at a clearing by the water— some stretch trodden clean by animals foraging near their drinking supply—that he could feel at ease in the dark undergrowth, not fearing that he was rolling on a snake or disturbing some jungle animal from its sleeping place. Once they had found a spot, he was torn between the physical urgency throbbing in his groin and the anger still flitting through his brain. When he first touched her, she had seemed to go along with him only reluctantly, as though he were expecting too much. But when he kissed her, she returned it—not a wet, ardent, anonymous act, but gently, as though she meant it. And he felt she did mean it—to hell with her reasons for doing it. But he was nevertheless consumed between wanting her and the perverse wish to humiliate her for trying to manipulate him.

In the soft light of the night sky her beauty was flawless—night was always the master cosmetician. He reached forward and undid the top button on her fatigues. She didn't move. He undid the rest—not kissing her, not touching her, just exposing her. She wore a cotton knit top, more like an undershirt than a brassiere; he remembered shoving it up under her arms the first time. He lifted it off, and she raised her hands, looking at him now with a little question in her eyes.

The trousers came down, and the little native silk pants. She stepped out of them gently, but the question was bigger in her eyes. He pulled off his own clothes, exhibiting himself cruelly, he felt—but she didn't look at his body, just continued to watch his eyes as though waiting for his tenderness. He took her hand and waded into the river. He was going to have her as he'd wanted to have her that first night when he'd heard the women splashing in the river.

But it didn't work out quite right. This river was only about a foot deep at its deepest. There was no water running down her, no flowing river about their hips. He took her out past the middle and then real-

218

ized it wasn't going to get any deeper. He felt ridiculous. And when he turned to her, he was suddenly swamped with guilt for trying to humiliate her, for making it crude and unpleasant. He felt awkward and so aware of his stiff penis arched up like some fat and ugly flagpole between them that he could feel it begin to shrink. He pulled her to him and kissed her. Her arms wrapped around him and pressed—gently—talking to him, gradually warming, telling him she was his the way he wanted her, any way.

It was fantastic lying on the bank after it was over. They had spread out their fatigues as a cover for the ground, and above them a sliver of the moon had started to climb through the trees. They could hear an occasional jungle bird, cawing distantly of some triumph or fear. It had never been better for him. Unlike the first time, it had gone on and on and on . . . and then the fevered exquisite delirium again. And as they had the first time, they had come together. Janowitz had collapsed on her—a mountain of sweating, flaccid flesh, he felt—but he never wanted to move again. And somehow her tiny body supported him; her lips opened and closed every now and again on his ear, his neck.

It was the realization that someone was probably watching that finally gave him the impetus to roll over and lie on his back. She was immediately in the crook of his arm, a kiss on his breast and then her head back, moving softly to and fro against his bearded chin and smooth shoulder, talking to him again, saying, he thought, that it had been as good for her, even saying thank you.

Yet as he lay there, the flashes of nagging doubt began again. He knew Thai would never risk letting him escape. He felt certain, too, that the stop had been picked deliberately for the little bend in the trail that would mask their departure. And that meant Thai would also have sent someone to make sure he didn't get away. But Janowitz was feeling so euphoric he didn't really care. It only amused him to think what agony their pleasure would have brought to some sex-starved onlooker. And then he found himself wondering how sex-starved the VC really were. Was she possibly humping for someone else? The presence of boxes of rubbers didn't exactly imply a life of celibacy. He was curious, suddenly; what *were* the communal arrangements? Like most GI's, he had been so used to just thinking of the Indians as wild men attacking suicidally it had never occurred to him to wonder about the nights they lay in the jungle thinking that nothing in the world could be more important than a luscious piece of ass.

But he didn't care. As long as they weren't humping Mỹ, he just didn't care. He smiled. The thought of his half-cocked theory about happiness flashed through his mind. Yet here he was, not a stitch of clothing on, a prisoner, his stomach only half filled by a little rice, facing an endless vista of disaster: He had no car, no booze, no fancy clothes, no records; his bed was a filthy fatigue uniform—he had absolutely none of the things you fight to get because they're supposed to make you happy, and yet it was bliss. Bliss city, comfort heaven. He looked down at Mỹ. Thank God she had boobs. Nice full boobs and that tiny waist. Yes, God made woman for man. It's so much we shouldn't ask him for anything more. He could stay right there the rest of his life as far as he was concerned.

It was only when they heard the first stirrings from the camp and the unexpected sound of Tack's roaring voice that he felt another wave of guilt. Not that he was lying there wrapped around a VC—but guilt because he hadn't used one of the damn French letters Thai had given him. They didn't want her to get pregnant because they'd lose a soldier. To hell with them. But he'd seen enough in Vietnam to know that he didn't really want to bring forth a child to that. Especially not to her. Whatever her motives in laying for him, she was too gentle, too loving, to have that happen to her. And he could almost picture a baby made up of him and her: soft, honey skin, with a fat little bottom to pat; a boy, longer and more muscular than most Vietnamese—maybe with huge brown eyes. He could see his mother with that grandchild. She'd love him. My God, how she'd love him. And the thought of that child in the pain and barbarity of this war hurt him even in the imagining. He prayed to God it hadn't happened. He would never do it again without one on. Never.

Big Tack had returned all right—and he'd brought Pershing with him. Mỹ slipped around to enter the group with the main body of VC, but when Janowitz tried to settle down inconspicuously beside Hill, Tack burst out in greeting.

"Hey, water buffalo!" he shouted. "You find a mare, okay?" He roared with laughter. "We build you for good Viet soldier yet! Okay?"

It was so goddamned exuberant and happy Janowitz couldn't help smiling.

"They've got Pershing over there," Hill said softly. "He looks pretty beat up."

Janowitz looked, but he couldn't see anything clearly beyond the turn in the path. Big Tack was still describing something colorful and amusing—at least to him—to the group on the other side, but there was no picking Pershing out among the dark blurs moving in the foliage beyond Tack.

Thai had them marching again in a couple of minutes, but Pershing was put up at the front of the line, and they were kept at the rear. They didn't get to speak to him all that night, and Janowitz got his first look at him only during the last break before dawn. His whole head was bandaged—around his forehead, down under his jaw—one arm was in a sling, and he sat so erect Janowitz guessed he was in some sort of cast as well. They'd really worked him over.

They marched all night. It was a long, tiring march, climbing gradually all the time, and when dawn came, it was welcome not only for its promise of warmth, but for the rest it augured. Janowitz's pack had come to feel like a boulder on his shoulders, and he wondered wryly how many VC secretly sighed in relief at the promise of American planes bombing the hell out of the trail all day long. If it weren't for them, the marches might have been even longer.

As it was, they continued for almost an hour past dawn before they came to a group of lean-tos perched below them on the side of a steep incline of pines. They were well out of the rain forest now and had been moving along the top of a long ridge, and again Janowitz was reminded of the Appalachians, because the ridge and the ones alongside it weren't high, like real mountains, like the Rockies, but they were up there, and they ran in ribbons stretching along, folding, dividing, reforming like rumples in a satin quilt. And up North, just this short distance, the character of the trees had begun to change. Besides the predominant pines, there were still a few giant teaks, kapok, scrubs of bamboo and rattan, but there were also occasional clusters of familiar deciduous trees, too, even big cedars that reminded him of home.

The lean-tos were well camouflaged from the air, but once you were near them, they seemed spacious and inviting. The incline was so steep none of them could descend it without sliding and clinging to trees for support, but the worst—and best—thing about it was the thick carpet of pine needles. It made the going difficult, but it meant there was almost no underbrush. There, in the early day before the heat had started to build up, it was like being in a mountain resort. A dozen little lean-to chalets, crisp, clean air, the smell of pine, a fabulous view across unspoiled mountain scenery. With a little advertising, he thought grimly as he slid to a stop against the side of one of the lean-tos, they could draw quite a crowd.

They all were bundled into the same lean-to. He had resisted the shoving long enough to get a look at Mỹ. She was watching him even as

221

he searched for her, and when his eyes came to rest on her, the wide mouth slowly blossomed, the eyes sang. Shit, he loved her! If she was acting, he didn't care. As long as she could react on cue like that, he was booked for the whole run of the show.

Inside, the lean-tos were just simple shelters. Long benches along the walls for sleeping, little stone pits for cooking. No one was in them, they were strictly transient, for units passing through, but there were iron pots for cooking, wooden bowls of all sizes, even three or four pairs of chopsticks. And there were several blankets. Hill held one up —navy blue with great white letters: U.S. NAVY. They all laughed—but even so, they were restless, waiting for Pershing to be returned to their midst, wondering why they had kept him separated, wondering how badly he was hurt.

"When you go for a drink, you mind if I go along to watch, Lieutenant?" Hill said as he flopped out on one of the benches. "I wanta learn what's so sexy about an officer licking up water from a mountain stream."

Janowitz grinned. "Sure, soldier, I don't mind your watching. Just bring along evidence you've attended the required VD courses, and I'd be glad to introduce you to manhood."

"I don't know how you got the energy for sex," Miller sighed, falling on one of the benches with a crash that shook the whole lean-to. "I'm so goddamned pooped if Sophia Loren and Brigitte Bardot walked in hand in hand begging for it, I'd turn 'em over to Russell."

"What the hell's the matter with *me?*" Hill said. "You even segregate your sex fantasies?"

"I segregate them against you, you bastard. You're so far ahead of the game, ordinary mortals like me and Russell'd have to hump like sparrows in spring to catch up!"

"Well, I *need* it more than you do." Hill grinned. "Hell, swinging around those trees in Africa, you'd be surprised how many young ones we lost to gravity every year. We just had to keep at it to keep the race alive."

Miller laughed. "Yeah, well, I believe you'd take it in a tree, you bastard, hanging upside down at that."

"Jesus, haven't you heard?" Hill exclaimed. "That's the *only* way, man! You've never had sex until you've had it hanging upside down."

They all laughed until tears rolled. "Fuck me," Miller finally said with a sigh. "When the hell are they going to let us see Pershing?"

Unconsciously all their eyes went to Evans. "I don't know," Evans said. "They brought him back to be with the group, that I do know. Why they've isolated him—" He shrugged his shoulders.

Big tits came along with some pine branches and started to build a fire for them. Hill cracked them all up by bounding off the pad and jumping to assist her in every move. She'd put a piece of pine down, and he'd pat it in place. She'd brush some dirt away, and he'd sweep at it like a lunatic with a thing about dirt. She lit the fire, and he blew at the flame to make it go. He made each move with exaggerated cavalier gestures and convulsed them all. As for big tits herself, she never looked at him, but she was grinning the whole time like a Cheshire cat.

She was awfully sexy. Even Janowitz, who was thoroughly hung up on Mŷ, realized he'd never turn this down if he got a chance at it. It was funny, it was her eyes and mouth as much as her boobs. Especially her eyes, which were big with heavy lids that always looked half-closed, languid, and willing. And her mouth just set them off. Too big, even a little brassy, but a wonderful, moist focus. And always on the edge of the picture the superstructure. He'd read once they had evolved as a sex stimulant as man changed reproductive positions in the trip from ape to man. And if anything rang true to him, that did. There was nothing else to explain the impact a pair of knockers had—especially in the hot jungle, Janowitz thought wistfully as he watched her bend before the fire, feeding it until it was going even and strong. She might have been lighting them up as well. It had the same effect.

Hill was still circling about her, barely managing to keep his hands off her, but fluttering them like antennae in the presence of some overpowering stimulant. She had a wise, experienced look—a little cynical, a little amused—that added to her impact. With those stimulants of hers she must have had guys charging at her from the time she was twelve, Janowitz thought dryly.

When the fire was really going, she left and then returned with a pot of water. She collected rice from each of them, Hill fluttering around her even more outrageously. When she'd gone to get the water, he'd tried to go with her, but one of the two VC they'd set by the trees to guard them had jabbed his rifle at him to stop him. And Hill had mimed a broken heart so effectively that even the guard had grinned—though he'd begun quite angry. Now, as she collected the rice, both guards were laughing at Hill's antics.

When she got to Janowitz, he held out his rice, and then just as she was going to take it, he pulled it back. She looked up at him and smiled slowly. *Bam!* She was a bomb all right.

"Hey, hey!" Hill yelled. "Enough of that! You got one already! Him no good fucker," he said, gesticulating madly at big tits. "Two women kill him dead." He mocked a heart attack. "Him circumcised bastard—once a month his absolute limit!"

Janowitz was grinning from ear to ear, but he held big tits' eyes, and she his. It made him wonder. He passed her the rice, and it seemed symbolic of something more.

"The goddamned Arabs are right," Hill muttered as she—and he—passed on to collect Russell's rice. "You bastards are out to take over the world!" Janowitz kicked him in the butt, and Hill went into one of his awkward, gigantic leaps. Surprised, big tits looked at him for the first time. "Him just shot his wad," Hill whispered to her, his eyes dilating in anticipation of something very energetic. "Now you belong to us." And he opened his arms to her. She turned quickly back to Russell, but there was a smile on her face as broad as the Mekong in flood.

She fixed their rice, chopping in bits of vegetables and fish that she contributed from her pack. And with Hill as her lascivious genie, she passed each his own bowl. She lingered long enough on each of them to make it clear she was aware of them all as individuals, and by the time she left they were sure as hell aware of her.

Hill escorted her as far as the guard would let him and then sagged with exaggerated limpness until she was out of sight. When he turned around and sighed, they all sighed with him.

"Man," Miller said, as he dug into his rice, "I've changed my mind. I'm not as pooped as I thought."

"Listen, you're married," Hill said. "I know you wouldn't think of doing something like that." And before Miller could do more than smile, Hill turned to Russell. "And you're a loyal member of the Ku Klux Klan, you bastard; you wouldn't screw anything that wasn't a white Anglo-Saxon Protestant unless it was a slave. He's out of it," he said firmly of Evans. "And you, Yid—sir," he said to Janowitz, "I know your Jewish schmaltz would keep you from breaking the heart of that little doll who gave herself to you not knowing what she was missing from me." He flopped down by the fire, looking out over the hill. "And that just naturally leaves big tits to little ole George Hill, valiant soldier, brave warrior—"

"Mental delinquent, physical misfit, and sexual deviate," Janowitz rounded off.

Miller and Russell guffawed, but Hill smiled beatifically. He was not to be disturbed.

By the time they'd finished a haze of heat had begun to rise over

224

the mountains and valleys in front of them. It was still relatively cool in the forest, and they all lay there, heads propped on elbows and hands, looking out over the rolling green mountains—colored here and there by a splash of red or silver. The noise of the dinner preparations was over throughout the camp now, and all was still—a silence made even more acute by the caw of a hawk circling somewhere over the pines behind them.

"The war seems a long ways away," Miller said pensively.

"*Hm*. So does home," Evans said reflectively. They all looked at him. It seemed an odd statement from him, but it was true right enough. The hills did look like the Appalachians, but there was nothing of home about them, and with their ridges stretching endlessly as far as they could see ahead, and as far as they could see left and right, it made "home" seem far beyond their wildest reach.

"You think you're ever going to be able to go home?" Hill asked. It was thoughtful and downbeat.

"I don't suppose so," Evans answered musingly. "But if someone had told me five years ago that one day I'd be lying in a forest in Laos doing what I'm doing now, I'd have recommended him to a psychiatrist . . . so you never know. But offhand, I'd say the chances are slim." He smiled bleakly.

"Don't you want to go back?" Miller asked—again, no needle to it, just a question.

"When I knew I could go back, it didn't make any difference at all. Except for missing the physical things—a wooden frame house, the smell of a drugstore . . . seeing my mother—I could have stayed in Europe for years . . . but once I realized I couldn't go back if I was dying to . . . I find I get very lonesome for it."

Janowitz glanced across at him. He had guessed from his tone of voice, and it was true—the guy's eyes were full of water. And he was supposed to convince *them* to do something that would get them into the same predicament. He's more of an optimist than he looks, Janowitz thought.

"In a good cause," Miller said with quiet irony.

Evans rolled so that he was looking at Miller. "Yeah," he said quietly.

Miller studied him without speaking; then he nodded slowly. "Yeah," he said, "I guess you are doing it for what you think is a good cause. The catch is I think we're fighting in a good cause, too."

Evans smiled. "I know. The whole problem in this war is to get two well-intentioned groups to see that the other isn't the devil incarnate."

He grinned again. "My eldest brother always used to say my whole problem in life was that I saw both sides to *every* problem—but I don't think even he anticipated the trouble it'd get me into." They all smiled—that was Evans all right!

It was the end of the conversation. In about twenty minutes Janowitz went out to go to the can and, hopefully, to catch a glimpse of Mŷ, but no one was stirring except a couple of guards. When he came back, all the others were asleep. He stretched out, looking across the hills in the growing heat . . . until he too dropped off.

It must have been hours later when he awoke. He was sweating from the heat, and the sky, which had been soft blue, was now azure and dappled with white puffs of cumulus. It was the sound of aircraft that had awakened him. The sound wasn't overhead but near, and the pass had been quick and low because the jet drone was already fading to inaudibility.

Evans backed into the lean-to, looking out over the hills in the direction of the sound.

"We're heading east tomorrow," he said when he saw Janowitz awake. "We're far enough north now." Janowitz just nodded. Evans walked to his place and stretched out again. "Pershing will be joining us tomorrow morning," he said, as though explaining his absence.

"Is he all right?" Janowitz asked.

Evans smiled unexpectedly. "Yeah. He's a lot better than I thought."

The sound of the plane coming back interrupted him. They both watched it as it came across, parallel to the ridge, maybe three miles out. Nothing in terms of airspace. It was a Phantom, and they could see all its markings in the sunlight. It looked silver and clean riding above the bright greens of the forest. They saw the rocket launch— and, long after, heard its swish and, later still, the explosion.

The black, red, and yellow ball of flame rose up from the jungle. It almost seemed absurd. All you could see for miles and miles was the green of jungle. There was no sign of human life at all—just the beautiful silver dart, flying over the equally beautiful forest. And then, before it had passed from sight again, they saw two more coming down from way up. And they joined in, the three of them making one pass, another, and still another—always bombing near the same spot. Once there was a string of light flashing through the green, followed inevitably by the delayed *boom-diddy-boom-boom* echoing in muted resonance across the hills. Another time the flashes of rockets, and a clear view of their arching trajectory—and then the rising smoke and flame. They had pulverized something down there, but all around the

226

spot the forest rose and fell over the hills, blanketing all in green, absorbing the loss. And as Janowitz lay watching the three planes finally climbing away, leaving the island of smoking ruin, he felt that the forest would be able to take it all, that one day you would be able to walk through its green dominion and never know the silver darts had been at all.

viii

It wasn't long before Tick came along to waken the others and they were all led out to gather firewood. When they got a fire going, little Toe came along with a big pot of rice and dolloped out a smallish portion to each of them. But he also brought a sack full of kumquats, sour as hell, but tasting marvelous just the same. Later, as they wandered about the lean-to, watching the orange tint of late sunlight spread across the hills, they saw that the others had gathered in groups for indoctrination sessions. It made them all turn to Evans. He shrugged.

"Part of the routine," he said.

"For us?" Miller asked testily.

"The military is the military, Miller," Evans replied, "in any uniform. I'll lay you five to one that someone is along in less than five minutes to see that I'm talking to you about something."

"How about sex?" Hill offered enthusiastically.

Evans pondered a moment thoughtfully. "I think I could do that, Hill. Something right up your line." While the others looked at one another askance, Evans went to his pack and pulled it open. They could see a stack of magazines.

"Is that what you've been carrying?" Janowitz said caustically.

"There are some other things in there," Evans said, "but I went through their library at the underground stop and found these."

"You got a *Playboy* there?" Hill inquired hopefully.

Evans pulled a couple of magazines loose and returned to them.

"What the hell have they got, a U.S. newsstand or something down one of those tunnels?" Hill demanded.

"They capture magazines, as well as rifles and mortars—and Navy blankets. They keep them all, and some they follow very closely," he said, and squatted down by the fire. "You know where we are, Miller?"

"Up shit creek?" Hill suggested.

"We're in Laos," Evans said, ignoring Hill. "And we might not be the last Americans either. It was split up in Geneva a little like Vietnam, between a free world side and a Communist side, dominated by the Pathet Lao. We've always claimed the Pathet Lao violated the treaty by allowing the North Vietnamese to pass through the country—kind of blithely ignoring that they were passing through to get at our troops, who were in Vietnam *also* in violation of the treaty."

Hill looked out at the dark night. "Well, from the looks of it there's plenty of room for everybody."

"Yeah," Evans said more seriously, "like an argument, room all around. There was supposed to be a coalition government, but—believe it or not—this time the *Communist* member was assassinated by *right-wing* thugs and the Pathet Lao withdrew. You can imagine the claims we made—some were probably even valid. But you can also imagine the claims *they* made." He had picked out one of the magazines and flipped through the pages. It was a *Newsweek*.

"They said the assassination was engineered by the CIA, that the U.S. was trying to support a corrupt government against the interests of the people. The usual shit." He held the magazine out to Hill. "You want to read this, or shall I?"

"If it isn't dirty pictures, the pleasure's yours," Hill retorted.

Evans shrugged and turned the magazine around. "It's the issue of October twenty-third, 1967," he said, "an article about the U.S. in Laos which begins by describing a flight from Bangkok to the Laotian capital of Vientiane." He scanned the article quickly. "Says the plane is loaded with betel-nut-chewing old women—"

"*Ahhh,* the sex at last—" Hill cut in.

"And squawking chickens," Evans went on, "and 'hundreds of pounds of gold bullion destined for the Vientianese gold market.' And what's gold used for in this neck of the woods, Hill?"

"False teeth?" Hill offered.

"Smuggling," Evans said, ignoring the laughs. "Usually dope. But now, the part *you're* waiting for—'of the handful of tourists who deplane at dilapidated Watthay Airport, most head straight for the capital's special charms: its openly flourishing opium dens, its hawkers of cheap hashish, and its legions of youthful prostitutes.' "

"How far are we from this place, did you say?" Hill inquired eagerly. He looked across at Janowitz. "I've always had an itch for a really experienced twelve-year-old."

The others laughed, but Evans turned to him very soberly. "We're a world away, Hill. A world. Because you see that's the 'free' world

228

we keep boosting. It's kind of easy to find hoards of youthful prostitutes in most of the countries we sup—"

"Oh, come off it!" Janowitz snapped.

Evans looked at him. "Sure," he said finally, and looked back down at the magazine. "It goes on to say that the *Newsweek* reporters met CIA agents who openly admitted they ran the place. One of their correspondents walked into the Laotian Army headquarters and found the commander in chief getting instructions from a group of U.S. officers. And the CIA, it concludes, 'is bountifully equipped with money and advice' to keep up the good work." He tossed the magazine on the ground below.

"Communist propaganda," he said sarcastically. "A corrupt government run by the CIA."

"Honest to shit," Miller exploded. "There are minutes—seconds anyway—when I almost think I could like you, Evans. You're put together about as back-assed-to as my brother, but you almost make it as a human being! And then you swallow shit like that."

"It's in the goddamned magazine," Evans insisted. "You think they're lying. You think the CIA isn't running things in Laos. You think Vientiane isn't full of prostitutes and dope dens and the conditions that create prostitutes and—"

"No, you silly ass!" Miller shouted back. "I'm saying what you know is as plain as the nose on your goddamned face: The United States is not—repeat *not*—interested in prostitutes and dope dens."

"Speak for your fuckin' self!" Hill roared.

Miller looked at him numbly, then turned back to Evans. "If the CIA is there, it's because they're trying to keep the Commies out—and nothing else."

"I know the United States doesn't go around *actively promoting* prostitutes and dope dens," Evans said sarcastically, "but—" He cut off as Big Tack came swinging around the lean-to. Seeing Evans squatting by the fire and the others lounging around the benches, a big smile spread across his face.

"Hey, Trach lonesome for GI comrades, okay? Tomorrow, maybe we have big dinner, okay? *Beaucoup* wine. Pretty girls dance for us. Okay?" He grabbed Hill's foot and twisted it with rough camaraderie.

"Okay, you big ox," Hill said, shoving himself free.

Tack grinned, whacked Hill on the side with one of his giant paws, then smiled awkwardly at the rest of them. He had obviously come to break up a fight and didn't know what to say now. He slid down, sitting on the ground with his arms on the bench just in front of Hill.

"Okay, okay?" he said in one dying gasp of sociability. Evans nodded at him in mutual discomfort and looked back at Miller.

"All I was really trying to say, Miller, is that we treat all their propaganda as so much bullshit. But it isn't. The governments we support around here *are* corrupt. And the CIA *does* have its nose in half of them."

"We feed half these fuckers," Miller returned in quiet anger. "If it weren't for U.S. aid, ninety percent of them would be flat on their ass."

"God, *Miller!*" Evans said. He took a deep breath as though he had repeated two plus two ten times, and the stupid student still hadn't got it.

"You mean we don't really give aid, eh?" Hill grinned. "Mother! When I think of all my income tax!"

Evans turned on him like a shot. "Sure we give aid," he said. "And as a big capitalist businessman you ought to recognize just what it's like. Because it's something like the aid we give to cities like Philadelphia. A lot of talk and a lot of bleeding for the taxpayers, and then if the people who live in the ghettos really get lucky, some small token might just filter down to them—if there's a riot or the threat of a riot!"

"You suggesting we haven't been giving all that wheat to India, for example?" Janowitz said. But his voice was careful. Evans had struck a nerve in everyone, and they all felt a little funny about it in front of Hill—the first time on the whole journey that race had produced any genuine discomfort.

"We got rid of a lot of surplus wheat that was costing us money to let rot in storage bins all around the country, yes," Evans replied. "And we've *lent* quite a lot of money to India, but most of the direct *giving* has come from private charities. The very great bulk—and I mean like *seventy percent* of our foreign aid—has gone to those three centers of international riot: South Korea, Formosa, and South Vietnam. And if you don't believe me, I'll try to find some figures from American sources you *will* believe! And even there it's a joke. I forget the figure, but I think our aid to South Vietnam was three billion last year. *Two* of those three billion came in manufactured goods produced and bought in the United States!"

He paused and got hold of himself. "Most of the people of America don't know what's being done in the world in their name," he went on softly, but with the tension still dancing in his words. "Not just in Vietnam, but all over. Our aid usually makes the rich richer and the poor poorer, and if you don't think that isn't obvious to every peasant being clobbered by a thousand-dollar bomb hurled from a multimillion-dollar airplane, you're crazy. Ask the girls in the whorehouses in Vientiane about our aid, Hill. They believe it—just the way the people in the ghettos in Philadelphia believe it. It's the same hypocritical bullshit."

There was a long, long silence. A bristling silence. Eventually Hill sat up. "It's my fault," he said rancorously. "I shouldn't have brought up sex." He stood up and walked to the front of the lean-to, kicking at the dirt.

"You're a real bleeder for poor, suffering humanity, aren't you?" Miller sneered at Evans. He stood up and walked over to Hill, holding out a flimsy VC cigarette to him. Hill took it, and Miller threw away the thin paper pack. It was his last. He lit it for Hill, and the two of them stood there alternating puffs on it without ever exchanging a glance. The brief twilight had passed, and the hills were now covered in darkness.

At long last, Hill turned to Evans. "What the shit do you want from us, Evans?" His voice was as penetrating as a knife—and as deadly.

"I want you to help me put an end to this insane war," Evans said quietly. For a second it stopped them all. They waited for more, but that's all he said.

"How?" Miller finally asked bitterly. "Making speeches about how our country is all fucked up and the VC are the real heroes of this thing?"

"No," Evans said. "That wouldn't do much good anyway. If you did make speeches—of any kind—people in America would just say you'd been brainwashed. No, it's nothing like that."

"What then?" Janowitz insisted.

Evans looked across at him. The fire had died to a glow of embers, and though their eyes were growing used to the dark, it was hard to tell his exact expression, but his voice was almost self-mocking. "It's not very grand," he said. "We shouldn't overestimate ourselves. Nothing any one of us could do as soldiers was likely to win the war; nothing any of us can do as prisoners—singly or together—is liable to end it."

He stood up and wandered to the empty bench opposite the opening. Finally, he sat on it and looked across at Hill and Miller. "It's like everything else we've done in this war. Maybe like everything soldiers do in any war. I'm not sure it'll work—if it works, I'm not sure it'll be worth it. All I'm sure of is that it's better than doing nothing."

"Maybe that's the way some of us were fighting the war anyway," Janowitz suggested. "I didn't particularly take to it like candy, but I felt if we won, it'd be over—and better for everyone all the way around, including the Vietnamese."

Evans smiled. "If we were going to win next month, I suppose we *could* live with it, and though we could never be proud of what we'd done, it'd be worth it just to stop it, but like I said, I don't think these people are going to give up any more than we would if they were marching through Iowa and Indiana shooting up our countryside."

"So *they* should win?" Miller asked sardonically.

"Nobody's won this war, Miller; nobody *will* win it. You've seen enough to know that. I'm only asking you to help stop the bleeding." He grinned self-deprecatingly. "Or rather, to help me in a step that might possibly be a move toward stopping the bleeding." He sighed. "I can't put it any higher. Let's face it, none of us is really much more important than that. We aren't the wheels or even the spokes, just little bits of grease that may help the wheels turn—or maybe get burned trying."

God, Janowitz thought. All upside down again. It sure as hell wasn't what he'd expected. It was worse because everything he'd thought of would have been easy to turn down. Help the VC? Whatever he thought of what they were trying to do, he just couldn't. Hurt the States, however wrong we might be in Vietnam, he knew he couldn't do that either. But try to end this fucking war?

Instantly—and in a funny, spine-tingling way—he knew that this was maybe the one thing in his whole life that he thought he just might be willing to put his life on the line for. And maybe all the time Evans had known it. He smiled grimly to himself—that fucking Shakespeare course: "There's a divinity that shapes our ends, Rough-hew them how we will."

Evans was staring at him. Had the fucker been waiting for always—since time began?

9

i

That night they crossed into North Vietnam. There was no way of knowing except that Big Tack came back in the line to tell them. He seemed torn between pride in the accomplishment and displeasure at the result.

"North Vietnam—*merde!*" he said descriptively.

"What's that?" Hill said to Evans.

"Shit," Evans replied with a laugh. "Trach is from the delta. They don't like Northerners. Don't trust them. It's like you Alabamans," he said to Russell. "The Northerners have more energy than the Southerners, or at least they have a reputation for having more energy—and craftiness," he added diplomatically. "And they're more modern, more factories and that sort of thing. The coal and minerals are all in the North. The South is slower, more relaxed."

"I knew I was going the wrong way," Russell said sorrowfully. Hill whacked him on the back and almost sent him flying.

Later they camped for their midnight lunch. Janowitz looked for Mỹ, but she kept herself busy. He found to his surprise that just looking at her, working next to big tits, filled him with an unpleasant sense of guilt. God, he hadn't screwed big tits; he'd just had the *urge* to screw her—why should that make him feel guilty? He remembered Hill's words: "And you, Yid—sir, I know your Jewish schmaltz would keep you from breaking the heart of that little doll. . . ." Man, what a disaster if it were true! He guessed that's what ultimately tamed the instinct for variety in men who were loyal—schmaltz, fidelity, whatever you wanted to call it; anyway, an overpowering sense of guilt for being untrue to someone they didn't want to be untrue to. But damn, he didn't want to feel it already. Maybe after ten years of marriage or something—or even one year! But not after a couple of wordless screws to a girl whose name he didn't even know. That was carrying even *Jewish* schmaltz too far!

There were two fires. The three musketeers shared theirs. But Pershing was kept with Thai and the other group. Janowitz's feelings were even more complicated looking at him. It was the first time he had got a good look at him since the fire. Some of his bandages had been taken off already, and though he still moved a little stiffly, he seemed as capable of taking care of himself as ever. Janowitz noted that they kept two guards on him even while he ate.

Boy, Janowitz thought, were you ever right, Pershing baby! Name, rank, serial number—not a syllable more. If they'd stuck to that, Morris might have died, but Morris had died anyway, and now—just as Pershing had predicted—there was no stopping it. They were in. If they tried to stop it, Janowitz felt sure the VC would execute the sentence against Pershing—and probably Evans, too. That alone was enough to keep them all in line. But it was worse than that. Now Janowitz didn't *want* to stop it. He wanted to know what Evans really had up his sleeve. The whole story. Maybe when he did, he'd still say no, but he knew that nothing Pershing or any of them could say to him now would stop him from finding out.

When they had had their chow, he sat next to Hill as usual, but when he looked up, he found Evans looking at him across the fire. Janowitz nodded to him. Man, it was screwed up all right. His heart wouldn't slow down—it was like those minutes in the locker room before a game, before you went out on the floor and actually got a ball in your hand.

Evans seemed to sense what he was feeling, that a big step had been taken. He turned easily to Russell.

"Do you know how close we are to China?" he asked.

"Well, I reckon we're too close," Russell answered in a tone that suggested he was giving the exact mileage.

Evans smiled with the others. "Probably," he said. "We're closer to China right this minute than Alabama is to Washington, D.C."

"Oh, hell, I ain't worried then." Russell smirked. "Back home we reckon Washington's the other side of hell."

"Well, some people are worried," Evans said. "They see a billion of them pouring down out of those hills with atom bombs in their hands, out to get every last one of us."

"Well, I hope someone sees them before I do," Russell said dryly, " 'cause I sure wanna get my ass out of the way when they do."

They all grinned. Janowitz looked out toward the north. It was funny to think of China so close. The forest seemed endless around them, and yet a couple of hundred miles north was a country bursting at the seams with people. He'd talked to guys who'd flown near the

234

border, and they'd said it looked just like North Vietnam—miles of nothing but wood and hills. But somewhere up there were the cities and the millions. And they were very close.

Marching across the hills, rather than along them, was exhausting. They kept to the valleys as much as possible, but mostly now it was up, down, and around, and he figured they'd gone precious few miles as the crow flies that night. The sun had hardly started to light the sky when Thai called the halt. Everyone was beat and more than willing to call it quits.

There weren't any camping facilities. They just stopped in a valley, still misty with night fog. As it gradually cleared, they saw dozens of little gushing rivulets of water running down over the rocks and turf of the hills and in the middle of the valley—the last to lose its shroud of milky haze—a stream, only about a foot deep and a couple of feet across, but running fast and clear.

They all were looking forward to being with Pershing again, but after the rice had been cooked and eaten, they split up into indoctrination sessions as usual—and Pershing was parked with Thai. His two guards were with him, but Thai just flaked out. The hills had obviously taken it out of him.

Tick, Tack, and Toe joined them, but it was Evans who was in charge again. It was obvious they didn't want to entrust another session to Tick, and as long as Thai was out of it, Evans was evidently expected to be instructor in charge.

"What about Pershing?" Janowitz asked curtly when he saw what they were in for. "You said he'd be with us at dawn. Well, it's dawn."

"I said in the morning," Evans said defensively. "The morning isn't over yet."

"Why can't he join us now?" Miller put it. "Are you afraid he might ruin your little lesson, like he did before?"

"I'm not trying to trick you, Miller," Evans answered soberly. "When you think I'm telling it wrong, say so. If Pershing thinks I'm telling it wrong, he can say so, too. You must have figured out by now that I wouldn't mind being wrong. I'd *like* someone to prove to me that we're pounding the shit out of these people for some *good* reason. If Pershing can give it to me, I'll sit the war out in the same camp you do."

"We'll see," Miller said belligerently—as though he felt Pershing would make a big difference.

"Okay," Evans answered. He tried to sound firm, but he was obviously shaken by Miller's animosity. He turned to the rest of them. "It

235

may sound strange after all the other things that have been said, but I don't think the people who sent us over here to pulverize this place did it for kicks."

"Awww!" Hill muttered with mock disappointment. Evans ignored him. "I think they're afraid. Genuinely afraid, and they're reacting as people do when they're afraid—blindly and stupidly."

"I think you're telling it wrong *right now*," Miller cut in acidly.

Evans paused, then sighed and went on.

"I confess that as a dropout from American hysteria about Communism I think the whole problem is the usual one of generals and politicians seeing everything in terms of the last war. I don't think a Chinese army sweeping across Asia is a *real* problem, any more than I think a horde of cigar-smoking Wall Street capitalists starving the world is a *real* problem. But if it is, I'll just take the word of most American generals and admit that if they do march, the only way to stop them is to use *our* strong points—our goddamned Air Force and our submarines and our rockets against the Chinese mainland. If they move, we hit. Not hit the soldiers streaming through the forests with their atom bombs—but back home in China, where it hurts. And we're well equipped to do that without chewing up the Vietnamese."

"You want fight Chinese?" Tack said with a big grin, looking at Russell.

"No," Russell said with a poker face. "Chinese vellee good fellows, me likee fightee you, but you takee my gun away." They roared with laughter.

"Okay," Tack said, going along with the laughter, not understanding a word. "You fight Chinese good. We let you walk up Vietnam. Free. No sweat, GI. Yankee fight Chinese, Chinese fight Yankee. In Vietnam we have big holiday!" And he laughed at himself, clapping Russell on the back, convinced the Americans all were laughing at his humor.

All the other VC were looking at them obviously wondering what the commotion was about. Janowitz saw Mỹ smiling at whatever was amusing them. Man, he loved her face when it was sober, but when she smiled! He decided he wasn't feeling all that guilty. Sometime that day he was going to have to go for a drink.

Pershing was looking at them, too—but frowning. Hill waved to him to indicate the laughter was on our side. Pershing nodded, but he still didn't seem pleased.

"All right," Evans said, grinning in spite of himself, "I give up, me vellee bad discussion leader." The poor sonuvabitch had probably

236

been preparing his pitch over every step of the night's march, Janowitz thought, and now the rowdies in class had shot the whole thing to shit. He almost felt sorry for him.

They sat in silence for a time; then Evans looked up at them, blew at the sweat beginning to bead his face, and smiled at Russell.

"What I was trying to get at," he said quietly, "was that the best guarantee we have the Chinese won't march through these countries are the people in them. They don't want the Chinese. There are a lot of Communists in Burma, but when some Chinese students put up a picture of Mao Tse-tung in Rangoon, the Burmese ran riot. Burned not only the pictures, but half the Chinese shops in Rangoon, too. And there are a lot of Communists in India, too, but you may remember what they did to the Chinese ambassador. And here in Vietnam—before we and the French came—all the battles they remember, as we remember Bunker Hill and Yorktown, were fought against the Chinese. Only one thing could make them turn to the Chinese—and that's for protection against *our* armies.

"What I meant to make you see was that if it's the Chinese we're frightened of, not only are we *not* doing the *right* thing by fighting in Vietnam, but we're doing exactly *opposite* to the right thing. Beat them badly enough and they may ask the Chinese to help. There are cynics who say that's what our military wants, so they'll have an excuse to bomb China's atomic capabilities now. If that's so, I think we've got no right to find our excuse over the dead bodies of the Vietnamese."

Clever, clever, clever, Janowitz thought. He gave up—yeah! He'd made the point six times more effectively than if he'd rammed it down their throats.

Evans had scrambled over to his pack. He took out a magazine and came back to them.

"*Look* magazine," he said, holding it up. "September nineteenth, 1967. I want to read just one bit of one article—and the session's over. Russell, you can march with Trach on China, and the rest of us can go to sleep.

"It's an article by the man who was the United States Ambassador to Japan from '61 to '66 . . . you know, just the sort of guy you'd expect to be a big left-wing propagandist." He looked at them all.

"Read the fucking thing," Miller said gruffly.

"Miller, just open your mind once. You don't have to believe what the man says; you don't have to believe what I say. But—"

"I don't!"

"But you just might learn how you're going to explain to your grand-

237

children why these people fought you to the death. You might be able to explain to yourself why your brother wouldn't go into uniform and fight under the—"

"Leave my brother out of this," Miller rasped hoarsely, "or you're going to need this whole fucking encampment to pull me off you."

Evans flushed and lowered his eyes to the magazine.

"He begins," Evans said, "by saying that when the decisions were made, we had two choices; one was fighting—which we did—and then he says, quote, 'The alternative was to allow Ho and his communist dominated Viet Minh to take over the whole of Vietnam. This would have happened early if the United States had made quite clear in 1945 that it did not approve of the revival of colonialism in Asia and would give it no support.

" 'It would still have happened if we had not given massive aid to the French war effort after 1949. It would have happened if we had been willing in 1954 to support the Geneva Agreements and had not tried to build up a permanent regime under Diem in South Vietnam . . . it would have happened if we had not steadily increased our military commitments to South Vietnam between 1960 and 1963. It would have happened if we had decided against massive participation in the war in the winter of 1964/65 . . . quite possibly, a unified Vietnam under Ho, spared the ravage of war, would have gone at least as far toward the evolution of a stable and reasonably just society as the divided, war-torn land we know today.' That's his joke," Evans said ironically. "He then says, 'I believe it would be safe to assume that it would have been a highly nationalistic Vietnam. By the same token, I believe it also would have been free of Chinese domination.' "

He leaned over and placed the magazine gently on the ground in front of Miller. Then he looked at Janowitz.

"At each stage you notice he doesn't say the war escalated because the Communists did this or Ho did that. Each time *we* were the ones who upped the ante. *We* were the ones who denied them the victory against colonialism they won long ago. That's why they fight. The Communists like Tho, the Buddhists like Trach, the rebels like Thai, who fight because they won't be dominated by anyone."

He got up and walked away, leaving them all stunned. Janowitz had never heard it laid on the line quite like that—not by somebody like a U.S. ambassador. So it was true that we were the ones who destroyed the Geneva Agreement, we who had kept the French fighting. And he was stunned, too, by Evans' implication that Thai wasn't a

238

Communist. It explained a lot if it was true. The bugging he got all the time from Tick—who *was* a Communist apparently. Jesus, wouldn't you know the bastard in the pack *was* the party member? When Thai's usefulness was over, who'd be boss then? As if he couldn't guess.

Miller had picked up the magazine and was looking at the article. There was a clipping attached to it, and Miller was reading it. "Listen to this," he said quietly.

They all turned, caught by his tone as much as by his words. "From the *Congressional Record,* the former Commandant of the United States Marines, General David M. Shoup. 'I believe that if we would keep our dirty, bloody, dollar-crooked fingers out of the business of these nations so full of depressed, exploited people, they will arrive at a solution of their own, that they design and want, that they fight and work for. And if, unfortunately, their revolution must be of the violent type because the "haves" refuse to share with the "have-nots" by any peaceful method, at least what they get will be their own and not the American style which they don't want and above all don't want crammed down their throats by Americans.' "

Miller stopped, holding the clipping, staring at it. Janowitz looked over at Hill. Hill shrugged and shook his head. Finally he stretched and roughed Miller's hair; then he walked over by the stream, away from Evans. Miller still hadn't moved, and when Janowitz stood too, he didn't seem to notice or didn't care to indicate he noticed. Janowitz touched his shoulder and then walked over and stretched out next to Hill.

Near the stream you could hear it rippling over stones and gurgling along the banks. It made it seem cooler, and that was already a desirable feeling. It also gave a feeling of privacy—covering their words in its swirling eddy.

"What'dya think?" Janowitz asked. He found it hard to ask Hill anything without a smile coming to his face.

"It sounds to me like we've been sold another bill of goods."

"By Evans—or Johnson?"

"Evans maybe—Johnson for sure."

Janowitz had to smile again. Hill's tone was sardonic, but he didn't seem very upset about it.

"And what'd you do if you were in charge?"

"Well," Hill said ruminatively, "I think I'd pay Muhammad Ali one hundred thousand dollars a year, and throw Johnson in jail."

Janowitz laughed, and Hill seemed pleased.

239

"You think I ought to say something to Miller?" Janowitz asked, twisting to see if those broad shoulders were still hunched stoically over Evans' magazine and the article on General Shoup.

"No. Miller's all right. I don't think Father Evans has converted that bastard like he thinks, and neither has General Shoup. I know my Miller baby. He's American Legion Republican through and through. I could turn into a snowdrop quicker than he could think the Reds were right—even if Christ and the Twelve Disciples were up there running the show in Hanoi and Evans was John the Baptist."

"Oh, yeah?" Janowitz replied skeptically. "And what do you think he's doing there now, praying for *Evans'* conversion?"

"No. He's got this problem, see. His young brother went to college —and he didn't. And when his brother wouldn't fight, Miller was half-afraid his brother was a coward and half-afraid the whole family would be taken for cowards. As far as he was concerned, everything his brother said about Vietnam was so much shit. They were Communists, and we were fighting for America. Simple as that. And one day he figured his brother would see the light.

"And now," he said, "Evans has convinced him his brother is never going to see the light. He hasn't shaken Miller, but he's gotten through enough so that Miller knows his family is always going to be split right down the middle."

Janowitz shrugged. "You figure, huh?"

"Yup. And it's even worse because right up until this morning he always had the secret belief that Pershing could put it all right. That he could twist Evans like a pretzel and have him with cold beer. And right now he's staring at those words, looking for the hole, and feeling inside that he ain't goin' to find it and that Pershing ain't either . . . That's my Miller."

"I thought you were buddies," Janowitz said. Hill's tone hadn't been derisive, but what he said didn't sound very buddy-buddy.

"I'd die for that baby, and he would for me," Hill said quietly. "Pershing, him, and me—we're family. Closer than brothers."

He looked over at Janowitz, a sly smile crossed his face. He was obviously amused at Janowitz's reaction to the paradox.

"But, dad," he went on drolly, "you take us out of these uniforms and put us back in the land of the big PX and I'd be stretched to think of a whitey I know who'd fight harder to keep his neighborhood clear of us jigaboos. Miller don't want us messing around with his wife or daughter, no, sir. And if you ever find me tossing Molotov cocktails, you can be damn sure I'll be slingin' 'em at a guy like Miller—just like Miller." He shrugged. "That's the way the bacon fries, man."

Janowitz tried to find something basic, some rock of truth, behind the mocking smile in Hill's eyes. He decided maybe it was all true—including the smile.

ii

It was a hot, hot day—even as high up as they were. Once he had settled down, Janowitz's mind played with what Evans might have in mind. But gradually his head filled with vague, sleepy thoughts of Mỹ. Now that he knew Thai and the others accepted—if they hadn't actually arranged—the meetings, the heart-stopping excitement was gone from them. But on the other hand, the feeling of certainty that he was going to get it, that it was just a matter of making his move at the right time, kindled a nice glow in his groin. He wondered if this was what it was like to be married and glance up at your wife across the dining-room table, knowing it was certain, yours for the asking. He'd never actually lived with a girl. He'd humped steady, as they used to say back at Michigan, but never really *lived* with one. Oh, there were lots and lots of things to look forward to—he hoped—as he stretched languorously . . . and finally accepted sleep.

He'd set a mental alarm, and when he awoke, he didn't know exactly how long he'd been asleep, but he knew the day wasn't over. One part of him wanted desperately to sleep on—the climb over the hills had taken a lot out of him—but the other part knew he had to pull himself awake or miss his chance. He rolled over and looked around. Everyone was sleeping except the two guards standing by Pershing. Even they weren't paying attention to anything beyond their own conversation.

Janowitz tried to locate Mỹ. Finally, he saw all the women grouped in one pool of shade. He stood up. Pershing's guards glanced at him, but no one else stirred. He stretched and moved a few steps toward the women. He'd half expected Mỹ to be lying awake, waiting for him, but no such luck. He couldn't make out which body was hers, and none of them seemed to be awake.

He took a long drink at the stream and splashed the water, rinsing his face. Nothing. He stretched and tried it again. Nothing. He started to walk into the woods to take a leak, and one of Pershing's guards moved toward him—not close, just keeping an eye on him. He went ahead a few feet, rattling the bushes going in, rattling them coming out. Nothing. He coughed and spat. Nothing. He took another gurgling drink at the stream. Nothing. The heat was impossible, and on top of it he was now wide-awake.

He went back to his place and settled down next to Hill, trying to fight the images flying around in his mind. He found that most of them were of big tits. Man, he wondered, could she possibly be as good as she looks? He rolled over. The warm grass on his loins was not a good idea; he rolled back, and as he did, he saw a figure moving toward the stream. He hunched up. It was Mŷ. She'd set her alarm, too; he smiled to himself.

He squirmed over to his pack and wormed his hand in until he got one of the boxes of rubbers. He slipped it into his pocket and sat up. His heart was already beginning to beat faster. Mŷ was just bathing her face in the cool water. He stood and walked to the stream, keeping his eyes on her, and bent down to drink. She must have seen the movement, but she still hadn't looked. Finally, she stood erect and turned to him. His heart thudded. He glanced at the guards. They were looking, but neither of them moved.

She smiled. Janowitz died. He jumped the stream and walked slowly toward the cover of the forest, not looking back at her or the guards. He figured they'd yell if they were going to stop him.

He got himself well screened from the camp before he turned around. It wasn't long until she appeared. When she saw him, she ran to him, smiling the whole time. Janowitz took her in his arms, sweeping her up off her feet and squeezing her while the pleasure of it sang through him.

But it didn't go well. The touch of her had roused him instantly to thoughts of endless intercourse. He could see them making it last for hours. But when they found a patch of soft grass, he found his mind wouldn't stick to the road but kept veering off out of control. She was exquisite and he loved her, but when he undid the top button on her fatigues, his mind fastened on big tits. For once in his life, he didn't want love, he wanted to nuzzle those great big boobs and plow that woman with the sensuous face. Mŷ's innocence seemed inadequate to the carnality of his desires. He wanted to be randy, to be animal— cruelly, wildly, without love.

He kept trying to push it from his mind, to concentrate on the beauty before him, to respond to the sensuality and warmth in her eyes and mouth. God, it was enough. But it didn't work. He felt awkward and even a little dirty putting on the rubber, and when she smiled dismissively about it when he turned back to her, he wondered how many times she'd seen that scene, and his mind got crossed between thinking of her as a whore and its dissatisfaction that she was too innocent for the mood of pornographic abandon big tits had induced in him.

In the end the only way he was able to arouse himself was to close his eyes and think of big tits. It killed him. The minute he'd finished, he felt smutty and full of self-disgust. The thought of big tits, so inflammatory seconds before, made him want to spit. And to make matters worse, they hadn't come together; he hadn't looked after her at all, just produced his own frenzy of assisted masturbation and let her look out for herself. And now she was looking at him, her eyes still sensual, but waiting and half-puzzled. She kissed him and tried to pull him to her again, but he knew it was hopeless. She was losers for this day.

He lay on her for a long time, and she stroked his head until she gradually relaxed. Her very gentleness made him feel even guiltier. He finally found the strength to look at her. Jesus, she was so slender of body, so beautiful. He felt like the prime shit of the Northern Hemisphere.

"Hieu," she said. It sounded French, her voice, a little high, very feminine.

"What?" He smiled.

"Hieu," she repeated, pointing a finger at her chest.

Janowitz got it. "You're Hieu," he repeated, pointing to her. She nodded. He pointed to his own chest. "I'm Hank." You Jane, me Tarzan, he thought.

She tried it, and it came out a little like Haunk. Janowitz smiled. "Do . . . you . . . speak . . . English?" he asked. She looked at him and smiled back. She obviously hadn't understood a word. *"Parlez-vous français?"* he tried. This time she shook her head quickly.

Great, Janowitz thought. It'll have to be sign language all the way. He pulled himself loose. God, messy. He hated rubbers. He'd used her —and that was it.

When they returned to the camp, it was even worse. The two guards were waiting for them. There were leers for her and promised violence for him. Their chattering woke Pershing, and he sat up and watched Janowitz and Hieu come into camp and then separate. His first reaction was disbelief, but then he studied Janowitz with cold reproof.

Janowitz flopped down. Man, life. Here he was with the ideal setup for any prisoner of war, and it wouldn't work out. He'd got a woman who'd satisfy ninety-nine and sixty-four one-hundredths percent of the men in the world, and he couldn't screw her without thinking of some *other* woman. And then an NCO looked disapprovingly at him, and he felt as guilty as an Eagle Scout who's forgotten how to do square knots and beats up old ladies for kicks.

iii

He felt no better when he woke again. A fire was going, to cook their rice, and the sun was already lost behind the hills. The sky was still light, though, and the heat told him that it'd be hours before they felt any relief from the muggy blanket of warmth.

They got chow from a central pot, and Pershing was allowed to join them at last while they ate. Up close they could see that he had really taken a beating. He was taped around the chest, and one eyebrow had almost been torn off. Evans had first thought he'd lost the eye. But it wasn't as bad as that. Pershing told them he'd also had a dislocated jaw, but that was all right now—at least temporarily, he said with a smile. And the VC had put his arm in a sling because they thought they'd fractured his forearm, but it had turned out to be only a bad bruise. "They're going to let it heal and try again," he cracked.

He seemed in great spirits. Not only was he pleased with the part he had played in the shellacking the Air Force had given the big VC camp back in the valley in Laos, but he was more than a little proud of the trouble he'd caused since then, too.

After his capture and trial, they'd fixed him up a bit and sent him on after the rest of them, but despite the fact that he could hardly move the upper half of his body and had one eye bandaged, he'd escaped twice. That's why they had the guard on him all the time now. The last escape had been outside the underground camp, and they'd been so afraid he'd manage to work up some kind of signal to indicate where the camp was that they had had more than three hundred troops beating the jungle for him. That's what Big Tack had been telling Thai about when they had finally caught up with the group. They had emptied those tunnels—everyone was after him. Men, women, and boys. Pershing laughed remembering it.

"I felt like a fucking VC," he said. "I could hear and see these bastards all around me. If I'd had a gun, I could have dropped a dozen before they even knew what area I was in."

"How'd they get you?" Miller asked, his face beaming. Pershing had raised *his* spirits all right.

"Goddamn dogs," Pershing grunted. He glanced at Russell. "I heard those damn hounds, and I half expected to see Russell and his dad closing in on me."

Russell shook his head. "Hell, as long as you stay out of our swimming pools, we won't bother you, boy."

Pershing reached across and tousled his head. The stretch obviously pained him, but he didn't lose his smile. Even Janowitz was beginning to catch some of the mood of buoyancy, though he dreaded the moment when Pershing would ask what had been happening to them.

It came during the long break for their meal during the night. They had marched for only a couple of hours when they realized why the VC had returned Pershing to them for good. The hills began to fall away toward a broad plain—a plain Janowitz knew stretched all the way to the sea. And as they descended, the forest gave way to terraced fields of rice, sugarcane, corn, and soybeans. Though they didn't see anyone, they knew there must be people around, and the chances for escape were infinitely less than in the jungle.

They had stopped in a stony field some five hundred feet above the plain, and for the first time on the trip the VC boiled the water they took from the rivulet that coursed beside the field before they cooked the rice in it.

Evans left them to talk with Thai, so they had a chance to speak freely. Janowitz guessed it was done deliberately, and he was a little taken aback that Evans should be so confident.

Janowitz did most of the talking. He knew it wasn't going to make him feel any better to dodge the issue or hide behind someone else's view of it.

He told Pershing about the loss of Morris, how Evans had saved them, and how Evans had come to be with the VC. He tried to explain that Evans had been trying to get them to see the war through the eyes of a VC and to some extent had succeeded. And that when you did see it that way, it looked a little different. He told him about the U.S. backing the French during the last two years of France's time in Vietnam, about the VC identifying us with the colonial powers because of it—and the governments we supported in Saigon. When you knew that, all our talk about being here to ensure one man, one vote and to repel an invasion from the North didn't sound too straight. Not when we did our damnedest to keep the whole place a French

245

colony and, when that failed, set up a government of our own making in the South.

Pershing didn't say a word during any of it. He kept his eyes calmly on Janowitz, as though listening to a tactical briefing, nodding his head occasionally.

"He hasn't made any converts to Communism or any crap like that," Janowitz finished wryly, "but he sure as hell has made me, for one, pretty convinced we're fighting the wrong war in the wrong place at the wrong time."

"You're going to become another Evans, is that it?" Pershing asked softly.

"No," Janowitz said, "I'm not. But to be honest, Pershing, I can't give you a *good* reason why not . . . except that I'm afraid it's not in me. Loyalty to the system is apparently more important to me than principles." He said it harshly, aware of Pershing's cold disapproval, and the instant he'd done so he regretted it. He had no right to talk to Pershing that way. He went on more moderately.

"Evans claims we were captured because he's got some cock-eyed plan to help finish the damn war. None of us has said anything—one way or another. But they've got you up on a death penalty, and Evans up on a death penalty, and if for no other reason than to prevent them from being carried out, I think we ought to find out what it's all about."

"I'm not worried about a death penalty, sir. Are you worried about Evans?" Pershing said it quietly, but the irony was savage.

"Evans is up because he saved my life, and Hill's, and Miller's—you're damned right I'm worried about him." He held Pershing's stare. "And even if I weren't, Sergeant Pershing, I intend to hear Evans out whether the rest of you do or not."

He felt better instantly. Maybe he'd been feeling so damned guilty because he'd been keeping his thoughts to himself. Now that it was out in the open, his head cleared. Pershing looked at him for a minute as though measuring his resolution.

"You turning in your bars?" he asked.

"I'm not giving orders if that's what you mean."

"Then that leaves me in charge?"

Janowitz thought it over for a second. Why not? But he knew what would happen. Pershing would say name, rank, serial number—and no matter what happened he'd stick to it, even if it meant *his* death and Evans'. With his hold on Hill and Miller, they'd probably go along with him. And he suspected Russell would, too.

"No, Pershing, it doesn't," he said finally. "I'm still the ranking offi-

246

cer, and I'm afraid I don't believe Evans is a traitor in the accepted sense of that word. I don't know what the hell he's got in mind, but I want us to hear him out. When it comes time to decide, I guarantee you each man will be free to choose as he wishes. I won't force a decision on anyone, and if they try force, I'll fight them no matter what my views."

"You ever hear about obeying orders, Lieutenant?"

Janowitz looked him up and down. The fire glow flickered over Pershing's brown face, tinting the grubby bandages with pink, making his handsome face even handsomer. He was a great competitor. Powerful of mind and body, ready to give—and take. Janowitz's combative instincts surged in response. It was like in a game when you were up against a guy who was great. You *fought*. When it was over, you might admire him more than anyone, but until then it was a *fight*—with no holds barred.

"I'm a Jew," Janowitz said coldly. "I've heard *a lot* about guys obeying orders. They fried six million people like me—obeying orders."

Pershing looked at him—hard. The will to fight was there, but nothing came. Finally, he turned away. They spent the rest of the break in silence.

iv

About half an hour after they hit the plain, they angled into a dirt road. It was hardly wide enough for one car, and was rutted and pitholed, but they suddenly saw more people than they'd seen since the big camp. There were carts, bicycles by the score, squads of marching troops, work gangs of men and women, and occasionally a truck would come honking along and everyone would move aside to let it pass. After the days in the jungle it was exhilarating to hear human voices again—singing, laughing, cursing.

As he watched the people go by—women with their conical rattan hats, men in uniform and out—Janowitz felt it was like coming home. They could be on the outskirts of Saigon from the look of the faces going by, the clothes, the way they used their bikes, the language. About the only real difference he could see was that the North Vietnamese had kept most of the French-style road markers, whereas down South the Army had replaced most of them with U.S.-type road signs. Must be symbolic of something, he thought.

Just before dawn the road started to clear as though by magic. What had been a teeming thoroughfare was now only a long country road with one or two isolated figures on it. The sky had turned light by the time they turned off on a path that led between two rice paddies to a little village of perhaps fifty mud and stone huts with bamboo, palm, and rattan roofs. People were already working ankle-deep in the fields, and as they came into the village, they saw two little kids taking turns pumping a huge wooden spoon contraption mounted on poles. They were scooping water from one field to another, and each time the thing filled, it carried them right off their feet. The whole group was smiling at it when one of the kids spotted them. He stopped in mid-flight, then dropped into the mud and, with his buddy, raced for the village. Whatever they were yelling was incomprehensible except for "Yankee!" That came through loud and clear several times.

When the group got in the village, there was a formal meeting between Thai and what Janowitz took to be the local chief—or maybe you said commissar up here. Tick stuck his two cents in, and then they were ushered toward two of the huts. The minute that happened the formal restraint of the village evaporated. Kids ran along grabbing at them, marveling at Janowitz's and Hill's height, jumping on their tiptoes, trying to get their heads as high as the shoulders of the Americans. Big Tack eventually had to shove their way through the ever-closing press of excited villagers—kids *and* adults. Inside the huts they were given straw mats to sleep on, and Janowitz remembered dozing off with the sounds of village chatter still in his ears.

None of them had had enough sleep when they were awakened, but they were given a wonderful dish with big hunks of fish and then marched out into the central square. The sun was still high, and it looked as if the whole village were gathered. Janowitz tried to see Mỹ—he couldn't stop thinking of her as Mỹ, even though he knew now that her name was Hieu. He finally found her in a group of women. She was still in uniform, but she'd changed her flopping Garbo fatigue hat for a light conical coolie hat—and to say that she was to the custom born was inadequate to describe the result. Her name might be Hieu, but she was a *mỹ* all right, a beauty. And with that round hat framing her face, no longer a female soldier—but a young girl. A delicate, almost frivolous girl, with sparkling eyes and a smile to send you dizzy. Big tits was only three or four feet away from her. She was wearing one of the hats, too, and there was no denying she looked like a smoky siren, but he was already wondering how he could have preferred her, even momentarily, to Mỹ. To Hieu, he corrected himself.

248

No, compared to Hieu, she looked coarse and ordinary. Hieu was a flower.

They had been gathered, the village had been gathered, to see a show. Janowitz had seen newsclips of similar North Vietnamese "entertainment" when he was in the Philippines. There were eight people in this one. Three of them played instruments, funny-looking guitars and different kinds of drums, and the others mimed and sang. One was the big villain, with a tall top hat with a multicolored dollar sign on it, and a crude U.S. stitched on his back. Another was a near midget, all done up in light gray, who zoomed around making airplane noises— getting encouragement from "U.S." and being shot down several times a minute by the three who evidently represented the valiant people of North Vietnam. One of these, a girl, kept stopping the action to sing songs that brought big grins to everyone.

Janowitz watched Hieu from time to time. She could have been seventeen standing there in the sun, giggling like a schoolgirl, sometimes turning her head away in modesty when something made her laugh helplessly. He wondered how old she really was—nineteen, twenty, twenty-one. She sneaked a glance at him once when something struck her as particularly funny—and was probably particularly biting about Americans, he thought. Except that she looked so familiar, he could hardly recognize her as the solemn-eyed, trudging veteran who had marched through the jungle and tended the wounded as though she had been doing it for decades.

His eyes caught Pershing's a couple of times, too. Pershing didn't rub it in, but he was obviously thinking, so you think this kind of propaganda is right? Janowitz felt embarrassed at first, but then he thought, what the hell, it *is* their country. If this is the way they react to getting bombed by somebody they don't know, tough shit—maybe if we stopped the bombings, they'd stop the shows . . . but, for all that, he regretted it.

After the show the commotion in the village didn't die down for a long time, but they were allowed to go back to their hut. It was dark when they were summoned by a cheerful Big Tack and fed again.

The village was asleep when they left. It smelled of animal dung— and human dung, too—but it was the first bit of normal life they'd seen in weeks, and Janowitz felt a twinge of regret as they moved along the path toward the road.

They marched all night. Five or six times they came to junctions, and there'd be little confabs before they'd march off on one or another of the alternates. At one of the junctions they separated from most of the group which had joined them after the fire at the camp in Laos. Janowitz couldn't tell how many left, but they took his mailbag and most of the load and headed off along the trail to their own destination.

The roads were little more than diminutive trails, but they all were busy. And the farther they got into the flatland itself, the more aware they were of activity on all sides—north, south, east, and west. When dawn came, they still hadn't reached their destination. But it wasn't as it had been in the forest. The minute the sky grew light, Thai split them in small groups, and they went ahead in threes and fours, widely separated. Janowitz was put with Evans and a guard . . . and Evans was given a pistol. Then, for the next couple of hours, the three of them advanced in careful stages, pausing, scanning the sky, and then darting ahead to the next bit of cover. Not once in the whole time did they see a plane, but the routine never altered.

Finally, they came to a little town. A church spire and rows of buildings set among trees. As they got closer, Janowitz could see that the whole place had been flattened. The church spire was seventy percent air and seemed suspended more by miracle than by the flimsy struts that remained. Below it, the roof was in ruins, and one wall had totally collapsed in rubble. And the rows of buildings were really rows of shells, a wall here, a doorway there, part of a roof, but everywhere rubble, stone, charred beams. The trees that lined the streets as if they belonged in some French provincial town were splintered and in some cases toppled right across the cobblestone street.

As they approached it, Janowitz felt like an extra in some old World War II movie. A French road marker, a French sign for the town, Yen Cai, they were moving single file along the highway, close to the neatly spaced sycamores, ahead of them a town gutted by bombardment. If he'd seen a German tank blazing on a street corner, he wouldn't have been surprised.

When they moved into the town, Janowitz could see that it was really just one long street, with two smaller intersecting streets, neither of which continued out for more than a block. Here and there Vietnamese were working in the rubble, taking away a piece of wood or a hunk of metal, but except for these scavengers, it was a ghost town. When they were almost at its center, little Toe suddenly appeared in the doorway of an elegant-looking ruin still bearing wrought-iron grillwork over the door. He signaled Janowitz and Evans to follow him inside.

They went through the opening, and there was the rest of what Janowitz recognized was now their own little group. They weren't many. Thai and the three stooges, the two women, two guards, Evans, and the five Americans. None of those whom they'd picked up in Laos remained.

Thai surveyed them all as though reappraising them freshly. Then he nodded to the women, and they went about preparing a meal. The rest of them he motioned over against a wall that had begun to be traced with bougainvillaea. The plaster was shattered, there were spots where pictures had hung and gaping holes where things had been torn from the wall, but the blue and white and little flashes of red in the bougainvillaea made it all fit somehow. It was like a painting in the early sun.

"We are at the end of our journey," Thai said. "At least for a time. Here we will grow strong"—he looked at the Americans—"and you must decide to atone for your crimes—one way or the other." He smiled and concentrated on Pershing. "Comrade Pershing, I must warn you that if you attempt to escape again, you will find you have tried our patience one time too many."

His whole attitude suggested that Evans had told him they were going to get the cooperation they were looking for. The threat in his voice was really not menacing in the way it had been, and he seemed to have switched his mind already from conversion to logistics. We call it counting your chickens before they're hatched, Janowitz thought.

"Yen Cai, as you see, has already received the attention of your Air Force. For us it is a convenience, because as long as we are not seen among them in any great numbers, even the Americans do not bomb ruins. There is a cellar in this building. Anyone who chooses may sleep there. Comrade Pershing *must* sleep there.

"Given reasonable cooperation, you may move about what is left of Yen Cai as you please—as long as there are never more than three of you together at one time. You will soon understand the reason for this generosity. Though deserted, Yen Cai is still the center of this district. You will find it difficult to go fifty yards from the town without meeting a peasant farmer, a buffalo boy, a soldier. To go a hundred yards would be even more difficult. Five hundred yards I should think would be impossible even for Comrade Pershing." He smiled. They had to, too. Even Pershing gave it a slow grin.

"I should add that this district is in the center of the training area for the Fourth Army of the Republic of North Vietnam. In the village councils, in the Army Order of the Day, the entire population has been made aware of your presence here. You will be treated as guests—as long as you act like guests."

They ate in silence. Big Tack kept offering more rice and slapping Hill on the back now and then. But the general mood was one of torpor. Janowitz was suddenly ready to admit that, however fit he was, his whole body was tired—pooped!—from the endless marching. And as the awareness that the journey was over set in, the others sagged, too. The sun rose, the flies and bees buzzed around the bougainvillaea, the rice settled in their stomachs, and their eyelids became heavier and heavier.

Janowitz watched Hieu from time to time, and several uncommunicative glances passed between them. Somehow the knowledge that this was now their group, their community, altered all their relationships. Especially the sexual ones. Even in the hot, lazy sun, new tensions seemed to flash around the little area of concrete floor where they sat. No move of Hieu or big tits passed without its appraisal by some masculine eye—calculating, cautious, cynical. Janowitz could see them—eyes in white skin, black skin, yellow skin—all windows for the same thoughts. And the two girls moved as though they were walking on a mine field. Their feminine antennae sensed it all. Only a woman would know, Janowitz thought, whether their reaction was fear or excitement—perhaps both. Outwardly they were as studiously noncommittal as politicians at a Fourth of July picnic.

After everyone had eaten and they had damped down the fire, they suddenly left. Maybe that was the solution, Janowitz thought. The women were going to live somewhere else. But it wasn't. They were back in about twenty minutes with two new packs. It turned out these contained medicine and bandages, and the women immediately set about redoing Thai's bandage. The activity became the center of everyone's drowsy attention, and Thai spoke once more.

"There is one more thing," he said. "We will return to sleeping at night—and working in the day." He looked around them all. "If you go to sleep now, you will not be awakened until *tomorrow* morning."

Janowitz didn't think he could sleep that long, but the heat was weighing on him more every minute. Twice, as Thai was being rebandaged, they heard planes, and when the girls moved to Pershing, a plane whipped over the horizon and zoomed past them about two "houses" down. The plane fired after it passed, but it was evidently at something in the fields beyond. They were screened by the two standing walls and a long hedge that had once run down the outside of the house. A plane would have to go almost over them to spot them, but the incident made Thai nervous, and he moved the two guards over against the hedge and the rest of them around the walls, so that a plane couldn't have spotted more than three or four of them on one pass, even if it went right over.

Janowitz sprawled next to Hill, and they both watched as Pershing was rebandaged. The women inspected the tape around his ribs but didn't touch it. They completely removed the covering from his head, though, and when they had, it was clear he'd been cut up in more places than the eyebrow. His head was covered with wounds.

"They worked my baby over proper," Hill whispered.

"They did that," Janowitz answered. The women proceeded with him gently, and they too seemed surprised at the extent of his injuries. They worked meticulously, and while Pershing wasn't comfortable, he obviously enjoyed their ministrations. Janowitz realized he couldn't have recovered as quickly as he had if the wounds hadn't been largely superficial. But it was plain luck. That beating hadn't been given him with any care—it'd been done in fury. That they hadn't killed him was as much accident as design. Damn, life was complicated, Janowitz thought. He wanted Pershing to go along. Pershing was the last man he wanted to fight. He loved Hill, but he knew that if he had to pick one guy in the outfit who was basically sound, it was Pershing. And seeing him battered like that filled Janowitz with shadows of guilt and remorse, for all his feeling that Pershing was persevering doggedly in a wrong cause. But at the same time he had to admit that deep inside himself the sight of Hieu so tenderly caring for that handsome Negro face sent shivers of discomfort up his spine. Yeah, life was complicated all right.

When the women finally finished, they went off to prepare their own meal separately, whispering quietly between themselves, as the men around them gradually gave in to the heat and went off to sleep. Janowitz remembered being vaguely aware of them squatting face to face, eating from their bowls and giggling softly; then he too slumbered off.

He awoke to savage hunger, the sound of Hill's voice—and the smell of eggs and bacon. Hill was at the fire. He had a long strip of metal rigged over it and must have had a dozen eggs frying. Hieu and big tits were hovering about him, torn between laughter and panic, and Hill was pouring out a torrent of ballyhoo like a fairground huckster.

"Welcome to the Black Power Kiwanis Club Breakfast, Lieutenant!" Hill shouted when he saw Janowitz sit up. "We citizens of the biggest little town in North Vietnam want you to come along an' join

253

right in with us here, just like you was a white man! And bring the missus! We've got white eggs and yellow eggs and black bacon and red power! And if the frigging natives ever find out what we been doing to their chickens, you're going to see some purple ass as well!"

The VC fluttering around him didn't know what the hell he was saying, but they were laughing as hard as Miller and Pershing, who sure enough did. And Hill was leaping around the fire in those Stepin Fetchit swoops attacking first the eggs, then the fire, and all the time mouthing obscenities in the same carnival barker's chant. "Yes, sir, look at that mother-fucking egg! It is the sweetest little seed this side of the Yangtze, and what you going to do with it, little Vietnamese boy? Why, you're going to turn it into a smelly ball of shit; that's what you're goin' to do to my sweet little old egg that is still fresh from the tail of the cutest damn chicken ever to tickle the fancy of a tantalized rooster! But do I hold it against you? No, man! I say take the fucking thing *before I drop it!* That's it, stupid, you managed it! Hurray for the ingenuity and intelligence of one half-assed member of Uncle Ho's Marching Society for the Provision of Night Soil to the far-flung hills of Vietnam!"

He got to them all—but none more than Pershing. Pershing's face was wet with tears of laughter, and he kept clutching his poor cracked ribs. And Hill just went on and on; the invention never ceased.

"Step right up, Lieutenant! We'll eat with you; we hold no grudges. This circumcised erection has never given pleasure to a chicken in his whole life, but do the chickens howl out against him? No! They are dropping double time at the sound of his name—Jaanowww-witz!" He made it sound as though he himself were producing the egg.

"There you are, *sir!* Smiling at you from her little yellow eyeball! Take another! Eggs is what your balls are crying out for, Lieutenant, fucker, sir! You have got to service this little ole Vietnamese girl, and the reputation of all us fuckers you represent calls out for eggsemplarary conduct *above* and *beyond* your regular little ole six inches! Don't disappoint her, Lieutenant! Disseminate the productive juices! That's it! You are living, Lieutenant!"

The two girls were helpless. He only had to raise an arm in exaggerated alarm at some move they were making, and they were corpsed. And through all the huckstering he was also forever shepherding one or the other of them hither, thither, and yon, grabbing a free feel now and again and whooping and waving his eyes wildly at Thai or Janowitz when he did so, as if he were some great queen doing his act at the local show bar.

254

Even when he sat down to eat, he kept it up. "Oh you juicy, fruity, Communist seed, come ease your way into papa's quivering, gold-toothed, capitalist hole. Oh, lovely, lovely, lovely!" And on and on and on.

As a matter of fact, the eggs were covered with soot and pieces of ash and flaked paint so that once they were dumped with the ham into a wooden bowl, the mess looked about as appetizing as a miscarriage. But the taste was indescribable. Janowitz wasn't even a lover of eggs, but he hadn't had one in months. And the smell and the taste with the ham and the French bread little Toe was passing around was enough to convince him there was only one thing better than Hill's sales pitch—and that was his food.

By the time Hill had finished his spiel and accepted the warmth of the sun he'd exhausted them all. Janowitz's sides ached from laughing, so he didn't know how Pershing stood it.

Hill finally flopped back with a huge sigh of satisfaction, his arms spread wide. "Hill," he said, addressing the sky, God, someone, "you're a fucking genius!" There was no one to disagree with him.

After that they just lay there in complete silence, punctuated only by an occasional groan of contentment from Hill or a giggle from one of the women. The sun was high; it was near noon, Janowitz could tell; they *had* slept the clock around. They heard aircraft two or three times, but always distant. In the aftermath of Hill's performance the whole mood of the place seemed tranquil and serene. Finally, Hill sat up lazily and looked across at Janowitz.

"Lieutenant," he said, "what'dya say we go see what makes this fuckin' town live?"

Janowitz grinned—and nodded his head. Hill stood and stretched; then he looked at Pershing.

"Okay with you, dad?" Pershing nodded slowly. "Want to come?" Hill asked. Pershing shook his head.

Janowitz found it hard to believe they'd really be allowed to go off on their own, but though all eyes were on them when they went through the smashed doorway, no one followed. They were hardly in the street when a plane came hurtling along above it. They both instinctively flattened against the wall. Right over them it let go with its machine guns, strafing the road coming into the town. They saw two guys on bikes running for the fields. The plane arched toward them, bullets tracking in an explosive race over cobblestones, bricks, ground. The cyclists dived for mud, the plane flashed over them, and they slowly poked their heads up from the mud and watched it for a time, then calmly wheeled their bikes back onto the road, scraped some of the mud off themselves, and pedaled on their way. Hill shrugged at Janowitz. They both laughed and walked out into the street.

There was damn little left to see in the town. From the remains they could tell most of the houses had been of pastel shades and once been quite substantial—bricks, cement blocks, big wooden beams, lots of wrought iron. Janowitz guessed it must have been a French provincial headquarters or something. Even in its present state you could see that it had all been clean and neat once, and most of the houses had been of two stories with six or eight rooms. That wasn't for peasants. Near one intersection there were three shells of what must have been the main shopping stores. Behind one was a long cement building that had been chewed up like the rest. It had probably been a warehouse or a market where the peasants brought stuff to sell. It had been painted with two large red crosses.

Janowitz had heard plenty of ambiguous stuff about bombing hospitals at the officers club in Bien Hoa. Some French paper had printed a lot of stories about how many hospitals our planes had wrecked in North Vietnam, and French TV had got permission to interview a number of pilots. Janowitz himself had found it hard to believe any Americans would bomb a hospital, but the French TV team had dozens of pictures of ruined hospitals, and they claimed they'd seen such bombings themselves. Then some of the pilots who were flying North got hot under the collar and said that sometimes the North Vietnamese Army mounted antiaircraft on hospital roofs—and if they wanted to do that, you're damned right they'd get bombed. Then a whole chorus of them claimed they'd drawn fire from NVA hospitals and that they had retaliated. And a fat-assed, shiny-cheeked PRO had piped up that the NVA were putting red crosses on warehouses and every other damn thing they didn't want us to hit. If they thought they could get away with it, he'd said, they'd slap a red cross on the whole damn country. That's when Janowitz decided an NVA hospital—with or without a red cross—was probably not the safest place to sit out the war.

This building had obviously not been built as a hospital, but inside there were several smashed metal beds and odd pots and pans that indicated it might have been converted into one. They kicked through the rubble and then went back outside and stood in the shade of a tree staring at it.

"That tends to piss me off," Hill said, looking at the red cross. Janowitz looked at him closely.

256

"You with me, Hill?"

"I told you, Lieutenant"—Hill smiled—"I don't volunteer for any-thing."

Janowitz shrugged. He had the feeling Hill wasn't against him.

As they walked on toward the church, another plane went over-head. It was a little like living near an airport. There always seemed to be something going overhead or something approaching from the dis-tance. They found they grew used to it and reacted only when some-thing was really on top of them.

"Did you steal those eggs?" Janowitz asked.

"You joking, Lieutenant? I wouldn't steal no eggs." He was grin-ning, of course. "But Tack brought in six. Now I suspect he *isn't* above stealing. So I just told him he was a goddamned failure; I could eat those six myself. He should go out and get us some *eggs*. Well, the son-uvabitch goes off and comes back with dozens of 'em and a hunk of ham the size of a telephone book. I coulda given him the Philadelphia Boys Club Medal of Dishonor with crossed handcuffs."

They both smiled. The breakfast was still warming their stomachs. Thank God for Tack.

The church was the one structure in town that looked as if it might still be in use. Several roof beams were still lying aslant from floor to ceiling, but the place had been cleared of rubble. It was a Catholic church, of course, and there were statuettes in the niches in the good wall and a stone altar that had a big silk cloth draped over it—in bright green and red. Fishes and loaves. And there were little candleholders all over the damn place with stubby candles in them and drippings all around, as if they had been burning last week or something.

Janowitz and Hill looked at each other quizzically as they walked through it. There was a big wooden crucifix below the spire. It had been splintered but was patched up and hung there suspended by two ropes. It was almost over the altar, but not quite.

When they left, Hill said, "Well, papa Pershing is going to be a lit-tle shaken up." And Janowitz thought, is this all part of the plan? Why *this* village? Because of the Catholic church? To get Pershing? He didn't honestly believe he could accept any of the American arguments for being in Vietnam anymore—except that it was a mistake and there wasn't any easy way out of it. But one trouble with going even a little way with an outfit run by Communists was that you couldn't trust them for the time of day. Was it a real church—or had it been arranged for their benefit?

They weren't long in finding out that even if it was real, it had

certainly been arranged to make an impression on them. When Janowitz and Hill returned, Pershing, Miller, and Russell were in a confab
and, after a second's hesitancy, signaled them over. But Thai muttered something to Big Tack, and Tack ushered them outside again.
They spent the afternoon wandering around the countryside, where
Tack showed them three little villages, the mud and bamboo huts so
buried among palms and laurel that they weren't aware they were
there until they were on them.

All the people seemed to know Tack and waved at him. Some
raised rifles in salute. But Tack wanted to show them the wounded.
And he took them to one hut after another and it seemed as if every
one of them had someone who was wounded, a kid, an old woman,
a man. They all were freshly bandaged, and none of them looked as if
he were going to die tomorrow—but for three villages there were
a fair number of them.

Lesson over, Tack took them back to Yen Cai. It was almost sunset. They ate rice and vegetables, and then Thai got them all together in one circle. He looked at Pershing.

"You have not been to mass in a long time. Tonight in Yen Cai
you are invited to mass."

Pershing looked over at Evans, then back at Thai—and nodded
slowly.

They all went. Thai walked with Pershing and stayed near him
throughout the mass. It was dusk when they arrived. There was still
some light in the sky, but you had to strain to see. They were soon to
learn that this was the favorite time in North Vietnam. Not just because it began to get cooler then, but because it meant the daylight
raids were over and it was too early for night raids. For these few moments they could feel free about candles and fires, even headlights on
trucks.

If the church looked like a ruin by day, it was a masterpiece by
night. It really consisted only of one wall, an altar, and some odd
pieces of superstructure, but when it was lit by the flickering, inadequate light of a few candles, it was transformed into something ma-
jestic. The expanses of nothing that made it seem fragile and hollow
in the sunlight became dark vaults that extended the dimensions of
the church frame far beyond its stone and wooden skeleton . . . into
the night—and into the imagination. The damn little village church
became some immense Gothic cathedral where the light of man flickered in only one tiny corner.

They stood outside on the grass that lay between what had once been the wall of the church and the cemetery with its stone crosses. The priest was in a robe that glittered with spangled thread exactly matching the silk of the altar cloth—the brilliant green, the ocher red. All the candles were lit—tiny ones in clusters along the standing wall, six huge ones on the altar. There were two altar boys in white . . . and, throughout, that slow ritual pace and formal repetition that men have always associated with their ministrations to the deity.

There were probably only fifty or sixty people actually in the congregation but there were half again as many watching outside. And when parts of the mass were sung, half of these people joined in tentatively, as though they had witnessed it so many times they half knew the words and music. Janowitz wondered if they had been reluctant Catholics when the French were there and were reluctant non-Catholics now that the Communists were in charge.

There were bicycles all around, and some of the girls looked stunning in their au-dais and glorious conical sun hats. Mŷ—Hieu—was in fatigues, but she looked as ravishing in the candle glow as she had the first night he had seen her like that. He wanted to go out and buy her an au-dai so the rest of them could see that she was as beautiful as any of them.

When it came time for communion, Janowitz was locked in thoughts of his own about God and man and all his religions of love and duty and morality—and how weak they were compared to the primitive drives to compete and destroy.

When the priest came down to the rail where they served communion, the congregation turned, and from the back of the church came a line of about a dozen people. Janowitz recognized some as the people they'd visited in the afternoon with Tack. The mass might be real all right, but they were going to make use of it.

There were all kinds of wounded, but the two that really got to Janowitz belonged to a kid and a young woman who was carrying him. The kid didn't look two years old. One of his arms was a bandaged stump, and the mother's face and neck had that purple, twisted blemish of burned flesh—as if someone had spilled scalding water on her. But the thing that was killing was the way the kid was chattering an incoherent blue streak in the otherwise silent church, wiggling around and pointing with his good arm to the candles and grabbing his mother's face to make her look at him as he tried to tell her about them. She kept trying to hush him, but nothing slowed him until she took the communion wafer—and then he stopped flat, stared up at the priest, and burst into tears, howling as if he'd been stabbed.

It brought titters from everyone. Janowitz looked at Pershing. Pershing lowered his head. Later, when the general congregation went up for communion, Pershing went with them. Evans did, too.

v

The next day they had their first work session. It was held in the corner of their "home," and all the VC conspicuously absented themselves, except for the two guards who just squatted by the hedge and kept a casual eye on the whole proceedings. Evans was in charge. He began very deferentially and avoided looking at Pershing as long as possible.

"General Giap has a motto," he began. "It translates something like this: 'Plan carefully, prepare thoroughly, strike unexpectedly.' "

"We aren't working for General Giap," Pershing cut in flatly.

"We are about to enter stage two," Evans went on, ignoring him. "And very soon you must either decide to prepare along with us or— or it will be too late, and other plans will have to be made . . . for Thai and the others, and for us."

"I think the crucial issue," Janowitz said firmly, "is just what the plan is. None of us are committing ourselves to anything until we know what we're being asked to do."

Evans paused. Then: "You've already seen what we've done to the country we're supposed to be saving. The plan is to do something that may save what's left."

"That isn't enough, Evans," Janowitz said.

"That's as much as I can tell you right now."

"Are you really so naïve, Evans, that you think because they've left a few Catholics around up here, the Communists are interested in some kind of 1776 independence and freedom?" It was Pershing. He was staring right at Evans. Janowitz had to admire him again. He had evidently decided that Evans had made an impact on them and that the way to combat it was with a head-on attack—but one without rancor. He'd overcome his own initial anger, and he sensed an emotional attack on Evans wouldn't work. It had to be a cold, logical dissection.

"Are *you* really so naïve as to think that anyone in Vietnam who isn't an outright profiteer is so afraid of Communism he'd die fighting it?" Evans shot back.

"Maybe." Pershing smiled. "If I were a Vietnamese, I might not

260

know much about a free ballot, but I think maybe I'd be smart enough to know that I didn't want my life run by a bunch of terrorists and murderers. I could be a pretty dumb Vietnamese and still figure that the time to fight the sonsubitches was when I still had the chance—not after they took over completely."

"And that's what you think the Liberation Front is—a bunch of terrorists and murderers?"

"Yeah, I'd say that's a fair enough description." Pershing grinned. "You going to tell me they get these villagers to go along by popular acclamation? Or that when they slice up some village chief and his family, those people just lie down for them and say, do me in, comrades, I've got an itch to see my ancestors?"

Everyone but Evans smiled.

"Well," Evans said, "our government has tried its damnedest to convince everyone the VC are nothing but terrorists and that's how they manage to keep their hold on the population."

"Well, they've *sold* a lot of people," Pershing said lightly. "But of course, that may be because the VC have been helping them by providing so many dead bodies."

"There're a lot of people they *haven't* sold, too!" Evans snapped back. Pershing was getting to him. "And I should think it would be obvious even to you that a dead Vietnamese wouldn't be able to see much difference between being killed by an American plane or by a 'terrorist' bullet. And when it comes to numbers slaughtered, the Liberation Front can't *begin* to touch us!"

"They're working on it, though, you'll admit that?"

"Pershing"—Evans sighed—"you were born to be a believer. I'll bet in catechism class you accepted Adam and Eve, Noah's Ark, and the Virgin Birth without an instant of doubt. If the nuns told you it was so, you clasped it to your little heart for life!" He was trying to hold his temper, but he wasn't succeeding.

"Sure—and I accept that Jonah spent forty days in the whale, too." Pershing laughed. "But what I *don't* believe is that even a failed priest from a highborn Southern family is a patriot when he's fighting against his country! Right about there my gullibility stops."

Hill burst out in laughter, Miller slapped Pershing on the back, but Pershing held his eyes right on Evans.

"Well," Evans said quietly, "the king's subject, George Washington, fought against Britain, Lee fought against the United States, and I've seen Negroes hurling rocks at the U.S. Army. I must be like all of them—because I think the word 'patriot' can be misapplied. I don't

261

happen to think that every sonuvabitch who goes round shooting up the countryside in the name of what he calls freedom is necessarily a patriot."

"And I don't think a guy who goes around killing teachers and local headmen is necessarily a revolutionary out to free his country," Pershing hammered back.

"The headman represents the landlord, Pershing," Evans answered angrily. "And the headmen don't like the Liberation Front, and the Liberation Front doesn't like the headmen. But I can tell you that when a headman is killed because he won't go along, the peasants don't always send up a wail of regret. In fact, it's often cause for a big celebration!

"And you talk about teachers—the 'well-trained' members of the so-called Revolutionary Development teams. Those people come—armed—into the villages to 'pacify' them. They come seeking information on suspected members of the Liberation Front. They come with American propaganda, American equipment, American tape recorders, film shows, cigarettes—everything! They're paid by Americans, trained by Americans, run by Americans. Now just what the hell is the Liberation Front supposed to do? Of course, they shoot them! Would we let the Liberation Front send teams into Saigon and Hue to 'educate' and 'pacify' *them?* This is a war, Pershing! Remember?"

It was the eternal priest flying, and Pershing was stopped, at least for the moment.

"I know plenty of Vietnamese who hate the Communists and hate the VC," Miller butted in.

"You're Irish, aren't you, Miller?" Evans asked, turning on Miller belligerently.

"So?" Miller bristled.

"Well, the English called the Irish Republican Army terrorists and murderers, didn't they? And sent the Black and Tans to butcher them. And the Irish quarreled among themselves. They weren't all one party or one belief—but they were all against the British!

"And you name it, Miller—Ireland, Africa, Kenya, Israel, China, they're all murderers if they have the gall to think it's wrong to let their children die of malnutrition and simple, curable diseases while others grow fat on their land and labor! Murderers, because they are willing to die—yes—*and to kill* to put an end to it!

"Well, now we've dubbed *these* people terrorists and murderers in

262

the same way. We have a society that doesn't get too shook up when a guy is hung up on a meathook for not paying off a loan shark, but we get real upset at these terrorists who won't accept our arrangements for running *their* country!"

The silence was absolute. Janowitz glanced at Pershing. What was going on in his brain? He knew Pershing wasn't calcified in his convictions the way Miller was. Pershing was too open to hang onto a belief that he couldn't honestly hold up to the light. Had Evans got to him? God, Janowitz hoped so. He was feeling butterflies again. Evans' fire made him all the more determined to go along—unless it was something impossible. But how he hoped he could take the others with him.

"Listen," Miller said, "I've seen pictures of a family the VC butchered. I don't think the Irish ever did that to their own kind."

Evans burst into laughter. Miller reached forward like lightning, grabbed his ankle, and pulled his legs out from under him. He was on him before any of them could do anything about it. Shots tore into the wall above them, and the guards came running, but Miller had smashed Evans in the face twice before Janowitz and Pershing could haul him off. The guards shooed the rest of them back with their guns.

Evans' nose poured blood, and he was going to have a welt on his cheek, but after a second he struggled to his feet. He said something to the guards in French, but they wouldn't obey. Then Big Tack and little Toe came scurrying in, drawn by the shots. Tick wasn't far behind. There was a big confab, with Evans trying to assure everyone everything was all right, but Tick insisted Miller's hands be bound, and for the rest of the session the three musketeers sat around behind them fondling their AK-47's.

Evans was forced to hold a hunk of bloody cotton to his nose, but at first he seemed almost amused by the incident.

"I laughed, Miller," he explained, "because my field of study at Louvain was the Renaissance, and one of the areas we covered was Irish history in the sixteenth and seventeenth centuries. Unfortunately it was mostly a tale of Irishman slaughtering Irishman in the most ingenious ways. Ireland was sort of Europe's Congo, and as the records tell it, one of the favorite pastimes of warring Irish soldiers was to rip the baby from a mother's womb and then stab it in front of her eyes."

"Bullshit!" Miller glowered.

Evans smiled again. "Then of course, when that group was domi-

263

nant, they did the same to the other side's women and children. Would *that* make sense to you?" His voice had grown harsh and demanding. Miller only grunted fiercely.

"Because that's what's happening here!" Evans went on, relentlessly. "The Liberation Front spreads around pictures just like we do, Miller. Pictures of women and children burned, maimed, *killed* by American guns and planes. And many of the men fighting have lost family of their own." He nodded to Toe. "Thao, whom you call Toe, would probably be a soldier in any era. He likes soldiering. But he will fight this war to the death because he once had a wife and a daughter—and both of them were killed in an American air raid on an undefended village. I don't think he hates any of us as individuals particularly. But America is an enemy, and he will fight on and on as long as we are here.

"And Tran Van Tho, whom you call Tick, is a Communist. He *does* hate us—collectively and individually." They all were uncomfortably aware that Tick—sitting behind them—could understand what Evans was saying. "His parents died in the war against the French. His sister, who was also a member of the Liberation Front, was killed in a B-52 napalm attack. His wife and *three* children were sunk on a sampan by a naval patrol boat.

"When people like Tick—and there are many—come upon the families of men who have been collaborating with Americans—and profiting by it—their mercies are often just as violent as those of the Irish warriors of the Renaissance.

"Of course, there are atrocities. After all the years of fighting, what would you expect, Miller?" He turned to Pershing. "What would *you* expect? If Negro children were being slaughtered by white bombs, white napalm, white pellet bombs, how would *you* react, Pershing? How would you treat the Uncle Toms then? And *their* children?"

"Don't pull that shit, Evans!" Pershing shot back harshly. "Keep off that! Negroes aren't being bombed, and we aren't bombing Vietnamese as Vietnamese either. We're bombing Communist gunmen, and their supporters—whatever their color. If they were white Russians, or white anything else, it wouldn't make any difference!"

"Yeah?" Evans smiled icily. "You want to think about that statement. You'd bomb Russian children, too, eh? Well, that *is* democratic. And Russian women and old men—the lot. Well, *you* aren't prejudiced!"

"That isn't what he meant," Hill said virulently. "You watch your ass, son, or we'll be having *you* for breakfast tomorrow."

264

Janowitz looked at him. Evans had overstepped. Hill had murder in his eyes.

But Evans came right back at him. "Well, if he's so concerned about children," he said with a nod to Pershing, "and what the terrorists might do to them, you tell him to get his ass out of Vietnam— and take the rest of his flag-waving patriots with him! Because the Communists may be short of a lot of things, but you take a look at the children in Russia and Yugoslavia and Poland—and even China— and you'll see they don't fry them or tear them to pieces with pellet bombs. The children do all right in those 'horrible' countries. They get food and medicine and education and lots of tender loving care! And if he's so concerned about kids, he should take his carcass out of Vietnam because he and his kind have made it about the worst place on the face of the earth to be a child of any age!"

"You're ranting at the wrong man," Miller said from between clenched teeth.

"*Am I?*" Evans hissed. "Well, I'll tell you, Miller, and him, too. You just leave these people alone, and you won't have to worry about their children *or* their teachers! You just look around you up here and you'll see more teachers than you ever saw in South Vietnam and more children, too! And they're doing all right. *When we're not bombing the piss out of them!*"

He had squelched them. Even Hill looked away.

vi

They ate their lunch in absolute silence. When they finished, Janowitz asked Pershing to take a walk with him. Pershing hesitated but finally stood up, and Janowitz looked over at Evans, half expecting to be stopped. But Evans just smiled that shit-eating grin of his. So Janowitz turned to Hill and signaled him to the door, too.

The three of them wandered silently down the main street, staying in the shade of the trees, only glancing up when a plane buzzed over. They kept looking back to see if they were being trailed—but they didn't see anyone.

They went as far as the church. Pershing genuflected toward the altar when they passed around the front. His face was locked in concentration. They finally settled down behind the church with their backs against a broken bit of the church wall and sat looking out over the flat rice fields to the haze of the hills beyond. Hill and Pershing lit up cigarettes, and then Hill spoke their first words.

"I'm going to fertilize me some North Vietnamese rice," he said soberly. When he got back, he grinned at Janowitz. "That's better. Now what've you got on your mind, Lieutenant?"

"I thought we ought to have a word without Evans around," Janowitz said, fighting his usual urge to smile at even the simplest question from Hill. Pershing nodded out in front of them. Janowitz looked. A buffalo boy was sitting on top of a water buffalo far across the fields, prodding it along with a stick as it slowly moved between two fields. A plane had broken from the hills, and the kid had just spotted it. He stared for a time, then slid off the buffalo, standing so it was between him and the plane. The plane buzzed low and passed on. The kid watched it for a time, then scrambled back up on the buffalo's back. Janowitz shook his head—he'd actually been worried.

"Well, there's another one we missed," Hill muttered in mock reproof. Pershing punched him on the shoulder.

"Pershing," Janowitz began tentatively—he felt at ease with these two, despite the hurdle between him and Pershing. "I get the feeling we're losing a lot of these arguments because maybe we're in the wrong."

He'd meant it to be mildly ironic, but Hill whooped. "You get that feeling, do you, Lieutenant?" and he slapped Janowitz on the back. Pershing was smiling, too, but not very enthusiastically.

"What the hell," Janowitz said, "it's not the end of the goddamned world. But I'm afraid that I, for one, think we've made one huge fucking mistake. We're beating the shit out of the wrong people—not even for the wrong reason, but for no reason at all. And I get the feeling that if we really dug what was going on here, we'd be cheering the VC." Pershing's face was thoughtful, pensive, but still half-frozen in a grin. "You can't win 'em all," Janowitz went on. "Most of the moves we've made in our history I think were right, but if this one is wrong, I don't see any advantage in hammering away at it until we've exterminated the whole damned country." He waited, then quietly asked, "Do you?"

"Well, Lieutenant," Pershing began, "there are things about this war I don't like." His voice carried the same note of light irony Janowitz had used. "But it seems to me there are ways of disagreeing and *ways* of disagreeing. Joining up with the enemy strikes me as sort of taking things to extremes." They all laughed.

266

"Well, we're in a rather difficult position to protest," Janowitz replied. "I don't think the VC are going to let us off for a parade down Pennsylvania Avenue."

"Well, maybe we just better wait until we get back then," Pershing said more seriously.

Janowitz looked at him. He wasn't stonewalling.

"If it were an argument, or a basketball game, or something like that," Janowitz said, "I'd be inclined to agree with you. But I don't think I'm put together in a way that I can go on watching these people getting chopped up just because we got our signals mixed."

"Well, sir," Pershing said, "I'm sure your intentions are all right, and maybe even Evans' are, too. But you want to remember that some of the people being chopped up are Americans. We've got guys down South right this minute who are being sliced with VC mortar, who won't ever walk right again, won't see again—some of them won't breathe again. I think before you do anything rash, you ought to give a little thought to them."

Janowitz looked at him closely. "You being straight with me, Pershing," he asked, "or am I supposed to take all that as sarcasm?"

Pershing's smile went on and off like lightning. "When I'm being sarcastic, you'll know it, Lieutenant."

"I'll keep my eyes open," Janowitz said offhandedly. Keep it cool, he thought. "Let's say we *are* here mistakenly," he began. "Won't you agree that you can't very well shoot people up, and then when they shoot back at you, say, 'Well, you bastards, now that you've got some of our guys, we're *really* going to get you!' . . . If we hadn't sent troops here in the first place, they wouldn't have got shot up." He shook his head. "Frankly, I'm kinda surprised to hear that they-killed-my-buddy stuff from you."

"Well, you say they got emotions; we got 'em too."

"Oh, come off it, Pershing," Janowitz replied. "A bunch of thugs come into your house and shoot your wife—you shoot one of them back, and *they* get mad because you killed their buddy. That's nuts. We get our asses out of here, and there won't be a death roll of GI's to get emotional about."

Pershing shrugged noncommittally, but Janowitz felt sure he had him. "Shit, I've always been embarrassed by that our-heroes-overseas routine," he said. "Bums, unemployables, and niggers back home"— Hill and Pershing glanced at him, but despite the quiver of unease, he knew he could call it as it came—"but big heroes once they're stuffed in uniform and sent over here. Jesus, you read the American magazines and they talk about our gallant Marines here and our poor hospitalized boys there. Lyndon Johnson talking about the Alamo."

He shook his head. "Do you remember when our dear Lyndon first brought that up? It was when the Marines were trying to retake Hue during Tet. Remember? Man, here are a few hundred VC—surrounded in their own country by thousands of foreigners hitting 'em with tanks, napalm, bombs, rockets; we've got planes, ships, helicopters, tanks, rocket launchers, everything, zeroed in on these bastards. And this little band of VC are holding out against it all—just like the Texans. And who brings up the Alamo? Our Lyndon! Only he's talking about our side, not theirs!

"Shit," he went on, *"we've* fought with courage; *they've* fought with courage. I hate to see any sonuvabitch cut up, but even by our figures we kill about ten of them to every one of our guys; we've plastered their country with several tons of bombs for every man, woman, and child in it; we've used defoliants, napalm, white phosphorus, gas —and then we've got the guts to talk about our gallant boys as though they were the only ones hurtin'. Fuck all the gallant Vietnamese men, women, and children . . . and the sick and the tired and the old. At least our guys are healthy, well-fed young bucks."

Pershing stretched out, putting his hands above his head, and grimaced at the pain it brought to his ribs. "Tell me, Lieutenant," he said softly, "if you got killed, do you think your mother would give a shit about all the gallant Vietnamese men, women, and children? Or would she think maybe you were her 'gallant son who died overseas'?"

"Man"—Janowitz staggered—"what the hell kind of question is that?"

"A straight one," Pershing replied.

Janowitz shrugged. He'd answer it straight. "Sure I'd be a hero to her, and I suppose she'd hate the Vietnamese at first. But shit, Pershing, when the Germans were shooting their way through Europe, don't you think German mothers felt the same way about their sons? I don't care how bravely we fight or how many die, if we have no right to be here, we should get the hell out. All we owe the dead is justice —not revenge."

"*I* want to get the hell out," Hill said brightly. "Not too soon, though. I want me one more tour in Saigon. If we're going to go along with Evans, I want a guarantee they won't stop the goddamned war in a day or so. Give me six months, dad, and they can do what they want with the country."

The smiles came back again, all around. But it was still uneasy.

268

The three of them just lay there for a long time, wrapped in their own thoughts, watching the buffalo boy slowly wend his way across the heat-hazed fields like some symbol of Vietnam—placid, unhurried, primeval.

"Well, Pershing baby?" Hill finally queried.

"Are you on his side?" Pershing asked.

"Dad, I'm on no side. You know that. But use that little ole noggin. If the war goes on five years, ten years, *twenty* years, where are *you* going to be? That's right, father. Rice and fish eyes for you until you're a bald granddaddy. Me, I'm a gambler. If Evans has got less chance than hitting the daily double of speeding this thing up by one day, well, it's still worth a fling, 'cause that's a day sooner I can turn in these GI gumboots on a Caddy convertible."

"Man, leave it to you to figure your own angle!" Pershing said acidly.

"Sure." Hill smiled. "What's buggin' me is the lieutenant's angle. He must have a real dolly back there in Detroit, because if they offered me his little piece and all the free rice I could eat, you'd have to haul me out of here with a herd of water buffalo."

Janowitz smiled, but he had an idea Hill was more vulnerable to Evans' arguments than he was making out.

"My trouble," Janowitz mused, "is this Communist economy. One woman at a time is just so far below my normal requirements I'm feeling deprived."

"Man, I knew those eggs would get him," Hill roared. "They've gone right to his imagination!"

Janowitz grinned, but he got back to the point. "Well, Pershing, what about it?"

"Lieutenant, I've got no personal ax to grind at all. My rank is as high as it's ever going to be; I'm lonesome to see my daughter and my wife. It kills me to see one Vietnamese kid caught up in this mess —and to be honest, my heart can even bleed a little for a VC when he hasn't got his sights aimed right up my ass. But for all that, what you're asking is impossible.

"Maybe these people are only being used by the Communists—let's say they are. I'm sorry. But we *can't* let them win. Communists in Vietnam are going to mean Communists in a lot of other places. Someplace we've got to draw the line. Rightly or wrongly my country has drawn it here. And I'm a soldier. I've just got to believe that for all the brutality going on now, there'd be more brutality if we quit. I don't mean in Vietnam. I'm not claiming the Communists would kill more people than the war is killing—but I mean in other wars in other places."

269

Janowitz stood. He stretched, glancing contemplatively at Pershing. It *was* better without Evans. There wasn't the bitterness; they all knew they were really on the same side. He picked up some pebbles and started tossing them out across the field. About twenty yards ahead the field sank a couple of inches and was marshy like the rice fields. The pebbles threw up little splashes of mud and water.

"Well, maybe that's right," Janowitz said speculatively, after he'd hashed it around for a while. "But it's very close to what Evans is saying, isn't it? We're using the Vietnamese people as a buffer against some distant possibility of aggression—just as the Russians used the Hungarians."

Pershing shrugged. "Like I say, I wish it didn't have to be."

Janowitz grinned and tossed another pebble. "Pretty rough on the Vietnamese."

"Yeah," Pershing conceded, "but I think there's a difference between us and the Russians."

Janowitz laughed. "Maybe. But it must be hard for the Vietnamese to see it."

Pershing nodded, but he was unmoved. Hill stood and grabbed a handful of pebbles. Janowitz threw; Hill tried to beat it. The pebble fell short. Janowitz grinned and wound up carefully. The splash was ten or fifteen yards beyond his others. Hill wound up grimly and fired savagely. He had aimed too low and the pebble sailed in only about thirty yards out.

"Great," Janowitz said.

"Fuck you, Yid," Hill retorted and fired again. It was good, but still short of Janowitz's last throw by at least ten yards. Janowitz grinned and lazily let fly another—as though he were only half trying. Hill grunted and threw with everything he had. It landed just short.

"Well, keep trying, boy," Janowitz deadpanned.

Hill gave him the finger, and they stood there—first one, then the other, tossing in a game Hill could never win.

Janowitz turned to Pershing between tosses. "I wonder if we're holding the line or just proving that a tiny country can take all the B-52's and napalm we can throw at it and still handle a half a million of us and another half million of our 'valiant allies.' Shit, *two* wars like this and we'd be flat on our asses."

Pershing smiled. "We ain't all *that* stretched."

"Maybe not"—Janowitz grinned—"but at the rate we're going here, a few tiny countries could immobilize our whole nation. It's obvious to us, and it must be obvious to everyone else."

270

Janowitz threw another stone. The more he thought about it, the more convinced he became that Pershing was wrong. "And anyway," he observed, "this isn't like 1939 and holding the line against Hitler. No one's *unprepared* now. In fact, everyone's bristling for a fight. But we can't have a war—a *real* war—and everyone knows it. We've got to find some way of living with the Russians—and the Chinese—*without* fighting. And before this damn thing blew up, it seemed to me we were inching toward that. I used to blame *them* for screwing it up, but now I'm not so sure. But I *am* sure that every month this goes on, it gets worse and worse. And the more dead there are on both sides and the more atrocities there are on both sides, the closer to the 'impossible' war we come. And then there *will* be some deaths; the whole world can look like Hue in five or six minutes. Is it worth that?"

Pershing looked at him thoughtfully.

"Look," Janowitz said, "we claim we want to end the war, too. Maybe what Evans has got in mind is something we can go along with."

Pershing laughed. "Why all this indoctrination if it's something we can go along with?"

"They may want to convince us it wouldn't be the end of the world if we did help them."

"Christ, they indoctrinate their own cats every damn day," Hill interjected. "Maybe it's just force of habit."

Janowitz kept his eyes on Pershing. "How many people are going to die today in Vietnam, Pershing? How many of ours, how many of theirs?" He nodded offhandedly to the church shell behind them. "Every Christmas"—he smiled—"you goddamned Catholics are shouting, 'Peace on earth, goodwill to men,' until it isn't safe to turn on the radio. What happens to all that jazz after December twenty-sixth?"

It was a contradiction that yet amused him. Catholics were always doing the good bit about love and understanding—until it came to Communism, and then it was all fury and ferocity. But he could see he had got to Pershing. He was thinking about peace on earth—maybe even goodwill to men.

"If Evans' plan doesn't involve killing Americans or making America look like hell," Janowitz said more seriously, "I think we ought to at least consider it. It won't hurt to find out what it is anyway."

"This sounds awfully familiar, Lieutenant," Pershing answered wearily. "Weren't you the officer who told me we could go along with their classes without worrying? They wouldn't get you, they wouldn't get me . . . and we could take care of the rest?"

Janowitz flushed. It seemed a million years ago.

"I—I still haven't done anything against my principles—or against my country," he mumbled. "And I don't intend to."

"We'll see," Pershing said with a slow smile.

"You'll hear him out then?" Janowitz asked.

Pershing nodded resignedly. "Only I warn you, Lieutenant, if I don't see it and you do, I'm going to give you so much static you're going to wish you never heard of John Andrew Pershing."

Janowitz laughed. He let fly with a pebble. It sailed far out—and made a small muddy splash.

vii

"So how come you didn't go to graduate school and get out of all this? Not enough brains, Lieutenant, sir?" Hill asked cheerfully, as he struggled to light a stringy VC cigarette.

They were parked down the street from their "home," watching the entrance from behind a crumbled wall. They had wandered through the countryside that lay beyond the church for a while. The natives were all siestaing, and those that were moving would look at them coolly—and smile if their eyes met directly—but they all fingered their guns like frontier farmers who'd just spotted a band of passing Indians. It was hot, and after a while they decided to go back, but once they were in sight of their "home" the thought of losing even their limited freedom chilled them all. So they went into the shell of one of the other houses and squatted down in the shade of the half-collapsed roof.

"Well," Janowitz answered patronizingly, "I thought of you struggling along over here on your own, Hill, and I said to hell with all this soft living. I was getting fat on malted milks and steak sandwiches, and I just figured I'd prefer squatting in the mud and eating rice with you." By the time the sentence was out he was half-sorry he'd opened his mouth. In this heat the thought of an ice-cold malted and a steak sandwich with crisp green lettuce was enough to make him wish he'd gone on for a PhD! Hill and Pershing looked as floored by the image as he was.

"The big truth is," Janowitz said with a sigh, "I didn't know what else to do. I'd figured I'd play pro ball for a few years, but the Army won't let you off for that." He smiled. "I'd taken biz ad—business administration to you slobs."

"Thanks, dad," Hill shot back with mocking gratitude.

"And I was planning on being a millionaire by the time I was thirty —or maybe thirty-one," Janowitz conceded imperturbably. "But the thought of another two years' studying management techniques and cost analysis and all that shit sounded grimmer than anything the Army might cook up." He chuckled with Hill's laugh. "Yeah—well, I was young and naïve then."

"Couldn't you have taught?" Pershing asked.

"I suppose I could have chiseled a high school job coaching and teaching athletics or something, but I hadn't taken any teacher training, and it would have been a dodge." He looked at Hill. "Anyway, you won't believe it, you sonuvabitch, but I *wanted* to join the Army. Not to fight Uncle Ho. That didn't figure in it one way or the other. But I'd been in the academic, practice-all-afternoon, study-all-night grind since I first went to high school. I had to work every vacation and count pennies until I had calluses on my fingers. I was ready to get out. I wanted to do something I could tell my grandchildren about, not just walk through life in one big predictable rut."

"Come on"—Hill smirked—"don't tell me when you were playing ball up there and gettin' your pictures in all the papers you had to work!"

"Listen, son, Michigan's one of those palaces of purity. You're fucking A I had to work. They helped fix me up with some summer jobs, and I got to eat at the training table, but there was no cash—and no fiddling the grades either. Why do you think I'm so damn bright, boy?"

Hill dusted his cigarette ash on him.

"Well, you sure are going to have something to tell your grandchildren about," Pershing mused.

"Yeah, well, maybe I overdid it," Janowitz acknowledged wryly.

"What the hell do you really want to do?" Hill asked. His eyes had narrowed, holding Janowitz in a sardonic grin. "When you finish slummin' with us coloreds, I mean. What's your big aim in life?"

Janowitz smiled thoughtfully. "I haven't got a clue," he said pensively. "I hated all that business administration shit. It's even worse than slummin' with you, Hill—sometimes. I always figured I'd make enough playing pro ball to set myself up some kind of business of my own, and even if I didn't like it, I'd know I was doing it for me. Being a slave to someone else's profit targets is not my idea of living."

"Isn't there anything you want to be? Banker? Doctor? Something like that?" Pershing asked. Janowitz could tell by his tone of voice that, like Hill, he seemed to think any college-educated white could call

273

his shots any way he liked. Pershing always appeared so level-headed, but now he sounded just like all the other urchins at the window. It all looked great on the inside—there couldn't be any problems there.

"I'd have to start college all over again to be a doctor—and I ain't got the stamina for that." Janowitz groaned. "And so what's a banker? Shit, I'd go mad. All neat and 'yes, sir' and 'no, sir' for forty years and most of the time you aren't making as much as a respectable street cleaner."

"Come on!" Hill cut in. "Man, you're a big college star; you got all that Jewish buddy-buddy stuff working for you. You'd be vice-president the first week."

"On those terms"—Janowitz laughed—"I'd think about it."

"Why, you pricks got the world by the short hairs," Hill said, leaning back luxuriously as though imagining himself in the same position. "You're a goddamned minority like us, but you got it all cornered, all the loot, all the interesting jobs, TV, the movies—"

"Dry cleaning, dressmaking, pawnbroking—yeah, all that interesting stuff," Janowitz added dryly.

"Yeah, but don't tell me you couldn't walk into any job you wanted," Hill went on undeterred. "Man, I thought about it plenty. I don't want to be white. I want to be a white Jew. It's your only animal."

"That's what Hitler thought." Janowitz grinned.

"Mere jealousy," Hill cracked. "If you can't join 'em, beat 'em."

They all broke up. Janowitz felt great. Man, there was so much you buried in everyday life. The Army was crap, but there were aspects of it he loved.

"Now come on, Yid, sir," Hill nagged playfully. "You going to tell me that after all you did for Michigan, you wouldn't be sort of a Jewish Pope—and could call your shots any way you want?"

"That's *exactly* what I'm telling you." Janowitz laughed. "What the hell do you think we got? Half my relatives aren't even speaking to the other half. You come around pulling that Jews-stand-together shit with them and they'd ram a flaming menorah up your ass."

"What's a menorah?" Pershing asked quickly.

"Never mind," Janowitz answered. "You get the picture!" And they all laughed again.

"I thought Jews always helped each other," Hill insisted. "That's the whole bit."

"Is that right?" Janowitz came back. "Well, I thought niggers always ate corn pone and practiced incest by the numbers."

274

Hill shrugged, a thoughtful grin still on his face. "It's wrong?" he asked dubiously. It broke them up again.

"I can't say for sure about corn pone and incest," Janowitz finally replied, "but when my old man died, he'd been a cantor in the local synagogue for about fifteen years. Everyone cried over my mother as if it were the spring monsoons. And some people did help for a while. But my mother had to sell our store—and she took a beating on it. To my second cousin. Then she needed a job, and she finally got one. No relative, but he's from our synagogue. He did her a big favor. She —and fifteen other women—decorate cakes for his bakery, from three in the morning to one in the afternoon, five days a week. Union rates." He grimaced philosophically. "It's all right. My mother *likes* decorating cakes, and she's good at it. But as I recall she didn't have to turn down the vice-presidency of the bakery to take the job."

He could see that Hill was genuinely surprised. It made Janowitz smile again. "Man," he said, "it may shock you after meeting a sensational genius like me, but Jews are people. They've been kicked around enough so that they've learned a little about sticking together when the going's rough, and they've been forced to learn that money and power can save them from a lot of unpleasantness, but if you think it's some kind of union with admission by circumcision you've got another think coming.

"Hell, I might get a shoo-in to a lot of companies—Jewish and non-Jewish—because I played ball at Michigan, but I'll bet my left nut against one of your gold teeth that if I didn't perform, the *first* outfit that would plant my ass on the pavement would be the Jewish one. That I promise you." He grinned with ironic conviction.

"Oh, I don't know," Hill groaned. "All my fucking illusions getting shattered. I shoulda stayed in Philly. Have you told that little VC girl you're Jewish?" he asked solemnly, as if he were talking about VD. Janowitz clubbed him in the chest with the back of his hand. Hill went into a mock attack of TB—coughing asthmatically until Janowitz was laughing so hard Pershing had to reach across and silence them both before they were heard down the street. Just as Janowitz acknowledged Pershing's warning, a little Vietnamese man, about ninety to judge from his wrinkled skin, peered over the wall at them from the house next door. He was hauling a big piece of timber he'd pulled from the wreckage, and he was staring at them as if they were from another galaxy. They all rolled around, trying to keep from laughing out loud, but reduced to hysteria by the round, immobile eyes that continued to stare at them in wonder and disbelief.

He finally lowered his head, and they could see the piece of timber bobbing off down the street. It took a long time for them to get back to where they could breathe normally.

"Jesus," Pershing said finally. "We'll probably look like that if Evans keeps at us a few more years." And they were grabbing their sides again.

"So come on, Lieutenant," Hill said at last. "Isn't there anything you wanted to be—like a big movie star, or a senator, or some jazz like that?"

"I wanted to play basketball," Janowitz said wistfully. "The only other job that's ever looked good to me was my dad's. We had a neighborhood bakery. I used to love the smell of the dough, the ovens heating, the grain of the wood on the tables, the stuff coming out, golden, warm, smelling like heaven. We were near a school, and guys used to come in for lunch—right into the baking room. And Dad served up bread and rolls straight from the ovens—my mother cut it up —with corned beef, hamburgers, pickles on the side, cupcakes, apple strudel for finishers. The guys loved it; I loved it; my dad loved it." He smiled at Hill. "He never made much money, mind you, but he loved it."

"So why don't you have a bakery then?" Pershing asked gravely.

Janowitz shrugged. "Maybe, for kicks someday. But you can't run a bakery like that nowadays. You can have a factory that mass produces baked goods—but a little neighborhood bakery?" He shook his head. "No, my dad was a baker, and his father—in Vienna. And before that the family were bakers in Czechoslovakia. Only it was all Austria then—the Austro-Hungarian Empire. . . . And me, I'm the Janowitz that's going to break the chain." He knew the absurd tinge of melancholy he felt about it was creeping into his voice, and he tried to shake it. "No, I think I'll start a new tradition, Hill. I'm going to learn your trade—pimping."

Hill looked across at him sharply. The smile came slowly, "Well, Lieutenant, it doesn't smell like a bakery—that I can guarantee you— but on the other hand, I don't see it ever being turned out in a factory either."

viii

When they finally went back to the house, they expected everyone to be waiting for them, but they got little more than a glance.

Big Tack was the center of a major operation. A fire had been lit in one of the corners, and Tack was sitting on a box near it like a king on a throne, his legs spread wide, his chest out—and his face covered with shaving cream. Big tits was shaving him, circling around him, and he kept grabbing feels from her, patting her butt, smooching at her with his fat, lather-covered lips. He'd got her several times because she had little patches of shaving cream on her cheeks and neck, her fore-head, even on her chin. She was enjoying it all, laughing, swatting at him with her hands, and flitting artfully—and familiarly—in and out of his arms. Now they *got* to be doing it, Janowitz thought. There was something about big tits' brassiness and Tack's earthiness that went to-gether like rice and fish. He wondered how he'd failed to notice it be-fore.

Hieu was on the other side of the fire shaving one of the guards. They both looked pretty subdued compared to Tack and big tits, but the guard was eyeing her as she moved about him solemnly absorbed in the job at hand. A flame of anger and jealousy went right through Janowitz. The guard said something with a nod to Tack, and Hieu burst into a smile as radiant as any she'd ever given Janowitz. It was torture. If she smiled like that at everyone, who the hell would ever leave her alone?

Only Thai and Tick had remained clean-shaven through the whole trip, but now, as Janowitz looked around, he saw that everyone had been shaved. Russell and Miller both looked ten years younger, and Miller's grim ruggedness had been transformed into a cheery rosiness. He looked like one of those beer ads. A thick-chested, beer-drinking man, shining with health and vigor.

"Hey, buffalo!" Tack had spotted Janowitz, and he spread his arms as though he expected him to run right into them. "Come with Trach. Okay? We wait for you, GI! Come here!"

He turned to the guard and yelled obscenities at him, shooing him imperiously off the other box, shaving cream and all.

"Hey, come, buffalo! Her mare wait for you, okay!" He roared with laughter. Hieu was busily rinsing the razor in the pot of water over the fire, but she glanced at Janowitz as he approached, and her face wrote books for him. She was smiling at Tack's performance, but her eyes said she was sorry for the fun being made of them, said the sight of him stopped things in her, as they did in him. Janowitz thought, my God, how can I ever take home a VC who doesn't even speak Eng-lish? No, Mom, she's not Jewish—she's Catholic. Oh, and Mom, she's Vietnamese—and she can't speak English. He grinned at the idea, almost laughed, and Tack roared again—he'd seen the exchange of glances between Janowitz and Hieu, and it was a language he recognized.

"Hey, buffalo," Tack roared, "there are one good mare, okay? Big eyes! *Amour, amour! Beaucoup* the little buffalos, okay!" He smacked his lips, kissing at Hieu.

Janowitz sat down on the box, and Hieu fixed him a pan of hot water to wash in and set a pail of cold beside her. Tack didn't stop; he was either jabbering lasciviously in Vietnamese at big tits—drawing laughs from her and fleeting embarrassed smiles from Hieu—or roaring obscenely at Janowitz in broken English.

The whole thing got to Hieu. She began to titter, and by the time she started shaving him, her face was a wreath of smiles. Tack was all shaved before she had finished. Sitting with big tits on his lap, he watched the two of them as if he were master of some great Oriental whorehouse showing off a prize new doxy to his best customer.

Hieu finished slowly and deliberately. When she went for the water again, Big Tack reached out for her backside, but she skirted around him. She brought more hot water, washed Janowitz's face, and dried it carefully with a cotton cloth, and then, with her hands still on the cloth, she tilted his head slightly and, in front of them all, kissed him flush on the mouth.

Tack bellowed! When Hieu pulled her face away, she held Janowitz's eyes as though they were alone in a world that had been totally depopulated. Janowitz was stoned. Maybe Hill was right—let the war last twenty years. Hieu and rice were all he needed.

Tack had sprung up and grabbed Hieu, and now he lifted her in the air, shouting something in Vietnamese, then plopped her down in front of Janowitz. "Buffalo, we make—how you say?—*don* for you! Trach make for you *un cadeau magnifique!*" And he picked her up again and started off with her like King Kong with Fay Wray. Big tits ran along beside him chattering delightedly, while Hieu just took it all with a dark, imperturbable smile.

Big tits came back in about twenty minutes, with a big smirk on her face. She finished shaving the guard that Tack had forced from Hieu's chair and then shaved Pershing and Hill. As usual, she lavished enough deliberate care on each to make them both ready to bite on the spot —and Hill gave her quite a time. But Janowitz was too preoccupied really to enjoy it. His stomach was churning from his response to Hieu, and his mind was racing with the realization that he was about to face Evans and say that—on acceptable conditions—they were ready to

278

go along with him. It was worse than pregame butterflies. It was like his first parachute jump.

By the time big tits had finished with Hill the sun was hanging like a great celestial orange over the hills to the west. Little Toe, looking even smaller and uglier without his beard, had brought in a bunch of vegetables, and big tits went to work preparing dinner. The food was getting better every day. They had carrots now—huge ones—and cauliflower and big hunks of onion in the rice. Fish was still a once-a-day treat, but Janowitz could remember many a daily special at the Student Union that hadn't tasted all that much better than the fare they were getting now. The smell of it cooking made him ravenous.

They were already eating when Thai, Evans, and Tick returned. They had brought bikes—one for each of them. Clean-shaven, Evans looked impossibly young. He brought his bowl over and sat across from Janowitz, smiling tentatively. He seemed to have something special on his mind. Watching him in the growing dark, Janowitz suddenly wondered how the hell the guy had done it. Without his beard he looked almost fragile, ineffectual, the last guy in the world to take on five GI's—especially five like this lot. Yet he had taken them on, and maybe he'd even won.

And then Tack returned. He grabbed a bowl and stuffed himself as he gabbled exuberantly to Thai. Thai glanced across at Janowitz a couple of times as Tack spieled and finally nodded consent to something. Although Tack's enthusiasm was infectious, Thai hadn't condescended to smile. He was tolerating, rather than participating. But Tack was not to be squelched; he held out his arms to Janowitz. "Buffalo! I make for you heaven!"

He motioned Janowitz up, and Janowitz stood.

"He's going to blow you, right here, for dessert," Hill said tonelessly.

All the GI's laughed, but Janowitz followed Tack as the big VC kept backing up, drawing him over to the corner where the fire was. He made Janowitz sit, placing him carefully behind the fire; then he stood erect and shouted in Vietnamese, clapping his hands together at the same time.

Janowitz heard the whistles before he could see anything. Then he saw Hieu coming toward him from beyond the fire. Had he not been so used to seeing her in the dark of night he might not have recognized her. Her hair had been fixed—fluffed around her face to frame her cheekbones in black—and there were loose bangs across her forehead. In the light of the fire it was as though her face were some glowing treasure set in black satin. The cheekbones, the mouth that sometimes seemed too big were part of a whole that an emperor couldn't fault. No wonder the French hadn't wanted to leave! She wore a white silk au-dai with a high collar and, down its side, a pattern of tiny stitched flowers that were repeated here and there across the dress. One rested just above her right breast like a demure medal.

She paused across the fire from Janowitz, but her eyes never left his. He shook his head incredulously.

Big Tack jumped into action. "Hey, buffalo—make something, okay!" He picked Hieu up and set her down right in front of Janowitz. Janowitz could think of nothing more than to thank God he was shaved. Tack pushed her toward him, and Janowitz wrapped his arms around her.

But it wasn't like before. With Thai and Evans there, he couldn't bring himself to ignore the others as she was doing, but he was so stunned by her he felt a sort of pride. Not quite of possession—but close to it.

He led her over to the big box where Tack had been shaved and sat her down formally. Tack clapped his hands; so did big tits. Then he got her a bowl and chopsticks and brought her her dinner. She was amused, but obviously uncomfortable. Vietnamese men did not wait on their women. Janowitz walked back and got his own bowl, ignoring Evans and Thai and whispering, "Piss off!" to Hill, who was groaning under a highly dramatized attack of masculine envy. As for Hieu, he thought, girl, just wait until all this is over and I get you by myself; then you can be submissive Vietnamese female and I'll be your dominant male all right—two times over.

But Thai and Evans had other plans. It had just about got to the point where the others were ignoring Hieu and Janowitz when Evans got up and walked over to them.

"We'd like you to make a little trip with us," he told Janowitz quietly. He glanced at Hieu fleetingly. "We ought to be back before midnight." It wasn't leering, but he obviously knew what was in Janowitz's mind. "You'd better come now."

It was as close to a command as anything Evans had ever said to him. Janowitz shrugged nonchalantly. "I'll think about it. Where we going?" One thing he did not intend to do—ever—was take orders from Evans. Cooperation Evans might win, but he was never going to command it.

Evans blinked; he dug the resistance all right. "Just for a bike ride." He tried to smile. "We had hoped to start before it gets too late."

That's more like it, Janowitz thought. He stood and kissed Hieu behind her ear. She rubbed her head against his. Boy, we'd better be back by midnight!

"Hey, buffalo, I keep him for you, okay?" Tack shouted as Janowitz started out the door.

"You keep him hands off her, that's what you do!" Janowitz yelled back.

He'd been aware of the night traffic in the street—their first evening it had even awakened him, and he'd noticed the sound of engines among the other noises—but this was his first real look at it. The trees that lay across the street all day, making it look as though the road were still blocked, were neatly stacked along the side of the street, and bicycles, carts, and a few trucks were moving freely through the town.

Janowitz got on the bike little Toe trundled out for him, and Evans and Thai got on the others. They were English-style bikes—thin tires, with the brakes on the handlebars—and they were damned good ones. It'd throw you eighty or ninety bucks for a bike like that in the States, Janowitz thought, and he wondered if the North Vietnamese made them or if they got them from England.

Thai led the way. They traveled due west, and because they were the only ones on the road without loads, they seemed to be flying through the countryside. Evans rode tail, but he didn't have a gun, and Janowitz thought fleetingly of his chances of escape. He didn't have the motivation for it he once had, but in many ways it would resolve a lot of dark doubts. But everyone else on the road carried guns strapped across his load or across his back. All Evans had to do was shout, and he would have two hundred guys shooting for him.

They cycled for an hour before taking a break, and Thai's pace was so fast that Janowitz was covered with sweat. He'd long since got his second wind, but it was hard work, and he was grateful for the chance to rest.

It still hadn't cooled off, but Thai unrolled the blanket tied under the seat of his bike and wrapped it around him. Janowitz decided he'd better do the same. He didn't want to stiffen up if they were going to cycle long like this.

They didn't speak for a time; then Evans smiled at him. He seemed more at ease when the others weren't around, as though he had something in common with Janowitz, and Janowitz suddenly remembered that first morning he'd awakened him: "I'm Evans. Heyward Lee Evans from Bluefield, Virginia . . . It's a name you'd expect from Virginia." God, that was a million light-years away, Heyward Lee

Evans—but in a funny way I don't know much more about you now than I did then.

"When I was in my infantry outfit," Evans said, "we always joked about how lazy the Vietnamese were. If we'd ever known how much work they do at night—" He nodded at the heaving backs pedaling and walking along the road.

Janowitz watched the procession for a while; then suddenly they heard bugles distantly—then closer—and there was a mad scurry to get off the road. All the loads had laurel branches tied all over them, and every hat and back carried them, too. There was frantic activity for about sixty seconds while bikes and carts were pushed and pulled off to the side of the road and everything arranged so that nothing but laurel showed straight up. The activity slowed and finally stopped, and when it did, Janowitz heard the sound of planes.

The whole countryside that had hummed with activity and then crashed into panic was now silent—with just the drone of the approaching planes hanging ominously over it. Flares went out. Yellow, orange, white. They must have been five or six miles away. They lit up an area of the sky, but the ground near the road remained shadowed and dark.

They heard the thud of bombs some distance off but couldn't see any explosions. The planes passed over them. Gradually the flares faded, and darkness returned. In a couple of minutes the road started filling up again. The activity was slower, and you were more conscious of the effort, but it didn't seem long before the traffic was flowing along as smoothly as before.

"You know, Evans," Janowitz said as they sat watching the stream go past like some procession of ants instinctively scurrying to and from some important task. "Something's been bothering me ever since you first spoke to me after we were captured. What did I ever say in that class in Manila that made you pick on me?"

Evans chuckled. "It wasn't much," he said. He was plainly amused that it should have been troubling Janowitz all this time. "In the first place, you said you'd toured Eastern Europe and part of Russia. I toured Eastern Europe, too. Not playing basketball—with a Christian study group. But I didn't really believe that any reasonable person who had seen life there could conclude that it was so much worse than life in America that it was worth slaughtering a nation of people like the Vietnamese over the difference. At least that was one thing."

"Yeah? So what was the other?" Janowitz pursued.

282

Evans ducked his head, smiling. "You bought an ice-cream cone," he said, and laughed at Janowitz's puzzlement. Thai laughed, too.

"What'dya mean, 'I bought an ice-cream cone'?"

"One hot day after you'd dropped out of class, I saw you in downtown Manila. It was on one of those side streets off the Escolta. You don't see many GI's down there—not in daytime. Anyway, there was an ice-cream cart on the corner and you went up and bought a cone—three dips, I remember."

"Is that a signal among international Communists or something?" Janowitz asked wryly.

Evans laughed again. "No. But watching you dig into it made me long for one, too. So when you walked away, I went over and ordered one."

"And you found a message from Mao in frozen chocolate sauce?"

"In a way." Evans grinned. "The vendor was busy. He made four cones while I stood waiting in the hot sun. Then he whistled at some kids in a doorway down the street and passed them around."

"So that makes me a revolutionary?"

"No," Evans said quietly, "but you'll admit that most Americans walk right by the short-changed in this world without a thought—never mind buying them triple-deck ice-cream cones. His voice grew more serious. "It wasn't much to go on, I know. But at least it showed you had the imagination to understand what it might be like to be a kid on a hot Manila street and not have the money for an ice-cream cone. I hoped you might be able to see what it felt like to be a Vietnamese, too."

"And that's how I got into all this?" Janowitz said incredulously.

"Not altogether." Evans smiled. "By accident your name was on a list of officers that fell into the Front's hands. I remembered the name; then I remembered the other things . . . and, from then, it all sort of happened." His voice had grown very still.

Thai studied Janowitz attentively, then smiled abruptly and started rolling his blanket. In a couple of minutes they were on the road again, cycling past the endless lines of trudging Vietnamese.

In about fifteen minutes they hit the first foothills and started to climb. It was hard work, but in another twenty minutes Thai stopped at a small village. Five black-pajamaed North Vietnamese were sitting by the road waiting for them. Only one of them seemed over twenty. He had a full mustache and looked like a Mexican—and he was obviously the leader. He spoke a few words to Thai and then led them out of the village on a trail that headed right into the side of a hill that overlooked the main road. Soon the trail ended, and they parked their bikes. They climbed a bit, then twisted behind a tall maze of undergrowth and were at the entrance of a huge cave.

When they stepped inside its limestone walls, the mustachioed leader lit an oil-soaked torch, and there was a blood-chilling whirl of activity as thousands of bats fluttered and screeched around them. The other members of the group struck torches from the first, and gradually the frenzied swirling of the bats was reduced to an occasional swoop and dart across the white, shadowed interior.

The place looked like a huge hangar. And that's what it was. The centerpiece was draped in strips of canvas, but even before the torches were placed in crevasses in the wall, Janowitz recognized the big Huey for what it was.

And he knew what they wanted him for.

Not the details. They really didn't matter. They had picked him to fly that big-assed bird. What for was not so important; at least he now knew why *him*. It clutched at his throat and washed him with relief at the same time. It wasn't esoteric and doctrinaire. It wasn't about Communism and freedom or capitalism and colonial underdogs. And it wasn't a mistake. They simply needed a helicopter pilot who could handle a Huey. It was so fucking simple. He wished Evans had said so in the first place. It would have saved a lot of anguish.

When they got all the canvas off, he could see that the bird was not exactly in flight-line condition. In the first place it was an old model, H-34C. The tail stabilizer was half shot away. The propeller on the rear rotor was chewed up, the nose-turret perspex was shattered, the shocks on the starboard side were gone, and the bird was being held level by a stack of mud bricks. There was a sickening bend in the nacelle paneling just to the rear of the air intakes that suggested the steel supports for the main rotor and gearbox might have buckled. But for all that, it was a bird, and given the proper attention, it looked as if it could do what it was meant to do.

"Well?" Evans began lightly. "Do you think it'll fly?"

"Not like that it won't."

"Assuming we could make reasonable repairs?" Thai asked.

Janowitz shrugged. He wandered over closer to it. He loved flying the cock-eyed things. He never thought he would love anything as much as basketball, but there were moments when he was fluttering some eggbeater across the treetops when his whole being exalted at the thrill of it. And he knew that he was good at it, just as he was at basketball. And even that smacked of false modesty. He wasn't just *good*—he was better than that. It was like handling the ball. Your genes carry some fluke equipment, you practice, practice, practice, and then one miracle day the goddamned ball becomes part of you. You own it. And the same with those birds. They say it's like patting your head, rolling your stomach, and dancing to different times with both feet. But he could make them talk. And standing there with the smell of it rousing memories of dawn takeoffs, of long sweeps along lazy Vietnamese rivers, of those early training days in New Mexico with cloudless days and a tarmac hot to the touch of the foot, he had to fight the urge to get in the cockpit and make the big puddle jumper hum. They mustn't know how eager he was—not yet anyway.

"Go on up," Evans said, as though he had a coaxial cable right to Janowitz's cerebrum.

God, I'm a great actor, Janowitz thought. Really had him fooled. But he climbed through the open barn doors and walked toward the cockpit. As he did, the memories of that first meeting with Evans rushed back at him, overwhelming, like a great wave breaking. Adnapoz. The last time he'd been in a chopper Big Tack had shot Adnapoz while Evans watched. And that kid on the gun in the barn doors. He felt half-sick. What was he doing helping these bastards? He wheeled angrily. Evans was getting to his feet in the cabin. Thai was just climbing aboard. Although it was dark inside the cabin, they could see the look in Janowitz's eye . . . but Evans' coaxial cable was still working.

"That was all accident," Evans said. "You must have seen that. The plan was to take you and your copilot and get out before anyone knew what happened. It would have worked but one of—Hill! It *was* Hill, wasn't it? Hill stayed in the chopper too long. We couldn't wait. And then, before we got a chance to tie him and the guard up, your copilot opened up the door, and from then on . . . it just happened."

His voice was tense and desolate, and Janowitz remembered how shaken he had seemed in that cave they took them to. Maybe it *was* an accident. After all, the VC got cut up pretty badly, too, and that village was a shambles. But what about the others then?

"You only wanted me and Adnapoz?" he asked skeptically.

"That's right," Evans answered. He smiled tentatively. "You both might have been hit on the head, but that's the worst we'd planned."

"If that's the case, why have you kept the whole group together? Why have you kept on at Pershing and Hill and the others?"

Evans hesitated. "Someday perhaps I'll tell you. I can't now."

Janowitz didn't move for a second. The flood of anger slowly passed, but with it went his enthusiasm for the chopper. He turned slowly and made his way to the cockpit.

The damage there was minimal really. The controls wouldn't move, but that was because the surfaces outside were shot up. Engine pitch, mixture controls, everything that mattered seemed sound. The radio was gone, and the gyro horizon was shot to shit, but if the support posts for the main rotor could be replaced and the tail assembly put right, the bird should fly.

Evans slipped into the copilot's seat.

"So what's the game?" Janowitz asked, keeping himself busy, deliberately avoiding looking at Evans.

"What's the story with Pershing?" Evans dodged.

Now Janowitz did look at him. "He's agreed to listen . . . and that's all *I've* agreed too."

Evans nodded. He sat there, seeming to weigh it all for a time. Finally, he said, "I think I can tell you what we plan—in general at least—tomorrow."

Janowitz's heart suddenly started tripping double time again. Tomorrow. That was soon. Very soon.

"Could you make a list of all that's needed to make this thing flightworthy—not just flightworthy, combat-ready?" he added hesitantly.

Janowitz's heart was going *triple* time. Keep cool, he schooled himself. "I could," he said quietly. "But I'm not going to until I know I want to go along with you."

Evans thought for a moment. "Could we compromise? You make a list tonight and keep it. If you decide you aren't going to help us, you destroy it."

"You're going to tell us what it is tomorrow?"

"Probably. It's a long cycle back here," he said lightly. "I hate to make an extra trip uselessly."

"All right, we can compromise," Janowitz said calmly. "I'll make the list tonight. But when you tell us, it has to be you alone—with all of us, and none of them—so if I want to destroy the list, I know I can."

Evans shrugged, as though amused at his distrust.

"And," Janowitz added, "if someone tries to lift the list from me before that time, you can forget the whole exercise. I won't fly anybody anyplace."

Evans handed him a notebook and a ballpoint. "It looks as if we've got a compromise," he said. Janowitz accepted the notebook,

286

and Evans added, "You're the only pilot we have on hand. You're in a stronger position than you think. No one is going to *force* you to do anything."

It took almost two hours. He went over everything once and was reasonably satisfied he had it all, but Evans had said they probably wouldn't be back, so he went over it again. This time he found the rudder bar on the copilot's controls was loose and needed new coils, and he checked everything all over again. Finally, he was satisfied he had it all, and they gave the cave back to the bats.

The trip back started like a shot. Going downhill, they raced along at a fantastic clip. Thai was expert with the bike, and by the time they hit the flats he was far ahead of Janowitz, and Janowitz was far ahead of Evans. Thai waited about half a mile farther on until they caught up and then they started on toward Yen Cai. It was getting cooler, and after the exhilarating coast, the first miles went by easily, but after a while Janowitz realized he had stiffened up. By the time they finally saw the trees and church steeple silhouetted against the night sky he was dog-tired and praying for the journey to end.

He hadn't forgotten Hieu. It was what had kept him going over the last four hundred miles of cycling. At least it seemed like four hundred miles.

The street was still full of traffic and two big trucks were pushing through when they started into their "house." He let the traffic distract Evans and Thai and slipped on in. He knew where Hieu slept—near the hedge.

Her sleeping bag was gone.

"Hey, buffalo, quick, *vite!*" Big Tack hissed at him from where the fire had been. Janowitz hurried over. The old lecher. He was probably counting on watching. He had Janowitz's sleeping bag in his arms, and he shoved it at him and pushed him along toward the hedge.

"Make one for Trach, eh, buffalo!" he said gleefully.

No, Janowitz thought, that I'm *not* going to do!

Bit tits was waiting at the end of the hedge, looking, in the soft moonlight, like a glowing marble statue. Goddamn, Janowitz thought on coming face to face with her, *she* looks nice in the dark, too! She took his hand and led him around behind the remains of the building next door and then through a path to the street. They ran along the buildings a good way, parallel to the street. She kept hold of his hand, and he couldn't help reacting to its gentle pressure, but the incredulous looks the two of them caught in the half-light from the characters trudging their bikes through the street were too comic to accompany any but the most lighthearted of moods. And Janowitz could just imagine what must be going through their minds: a huge Yank running down a bombed-out street miles north of the DMZ and one of their own ripest trotting blithely at his side. No wonder they stared!

She finally turned into the street and pulled him through the passing stream. Someone muttered something, and she turned around and called back a mouthful of curses that made him wish he'd learned Vietnamese.

She led him right to a ruin with a big double door—or at least the frame of a double door. Then she turned around, gave him a wise look of humor, conspiracy, and flirtation, reached up, kissed his cheek, and ran back across the street.

Inside, no remaining part of any of the walls was higher than three feet, but he couldn't see Hieu. He walked farther in—and then he saw her. Lying against a section of wall in the next "room." She was in her sleeping roll, wrapped in the night like a true VC, Janowitz thought ironically.

He moved to her side. She was asleep, but the moment he stepped beside her, her eyes opened. A split second of confusion, then a smile the darkness couldn't hide. Janowitz sighed. If it was a plot, this is what Mata Hari must have been like. Pure sex could get a guy excited, but no one was going to betray himself or his country for it over any given four-hour stretch. But for a smile that made you feel you were the sun and moon, the stars and all the heavens . . . for that, you could be a sucker.

He pulled her up, and she wiggled out of the sleeping bag. She was still in the au-dai. It was wrinkled, and she looked less like an exquisite porcelain figurine, but with her hair mussed and the dress rumpled and clinging, she looked about twenty times as sexy. He held her at arm's length. She watched him tentatively, questioningly—did she please? He shook his head with an irrepressible grin. Goddamn— *did* she please!

He rolled his sleeping bag in hers, clutched both to his chest, grabbed her hand, and pulled her along out of the house. He wanted to get away from that street and the columns of bikes. They ran along behind the row of houses, scaring the hell out of a couple of cats, until they came to one of the little side streets. They jumped and hopped through the rubble of a small building to the street itself. Janowitz planned to take her out into the countryside someplace, to find a quiet spot on one of the paths between the fields, but as they ran down the path between the housefronts and trees, he saw, across the way, the

288

last house on the street. There were trees along the front and down the side, and about half the façade still stood—light-pink stucco with a white window box hanging askew from the burned and blasted window frame, strands of bougainvillaea clinging to the wall. As the real estate men say, it had the look of a happy home.

He led her across the side street. Even here the noise of the traffic on the main drag was more than half lost in the night—diminished by the square of the distance, Janowitz remembered frivolously. He was feeling great, like the intoxication after a good ball game. Was it because he knew they only wanted him to fly? He didn't know, he just knew he felt like celebrating from his toes up, and Hieu had caught his mood. They were like kids at the lake in summer—running from the goddamned adults, from friends, from the world of rules.

When they reached what had once been the patio, Janowitz stopped and tossed the sleeping bags into the "house." He picked up Hieu. She didn't understand, and her exhilaration turned to a baffled query. Janowitz laughed.

Down below the remains of the wall, the world was theirs. Beginning, middle, and end. One great thing about a bombed-out building —the sky made a spectacular roof. He had had her once with the au-dai on, just pulled the damn thing up, and it was marvelous. Then he undid each of the little hand-sewn buttons, and they crawled together into his sack and watched the moon and falling stars and even laughed together at a satellite that slowly stalked across the horizon. They were growing used to each other, and the animal pleasure of just lying body to body in the clear air, huddled down out of the sound or sight of anything else in the world, was so liberating and total Janowitz found himself wondering if that was what Eden had been like. He didn't see how it could have been better.

The sound of a jet—distant, but carrying far over the flat plains— reminded them it wasn't Eden. They made love again—long and personal, not just any two bodies, but his and hers, mind and body and eye. And still warm in the luxury of it, Janowitz went to sleep.

ix

Evans took them to the church graveyard. It wasn't a macabre joke; it was just that it was about the only place they could go to be sure they wouldn't be overheard or be up to their asses in mud. All the fields around the village were irrigated, and only the paths between them free of water. It was Janowitz who suggested the spot. He had his list —he'd checked with a shiver of doubt before he left Hieu—and he wanted to make damn sure no one got it from him until he knew in his own mind what he wanted to do.

The morning had been an embarrassment. Right after dawn he and Hieu had been awakened by aircraft. Far from being satisfied, he felt as if he hadn't touched a woman in aeons, and her body next to his was aphrodisiac par excellence. By the time they'd finished her face was ruby from his beard, and they could hear Tack shouting up and down the main street for them. They got dressed quickly and slipped back across the side street, darting along under cover until they reached "home." As they ran across the main street, Tack had spotted them and bellowed out his welcome, charging down the street toward them.

They had tried to slip in unseen, but the looks they got were as hard to confront as the promise of Tack's ribald enthusiasm. Evans grinned as though he were embarrassed; Thai was coldly emotionless. Tick and the guards would obviously have liked to have held a public castration, and they didn't look too pleased with Hieu either. Hill rolled himself in a ball and groaned. The sight of Hieu in that rumpled silk had obviously stabbed him, and the reaction was real, even if exaggerated. It all convinced Janowitz he was going to have to think of a way to organize their morning entrances so they were a little less conspicuous.

But it was too late for that day. Tack bounded in, glowing as if he'd been doing it all himself. He looked at Hieu and went over and rubbed her pink, abraded cheeks—and leered as if she'd just invented sex. Then he squeezed big tits around the waist and roared like a bull in heat.

It didn't stop through breakfast, and only Thai's evident dislike of the whole thing kept it subdued when the women shaved them. Tack had deliberately kept Janowitz away from Hieu—as though they'd explode on contact. So big tits had shaved him, while he watched Hieu do Hill. Hill's eyes were as eloquent and quick as his tongue, and he had her giggling most of the time. Janowitz was mad for her.

But after they were shaved, they were split into groups, and Thai's tone of voice left no doubt that the clowning was over. Tack looked a little hangdog, and at first Janowitz felt awkward himself, but he thought, shit, it's probably your idea, so don't go making me feel

290

guilty about it. And by the time Evans asked him where he wanted to go to discuss the next step, he was feeling belligerent by way of reaction.

As they paraded through town, Pershing walked along beside him, "That free tail hasn't had anything to do with your 'conversion,' has it?" The question was rhetorical.

Janowitz regarded him acidly; then he thought, fuck it—you pay for everything in this world. This was part of the price he was going to have to pay for Hieu. "Yeah, maybe it has," he said stiffly. "It's convinced me that even the VC are human."

"From the waist down anyway," Pershing said. He wasn't exactly antagonistic, but he plainly felt Janowitz belonged on the defensive and didn't mean to be put off by curtness.

"Pershing," he sighed, "you don't know me, I know. And it's no good my telling you that screwing a hundred women wouldn't have affected my attitude one way or another." He grinned despite himself. "If I'm driven by sex, it's all sublimated *and* subconscious. I'm not about to betray my country for a piece of ass. Not now. Not ever."

By the time they reached the church he was half-sorry he'd been so brusque. Much as he resented Pershing's assumption that tail would affect his thinking about something so fundamental, he realized Pershing *didn't* know him. And they weren't exactly playing chess. They all had a right to know what was swaying any of them.

Evans didn't start with much assurance. He seemed to understand that the way he told it was maybe as important as the thing itself.

"Last night," he began, "we took Lieutenant Janowitz to inspect an American helicopter." Shrewd, Janowitz thought. The word "helicopter" made them all sit up, and it was the first time Evans had ever called him Lieutenant—that shook them, too.

"Just east of Pleiku the Arvin have a prisoner of war camp," he continued. Janowitz was as attentive as the rest now; from here on it was news. "In it is a man who—before his capture—was a member of the Central Committee of the National Liberation Front."

"A Communist?" Pershing cut in.

"A Communist." Evans nodded. "He is a Southerner, but in the days before there was a North and South Vietnam he was a division commander under General Giap in the Vietminh. He served at Dien Bien Phu. He comes from a family of wealthy Vietnamese landlords and has contacts—if not friends—North and South."

"And we're supposed to spring him," Pershing said bluntly.

"Yes, Pershing," Evans said resignedly, "we hope to spring him." He looked at Janowitz. "And we have reason to hope you will help."

"If he's so important," Janowitz asked, "why don't the VC get him themselves? They've broken prison camps before. They don't need our help." He asked it straight, for information. He wasn't following Pershing's line—in fact, the more contentious Pershing was, the more determined Janowitz was to hear the whole story and hear it Evans' way.

"The answer is that he's not important to everyone. He's only important to some."

"He's not important to me—that I'm sure of," Pershing said.

"He could be," Evans said softly. "As a matter of fact, I think he is."

"Well, when I get out of here, I'll go down and have a word with him. But I know that no VC is worth my taking part in any raid against Americans."

"Pershing," Janowitz said sharply. "You agreed to hear what the hell Evans had to say and—"

"I've heard," Pershing interrupted.

Janowitz held his breath. "Then why don't you take a walk?" he said coldly. "The rest of us would like to hear the whole story—without the benefit of your interruptions." Pershing—none of them—had really seen him angry, and he could see the surprise in their eyes, but it didn't cool him down.

"You pulling rank?" Pershing asked with a tight smile.

"You agreed to hear Evans out," Janowitz answered. "If you didn't mean it or were afraid of the impact he might have on the rest of us, you should've told me straight then."

"Oh, I'm afraid of the impact he's liable to have, you bet your butt I'm afraid of that, Lieutenant, but I'll hear him out—though I can tell you from what he's said already just exactly what my answer's going to be."

He held Janowitz's eyes. "Okay," Janowitz said. "Only save your hostility until you've got an argument. And if it's my sack sister that's bothering you, maybe it'll ease your mind to know that she doesn't speak English *or* French. We grunt," he explained derisively, "and I can assure you it hasn't affected my stand on anything more earthshaking than the pleasure of grunting." Hill laughed, and some of the antagonism dropped from Pershing's eyes, but he was not relenting.

"When you've finished listening to Evans," he said, "I assume I'll get a bit of say, too?"

Janowitz smiled, shaking his head. "Pershing, you're a lot surer than I am that anything Evans is ever going to say will make sense to me."

292

Pershing snickered. He turned to Evans and nodded, as though to say, "All right, buddy, let's hear it."

Evans had been leaning against a headstone, listening. He slid down against it, sitting on the grass and weeds. All of them were sprawled around on the ground, Miller on a little grass mound, chewing a stalk of grass and watching them all with an edge of tension, Russell and Hill leaning against a monument built like a stone catafalque. The sun was already getting hot, and Janowitz had the urge to move to the shade of one of the tombs, too, but he was aware of Pershing's eyes glued on him, and he'd be damned if he'd move.

"Well," Evans said slowly, "you know and I know that only one man really calls the shots in North Vietnam. He doesn't have the sole voice in the South, but he has a big one there, too."

"You talking about Uncle Ho?" Janowitz asked. He wanted to break the tension and get it back to a discussion. Fuck Pershing anyway. Or maybe it was Evans. Why couldn't it be like the other day with him and Pershing and Hill?

"Yes"—Evans nodded—"Uncle Ho. But of course, it's not that simple. In the first place, I understand it's not an absolute dictatorship, there's a Central Committee, and evidently others have some power, too. True or not, I don't pretend to know, but it's obvious that a leader, no matter how powerful, can't make all the decisions. He has to delegate power—and he has to listen to advisers . . . because things happen, conditions change, money becomes available or money is lost, allies get stronger or weaker, armies gain morale—or lose it. And it is only through other people that he can know these things—or control reactions to them.

"And even in the most absolute kingdom—royalist, Communist, or Republican—factions grow up. Well, it may or may not surprise you that that is as true in North Vietnam as it is in Washington or Delhi or Moscow—as it was in imperial Rome.

"Right now the most powerful faction in Hanoi wants this war to go on until America is driven out of Vietnam as the French were driven out. If it takes eighty years—as it took against the French—they are prepared to fight eighty years.

"But there is another group—not so powerful, more divided. They don't want America here, they don't want a divided Vietnam, but they wonder if America can be equated with France . . . and maybe even more important, they don't want their country to go through another ten years like these last ten. Like many Americans, they're ready to scream 'enough.'

"They're not extremely popular," Evans continued, "but most of them have earned their spurs fighting, losing family of their own, making sacrifices most of our families wouldn't dream of—so they have a voice, as well as the courage to open their mouths."

"And the guy you want us to get is one of them," Janowitz conjectured.

Evans laughed. "Well," he said, "it's not quite that simple. I told you we aren't all that important. We aren't going to make or break the war—whatever we do."

"Don't tell me he's on the *other* side," Hill said.

Evans shook his head. "Nobody's certain," he replied. "At the time he was captured he was among those who wanted to fight on . . . and it's a good thing he was or none of this would have been possible. The support that has been gained for this mission came only reluctantly and then only because some of those whose help was needed believed it would backfire.

"But if the man *has* changed his mind, he might have a big influence. General Giap is the strongest of all the voices for the long war, and this man is probably closer to Giap than any man alive. He was his protégé, his friend, probably his only confidant. If anyone might be able to modify Giap's attitude, or influence those around him, it's the man sitting in Pleiku now—in, I might add, a maximum security concrete bunker."

"But I don't get it," Janowitz said. "What makes you think this guy may have changed his mind?"

"His son," Evans answered. "His son served under him, and before the engagement in which his father was captured, the son alleges that they toured a district cleared by the Air Force. The Liberation Front was using it, but it was mostly charred forest, and what hadn't been burned had been destroyed by chemicals. The villages were obliterated, but worst of all, the people had no source of food at all. They were scavenging in the woods for nuts, roots, anything. They ate bark, dogs, insects—"

"Thai," Hill said apocalyptically.

Evans nodded. "That's right," he said looking at Hill. "I'm talking of Thai's father. That day you made the crack about betting five bowls of rice to two was only two months after he had seen children—half-wild—digging for bits of root. The anger he felt that day was over that—and for his father's capture."

"Thai is this guy's son?" Pershing repeated incredulously.

"Yes," Evans repeated. "Thai had been a company commander

294

under his father. After his father was captured, Thai reported that before the battle his father told him that some means had to be found to end the war. The Liberation Front was not losing—but Vietnam was."

"And that's all you're going on?" Janowitz asked.

Evans nodded his head. "That's the most important. There are other things. Thai's father is a Communist—but the family is Buddhist. In fact, his father is still a Buddhist—as well as a Communist. But many years ago under the French, he met a young American officer, an adviser with the French Army—liaison officer he was called officially. They got on very well. Thai's father was working underground, but he was circulating as a leading member of the Buddhist Struggle Movement.

"Just after Ky and Theiu came to power in the South," Evans explained, seeing their uncomprehending looks, "they faced an armed rebellion in Hue. That time it wasn't the Liberation Front. It was a purely Buddhist group called the Struggle Movement. When the Liberation Front took Hue a few months ago during Tet, they expected that group to join them. But they didn't. Most stayed aloof. They are educated and rich by Vietnamese standards, and they don't really relish the kind of economic equality practiced in the North. But anyway, that group is a power. They are against rule by the military—against the present Saigon government—but they are also non-Communist. It is possible that they could form a government in the South that could negotiate with the Liberation Front—could even share a government with them. They've proved they won't collapse to Communism, so they might be acceptable to Washington. They're anti-imperialist, anti-American, so they might be acceptable to the Liberation Front.

"Thai's father has many links with them—by family and from his youth. So do lots of North Vietnamese who were educated in Hue—including Ho Chi Minh."

"So where does the American officer come in?" Pershing asked.

"Well"—Evans smiled—"there's a double problem. No one in North Vietnam believes the Americans; no one in America believes Hanoi. This American officer is one of those rarities our military sometimes tosses up. He's from Oklahoma, he's stubborn, he speaks his own mind, he knows about twelve different languages, he's been in hot water most of his career, and even now he is only a lieutenant colonel."

"Jesus, Mary, and Joseph!" Pershing exclaimed.

295

"That MAAG light colonel in that village," Hill added with the same thunderstruck tone.

Evans nodded. His face was deathly serious. "For fifteen years that man has evidently been telling everybody, whether they'd listen or not, what was really going on in Vietnam. He was ignored, put away, frozen. Then finally—after we had ripped this country apart by the roots—and the Front still wouldn't give up, some sonuvabitch in the Pentagon decided that if a first-rate power like us couldn't beat a fifteenth-rate power like them, it might not be because there was something wrong with *us*—just maybe there was something *right* about the Vietcong and what they were fighting for. And he happened to remember a certain pig-headed lieutenant colonel.

"And they're so damned desperate in Washington for any straw, they actually listened to him, and they sent him out here. Essentially, they wanted him to make recommendations about land reform—as though there haven't been enough recommendations about land reform—but secretly he was to find out if the Buddhist movement would make a workable alternative to the Ky and Thieu regime, if those bastards continued to refuse any workable compromise with the Liberation Front."

"And you kidnapped him," Pershing said ominously.

"I helped," Evans said, blinking, suddenly defensive and flustered. "But they were going to get him anyway. The word had leaked, both that he was coming and where he was coming. It was Thai who convinced me something worthwhile could be made of it."

"Quite a few people died in that little foray," Pershing said coldly.

"Quite a few people die in all the forays, Pershing," Evans came back somberly. "Don't make the dead an excuse for more killing. That raid was murder, I know, but you don't plan raids *not* to work, and to take that force before the jets came in, they had to strike fast and hard. What we want to do is put an end to all the forays . . . on both sides."

Pershing held his eyes for a moment. "All right," he said neutrally, "let's hear the rest of it."

"It's not much," Evans said. "Thai believes his father wants to try to stop the war. He also believes his father's voice is strong enough among the hawks to matter, to be able to change some of their minds. If he can influence Giap, it will make a big difference. Perhaps a crucial one.

"But no one in Hanoi or in the Liberation Front—including Thai's father—wants peace alone. They could have had that anytime in the

296

last twenty years if they'd just given up. It happens they *believe*—every one of them—that unification and the form of government they choose are their own sovereign decisions—not to be dictated by us or puppets we support."

"So what's the point?" Miller said. "You're back to square one. The bastards won't negotiate and never will."

"That's where Colonel Bussko comes in," Evans said calmly, refusing to be drawn by Miller's hostility. "Thai and I hope that if we bring them together, Bussko could convince Thai's father that America would accept a kind of independence for Vietnam now. That if those generals we're backing down there won't compromise, it's not just another American trick. That if they refuse to budge, America might be convinced it should shift its support to an independent, non-Communist group—a group the Front could accept."

"The Buddhist Struggle Movement," Janowitz said.

Pershing laughed. "We're supposed to just walk out on the South Vietnamese Army, is that it? Is that what you think this Colonel Bussko is going to propose?"

"No," Evans replied. "It's not a matter of walking out on the South Vietnamese Army; it's a matter of determining who *controls* the military—and therefore life—in the South. It could be the Liberation Front, it could be the people we have put in and profit from us—or it could be a group independent of both."

"And the North Vietnamese would accept that?" Janowitz asked slowly.

"I don't know," Evans said. "It's possible. For one thing the Buddhists have never been in the pay of the French or the Americans; that alone makes them acceptable as true Vietnamese—rather than puppets. If Hanoi or the Front will accept any compromise, this seems, at least to Thai and me, the most likely."

"If we just ignore our commitments," Pershing said acidly.

"Knowing what Bussko's mission was"—Evans smiled—"I have a suspicion, Pershing, there are parties in the Pentagon who are so eager to extricate their asses from this mess they've created that they might very well 'reexamine' our commitments. Anyway, our basic claim is that we want peace and independence for Vietnam, too—that doesn't necessarily mean military rule.

"There's something else, too, that *you* might appreciate, Pershing," he continued more soberly. "In the North they look at America's strength, at American military, naval, and air power, they see where Americans are and where the Russians are—and our panic about

Communists in Vietnam just doesn't make sense to them. It seems nothing but an excuse for colonialism—like religion used to be in the old days.

"Bussko might be able to convince them, through Thai's father, that we aren't colonialist in the French sense. He and Thai's father are close, very close. They have fished together, hunted together, talked for hours. They like and trust each other. And they are both military. If anyone could, Bussko could best convince him that we don't want Vietnam in the way the French did, that it would be to everyone's advantage if the North took into account our fears, too."

He looked at them all for a moment. "You see," he said bleakly, "I told you it wasn't much. It's not a miracle . . . we are only grease on the wheels. It may even be that the POW camp has hardened Thai's father. Or it's possible that even if Bussko is willing to argue for this compromise back in the States, it will be treated like all his other suggestions—if they want to stop their country getting the hell beat out of it, let the VC turn in their arms and the North Vietnamese go back home, as though they all would just abandon what they'd been fighting for for almost *eighty* years because our State Department wants carte blanche or nothing.

"No, it's not a miracle," he continued quietly. "It is only a chance we could take. But that is what soldiers do—take chances. But this one would not be meaningless or taken *against* anyone. It would be done to do what I first said it was meant to do—to put an end to this insane, brutal war."

They all lay there for a time, not moving. Janowitz finally looked up at Pershing. Pershing shrugged noncommittally. It was like a signal. They all stretched thoughtfully, moving about, getting into a bit of shade. Janowitz was less sure of what he wanted to do than he had been when he didn't know what the damned mission was. Evans was right. It certainly was no miracle. Even as a chance it wasn't much of a bet.

"Why won't the VC do it?" Hill asked at last.

"It's a dangerous raid. There's an Arvin headquarters in Pleiku, besides all the American units, so they can deluge the place with planes and artillery and reinforcements in minutes. If this plan hadn't been hatched, no one would have considered it. And even then its been an uphill fight to get support. If Thai's father had fewer friends, it would never have been given. You see, they don't need him to fight the war. He's only needed to help *stop* the war—not a highly popular

298

cause among the military high command on their side, any more than it is among the military high command on our side."

"And what *is* the plan?" Pershing said bluntly.

"I can't tell you all of it. But one essential ingredient is to use an American helicopter with an American pilot to get over the camp. The rest of the attack force also works by surprise. *How* is more complicated."

Nobody said anything, but Janowitz's heart jumped. He could almost feel it happening. No wonder they had taken special care of him. The whole idea sent charges of excitement flashing through his nerves. Why had he seen so goddamned many movies? But damn, him and a chopper coming in over a camp—daring to pluck their prize chicken from the roost, right in front of their eyes.

"It is an *Arvin* camp," Evans emphasized. "It won't involve Americans—unless we goof. And if that happens, they'll just be shooting at us, not the other way around."

He looked across at Janowitz. There was a stone ornament between them, Janowitz could see only part of his face, but the eyes were on him, steady and personal.

"And there's one other thing," he said evenly. "Ky once said he had but one hero—and that was Adolf Hitler. This camp is a living proof he meant it in more ways than one. It is one of the main sources of intelligence on the Liberation Front. Human beings do to other human beings what no animals would do to their kind. The art of the Gestapo has been refined by the hatred of a civil war. Men —and women—like the ones we've marched with live in terror of the next moment . . . every moment. When the Arvin threaten prisoners with it, when they refer to it among themselves, they call it by its nickname. Dachau."

Janowitz could feel the blood drain from his face. He kept staring at Evans, but his eyes went out of focus. He didn't really see him. Where before he was all excitement and tension, now he was jelly. He couldn't believe it would affect him this way. That goddamned priest training. Evans had caught him, caught him beyond expectation, beyond his own understanding of himself.

"It doesn't sound very promising," Pershing said skeptically. "We've already offered those bastards every chance to negotiate."

"Crap!" Evans said bluntly. "We keep claiming we want peace, but our money, our guns, and our Army are backing a regime in Saigon that won't have peace with the Liberation Front at any price. Well, that means we're liars—as some North Vietnamese say we are—or it means that when we say 'peace,' we *mean* defeat for the Liberation Front."

Pershing was going to speak, but Evans stood and cut him off. "And I don't think what we're asking you to do will hurt in the North either. It takes guts to be for any peace short of victory up here. They've had their cities bombed, their children slaughtered, their country razed. It's not easy for anyone to say let's make a deal with the Americans. But someone on both sides has to have the nerve to make a genuine move—even while people are shouting traitor at him. That's what you want to shout at me, Pershing.

"Well, I can take you calling me traitor till the end of my god-damned days. Because I know I'm not being traitor to anything but phony hysteria and the flag-waving of politicians we can't believe, a military that is glorying in the war, and a State Department that tries to manipulate other nations as if they were chessmen in some private game.

"But I'm not very important. If the whole world thinks I'm a traitor, it doesn't mean shit! But if Thai's father risks being called traitor, it just might mean something. He has guts, and he's not grease on the wheel like us. He *is* a wheel.

"In any case, it's better than closing our eyes to what the Vietnamese have gone through and what *they* believe, and shouting we're for peace, and wringing our hands while the slaughter goes on—theirs *and* ours!

"That's what *I* think, Pershing. Now you chisel away at that all you want!"

"You mustn't mistake me, Evans," Pershing replied quietly. "A lot of what you've said makes sense. And believe it or not, I have a feeling I have as much sympathy for the Vietnamese as you do. And I'm *certain* it shakes me up a lot more than it does you to see a GI crumpled around a hole a VC bullet has put in him. I'd like the war to end *now*. But I sure as hell don't believe the way to bring it about is to start fighting it according to someone's own private plan."

Evans smiled. "Pershing, we both took an oath—to fight the enemies of the United States. I have seen some of our 'enemies'—children, women, peasants, who think Cuba is as big a country as France, that the United States is a huge island off Europe, that Russia is a land of rich peasants and reindeer and perpetual snow. I will fight America's *real* enemies anytime. But because someone points a gun at these people and declares them to be our enemies, I am not going to take their

300

word for it. We are too rich, too big, too powerful to go on killing the Vietnamese as enemies of the United States. The world despises us for it, and *I* despise us for it."

"And what if every soldier started making up his own mind that way?" Pershing asked.

"The war would be over," Evans shot back.

Pershing's look of sarcasm wasn't bitter, but it made its point loud and clear.

"What about this Colonel Bussko?" Miller interrupted. "Where is he? What does he think about all this?"

Evans hesitated; then he shrugged. "He's at a village less than fifty miles from here. He still doesn't know why he was captured. He won't until we bring Thai's father to him."

"So all this is your idea—and no one else's," Miller said coolly.

"The idea of a raid was Thai's and his uncle's. His uncle is a wealthy Southerner—who, like lots of wealthy Southerners, pays certain 'taxes' and does some other things for the Liberation Front. The two of them got some support for the idea, but not enough. I was exposed to the problem and suggested that a relatively small force might be able to do it—if they used surprise and the force included some Americans . . . and an American helicopter."

"Well, you can count this American out," Miller said categorically.

"That makes two of us," Pershing said. He turned to Hill, who was watching them all with amused detachment.

"Well, Hill?" Evans asked.

"Well, shit, don't look at me," Hill said pleasantly. "I just been lying here thinking what a great place this is to sit out the war. I just hope Thai's old man is feeling the same."

Pershing laughed. He had Hill.

"Russell?" Evans said dully.

"Man, all this shit is too complicated for me," Russell drawled with a deliberate show of dimwittedness. "All I know for sure is I'm American, and they're Communist. One of us gotta give, and I don't reckon it's going to be me—not right off anyway."

Evans looked across at Janowitz. Janowitz had been chewing a blade of grass, staring noncommittally at the ground, but now he knew all their eyes were on him. He needed a thousand years to think, but finally, he looked up at Evans.

"Well," he said slowly, "you've got yourself a pilot. It's going to make one helluva story to tell my grandchildren." He glanced over at Pershing. "I'm sorry, Pershing. But I think the man is right—none of us is very important. And this isn't some betrayal that's going to make America look sick. If it works, it may do some good; if it doesn't, I can't see it'll do much harm. And if I get dubbed a traitor, there'll still be fifty stars in the flag—if I live to hear people calling me one, I'll know why I did it, and I think I can live with it."

"Traitors are sent to prison," Pershing said firmly, "and sometimes shot."

"Patriots are sent to prison, too." Janowitz smiled. "And sometimes *they're* shot. Ask Evans about Nathan Hale."

Hill laughed. Pershing seemed a little confused.

"Well, sonuvabitch," Hill said, stretching out to his full length on the grass. "I don't see how the lieutenant can fly a big-assed bird right in over the 'enemy' without a copilot to see him through."

Pershing turned on him like a shot.

"Why, fuck, Sarge," Hill said innocently, "you know I always wanted to be a copilot. Shit, I might even win me my wings. Might even get promoted to an officer. Lieutenant Hill. Man, think what that'd do down in the Thirty-eighth Street branch of the Philadelphia Boys Club. It won't bother those babies that it's in the VC Air Force."

"Skip the humor," Pershing snapped brusquely. "If the lieutenant wants to stick his ass in this, that's his business, but you aren't going anyplace."

There was an edge of violent anger in Pershing's voice, and though Hill was still smiling, his eyes froze the way they did when someone pushed him.

"Sarge," he said coolly, "you know I've been looking for an excuse to take a potshot at some Arvin ever since I came to this shithole of the East. Now don't deprive me of the one chance I get."

"Forget it!" Pershing growled.

"Now, dad, you're all excited," Hill answered. "The man just wants us to go for a little ride and pick up a friend. All you have to do is stay here and count your rosary beads and leave it to little George Hill. We'll do a lot better with you praying for us."

Pershing looked as if he might choke. Hill held his eyes for a moment and then stretched again.

"Do I get flight pay and hazard pay for this little job, Evans?" he asked blandly.

"I'll try to get an extra fishtail in your rice," Evans retorted.

"Fishtail I'm not so interested in," Hill remarked, looking up sharply at Evans, "but it seems to me if I'm going to give my all for these shoeless pirates, a little of the kind of tail the lieutenant's getting ought to

302

be right in line. Yeah," he said, rolling on his back, "you can just let ole big tits there know where her duty lies. I'll run her up the flagpole a few times and teach her all about the dangers of escalation."

"Whatever this guy tells us, Hill," Pershing said, his voice choked and tense, "Russell is right. *They're* Communists, and we aren't! And as long as I'm alive, we aren't ever going to be. You help them to do anything—if it's only to wipe their ass—and you're damaging our country . . . for the good of Communism!"

"*You're* damaging America," Evans said flatly.

"Shut up, Evans!" Pershing barked.

"America means liberty and freedom from oppression"—Pershing wheeled on him, but Evans went right on—"and, nigger, you ought to know all about liberty and freedom from oppression." It stopped Pershing cold.

"Except for the slaves they tied in boats," Evans continued acidly, "our ancestors came to America to get away from oppression—*economic* oppression in nine cases out of ten! And our Revolution was about economic liberty, too—the fight started over the *stamp tax,* remember? What kind of tax do you think these people pay on their homes, their lives, their ambitions. You ought to know, nigger! You ought to know just how free a man is to open his mouth when he's up to his eyeballs in debt to his landlord, the grocer, or a banker. How free is he when he hasn't got an education and no hope of one for his children?

"You yell about Communism! Why aren't the schools in Watts as good as the ones in Moscow? Why do the Russians turn out four times as many doctors a year as we do—they've got a country that has been bombed out and ravaged twice in this century! Torn right to shreds, they started poor and ignorant, but there isn't one of them that isn't rich compared to a sharecropping nigger in Alabama in rich, free enterprise America!

"Why? I'll tell you why! Because the white sitting in his fancy suburban home that you are over here dying for, with his shining car, his nice school for his kids, his company health insurance—he's not going to pay taxes for *you!* A few million for a B-52? Sure! Bomb the piss out of the Vietnamese and keep the world safe for profits. Glad to! But a few million for housing niggers. You out of your fucking mind, man? Never! That's the system you're fighting to defend, Pershing. And if you think you're doing America any good trying to pretend it's God's answer to the problems of the world, you're deluding yourself—and you're not helping America either. Because until we wake up to the fact we haven't got all the answers and we're no prime model

303

of virtue in a world of black devils, we're going to be in for a lot more trouble in Vietnam, in America, and everyplace else!"

Pershing was stopped. And Evans had used the one course that would keep Miller out of it, too. But he wasn't finished. "And *you've* got a lot of guts to talk about freedom. The reason Communism got such a hold here—and keeps its hold—is that it offers economic freedom like these people never dreamed of. Well, Pershing, you blacks enlist in the military by the thousands—why? To fight for liberty? Save that shit for your aunts and uncles. Most of you guys are running like scared cats from the 'freedom' outside. The freedom to pound the pavements for jobs, the freedom of niggers like you to take the second-rate in houses, schools, food, jobs, everything. You have gladly swapped your freedom of choice for freedom from starvation and insecurity . . . well, a lot of Communists have done the same thing, Pershing!"

Pershing stared at him, his eyes bloodshot with rage. His whole body was shaking. "Come on, Miller, Russell," he rasped. "Let's get the hell out of here!"

Janowitz watched as the three of them walked out of the churchyard, Pershing not even turning to see if Miller and Russell were following.

Evans stared after them, panting from his tirade; then he looked at Hill and buried his head in his hands. "I'm sorry," he stammered. "I'm sorry, I'm sorry, I'm sorry."

Hill glanced at Janowitz. Janowitz raised an eyebrow. They both stared off at Pershing. He and Miller and Russell were already almost out of sight, moving down the main street.

Hill finally rolled over, gazing up at nothingness. Then he glanced over at Janowitz, and Janowitz signaled toward the back of the church. They both got up quietly and walked off through the tombstones to the path they'd taken on their walk the day before.

They wandered through the fields for a long time in silence. It was very hot, and after a while they took off their shoes and waded in the mud of the rice fields. Finally, they saw a plane sweeping toward them across the flat plain, and they scrambled for cover behind a path. The plane whizzed past. They turned around, watching it fly on until they could see it no more. Then they rolled over and just stretched out on the embankment of the path—their feet in the muddy field, their backs against the bank.

"Did that get to you?" Janowitz asked at last.

Hill grinned. "It's not news, dad . . . Most of us figured it out when

304

we were about three." He looked at Janowitz, the grin genuine, but his voice laced with philosophic bitterness. "But don't let it shake you . . . what I didn't take to was him cutting up papa Pershing like that."

Janowitz peered at him. Shit, he liked the sonuvabitch. He fractured you one minute and broke your heart the next. "You know, when we were back at camp," Janowitz said, "and you could get those broadcasts from the North, and they kept on about the Negroes being exploited and fighting a white man's war for him, I always wondered if it ever got to you guys. I didn't know any of you well enough then to ask."

"Well, if we were the only ones fighting," Hill answered soberly, "if there weren't a few whiteys around, I suppose it could've made us a bit itchy. But the Army's fairly straight, and we aren't fighting *all* by ourselves." His smile appeared. "Once in a while one of you fuckers gives us a hand."

"Yeah, well, we don't want you to get all the credit," Janowitz replied. They both grinned and gazed out at the hot fields with the ripples of haze undulating above them. "But guys like Pershing," Janowitz went on, "they must see that ninety percent of this war is being fought by Negroes and the poor, the guys who are the real losers in our system. And yet he defends it like he was a stockbroker."

"Well, papa Pershing is a big believer. He's a lot better off than his old man was, and he thinks his kids are going to be a lot better off than he is. He sorta chews into that American dream bit." He smiled again. "He ain't noticed he's got the wrong color kit."

Neither of them said anything for a time; then Hill spoke again as though he'd been thinking it all over. "I guess most of the guys fight because deep down they *do* dig the American dream. Maybe it's all the advertising or all the crap you get in school, but inside every black power boy, you really got a big, sticky-fingered patriot sucking a red, white, and blue lollypop. They want to be American. . . . And lots of them think if they earn their spurs here, they're going to make it. Pershing, he believes in one long evolution, and this war is a big jump forward. Sure we're fighting the war for the sugar daddies in the suburbs—and ole John Andrew thinks in the long run they're going to be grateful. They'll let his sons screw their daughters—or his grandsons screw their granddaughters." He grinned sardonically. "And then there's us lads who are here because we're here—and because the fucking draft board sent us here."

"And Charlie gets to you?"

"Shit, Charlie's like Evans. So he thinks he's telling us something we

305

don't know. Man, our little cotton-pickin' brains aren't that slow. It's been like a hundred and fifty years now, ain't it? But what the fuck are we supposed to do? Desert?—Where? Shoot?—Who? Big pricks like you? Jesus, man, we wouldn't get anything out of that but one big trip to cloud nine. And then somebody'd come in with the fucking bill."

"Oh," Janowitz answered with mock enlightenment. He rolled over so that he was looking right at Hill. Hill spit out a piece of grass as if he were calmly sizing up Janowitz for that last walk down Main Street, gun to gun. They both were suppressing grins, ciphers of understanding between them that could never be articulated, for which there are still no words. "And what about the prize of the Thirty-eighth Street Boys Club?" Janowitz asked. "Is he a black power boy ready to lower the boom on all us whiteys when he doesn't have to pay the bill?"

Hill laughed.

"Dad, they ain't invented the world where you don't pay the bill," he said mordantly. "No, I hear those cats saying we're going to make us a Vietnam in Philly—and another one in Detroit and Chicago and St. Louis. And old Uncle Sam is going to be so busy taking fire-crackers out of his ass he won't notice we're sticking 'em in his ears, nose, mouth, and belly button. And the prize of the Thirty-eighth Street Boys Club, he just lies back and says, 'Baby, baby, baby, maybe all them stories about the apes are true.' And the little chillen gather roun', and they say, 'Tell us true, papa, tell us true.'

"An' I rocks back, and I say, 'Now lissen to me, hear? This ole daddy's gawn to preach you da trooff.' " He'd slipped into it without any change of expression, and Janowitz had to fight breaking into a laugh. "I say, 'Chillen, over dare in dat Vietnam, yo Uncle Sammy he up shit crick. But that's acause he cainnot tell da gooduns from de baduns. Sho nuff he cain't beat dat li'l ole VC, but I'm here to tell you he could still whallap them Russians, yo bet yo sweet potaters he could do that! Now *why* is dat, chillen? I'm gawn to tell you why! Acause he knows were dem Russians are! An, he can zap dem people with hy-drogens and rockets and submarines, and dey gawn to be dayd! Hear me, chillen—*dayd!* ' "

Despite Janowitz's reaction, Hill didn't budge out of character—not a smile anywhere, only corncob wisdom and profundity. And that made it worse—or better.

" 'No, sir,' I says, 'don't yo'll go an' underestimate yo big Uncle Sammy jus' 'cause he got his ass in a sling in dat li'l ole Vietnam, I say. He is a big, pow'ful Uncle Sammy jus' the same.

306

" 'An' in case you ain't noticed, bruvvers, dat Uncle Sammy is white as a snowdrop an' he got ten ob his whites for every movverfucking one ob you black boys. And jus' to make things completely fair for de white man, he also got de poe-lice, he got de Army, he got de Navy, he eben got de fuckin' Marines!' "

Janowitz cracked up. Hill was undaunted.

" 'And den to hep him out a liddle wen he feelin' blue, he own all de jobs, he run de fuckin' Congress, and maybe you noticed, dey ain't no black President! Hell, man, he own de fuckin' house you lib in, de stores where you git de groceries, and to keep it all clean and on de up-and-up, dat white fukker eben owns de farms where de groceries *come from!*

" 'Now *how,*' Ah says, 'is you gawn to make a Vietnam like dat? He gawn to blow de piss out of you, man. And he know *who* you is and *where* you is! It's not like with dem VC cats. He can tell you is black, black boy. It's like magic, jus' one look an' dat cat *knows.* So he ain't gawn to have no problem pickin' you out. And findin' you? Man, it ain't goin' to be like lookin' in dem jungles for dem VC. No, movver fuckers! He got you *downtown,* where he know where you be! He don't wanna sweat out his ass findin' yo'all.' "

Janowitz had given up. He was rolling around gasping, tears running down his cheeks. But he kept from laughing out because Hill was just pouring on with it.

" 'No, sir,' Ah say, 'you fo'get yo' fuckin' Vietnam in Philly. You gawn to gib dat white man da chance to do you da same favor he did fo' da Indians. Yo watch. In two thousand sixty-eight, da late night movie it gawn ta be on da U.S. Air Cavalry coming to da aid ob a white nurse wid big tits and her li'l ole bright-eyed bruvver of four when dey is surrounded by da last libbing tribe of black—led by Stokely Carmichael. And yo'all *know* who gawn to *win* dat battle! Dey only gawn to preserve enough ob us blacks to keep dem in a supply of extras for dem movies. And when de white man he discovers a paint dat make him look really black, why Equity gawn to pull de trapdoor on dat one, too.

" 'So yo' lissen, chillen, yo'all fo'get yo' Vietnam in Philly. Yo'all do like yo' pappy do. You find yo'self a li'l ole corner ob graft dat no white man he really wants, hear? And you go along whistlin' in the sunshine, dat's what you do. Acause he got all de cards, boy. You jus' clean up de ashtrays and rob de beer from de icebox and count yo' blessings. Dat's what ole papa tells 'em.' "

Janowitz was exhausted. It was so true, so funny, so bitter, and yet so free of malice. Hill was smiling, staring out at nothing, a little pleased, as always, at the impact of his humor, but aware too that Janowitz understood the spiky, somber truth beneath it all. Finally, Janowitz sighed, getting his wind back. He brought his doubled fist down on the top of Hill's head. Hill grinned, but he didn't move. They lay for a long time, perking their ears up only when they heard the sound of distant bombing. It lasted a fair time—some village or bridge getting it, Janowitz thought, because the attack was persistent and they could hear rocket fire chattering through the louder echoes of the bombs. They twisted to see if they could spot it, and finally, Hill pointed toward the hills in the distance far beyond Yen Cai, off to one side of its fractured spine hanging in the sky as if on some invisible thread. Rising above the heat haze they could see clouds of smoke, but they were too far away to see any of the aircraft. They settled back and thought of themselves.

The bitterness of the clash between Evans and Pershing had washed right away. Janowitz felt a contentment as full as he'd ever known. He had been right to come in the Army. It'd always been go, go, go until he enlisted. And then in the Philippines, in camp—even here as a POW—he had got his crack at just taking it easy and watching the world go by and even thinking about it now and then. It was a good feeling—even if the price was a little high, he thought flippantly. He glanced over at Hill. He loved the bastard.

"You sure you want to go along on this junket?" Janowitz asked quietly. "I can't tell you exactly why *I'm* doing it . . . but I've probably got better reasons than you. And I can handle that bird by myself if I have to. So you've got nothing to gain by going. Evans will get his try with or without you. And even if we succeed, you've got a lot to lose if it ever gets out how it happened."

"Will you listen to that? Trying to deball me right out of my sense of importance. Why, fuck you, Lieutenant, sir. You get that whirlybird up over a bunch of Arvin shootin' away at you with everything from 155's to slingshots and you're going to be praying for Big George Hill at the top of your fucking lungs. Like any dumb-ass officer, you can get yourself in there, right in the middle of the shit, but who the *hell* do you think is going to pull you out? Man, they must feed you guys on Wheatie ads at OTS; every one of you shits think you're a walkin', talkin' Mighty Mouse."

Janowitz grinned. They were in it together—for keeps. He felt better. Much better.

308

Evans wasn't in the churchyard when they got back. They headed down the main street and were suddenly confronted by Pershing, Miller, and Russell.

"I want to talk to Hill," Pershing said.

"Talk, dad." Hill grinned.

"Alone," Pershing insisted with a challenging glance at Janowitz. Janowitz looked at Hill. Hill just shrugged benignly.

"Miller and Russell coming with *me?*" Janowitz asked. Nice, Hill thought. The lieutenant's going to take care of me; he isn't going to let the three of them get to me alone.

"Sure, Lieutenant," Pershing answered.

Janowitz seemed to relax. Man, he didn't know papa Pershing. But Hill didn't mind. He'd come to his decision, and even the supersarge wasn't going to shake him.

Pershing led Hill into the ruins of a small house. Three walls were still more or less intact to the roof line. The other wall and the roof had collapsed in a heap of rubble that sealed off one side of the central room as effectively as the three walls did the others. When they came in, they roused a dog, and it growled savagely at them. Pershing moved Hill away from the shattered entrance, and given his chance to run, the dog put his tail between his legs and scurried out.

Pershing moved back into the door and faced Hill. "I'm not going to let you do it, Georgy boy."

Hill grinned. "Now come on, dad," he said, "you're always telling us a good soldier takes the initiative."

"Fuck around all you want, son, I'm not letting you."

"And how you going to stop me?" Hill smiled.

"This war isn't going to last forever, and we may not be able to beat the VC, but one thing is for damn sure, they ain't never—not in two thousand years!—going to beat us. You remember that. And you remember that when it's all over, I'm going to be there to point the finger at you. And, son, LBJ is paradise compared to what they're going to give you at Leavenworth."

Hill appraised him silently for a moment. Then he broke out in laughter.

"You're never going to split on me, dad. No more than you would in Saigon. When I start breaking old ladies' legs for kicks, then I'll worry about you bad-mouthing me to the law. But not for this, papa." He had him, and Pershing knew he had him. "I don't even think you'd split on Evans," Hill went on flippantly. "He ain't no traitor, and you know it. And the great thing about you, Sarge, is you know just how hard-assed and stupid the law can be. When you're policeman, judge, and jailer, then you believe in the law. When you ain't, you show just a surprising amount of common sense."

But Pershing's determination didn't alter one iota.

"Only here I *am* policeman, judge, and jailer. And you're not taking part in anything."

"Dad, I love you, but don't get hysterical. Like the lieutenant says, if worse comes to worse, what harm have we done?"

"Every guy you let out of that prison could end up killing ten GI's—that's what harm you can do. And some bigwig in their Security Council might be useful. Very useful—to *them*. How do you know Thai's old man will even go along with this shit? Even Evans admitted being a POW might have changed his mind plenty. And since it's an Arvin camp, you can bet your ass he's going to come out of there after blood—American blood, as well as Arvin blood."

Hill shrugged. "Maybe . . . and maybe not. Now, come on, I'm getting hungry." He started for the door. Pershing shoved him away. Hill looked at him coldly, then laughed again.

"Now come on, dad. I'm not going to fight you."

"Good. Then stay here until we've talked this out."

"We've talked it out—and I'm hungry." He had no intention of fighting, and he couldn't help finding Pershing's grimness amusing. He moved toward the door again. Pershing shoved; Hill danced back lightly. "Come on, don't be crazy," he mocked. "I'm going."

"You're not."

Hill turned resignedly from the door, then darted suddenly to go around. Pershing swung with him, but Hill twisted and, using Pershing's own momentum, shoved him along the wall. But he didn't make it out the door. Pershing brought him down with a tackle before he was halfway through. Hill got up, slow and pained—but tolerant. Pershing shoved him back, clear of the door.

"Goddamn, you're stubborn," Hill said. He was grinning as broadly as ever. He bent to dust himself and, in a sudden, flashing blow, brought his fist thundering into Pershing's kidney. Pershing doubled over and went down on his knees. Hill stood over him—no grin.

"Look, dad, I fight dirty, you know that." He started around Pershing, but Pershing, even in his pain, reached out and clung to a leg. "Sonuvabitch!" Hill muttered, and swung at the side of Pershing's head. But this time it was Pershing who faked. He twisted away and, using the force of Hill's own blow, brought him crashing on to the ground. Pershing scrambled to get on top of him. Hill shoved him away, but Pershing's strength was gradually coming back, and he hung on. Hill was more annoyed than hurt. He shook his head in disgust and clapped both hands hard over Pershing's ears. In a paroxysm of pain Pershing released his grip, and Hill shoved him off.

He made for the door again, and again Pershing had him around the waist before he could get out. Only this time, when Hill turned, he met a fist coming at him. It stunned him, and he went down. Big daddy was mad!

By the time Hill scrambled to his feet Pershing's fist was coming again, and it caught Hill in the gut. As he folded, his cheek took the cross coming the other way. It knocked him flat. That little fucker can fight, he thought dazedly. He caught his breath, started to rise, bent quick to pick up a hunk of rubble, and, as he figured, it made the sarge attack and he swung at him coming in, but Pershing took it on his elbow, and there were three fast blows, one to the body, two to the head, and Hill was on his ass again, bleeding and stunned.

Man! Hill thought, shaking his head to clear it. I'm going to have to fix you, Sarge. He scooted over to one of the walls and slid up it. Pershing came at him. Now, Hill prayed, you be as fast as I think you are, dad. He pushed off against the wall. The force of his launch robbed Pershing's first blow of its sting, and Hill's punch landed at the same time Pershing's second did. But as he figured, Pershing kept coming, and Hill backed against the wall again. Now, daddy, stick with me. Step one, against the wall, and push—that's it, you're ready for me. *Oww.* Retreat to the wall again . . . get ready, Sarge . . . push . . . he could see Pershing's legs pivot with the blow—it was coming right from the floor—now *sink!* . . . and Pershing's fist flashed by his ear, crashing into the wall with a sickening thud. As it did, Hill straightened from his crouch, slamming the top of his head into Pershing's face. And on the instant both fists hammered into Pershing's gut.

Pershing collapsed onto the floor, his hand and face bleeding, his body doubled in convulsive pain . . .

"I'm sorry, dad," Hill said numbly. "We learn it kinda rough up East." He wiped the blood from his mouth and shuffled slowly to the door. When he turned to look again, Pershing was still on the ground, trying to heave—little bubbles of puke already slithering down the side of his chin.

"You belong, papa," Hill said quietly. "I gotta play it by ear. That red, white, and blue flag has only meant one thing to me—the county courthouse . . . and some fuzz beating the shit out of me." He smiled grimly. "I got this weakness for kickin' back once in a while—but you don't need to worry. I'm not going to be a hero in anyone's cause—" He looked away dejectedly from Pershing's trembling body. "I love you, dad."

When he crossed back into the road, he could hear Pershing finally making it; the heaves came up full and hoarse.

Part II

10

i

Quang Khe is on the coast of the South China Sea. Janowitz savored the name; he could even still thrill a little to the idea of being on the South China Sea at all. It was a long way from Detroit. And he confessed that being a long way from Detroit was always dream and ambition—though neither had even been vaulting enough to conceive that one moonlit night he'd be riding a Russian-made truck up a rutted road to a harbor he'd never heard of, a hundred miles or so from a town as remote as the Forbidden City. In fact, Hanoi *was* the Forbidden City for his generation.

The Air Force had flattened Quang Khe. But it wasn't like Yen Cai. They hadn't left it alone but had come back again and again—until now the town was really nothing but rubble. But all the bombing couldn't destroy the harbor nature had etched from the meeting of river and sea. So the North Vietnamese went on using it, and the Air Force went on bombing it.

The Northerners had found ingenious ways of keeping open the two roads leading to the harbor. They had built huge platforms of houselike rubble, which they pushed over the road in the day, and other platforms surfaced like road, which were put over the real rubble of houses. But the most ingenious of all was the sand. Sand dunes lined the coast and the coast roads. And when the wind shifted off the sea, lines of peasants tossed sand in the air to let the wind hurl it across the flat plain. In his mind's eye Janowitz could see the result from the air. The sea, and a sweep of sand three or four miles wide. And somewhere in that sand were two roads. Your chances of ever hitting one of them were pretty damn thin. Infinitesimal. And the method had been used all the way from Quang Khe to Dong Hoi fifteen miles south— and maybe even farther for all he knew. And at night, once the first trucks were led through, their wash marked the path of the road. By dawn the little macadam tracks, glorified with the names Route 1 and

Route 2, were almost clear. But by then the coastal wind had started to rise, and the endless line of peasants would be there again, tossing sand to the wind, obliterating the roadway until the next night.

It was almost eighty miles from Yen Cai to Quang Khe, but they'd made it in one night. When Janowitz had returned to the "house" after leaving Hill and Pershing, he decided it was time to give his list of damaged parts on the chopper to Evans. The formal declaration. Neither Miller nor Russell had spoken at all as they walked along, but their silence felt more like embarrassment than hostility. They had even grinned weakly at him a couple of times, and Janowitz had smiled to himself. If Evans hadn't converted them all, at least he had revealed how morally ambiguous the situation was. Even Miller wasn't ready to call him a traitor.

Evans, Thai, and Tick had been in close conference when he brought the list over. Evans thanked him, Thai nodded, and Tick sneered. It was a little anticlimactic. He'd thought they might show more enthusiasm. Thai invited him to sit with them and signaled to Hieu and big tits to prepare them tea.

It was then they had told him they would be leaving for Saigon that night. If they'd said Washington, he wouldn't have been more surprised.

"You will be well guarded at all times," Tick said bluntly.

Janowitz shrugged his unconcern.

"We must obtain the correct parts," Thai said, tapping the list, "and you are the one who must see that we have them. Among thieves and blackmarketeers"—he smiled—"there is very little honor."

"You think you're going to get *those* in Saigon," Janowitz said.

Thai only smiled and pocketed the list. "Tonight," he said, "we will leave for the coast. Tomorrow night we shall be on our way. I hope you are not subject to *le mal de mer*."

Seasickness didn't worry Janowitz in the least, but within seconds another kind of sickness had struck him. Hieu came with tea, and as she did, Tick made a conspicuous show of shifting the paper before him to his pocket. At first the significance of the performance didn't register . . . but then Janowitz saw it was a list, his list. Thai still had his original—that could only mean that someone had made a copy. He glanced up at Hieu. She was flushed and disconcerted and avoided his eyes. Sometime during the night she must have taken the list from him and passed it on to be copied, then slipped it back so that he might never have known . . . had Tick not been one of nature's spoilers.

His first reaction was to feel sick, his second anger. Screw them. He had warned Evans if they tried to take the list from him, they could write him off. But he could feel the presence of Miller and Russell behind him, he could read Evans' plea on his face—and he knew it would be a pointless, petulant gesture. He was committed. If they'd got the list from him, it was because he was an ass. He looked at Hieu again, and the sickness returned. So this was what a betrayed husband felt, he thought—empty, dead.

He tried to tell himself that he knew from the beginning that part —or all—of what she had done had been on orders, that he knew she was one of "them." But none of it did any good. Inside he had felt there was a link between them that superseded the tribal loyalties.

Even Hill could not revitalize him. Hill had returned alone, and when he heard that a group was leaving for Saigon, he had begged to be included. Evans had laughed and said they'd have enough trouble keeping an eye on Janowitz; Hill would require a regiment. Hill got down on his knees, a lascivious grin from ear to ear, and swore they could count on him; they wouldn't have to guard him at all; hell, he'd guard them! But despite the amusement it caused, it was to no avail.

About five it had started to rain hard, and Thai had evidently taken it as a good omen. There'd be no planes out in this; they could start early. He called Tack over to him, and when he did, Hieu went to his side, too. She spoke intently to Thai, nervously fluffing the hair from her face time after time. Tack had just stood beside Thai, listening, grinning, glancing with an occasional laugh at Janowitz, until Janowitz felt he could gladly kill them all—or himself.

After that Big Tack and little Toe disappeared but were soon back bearing long brown plastic capes and riding two more bikes they'd commandeered. Thai gave one of the capes to Janowitz—and one to Hieu. He then led them off on the bikes. Thai rode in the lead, Janowitz just behind him. Evans, Hieu, and Tack were strung out behind. Hieu had looked at Janowitz several times as they put on their capes and said good-bye to the others, and each time he'd glared at her with as much loathing as he could muster.

As they cycled out of town through the downpour, he caught a glimpse of Pershing standing stoically in a path between the fields, not moving, letting the rain drench him. He looked as forlorn and empty as Janowitz felt, and Janowitz wondered what had passed between him and Hill. But his own malaise was as isolating as the rain around him, and he pedaled on, conscious only of the continuous movement of his legs, the wheels splashing leadenly through the dark puddles, the muddy trail left by Thai's bike before him.

They had cycled for about an hour before traffic began to build up. The rain was subsiding by then, but night was closer, and evidently all the links in the whole chain decided the extra hours of movement were worth the risk. They dodged in and out around carts and men and women struggling with their camel bikes, sometimes getting separated by large distances. Just as night was really settling in, they reached Long Dai. Thai had got well ahead of Janowitz, and he was waiting at the roadside just by the sign that identified the city. It was like Yen Cai. No building was left whole in it, but it was much bigger, at the intersection of four roads, and was a rendezvous where considerable transferring of loads and cycles took place.

When the others had caught up, Thai took them to one of the intersecting roads and they waited in the drizzle, hunched on the ground, their capes wrapped around them like Mexican ponchos. Janowitz glanced at Hieu only once, when she got off her bike. She was wearing a coolie hat, and her face was the only part of her that you could see from the top of its crown to the bottom of the long swirling cape skimming along the ground. She looked like a china doll. Janowitz was stabbed with pain, and the melancholy settled on him even more fiercely.

It seemed hours later when a truck came slowly in through the traffic. It stopped opposite them, and boxes and bags were unloaded by dozens of cyclists who suddenly appeared from behind the walls of one of the demolished buildings. When they'd finished, the truck turned around in the road, the driver hooting the horn again and again as though he thought no one knew what he was doing. Thai signaled him, they had a brief word, and then all of them piled in the back, bikes and all. The driver made loud clucking noises at Hieu. Thai tried to cut him with a look, but the guy was undaunted; he banged the side of his door to draw her attention and clucked like an old hen. The North Vietnamese mating call, Janowitz decided. You can have her, Mac, he thought to himself, but he knew if the bastard got out to "help" her aboard, he'd get the full benefit of his own turmoil. Punching someone in the nose was just the antidote he needed.

The ride north to Quang Khe had seemed interminable. They'd just get a little speed, and then they'd crawl. Sometimes the driver would honk his horn with nagging insistence, and at other times he would poke along at two miles an hour with what seemed like divine patience.

At first, it all drove Janowitz mad. If the driver honked, he wanted to go up and kick his teeth in, but if they crawled along for five minutes and the driver didn't honk, Janowitz wanted to climb on the truck and shout at whoever was causing the holdup. But he finally accepted that what was really getting him was the presence of Hieu only three feet away, staring at him unremittingly. Sure, worm your way back, he felt acidly. You never know, you may be of some other use to them. But he finally got sufficient hold on his bitterness to realize he was only damaging himself by dwelling on it. And he tried to force his mind to something else.

It was then that he began to watch the countryside and the faces trudging along behind them. He remembered reading someplace that all the North Vietnamese wore the same dull-blue suits. He wondered where that story got started. The rain had stopped altogether, but some of the cyclists were still moving along with their capes spread across their handlebars—and he could make out yellow ones and black ones and others with shades in between. There were men in light uniforms, women in black ones, and still others in baggy slacks with white blouses and patterned neck scarves, abstract, striped, and checkerboard. The only things they all wore that was alike were the conical coolie hats of the women and the broad-rimmed topees of the men—and their guns. Walking, riding, cycling, they each had a rifle slung across the shoulder.

It was the sight of an exception, an old man in a cap that looked like a golfing cap from the Roaring Twenties—and no gun—that had made him think of Detroit and how his life had turned away from the predictable and expected pattern in a way that had been beyond calculation . . . and, whatever the consequences, he knew he was grateful for it. Even tomorrow wasn't predictable, never mind next week or next year. And not in any small way either. It could be over tomorrow, the whole pattern of his life. He didn't believe it would be—that's why he could relish the danger of it—but the possibility was real, and he admitted there was a saltiness in the fact that even made the NCAA finals seem flat. And inching along this tiny, bumpy road with a half moon glancing now and then between the thinning clouds, watching the faces of these small, brown, beautiful people, he laughed at how distant and exotic Boston and San Francisco and New Orleans had once sounded to him.

The gray of dawn began to illuminate the eastern sky before the moon had settled in the west—it was like a false dawn. And it was then he saw the long line of peasants standing on the dunes with their small leather baskets, stirring over the wet sand, tossing the dry to the winds.

They had entered Quang Khe and crossed right through to the river. And the whole tempo changed from the dogged, unhurried progress of the night. People shouted and cursed and cast anxious looks at the sky—and Janowitz suddenly felt himself too easy a target sitting in that truck. There were three ferry barges working on the river which widened dramatically about a half mile from the sea, making a broad, turbulent harbor, and they finally made it on one of them. Once on the other side, Thai and Tack hurled down the gate of the truck, and they all jumped off. The driver yelled obscenities at them for every second they took and then pulled the truck away before they even got the gate back in place.

Light tinges of predawn color were already appearing in the sky by the time Thai headed them at full speed down a little trail over which a thinning crowd of Vietnamese were already scurrying. There were no buildings on this side of the river, just a flat, sandy, windswept plain. Janowitz dodged around people, often going off the trail, bouncing up and down over ruts, trying to keep pace with Thai.

He went as fast as he could, but Thai was always lengthening the distance between them. He wondered how the hell Hieu would ever keep up, and when he heard the first sound of aircraft, he was overwhelmed by the need to go back to her.

He cut off the path and pulled up, looking back across the wild bamboo and tall, silvery grass that was spotted across the barren coastal strip. Tack was only a few yards behind him, but Hieu and Evans were far back—maybe two hundred yards—and there were thirty or forty people between them. He turned his bike and started back when Tack came angling at him on collision course.

"Down, buffalo! Get down!"

And Tack smacked right into him. They both went down—and before Janowitz could get up, he heard the first bombs go in. The planes sailed over, machine guns chattering. Janowitz didn't see or hear anything go in near him, and the planes—three of them—had hardly passed when Tack and the rest of the Vietnamese were on their feet. The mob kept running—away from the river, away from the harbor area, toward the line of dunes that lay another quarter of a mile away. Tack grabbed him.

"Go, buffalo, quick!" He jerked Janowitz's arm around in the right direction. Janowitz was thinking of the pilots upstairs. How many targets did they have? From what he'd seen just minutes ago in Quang Khe there *must* be activity there—and the ferry barges, they'd have to go for them. The real worry was that as they came in off a pass, they'd machine-gun anything moving. He glanced back again. Hieu and Evans were back on the path—not riding, but running with their bikes.

"Buffalo!" Tack hit him on the shoulders. Resignedly Janowitz swung his bike around and started to run, too. The planes were sweeping back, but they were coming in on Quang Khe, and their angle wasn't going to bring them overhead. The Vietnamese seemed as wise as he about it because they just kept running and cycling toward the safety of the dunes. He heard antiaircraft fire and saw puffs of flak, but he couldn't tell where it was coming from.

Once more, before they hit the dunes, they had to go into the sandy dirt. But as must have been clear even from the air, the dunes were shelter. Caves had been dug underneath them, and they were engineered. Concrete walls, electric lights, even steel racks for bikes. It would take a big bomb to penetrate—and then it'd have to hit in exactly the right place—but even then the damage would be limited, absorbed by the concrete, deadened by the sand.

Janowitz put his bike in a rack in the first big tunnel by the entrance and turned back just as two Vietnamese dragged a wounded cyclist down the concrete incline. It made him even more concerned for Hieu, and he started back up the incline before Tack could stop him. But then he saw her, with Evans, scrambling across the sand toward the bunker. He knew they'd make it, but with the sound of the jets reverberating through the entrance chamber, he had to keep himself from running up the incline, smothering her in his arms, and carrying her to safety. Even the thought of holding her somehow lightened his gloom. But he forced it from his mind, and as she neared the concrete passageway, he turned to follow Thai down into the wide main corridor that ran under the dunes.

Goddamn, he reflected with baleful incredulity, I must love that sonuvabitch, really love her. He had always taken for granted that love was no more than the excitement, the uncontrollable pounding of the heart on sight of the familiar face, the silhouette coming at you across campus, the elation you got from holding one hand that was different from holding any other—all that he'd experienced, been delightfully sick from, many times. But Hieu had betrayed him, made him feel diluted, without marrow or even the will to have marrow—he hated her. He had never felt as deceived and taken in in his life. He distrusted her, despised her—but at that moment it didn't mean anything.

As they went along, he remembered seeing *The Blue Angel* once.

321

Emil Jannings made fool and derelict by love for Marlene Dietrich. Joke, but powerful beyond belief. And as overwhelmed as he had been by Jannings' performance, he felt it could never happen to him. Let a woman treat him like that and he'd walk away from her. He couldn't believe he had fallen victim to one he couldn't walk away from—regardless of what she did. He heard her voice behind him, talking to Tack. If she so much as touched his hand, he'd take her in his arms.

The underground complex was long, with a couple of offshoots that seemed to go nowhere. Thai finally stopped at one of them, a narrow entranceway; he checked to see if they all were still following and then started in. The lights were few and far between, and the tunnel was much too small for Janowitz. He had to stoop the whole time, and before long his back ached and his thighs screamed for a chance to stand erect. He would have stopped for a breather, but he could hear Tack and Hieu and Evans behind him, and he wasn't going to be the first to cry halt.

The tunnel wasn't deep because there were times when they could hear the muffled roar of jets over their own breathing, but it was long; that Janowitz was willing to concede—long, long, long. At the other end it opened into a large vaulted bunker filled with stacked oil drums, engines, machine guns, and odd parts from ships—rudders, mooring pins, steel cable, pulleys. Half a dozen men were working in the place. When they spied Janowitz and Evans, they turned openly from their work and stared with undisguised hostility.

Thai ignored them. There was an incline from the tunnel to the vault, and when Tack, Hieu and Evans had run down it and caught their breaths, Thai led them up another incline to a blank wall, a turn . . . and they were in daylight. They were downriver from Quang Khe, about two miles, Janowitz estimated. There were trees along the river here, and they had come out near a small group of mud and thatch huts. There were about eight fishing boats moored off the village, and across the river they could see a false hillock about twenty-five yards long, masking a concrete-domed anchorage.

Thai checked for planes and then led them at a trot along the riverbank to one of the huts. It was half dwelling place, half boathouse. Thai was greeted affectionately by a man of about thirty-five. The man nodded to the rest of them, but the look was cold and uncompromising. In the hut there were three small children and two older women. Food was cooking, the man gave instructions, and the women and two boys and little girl immediately started to serve. The

322

eldest boy—nine, Janowitz guessed—had lost a hand, and he maneuvered his stump quite unconsciously, but Janowitz wondered if this
accounted for the hostility they all showed to him and Evans. When
they were given their bowls of rice and fish, the two of them retreated
down the hut toward the empty boat slip. Janowitz took his shoes off
and sat on the hard mudbank, dangling his feet in the water and looking out through the open entranceway to the river.

"They don't much like us," he murmured to Evans.

"Listen," Evans answered.

Janowitz could hear the planes. No bombs, just the planes—no,
there was a rocket . . . and another. It was distant, but it was to go on
all day.

Sometimes a plane would hurtle down the river at treetop height or
dive out of the sky with startling suddenness. Not once did they bomb
or strafe the few huts, but three burned-out hulks in the group were
testimony that this wasn't always the case.

"These people are under a lot of strain," Evans observed. "The
dogma is to hate the few who are responsible—not the American people as a whole—but it's been a long war, and the dogma is growing
thin. There are a lot of people who have just come to hate Americans—all Americans."

Janowitz glanced surreptitiously at the women. Mother and daughter obviously. The daughter might have been the wife of the guy who
greeted Thai—she was about the right age—but there was nothing in
the way he acted to her to indicate she was. The other woman must
have been sixty—but not so wrinkled and dried out as some of the
older women looked. She still had her features and was plump. Enough
to eat, he thought. The river is probably a good provider. Hieu had
joined them in serving the food, and having shed her cape like the rest
of them, she looked diminutive and built again. And as if to goad him,
domestic and loyal and feminine.

"I'm still reserving the right to back out on this," he muttered harshly to Evans. Evans was taken by surprise; he looked at him
in open bafflement. Janowitz nodded toward Hieu. "I warned you that
if you took that list before I agreed, I was out." There was no keeping
the anger and bitterness out of his voice, and Evans was visibly shaken
by it.

"I didn't want that to happen," he said earnestly. "But try to understand Thai's point of view. It's his father who's in that camp. And the
chances are he's being tortured by every device they can think of—

323

modern *and* ancient. If you failed us, we'd have had to start from scratch again—and without some sign of progress he might never have got permission."

"So she was set up to take it from me even when you personally guaranteed that the choice was mine."

"No," Evans protested, "that's not true. It was only after we had come back that Thai told me he was going to have Hieu do it. I argued —not much I admit, because I knew what was in the back of his mind —but it wasn't premeditated. After all, we didn't know before we went to the mountains that you'd make that reservation about compiling the list."

"So when was she told?" Janowitz said skeptically.

"Tuyet"—he was talking about big tits—"was sent to find you. Tho went with her to make the copy." Tick, that bastard. Seeing them lying together like that. It almost poisoned it all. Thank God they'd crawled into his sleeping bag.

"And Hieu agreed, of course," he said bitterly. Evans looked up at him in surprise. Shit, he'd given it all away. He could feel a blush begin to rise.

"Hieu," Evans said with obvious relief, "is a soldier in a cause she believes. And like a good soldier," he added ironically, "she does as she is commanded to do." He smiled; it was friendly, almost comradely. "But like most human beings," he went on, "there are some commands she prefers to others."

Janowitz was embarrassed and levitated at the same time. Hell, if she were his prisoner and had information he needed, of course, he'd take it from her, without feeling he was betraying her, not necessarily even feeling he was using her. He felt as if the sky had opened. But he couldn't take Evans' benign solicitude and turned away. He glanced across at Hieu. My God, he wanted to touch her. He could feel himself swell. He wasn't even thinking about that—just her—but *something* in him was thinking about that! He stood in the boat slip—it was only about a foot and a half deep—and he waded across it and out into the river, clear of the thatch roof. The water deepened sharply a couple of feet out, so he waded along parallel to the bank. Mentally he was pleading, please, Thai, let me go, I can't get away, just let me wander— and Hieu, goddamn, woman, come after me!

The sun was already warm in the patches of light that filtered through the trees on the bankside. Just past the huts there was a big field where the ground was packed hard. Stacks of rice sheaves were placed all around it, and at the far corner of the field a group of women

324

were threshing it by hand, while others tied and stacked the straw in small bales. Occasionally they would turn to look apprehensively at the sky when the sound of a plane obtruded with unusual ominousness, but otherwise, their movements in the early heat were as regular and stately as their ageless chore. Janowitz leaned against the bank, eating from his bowl with his fingers and relishing the feel of the water about his ankles. He kept looking back at the hut. No one had followed him, so he was free to wander. But Hieu, Hieu—where was she?

He had finished eating and was washing his hands in the water when a movement at the hut caught his eye. He looked up, and there she was. She just stared. He smiled. She still didn't move. Damn her. He raised his hand and with one finger signaled her to come—like schoolmaster to pupil. She started slowly toward him—up on the bank beside the house—but then she started to run, along behind the trees, her face in pain; she went faster and faster, finally sliding down the embankment at him and clutching him around the waist. She slammed her head so hard into his chest that he had to step back a foot to keep from falling backward into the river. But then he turned her face up to his and covered her with kisses. Every squeeze of her arms around him was a further release from the weight of gloom and melancholy he'd been toting around since Tick had revealed her "perfidy."

They spent the day in a field beyond the threshing ground, near the river. There were shocks of rice stacked about the field here, too, and they broke one open to make themselves a bed and a cover, bending over a strand of bamboo that stood at the edge of the field and placing sheaves over them. When they first made love, it was like nothing Janowitz had ever experienced before. He wanted her, but emotionally it was quite different from any sex he'd ever had before— even with Hieu. It was as if they had been sealed together, and when Tick had pulled them apart, they were simply waiting for release to fly back together again—impelled by some irresistible necessity as much as by desire. They *had* to be together. And as Janowitz poured over her with hand and mouth and body, he knew he could never express all he felt—not verbally, not physically.

Lying later with her in the crook of his arm, her black hair trailing across his chest, he thought again of *The Blue Angel*. It was true: she could hurt him, cut him, fail him, and still he was tied to her as he never thought he could be tied to anyone who didn't conform to his ideas of loyalty, trust . . . faithfulness. Not that at the moment he doubted her; it was just that it wasn't relevant. If she weren't "faithful, loyal, and true," as he saw it, he knew he couldn't turn her off anyway. It was a perilous feeling, and he frankly wished it weren't there, but the commitment carried its reward even now. Man, someone said, is a mating animal—play around all he likes, he was destined to be paired. Without really choosing, without willing it or even being aware of what was happening, Janowitz was afraid that wildly, unpredictably, calamitously, he had found his pair. She pushed her head against him, and her arms pressed gently around his back. He tipped his face down and kissed the top of her head.

iii

"Buffalo! Buffalo!" Tack was working his way along the river, swinging from a tree here, crashing over another. Janowitz had heard the sound vaguely in his semisleep when Hieu had wakened him. They'd turned and could see him coming along, more water buffalo than I, Janowitz thought. He was exhausted from sex, but as Hieu huddled down with him, grinning and amused at Tack bellowing good-naturedly for them, he felt, with a wave of delicious frivolity, that he just might be able to swing it again. He curled over, half on her, and in the pink half-light of the setting sun they watched Tack come even and then pass on beyond, mixing an occasional *Merde!* at some obstacle with his leering, full-throated calls to Janowitz. They had one more short but, at the moment of climax, agonizingly intense union—buffalo boy and buffalo girl. Janowitz sagged on her, sweating, exhausted, sunk in a bottomless well of love. She gnawed at his chest playfully, and grinning, he finally found the energy to roll off her. She looked at him with amusement—and he felt twelve to her nineteen. Finally, he bumped her nose with his hand and sat up and slipped into his fatigues. She climbed into hers, and he took her hand and raced to the river. Before she knew what he intended, he had pulled her into the water and lunged out toward the middle.

She swam well, short strokes, fast and sharp with her head out of the water, and while the air in their fatigues bore them up, it was fun, but then the cloth got more and more soaked, and it began to be work. She got up close to him, and they tread water together, grinning at the exertion and the pleasure of the cool water. As Janowitz expected, Tack heard them and was pushing his way back along the bank. When he finally spotted them, he let out a roar, tossed down his rifle, and took a beautiful, racing dive into the river. He swam up to them, and

326

the three of them linked arms, laughing, treading water strenuously in the darkening twilight.

Hieu was treated with more scorn than he when they returned to the hut, and the women would not let her help with the meal. Janowitz knew there was a limit to how open they could be, and though he felt the urge to go sit by her and defy them all, he knew it was best to ignore it.

It was dark by the time they finished eating. The Vietnamese man left the hut but came back in seconds. He nodded to Thai, and Thai said it was time to go. They rolled their capes; the women gave Tack a basket of dried fish and raisins and two long rolls of French bread. They waded out into the river. In midstream opposite the underground anchorage, four oarsmen were keeping a large fishing boat in place against the flow of the current. Thai swam toward it, and the others followed. There was a rope ladder over the side, and Thai went up first, taking the basket from Tack. Evans went next. Janowitz maneuvered around to let Hieu up, but Tack muttered quietly, "No, Buffalo —her and me—we stay." He smiled. "Is only *à bientôt,* okay? You come again here soon, okay!"

Janowitz reached out for Hieu. She clutched his hand, and he was torn between anger and resignation. He squeezed back and started up the ladder. Once on board, he tried to watch her for a time from the stern, but the current soon carried them out of sight.

iv

The fishing boat had a crew of eight, plus a captain and his wife. The woman was a real crone, tall for a Vietnamese, with a face that looked just like Lee Marvin's—only Lee Marvin in drag *and* with weathered skin and bad teeth. But she looked about as strong as Lee Marvin, too, and as they raised the huge lateen sail, she was as useful as any of the men.

They ran under sail and engine, and at first Janowitz couldn't get used to the dark, but gradually he could see that they were moving along just offshore. He knew you couldn't trust distances over water, but he'd have guessed they were less than a mile out. They were one of a stream of ships when they cleared the harbor at Quang Khe, but in almost no time they were alone—just the wind in the sail, the dark mass of the land on their right, the smooth throb of the engine, and the rush of water along the sides of the ship—only the stars shared their isolation.

They walked the deck for a time, each to himself. The fact that they were going South, into "American" territory, kept Janowitz on edge; he couldn't relax. Thai finally wrapped himself in his cape and sat on a pile of netting. Evans soon settled beside him, and after a while Janowitz plonked down with them. No one spoke, and then, suddenly, the engine stopped.

"It's all right," Thai said calmly. "Here in the North there are radar stations all along the coast. We stay in close to be in their line of sight. When they pick up an American patrol boat, they radio a warning, and the motor is cut until it passes."

"What if it doesn't pass?" Janowitz asked, scanning the black sea away from the shore. There was no sound of another boat, just the rustle of wind in their own sails.

"They won't come in this close," Thai said confidently. "They've learned to respect our shore batteries—but we don't tempt them."

Janowitz sank back on the netting. They seemed even more removed now. The wash of the water on the hull registered more clearly, but with the motor silenced, the world seemed to have been silenced, too. The wind was fresh, and he slipped his cape around himself. The boat was wooden—thick and sturdy-looking—and there was a sensation of moving even faster under sail than when the motor was running. Janowitz watched the white glimmer of their wake for a long time. Finally, he turned and looked at Thai. Thai raised his eyes to him and smiled softly.

"Your father seems to have quite a few friends," Janowitz said. Thai shrugged disparagingly. Janowitz studied him for a moment. "If we do manage to get him out, do you think he may have changed his mind?"

"It is a risk," Thai said. Then he smiled again. "A risk for you. I, of course, will be happy to see him free whatever his attitude. But I do not think what happens in a prison camp is going to come as a surprise to my father," he continued more solemnly. "There was a time when he believed American statements about democracy and he made the mistake of acting on them under the rule of Diem. Techniques in handling prisoners may have 'improved' since then—though I doubt it.

"Nonetheless, I think my father will do a great deal to see the war stopped," he added reflectively, "but he will need help—and not all of it can come from our side."

328

"Meaning?" Janowitz queried.

"Meaning that even my father will not seek peace at any price, and your country has not shown much enthusiasm for peace on any other terms."

"Well, the terms you cite always sound a bit like those offered a *defeated* enemy," Janowitz replied.

"I'm sorry," Thai answered with the same easy mockery, "that you should regard the evacuation of my country by American troops as a sign of defeat. You also apparently feel it a loss of face to stop bombing the northern half of my country. You must forgive our Oriental quaintness in not regarding these American 'rights' as sanctified as your government does."

Janowitz laughed.

Thai's voice lost its note of raillery. "You will have to take my word," he said, "that my father and most of the men like him are patriots who are fighting for *their* country against foreign invaders—and they will never surrender while the invaders are still here."

"We aren't invaders, Thai," Janowitz replied soberly, "but nevertheless, you can't expect the United States just to walk away from Vietnam."

"No," Thai said ruefully, "that we cannot expect."

"Then what?" Janowitz insisted.

"I don't think my father—or those like him—will ever accept what your present government wants," Thai declared. "They won't accept a divided Vietnam. My father and some of the others even more so are politically conscious men. They know what such a division leads to. West Germany, South Korea—they can envision its happening, too, in the South . . . a heavily armed country, with the United States paying the bill for a vast army. A permanent division, hardened by propaganda, perpetuated by American military force. That they will never concede. Their view of history is too long for that.

"But you say your troops are stationed in Europe to protect it from the Russians. Well, I believe my father might be able to get a majority to agree to undertakings that neither Russian nor Chinese troops will ever be allowed in Vietnam. As a sovereign nation one does not like to be *forced* into such undertakings, but it would be worth a little loss in national face to stop what American forces are doing to our country, and I can assure you no one *wants* Russian forces or Chinese forces here."

Janowitz shrugged. "That may seem a concession to you," he said, "but I'm afraid it won't exactly make headlines in the United States."

"One can get quite bitter about the expectations of the United States," Thai remarked wryly. "There are times when one feels they have almost asked enough of Vietnam already."

"Yankees are human too." Janowitz smiled. "Just to go home and say we've made a mistake would be difficult for the best of us; for politicians it's impossible."

"Even if you *have* made a mistake?" Thai asked.

"*Especially* if we've made a mistake," Janowitz shot back.

They laughed easily, Evans with them.

"Well," Thai went on, "it is my uncle's hope and *my* hope that if America would agree to withdraw its forces and its support for the militarists, the Central Committee would agree to a government in the South in which Buddhists and the Liberation Front would take part in some form or another. If, with that, there is a provision for a plebiscite on unification at some date—" He shrugged. "Even that would be difficult because as you know there has already been one such agreement—an agreement the United States thwarted. But if the United States makes a *public* declaration, and we can keep American troops —and the CIA—out of Vietnam, enough people may believe you will not flout world opinion a second time."

Janowitz turned to Evans, and he was sure Evans sensed he was having second thoughts about his commitment to the whole mission. For what he was now undertaking, he had to believe there was some genuine prospect of success. But it was hard to believe that what Thai was suggesting could lead to that.

"Thai has left one thing out," Evans observed carefully. "It's almost certain the Central Committee would make some formal guarantee that there would be no physical retribution taken on the present government in Saigon."

"Big deal," Janowitz scoffed.

"Well," Evans replied testily, "our press always makes a big deal of it! The bloodbath that would follow if American forces left. It's part of the big myth, isn't it?"

"Well, some of the massacres," Janowitz said, "haven't exactly been mythological, have they?"

"It is wartime," Evans enunciated insistently. "There *have* been massacres of people they regard as collaborators—brutal ones, as brutal as some of our ravages. But there were atrocities in Algeria and Palestine and Africa, too. And there were the same threats of bloodbaths in all those places—if French forces left, or the British forces, or the Dutch forces. And the only place where there *has* been a bloodbath is in Indonesia, where *several hundred thousand* so-called peasant Communists were killed by an army *we* supported!

"But there isn't going to be any bloodbath," Evans went on. "My God, look at North Vietnam. Do you see terror and prison camps and people living in fear? Fear of us, yes! But fear of the government? It's a statement with no visible relation to reality.

"For once in our history," he added reflectively, "we are losers. Not in the sense that Germany was a loser in the last war, or France was at Waterloo, or anything like that, but not winners who can dictate the terms of peace. And it *isn't* going to be easy to accept. But it's that or an endless progress of catastrophe and pain—in a bad cause. There is just no other way. There is no miracle."

"You don't think they would accept even a token force of Americans?" Janowitz asked Thai.

Thai shook his head. "*I* don't think so," he said. "It would be like accepting a token force of French—after we won that war. And," he added slowly, "we don't trust your country in the way it was once trusted. Your words say one thing and mean another. We want you, your Army, your CIA, to go. Have your cold war somewhere else. You have your 'token' forces in Formosa, in the Philippines, in Japan. You will not have them in Saigon."

Thai's voice had become as cold and hard as steel. And Janowitz knew if that was Thai's attitude, it wasn't likely to be different among older, more hardened men who had been fighting for as many years as Thai had lived.

"I am not an optimist," Evans said, as if responding to Janowitz's growing feeling of hopelessness, "but I am not as pessimistic as you are. There are a lot of people in America against the war—totally. Sure there may be more for it—but not a great many who are for it *totally*. People want out. And if there are enough doves even in the Pentagon to send Colonel Bussko over here, there is hope.

"I suspect those sonsuvbitches sitting there in Foggy Bottom are beginning to understand that if they don't get their asses out of here before thousands more Americans are killed chasing their false dreams, the public is going to turn on them in a big way and take all their little toys and bottomless budgets away from them."

The motor suddenly coughed and started again. Two of the crew ran across the deck to adjust the sail, hauling anxiously at the ropes holding the long boom. The sail fluttered wildly for a few seconds, then snapped taut. Janowitz stood and grabbed the stay that ran from the bow to the tip of the mast. The air was chillier when he stood up, and he shivered involuntarily. He could see inland now to where the mountains rose behind the plain. Not a light to be seen anywhere. Except for that, it could be any country. But this was a land full of people who obeyed the rules, who lived in darkness at night because our planes punished them if they didn't—and maybe because someone else punished them, too. He hoped Evans' optimism was justified. He sure was investing a lot in it.

He crouched back down again to get out of the damp breeze and curled up in his cape. "Are you a Communist?" he asked Thai at last. "I don't mean a party member—but you know, a believer in the system?"

"No, I am not a believer in the system," Thai answered. "But when I do not feel murderous about it, I am amused at your Yankee faith in the other system, in your capitalist democracy. You seem blinded by some apparition that fails to appear to the rest of us, no matter how desperately you rub your crystal ball."

"Come on now"—Janowitz smiled, wrapping himself even more snugly in his cape—"it's not all that difficult. We're the richest nation on earth. There must be *something* to our system."

"Ah, yes, but I am a poor Asian," Thai answered with mock humility. "Very provincial really. And though I confess your system gives a great deal of buoyancy to a land as rich, as uniformly educated, as economically democratic as the United States, I find its application to Asia just short of lunacy. And I am afraid," he added tauntingly, "your efforts to push it down our throats have—in my poor opinion—crossed over that line."

Thai's mocking tone was more playful than provocative, and Janowitz smiled in response. "The trouble with democracy," Thai went on, "even when it is separated from capitalism and so-called free enterprise, is that it is like a tree planted in the sand: It must be protected and fed for a long, long time, before it can stand on its own.

"You Americans talk about it as though everyone accepts its values—and ignores its problems as you do. But outside Europe—or places where Europeans have settled—there has never been democracy. Russia, China, Asia, Africa—none has had any experience with it at all, much less the long tradition you have. I studied for two years at the Sorbonne, and do you know what most amazed me?"

"Other than the girls, I can't imagine," Janowitz admitted.

"Other than the girls," Thai continued, "it was how Roman France was. Not just the Roman remains all over the country—the arenas and temples and aqueducts—but the Roman character of French monu-

332

ments and traditions. Napoleon and Caesar—Napoleon's tomb, his victory arches, everything, it is the same. And De Gaulle, he too is cast in exactly the same mold. And the law, the institutions of government —Senate is even a Roman word. So is justice. You all are raised in a tradition of democracy so strong you are not even aware of it—or how long it has been with you. But to us it is remarkable. *All* of it goes back to Rome—and ultimately to Greece. Two thousand years of emerging forms and traditions. The rest of the world has witnessed only perverted offshoots in the form of colonialism—and that for only a *hundred* years. You expect too much of us with your instant democracy. I do not think any of us are up to it. A people's democracy like that in Yugoslavia is better than the democracy in India, and far better than the corrupt 'democracy' of Venezuela or the Philippines. The solutions America keeps offering so hysterically to the world just won't work at this moment in history. One need not be paranoiac about it; one can regard it quite calmly. But I suspect the hysteria rises because you can see that it is true and simply will not face it."

Despite all the dry needling in Thai's argument, Janowitz felt a wave of pleasure. He was no scholar, but he loved to learn, loved the sensation of a new insight. He nodded to Thai, patronizingly—as though, "an amusing idea, young man." It wasn't in the nature of their banter to let Thai think he'd really scored.

For a time none of them spoke; just the even pulse of the motor and shriller rustle of the wind in the sail sounded about them. Finally, Thai spoke again, his voice reflective and without bitterness or irony. "What sort of democracy do you think there could be in the southern half of my country? Do you really think, for instance, that the peasants would vote in their own interests—or even know what their interests were? Do you think the influence of the landlords and monks and priests would be circumvented? Or that the wealthy would willingly give up their land and their power, that they would not manipulate the people and the legislature and the courts in their own interest? I will tell you—the answer is no. At best you would create a feudal democracy—like the Philippines. A mockery. The rich would remain rich, powerful, and corrupt; the poor would grow poorer—fed on the illusion that a choice between a few names selected for them on a ballot every few years represented 'freedom.'

"Perhaps," he continued with sudden drollery, "in *two hundred* years or maybe *three* hundred years there would evolve a condition something like you have in America. But not tomorrow, Lieutenant Janowitz. Or the day after. Not even," he said, grinning provocatively,

333

"in the fifty years it took Russia to go from feudalism to the moon—despite the cost of two wars and a revolution."

"I thought you weren't a Communist," Janowitz said.

"I'm not," Thai answered.

"Oh? Well, there are people at home who might say you'd do for one until the real thing comes along," Janowitz insisted.

"Ah, well," Thai sighed. "People at home are the bane of one's existence." He was staring right at Janowitz, and suddenly his face opened into a forthright laugh. "At times you are very serious, Comrade Janowitz."

"Am I?" Janowitz smiled. "That's only when a convinced non-Communist like you calls me Comrade. It confuses me. I think maybe he's taking me for a ride—one way or another."

Thai laughed again. "Quite right," he said. "But, you see, we use 'Comrade' as a revolutionary term. Why even Chiang Kai-shek used it, for he too was a revolutionary. It means," he said banteringly, "that we are equals."

"Oh," Janowitz replied, "that's what it means. I had the feeling it just might mean you *were* a Communist. You do such an excellent job of defending them. I kind of shudder to think how convincing you might be about something you *really* believe in."

Thai burst out laughing. "I will tell you," he said finally, "that that is my whole trouble. I do not *really* believe in anything. Except perhaps that it is wrong to believe too much in anything. Yes, I think that is what Comrade Evans and I have in common, a universal skepticism. Right, *Comrade?*"

"Amen," Evans intoned.

"No," Thai went on, "unlike the Communists, I do not believe man has produced any system with *all* the right answers. I do not even believe he ever will. All I think he can do is keep an open mind. There are enough problems around for *all* the solutions we can find. That is my faith, Comrade Janowitz."

"Then I would say," Janowitz observed, "that a skeptic like you would fare much better in our society than in a Communist one."

"I don't think so," Thai replied. "I doubt whether I would really be very free in the United States to say I thought the Communists had many of the right answers. And like most Americans, you do not recognize the freedom to criticize that exists in Communist states—the satiric nightclubs in Hungary and Czechoslovakia, the church in Poland, the humor magazines in all the countries, and, most important

334

of all, the critical power of the workers' committees themselves. How do you think so many reforms have come—even to Russia? Like all believers, you have closed your minds to the evidence.

"And everywhere in the world your country stands against the kind of progress I *do* believe in: the right to eat, the right to be free of foreign domination . . . and *economic* domination in one's own country—all these I am afraid I consider more important than your Roman worship of debate."

"And things like concentration camps for those who *do* debate—you can stomach that, can you?"

Thai smiled. "I don't *favor* them. But the Communists didn't invent concentration camps. Russia knew all about the things you ascribe to Communism long before Stalin was born. The Czars transported populations; they filled concentration camps in Siberia, tortured dissenters, and built up a ruthless secret police. Those things were an age-old part of Russian history. And it is the Communists who are at least beginning to put an end to them. Stalin—who would have made a good Czar incidentally!—was no help, to put it *mildly*. But neither is their fear of attack by the West. But do 'debaters' fare so well in what you call the free world? I'm told there are concentration camps in 'free' capitalist Greece, and how many political prisoners are there in Saigon now? And in Spain and Portugal and South America?"

He had grown serious, but now he grinned at Janowitz's sober frown.

"You Americans and your crusade against Communism." Thai sighed. "Ready to blow up the world and you really don't understand what you're fighting. Of course, the Russian Revolution led to vast excesses—as the French Revolution did, as *your* revolution did . . . though of all the revolutions, I confess I think yours the best.

"But the Russians destroyed a whole way of life—a brutal, inhuman life that regarded peasants as property to be bought and sold. In *this* century, in 1914. Of course, there were excesses in bringing it to an end! And you Americans are still diligently resisting them. But look at socialist society in Russia, or Yugoslavia, or Rumania—or *North Vietnam*. For the ordinary man, it is a thousand times better than it was before the revolution. It is not paradise. But do you really have paradise in the United States? I am inclined to think not."

Janowitz studied Thai—and he was shaken. Not so much by what he had to accept in Thai's arguments; those were verbal and ultimately debatable. It was Thai's attitude. He wasn't uninformed and he wasn't doctrinaire, and yet it was clear that he really didn't see any advantage in freedom, as Janowitz knew it, over Communism as Ho Chi Minh knew it. Not any advantage at all.

In a strange way it was more disturbing than all the words, all the reasons put together.

v

They were called below by the captain's wife about an hour later. It was surprisingly spacious belowdecks for the size of the boat. Only one swaying storm lamp lit the whole area, but they could see there were bunks in the bow and an open galley amidships. The captain's wife had placed their food on a wooden table that swung down from the bulkhead by the galley. It was low, and they sat on mats placed on the deck. Besides their own food, they were offered hot cauliflower with an aromatic cheese sauce, grapes, apples, and a rich red wine. Janowitz was sometimes as floored by the Frenchiness of the Vietnamese as Thai had been by the Romanism of the French. The moment they came down, the rest of the crew went up on deck, and only the captain's wife stayed below with them, busying herself about the galley as though they didn't exist.

"Tell me," Janowitz asked Thai, "is Tick—Tho, that is—is he *for* this mission or against it?"

"He is for the attack on the prison camp. He is against any negotiations with Americans," Thai answered. "He is even against the participation of Americans in the raid."

Janowitz frowned. "Why was he chosen then?"

"I think you call the system checks and balances." Thai grimaced. "Those who supported the possibility of negotiations were strong enough to get the mission approved—it is a very small mission, after all—but those who are against negotiations of any kind were strong enough to get Tho assigned as political officer to the mission." He shrugged philosophically.

"Is Hieu a Communist?" Janowitz asked slowly.

Thai hesitated. "She belongs to the Communist Youth League," he said after a moment. "Eventually she should be accepted into the party. Women tend to be the staunchest believers . . . in any system."

It fit, Janowitz thought. Hieu, conscientious, trusting, earnest—she'd

336

belong to the Communist Youth League all right. He was tempted to ask if Thai had ordered her to provoke the lovemaking that first day, but he wasn't sure he wanted to know.

He drank quite a bit of wine and felt very sleepy after their meal. The captain's wife indicated the bunks in the bow, and Thai said he was free to use one if he wished. But he still felt too nervous about moving South to feel he could drop off, so he returned to the main deck with Thai and Evans. They sprawled on the netting again, and Janowitz dozed fitfully, but a wind had come up and he felt chilly. He wrapped himself up in his cape again, but he still couldn't sleep. Finally, he decided he'd be more comfortable if he got away from the chill breeze and went below and crawled into one of the bunks. It was warm there, and the sound of the waves lapping on the hull was soporific. He finally went off to sleep thinking of Hieu, sitting bright-eyed and attentive at a Communist Youth League meeting, singing Red songs, believing every word. Even that thought made him smile. He loved her. He'd have to teach her "The Star-Spangled Banner."

vi

He snapped awake when the engine stopped. He knew he was on the boat, but for a second the surroundings of the bunk confused him. As soon as he recalled where he was, his pulse slowed down a little, and he sagged back, trying to go back to sleep again. He'd hardly closed his eyes and accepted the slower tempo of the wash on the bow when there were excited shouts from the main deck, and almost immediately the motor thumped into action again. He jumped out of bed and had reached the steps of the companionway when he heard the roar of a plane flashing overhead—and before his hands could grab the rail, there was a muffled explosion, and the boat lurched crazily. Ropes, pans, bowls, and drums of gasoline crashed around him, and water rushed down the companionway. He fought to get to the hatchway, but a second wild lurch pitched him head over heels. Before he could regain his feet, the boat swung back crazily, and he was sent sprawling into a lake of water on the lower deck. The boat rocked back and forth, but he managed to scramble to his feet. Outside he could see the weird glow of flares, and he heard another plane coming in. He grabbed the rail. The plane seemed on his head, wing cannons thundering. Wood flew around him; there were more shouts from the deck, the whoosh of an explosion followed by a wave of cascading water. But only the splash got them, the bomb itself had missed, and he fought his way up on deck.

Three flares were hanging in the sky, swinging on their chutes, making everything orange and pale blue. Janowitz couldn't tell how many planes there were. Another came whistling in at them seconds after he made the deck. He went down on his face, and it shot over, only inches above the mast it seemed. Two rockets had flashed at them as the plane closed, but they both were short, slashing into the water and sending up whirlpools of foam.

The crew were instantly back on their feet, two machine guns were pulled from beneath canvas and slapped into place, one at the bow and another in the stern just behind the tiller. Another plane was coming at them from way up, like a dive bomber. The crazy bastard, Janowitz thought, he thinks he's flying a Stuka, not a Phantom. But the guy made up in caution what he lacked in brains. He broke his dive fully a thousand yards above the boat and fired a pair of rockets that landed half a mile from them. The boat crew didn't even bother to fire back at him.

But they had their troubles. Another plane broke out of the dark, just off the bow, about fifty feet above the water, and it was going to get a long, full shot at them. Both machine guns on the boat poured lead at it, their tracers seeming to hit it again and again, but the plane kept closing. Janowitz buried his head in his hands. The rockets came first. He heard the explosions and wood cracking all around him; then the plane thundered over, shaking the boat in its wash—and then *wham!* The deck heaved, and Janowitz slid, clawing for a hold until he finally got a metal stanchion. Wood ripped, and part of the sail slashed down on him, pinning him to the deck. There was more machine-gun fire; another plane zoomed overhead. Janowitz clung desperately, but there was no explosion. At last he felt hands tearing at the sail, and Thai and the captain's wife pulled him free.

The boat was racing for shore. Janowitz wished to hell the guy on the tiller would take some evasive action, but before the next pass, he knew what was happening. Courageous Joe up above was trying another bit of long-distance dive-bombing. He started in his dive, and the whole shore line suddenly blazed. A curtain of ack-ack surrounded the plane. Immediately the pilot broke his dive, swept into a turn, and headed for the open sea. There was one laddie, Janowitz thought, who had every intention of living this war out!

338

One of the other planes started in at them just above the water. Janowitz went down again, Thai right beside him. But the shore batteries had the range now, and the plane was in a stream of flak to within fifty yards of the boat. It swept over, taking it from the machine guns and flying right on into another wall of flak when it had passed—and the pilot hadn't fired cannon or rocket or dropped a bomb. Janowitz wondered if the guy had been hit or just disconcerted. He did a sweet low-level turn and barreled out over the water—close to the surface and soon out of range, so Janowitz assumed he hadn't been hurt too badly, if he'd been hurt at all. It was the last they saw of the planes.

First one of the flares, then another sank into the sea. The last hung for a long time as they putted along more slowly very near the shore. Two of the crew had been hit. One was dead. Thai, the captain's wife, and a muscular young kid were tending the other. Janowitz watched them carry him below, then moved up to the bow to see if Evans was okay. He found him hanging on a spar, looking more than a little worse for the wear.

"Jesus," Evans groaned, "I almost went over the side."

"That makes two of us," Janowitz replied. Evans stared at him blankly for a second, then took a deep breath, as if he were just getting his wind back.

"It's funny," he said, "I can get scared in a fire fight on the ground —I guess I'm always scared in one. But on a ship I feel helpless. Like *they're* against me, the sea's against me—even the boat's against me."

Janowitz laughed, and Evans smiled bleakly. "It's weird," he said, "I don't feel that way in an airplane. I figure the sky's neutral, and the plane's with me. But on a boat—" He shook his head. Janowitz grinned, but then their eyes were caught by the activity at the stern. They were wrapping the dead crewman in canvas.

"Too bad," Evans said solemnly. "At least he'll be buried with his ancestors. It's become a rare privilege for those who die young."

Off the stern the last flare swayed back and forth near the surface of the sea and finally sank. The night was black again—after the sudden light, even blacker.

The motor revved up a bit, they started to move faster, and some of the crew returned to the deck, clearing the ropes of the sail, trying to salvage as much canvas as they could. The mast was shorn about three-quarters of the way up, but that was all the damage you could see in the dark.

"How did they spot us?" Janowitz asked quietly.

"Just routine," Evans shrugged. "Could have been a sonar citing by a sub or an SOP flare drop to see what they could see."

"But why us?"

"No reason. They'd do the same for any fishing boat. Why do you think the boats go out at night?" Janowitz looked at him with sudden understanding. Evans smiled grimly. "It's a great little war," he said, sprawling out on the tarpaulin. "It's a small, backward country. We've already dropped more bombs on it than we did on all of Europe during World War II—Germany, France, Italy, Holland, Rumania, Hungary, Czechoslovakia, all of them put together. What do you think we're bombing? Military targets? Sure, if a fishing boat supplies fish for the Army, it's a military target. If a harvester has a gun, he—or she—is an armed combatant. They all get shot at." He looked at the crew working on the sail. "They honestly believe we intend to destroy them as a race. A thousand missions a week, week after week, for the last *three* years, shelling by the Navy, fragmentation bombs used on villages, little extra raids by B-52's. And it's a *little* country—smaller than Idaho, for Christ's sake. What would you think?"

Janowitz didn't answer.

"It's funny," Evans said glumly, "it's not really the killing that bothers me so much as the deceit and arrogance of it all . . . like Hitler . . . only it's my country doing it."

"It's not altogether like Hitler," Janowitz corrected.

"Why? Because we let the Arvin torture instead of doing it ourselves? No, that isn't fair," he said. "It isn't like Hitler. There are many people trying to do the right thing. I suppose it's the government that gets me. . . . It seems like, I don't know, when I was in high school—ten years ago—we could trust what our own government said. We knew that 'they' were the liars, the deceivers—not us. And in ten years it's all gone upside down.

"Only Reds lied; now we not only lie, but lie louder, more obviously, more brutally. Once only Reds overthrew governments with spies and provocateurs; only Reds were guilty of political assassination. Now we know our CIA is capable of anything they are. Whatever gains our geniuses in Washington think they've made, they've lost, lost because now everything we say in the world is as suspect as what Russia said in Stalin's time. Only maybe it's worse—because those who once trusted us are disillusioned, twice deceived because they didn't expect it."

340

Janowitz rolled over on his stomach. He could see the shore now; his eyes were getting used to the dark again.

Evans rolled over, too, both of them looking out over the bow, the rush of wash just below them. The cold wind had died, and the air rising from the sea actually seemed warm.

"The big lie," Evans said caustically. " 'We are in Vietnam to repel invasion from the North.' Our President has said it; our Secretary of Defense has said it. I don't think anybody in the world believes them, but they keep saying it—as Hitler used to say the Sudetenland is German. And the theory is if you say it long enough and loud enough, it will become a truth—like the real truth." He put his head down; his voice was strained and emotional. "And what do you think *that* sounds like to the Vietnamese?"

"Well, it may be a bit off-color," Janowitz answered, "but you're not going to deny that the North Vietnamese *are there* and have been for a long time!"

"No," Evans replied sullenly. "But they're there in *response* to what we were doing in the South, not the other way around. Hell, did we support the French because of an 'invasion from the North'? Crap! The truth is that for the first year after the Geneva Conference, Ho evidently believed there was going to be a referendum, and no one of the old Vietminh—North or South—did anything. And by the time Diem announced that he had no intention of running for an election of any kind, *we* were already thick on the ground in South Vietnam, and Diem's government would have collapsed in a week without our financial support."

"Damn." Janowitz sighed. He watched the bow chop through the rolling waves. "How the hell did we get in this mess?" he said at last. "I know we've lied, I know we've deceived, I know we've been brutal, and yet I know and *you* know that isn't America. It's not our thing."

"Jesus," Evans puffed remorsefully, "how I wish I could understand. I know it's fear of Communism basically, but even given that how can people watch our country do it and continue to work in factories making arms, send their sons marching off to get killed, and all the time wave their flags and sing 'God Bless America'? I wish I knew.

"You know," he said pensively, "it amazes me that people in America can't conceive how that mess in Tonkin Bay looks to the North Vietnamese. Our President says two small American ships were innocently cruising in the high seas off North Vietnam and they were savagely attacked by North Vietnamese torpedo boats. And in response

341

to this wicked act of provocation, we started our bombing of the North, we built up our armed forces in the South from about twenty-five thousand 'advisers' to half a million combatants. And now, *years* later it finally comes out that those two innocent little American boats were supporting an Arvin raid on Northern radar installations, that they'd been warned off, and that maybe two torpedoes were fired at them—but maybe none at all.

"But the North Vietnamese have known the truth all along! They knew no one torpedoed 'innocent American ships sailing in international waters.' They knew from the beginning we manufactured an excuse to bomb—and we bombed. And they know we screamed our excuse to the world through the mouths of the highest men of our government—and after all that *we* say the North Vietnamese are not to be trusted! Jesus, after his past experiences trusting the West, after the way he has seen our government use the big lie, how can people even wonder why Ho Chi Minh says he doesn't trust *us?* I wouldn't trust us with a used beer can."

Janowitz sat up. He was beginning to think it all was hopeless again and wished Evans would shut up. The crew were still clearing away the mess on deck, but the captain's wife and a couple of crewmen were already at work stitching the sail. She was near the stern, with a big kerosene lamp swinging beside her. Her face looked stupid and harsh. He wondered what the hell she knew of Tonkin Bay and statements by Presidents and that crap. She looked as if it wouldn't make any difference to her whether the Japanese or the French or anyone else ran her country. If an American general set up house in Hanoi next week, she'd probably move down the coast with a cargo for him just as willingly as she was doing for Uncle Ho. Of course, the way these people were indoctrinated, she probably was forced to know a lot more about things than people like her ever had before—but there was something about that hard, stoic face that convinced him it would all be like water on a duck. It was the winner she was interested in.

They both slept off and on until just before dawn. Then Janowitz awoke, feeling stiff and aware of murmured conversations. An angry shout echoing across the water turned his head. Through the dark, off the starboard side, he could see the shadowy outline of a whole flotilla of boats slowly closing on them. That was the source of the murmured conversations. He could hear them now, clearly, across the water, people talking, giving directions. He sat up. The crew was lined up along the deck rail, two of them held grappling hooks. As he

342

watched, the captain's wife made a weird, birdlike call through her cupped hands.

Evans stirred, stretched, and sat up. He started when he saw what was going on, but he threw a quick smile at Janowitz. "Well," he said, "you're back in South Vietnam—or at least the waters of South Vietnam."

Janowitz peered harder at the boats approaching. He could tell now they all were fishing boats—similar to the one they were on. All had the same tall mainmast, the lateen sail, the small mizzenmast astern that he assumed was used as a hoist for nets. His stomach started feeling queasy again.

"Where are we?" he asked.

"Not far off Hue," Evans replied. "This fleet is from Quang Tri."

They watched as one of the boats came alongside. The grappling hooks went out, and Thai, who was standing with the crew, jumped across. The ships drifted apart for a time; then Thai appeared on the deck of the other boat again, and they drew alongside once more.

"Come along," Thai shouted to Janowitz and Evans. He was smiling and seemed buoyed up by something. The grappling hooks went out again. Janowitz grabbed his cape and leaped across. He turned to wave at the other crew, but they simply watched stoically as the two boats drifted apart again.

On board the new boat the atmosphere couldn't have been more different from the North Vietnamese boat. There were smiles everywhere, and the crew kept looking at Janowitz and Evans and nodding their heads like teen-agers whose party had just been crashed by Paul Newman and Warren Beatty.

Thai took them below and showed them where they were to hide if the boat was searched. Two false panels in the bow, covered with half-rotted bait. Janowitz realized what a chance they were taking with him. And from the way Thai looked at him, so did he. If they were searched, all Janowitz would have to do would be to make a rumpus— and that would be the end of mission, of Thai, of Evans. But they were right to trust him. It was beyond him now to betray Thai or Evans to a search party of Arvin—or even of Americans. It wasn't that he'd switched his loyalties, he knew that—he'd only expanded them. He was still loyal to that cluttered flag, but he was loyal, too, to Evans and Thai—even to the mission. And he was half-amused to realize he no longer found those loyalties contradictory.

Dawn came as in a storybook, a huge orange globe rising slowly out

343

of the sea, clearing the mist before it, looking like some massive, benign observer from space on our frenetic little escapades down here below. They remained on deck for a time, watching the rest of the fleet materialize from the gray-pink predawn haze, seeing the shoreline emerge from the wraiths of mist and gradually solidifying into a copper and green border on the endless expanse of gray-blue sky. Janowitz felt strange looking at it. There were Americans there, getting ready for the day, writing letters, thinking of home. The first little puffs of cumulus began to evolve above the land, culled from nothingness, like magicians' rabbits, when a call came from below and they descended to find a grinning, widemouthed boy of about twelve.

He had prepared the three of them an "American" breakfast and was proud beyond containment. There were eggs and strips of fat bacon and a big box of Kellogg's Corn Flakes. Janowitz and Evans both laughed. American breakfast cereals weren't rare in South Vietnam, but somehow this all-American culinary display made the war, the mission, and everything else seem ludicrous and inconsequential. Janowitz tousled the boy's head, and the kid's face shone. Thai didn't get the joke, but he was more than willing to join in the fun. When it came to eating, it was more difficult. The kid produced a jug of milk for the cornflakes, but there was no sugar, and when they tasted the first mouthful, Janowitz knew something else was wrong, too.

"Goat's milk," Evans whispered.

Janowitz had never tasted it before—and right away he knew there was a hell of a difference between goats and cows. But they couldn't disappoint the kid, and they plunged manfully in—and the worse it tasted, the more they had to grin . . . until by the time they finished they were laughing out loud at almost every bite. And the kid was delighted.

Thai's own lightheartedness grew from a bit of luck. Nine times out of ten the fleet was accompanied by a naval patrol boat—usually manned by Arvin types—and an elaborate meeting and parting in the night had been planned, but a raid was being staged somewhere along the coast, and all the patrol boats had been assigned to it. Not only did it mean the transfer was easy, but they'd also be able to head south at full speed without any pretense of fishing along the way. The fleet would fish now for about an hour, then dump all the fish on the three fastest boats—of which this was one—and send them on their way. If they were stopped, they were only an eager unit separated by ambition from their lazier brothers who had stayed around Hue.

344

"And if one man in the whole fleet opens his mouth, we're cooked," Janowitz commented.

Thai grinned. "In most of this war if one man were to open his mouth—in a village, in Saigon itself, in many fishing fleets like this—the Liberation Front would be cooked."

"And you're telling me that isn't managed by terror?" Janowitz asked cynically.

"Oh, I would not want to be an opportunist who had sold information to the Americans," Thai replied, "nor would I care to be a village chief who had decided his bread was best buttered by the Americans—to use one of your expressions. But if all the peasants, or fishermen, or villagers were against us—even if many of them were against us—we could not survive. You forget this has been a colonial country for many generations, and my people learned long ago to turn a blind eye to the activities of those who resist the white conquerors."

Thai smiled. "You have no friends in Vietnam, Comrade Janowitz. Not even General Ky *likes* Americans. . . . But take your planes and your tanks and your flamethrowers home," he added, "and come back with your cameras and your wives. Then you will find friends in Vietnam."

Back on deck they watched the crew fish tirelessly. The nets went over the side again and again. All the other ships were some distance from them and fishing just as strenuously. Janowitz helped toss a few baskets of fish into the hold, and the crew all grinned broadly at him. Why, he wondered? An American on their side? Or because Thai's uncle had bribed them all heavily and he represented a big catch? Or was it just because the sun was up and the sea smelled good and it was hard to be angry at anything?

Finally, the master of the ship, a thin, bald man with a little goatee and a mustache, rang the ship's bell, and the other boats hauled in their nets and started to close on them. They took turns dumping fish aboard—and soon all three of the fastest boats had fish piled and leaping about their decks as the crews worked to fill the holds. Janowitz, Thai, and Evans plunged into the work with the rest, and the crews on all the boats laughed and chattered about the working Americans. Finally, the three boats were loaded and headed off toward the south, riding under sail and motor and moving at a good clip.

Janowitz stood with Thai and Evans in the stern until they could no longer see the rest of the fleet. Then Thai turned and put his hand on Janowitz's shoulder. "If we are lucky like this on the whole trip, we will be in Saigon in three days. You see," he smiled, "we can travel openly in authorized boats during the day and illegally at night in boats of the Liberation Front. Your planes will not bomb us during the day"—he nodded at the identifying flag at the stern—"and at night they will only bomb us if they can see us. Perfection, *n'est-ce pas?*"

"American Express couldn't have arranged it better," Janowitz said. Thai laughed. "You can see the advantage if we invaded the North as some of our generals want," Janowitz continued lightly.

Thai's smile died. "There are many who wish you would," he said coldly.

"Why the hell do you say something like that?" Janowitz demanded.

Thai relaxed, and his face lost its edge of astringency. "Mathematics," he explained. "You have half a million men fighting approximately one hundred and forty thousand in the South. We have an army of almost half a million in the North—and a trained civilian militia three times that size. And in addition, every civilian is armed and ready— mentally, as well as militarily. Some of my father's more ambitious friends hope you will attack. They believe you would then be faced with outright military defeat or with the need to raise an army of four to five million to fight little Vietnam. Actually they are convinced you would not *win* if you sent an army of ten million. And who can say they are wrong?"

"It might be a dangerous gamble on both sides," Janowitz said. "I can hear some of *our* generals shouting atom bomb in a situation like that."

Thai shrugged. "It is *all* 'generals' talk' to me," he said. "They talk of deaths as they do of mortars or typewriters—you only count them. To me it is all madness. But they would answer you that if America did use an atom bomb, America would soon look like Vietnam, because by our defense pact with the Russians, they would be forced to retaliate."

"Well, pacts have been made, and pacts have been broken." Janowitz smiled. "I don't want anyone using an atom bomb for any reason, but I don't really think, Thai, that the Russians are ever going to risk Mother Russia for all the rice in Vietnam."

"At the end of World War II," Evans interjected, "the historians discovered that that was exactly how Hitler reasoned when he attacked Poland. England and France were never going to risk their people and their homes for distant Poland because of a scrap of paper. So Hitler marched—and World War II began." He shrugged. "The human mind is never utterly predictable."

346

They made good time until late in the afternoon when a patrol of three PT boats appeared far astern, closing on them fast. An alarm bell clanged, and there was much frantic shouting back and forth. The fishing boats were slowed gradually, but the nets were lowered immediately to give the appearance they were trawling. In a few minutes the boats were down to genuine trawling speed, and the PT boats were near. Janowitz and Evans were hustled below, and Thai took up a station at one of the nets.

It was smelly, hot, and close in behind the false paneling. The area was really only big enough for someone about five ten, and Janowitz thought he'd die of backache if he had to stay there more than ten minutes. But when he heard the roar of the PT boats pulling up alongside, he forgot all about his aching bones. His heart was pounding. He thought of Thai on deck, and that crew. What would their faces give away?

He heard boots on deck, and then everything was quiet for a time —then boots coming down the stairs into the hold, some cursing in Vietnamese, more footsteps, then the boots going back up. He breathed a sigh of relief. But too soon. The cursing grew louder on deck; there were shouts and then a burst of machine-gun fire. He almost burst out of the panel. Thai? If some fucking Arvin had shot Thai, he'd join the goddamned VC himself—totally, no reservations! The engines of the PT boat roared again, and he could hear one of the other PT boats. What was going on? Were they taking them all in?

He waited and waited. The motor continued to idle. Nothing happened. He was drenched in sweat, and he felt he was going to die of suffocation. Then the boat started to move again—slowly. They're escorting us in, he thought. What now? If they go over these boats and find Evans and me . . . Traitors? Or prisoners? Shit, he thought, he could make anyone think they were prisoners—they hadn't shouted out simply because they had been threatened with their lives if they did. All right, let them find him . . . but what had they done to Thai?

Then suddenly someone was loosening the panel. It was Thai— barefooted like the rest of the crew, smiling and looking very pleased with himself. Janowitz sagged back against the hull. He didn't even want to move. Thai pulled Evans' panel loose, and Evans came out, looking white from the heat and confinement.

"What the hell happened?" Evans said.

"The glorious Navy of the Republic of South Vietnam." Thai

347

smiled. "They asked a few questions, believed no answers, hit a couple of men, fired some threatening shots at our little cook, and then left. They sensed something was up, but I don't think they really wanted to pursue it too far." He took Janowitz's hand and pulled him gaily out among the fish.

Janowitz stared at him incredulously for a second, then growled, "Fuck you!" and staggered belligerently through the quivering fish to the gangway ladder. Thai frowned in bafflement at Evans, but Evans was as much at a loss as he.

Up on deck Janowitz could see that the boats were trawling again and heading east. Thai and Evans came up and stood tentatively beside him. "We figure they picked us up on radar," Thai explained, "so we must be too close to shore. We're going to run out to sea for a time before we get up speed again." Janowitz flopped out on deck. The breeze felt wonderful. Wow. He'd heard of torture by the box, and that was as much of it as he ever wanted. Now that his anxiety was over, he was aware of every aching muscle and bone in his body—and from the way he felt they all were aching.

Evans sprawled beside him, and Thai sat, Oriental fashion, at their feet. Janowitz had his hands over his eyes; he lifted them a little to glance at Thai. He had to smile. "You don't like the Arvin?" he asked archly.

Thai shrugged. "When I see them, armed and uniformed in equipment bought by Americans, in boats and tanks supplied by Americans, I want to strike them down," he murmured quietly, the gentleness of his tone belying his words. "But when I think of how they became what they are and the nights of doubt and fear they must have, I feel sorry for them."

"So how did they become what they are?" Janowitz asked.

Thai stared at the deck, as though seeing it all before him. "Some come from families who have a tradition of serving in the French forces. Ky is one of those. But ordinary soldiers, too. It was a way to make a living. And then there are the bullies and Fascists—every country has those. The Arvin makes a comfortable home for them as well —but they know that one day there will be a reckoning; Americans will not be here forever, so all those who are not insane act with some moderation."

"You're more generous toward them than Hill." Janowitz grinned.

Thai looked up at him. "They are my countrymen," he said softly.

11

i

       As Thai had predicted, it was just after dawn of their third day that they rounded Cap St.-Jacques into the estuary below Saigon. The run, with its changes every twilight and every dawn, had been smooth and fast with only one time of real anxiety—when the daylight hours were running out on them opposite Cam Ranh Bay. The little fishing boat they were on was plowing through streams of American shipping—commercial and naval. Planes and helicopters were passing overhead all the time, and Arvin PT boats flashed along the coast in forays to and from the big harbor. It seemed certain someone would stop them, but it was probably the very audacity of their brazenly sailing through it all that saved them from danger. They continued on, even a little after dark, to the port at Phan Rang, where they transferred to a VC sampan powered by a giant Evinrude with an underwater silencer and a hand-painted water skier on its flashy hood. The rest of the run had been easy, with the greatest danger always at night when the fear of some sudden flare lighting them up for shore batteries or American sea and air assault was always with them. But the VC were confident, and twice they had casually pulled in under cover after being warned in advance of patrols—and calmly played cards until the search ships passed. Janowitz found it a bit too unnerving and always drank as much wine as possible at dinner and tried to sleep the night through.

      Before dawn on the third morning they had transferred to a big fishing launch with Saigon registration and the English name Lynda Bird gaudily painted on bow and stern. The crew seemed more American than Vietnamese. The captain wore a GI fatigue hat that had been dyed blue and looked like a yachting cap. He was sort of young, maybe twenty-eight, and trim and muscular, with a small layer of fat that suggested a few too many beers. The whole crew wore American

349

sneakers of various ages; the captain had a brand-new pair of blue and white Keds. And all their clothes were American, too—torn T-shirts, sawed-off khaki pants, polo shirts. The cook—a guy with thick glasses and the precise air of a lifetime civil servant—had a sweat shirt with "University of Pennsylvania" stamped on it, escutcheon and all.

The whole atmosphere reeked of a sort of prosperity Janowitz hadn't seen since he'd been captured. It was like walking from nineteenth century to twentieth century in one step from sampan to diesel-powered fishing ketch. Even the boat looked as if it wouldn't be completely out of place sailing into the harbor of the Detroit Yacht Club on Belle Isle. It was freshly painted, the decks were clean, the mainsail was synthetic fiber rather than canvas, and the tiller was housed in three-quarter-glass shelter.

They were hurried down belowdecks, and the captain told them to remain below until he himself gave them explicit instructions to do otherwise—no matter what happened. They didn't really need the warning—not this close to Saigon. But things had changed. On the rest of the trip everyone had treated Thai with deference, but this guy looked—and acted—like the captain of a charter boat who wasn't going to let the customers be boss. It was all pleasant and convivial, but no-nonsense either. He shook hands all around and trotted up the companionway. In a few seconds they were bouncing across the choppy waters of Cap St.-Jacques at full speed.

Down below it was as spit and polish as up above. The dining table was burnished with wax and elbow grease; there were benches on each side and, in the ceiling, gleaming fluorescent lights powered by the engine. The cook gave them a breakfast of fish and eggs, French bread, and tea. Then he led them to a forward cabin that had four bunks equipped with plastic foam mattresses.

"Goddamn, the twentieth century, Thai!" Janowitz remarked brightly. "You can't knock it."

Thai smiled, and Evans flung himself on one of the bunks. "Jesus," he exclaimed, "the next war I hope to hell I can stay on our side!"

Janowitz laughed and climbed into the bunk above him. It gave him room to stretch his feet over the end. Thai muttered something in Vietnamese to the civil servant cook, and the guy bowed with the supercilious acquiescence of civil servants and went out, closing the door behind him. Thai took the upper berth opposite Janowitz. There were small portholes on either side just about at the line of the upper bunks, and you could lie with your head pushed down on the mattress and look out at the passing scene.

"This guy looks as if he's really got the system sewed up," Janowitz observed as he looked around the cabin. There was a Playboy calendar on the door, American cigarette butts in the ashtray at the side of the bunk, and a bottle of VO, a bottle of Black Label, and a bottle of Gilbey's Dry secured in the rack below the life preservers.

"Some people are to the manner born," Evans remarked.

"What's he doing," Janowitz asked Thai, "playing the black market with one hand and making sure he keeps in with you guys with the other?"

"He is probably cautious," Thai answered thoughtfully. "He would not betray us because he knows that might lead to an unfortunate accident, but I do not really think that surrounded here by thousands of Americans and seeing all your planes and guns and ships, he believes the Liberation Front is ever going to win—not in Saigon anyway. There is a whole body of shopkeepers and entrepreneurs—you would call them middle-class people—in Saigon who do not think the United States will ever be forced out of the large cities. They may have perhaps a ten percent doubt—but when they look at the roads you build, the ports, the huge warehouses and landing fields, the offices and housing, they do not believe you are ever going to simply sign a piece of paper and walk away.

"I would say our captain is one of those people," Thai added. "He has made himself American and will try to improve on the process. As for his treatment of us—that is simply American regard for the customer. We are a very good customer of his. We pay good prices, and we pay in advance. He only hopes the war lasts long enough for him to build up enough capital so that he may transfer to some more legitimate business. I suspect he is really long past that point, but he has absorbed the American drive to exceed last year's goals with even new records this year." He was grinning at Janowitz, a combination of amusement and mockery lighting his face.

"I take it," Janowitz replied wryly, "that you're trying to tell me again that the VC buy in the Saigon black market."

"I'm telling you that the *Liberation Front* buys in the Saigon black market," Thai corrected.

Janowitz nodded. "Of course, my mistake. But do you really think you can buy *American* stuff?" Thai laughed, and Evans joined him. "I'm not talking about PX knickknacks," Janowitz went on testily. "I mean something that matters—like a prop for a helicopter?"

Thai shrugged. "We might have to steal that—or arrange to have it stolen. But almost everything else—" He smiled and spread his arms

351

in a gesture of amplitude. "We will probably be able to choose from rival sellers."

"Have you ever been down to the docks?" Evans asked.

"Nope."

"Well, it's not all military, you know. There are several hundred free-lance American businessmen down there running short-haul transfers, wholesaling, shipping. They're here to make a profit—not because they love the smell of Saigon Harbor. The military's their big customer, and none of them is going to risk losing that business, but if you provided enough cover for them, they'd sell you the *Enterprise*—and all the planes to go with it."

Thai was still watching Janowitz tentatively. "You see," he said, "they too believe America is bound to win, so they feel that a little profit to them will hurt no one—and if they don't question too deeply where the items go, they can declare with some honesty that they had no idea the material was going to the Liberation Front." He grinned. "And so, you see, the half lie does not always work in your favor, even in Vietnam."

"It's not all a joke," Evans said with sudden asperity. "The Front buys on the black market—in big quantities—and it sends the price of everything up." He rolled out and leaned over his bunk to look up at Janowitz.

"The first time I was sent to buy for the Front," he said, "I went as an American civilian, and after going through a chain of about forty people—Vietnamese, French, Chinese, English—I finally ended up meeting an American warrant officer. He had steeled himself with several shots of whiskey and was three sheets to the wind when I met him at a bar down in Cholon. He kept laughing and saying, 'Hell, I'm not doing anything anyone else wouldn't do if they had the chance. Boy, everybody's making money off this war,' he'd say, 'all them people back in the States, those civilians working downtown in offices, the Philippines, the Japs—why shouldn't we, eh?' And he'd poke me and take another drink.

"And finally we made a deal. I paid him a fortune, and a smaller one for two GI drivers who were to haul the stuff from the port area to a warehouse in Gia Dinh. It was meat and canned goods and about a quarter of a shipload of fresh lettuce heads, all neatly wrapped in cellophane. The warrant officer was procurement officer and assistant head of a mess hall at Tan Son Nhut. When we'd sewn up the deal and I'd dropped a few pointed hints about what would happen to him if he didn't come through with the deliveries, he got real maudlin, almost

352

crying in his beer, and he said I didn't have to worry, he wasn't doing this just to make a killing. Hell, he was bleeding for those poor fucking Vietnamese. So he had six thousand guys to feed; well, fuck it, if he couldn't steal enough to feed another six thousand Vietnamese without anybody knowing the difference, he'd wasted twenty years in the Air Force. No, sir, he wasn't doing this just for money; he felt these people deserved a break, and if the black market was the only way to give it to them, then he'd use the black market."

"Real humanitarian," Janowitz commented dryly.

"That's right," Evans agreed. "He was going to do about three more deeds like this for the struggling Vietnamese and then take his retirement, move to Arizona, collect his check from Uncle Sam every month, and vote to preserve law and order. He had a whole life of public service already mapped out."

"Well, I wouldn't get too cynical about it if I were you, Evans," Janowitz admonished. "I kinda feel he wouldn't exactly approve of the way you've got your life mapped out either."

"No, I'm sure he wouldn't," Evans said. "But what really got me about the whole experience was that I felt the guy was sincere. He was rationalizing sure, but he really did believe he was helping the Vietnamese. And maybe it was the whiskey, but I began to believe it too." He glanced severely at Thai. "But then I saw what the Front did with the stuff. The canned goods were sent down into the delta to combat units there, but the meat and lettuce were sold on the black market—not to the poorest, the hungriest, and the neediest, but to the highest bidder. The French colony, the Chinese merchants, and the Tu Do Street bars had fresh lettuce and thick steaks for two weeks."

"It paid for bribing your mess officer and for the canned goods," Thai said flatly.

"And a good deal more," Evans cut back.

Janowitz glanced from one to the other. Well! Life did have its surprises.

"So in the end," Evans said, "I decided the drunken warrant officer wasn't such a slob after all. He was looking out for number one, but he had some concern for the people around him. And the Front—whose business is the people—was only concerned with making the deal pay."

"We have a war to finance," Thai said.

"I wouldn't be here with you now, Thai, if I thought war was a justification for shedding your principles," Evans replied quietly.

It put an end to the conversation. None of them even moved for a time, too embarrassed by the tension the story created. Finally, Janowitz rolled over and watched the shoreline slip past. The occasional sight of an American truck would flip his heartbeat up, but it wasn't long before he dozed off.

It was a ship's horn—raucous and ill tempered—that finally woke him. He shook his head and looked out the porthole. They were nearing Saigon, and the river was crowded with traffic—sampans, powerboats, a few fishing ketches like the one they were on, PT boats. He couldn't see the boat whose horn awoke him—passed on the other side, he guessed. It was stifling hot in the cabin now, and he was wringing wet with sweat. At first, all the activity on the river made him nervous, but then he accepted that no one was paying attention to them. He fumbled with the porthole, trying to open it but couldn't get his hand on the latch.

"Here, maybe I can do it from down here." It was Evans. He knelt on his bunk and shoved at the porthole, and it opened to about forty-five degrees, letting in a reviving stream of air.

The stench was awful. They weren't far offshore, and as far as the eye could see, little tin and steel shacks huddled together in the hot sun. The shore was lined with people emptying slop pails of excrement, and there were rivulets running down the little alleys, rivulets whose stinking loads flowed right into the water.

Fortunately they passed another tongue of the estuary and swung out from the shore and were in clear water again.

"Look!" Evans called.

Janowitz turned back to the porthole. Evans was kneeling on his bunk peering out, and Janowitz followed his line of sight. Down the other tongue of the estuary he could see a Hovercraft buzzing down the center of the waterway. Foam flew around its base, creating little rainbows all around it, and as it got closer, its great humming roar obscured all the other sounds of the river. He could see the people in sampans and houseboats, women washing in the filthy water, turn and watch it—they were immune to interest in anything else on the river. As it came closer, he could see the guns mounted fore and aft and the Navy crew perched, arrogant and self-satisfied, in the breeze. In a strange way the Hovercraft separated them by more than a century from the Vietnamese. It belonged to the day after tomorrow—more mysterious, more awesome than the familiar Western instruments, no matter how complicated or savage they were. He could imagine himself an uneducated Vietnamese watching a Hovercraft—and he

354

guessed that maybe that would make him feel more hopeless than all the B-52's, the napalm, and helicopters put together.

He glanced over at Thai, lying on his bunk, looking slight, almost frail. The guttural roar of the Hovercraft had awakened him, and he opened his eyes without moving. He smiled at Janowitz and then closed his eyes again, slipping back into sleep. Well, *he* was calm enough.

Their boat continued upstream for another five minutes or so, and then the motor began to idle and the anchor was dropped.

"What now?" Janowitz asked.

Evans glanced at his watch. "We wait for a time," he answered. "It shouldn't be long."

They were about sixty yards from shore, another flat, muddy stretch covered with hundreds of shacks. It was near midday, and few people were moving in the heat, but Janowitz could see three or four gangs of kids playing as if they were in a park. Just give them enough food so they weren't absolutely listless, he thought, and kids would roar through life on a garbage heap. But he was glad he wasn't stationed in Saigon. Out in the country you saw the beauty of the place. If a village was bombed out, it was still surrounded by greenery and water and shaded paths. But it would have killed him to have seen these people every day, dirty and underfed, baked in miles of squalid ovens. Hell, some of them must have to walk through twenty minutes of it even to get to a road—twenty minutes of walking through shit to your first breath of fresh air—if a hot tarmac surrounded by shacks could be called a source of fresh air. He wondered why suicide wasn't one of the biggest problems of the war. It'd sure depress him—and what it would do to a woman who couldn't get out of it, he shuddered to think.

There was a howl across the water, and he saw a couple of the kids fighting. A skinny, wrinkled old woman hobbled out of one of the shacks shouting and waving a bamboo stick at them. The kids ran— victim and victimizer alike. Janowitz rolled over on his back. It was then that he first became aware of the rumble. Just the deep-throated hum of a powerful motor, very close and drawing nearer.

"Evans!" he whispered.

"Yeah?"

"Do you hear—" But before he could finish, they heard and felt the bump of a boat alongside. He squeezed down to the porthole, and inches from him was the dark-blue hull of a boat of the harbor police. Evans was on his knees looking out, too, so there was no need to say anything more. Janowitz pulled himself back and sat hunched up with his back against the bulkhead. He didn't want to take any chance on them seeing *him*. All of a sudden he wondered how smooth the boat captain really was. *Lynda Bird*. He should have named the damned boat *General Ky*.

There were footsteps on deck, and then others, coming down the companionway. Voices, social laughter—and then the door to the cabin opened. The civil servant cook was holding it back . . . and in walked two white uniformed police. The "White Mice" of Saigon. Janowitz stared—too stunned to do anything but gape. The fucking captain had sold them out.

The police looked around at the three of them, nodded toward the still-sleeping Thai, and then walked back out. The cook shook Thai's leg, and Thai sat up groggily.

"Police—" Janowitz whispered.

Thai glanced out to the main cabin. He jumped down and followed the cook out, closing the door after him. Evans slipped out of his bunk and stood looking at Janowitz.

"What the hell gives?" Janowitz asked.

"Just wait," Evans said tensely.

The door reopened, and the cook signaled them out. As soon as they moved into the cabin, the police slapped their hands behind them and handcuffed their wrists. "All right," one of them said in thickly accented English, "move along." And he shoved Janowitz toward the companionway. What is this, Janowitz thought? Has the captain betrayed us, or has Evans betrayed me? He was "encouraged" up the companionway, and on deck another pair of White Mice shoved him toward their boat. It was a PT boat with a spacious cabin abovedeck, and as he was pushed into it, he saw Thai coming up to the deck of the ketch and being roughed up and handcuffed.

There was a conference between the head of the White Mice and the boat captain and thirty seconds later the police boat roared away from *Lynda Bird*.

The three of them were lined against a bulkhead and secured with a chain to a steel rail. Janowitz looked at Evans. It looked as if Evans were going to say something, but one of the White Mice slapped a thick cloth blindfold over his eyes and nose. And a second later Janowitz got the same treatment. It wasn't tied too tightly, and by tipping his head a little, he could get a glimpse across the deck. He watched the feet and, when no one seemed right in front of him, twisted to look aft. By tilting his head, he could see over the low gunwale. They were sweeping past rows and rows of small houseboats, moored side by side, most of them nothing more than sampans with rattan housing over

356

the hulls. No one was moving in the midday heat, not even to watch the surging police boat. But from the way the boats were packed together, Janowitz knew they were being taken into the center of the city.

He was suddenly aware of a foot close to him. Shit, he was going to get a good clout. But the foot moved on. And then he realized it all might be part of the plan!

"Evans!" he yelled over the motor's roar.

"Be quiet!" Thai shouted back.

Well—maybe yes, maybe no. He tilted his head again—still acres and acres of the little rattan houseboats crammed together. The river was curving; he could see trees distantly. God, they were taking them right in. They'd be in the waterfront area soon. Down in Soulsville, Hill's own stamping grounds. He got a hard, sudden cuff on the side of the head. He brought his face down. The feet stood in front of him but, when he didn't try to tilt his head again, moved on.

In a few minutes the boat subsided in the water. Janowitz could hear shouted instructions; they slowed down even more. One of the White Mice hurriedly undid their chain. "Down! Down!" And they were shoved to the deck. Then suddenly the boat surged ahead again at full speed. There was a sharp turn, another; then it slowed, and even before it settled in the water, someone was yanking at their blindfolds. He could feel other hands undoing the handcuffs. When he rolled free, Thai was already on his feet. They were idling beside an elaborate houseboat—with awnings and floral deck furniture.

"Hurry!" Thai commanded, and ran to the side of the boat and leaped onto the houseboat. Janowitz jumped after him, and Evans scrambled along behind. They were on a bay with big houses, private docks, and, here and there, a fancy houseboat, like the one they were on, moored to a dock. The police boat backed away slowly, swung around, and roared off.

Thai pushed Janowitz through white louvered doors into a shadowed central room on the houseboat. It was high-ceilinged, and all the walls were louvered; there were two hammocks covered with mosquito netting strung across one end and wicker chairs and a wicker liquor cabinet in the other half of the room. Thai ran immediately to the louvers on one side and twisted his head to look out. Evans went opposite and did the same thing. Janowitz sagged into one of the chairs.

Evans finally turned around and grinned broadly. "Welcome to Saigon," he said, "the Jewel of the East."

Janowitz grimaced.

"She's coming," Thai said quietly.

Evans moved quickly to his side. "She should have waited."

Janowitz could hear footsteps moving up the wooden dock.

"It's siesta," Thai reasoned. "Maybe it's best to be quick about it."

The footsteps jumped from dock to houseboat, and in a second the tall louvered doors opened. In the doorway stood a girl of maybe eighteen, nineteen, with a long muddy-blond ponytail. She was in a bikini and had the tan of someone who spent hours in the sun—regularly. She slipped in and closed the door behind her.

"You were supposed to wait," Evans said sternly.

The girl smiled. "I couldn't," she said simply. She was staring right at Evans, her eyes—big and sort of washed-out blue—dancing with pleasure. Janowitz looked at Evans. He could hardly believe his eyes. Evans was trying to look disapprovingly at her, but his face was glowing; he might have been a supernova about to explode.

"Welcome to our home, Thai," she said, extending her hand to Thai. She had a bath towel draped over her shoulder, and as she passed Janowitz, it flowed back and forth. At the same instant he got a whiff of her perfume. Damn, he thought, maybe a harem is the only answer for me, after all. The girl shook hands with Thai in the French fashion —the gentle little pump rather than the clasp, squeeze, and isometrics of the American handshake. And that made him realize she had spoken with a soft French accent—very like Thai's. He'd grown so used to it, it had slipped right by him.

"Jeanne-Paul, this is Lieutenant Janowitz," Evans said, directing her to Janowitz. "Jeanne-Paul Delambre—Henry Janowitz."

She shook Janowitz's hand. Face to face she wasn't as pretty as she had seemed standing in the doorway. She had a band of freckles that ran across the top of her cheeks and right over her nose, and the bone structure was nothing like Hieu's, not handsomely featured at all, and a little round and fleshy, but it was an open face, direct and sunny. He thought she might be only seventeen. In any case she was ripe, a girl just beginning to sense the power of her sexual attraction and liking it—not lubriciously, but joyfully—and somehow that made her even more attractive.

"You're very tall, Henry Janowitz." She laughed.

"He's a very famous basketball player," Evans said. "They stitch thirty centimeters onto their legs when they're young. It's an ancient ritual in our northern states."

Jeanne-Paul giggled and poked Evans with her elbow. She moved

358

across to the liquor cabinet and opened it carefully. "Here," she said, tossing a pair of swimming trunks at Evans. Then she placed three others on the chair next to her and turned to Thai and Janowitz. "I hope you can find two that will suit you," she said, and walked to the louvered doors. "I will take the boat out for about five minutes. You change, and when you hear me coming in, slip under the dock, and then we will all go into the house together." She held Evans' eyes for a second and then slipped outside.

Janowitz looked across at Evans . . . and Evans was suddenly disconcerted. He started to blush. But he and Thai moved quickly to the wall and peered apprehensively through the louvers until they heard the boat pull away. Then they exchanged a smile: They seemed to have made it.

When they heard her boat returning, they all slipped out the door, over the side, and swam under the dock. The boat was an open Chris-Craft. She brought it right into the dock beside them and threw a pair of water skis over the side. Evans dived under the boat and went for the skis. When she cut the motor, Janowitz and Thai followed him. Evans was paddling toward shore with the skis, and she was tying the boat up when they surfaced.

"Hurry, or he'll finish all the food!" Jeanne-Paul called brightly. Thai splashed at her, and she shrieked. Near shore Evans slammed the skis on the dock and hopped up beside them. Thai scrambled up, too, and Jeanne-Paul knew what was coming. She started to run for the houseboat, but Thai grabbed an arm. Evans was almost on them. Jeanne-Paul twisted and pulled, and she and Thai were whirling toward the end of the dock when Evans charged right into them, sending all three crashing into the water. Janowitz glanced around the bay. If anyone were watching, it would be hard to believe they weren't just three youngsters frolicking in the midday heat. But as Janowitz pulled himself out of the water and stretched out on the dock, he was amazed at how much more than an act it was. Thai had become a facet of war to him. The idea that he was really a young man capable of play and fun, just for the hell of it, had never really occurred to him. But Thai was hardly an adult, younger even than Janowitz. It seemed incredible. Yet splashing there in the water with Evans and Jeanne-Paul, he looked easily the youngest and weakest of the three. The little Vietnamese friend two Westerners had invited for a swim.

Jeanne-Paul scampered up the ladder first and ran right over Janowitz, up the dock, toward the big screened and porticoed wooden house. Her legs were a little too heavy, and one day her bottom was going to be too much—but now at seventeen or nineteen, whatever the hell she was, it mattered not at all. She looked like every college boy's idea of a swinging summer.

Evans and Thai started to climb up the dock, and halfway up, Thai pushed Evans back in. Evans yelled and, when he surfaced, managed to get hold of one of Thai's legs. They were pulling and tugging at each other when Janowitz calmly got up and, putting both hands under Thai's chest, hurled him out in the water over Evans' head. They both were shouting at him as he walked up the dock to the house.

Jeanne-Paul was waiting for him at the porch door. She handed him a towel and welcomed him in. Coming through the door of the house was a smallish, middle-aged man in a striped seersucker jacket over a checkered open-necked shirt. He looked sleepy, as though he had just awakened, and his hair, which was very thin just in front, but thick on the back and top, was still disheveled, but he had a big smile, and his hand was already out in greeting.

"This is Lieutenant Janowitz, Papa," Jeanne-Paul said with schoolgirl formality.

"I'm very glad to meet you, Lieutenant." He had bushy eyebrows and a broad mouth with firm, straight white teeth, and his smile communicated both wit and warmth. It relaxed Janowitz completely. "We're going to have a little trouble fitting you into my clothes," he said with a laugh. "But apart from that, we hope you'll enjoy your stay." His hand was strong, and his fingers were long for a smallish man. Janowitz got one of those sudden stabs of remorse that came to him—erratically, unpredictably—shit, I wish my father had lived.

Evans and Thai came running up the walk, laughing and pushing each other. They sobered on seeing Jeanne-Paul's father, and Evans came through the door cheerfully, but with a manner of evident respect and restraint.

"Dr. Delambre."

"Heyward—we've missed you. And Thai. Welcome to our home. Your uncle will be very pleased you are safe."

He marshaled them quickly into the house and then went back out on the porch himself and took a long look around. When he came back in, he nodded to Thai and Evans.

"No obvious trouble," he said. "We tend to have a tolerance for neighborhood irregularities here. None of us is so guiltless he can afford to do otherwise." He smiled, and then said more seriously to Thai, "The watch has been set on the road. We'll be warned if anything happens." He took Thai's arm, directing his attention from the bay and ushering them all into the interior of the house.

Inside it was a very Catholic home. The furniture was heavy and French, and the windows were hung with brocaded drapes and thick curtains, and it was almost impossible to move without seeing a crucifix or a picture of the Virgin Mary or a prayer book on a table. Janowitz was taken to a large bedroom that overlooked the little bay they were on. There were twin beds with a crucifix over each. Janowitz grinned to himself. Nice that Christ was a Jew, he thought, or I'd feel a bit hairy about now.

Evans shared the bedroom, and he promptly went to a big louvered door on the wall facing the bay and pushed it open. It led to a screened-in balcony that ran the length of the house, and they both wandered out on it. They were in the French quarter—that much Janowitz recognized. The houses looked French, even in the Vietnamese setting. Out on the bay a man was water-skiing. Two girls were driving the boat, and the whole scene might have been animated from a travel poster. It was pretty difficult to believe it was taking place in the one piece of Asia *he'*d come to know.

"The French have sure got it made in this war," he commented wryly.

"They have now," Evans agreed. "It's a false paradise, but there's no getting around it, those who stayed have done all right."

"What about Delambre? Is he a medical doctor?"

"Yes. He works at the Catholic Hospital. He has since 1951. Jeanne-Paul was only a year old when she came to Saigon, and she's only had one trip to France since. And she was only seven *then* . . . so you have met yet another kind of Vietnamese."

Janowitz smiled. "You sort of go for the Vietnamese, don't you?"

Evans laughed, and they went inside.

Within half an hour they were having a fabulous French lunch. Jeanne-Paul's mother was a woman fighting desperately to avoid being heavyset . . . or maybe the fight wasn't so desperate—she seemed to enjoy her food as much as the rest of them. But she was pleasant and outgoing once the first formal introductions were over. Of course, Janowitz's condition rather helped make everything informal. He couldn't get into anything in the house other than a pair of stretch swimming shorts and a terry-cloth bathrobe of Dr. Delambre's that looked more like a three-quarter beach robe on him. The inevitable view of his long, rather hairy legs reduced Jeanne-Paul to giggles the moment he walked in, but Janowitz felt she was in the mood to be amused by anything anyway.

They described their trip South, and somehow, in that atmosphere, everything about it seemed more funny than exciting. The Delambres spoke a little of the Tet offensive and the strain it had put on the hospital, and Dr. Delambre mentioned with studied casualness that it had changed some of the views on both sides. Janowitz saw a look pass between him and Thai that was the most solemn of the meal and wondered what it meant.

He was really stunned by Evans and Jeanne-Paul. He didn't know why. There was nothing about Evans that suggested he was sexless. He just seemed so preoccupied with other things, but he really grew both witty and boyish around her, and Jeanne-Paul obviously accepted him as her own.

By the time they'd finished the meal the burning heat was out of the sun and the shadows were lengthening. A few minutes later Thai left with Dr. Delambre. Thai shook Janowitz's hand before going, taking him to one side in the entrance hall.

"It is difficult to say unpleasant things at a time like this," he said. "But I will be gone until tomorrow—or perhaps the day after—and you will appreciate that you have been exposed to knowledge that could not only destroy our mission, but destroy all of us here as well . . . and make difficulties for many all the way back to Quang Tri." He paused as he saw the realization of what this implied spreading on Janowitz's face. "It is like taking a step off a cliff," he added with a little smile. "A half step is as good as a whole—and once you have made the first, there is no going back.

"Dr. Delambre has a cook and a gardener," Thai went on quietly. "They know how vital it is that you do not leave this house until I return. And they know what it would mean to Dr. Delambre and his family if you did. I do not think they would let you leave alive. In the houses on either side of this house there are also cooks and gardeners, and a few have chauffeurs and housekeepers, too. You would have to pass many houses before you came to one where"—he shrugged—"where you could walk in safety. And as you see, across the road they are building a new home. It would be a mistake to go in that direction —by day or by night. As for the bay, the houseboats at the far end are there especially in honor of your visit."

"Well, it looks like I'm sewed up." Janowitz smiled.

"It is a stupid safeguard," Thai said with a note of apology, "but

362

there is so much at stake, should you change your mind, that some measures were necessary. This way perhaps you will be able to relax and enjoy yourself. At least you can tell yourself that without any possibility of escape, you were not remiss in duty in not seeking it."

Janowitz was full and happy and a little gay on the cognac that had been liberally laced through their postprandial coffee. Escaping was not on his schedule, and he was amused at the thoroughness of Thai's precautions. "Thai," he said, "a good helicopter pilot doesn't really *need* a helicopter. If I had wanted to get out of here badly enough, I could have flown off the front porch while you were changing clothes —so don't panic, lad."

Thai regarded him soberly for a minute, then smiled and went out to Dr. Delambre, who was sitting in the drive in a little Renault 16. Janowitz felt like kicking himself. Thai had been subtle and pleasant —and he had been gross and flippant. Shit, there were times when it was difficult being an American.

He and Evans went up to sleep for an hour or so after Thai and the doctor left. Janowitz had forgotten the pleasure of showering and then sleeping on a real bed between clean sheets. Man, Evans was right —the twentieth century had its advantages.

When he awoke, the sun was almost down, and lying in bed, he could see the bay—steel blue, with tints of yellow and crimson reflected from the sky. It was laughter that had awakened him, and he could hear it again now. He sat up and peered out. Evans and Jeanne-Paul on top of the houseboat. A diving board was set diagonally across the forward corner, and Evans had Jeanne-Paul in his arms and was trying to walk out on it. She was laughing and kicking—but carefully. She looked as frightened as he did unsteady. He finally made it to the end, but instead of jumping or throwing her in, he kissed her. Janowitz looked away. It was like peeping through someone's bedroom keyhole. Eventually he heard the splash, followed by more laughter. Well, Evans was being bold enough about his presence here. It was probably the best approach. You sure wouldn't guess there was anything to hide from the way he was acting.

After a good, long stretch, Janowitz got up and decided to go downstairs. They'd had plenty of sleep these last few days, and had it not been for the cognac and the bulging stomach, he probably wouldn't have napped. As he came down the stairs in the apparently deserted house, a voice startled him.

"I thought I heard someone," Dr. Delambre said, appearing from the living room. "Come join me. I'll offer you a genuine American drink. A little white rum and Coca-Cola—very pleasing at this time of day."

He'd gone back into the living room, heading straight for the liquor cabinet. Janowitz ambled after him, still a little self-conscious in his abbreviated bathrobe. "That sounds fine," he said.

Dr. Delambre mixed the drinks and handed him one. "To your health," Delambre said, raising his glass. They drank and stood for a moment in silence. The laughter outside drew their eyes to the dock, and they both watched Evans and Jeanne-Paul for a time without speaking.

"It's strange," Dr. Delambre said at last, "but only when they're playing do we realize wars are fought by youngsters." He shook his head. "But this is not the time to be glum. Why don't we wander conspicuously out on the porch? Once they realize their privacy has been invaded, perhaps we can feel less like peeping Toms."

Once outside, the doctor plumped down in a wicker rocking chair, and Janowitz draped himself on a big swing that was set across one corner of the porch. It was covered with a thick mattress of foam rubber, and lying there, gently swinging to and fro in the warm sunset, sipping a drink, Janowitz thought he'd probably feel sybaritic even if he weren't in the middle of a war. If an MP walked in, he'd be hard pressed to explain what he was doing and how he got there, but the doctor seemed intent on burying his nervousness, and Janowitz decided he should do the same. He watched Evans dive from the top of the houseboat. It wasn't Olympic standard, but you could see that the rich kid had had coaching in all the little pastimes of life. Janowitz turned back and found Dr. Delambre staring at him with a fixed, inquisitive smile.

"You're taking quite a chance," he said after a moment.

"So are you," Janowitz answered calmly. The doctor held his eyes a second, then laughed and took a long drink.

"I guess I am," he said at last. "But *I'm* not an American."

"Well, Evans has convinced me that doesn't make much difference," Janowitz said matter-of-factly. Then he blinked and shook his head as though there must be something wrong with that statement, but he couldn't quite put his finger on what it was. The doctor enjoyed it. They both drank again, searching for conversation.

"Have you known Evans for long?" Janowitz asked.

"We first met Heyward about eighteen months ago," Dr. Delambre answered, glancing out toward the houseboat. "He showed up at the

364

hospital one day asking if he could be of any help. From time to time American soldiers have come and offered their services, and we have always welcomed them. But Heyward was a special case because his French was fluent. He became very useful . . . Then I discovered he was an ex-priest—or I should say an ex-candidate for the priesthood." He laughed musingly and turned back to Janowitz. "And ex-priests or even ex-candidates for the priesthood always have an irresistible attraction for Frenchmen."

"Then one day," he continued more seriously, "after everyone in the family had come to know and love Heyward, he disappeared. We thought he had been called away from Saigon, and I checked with his unit. It was true, he had been sent out, and so we expected he would write or return. But there was nothing. Then we discovered that he was missing in action." He grimaced. "We were a very unhappy household for several weeks. . . . And then one evening I was asked to do a small errand for a friend in the Liberation Front . . . and when I arrived at the appointed rendezvous—*voilà,* Heyward!" The doctor drank from his glass, his face relaxed, genial. "We were surprised at first, but when we came to think about it, it was quite inevitable.

"Of course, separation is rumored to do all sorts of things to the heart," he continued drolly. "And if my daughter can be regarded as a statistical sample, I must say the proposition is proved. They were bickering playfellows before he was presumed lost. But when I brought him home, alive and rechristened as it were—" He shrugged eloquently.

Janowitz smiled and sipped his drink. The house, the houseboat, the drink, the conversation—you'd think they were in Grosse Pointe with the Fords off on one side and the Knudsens and Chryslers on the other.

"I suppose you have to spend a lot of time at the hospital," Janowitz said. It couldn't *all* be like this.

The doctor looked at him closely and then nodded amiably. "Yes," he said. "I spend a fair amount of time at the hospital. You must appreciate that Vietnam was not always at war. Sometimes one feels guilty about this house, this way of life. But except for the little political gestures one might make," he said with a puckish grin, "there is nothing very practical one can do. To sell your house only provides another nice piece of real estate for American officers to buy. And that, of course, is not the sort of gesture one wants to make."

Despite the deliberate lightheartedness, it all was a bit strained, but Janowitz could sense the man reaching for some real contact.

365

"It must be a little rough being a doctor in Saigon these days," he said more personally.

Delambre shrugged. "Yes—and no. At least a doctor can do something. It is a privilege few other people have."

"From what I've seen, they could use about ten thousand more of you."

Delambre frowned thoughtfully. "Yes. But it would only be first aid. We can mend wounds, we can treat the dying, but no quantity of doctors could ever make this city healthy." He swirled his drink and glanced at Janowitz with a teasing smile. "To do that would probably cost as much as one whole squadron of your bombers, so of course, it is out of the question."

Janowitz studied his own glass a moment. "Is that why you help the VC?"

"No," Delambre said, shaking his head. "I do not like what America has done—and is doing—in Vietnam, but I did not like what our government did either. But in my case, and perhaps in my wife's case, it is what your allies have done that has forced us to be on the other side."

"The Vietnamese?"

Delambre nodded. "For a doctor in a voluntary hospital it is especially difficult. One knows how hard it is to raise funds and then to have to bid in the marketplace for medicines that have been sent 'free' by some charitable organization in America or Europe is sometimes—" He shrugged bitterly. "You would be surprised how often I have had to bribe senior government officials to get delivery of medicine sent by American churches.

"For a time," he continued, "I waited for reform. I watched as your government shifted its support from one group to the next—always insisting your latest allies among the Vietnamese handle your money and aid. A face-saving pretense for you—but a great temptation for the Vietnamese," he grinned. "We have a saying here, 'American aid is like a long pipe with many holes—and only a small dribble ever reaches the end.' It is very true," he said wistfully, "and I watched as the pipe grew larger and larger, and the holes bigger and bigger—but the dribble at the end has always remained the same. At times I was encouraged by the hatred of corruption some of your officials showed—but *dis*couraged by the corruption of some of your own businessmen when they saw the profits to be made. In the end it was something quite trivial that started me on my path of perfidy." He laughed and finished his drink.

366

"Would you have another?" he asked. Janowitz nodded and finished his off.

"They're very good."

"Peaceful coexistence!" the doctor explained as he stood and took Janowitz's glass. "The rum is from Cuba, the Coca-Cola you know about."

By the time he returned Janowitz had become aware that nightfall had come. He could see a few stars glimmering between the interstices of the screen, and house lights burned here and there along the bay. Just as Dr. Delambre sat down, a light in the houseboat went on.

"*Ahh,*" the doctor breathed, "for a father, that is a reassuring sign." Janowitz laughed along with him. You still couldn't see through the louvered shutters of the houseboat, but the light spilled out over the water.

"I hope it's not too late," Janowitz hazarded good-humoredly.

"I know you do," the doctor shot back, "but you are moved by simple masculine jealousy. For me, that is only a tiny, complicating factor!" And they laughed again. It was nervous laughter, but the liquor was helping them both relax.

"I was at the hospital one day when Thai's uncle came to me," the doctor said, picking up the thread of his conversation. "We had met many times in a semiformal way, but at that time I didn't know him personally. He asked me if I would come to his house. There had been an accident, and a doctor was required urgently. . . . Naturally I suspected. But I went. Just before we reached the house, he told me in so many words that the man in his house was an important officer in the Liberation Front—and said that if I wanted to keep aloof, I should say so then. Once I entered the house, it would be impossible to be entirely free again as long as I was in Vietnam."

He was speaking reflectively, staring out at the shimmering light around the dock, recalling the moment dispassionately. "I remember we were in the midst of a summer thunderstorm. The rain was pelting down, and it was one of those times when there was a seven o'clock curfew. It was past seven, and I could see car lights distantly in the rear-vision mirror. An American patrol or an Arvin patrol. I had all of three or four seconds to make up my mind. Concern for Jeanne-Paul produced my only real doubt. I gave her three seconds of consideration"—he smiled—"and then drove the car on." He drank reminiscently, but his face showed no regret.

"After that I received a call now and again, or I was given a message to convey . . . and slowly it has become my avocation."

Janowitz sipped his drink, and now he was the one who was studying the doctor with an inquisitive eye.

"Doesn't it worry you that your 'avocation' will probably lead to the Communists running the whole country?" he asked.

"In a perfect world it would," Delambre answered. "But the alternate is that the country will be run by the landlords and American business—and the American military. I think a truly Vietnamese government of any kind would be better than that."

"Well," Janowitz said with a whimsical glance at the house and the bay, "at the risk of sounding like a red, white, and blue materialist, may I say that it's liable to lead to quite a reduction in your standard of living!"

Delambre smiled. "No, I think not," he said. "Doctors do all right in Communist societies. I don't think we'll suffer all that much."

"You *are* Catholic?"

"Yes," Delambre said. "But *French* Catholic. Very anticlerical. I'm afraid I think the Russian church got what it deserved in the Revolution. It was a playground for the rich and depraved. It owned vast estates, its leaders were pawns of the government, and it taught that obedience to the Czar was God's will, and to deny it was a sin. Of course, the Communists—or anyone else who really wanted to change Russian society—had to attack it.

"But for all their attempts to teach atheism, they haven't destroyed a belief in God. I don't think that's possible in man. And their attempt to do it is just one episode in church history. A mere flick of the eye in the life-span of the Bible . . . or the church."

"But you're living in that 'flick of the eye,'" Janowitz reminded him.

"Ah, but the eye is opening a little already," the doctor said expansively, "and in any case I'm living in Vietnam. The Communists haven't burned down churches or attacked nuns and clergy here. They *have* put the church back in the business of religion. When we ran things, the church was one of the largest landholders, owning whole villages, charging forty percent on loans like everyone else, and getting very rich on the proceeds. That has stopped in the North, but mass goes on. As it does in Poland and Hungary and Yugoslavia." He shook his head in good-natured reproval. "There are more priests in Poland today than there were in 1939—*and* more churches. Did you know that?" And Janowitz shook *his* head.

"No," Delambre continued, "I won't welcome the Communists,

but I imagine my life will go on very much as it did before your people arrived."

He sipped his drink, studying Janowitz's reaction with a look of amusement.

"Heyward says you've been to Eastern Europe," he said.

Janowitz nodded.

"Didn't you see people going to church—and leading normal lives?"

"Lots of them—but I was suspicious," Janowitz added with a grimace of leering wariness.

The doctor laughed, and his wife appeared in the doorway, staring at the two of them inquisitively.

"Are you two all right?" she asked.

"We're just fine," Dr. Delambre answered. She shrugged, shaking her head at them affably, and went back inside. In a second the dining-room light went on and Janowitz could see her and the cook, a little wiry man of about fifty, setting the table for dinner. She was acting as calm as the doctor, but you could see the strain she was under.

"Did you think all those Eastern European mini-skirts and ski resorts, the traffic and television were all put on for your benefit also?" Delambre queried.

"It wasn't quite what I expected," Janowitz conceded, "but I kept seeing soldiers everywhere, too. And it reminded me of what I'd read about all those places Evans hates—like Greece and Spain and Formosa."

The doctor stared into his drink for a time, still smiling thought-fully. Finally, he spoke. "I know what you're getting at, of course. It's why I've managed to keep from hating Americans. You're doing all this because you're convinced the 'Reds' are out to conquer the world. And *you're* going to save us." He looked at Janowitz.

"It's why I admire General de Gaulle. His politics are not mine—he's conservative, right-wing—but he is the first Western leader to recognize that we are no longer living in Stalin's day, that all those soldiers you saw are not out to conquer mankind.

"While your Pentagon is still frantically devising schemes against a Communist world take-over engineered by the Russians, the world has changed. In the first place, the Russians are interested in Russia. A secure Russia to be sure, with a ring of safe socialist countries around them, but they don't want conquest; they want refrigerators and stoves, leisure, sports, days in the sunshine with their grandchildren. And if they don't feel threatened, no one in the world is going to drive them into a world-conquering hysteria. They have had enough of war."

He shook his head solemnly. "I don't think you in America can quite imagine what it has been like. You make much of your dead here. The Russians lost seven *million* soldiers in World War II . . . and God only knows how many fell in World War I and the Revolution, soldiers *and* civilians. Talk to a Russian—they want peace—desperately."

He looked at Janowitz warmly. "As desperately as you do," he said. "So I don't feel the least bit unorthodox or shortsighted in doing what I'm doing. A victory for the National Front in Vietnam will not be a victory for Russia. Ho Chi Minh is as independent as Tito, and his Communism will look quite unlike anything we've seen elsewhere. I shall grumble at it a good deal, I know. But I don't fear it in the least."

He smiled suddenly. "I'm much more afraid," he said, "that American business will turn the whole world into a vast supermarket for selling their wares than I am that Russia will march on us all."

"I noticed those were American sheets you had on the bed," Janowitz replied dryly.

"Well, better an American sheet *on* the bed than a Russian *under* it," Delambre acknowledged with a grin. "But one is a real danger, and the other I think pretty remote."

"I'll check under the bed the next time I go up." Janowitz smiled.

Later, when Janowitz was shaving, the conversation with the doctor kept hanging in his mind. It was strangely unsettling, and he couldn't help recalling that Thai's attitude had had the same effect on him— and for the same reason. It wasn't the ideas themselves; they could be accepted or rejected, argued, modified. It was the fact of belief that was so disturbing. The doctor, who, like Thai, was not uninformed or ideologically blind, really planned to live under Ho Chi Minh and did so without qualms.

And for Janowitz, the doctor's calm, everyday approach to this prospect was as testing to his view of the world as all that Evans had said during the whole length of the trip.

ii

Janowitz was standing on the balcony and Evans had just finished shaving when Dr. Delambre knocked. The doctor spoke quietly for a moment with Evans, and then they both hurried downstairs. Janowitz went out into the hall and peered out at the driveway in back, where he could hear voices. The window he was at was open, but it took a little time before his eyes could adjust to the dark sufficiently to recognize Thai in a group of six men conferring with Evans and Dr. Delambre. He caught an occasional word, but they were speaking French —very fast and a little heatedly—and he couldn't follow it. He was surprised to see an unmarked jeep in the drive; Delambre had said something at lunch about the curfew's being very strictly enforced. Finally, Dr. Delambre turned and came back hurriedly toward the house. Janowitz stepped from the window. When he started across the hall to his and Evans' room, he saw the gardener sitting on the stairs leading up to the cupola that sat on top of the house. In the dark his brown skin almost seemed a part of the staircase. He was sitting about ten steps up staring at Janowitz. When Janowitz recovered, he grinned and nodded his head. There was no reaction whatsoever. He could hear Evans coming into the hall below—so he shrugged, waved his hand in farewell at his silent guardian, and went back into the bedroom.

When Evans came in, he seemed nervous, but he told Janowitz with studied casualness that their arrival hadn't been reported but that later that night he was going to have to go out for a few hours. Janowitz asked if he was to go, too, but Evans shook his head. "You're more valuable than I am." He smiled.

Before dinner, Mrs. Delambre brought a pair of khaki shorts that Janowitz was able to wear with only minor discomfort. They had been long trousers, but she'd cut them and stitched an uneven hem around the bottom. Janowitz felt almost as ridiculous in shorts as he did in a robe, but at least they gave him the feeling of being dressed. She'd also produced an Orlon sweater that he could get into and in the cool of evening wasn't impossible to wear.

When they went downstairs, he thought he'd probably get another laugh with the outfit, but Dr. Delambre was on the phone and only nodded as though everyone he knew wore that sort of combination. Jeanne-Paul smiled a greeting when he came into the dining room, but her eyes were preoccupied—and all on Evans.

When Delambre was finished on the phone, they all sat at a table shimmering with china and silver and candlelight, and Jeanne-Paul said grace. It was a simple, inoffensive thing—about being thankful, God, for daily bread or something. Without creating any atmosphere about it, they had taken into account that Janowitz wasn't Catholic.

Jeanne-Paul was wearing a thin silk dress and bright earrings that emphasized her femininity—and there was a lot of that about, Janowitz observed. But knowing she was Evans' had killed his urge for a little harem making—maybe he was getting old, he decided.

"Are your parents alive, Lieutenant Janowitz?" Mrs. Delambre asked, cutting conversationally across the tension as they settled into the ritual of passing and serving. Her accent was more marked than Dr. Delambre's, but her vowels, like her husband's, were flat and American compared to Thai's and Jeanne-Paul's.

"My mother is alive," he answered.

"Perhaps you would like me to write to her—it would have to be somewhat vague, but it might reassure her."

In Yen Cai, Evans had told Janowitz that he had been listed as a prisoner of war through the Red Cross, so Janowitz knew his mother was aware he was alive. He'd written twice from up there himself, but he had no idea if the letters had ever been sent or how long it took the Red Cross to deliver mail from Hanoi to Geneva to the States.

"Yes, I would like that," he said honestly. "If you only tell her what sort of food you're giving me, she'll know I'm in good hands," he added with a grin.

"Food perhaps, but I'd better not tell her how you're dressed," she replied. Her eyes twinkled. "When we were very young," she continued, "my husband studied for two years at the school for tropical medicine at the University of Southern California. We saw a number of basketball games then, but I don't remember any of the players being *quite* so tall."

"Mama!"

Mrs. Delambre looked at Jeanne-Paul. Jeanne-Paul wasn't objecting to the reference to Janowitz's height. What bothered her apparently was her mother's attempt to establish an ordinary flow of dinner conversation.

"Look," Evans said, "every day since I was last here, I've lived in much more danger than I'm going to be in tonight." He was looking right across the table at her. She tried to smile, but her eyes filled with tears. Her concern obviously pleased Evans as much as it annoyed him, but he seemed determined to put an end to it. He turned to her mother.

"The appalling truth, Mrs. Delambre, is that in today's generation of basketball players Lieutenant Janowitz is a shrimp. The really big ones run seven feet and over."

"Really, Heyward!" Dr. Delambre laughed.

"It's *true*—isn't it?" Evans demanded of Janowitz.

"I'm afraid so," Janowitz agreed. "I wasn't the tallest man on Michigan's team. Not by a good ways."

"Ah, America! It's extraordinary!" Dr. Delambre exclaimed. "Seven-foot basketball players and nonstick frying pans. No wonder you hold the world in fief!"

And so it went, with the doctor and Mrs. Delambre trying desperately to make the dinner an interlude of normalcy in an atmosphere of madness. On the surface it worked, but when Dr. Delambre finally rolled a slender cigar between his fingers to signal the end of the meal itself, Evans and Jeanne-Paul had long since fallen from the conversation. The doctor winked at Janowitz and suggested to his wife that she bring them coffee and cognac out on the porch. They rose and left Evans and Jeanne-Paul to a more real conversation of their own.

Outside, Janowitz could see that several of the houses on the bay were lit up now, and two houseboats at other docks had lights shining from them. Over the water you could hear people playing and swimming. He was stuffed, but the beauty of the setting and the sounds of splashing and laughter made him wish they could take a swim. Maybe later—after the duck had settled, and pastries and the orange and spice-flavored dressing. But immediately the thought reminded him that Evans would not be swimming—at least not there, not among houseboats and laughter.

And as if in response to his thought, Evans came out of the house and joined them. He placed a pillow against the wall and sat on the floor with his back against it, and when Dr. Delambre took his wicker rocker, Janowitz stretched out gratefully in the swing. For a time they looked silently out over the water. You could hear the deep background rumble of jets—like continuous, rumbling thunder. Finally Jeanne-Paul and Mrs. Delambre brought them coffee and brandy.

"There are two things that make me believe in God," Evans said reflectively as they all sat looking out on the bay. "One is the sheer discomfort of guilt. When I tell Jeanne-Paul she's the most beautiful girl in the world *and* a better cook than her mother, I'm uneasy for days." Jeanne-Paul had put a pillow next to his, and she wriggled away in mock displeasure. "And the other is man's perverse, unreasonable sense of justice."

The sound of the laughter on the bay rolled up to them and mingled with the distant throbbing thunder of the jets. "Nature is so indifferent to justice," Evans continued contemplatively. "She kills, maims, destroys—without reason or mercy. . . . But man, her child—" He shook his head. "No animal cares, but cruel, stupid, stubborn man— he cares. It may kill him if he acts on it, but it kills him inside if he ignores it.

"If I could understand why—*without* believing in God," he added wistfully, "I'd be the perfect agnostic. Unfortunately . . . unfortunately I shall just go on suffering for my lies to Jeanne-Paul." She swatted at him.

"All men are impossible," Mrs. Delambre pronounced categorically. She had placed a pillow on the floor and was leaning against her husband's legs. "They will gladly spend their lives exhaustedly searching for reasons *not* to believe in God, call Him anything but God— order, physical law, morality, justice, even sex—but they will not relax and admit that they personally did not create the world."

"You're right, my dear," Dr. Delambre mumbled. "Our mistake has been to see God as a man—He's obviously a woman." His wife smiled, but she pinched his ankle.

No one spoke for a time. Janowitz sipped his coffee and brandy; it was a drink he'd never had before, and he found himself liking it more all the time. At last Dr. Delambre glanced at his watch and looked across at Evans. Evans nodded imperceptibly.

"Where does your God go, Evans, if the Vietcong win down here?" Janowitz asked quietly.

"He hangs around," Evans said. "I worry more about His survival back in our homestead."

"Oh?" Janowitz muttered doubtfully.

"We've made it kind of difficult for God." Evans grinned. "We've used His name pretty freely and then built a society that finds its driving force, not in brotherhood or love, but greed and envy. Discontent is its very wellspring. No matter what you've got, you've got to get more. Otherwise, the whole system falls apart.

"We say our material wealth proves the correctness of the philosophy, but I'm not sure God would be all that impressed with that huge gross national product of useless chrome and multicolored plastic and pointless gadgets, of military equipment and a quota of civilian conveniences. I'm fairly certain He would be disinclined to think it justified all the squalor, violence, and harsh frenzy that goes with it. And being God, I guess He would recognize they go hand in hand, because violence and inequality are the *logical* products of competition.

"Of course, our generation is revolting—on God's side," he said

374

with a teasing grin at Janowitz, "but we hardly know where to begin or what exactly we're revolting against."

"As a messenger of the Lord," Janowitz said, "you really believe all that, do you?"

"I do," Evans answered. "We talk about race riots, the breakdown in family life, crime in the streets, crime in big business, graft in state governments—we see the ugliness of our cities, the rape of our rivers and forests and the very air we breathe . . . and they're all looked at individually, treated separately as though each were a separate, particular disease.

"They're *not* individual diseases—they are all symptoms of *one* disease. The cancer of the acquisitive philosophy that motivates our society—not freedom, not the pursuit of happiness, but the get, get, getting of wealth and the symbols of wealth. The golden calves—and God has heard of them.

"We haven't made a society for man," he continued. "We've made one for business—where man and all his attributes must serve in the marketplace and are measured only in dollars and cents. 'Competition within the free enterprise system,' the best of all possible worlds."

He was staring now out across the bay, and he had slipped into a sermon—his real gift—and, even for Janowitz, he did it with a rhythm and emotional grab that was irresistible. "It's only a *partial* truth that man is acquisitive," he continued quietly. "He is also a lot of other things—like generous to those he likes and loves, concerned and sympathetic sometimes even with those he does not know—an animal that pleasures in play and physical contact. And above all, a transient who knows that even his time to *acquire* is limited—and who needs moments of peace to wonder at his coming and going. And it is possible to conceive of a society that prized these other facets of man, too, that didn't deify the one aspect of his nature that was most rapacious, most destructive. We might even find a way of life that reminds us that the child who became a man will one day soon become an ancient to whom the feel of the sun through a western window will mean more than all the goods and things he has accumulated and whose most treasured memories are not likely to be the moments of conflict and hate, but the moments he held out his hand to another like him."

His voice hung in the air. Finally, Jeanne-Paul leaned over to him and kissed his cheek.

Mrs. Delambre stood. She turned her eyes from Evans and, with a triumphant glance at Janowitz, went into the house.

Janowitz grinned. "I'm surrounded by enemies—"

"Ah! *Brotherly* enemies," Dr. Delambre hastened to assert.

Janowitz nodded. "The worst kind," he agreed wryly. The doctor laughed, and Evans glanced at his watch again. Janowitz was half-amused that Evans' preaching seemed so much less irritating when you knew that in a few minutes he was going to risk his neck for whatever it was he believed in.

"Are you a new leftist or an old one, Evans?" Janowitz asked lightly.

Evans smiled. "Neither," he said evenly. "I'm an old-fashioned Jeffersonian democrat—hopelessly behind the times. I don't like bureaucracies, state or private, and I don't think the pursuit of happiness a frivolous goal for *any* society. But I have not yet been hoodwinked into thinking freedom and free enterprise are the same thing. And I try to remember once in a while that the first civilization came to this globe of ours, not when our ancestors learned to club each other on the head, but when they learned to hunt together, to build and work together. It was *cooperation,* not competition, that marked the beginning of man . . . and I suspect God knew something about that, too."

Jeanne-Paul looked at her watch for the third or fourth time; only now the anxiety was getting harder to conceal, the conversation more and more unreal.

"Jeanne-Paul," her mother called from inside the house, "bring along the coffee tray before Lieutenant Janowitz corrupts your father any further."

Jeanne-Paul picked up the tray. Evans' eyes were on her the whole time, and she sensed it, but she only glanced at him once before going through the door into the house.

"When do you leave?" Dr. Delambre asked Evans once Jeanne-Paul was out of earshot.

Evans glanced at his watch. "Half an hour. Thai's uncle has been 'temporarily imprisoned,' " he added softly.

"Are there charges?" Dr. Delambre asked with concern.

Evans shook his head. " 'Protective custody.' They know he's sympathetic to the Front, but Thai doesn't think they have any actual information."

"What does it mean for you?"

"Thai isn't sure. The money is safe. Half of it in military green, half in actual dollars. We should be able to go ahead, but we can't be sure there isn't an informer someplace."

"Wouldn't it be safer to wait?" Delambre said thoughtfully. He had risen and was looking out over the bay, his back to Evans.

376

"Not if they don't really know what's going on. If they do, it won't make any difference anyway."

Dr. Delambre turned back to Evans. "The people are terrified of the planes. You can't know how terrified. Every day in the hospitals—with the conscious and the unconscious—it is the same thing. Thai is wrong. The Americans may never win in the countryside, but the villagers will never dare to let the Front win. Tet proved that. The Americans are in a stronger position to bargain than Thai realizes, than his father realizes. They won't make a compromise Thai's father can accept. They don't have to."

"The Americans here aren't the only ones who will decide; there are voices in America, too," Evans replied.

"Heyward," Dr. Delambre pleaded, "you're wrong. The American military will not leave South Vietnam unless it is in the hands of an army they can control. Believe me, when the time comes, theirs will be the voice that matters. And here they have won a 'victory.' They have bombed so many thousands of times no one cares anymore. They can destroy every village in South Vietnam, and it will get no more than a half column on the back page of the New York *Times*. What they do in the North is still worth a headline, but no one speaks of what the planes are doing here in the South. But people will not resist them anymore. They are beyond it. You must tell Thai before you go on, while there is still a chance to get out. If the mission is not worth it, you have to stop before you all are lost."

Evans nodded slowly. "I'll tell him," he said stoically.

"Heyward, I mean it," Dr. Delambre said gravely. "I'm not trying to protect you. I'm not being emotional. I am telling you clinically."

"I know," Evans replied. "I will tell Thai."

Delambre sighed with dissatisfaction. He sat back down in his rocker and chewed at his thumb.

"The choice is to do something—or do nothing," Evans said reflectively. "I can no more do nothing than you can."

Delambre squirmed uncomfortably in his chair. "Jesus, Mary, and Joseph," he said abjectly, "what an insane world we live in."

"That it is," Evans agreed.

iii

It was more than two hours later when Jeanne-Paul came out to the houseboat to get Janowitz. He'd been swimming beyond the end of the dock. It had been muggy and hot in his room, and even with the little desk fan pointing right at him, he'd got no relief. It was sticky and uncomfortable on the houseboat, too, and the shimmering light that looked so beautiful from the house was alive with millions of gnats and bugs of every description. But in the water it was all beauty again. Lights were still burning in one or two houses along the bay, and even the endless throbbing of jets in the distance couldn't mar the feeling of private luxury that came with turning, twisting, gliding through the cool, welcome water.

He knew there was trouble from the way Jeanne-Paul ran out on the dock. Her whole body shouted anxiety and panic. Dr. Delambre was already in his little Renault waiting by the time Janowitz had dressed. He had debated for a time whether he should wear his fatigues and in the end decided it was best. When he came back down into the hall, Jeanne-Paul was talking nervously with a thin Vietnamese kid who looked about fourteen. They were speaking in French, and Janowitz could tell little except that she was overwrought and the kid was reluctant to talk. When Janowitz appeared, the boy mumbled something apologetically at her and went out to the car. Jeanne-Paul pulled herself together and put her hand on Janowitz's arm. She forced a smile.

"Do be careful, Henry Janowitz," she said, guying the brief formality of their relationship by dwelling on his full name.

"I will, Jeanne-Paul Delambre," he replied in kind. He knew her concern was real, however bantering the words.

"And . . . tell Heyward to be careful, too," she added, tears flooding her eyes with a rush she ignored.

"I'll do that, too," Janowitz answered. He leaned down and kissed her cheek, wrapping his arm around her shoulder and squeezing as reassuringly as he could.

The next four days were a harrowing nightmare of heat and fear and filth. The doctor had driven them into the Cholon district. He'd taken along his bag and they were going to claim he was on a call if they got stopped by a patrol, but they knew it was a weak story, and there was little chance of getting away with it. The kid had crawled in back, under a rug, and he was going to be a stowaway they were supposedly unaware of, but even though they spent the whole trip kicking around ideas, they could think of nothing to explain Janowitz —without identification, proper clothes, or sufficient ability to speak French to claim he was a relative or worker at the hospital.

They drove with only parking lights, and twice they pulled into the curb at the distant sight of patrols and buried their heads as the jeeps rumbled by. Each time the car was swept with a spotlight, and each time Janowitz thought his heart was going to beat right out of his chest. He'd never experienced such tension. If they'd been sweeping the car with machine-gun fire, he knew he wouldn't have experienced the sheer terror he felt as the lights passed silently back and forth above his head.

And the next days were to be filled with a dozen similar terrors. The equipment was being assembled in a ramshackle godown in Gia Dinh, and each night Janowitz was smuggled back and forth to inspect it as it came in. After that first night he didn't see the Delambres again. He was shunted from one hiding place to another, rarely staying in one spot for more than four or five hours at a time. And in the whole four days Thai was the only one he spoke with. Of the scores of people who passed him back and forth, no one spoke English, or even rudimentary French—or, as he really suspected, no one would admit to speaking English or French.

Everyplace he encountered the same sullen, silent faces. He slept on mud floors under corrugated roofing in midday heat that was suffocating. He grew filthy—and found lice in his hair and sores on his body which wouldn't heal but became ulcerated and pus-filled. The food was unspeakable, but always so inadequate that he was never without hunger. And everyplace he went, his presence brought manifest fear and alarm. No one wanted him; no one wanted to see him, talk to him, feed him.

One terrible scorching midday he had been in a hut in one of those vast hives of huts and shacks sprawling endlessly between the little muddy tributaries that feed the Ben Aghe. The hut wasn't more than ten feet by eight feet, and three women and an elderly man were packed in it with him. Two of the women were a gaunt, wrinkled middle age, and the other was a girl of about sixteen, feebleminded and slightly deformed. They all were terrified of Janowitz, and even the retarded girl picked up the atmosphere of dread fear from the elders. She would gibber at Janowitz, scolding and frightened, and then cower behind one of the women. And Janowitz had suddenly had to take a shit. It was unbearable. He'd eaten nothing but rice and crap since he'd left the Delambres, and all at once it had knotted in his bowels, and he had had to do something. He tried to make his need clear to the old man, but the man kept shaking his head as though he didn't understand, and he wouldn't meet Janowitz's eyes—just wouldn't look at him. Finally, Janowitz was in such pain he went out of the hut.

And there it had been like a slow-motion nightmare of horror. It had been muggy and stifling in the hut, but outside, the sun was blistering and harsh—and the sight of Janowitz stopped everything. Faces turned away; people vanished into shacks—silently as though by magic—kids stared, looking even more frightened than the adults. No place he turned was there ever one adult looking at him, just narrow passageways, brilliant in the white intensity of the sun or spotted with the terrified, frozen faces of kids. He was going to give up, but he couldn't. So he started to walk.

It was more dreamlike than real. He could hear the distant buzz of human life all around him, but everywhere he moved he seemed to bring death and silence. It was as though the area right around him were always populated by a legion of cadavers, staring impenetrably at the sky, the walls, the ground, with only the dead infants staring at him. All around his feet lay the swill of their excrement. Little piles by the walls of the shacks, wooden buckets full of it, and everywhere flies buzzing in the heat and stench. At every turn it was just an endless expanse of the same. Finally, he could take it no more, and when he saw a plywood wall with a neat bucket beside it, he crouched over it and buried his head in his hands, trying to ignore the deadly fear which gazed at him with the same silent, burning intensity as the sun beating on his back.

At night it was always another kind of horror. In the city the patrols were easy to avoid, but outside the central area of town the Air Force kept the sky alight with flares all night long. Every night. Covering the two or three miles to Gia Dinh could take four or five hours—all of it spent in fear, with patrols prowling almost within touching distance, or dragon ships chasing across the sky, their tracers crashing all around you and bringing the ground troops converging in. And always Janowitz was pushed and pulled, shoved into the ground one minute, yanked up to run breathlessly another, with no one ever saying one word to him.

And Thai. All the confidence that had swelled in him as they had neared Saigon had gone. His face was lined, and his eyes looked as though they'd known no sleep at all since Janowitz had last seen him. He tried to be friendly each time they met at the godown, but his concern was overpowering. And once, when Janowitz discovered they'd been sold a faulty oleo strut for the chopper, Thai lowered his head in his hands in such exhaustion and despair that Janowitz thought he was going to cry. But when he ultimately looked up, his glance at one of the men with him was a death warrant for someone. It burned with a cold hatred Janowitz had never seen in Thai—ruthless and beyond appeal.

Evans he saw not at all. That something had gone terribly wrong was only too obvious, but the material kept coming, and Janowitz knew that it was Evans who was somehow producing it. He could almost see him—that blinking, shit-eating expression on his face, taking chances that even Hill or Pershing would demur at. There was no abundance such as Thai had so confidently anticipated, but gradually it all came—some neat and new, some fresh from maintenance, quite a few with the red HI-VALU sticker that meant they'd only just been flown in air express from the States.

On the fourth night, instead of being taken back toward the center of Saigon, Janowitz was led south. They traveled till dawn, and then Janowitz was put in the bottom of a sampan and poled down a river he did not know, until late in the afternoon. He knew he was in the delta area because he could hear the activity of the river life grow around him. They finally pulled into a little village parked just above the convergence of two wide streams. Janowitz was led to a hut raised over the muddy subsoil on thick wooden stilts. He was given rice and fish and vegetables—a meal. And then he slept on a rush mat while a party of Vietnamese jabbered around him, the first smiling faces he had seen in days.

It was well past dawn when he awoke. Evans and Thai were already there. Both of them were nervous and lined with fatigue, but Evans took him over the mud to a group of thatch mounds. Beneath them lay all the equipment they had been gathering. It had been sent down each night after he had approved it. The last shipment was due that day. Once it had arrived safely, they would move on through the delta to the coast. The first boat was already waiting for them at My Tho . . . and they would begin the trek north again. After the tension of the last few days it almost sounded easy.

12

i

They weren't expected at Yen Cai. When they arrived, only Tick and big tits were at their "house." Big tits was cooking, relaxed and unconcerned, as though she had the whole day. Tick was writing furiously, but Janowitz sensed that his intensity was dictated more by his nature than any genuine urgency in the matter. Big tits exclaimed in delight at the sight of them and couldn't mask her special pleasure at seeing Janowitz again. She ran to them, then stopped about five feet away and bowed, holding her hands together in the traditional restrained gesture of greeting—but her face was alight. Tick put on a show of welcome, and he did seem to be relieved, but Janowitz had no faith in the honesty of the performance.

Thai talked with Tick for a time in quiet conference, and then he said something to big tits. She had been waiting at one side, and when the words came, she moved quickly to Janowitz and took his hand, leading him out of the house and down the main street. Once out of Yen Cai, they hurried along the paths between the swampy fields, big tits squeezing his hand occasionally and beaming at him as though he were some prize she'd found at the local fair.

Hieu had never completely left Janowitz's mind. Even in the horror-filled days in Saigon he'd seen tiny aspects of her in the faces around him. There were times in the fetid squalor of it when he had felt that had he not loved a Vietnamese he could not have stayed with the mission—even for a few days. The stench, the filth and heat, the noxious sores were too nauseating. But time after time he had seen a pair of eyes like Hieu's, a profile that was hers, a little toss of the head . . . and he could see her in it, feeding her babies, trying to survive and make order in that fulsome sty. And each time it stiffened him.

He thanked God for the Delambres, too. What he was going to do

382

with Hieu, where he was going to take her—if ever the war was over —had already begun to worry him. Where would they be able to make their transition from American boy and Vietnamese girl to man and wife? The States was the quick reply, but how could he take Hieu to the States? And now he knew the Delambres were the real answer. He knew that if it were ten years before they met again, it would be as if they had never parted. And he knew if that was what he wanted, he could come to them with Hieu, and the million difficulties in everything from language to cooking that might beset the two of them could be transformed into *divertissements* that cemented them together. It would mean delaying his return home. But even that would have its gain. The place for his mother to first meet Hieu was at the Delambre's, too, with Hieu in an au-dai, supported by Jeanne-Paul and Mrs. Delambre and the doctor, to make it all seem natural and fortunate and right.

At last he saw a field ahead of them where several lines of people were working, ankle-deep in the mud, planting shoots of rice; most of them were women, their conical coolie hats protecting them from the morning sun. His heart quickened with the thought of her, but he could not bring a picture of her to his mind. He heard giggling and laughter, and then, in the midst of the group, he singled out Hill's tall, loose, broad-shouldered frame. He too was wearing a coolie hat, and he was groaning and bending, then rising and holding his back dramatically and groaning some more.

The group had their backs to them as Janowitz and big tits approached, and when the two of them were only twenty-five yards or so away, Hill altered his style, getting down on his knees in the mud and hobbling along like a broad-shouldered Toulouse-Lautrec. The laughing and giggling turned to hysteria. Janowitz was grinning like a member of the party himself. The damn clown! Even on his knees, he was as tall as most of the others, and in that GD coolie hat! But the girl next to Hill turned to get more seedlings, and Hill sprang to his feet and ran to the stock basket, presenting her gallantly with a new bunch. As she accepted them, she blew the hair from her face—and Janowitz not only recognized Hieu, but saw the smile of delight with which she accepted the proffered seedlings. It was as though a dagger had been driven into him. She was more beautiful than his fondest recollection. And to see that smile, those shining eyes, glowing at Hill.

"Hieu!" big tits called out.

Janowitz saw her turn. Hieu stared at him but didn't move. She didn't even smile. For an instant he thought she was scowling to cry.

"Hey! Lieutenant! Comrade!" Hill was galloping awkwardly through the mud to greet him. Janowitz held out his hand.

"So you came back! You're a failure! Where's your patriotism? Did you bring us some PX firewater?" he yelled, and he dragged himself up on the path and took Janowitz's hand.

"I brought *you* a good case of the clap," Janowitz cracked.

"Ah, Saigon, my baby ain't changed!" Hill peered into Janowitz's eyes, and instantly he read the reservation Janowitz was trying to hide. His own eyes clouded for a second, and he lowered them. Then unexpectedly they were back on Janowitz, glowing as before. He glanced fleetingly at Hieu. "Hey, dad," he said, "you aren't worried I'm stealing from your icebox, are you?"

"What?" Janowitz stammered stupidly. Hill burst into laughter.

"Come on, you stupid officer sonuvabitch," he yelped, and pulled Janowitz through the mud toward Hieu. "I'm surprised your mother ever managed to teach you to wipe your ass, Lieutenant, *sir!* There!" he said, stopping in front of Hieu and gesturing toward her as if she were the menu for the day. "Rape her I would! Screw her I would! But she's got a great big Star of David chastity belt wrapped around her ass, you Jewish get—*sir.*"

The whole group of planters stood gaping at them. They obviously couldn't understand a word of what was being said, but they gathered it was sportive because they all were grinning like the north ends of water buffalo moving south. Hieu's face was red and pinched. Tears were streaming down her face.

"Smile at him, stupid!" Hill encouraged her. But she only bit her lower lip, and her face grew even redder and more contorted. Janowitz moved toward her. Now he was smiling—really smiling. My God, Hieu, you *own* me. He reached forward to touch her, and she allowed him to pull her to him. When he kissed her, he could taste the wet salt of her tears. Her hands clung to him with more strength than he believed her slender body capable of. His mind was singing. Big tits started to applaud—the little, excited Vietnamese clap. The rest of the group joined in.

"Come on now," Hill muttered irreverently, "don't you give her *my* case of clap." Janowitz had to laugh, even as he kissed Hieu. He forced his mouth back on hers. Sonuvabitch, he was home. It was a fucking North Vietnamese village, but he was home.

384

They stayed in Yen Cai only that one day. Janowitz stayed with the planters until noon, walking beside Hieu in the mud, telling Hill what had happened on the trip down and in Saigon. He knew the equipment had gone on to the cave where the chopper was stored, and now that they had it all, Thai had told him they would get a crew of technicians from Hanoi to assemble it. Janowitz told Hill he'd never seen Thai so dynamic. Once they'd got north of Hue, his spirits had rebounded with a vengeance. They all had slept long and well on the boats coming back, and they'd eaten like purebred hogs, but that alone couldn't account for Thai's elation. It was *his* energy that supplied the driving force to the mission now—not Evans'. And for the first time, Janowitz felt the mission had a genuine chance.

When they returned to the village for lunch and siesta, Big Tack came running out to greet them. "Buffalo! Buffalo!" he called to Janowitz, whacking him on the shoulder. He had a big congratulatory kiss for Hieu, too. Once she'd stopped crying, the blotches of pink and red had disappeared from her face, and she glowed. Janowitz had to admit there was something down in your guts that loved that submission of woman to man that the East took for granted. She walked beside him, as exquisite as a flower, but not as his equal. She was his woman. And from that she derived her pride, and paradoxically that increased his pride and his respect for her.

Tack was irrepressible. "Hey, buffalo," he exclaimed, "you be my flying buffalo now, okay? We teach those Yankees, okay?" Okay, you big tactless sonuvabitch, Janowitz chided mentally. Tack kept squeezing him with one arm and Hieu with the other. The great bear was so powerful Janowitz wondered why Hieu didn't crack.

Even little Toe was waiting for them, leaning on the sign that read "Yen Cai." His ugly face was screwed into a smile as he stepped forward to shake Janowitz's hand. And Janowitz was feeling so good he was even a little pleased to see Toe.

At the "house" Pershing, Miller, and Russell were already eating with two guards and big tits. Janowitz rushed over to Pershing before Pershing could get up. The jubilation of his homecoming was complete at seeing that handsome brown face. Pershing had lain in the back of his mind like a troubling guilt, unatoned. Janowitz had feared he would be taken away, sent to some camp in the North to go through God knows what. And however right Janowitz felt about what he was doing, nothing could make him feel Pershing was wrong. And Pershing seemed to understand how he felt.

They clasped hands and pounded each other on the back. Miller and Russell shook hands, too.

"Well, you made it, Lieutenant," Pershing said smilingly. "I take it you didn't find Saigon completely occupied by VC."

"I sure didn't!" Janowitz laughed. "We may think we got problems down there, but sonuvabitch, you should see the problems *they* got!"

"*Ahh,* well"—Pershing grinned—"the news isn't entirely black then." Janowitz tousled his head; thank God they didn't have to fake to each other. It was disagreement without malice.

"What gives?" Janowitz asked, nodding to their food and the guards. Thai and Evans had come over by them and were hanging closely on the conversation. Janowitz didn't mean to be put off by them. He knew they both understood how committed he was, but he also knew that they needed him more than ever before, and he had more power in the group than anyone. He wasn't going to be obstructive—but he sure as hell was going to see that matters that concerned him went the way *he* wanted them to go.

"Well," Pershing replied deliberately, "we had a bit of a hassle while you were gone. But we've come to sort of an agreement. You can thank that big spade behind you for that," he added with a nod to Hill.

"Come on, dad," Hill said. "It was nothing more than the sweet power of reason."

"When he talks like that, I know there's got to be graft someplace," Janowitz said.

"You getting to know the man, are you, Lieutenant?" Miller said with a mock-sour look at Hill. But even in joking, there was an edge between them now—indefinable because externally the attitudes were what they always were—but it was there.

"Well, I'll tell you, sir," Pershing said blandly, "that *ex*-specialist fifth class over there with the coolie hat sort of dug his heels in. And he more or less convinced me that we weren't going to talk him out of playing this little game with you all."

"And I got the scabs on my knuckles to prove it." Hill laughed.

"So"—Pershing shrugged—"the three of us decided that since we were outnumbered up here by seventeen million or so, there wasn't much object in our fighting the system." Janowitz laughed. "And to be honest, I got no objection to putting an end to this damn war. And neither has Miller or Russell. We aren't 'capitalist warmongers,' you know." Janowitz nodded, benignly taking the sarcasm. "So we're going

386

part way," Pershing went on. "We aren't taking part in any raid on an Arvin camp or any other camp. But if you get Thai's old man out, we've got no objection to doing what we can then."

He stared at Janowitz firmly. Janowitz smiled and put his arm on his shoulder. "Pershing," he said, "I have no regret whatsoever for doing what I'm doing when I think of Johnson, or Nixon, or J. Edgar Hoover, or my mother, or my high school principal—or anyone except *you*. You're the one blight on my conscience. And I can't tell you how glad I am that you've been able to go as far as you have."

Pershing shrugged. "Don't thank me, Lieutenant. It's just one fucked-up war. I guess all any of us can do is the best we can." He held Janowitz's eyes, and Janowitz felt the surge of respect for him he had so often in the past.

Lunch passed quickly and pleasantly. Janowitz told them a little about Saigon—not mentioning the Delambres at all. He had told Hill, but somehow that was different. And even with Hill he'd been careful not to mention their name. Little Arnie Russell had sat bug-eyed through the whole meal, watching Janowitz with a combination of amusement and wonder. Janowitz could see that all his hunting instincts had been aroused. Russell was really the type to prefer the sort of fighting the Vietcong were forced into. The sharp, crafty strike—that was his métier.

After they ate, Pershing, Miller, and Russell went with Tack and the two guards out to the fields again. They were helping build an irrigation ditch near one of the smaller villages, and when Pershing told them about it, he laughed and said the only trouble with it was that the goddamned American Air Force thought any group of four or five men working together was cause for a big target-practice session. They'd eaten more mud in the time since Janowitz had gone South than any man should have to in a lifetime.

They spent the afternoon packing up the accumulations of their stay. At first Janowitz had hoped he could get away with Hieu, but it was soon evident that wasn't going to be possible, and they both relaxed and enjoyed just being near each other.

As soon as darkness set in, they started cycling toward the hills in the west. Janowitz had expected to see Pershing and Miller and Russell again at the evening meal, and when they didn't show, he had decided they were being held away deliberately. He had gone to Thai and asked bluntly what was going on. Thai claimed that nothing was going on, but that the others would be moving out to meet them all at a rendezvous point in the South later. It was only a matter of logistics.

387

Janowitz could sense that Thai was no longer the complete master. Tick had sat listening to them, and Janowitz had remembered that Communist Tick was not in favor of the mission, and somehow Thai had to keep him in check. But Janowitz intended to have his say about the others. So he had blown his stack, but very calculatedly.

"This mission has already cost a lot," he said, "in lives, in money, in time. It would be a crime to see it all go down the drain over some petty abuse of power. But I warn you—all of you—that if I find that Pershing or Miller or Russell are ill-treated in any way, I won't fly that chopper half a mile." He glanced severely at Evans. "You know me pretty well now, Evans," he said firmly, "and that's one promise you know I'll keep. You'd better know it, if you don't."

Shortly afterward, Thai and Tick and tailender little Toe had gone out and returned with three bikes. They left again immediately and were soon back with three more. Then six of them—Janowitz, Hill, Evans, Thai, Tick and Hieu—had set off for the hills to the west.

The trip seemed much longer to Janowitz than the first time. He was relieved they had included Hieu in the party without his having to ask—or insist—on it. Evans had told him during their wait for the bikes that the general plan was that while their group were repairing the helicopter, the others would move over the trail to their rendezvous in the South. Janowitz had assumed that Hieu would not be included in their group, and that if he was going to have her with him, he was going to have to make an issue of it—but they had apparently decided to keep him happy. Those masturbating, calculating sonuvabitch Colombos—thank God for them! Tick, he would gladly have done without, but one gain, one loss—that was life.

They cycled and cycled without any deliberate break, though twice they were driven off the road by aircraft. Both times flares illuminated stretches of the sky near them, but they were never in direct danger. All the strafing and bombing occurred two or three miles away.

By the time they finally reached the village near the cave they had ridden into a blanket of mist, and they all were wet and exhausted. A patrol was waiting for them and they were led off to their sleeping quarters. Hieu was taken off by two women, and Janowitz's heart sank. He and Hill and Evans slept together in another room.

iii

The days in the hills passed very quickly. A team of four mechanics had already arrived at the village, and though they didn't know the Huey, they knew their engines and aircraft. Janowitz was not strong on the engineering aspects of flying. It had never excited his interest. He flew the old-fashioned way, by the seat of his pants. It was one reason he was so glad he had chosen to fly helicopters and not try for jet school. Half the time in jets you had to ignore your senses and obey the instruments. When he got in a chopper, he used the instruments as guides, but *he*—not the instruments—flew it.

The first day after their arrival there had been a general meeting. He was present, but it had been conducted in French, and he hardly understood a word. He kept hearing "because" and "it's necessary" and a few mispronounced English derivatives like "helicopter" and "organization," but as for making any sense out of it all, he was lost. There were two North Vietnamese officers who seemed to have the commanding voices, and there was a civilian who apparently held the same position relative to them that Tick did to Thai. He struck Janowitz as equally repellent, and from the way the conversation went, he seemed to be equally obstructive. Finally, some sort of agreement was hammered out—and everyone at the table, except Janowitz and Evans, put their initials to it.

When they rose to go, the North Korean officers shook hands with Janowitz. They both were small but looked hard and muscular—better fed than any of the people he had seen on the trail. There, only Tack seemed to have a genius for cornering enough food to keep himself in solid, muscular flesh. They didn't show any great liking for Janowitz, but there was a sort of professional respect in their attitude.

The same could not be said for Tick's friend. He was openly suspicious and disdainful, but he managed to smile when he bowed goodbye to Janowitz. Sewing things up just in case his judgment might be wrong, Janowitz felt.

Later, when Thai and Tick dallied to discuss the details of the meeting, Janowitz and Evans wandered ahead toward the cave. It was past midday, and the sun was very hot, but the view down across the plains to the sea was breathtaking. Above the villages, too distant for them to tell a ruin from a native masterpiece, it was hard to believe they were looking at a land that had been more bombed than any nation in the history of the world.

389

"You know what bothers me most about doing this," Janowitz said discursively, "Tick—and the likes of Tick."

Evans looked at him searchingly. "Me too," he answered. "As long as people like Tick have power, any freedom that comes here or anywhere else today can be taken away tomorrow. That isn't freedom—and I hate it."

"Not enough, though, huh?"

"Enough," Evans contradicted. "But they've never known any other kind of freedom. At least the system they've got now has a built-in flaw. Once you educate people, they're going to kick back at the likes of Tick—ask Khrushchev. But how can an illiterate peasant ever hope to kick back when he's enslaved by debt and need to a rich, powerful, educated landlord?"

"Beats me," Janowitz said bleakly.

"Me too," Evans replied easily. "I don't think Communism is going to be the end of freedom for any of these people—here, in Eastern Europe, in Russia itself. It's the beginning. And I think we ought to be encouraging its opening up, not trying to beat it into the ground or scaring it into a deep freeze."

They had reached the limit of the village, on the hillside road that led to the cave. It curved out there, and you could see both south and north for miles and miles, the little ribbon of yellowish brown near the horizon marking the end of the land and the beginning of the endless sea that ran right up to the sky and melded with it. Evans stopped, and they both looked. Down on the plain just below them people were working in the fields; farther away the patterns of cultivated fields diminished in perspective until they seemed like a child's checkerboard and humans figured in the scale not at all.

Janowitz felt like saying something—nothing in particular, just something—but Thai and Tick had caught up and were only a few yards from them, Tick unburdening himself while Thai listened. Poor Thai, Janowitz thought, he and Hill would have to put the needle to Tick. They ought to be able to make life unpleasant enough for him so that he didn't have the time to harass Thai quite so much. He smiled at the thought—and Tick innocently, unctuously returned it.

Later that day they met with the crew that had been working on the Huey. They had rigged up a system to supplement the fuel tanks. The bird's range wasn't great, but neither was the trip long. Three hundred miles would cover them safely, and the fuel capacity only had to be increased about fifteen percent. But they wanted Janowitz to be satisfied. He went over what they'd done, and as far as he could figure, it would have passed inspection at the Sikorsky plant itself. But the crew were insistent he inspect every joint and tube in the system, and it took the whole afternoon to satisfy them that he was satisfied.

Each following day Janowitz and Hill spent as much of their time as possible in the cockpit, trying to expand Hill's knowledge and reactions. And it was a problem. Hill had a certain agility and was smarter than hell, but he just had not been born with the kind of coordination Janowitz possessed. Trying to do one thing with his right hand while his left did another and his feet worked independently tied him in knots. Janowitz would set up exercises, and they'd both go through them, and Hill would fuck up and then fall around laughing at himself, cursing, socking the instruments, and giving the finger to Janowitz all at the same time. His mind could function *six* different ways at once— but not his muscles. It was a lot of fun, but Janowitz realized it'd take months of flying to get him to the point where even the simplest maneuvers came as second nature. If anyone was going to get that chopper in *and* out, it was going to have to be him. He spoke to Thai and Evans about it, and they had the mechanics load the floor and paneling around his position with extra steel plating, but he knew that when the shoot-up came, if he lost the use of even *one* limb, they were in trouble.

Every day Hieu brought them breakfast and lunch, but they ate together with the whole group in one of the larger buildings of the village in the evening. Twice during lunch hours when they had been standing together near the cave entrance, the touch of her had been irresistible. They had kissed often, but on these two occasions he had wanted her uncontrollably, and they had slipped up the side of the hill above the cave and made love with a desperate urgency. The ground was pitched at a weird angle, and they were afraid of being spotted by villagers or the workmen on the chopper. It wasn't particularly enjoyable—just necessary. The rest of the time Janowitz was satisfied just to be with her. He felt they were going to have a lot of time to make love—lots and lots of time.

One day when the chopper was almost ready—it had been taken out of the cave, and the props were put on the next day—the mother and father of thunderstorms broke over the hills. After listening to it and feeling the cool breeze from it pour into the cave for twenty minutes or so, Janowitz and Hill gave up their practicing and went to the cave mouth to watch. It was a terrifying, thrilling display. Hailstones pelting the side of the hill, blackness deeper than night—and sudden crackling, paralyzing sheets of lightning. The storm finally rumbled and thundered on, back beyond the hills, leaving little patches of light-blue sky and glimpses of the puffing white cloud tops that were the beautiful mantle for all that anger and violence and explosiveness beneath.

Hill cut a wet reed and made a whistle from it, and for a time they sat in the cave mouth, letting the warmth return to them after the chill of the storm. For the first time Hill asked Janowitz if he had had any second thoughts about the mission when he'd been down there among his own kind in Saigon.

Janowitz smiled and shook his head. "No," he said, "if anything, I've hardened. I'm more sure than ever that we don't belong here. Of all the people in the world who don't deserve what we're doing to them, it's the Vietnamese."

"Course you got a special interest there." Hill smirked.

"Yeah, but you know and I know that a piece of tail doesn't mean anything one way or the other." They both laughed. Then Janowitz *did* have a second thought. "Are you having doubts?" he asked.

"Oh, hell, man, I'm just going along for the ride. If we can shoot the piss out of a few Arvin, I'll call it a day well spent. I'm saving all my political fervor for a *real* piece of ass."

Janowitz laughed as expected. He sighed a bit. "No, we had quite a little trip. And there was a lot of time to think. You've got to be pretty fucking convinced that Communism is awful, awful bad, and we're an awful lot better to do what we're doing to these people. Somehow being in that great big polluted PX, Saigon, doesn't make that proposition sound any more sensible than it does way up here in the jungle."

Hill blew aimlessly on the little reed whistle. "You should hear how it'd sound in my part of Philly," he said finally. "I'd rather spend a year in Yen Cai than a lifetime in Philly." He shrugged cynically. "Course there aren't many people who'd believe that once you get east of Honolulu."

As always, Janowitz was struck by the poignancy of Hill's hard-soft posture to life. "No"—he smiled—"I guess there aren't." He poked Hill on the shoulder. "Never mind, son, I'm with the fucking mission. Even if I have got a copilot who doesn't know his ass from a hole in the ground."

"Listen, baby, when the money's on, you see who's going to save your cookies for you!"

"Yeah, sure." Janowitz laughed. "Come on, let's get back in there and see if I can teach you your right hand from your left."

"You got a prayer," Hill said mockingly.

392

Two days later they had their first test hop. They waited until twilight, and there were lookouts posted on the surrounding hilltops. Janowitz took it up for only ten minutes, and he kept the maneuvers simple and smooth. When he came down, the mechanics were more dissatisfied than he was, and the next day and a half were spent in further repairs. Then he made another flight. Everything functioned better. He hadn't realized how stiff and contrary the bird had been on the first go until he felt its response on the second. He was more adventurous and stayed up a full half hour, giving the chopper and himself a fair workout. It was so dark when he came down that he had to be guided in by lights.

Hieu was there when he brought it in, and he experienced a wonderful feeling of elation. At first he couldn't put his finger on why. It wasn't only that he was the center of attention or that what he was doing was glamorous—he'd been up too many times for that. But then he realized that never since he'd known her had he been anything but a passenger—he'd been fed and bedded, he'd had his play and even his booze, but he hadn't done a day's work during the entire time. At last he was functioning—doing what he could do, as well as he could do it.

The mechanics worked all the next day. Janowitz had hoped to give it a third trial in the evening, but at noon Thai came to him and said they were to fly that night. It was a flat statement, but Janowitz could tell by the look in Thai's eye that if he objected strongly, he could delay it. Janowitz asked him if the mechanics were coming with them, and Thai answered only one. So Janowitz asked him to see what the mechanics said about moving off that night. Thai shook his head. "We must go tonight," he repeated, but his tone still said, "It's up to you." It was one moment in his life when Janowitz wished he knew more about engines, more about stresses and loads and torques. But his basic faith was in his own ability, and he finally nodded assent to Thai, breaking out into a smile. Thai was patently relieved and hurried off without so much as a thank-you.

About three in the afternoon a bank of thunderheads built up over the valley floor and came rolling slowly toward them. Janowitz felt a little sorry. Once he'd accepted they were going, he'd been eager to get moving himself. But he wasn't going to fly a helicopter through a thunderstorm. And neither would any other pilot.

By the time they took their evening meal, thunder and lightning were crashing all around them, and the rain was pouring down in buckets. Thai seemed totally unaffected, and when Janowitz told him it was impossible to fly in such a storm, he had only smiled benignly. Well, let him dream, Janowitz thought.

When they'd finished eating, Thai marched them all through the pelting rain to the field where the bird was covered with straw. A team of villagers loaded it with barrels of fuel, a supply of guns, some spares the senior mechanic selected carefully, and a couple of sealed crates. Janowitz supervised the loading. That *was* a job he knew well. He knew how he wanted the weight distributed, and he knew how he wanted it secured. Whatever Thai thought, they wouldn't fly in the storm, but it would be worth the trouble to give the chopper a test flight with a full load once the weather cleared.

After everything was secured as Janowitz wanted it, Thai led them back to the village again. They drank a toast in Russian liquor that the mechanics had brought from Hanoi, and then the three mechanics who were not traveling with them ceremoniously shook hands with Janowitz and Hill and bade farewell to Thai.

Janowitz just grinned and stretched out on a bench with his feet on a bamboo window ledge, while the storm rumbled on above them and the rain beat on the thatch. He wasn't moving. And to his surprise Thai didn't seem to expect him to. Thai quietly sat down on a mat on the floor, and the rest of the party slumped with him. Hill shrugged and stretched out beside Janowitz.

They had been waiting for about twenty minutes when the mustachioed boss they'd met on their first visit to the village arrived, spoke hurriedly to Thai, and handed him a sheet of printed type that looked like a telegram. Thai rose and smiled at them all. "I think we shall go now," he said.

Outside Janowitz studied the sky. It was still raining, but the center of the storm had moved farther west, over the hills. The rain they were in was steady and warm—and that meant the clouds immediately overhead were no longer thunderheads, but a layer of stratus. Thai walked along beside him. "You must remember that what is good flying weather for us is also good flying weather for American planes," Thai explained. "We have tried to pick the *best* of the *bad* weather."

By the time they were in the chopper and the engines were revved over Janowitz was damned impressed with their Metro. There seemed to be no break in the clouds to the east, and the cover was low. The base was maybe four thousand feet, but the mountains ranged from two to six thousand, so no jet was going to play around in them.

394

"It's good planning all right"—Janowitz grinned—"but how are we supposed to navigate? By radio?"

"When we are in the mountains, we will use some radio beams for a short distance," Thai said mysteriously, "but most of the way, I will show you where to fly."

Janowitz laughed spontaneously. It was a nonflier's remark, innocent and well intentioned, but even so the idea of someone familiar with the ground route leading them over those mountains from the air—in the dark of night—was so ludicrous the reaction was inevitable. Even Hill laughed, and Janowitz was glad—perhaps it would convince Thai of the hopelessness of what he was suggesting.

"Be patient with me," Thai insisted. Janowitz saw Hill looking at him. They had been playing a regular game with Tick every time they saw him, and they'd got so a glance between them was understood completely. This one of Hill's read, "Let's take the idiot up and lose him." It was tough on Thai, Janowitz thought, but it would give the Huey its test with a full load anyway. He glanced at Hill and shrugged. "Okay, we're on."

Hill signaled to the mustachioed chief to release the chocks, and Janowitz indicated that Thai and the others in back should sit on the floor and put their backs firmly to the cabin wall.

"All right, star," Janowitz said flippantly to Hill, "do you want to do it, or shall I?"

Hill looked at him stonily. Then he set his jaw, turned to the controls, and gave the throttle full power. Slowly, rockily, they began to rise. Janowitz was only half-amused. He kept his hands lightly on the controls, knowing that the first hundred feet off the ground were the most dangerous. Hill might be scared, but he was scaring him even more.

"Okay, papa," Hill shouted when they were about twenty feet up, "I've done the hard bit, *you* take it!"

"Easy! Easy!" Janowitz cautioned, slowly taking a firm grip on the controls. When he finally felt he had it, he yelled, "All right, hands *first* . . . take 'em off! Okay . . . feet!" Hill spread-eagled on his butt—hands aloft, feet aloft.

"Okay, hotshot," he hollered, "great, eh?"

"Sensational," Janowitz returned. Now that he had the controls, he resolved never to challenge Hill like *that* again. He had to think so hard to get one movement right—never mind a lift-off in a breeze, with rain on the windows to distract him, and the prospects of a burst

395

of air coming over one of the hillocks on the mountain to spill him. It was lucky the goddamned jerk hadn't killed them.

"What am I supposed to do, sit here like this all night?" Hill complained.

Janowitz laughed. "I got a feeling that's the safest thing you *can* do! Get out of that harness and get Thai up here. I want to see his face when he tries to navigate two miles past the village in this shit."

Hill unbuckled and went back into the cabin. A moment later Thai came forward and leaned over Janowitz's seat. They were about five hundred feet above the village now, and even with the windscreen wipers working full speed, you could just barely make it out. Janowitz didn't even want to screw around for fun. Even he could get lost ten miles out on a night like this.

"I think we'd better pack it in, Thai," he said.

"Which way is west?" Thai asked.

Janowitz snorted. God, he couldn't even get them started! He pointed with his left hand. "Off that way—where it's good and dark."

Thai put his hand over Janowitz's shoulder, and Janowitz saw that he held a powerful flashlight. He signaled with it several times in a westerly direction. For a short time nothing happened; then a light appeared on the ground, then another, and another, and another . . . until there was a whole line of lights, some very close to each other, some spread a good distance, but a line of them winding up and over the hills into the mountains ahead.

"There," Thai said, pointing. "*That* is the way over the mountains."

Following the lights over the hills was almost like following Japanese lanterns through a garden. After they'd flown for about ten minutes and were well away from the coastal plain, Thai told Janowitz to put on his running lights. When he did, more lights gradually came on, circling through the hills. Thai watched them appear, then proudly explained that it was really quite simple. For a week every unit that had gone off along the trail had carried lights for the back of their packs. The signal they waited for: the running lights of a helicopter. When the helicopter passed overhead, the lights were extinguished.

Janowitz hunched up in his seat to twist around to see. He could see the lights going out as they passed over. A curving stretch of lights, and bang, one after another, the lights would go out. It was fantastic: simple, beautiful, almost infallible. The trail wound through the valleys, if they just stayed over the lights and watched carefully for the dark hulks of the higher ridges, they'd go right through those mountains as though it were daylight.

396

And later it got easier. As they began to catch up with the storm, the sky ahead would flash with lightning and they could see the valleys in the two or three seconds of afterlight. When the little streaks of orange ribbon first began to flash across the sky far ahead, and they could pick out the dangers more easily, Janowitz asked Thai if he would send Hieu up to see. Thai touched his shoulder and went back into the cabin.

"Too bad Pershing can't see it." Hill laughed. "He's convinced American GI's are the only military in the world with ingenuity." Janowitz smiled. He wondered how the others' trip South had gone. He knew they had left in plenty of time to be at the rendezvous point by the time the helicopter arrived. He could almost see Pershing and Big Tack puffing along, trying to outdo each other over that trail.

Hieu came forward and stood nervously behind him. The sight of the lights gradually springing on before them, winding like the line of some Chinese print through the hills, was so beautiful to him, he thought she was bound to react to it as he did. But she was terrified by every little lurch of the chopper. When lightning etched the dark ahead with crimson and rose, it only increased her terror. It got to be funny, and both Janowitz and Hill cracked up at it. Though she tried to share their amusement, she remained miserable.

Finally, Janowitz told Hill to take her back and let her sit down. When they moved out of view, he was unwillingly reminded of that night back at the VC camp when Thai had taken them to see that Laurel and Hardy thing. It reminded him again how very different Hieu's background was from his. She had braved every conceivable danger on the trail, worked harder than most of the men, proved to be a woman of infinite softness, but there, on the floor of that heaving chopper, she was an awkward stranger from a different world. He shrugged. Ten flights in a jet can change that—but he was uncomfortable from it for several hours.

Twice in Laos they used VHF radio to confirm their position. Thai had brought the crystals for the frequencies with him, and the radio operators spoke English fluently—at least air traffic English. Their airspeed for the whole trip was very low; it had to be, flying as low as they did in those mountains. But after about five and a half hours' flying time, most of it running south along the length of the storm, rather than west into it, a string of red lights appeared ahead. Thai said that meant they were only ten or fifteen miles from their landing spot—east again. Janowitz banked, and for a few minutes they were in total darkness; then they saw another line of lights come on about three miles off to their right and he angled over to them. They ran along them for only a couple of minutes, when they saw a large square appear through the drizzle, marked by a run of lights on each side. As they started down, Janowitz was struck again by how small Vietnam was, what a tiny area this "great war" was really being fought in. Any college kid in a 1958 MG would be ashamed of his average speed for the trip, and yet inside six hours they'd flown from the heart of North Vietnam, to the heart of South Vietnam—going the *long* way around!

iv

When they landed, their rendezvous point turned out to be a tiny hamlet deep in the forest about twenty-three miles northwest of Pleiku. Thai showed Janowitz briefly on a map. It was near the meeting of the borders of Laos and Cambodia and South Vietnam, but deep enough in South Vietnam to have been left alone by the Special Forces units that periodically swept up and down the border areas and either moved villagers out to the camps in Saigon or Da Nang or burned the places down . . . or both.

As soon as they landed, a party of uniformed VC came in and unloaded the Huey. It was then pushed farther into the forest and camouflaged. Thai had words with the leader, and Janowitz sensed some jockeying for position. And then to his surprise, Big Tack appeared among the work party, and he provided the real catalyst for Thai's ascendency. When the leader looked as if he were going to contest Thai's orders, Tack saluted Thai smartly, grabbed the guy by the arm, and, chattering good-naturedly, half carried him off—finishing with a little shove that sent the guy staggering for fifteen feet before he could get his balance. That was the last time for the whole of the mission that Thai wasn't obeyed without question.

Janowitz, Hill, and Evans were taken through the rain to one of the houses. When they got there, they saw Russell already asleep on a mat on the floor. A man, his wife, and two kids were also asleep on little rattan benches that hung out from the wall. The man awoke when they entered, nodded politely, then turned his face to the wall. Hill shrugged and laughed. "Just like home," he whispered. They spread their gear out on the floor. Janowitz crawled into his sleeping bag because the rain was cool in the forest. He remembered going off to sleep to its steady fall on the rushes of the roof.

When he awoke, he was still conscious of the sound, but the sun

398

was glittering in his eyes. He shook his head and sat up quickly. The sun was coming through the open window. After a second of listening he identified the sound of water as the stream they had crossed coming to the house. Russell was gone, but Hill was still sleeping soundly. The woman was kneading a corn mash in a wooden bowl. She was rather heavyset, but handsome, and she smiled at Janowitz pleasantly, though she was very tentative and cautious about it—ready to look the other way as though she hadn't seen him if he didn't respond. He smiled back and stood, running his fingers through his hair and feeling his rough beard—his mouth needed a good washing out, and he knew he looked as much a bum as he felt. He grimaced at her in self-distaste.

The woman laughed and pointed outside. He turned and wandered out to the porch. He hadn't really seen the hamlet the night before, just dark shadows in the rain. But now he could see all there was to see. There weren't more than ten small thatch-roofed houses in the whole place. Their walls were made of adobe, and Janowitz was to find them surprisingly cool, even in the warmest hours of the day. They each had porches with wooden pillars draped with bougainvillaea, and long, open windows on all sides, with wooden shutters that closed against the rain. There was a tiny cemetery, filled with ornaments and a central temple smaller than a decent double-garage, but it looked imposing in that setting. And there was shade everywhere and fantastic greenery, from dark emeralds to light yellow-greens. And in the forest, giant trees of huge maroon leaf. It was a jewel.

Janowitz heard laughter and stepped out to see where it came from. Some ways down the stream a group was gathered around a bridge made of splintered logs. Tack and Pershing were on the bridge, Indian wrestling. Janowitz wiped his face with a handful of water and ran along toward them—*this* he didn't want to miss.

Tack was heavier than Pershing—and far too confident. They stood foot to foot, hands clasped, pulling and pushing, each trying to throw the other off-balance. Tack heaved and pulled with quick, powerful thrusts, but Pershing moved even faster and had surprising strength when he was forced to use it to save himself. Both were pouring with sweat when Janowitz arrived, but Tack's optimism was unflagging. He was grinning as if victory were his the minute he really put the pressure on.

There were people on both sides of the river. Miller and Russell, big tits, Hieu, little Toe, half a dozen or so of the uniformed VC, one or two men Janowitz took to be villagers, and about ten little kids, bright-eyed, brown, and saucy, yelling in Vietnamese—though every once in a while Janowitz would hear "GI" and "Yankee" in the chorus of high-pitched gibbering. Janowitz slipped in behind Hieu and wrapped his arms around her waist. He'd only watched for a little while when Tack spotted him.

"Hey, buffalo, Trach dump her for you, okay?" And he pulled at Pershing with a great yank.

Pershing resisted, held, then gave way and jerked, and jerked again —hard. Tack was suspended for a second; then he toppled incredulously—as Goliath must have done to David. His eyes were still wide in disbelief as he crashed into the water. Pershing stood on the log bridge, staring down at him, panting, a tight grin on his face.

Tack stood up in the water. It came just above his waist. He looked at Pershing with arms akimbo for a moment, then turned to Janowitz. "Hey, buffalo. You take those Yankee home, okay?" Evans and Miller laughed, and Pershing looked more triumphant. Tack made a face at him, then lunged out on his back and swam backstroke, lazily, loftily downstream.

It was their first moment of relaxation at Megu, as the people called their hamlet—and it turned out to be the last. By the time Hieu had shaved Janowitz—before he'd eaten breakfast—several small VC units came into the area around the houses. They kept in self-sufficient groups, preparing their own food, holding their own indoctrination sessions, communicating only with Thai.

That many of the men were battle-weary was only too evident, and Janowitz was struck with the recollection of Thai and the others when he had first been captured. How they too had looked tense and hard and harried. Their furlough from battle had done them a lot of good. It was hard to think of them fighting year after year—even one year seemed long enough for our guys. How goddamn discouraging it must be for a VC to see new, fresh American units pour in month after month. No wonder they needed so much indoctrination.

But in the relaxed, shaded atmosphere of Megu the VC troops, like everyone else, found the temptation for horseplay and indolent lounging irresistible. Little groups of four or five were always splashing about in the water while other flaked out on the banksides or ambled about through the woods. But all of them regarded the Americans with suspicion. A smile would be returned, a piece of bread shared—but they didn't remain in Megu long enough for their basic reserve and doubt to be eroded.

Thai sensed the uneasiness, and since the arrival of each new unit

400

increased the buzzing questioning and rumor—as well as the tension
—he isolated their group in the houses encompassed by the Y of the
two streams which met to form the larger river in the center of Megu.
The rest of the VC were ordered to stay downriver—and most of the
time they were lost from sight in the vegetation, unless they were actually swimming.

Pershing told Janowitz and Hill at their first breakfast that he and
the others had been at Megu for two days—adding facetiously that
he was already dickering with the chief to buy a plot on the other side
of the river for his retirement. He had been parked in the chief's
house, and the thin, wizened old boy had fixed him up with a hammock and a supply of native booze that tasted like cider but kicked like
corn liquor. It got to him a lot faster than any of Evans' talking, he
cracked.

Evans smiled, but he was not to be goaded. He and Thai were busy
as hell with each new unit coming in, and Evans seemed to have lost
interest in Pershing one way or the other. It was a funny thing,
Janowitz felt, but for all Evans' bleeding for masses—something he
knew was genuine—you could tell that old John Bircher Miller cared
more in his guts for Pershing and Hill than Evans ever could. Evans
had that patrician attitude of the Southern gentleman—as though Pershing and Hill were his darkies and he'd feed, clothe, and protect them,
but treating them as though their skin was as much like his as their
blood was, as though no difference existed at all—the way Miller did
—was just beyond him. Evans was a liberal, but when it came to Negroes it was intellectual frosting on a Southern gentleman cake. Emotionally he could turn Pershing and Hill off as if they were light
switches—or darky boys fanning the flies away on a warm night.

Janowitz asked Thai how the people in the hamlet felt about having their place used as a rendezvous point—considering what it could
mean for them if anything went wrong.

Before Thai could answer, Tack burst out in a loud laugh.

"We have the good friend!" Tack chortled grandly. He pointed to
the sky. Janowitz remembered that he had heard jets a couple of times
already that day, but the sound was so customary it hadn't really registered. "We speak with the headman. We tell her if some comrade
shoot to our good friend in the sky, our good friend, she comes with
bombs and fire and *c'est perdu*—her house, the villagers, the grain.
Tout! Everything!"

Janowitz looked at Evans. Evans shrugged. "They could threaten
the villagers with their own guns," he said, "but they're more afraid of

the planes. So they say if there's any trouble, they'll shoot at the planes."

"Sometimes maybe we shoot anyway, okay?" Tack grinned.

"What's he mean?" Pershing demanded.

At first Evans didn't answer, but Pershing kept staring at him. Finally, Evans looked up, uncomfortable, his eyes blinking his old shit-eating way. "If they fire at American planes, the village is raked. They shoot the hell out of everything. If the VC really want a place shot up, they shoot at a plane, and then when it's going past in the opposite direction, three or four of them stream out toward the woods— so the pilot will see them but can't maneuver fast enough to get them. That convinces any good squadron commander the village is a VC village . . . and that's the end of the village." He stared at Pershing, that funny edge of defiance dancing in his voice. "And such is human nature, that when their village is hit again and again and again by fragmentation bombs, by napalm, by five hundred pounders, and raked with machine-gun fire, the villagers forget about the fact that it was soldiers of the Front who started it all. They only hate the Americans. So from the Front's point of view, people from an untouched hamlet like this are 'doubtful.' But villagers from a destroyed hamlet will always be theirs. Whether we pick up the refugees and move them to Saigon, or they take off into the woods. . . . That," he added numbly, "is why sometimes soldiers of the Front fire at American planes even when the villagers have done nothing against them."

"Jesus!" Pershing hissed between his teeth.

Evans looked at him—and then got up and left. It made everyone a little sick, but Hill was staring defiantly at Pershing.

"So who the hell's worse, dad?" Hill said sarcastically. "The VC for shooting at the planes, or the Air Force for letting off a couple of tons of TNT in retaliation for a few rifleshots? It's their country, not ours."

Pershing glared back at him, but then he lowered his eyes and went on eating.

With what was left of the morning Janowitz and Hill checked the chopper with Suu, the mechanic they brought with them. Everything seemed to have stood up all right through the flight. The only things in bad shape were the tires. Janowitz kicked himself for not thinking about them in the cave before they went to Saigon. They looked all right, but they were bound to have been affected by the months of sitting in a damp cave. The landing at night had cracked a seam on one of them, and the one at the tail looked ready to go any time someone shoved a boot into it. But aside from that, the bird was ready for action.

All through lunch Janowitz and Hieu had exchanged furtive

glances. He knew what they were going to do during siesta. It wasn't the sudden sexual need that had possessed him when they were working in the cave. He wanted to make *love* to her. It had been building up in his mind ever since he had first put his arms around her tiny, supple waist. And the feeling had been growing all morning. And with her too apparently, because each time she looked at him, her eyes smoldered.

They had eaten on the porch of one of the houses, and she and big tits had helped the woman serve the others. When all the men had eaten, they sat to one side and had their food. Janowitz poked Hill. "I'm off, lad," he whispered.

"I'm going to cut it off for you if you don't stop waving it in front of me," Hill muttered.

Janowitz slammed an elbow in his ribs and slipped out of the house. He knew he wasn't fooling anyone, but it was better than making a big scene of it. He went up along the stream and stretched out under a giant tree. In its shade only a stubby sort of elephant grass could grow, but it made a soft, aromatic bed.

He saw Hieu before she spotted him. She had stopped to pick up a giant pink and white flower and was walking along smelling it occasionally, turning her head to search the woods for him, moving with the erect grace of women trained to carry things on their heads. Going to teach that to all my daughters, Janowitz thought to himself. He slithered around behind the tree, then stood up so she couldn't see him. He waited—her footsteps were so damned light in the grass he couldn't hear her. When he figured she was about even with the tree, he hopped out and faced her—only she wasn't there. Stupid schnook, she'd gone the wrong way. He peered into the forest and couldn't spot her. She wasn't farther upstream. He sighed in exasperation and started into the woods. He hadn't taken three steps when a hand was clamped around his mouth, a leg slipped between his, and he was toppled to the ground. He landed hard on his shoulder, and when he rolled with both hands up by his chest ready to shove his attacker off, Hieu slipped down between his arms and kissed him hard on the mouth. You fucking VC. Janowitz grinned to himself as he pulled her close. His heart was still pounding from the surprise, and his breath was short. He had to push her face away for a gulp of air. He looked at her reprovingly, and she laughed and snuggled down in his arms. He could feel her breasts pushing against his chest, and her hips were lying right on him. He began to swell, and he knew she could feel him, full and growing. She looked up at him, and her smile was gone. Her eyes were molten. He put his arms along her back and held her tighter. He gently worked his hand under the blouse of her fatigues. She was wearing nothing under the fatigues at all. He spread his hand on the ample softness of her bottom. God, it was too much. He bent for her mouth, and they kissed gently as he pulled her even closer to him. Then he felt her hand unbuttoning his fatigues, and working down slowly, easily, rubbing his flesh, squeezing it with the slightest of pressures . . . until she put her hand on him. She held him firmly and he was mad for her—but he made himself keep it slow and tender. She kissed his body with all the affection and wonder that he did hers. And they made love as though they were one—each giving to the other, belonging to the other, his body hers, and hers a part of him.

That night after supper, when Evans, Thai, and Tick were busy with the VC units, Pershing shared some of the headman's hooch supply among them. All the Americans sat together in the headman's hut, and Miller and Russell told them of the trip South along the trail. As Janowitz had anticipated, the whole trek had been a contest between Pershing and Big Tack. Who could carry the most, who could march longest without break, who could climb the steepest trail. They'd used a different trail than they had going up—it was more difficult and less heavily trafficked. Tack had proved surprisingly agile, and Pershing had lost as many of the silent battles as he'd won. Russell told of the final debacle with real country relish. They'd been in a small village on a plain in Laos, and Tack had challenged Pershing to a race on water buffalo.

"It was early morning," Russell drawled, "and we'd been trampin' all night, but we'd jus' had breakfast and we was all feeling kinda vinegary. These damn buffalo were saunterin' around with kids on 'em, right past the little spot of village grass we were lyin' around on. Ole Tack, he stands and says, 'Come with us, Yankee friend, we make race, okay?'" Russell chuckled at his imitation of Tack, and they'd all had enough booze to think it was pretty funny, too.

"The kids, they'd been grinnin' like monkeys at us the whole time anyway. And when Tack he jabbers to them, they start laughin' and hollerin', and quicker than you could chase a fly from your nose, the whole cotton-pickin' village was out there, jumpin' up and down, yellin' and grinnin'.

"Well, Tack he comes back and tells us the race is all set, and we're going to have it over on a straight stretch near where they're working. Now any ole possum would know somethin' was up, but we couldn't rightly figure what it was. Ole Sarge Pershing here, he was thinkin'

404

they were going to give him a wild buffalo, so he kept his eyes on the ones the kids were riding and got his mind set on a sweet ole baby that looked about as docile and lazy as my pappy's mare.

"Well, we get on this path by this muddy ole rice field, and Tack he shows the sarge where they're racing to—another path on the other side of the field, about a couple of city blocks down. Then ole Tack he tells the sarge to get on this one buffalo. But the sarge he ain't buying that shit. He shakes his head, and he points to the buffalo he's set his mind to.

"An' Tack is as obliging as he could be. He brings this buffalo over by the nose and helps the sarge up. An', man, those fucking things don't half stink. And flies! And ticks! Jesus, you can see why they're always washing the sonsubitches. But it don't do much good, ole sarge here'll testify to that!

"So then Tack he gets on this other buffalo he'd offered to the sarge. And already the sarge is in trouble. 'Cause his ole buffalo is turnin' and twistin' and stretchin' its neck like it don't want nothin' to do with whatever the shit that is on its back. But the kid that's been ridin' it, he takes it by the nose and lines it up with Tack's. And the fuckin' natives are going wild. Jumpin' up and down and laughin' and screamin'. Tack says to the sarge, 'Okay?' The sarge nods his head, and about six guys swat the butts of both them buffalo." Russell had to stop. The tears were streaming down his cheek.

"And, man," he finally went on, "the shit flew!" And that collapsed him again, *and* Miller, *and* Pershing.

"This fuckin' field," Russell staggered on, "had just been fertilized with cowshit, humanshit, dogshit, buffaloshit, every kind of shit in this goddamned world! You couldn't see it lying under that little covering of water they put on it, but, man, it was *there!*

"Tack's buffalo it lit out one way, and the sarge's it jumped off another. Ole Tack didn't have no easy time staying on at first, but he did. But the sarge he hadn't gone five jumps with that goddamned thing and he was tossed about fifteen feet in the air and slithered to a nose-down crash landing right in this goo!" Russell shook his head ruefully, still grinning like a banshee. "Right about there the sarge he would have packed it in, but them villagers were out there in nothing flat. Hordes of 'em. Some of 'em caught that buffalo, and the rest lifted the sarge out of the muck, and before you can say Jack Robinson, they got him mounted again. And off he went!

"Well, I'm telling you that happened *sixteen* times if it happened once! The sarge would go flying through the air and come to a three-point landing, and before he could raise his face from the goo, there were eight guys puttin' him back on old Whirlaway! Well, Jesus-at-the-roadside, I'm tellin' you the sarge he got so fuckin' *mad* I thought he was goin' to pick that goddamned buffalo up and *carry* the fucker across the line!"

Janowitz howled. Pershing was laughing now, too, with the tears streaming down his cheeks, but the memory was plainly a mixed one for him.

"An' ole Tack, he was riding alongside, bustin' a gut at it all and encouragin' the sarge the whole time. Finally, the sarge all but throttled that fuckin' animal he was so *determined* to hang on! Well, the fucker heads off the wrong way, and all the goddamned villagers are waving their arms at it and trying to chase it across the line, and finally, the ole buffalo gives in and lunges off the way they're trying to shoo it, and it tosses the sarge right off his perch. An' there's the goddamned thing lurching along and the sarge hangin' on under his neck for dear life. If he'da let go, the fuckin' buffalo woulda trampled him to death, and his hands are so slippery from all that shit, he's losing more of his grip every second.

"Well, I'm tellin' you, the expression on his face was worth the whole goddamned war! He was covered with wet crap from his toes to his eyebrows—but he was not about to give in. From the look in his eye, you'da thought he had that damn animal at *his* mercy! Ole Tack he finally stops the cow and pulls the sarge to his feet. Man, if looks coulda killed at that moment—I'll tell you the VC would be less one fat sonuvabitch!"

Janowitz wiped the tears from his eyes and looked at Pershing. He was grinning, but you could see the anger, too. Now Janowitz understood something of his expression when he'd been Indian-wrestling Tack on the log bridge. No wonder he'd wanted to win so badly.

"It took us about four hours of washing to get the sarge so we could stand the smell of him," Miller added. He was looking at Pershing and smiling, but Janowitz sensed that he shared some of Pershing's anger at Tack, along with his appreciation for a raw but funny practical joke. And he sensed that Pershing knew he did, too.

iv

The next morning the largest of all the VC units arrived. It was led by a guy who looked even younger than Thai. He and Thai clasped

406

each other like brothers, and had they not looked so little alike, Janowitz would have thought they *were* brothers. At lunchtime Janowitz could see from the house where they ate that all the VC were gathered downriver for a meeting. Thai and Evans both seemed tense and excited, and Tack and little Toe were running back and forth between the groups like squirrels tending their hoardings.

After lunch Janowitz took off into the woods again, and Hieu followed him shortly afterward. She was walking free again, like a girl, without her rifle. In fact, she was more often without it in the hamlet than with it, but her playfulness had deserted her, and she looked sad. Janowitz wondered if she had some information he didn't. From now on he was going to push Evans for more details of what was going on. Hieu seemed to want to walk, and they walked hand in hand for a long time up the stream. They eventually came to a tiny waterfall—two feet at most—but the sound of its rushing water beguiled the midday heat of its vehemence, and Janowitz trampled an area of undergrowth near it for a place for them to lie down. There had been planes overhead all that day, and they were careful to stay under the cover of the leaves.

Hieu was affectionate but remained curiously restrained, and Janowitz wondered if he had done something yesterday that had hurt or offended her. He could hardly believe it. They had loved and parted in the closest thing to rapture he had ever known—but something was wrong now. It was a full twenty minutes of doubt and confusion—even a little anger—before she was able to make it known to him that she was menstruating. He was so goddamned relieved he just collapsed on her. But despite his smiling and gentle teasing, she was genuinely embarrassed, even a little ashamed.

In a strange way it made him feel even closer to her. He held her in his arms for a long time, amused by her embarrassment, feeling for the first time that she *needed* his protection, his reassurance and affection. After a while they followed the river farther upstream, wading a little for a time in it after it had grown shallow. Hieu clung to him and gradually lost her solemnity. She would blow her hair away and smile up at him, and he would peck playfully at her nose.

It was long past siesta when they returned. They could see movement in the hamlet as they approached, and before they lost their isolation again, they stopped by a tree and kissed, at first with tenderness and then with an intensity that went beyond that. Janowitz encircled her in his arms and lifted her off the ground. He was filled with a kind of choking elation. Several times he whispered, "I love you, I love you." He knew she could tell they were words of endearment, but he wished he could tell her that he had never used them before. It was one of his things. For all his dizziness with girls, for all the things he'd told them when he wanted them badly enough—those words he'd saved.

v

That night he cornered Evans and tried to find out what was going on, but Evans was obviously up to his ass in planning, and when he tried to evade a discussion, Janowitz was fairly sympathetic. Evans promised that he'd have a very thorough briefing before they left the hamlet. Even the way he said it didn't make Janowitz realize how soon it was to be.

When he awoke the next morning, he was startled at how quiet everything seemed. The place had never been noisy, but now an even greater calm had fallen over it. Hill was up and gone, and so were Russell and Evans. The little kids were sleeping, but both mama and papa were already out of the house. He got up and went to the door. Hill was walking back from the stream.

"Well, it's gettin' near, dad," he said soberly.

"What do you mean?" Janowitz asked.

"The VC have pulled out—all of them. It's only our own little band of brothers and the villagers now."

Janowitz looked quickly up and down the stream. The village kids and a couple of elders moving among the houses were the only ones he could see.

"Miller said he got up in the middle of the night to take a piss, and they were already moving out," Hill added as the two looked out at the near-empty hamlet—its silence suddenly ominous and frightening. Janowitz felt his blood racing. It *was* getting near—and suddenly, it was no longer a gamble or a lark. He was scared and nervous and tense.

"Let's find Evans," he said sharply.

But Evans was not to be found. And neither was Thai or Big Tack. They found Tick but ignored him. Only when they couldn't find the others did they go back to him.

"They are having practice," was all Tick would tell them. He smiled in his supercilious way and waved his arms at the hamlet. "Make enjoyment for yourselves," he said.

408

Janowitz didn't feel like eating at breakfast, and Hill didn't either. Pershing stared at them both, an enigmatic smile on his face. Janowitz kept waiting for him to say, "Well, you can still say no." But it never came. Pershing just kept them under the steady pressure of his gaze.

It didn't help that Hieu and big tits were as nervous as they were. Hieu touched Janowitz every time she came near, but they were anxious gestures, full of concern and worry. Janowitz knew he had to snap himself out of his tenseness or he'd be a wreck by the time they had to fly.

Hill was his only safety valve, but even Hill's face was steel. The firmness of it was reassuring. It had the mark of someone who knew how to take care of himself when things got sticky, but it was tense—ready for the action now. And several hundred basketball games had taught Janowitz you can't perform if you spend a day or two in that kind of tension.

After pecking at breakfast, he and Hill wandered out of the house and started to amble along the river, and Janowitz saw his release. It had been one of the first things he'd noticed about the village. A small round communal oven. At every meal they had had fresh bread, but it had been a hard loaf, round and tough.

"I'm going to bake us some bread," Janowitz said suddenly.

Hill looked at him doubtfully. "Well, shit, man, I just can't think of anything I'd rather have," Hill deadpanned. Janowitz hit him.

"Come on," he said, "this little lesson is going to be worth a fortune to you."

"Yeah, I can see the possibilities all right," Hill said good-naturedly, "the first black baker in Vietnam. Shit, I can't lose!"

When Janowitz found the fat old woman who baked for the village, she seemed to understand immediately what he intended, and she grinned and nodded her head in pleasure. Given the taste of the bread she baked, Janowitz didn't wonder!

She took the two of them to the back of her hut, where the flour was stored in the hollowed trunks of four huge trees. Janowitz raised the flat stone lid on one and sifted a handful of grain through his fingers—and he knew one reason the bread was so poor.

"All right, son, I'm putting you to work," he told Hill. And with Hill's help he filled a basket and took it to the large, round millstone where the grain was ground.

"It's gritty," Janowitz explained to Hill. He squatted by the millstone and, taking the flat pestle, started to regrind the flour. Hill took

409

another pestle and followed his example. They ground silently for about ten minutes—each of them glancing from time to time toward the woods downstream and both pretending they didn't notice the other doing it.

Then a kid running by stopped dead in his tracks, stared at them, and ran off again. In a couple of minutes he was back with three more kids. *They* stood and stared.

"Maybe there's a union or something," Hill whispered. "They're waiting for the gang to arrive to give us the workover a couple of imported blacklegs deserve."

"I wouldn't be surprised"—Janowitz smiled—"look at that." He nodded to the baker. She was sweeping out her house, paying no attention to them at all—as though GI's came through every day and ground a bit of flour for her. "She sure isn't acting very worried about us stealing her job."

Hill laughed. "Maybe she knows what kind of baker *you* are."

Janowitz tossed a fistful of flour at him, and the kids laughed. Hill grimaced, and he tossed a fistful back at Janowitz. The kids giggled again. It broke the spell. A couple of them ran off shouting, and in five minutes every kid in the village was grouped around them, staring and chattering as Janowitz and Hill ground on. For the first time Janowitz noticed there wasn't a kid over twelve in the lot. He wondered if the older ones had already gone to the VC—or if they were hiding so the VC wouldn't "enlist" them. It set the triphammer in his heart going again—and he concentrated on grinding until he could look at them without glancing downstream, without thinking about the departed VC.

In twenty minutes three or four of the older men from the village had joined the group, and finally Russell peered around one of the huts.

"Hey! Come on, Russell, show these ignorant natives how a Ku Klux Klanner works," Hill yelled. Pershing and Miller had emerged behind Russell, and they all ambled over to the grinding stone. The two guards walked behind them. They never gave the three of them much berth these days—too close to home. And old cynic Hill had muttered to Janowitz that he was glad. He didn't trust Pershing's giving up the good fight for one minute.

Russell submitted good-naturedly to Hill's encouragement. He watched Janowitz demonstrate and then ground away furiously for a short spell before collapsing with a great show of exhaustion.

"See that, chillun," Hill observed disparagingly. "He'd be lost with-

410

out his fucking slaves. Come on. Miller," he said, tossing the pestle at him, "show us what a real white man can do."

Miller came on strong, sending the grain flying everywhere, and the kids buzzed hilariously around the great flat grinding stone, scooping up the fallen grain and hurling it back in place—until Miller sagged, winded.

"You're a fucking failure," Hill admonished disgustedly. "A pale nigger, that's all you are—slow, stupid, and lazy!" Miller grinned and raised the pestle as if to hit him with it. Hill grabbed it and held it out to Pershing. "Come on, papa, show these cats what a man can do."

Pershing still seemed moody, but he finally took the pestle and ground away meticulously and efficiently to Hill's extravagant praise until one of the toddlers wandered to his side, staring at all the grinning faces. He absently wrapped his arm around Pershing's leg and stuck his thumb in his mouth, hugging a ragged straw animal in his other arm, trying to figure what it was all about. The grinning turned to laughter, and Pershing had to quit. He picked the kid up and held him, but the kid just sucked away and stared at everyone else. Finally, he turned slowly and stared at Pershing—and did a sort of languid double take, like who the hell are you? And everyone *did* howl. Pershing lowered him and patted his round, tight little bottom and the kid wandered back among the others, still puzzled, still calmly sucking that thumb, and clinging to his straw animal.

Janowitz at last was reasonably satisfied with his flour, and he and Hill carried it ceremoniously to the little dome-shaped oven. Janowitz directed the kids to bring some logs from the stack near it, and one of the old men started a small fire in the oven's base for him. The baker had trailed along and she began to throw in more logs, but Janowitz stopped her. She looked puzzled, but Janowitz just grinned and made motions with his hands in the grain, repeating, "Milk . . . *du lait* . . . salt . . . *sal* . . . yeast." She knew what he meant but looked at the tiny fire in the oven and shook her head resignedly. He was going to make a mess of it.

When she came back, Hieu and big tits and two or three of the village women came with her, all bringing something for the bread. The operation had now become the center of everyone's attention, everyone still there in the hamlet. Big tits was carrying a jug of milk, and Hill ran to help her. He wouldn't take it but insisted on wrapping his long arms half around her and half around the jug. Well, at least he was getting *his* mind off that meeting in the woods, Janowitz decided.

Janowitz made inventory of all they brought, including some messy-looking fat. While everyone sat and watched, he heated the milk on the oven, then sprinkled a bit of the yellow yeast onto it and added some of the mixture to a portion of flour. He added salt and a few dabs of the fat and mixed it all again. Then he laid the thick roll of dough on one of the wide wooden spades near the opening to the oven and repeated the process with another batch.

"Man, you're really making this scene, aren't you, dad?" Hill commented.

"Just pay close attention, son," Janowitz retorted loftily. "You are going to see the difference between a baker and *a baker!*" He warmed the dough in the oven and then took it out, kneading it all again, sometimes adding a little flour. By now his deliberate movements had cast that hypnotic spell over his audience that a craftsman's technique always establishes. Even the baker had squatted on the ground to watch him, more mesmerized than critical.

He had the kids get another roaring blaze of dry, fast-burning twigs going in the oven, and its sides had grown pink by the time he finally had his finished loaves placed on the wooden spades. The baker had long since lost her cool. She looked at the men and gesticulated wildly to the oven, admonishing them all that this long-legged idiot was going to ruin the communal oven.

"Listen, dad," Hill said, "you aren't going to blow up their fucking oven for them, are you?"

Janowitz sighed with the martyrdom of the wise. He rose and indicated to the men to open the oven. When they did, you could see that most of the coals had already died. Hill shrugged; Janowitz shook his head balefully. He motioned the men to rake the coals out, and then he got flat on the ground and slid the wooden spades carefully into the oven, placing each as though he were adjusting the tuning on a piano. When he had them spread to his satisfaction, he closed the oven door.

"Now," he said to them all, as though everyone understood him, "we will all take a swim." And he marched imperiously toward the stream. The kids followed him, and eventually most of the others went, too.

Twice Janowitz left the water to check his handiwork. Each time the baker was still sitting there, and each time she hunched down and peered over his shoulder into the oven. Janowitz carefully switched the wooden spades around, trying to get an even brown on his loaves. And each time he closed the oven door again the baker looked at him with a scorn she was finding more and more difficult to sustain.

The loaves had baked for almost an hour before he was ready to withdraw them. Most of the loaves were golden and had risen fairly evenly, and only one or two had browned too much on the edges. Hill slapped him on the back, and the whole company chattered in excited approval. Janowitz felt better. The smell of the oven, the baking of the bread, the sight of the golden loaves *had* restored his nerves. He had had to work at it, but now he felt fit—and ready. He could play basketball, he could bake a loaf—and he could fly those birds, even when the heat was on. It wasn't a very impressive list, but in a perverse way he knew it was enough to satisfy *him*.

vi

Evans, Thai, Tack, and little Toe didn't appear at lunch. Hieu and big tits prepared a special rice dish smoked in large green leaves, and they carried a tray of it and a huge bowl of vegetables off into the woods. Janowitz gave Hieu a loaf of his bread to take with her. He knew she'd explain where it came from.

Afterward Janowitz walked along the river again. Hieu came in a few minutes, and they wandered to the spot by the waterfall. He held her in his arms for a time, feeling warm and good, but also beginning to feel butterflies again and wondering when Evans would return and when he'd know the whole plan. Without really being aware he was sleepy, his eyes grew heavy. He closed them for a second—and slept soundly until Hieu woke him. He was sweating and groggy. She felt so soft and looked so loving he wished they could make love. But he stretched and stretched and drove it from his mind. She seemed to want to get back, and he got up and washed his face in the stream. The sun had disappeared in a mass of clouds, but it was muggy and oppressive. About halfway back he took off his fatigues, waded out into the middle of the stream, and swam along as she walked beside him on the bank. The water was cool and the current fairly fast, and he had the marvelous sensation of swimming at great pace without any effort. He didn't quit until he could see the Y ahead, and then he crawled out and slipped back into his fatigues. Hieu buttoned him up and kissed his chest, wrapping her arms around him and clinging with a smile as lazy and warm as the afternoon.

When they got to the hamlet, Evans was waiting for them. He was in the uniform of an American light colonel. Janowitz laughed.

413

"Part of the exercise." Evans smiled self-consciously. "The Arvin are always impressed by American brass."

"Looks like they're not the only ones," Janowitz replied wryly. Evans blushed.

"I've been waiting for you," Evans said. "We thought you might like to hear the full plan now."

Janowitz nodded soberly. The butterflies fluttered again. The time for idleness was passing quickly. Well, at least he'd found an outlet. If it were to be tomorrow, he'd bake another batch of bread in the morning, concentrate on getting the loaves to rise more evenly, and fly like a pro when the time came.

Hieu had squeezed his hand and melted away the way she did when matters didn't concern her.

Evans said Hill was waiting for them downstream. They started off through the village. Pershing, Miller, and Russell were sitting on the chief's porch. Janowitz nodded as they went by, but Pershing's return wave was only perfunctory. He didn't mask his disapproval, and for all his conviction, Evans seemed disconcerted by it, perhaps because he was wearing a uniform he hadn't earned. It stiffened Janowitz. He was not ashamed of what he was doing, and though he could understand Pershing, he wasn't going to be bullied by Pershing's attitude of moral rectitude. The moral rectitude Janowitz felt was on his side.

"The colonel here doesn't mind if you boys don't salute," he hollered, "but I'm only a fucking lieutenant and *I* care."

His tone of voice was just ambiguous enough to make Pershing uncertain. He hunched up from the little wicker stool he was on and started a halfhearted salute. Janowitz kept his eyes fixed right on him, and slowly Pershing stood erect, and Russell and Miller followed suit— all looking embarrassed and even a little befuddled. Each managed a salute of sorts—and Janowitz returned it smartly, as if he were passing in review. He could see Tick and little Toe and the two guards watching them from the side of one of the other houses, and he wondered what the hell they were making of it.

"Thank you, Sergeant," he called out, keeping his voice harsh. "That's better," he whispered brightly to Evans. "You should've returned their salute, Colonel." Evans smiled, but he was walking more rapidly. Pershing obviously bothered him as much as Janowitz bothered Pershing.

Hill was waiting on the steel bridge that was buried deep in the woods. It bore a cast "D'Erlanger et Fils." The area must have be-

414

longed to a French planter once, Janowitz guessed, but now the foliage had grown around the bridge so thickly that he didn't even see it until they were almost on it. Hill was looking grim again, and Janowitz wondered if he were having second thoughts now that the action was drawing near. It was one thing to agree to an idea of distant risk; it was another to be face to face with getting laid out, right now—or worse, badly wounded with only the kind of care the VC could give you. And suddenly Janowitz himself was wondering if there was a doctor in one of those units that had come to the hamlet.

Evans took them on into the woods beyond the area where most of the VC had camped. About six hundred yards in, there was a clearing that was covered on top by a lacery of leaves from the giant trees surrounding it. Tack was waiting for them, his face wreathed in a big grin. Behind him they could see a mud and twig structure that looked like a bunker of some sort.

Thai and Suu, the mechanic, came out of the bunker as they approached. Thai nodded politely to them, but his face looked as grim and tense as Hill's. Thai said something to Suu, and the man smiled his agreement. He walked over and shook hands in greeting with Janowitz and Hill and then left at a half trot through the woods.

Only the five of them were left. Thai squatted, and the rest of them automatically slipped into a semicircle round him. The area had been flattened by lots of footsteps in the past few days, and Thai pulled a few tufts of grass and weed loose so the ground just in front of him was clear. Without saying anything he drew an outer perimeter—almost a square, but with one corner ballooned into a semicircle. Then he etched a number of squares and rectangles within the perimeter which Janowitz took to represent buildings. Finally, Thai drew one long, curved outline that Janowitz recognized had the shape of the structure in front of him. Thai thrust the stick he had drawn with into the center of his sketch. Then he looked up at Janowitz and Hill.

Almost on cue it started to drizzle. Thai turned his face up. For an instant he frowned, but slowly it changed into a quiet smile. He turned back to Janowitz and Hill.

"Perhaps you would like to know what we all are expected to do?"

"Yeah, perhaps we would," Janowitz replied.

Thai nodded to Tack, and Tack took a vinyl envelope from his fatigue jacket and handed it to Janowitz. Inside there were several pictures of dead VC lined up on the ground before some sweating American troops toting automatics and M-16's. All the GI's were huge and had thick, muscular arms. There were also pictures of scrawny kids holding their hands out for food and a really great one of a rat gnawing at a rotted human skull.

Tack leaned over and translated the Vietnamese captions under the pictures in his imperfect English.

" 'These ones are Vietcong killed by American soldiers. Ho Chi Minh makes speeches of the war to last five, ten, twenty years. Are you to be alive when it ends?' 'These children are to beg for food. Is it that your child he is together with them? Your brother? Your little sister? Your cousins? How many are your rations? The Americans eat much. Your little ones those have already lost, are you also to lose the fruit of your sweat and tears?' " And under the one of the sickeningly rotted skull and its scavenger: " 'Is it that this is being the way you are sometime to die? Is it to be your body is being preserved and is being buried with your ancestors, or is it that sometime it is to feed the rats from the field?' " At the bottom of each were the words *Chieu Hoi*. " 'The "open arms" of the Republic of South Vietnam and her allies it is able to wait to greet you,' " Tack translated. " 'Depart the revolution of the godless Ho Chi Minh and come to join with your brothers which are to be well fed and secure.' "

Tack laughed and then pulled a last document from the vinyl envelope. He held it up, and Thai nodded at it.

"If members of the Liberation Front are touched by these pictures and the appeals that go with them," Thai explained, "they are provided with a pass of safe-conduct to certain specified headquarters."

"In Tet"—Tack laughed—"their comrades he dropped more—" He was stuck, and he turned to Evans to help him out.

"The Air Force dropped more than three hundred *million* of those things during Tet," Evans said solemnly. "Almost a couple of thousand for every man, woman, and child in the Liberation Front."

"Okay!" Tack exclaimed, nodding his agreement. "Number one time we have toilet paper from many years!" And he roared at his own joke.

"The relevant point to us," Thai continued, "is that the military compound at Pleiku is one of the specified headquarters where *Hoi Chanh* —the returnees—are sent.

"Members of several of the units that were here for these past days have taken these passes, and at a given time they will present themselves at a number of roads and checkpoints around Pleiku.

"The timing will be fairly exact"—Thai smiled—"so that no one will be alerted. One or two men here, one or two men there. But, in total, a considerable number—a fact we hope will not appear evident until they are in the center of Pleiku. As they begin to arrive at the base, a group of native workers in the American sector will disappear from their places of work—very quickly to reappear as armed soldiers of the Liberation Front. They will not only release the *hoi chanh* from their guards but supply them with arms from hidden caches.

"When the fighting inside the base has begun, other units will begin a concerted attack at the northeast perimeter. When forces rush to repel it, another attack will be launched in the northwest." He looked directly at Janowitz.

"That is when we will fly over the prison area. It lies in the southeast sector of the military complex. It looks like this." He referred to his drawing. "My father is here." And he touched the area shaped like the temporary bunker. He looked up again at Janowitz.

"You will drop us down sixty meters from that at this spot." He indicated a small square. "This is the command post of the security section. At that point Comrade Evans and I will present ourselves as a party to secure the safety of their important prisoners. Given the confusion and the ranks we will bear, the American helicopter and the presence of two obviously American officers flying the helicopter, we have no doubt that our word will be accepted without question. We will take my father into the helicopter and—"

"Wait—wait a minute!" Janowitz interrupted.

Thai paused and looked at him patiently. The drizzle had turned to genuine rain. It was steady, and even with the cover of leaves, they all were getting wet, though it was hot enough that none of them paid attention to it.

"Have you got any idea of the kind of air traffic they've got at Pleiku?" Janowitz asked Evans incredulously. "Just how the hell am I supposed to get that bird over the camp without clearing traffic control and without explaining who the hell I am?"

"The timing is intended to be very exact," Evans said calmly. "In the first moment of the battle, three things must happen at the air base. The power supply and the emergency power supply at the tower will be destroyed. The explosive is already in place. Two, the central control room in the operations building will also be subject to an explosion. Third, the complex of radar screens will be damaged by close mortar fire. Since the radar screens are the most valuable of all these, the assumption is that the immediate reaction will be to protect them. The tower and operations building may not be functioning again

417

for five—perhaps even ten or fifteen—minutes. And when they resume functioning, an unidentified American helicopter will not be their *first* concern. We are assuming you can get in and get out in just under fifteen minutes. It should be enough."

Janowitz leaned back thoughtfully—and skeptically. Man, it was cool all right, but sonuvabitch, the tower would be screaming for identification when he was eight, ten minutes out. And if they blew the power that soon, that'd mean the Air Force would be after them before they began to clear the area once the action was over. And one jet could make a helicopter just a little bit defenseless.

"We're assuming," Evans said in response to the expression on his face, "that you can bring it in very low and can delay their identification inquiries."

"That's what we're assuming, is it?" Janowitz replied doubtfully.

Evans smiled. "We have the VHF crystal for the area. Suppose you were shot up and breathing hard and unevenly," Evans suggested, "don't you think you could fool them for a time?"

Janowitz shrugged thoughtfully; it might work.

"Once we are out of the immediate area," Thai went on, "we will return here. It would not be safe to fly the helicopter farther, and from here we can move in a very short time into either Laos or Cambodia, depending on the direction our pursuers take. In this area we will be led by my younger brother. He knows the terrain," Thai added with a grim smile, "rather better than anyone who is liable to be following . . . and he will have the men to ambush and delay any large-scale pursuit."

Hill looked at Janowitz, a lazy, irreverent grin on his face. "It sounds like quite a rumble," he said. Janowitz could tell that half of Hill's pleasure came from the chance to knock the piss out of Complacent Authority. But he was also obviously as relieved as Janowitz that the plan sounded workable, and believing a plan was workable was almost as important as the plan itself. The only thing that still bothered Janowitz was that it seemed like a helluva shoot-up to spring one man.

"And your father is all we're going to get out of all this?" he asked Thai quietly.

"There are five others in the security block," Thai said. "They are important to others. Our purpose is to get my father."

"It sounds like a lot of people are going to be dead at the end of the day."

"Yes," Thai answered solemnly. "There is hardly a day in Vietnam when there are not a lot of people dead at the end of the day."

He looked steadily at Janowitz, and Janowitz nodded, but the doubt was still in his eyes. "And from our point of view," Thai added dismissively, "any successful raid on the *inner* defenses of a major installation like that at Pleiku is an important psychological victory—more damaging to the enemy than could ever be accounted for just by numbering his losses."

"And the American losses—how are they justified?" Janowitz insisted.

"The bulk of the attack is going to be on Arvin units," Evans cut in. "American units will undoubtedly engage in the counterattack and pursuit . . . but I can assure you that at the end of the day the headquarters in Saigon will be able to report their usual gloating totals of several hundred losses to the Front for every American killed or wounded."

Janowitz looked away. He couldn't contradict Evans on that. And what the hell, he knew they couldn't take a place like Pleiku with a slingshot. He'd known that from the beginning. It was going to be a battle. But it sounded like they'd make it—if nothing went wrong. And perhaps the fact that Americans made his release possible would make Thai's old man *more* willing to argue for an end to the whole thing.

"Are we going to be in contact with any of those units on the ground?" he asked. Thai shook his head. "Well, what happens if somebody goofs and they don't get the tower like they're supposed to or some American unit with about fifty tanks just happens to be going by the prison when we land?"

"Once the battle is engaged," Thai said fatalistically, "we are no longer in command. It is up to the gods to fulfill our plan—or to play tricks with us as they do the crops in the field. All we can do is to prepare well, and strike boldly. . . . We dress to enact our fates—we do not write the scenes."

Janowitz glanced at Hill. For some time Hill had been listening with a no-nonsense attentiveness that was spiced with a morsel of relish for the little twists of Thai's plan. But this last remark seemed to strike right at Hill's own basic fatalism, and he was staring at Thai with a tight smile of admiration.

Thai rose. "If the command post at the security area is heavily manned, we may ask you to enter with us, Comrade Janowitz." He gestured toward the mud and stick copy of the prison bunker, and Janowitz got up and followed him to it.

Inside there were eight small cells, all below ground level. The

419

guards had a desk and a walkway at ground level that allowed them to look down into the cells.

"We do not know which cell my father is in," Thai explained, "but we do know that no one guard has the key to more than three cells and that there is no master key. If there is resistance, all the guards must be killed and the keys taken from each. There is also a means of blowing up the entire block," he added with a wry smile, "but that need not concern us."

"It's okay, Lieutenant," Hill said, "if they blow you up, you know I can take care of the helicopter. Christ, I can probably even bake me some bread if things really get rough."

"Delightful." Janowitz nodded ironically.

Thai led them back out into the clearing. For the first time they were forced to take heed of the rain. It was fairly heavy now, and the cloud cover had lowered. It was still up four or five thousand feet, but Janowitz knew it was a depression moving in, and it'd get a lot worse before it got better. He'd like to have seen a weather chart. Was it a matter of a few hours—or was it a real blow? A big depression in this country could turn into a small monsoon that lasted for three, four, even five days.

"Is this thing scheduled for a particular time," he asked Thai, "or do you just wait until you hear everyone's in place?"

Thai glanced calmly at his watch. "We must leave within forty-five minutes," he said.

Janowitz stared at him openmouthed. "Forty-five minutes? Today?" he finally uttered.

"It is only a five-minute walk to the helicopter," Thai replied innocently. "Unless you have some further question about the plan?"

Janowitz was caught totally off-balance. His first thought was of Hieu, and before he could even weigh how it would look, he gestured toward the village. "What about the—"

"The others will be waiting and ready to move out when we return," Thai answered. "In a plan of this sort the number of people who know its details must be as few as possible—and those who are eventually told must be told as late as possible." His voice was sympathetic and his logic irrefutable.

"What about this stuff?" Janowitz asked, pointing to the sky.

"I don't know," Thai answered. "The plan calls for the attack just before sunset. The advantage of darkness once we are free of the base is obvious. Unfortunately we do not have a meteorological report, but being Vietnamese, we consulted my horoscope and my father's.

The day is right for us. Perhaps the weather is wrong for the Americans and the Arvin."

Janowitz was almost ready to argue, but he'd been in Vietnam long enough to know how seriously even the best-educated people took their horoscopes, and besides, there really was no way of telling how bad weather *would* turn out. It could be their biggest asset.

vii

Suu was at the helicopter. He checked everything over with Janowitz. Janowitz couldn't find anything that bothered him. That raised his spirits—as did Suu's bright confidence. Shit, maybe it was best to start now. No time to worry. It was a good plan. Let them get in there and get out . . . and besides, he thought wryly to himself, there's Thai's horoscope and his old man's. He wished some smart ass had bothered to make *his*.

There was a good map in the cockpit. Regular USAF. The run was going to be ridiculously quick. Shit, twenty-three miles. Fifteen minutes if they loafed along. Fifteen minutes! His heart started thumping, and his hands began to squeeze reflectively. Hill looked like ice. Whatever was going on inside him didn't show one ounce. You could see he wouldn't fail because he froze or didn't dare make his move.

Thai kept checking his watch over and over again. He had changed into the uniform of an Arvin colonel. Hill and Janowitz had changed, too, into flight fatigues. Janowitz's had captain's bars. Hill's a first looey's.

"Well, sonuvabitch"—Hill had grinned as he crawled into his—"I *knew* I was officer material from the first time I hit the fuckin' draft board! You wouldn't have a camera or anything, Lieutenant?"

Janowitz had shoved him, and with one leg already in the air, Hill had toppled over.

"Goddamn," he said as he dragged himself up, "now you muddied up my official officer's uniform here. It's a good thing they made you a goddamned captain, or I'd have to lace your ass."

Janowitz had grinned at him. It was funny, but it had never occurred to him before, he wondered if Hill could "lace his ass." He was faster than Hill, and more coordinated, but— He decided maybe it was just as well to have Hill on his side.

"How long will it take?" Thai asked when Janowitz was settled in the cockpit.

"It depends on the wind," Janowitz said automatically, but then he realized that the rain was coming almost straight down. There wasn't enough wind to matter. "Make it fifteen minutes, Thai. We could slow it down, but I don't think it's wise to be in the air any longer than we have to."

Thai nodded and checked his watch for the six hundredth time. Janowitz had long since been parted from his navigational watch, but there had been another in the flight suit. And one in Hill's. He took Thai's arm to check that they'd been synchronized.

At five ten Thai ordered Suu and Tack to clear the camouflage. At five twenty-five he had Evans and Tack come on board. At five thirty-five he told Janowitz to start the engines. As Janowitz leaned forward to the starter, he said a quick prayer—him, his mother, Julie, Hieu. He wondered if the others did, too. At five forty they lifted off.

As they rose above the treetops, Janowitz's heart was racing in excitement and tension. He wheeled on course and tried to get a glimpse of the hamlet, but you couldn't see a thing even that low—just an endless spread of leaf.

They hadn't reached two hundred feet when a jet whistled over them, waving its wings and bumping them in its wash, sending eddies of rain across the windscreen. Five minutes later the sky seemed full of planes. Janowitz wished he had landed at Pleiku before. He knew the place was big and loaded, but he'd never seen it and wished the hell he had. From the chart, Thai's description of it was accurate, but he knew Hill couldn't navigate from the barracks to the shit house without getting lost, and if there'd been heavy reconstruction or something recently, they might fly themselves into one helluva reception.

Once they were airborne, Thai repeated the whole plan to them. He and Evans and Tack standing just behind Janowitz and Hill. It steadied them all. But once he'd finished, Janowitz switched in on the Pleiku tower. It was a fucking shock to hear that American voice calmly moving things around that field. "You are cleared for takeoff, Roger Delta Five . . . Charlie Zulu twelve, proceed along taxi strip three niner two to runway seven . . . Roger, Able Oboe seven, ceiling is eighteen hundred feet, landing visual, barometer two niner niner two, visibility five miles in rain, wind speed three knots from zero eight zero. . . ." Startlingly it reminded Janowitz once more that he was about to start fighting for the wrong side. And in an equally striking way it made everything the VC did seem feeble and crude and ineffectual. God, that one tower operator moved more high-powered equipment around in a day than the VC had in the whole war. The mission that had made so much sense back there in the jungle suddenly seemed a fragile and wild gesture against a giant that could crush them as easily as a GI crushed a beer can.

At five forty-six the radar screen picked them up. The tower operator said simply, "Chopper approaching from two eight zero, identify. . . ." It meant they had their range *and* speed because he knew it was a chopper. The operator paused and then busied himself with other traffic. Janowitz dropped to a hundred feet, but about half a minute later the tower operator tried again, that same emotionless twang: "Chopper approaching from two eight zero, identify. . . . This is Pleiku Tower. Do you read me? . . ." And again there was a wait, and he turned to other traffic. Janowitz felt that was the last time. They'd send something out for a look next time around. There was too much in the air to let a stray chopper wander around near the approaches to the landing strips. It came about twenty seconds later. "Chopper approaching from two eight zero, identify. . . . Do you read me?" Janowitz waited until he repeated it . . . and then waited until he dared wait no longer.

"Pleiku Tower, this is Air Force Sugar Delta Baker." He paused and pinched his throat, trying to make his voice rasp. The tower came back, twice. He didn't answer. Then he pulled it again, "Pleiku Tower, this is Air Force Sugar Delta Baker." He waited again. Another voice came on, asking if they were in trouble. It was the same flat, competent tone, but Janowitz knew they'd be stirring up there now. It was five forty-eight. "Roger, Pleiku Tower . . . we've been—" He paused again. "Pleiku Tower, this is Air Force Sugar Delta Baker. . . . Are you reading me? . . ." And he repeated it quickly before they could reply. Finally, he added, "We've been shot up, request emergency clearance to helipad." It was five fifty-nine and a half.

As he hoped, they didn't ask him from what base he'd come, though by now they were bound to know he wasn't one of theirs. He could see one of the radar screens, a huge thing, towering up over the horizon. And down below the forest was disappearing from under them. The land ahead was a sprawl of GI buildings in a moonscape of orange-reddish clay. Wet, it was an ugly mess; in the hot sun it must have been a dusty, sweating hole.

"Air Force Sugar Delta Baker, do you have wounded? . . ." Janowitz looked at his watch. Five fifty. He glanced up at Thai. When was the goddamned power going to be cut? Thai stared back at him impassively.

"I'm losing you, Pleiku Tower," Janowitz said. "Would you repeat? Do you read me, Pleiku?"

The tower confirmed that he was coming in strong and asked again if he had wounded.

"Pleiku Tower, this is Air Force Sugar Delta Baker," he replied, getting every second from it he could. He could see the field ahead now. He dropped to fifty feet. He wanted to keep out of their sight as long as he could. The rain was heavy, and everything looked gray, but he could see the runway, see the tower, see twenty-five jets at least along the tarmac. When the hell was it going to blow?

"We are not carrying wounded, but—" There was a burst of static, a crackle, then nothing but static. It was five fifty-one. Hill spotted an explosion off to the left and pointed to it.

"On time?" Janowitz demanded of Thai.

"One minute late," Thai answered.

"There!" Evans shouted, as he saw the first mortar fire land right in the maze of the giant radar screen. Flashes of electricity exploded across it, igniting the rain in puffs of fiery haze.

Janowitz cut the radio. It had continued to static furiously, but there was nothing from it—and wouldn't be, he hoped. They could hear shelling now, but they couldn't see anything. The base was so goddamned big. He was going to have to go around that huge radar screen. It was flashing fire again and had taken another round. The damn thing was immense. Ten, fifteen stories high—maybe more. They could see trucks and people flying around it and the smaller screens set at angles around it.

He swept up, opened the throttle, and started to circle. He could see Evans and Thai hang on out of the corner of his eye. When he was up to a hundred and fifty feet, he could tell that the shortest way to the Arvin sector was through the crease between the big radar screen and the airfield. With all that jet traffic in the air, with no tower control and a ceiling under two thousand feet, he knew the only other way was to circle the runways altogether—giving them a wide, wide berth. And they didn't have time for that.

He dropped it down again, diving for the crease. Tack almost pitched through to the plexiglass in the nose. Hill held him with one hand, and Evans got another on him.

"Get your asses out of here and get down!" Janowitz yelled. Thai, Evans, and Tack scrambled to the cabin as best they could.

There were some tar-paper buildings lined up along the taxi strip just behind the radar screen, and Janowitz went right in on them. Then he swung over and used them as cover. He wasn't ten feet off the ground, and he was doing more than a hundred. He could see Hill was scared shitless. He was pushed back against his seat, holding his hands out as if he expected to collide with something any minute.

"Keep your hands off that yoke!" Janowitz commanded. It penetrated, and Hill remained frozen. Guys were running all around them. Some of them dove in out of panic. A truck was barreling along beside on the taxi strip, the driver waving his hand at them frantically, but none of that bothered Janowitz. His mind was on what was in front of him. What worried him most was the chance of a mortar lob coming through that big radar screen. It filled the sky on their left, and he could hear the flashes of electricity as it was hit, and the light from them was blinding and disconcertingly unpredictable.

But they whipped past it and lifted to go over the approach lights to the field. They flew straight out the glide path at an altitude of never more than twenty feet. No jet was going to bother them there. But now that they were free of the radar screens, Janowitz could see that the sky was full of jets. Some were attacking the VC, and he could see their rocket flares, but he couldn't see any of the fighting.

They crossed a main road and lifted to about fifty feet. Trucks and jeeps were racing *both* ways on it. Except for instinctively ducking their heads, the GI's paid no attention to them. He knew the Arvin camp was to the right now, across another road. He banked and swept on. More trucks, more people running around below him.

Then dead ahead he saw a road crammed with vehicles, and right behind it a big Arvin signboard. They'd swallowed everything American, even when it came to announcing a base with a big billboard and a cartoon mascot.

"What's up above?" he yelled. Hill had got used to the speed and, now that they weren't barreling between obstacles on three sides, had regained his cool.

"Jets, but high!" he shouted back.

Janowitz flipped the bird up another hundred feet. The camp looked exactly like Thai's drawing. He spotted the security block. The only surprise was that the fence around it and the building itself were painted white—better background for a target.

He slid over to it, hovered a minute over the control hut, and eased the chopper in. Two guards snapped to attention as he idled the rotors, and a tall, thin Vietnamese officer came out trailed by an adjutant.

425

They were in all-white uniforms and ducked fastidiously from the wet spray of the rotors, but the officer looked eager to do service. There wasn't a hint of suspicion on their faces.

Thai, Evans, and Tack were already on their feet in back . . . moving unsteadily to the barn doors. Tack was dressed in neatly pressed suntans bearing the stripes of an Arvin master sergeant. There was no sense making Tack an officer; *that* no one would believe.

Thai doubled back quickly and glanced over Janowitz's shoulder at the whole security area. More guards were pouring out into the rain. They were wearing white plastic ponchos and looked alert—but more as if they were expecting an inspection than a raid.

"You'd better come with us, *Captain*," Thai said. Janowitz shrugged.

"You can keep this thing idling, can't you?" he demanded of Hill as he unstrapped himself.

"Listen, after that ride, that's *all* I'm going to do—ever!" Hill said.

When they stepped out, they were face to face with the commander, his adjutant and an escort of six MP's, all toting M-16's. It didn't bother Janowitz until they were inside the wire fence. Somehow with the Huey at his back, he hadn't felt outnumbered. But once locked inside that fence and surrounded by a couple of dozen guards, he knew that one false move and they were finished.

The commander had bought Thai's story like an Arkansas farmer buying the Brooklyn Bridge. Thai had done it skillfully, pandering to the guy's Vietnamese pride by saying that it had been his idea and that his American counterpart, the colonel (Evans), had agreed. With the area under attack it was best to get these valuable prisoners out—and the one place the VC couldn't touch them was in the air. They could hear firing all around them, and the thunder of jets made it necessary to shout every word. They all were soaked with rain. The commander led them into the compound and marched them straight to the security bunker.

Inside, the place smelled to high heaven. Janowitz tried to guess which was Thai's father as the prisoners were dragged up the stairs, but all he could see were sores and bruises and hollowed eyes. The guards scrambled about, shoving the prisoners forward, trying to act efficient, showing the kind of response their shouting induced from the haggard bodies they guarded. The commander ordered them out to the helicopter. That was when the first hitch developed.

The commander turned to Thai and said he imagined two guards would be enough to take along for each prisoner. That was something Thai *hadn't* thought of. He stared at the commander for a second.

"Fine. Two will be fine," he said. Then, taking the commander's arm, he said, "And I'd like a list of their names, too, of course." He indicated the guard desk. When the Commander turned to it, Thai nodded quickly to Tack. All the prisoners and guards were out; only the supervising NCO, the commander, and his adjutant remained. Tack pushed the door slightly to. One of the guards on the outside held it with his arm and stuck his head in inquiringly. Tack smiled at him and motioned him in. The guard moved forward, and Tack grabbed him by the neck, drove a knife into his stomach and ripped it right across the guy's guts, pitching him down into the well between the prisoner's cells. The commander turned, and Thai knifed him savagely, driving the knife deep into his neck. Even as he was falling, Thai withdrew the knife and drove it into the back of the NCO as the poor bastard reached for an alarm behind his desk. Thai lunged again, and again, grappling the man's body away from the wall and kicking him into the concrete well. The adjutant stared at them in frozen horror. Before he could move, Tack pounced on him like a great cat. His arm flashed, and the guy choked and fell like the others, ugly red stains of blood spreading grotesquely across his immaculate white uniform.

It was ten seconds of pure horror such as Janowitz had never seen, and it left him stunned and immobile. Evans took his arm. "Come on," he said.

They went outside into the rain and along the concrete walk to the command post. Thai stood in the door to the bunker, his back to the outside, talking calmly as though to the commander. The rest of the guards were too damned rank-conscious—especially with the Americans around—to do more than stand stiffly at parade rest. When they reached the chopper, Evans irritably ordered the guards who had gone on board with the prisoners, off the ship. One of the NCO's looked dubious, but Tack said something sharply to him in Vietnamese—and he moved. Outside, the NCO kept peering through the rain at the bunker, obviously expecting his commander to appear, but he didn't do anything but line his men up beside the helicopter and put them at parade rest.

Janowitz had already reached the cockpit when he saw Thai salute the air inside the bunker, close the door, and walk slowly up the concrete walk to the gate. Not a guard inside the wire moved. When Thai passed the line of guards outside the chopper, the worried NCO

427

glanced again at the bunker for sign of his commander, but Thai barked at him, and he promptly brought his group to attention. He saluted Thai. Thai returned his salute . . . and boarded the chopper. Tack followed smartly and closed the barn doors. Slowly Janowitz lifted the bird off the ground. He was still feeling sick, his enthusiasm for the mission spilled across the floor of that animals' cage.

They climbed to a hundred feet, and he swung it for the forest —away from the airfield. It was eight minutes after six.

viii

They flew as fast and low as Janowitz dared. They were heading almost due south, and according to the plan, all the ground fighting should have been at the other end of the base, but they could see jets strafing and mortar explosions on each side of them. Coming off the perimeter, they crossed another major road, and a line of trucks had piled up on it, but they could see it had started with a crash on the slippery road surface. GI's were running all around the place.

Janowitz knew the sooner they started heading north again, the sooner they'd be out of danger—but he wanted to get well clear of the base before he swung around. And he wanted to get over the jungle. If they were forced down, that was the place to be. The sky was already dull with twilight, and they might get away even if they had to go in far short of Megu.

It seemed many long minutes to him before they passed beyond the barren, scorched earth that surrounded Pleiku, and when they finally reached jungle, it was too scraggly to provide cover for minutes more of flying. Several times they spotted American units moving toward the base, and occasionally someone would wave a rifle to them in greeting. Finally, Janowitz thought the jungle dense enough and started his wide sweep north.

They were almost due west of the field before the tower came back in again. Janowitz had turned the radio on the minute they were airborne, but there had been nothing but static. There must have been one helluva fight at the field, because it'd been out for almost half an hour.

When it first blurted in, "This is Pleiku Tower. Pleiku Tower calling Squadron Nineteen!" Janowitz knew they weren't going to be wor-

428

rying about him for some time. The operator had lost his cool, and he was interested only in the fight on the ground. If the radar screens were still functioning despite the mortar bombardment, they might pick him up eventually—but it'd be too late then.

Ten minutes later he was worrying about finding Megu. It had grown quite dark, and the clouds in the west had lost all their reddish twilight tint. Ten more minutes and it would be black. It was great for getting away, but he wished they'd arranged some signal to aid their return. Every once in a while they would see jets zooming above them and choppers, as low as they were, searching for the fleeing VC. They heard the instructions go out—and, occasionally, the voice of a pilot who'd spotted something and was giving it hell. Any light on the ground for miles around would draw its own private holocaust that night. He knew from the way traffic control was working that the radar screens were still functioning in part, but they must have assumed he was one of the search choppers. They'd sent so many out it'd be some time before they got every one identified and plotted.

At least the flying and anxiety took his mind off the slaughter back there in the bunker. He had caught glimpses of Thai and Evans and Tack moving around among the prisoners in the cabin. They were using first-aid kits to bandage some of them, and he saw that Thai had a drink of some kind he was passing around.

When he figured they were three minutes out, he sent Hill back to get Thai.

"How we going to find it?" he asked when Thai leaned over his shoulder, indicating the dark forest below. It spread in all directions as far as the eye could see and was fast growing a uniform gray.

"Are we near?" Thai asked.

"Near," Janowitz answered, "but we could be five miles from it in any direction." Thai looked at him with critical disbelief. "That's good navigating, Thai," Janowitz snapped. "As good as you get without a radio or visual checkpoints."

Thai was properly chastened. "You haven't seen the river?" he asked.

"No. I've been looking for it," Janowitz replied. "Is it the only one in the area?"

Thai was stopped. He didn't have to answer; his face relayed his uncertainty.

Hill suddenly reached across and touched his arm. "Hey!" he said, pointing about forty-five degrees off the nose. Janowitz looked. Nothing. Then a light went on—and immediately went off. He hovered. The light went on and off again. He banked toward it. They flew on—and on. No light.

"We must have passed over it," Hill conjectured. Janowitz swung around and hovered again. The light went on and off again. Janowitz followed it right down to the treetops . . . and held it steady. It was so damn dark. Then the light went on again right in front of them—and stayed on for two or three seconds. He moved in—and then, there it was, just on their right. Their landing area. He brought the chopper down slowly. They landed—and the tail wheel tire exploded. Janowitz laughed. He knew those goddamn tires wouldn't hold!

When he cut the motors, he could hear the barn doors opening in back. Sonuvabitch. They'd done it. He leaned across and poked Hill. "Well, son, you flew a good mission," he said.

"If I hadn't been around to spot that light, you'da missed me, mother. Don't think you wouldn't."

"Who the hell was it?" Janowitz asked.

"Suu, I think," Hill replied. "See, just over there. The tree next to the evergreen. He's climbing down. See him?"

Janowitz finally sighted the dark figure moving against the somewhat lighter sky. Thank God there was someone around who knew something about flying. But it was his goof. He should have made some provision before they left. But it didn't matter. They'd done it. He couldn't believe anyone could catch them in the jungle now; it would have been tough enough even in daylight.

"Hill baby"—he grinned—"we got us a present for Colonel"—for a second he forgot the name— *"Bussko!* And I think maybe we're going to have us a little R and R up in Yen Cai."

"Yeah"—Hill smiled back lasciviously—"I got the feeling old big tits is just about ready to go into business with me. She's finally made it. You don't mind if I tell her I flew this baby in and out for you, do you? . . . I mean, you got yours all sewed up!" he added as Janowitz laughed.

"Come on, you goddamn thief," Janowitz said, freeing himself from his harness, "let's get this thing covered up. We got a long walk ahead of us."

"Damn. Officers don't have to camouflage," Hill complained as they walked back through the cabin. "Now that I'm a copilot, I thought I'd left all that behind."

When they jumped down, Thai was waiting for them. Beside him stood a short, gaunt man who might have been fifty. Even in the dark, the shape of his head, the eyebrows and hairline showed how clearly they were of the same genealogical stamp.

"Comrade Janowitz . . . Comrade Hill," Thai said proudly. "This is Colonel Tan. My father."

"I am proud to make your acquaintance," Colonel Tan said, and then he smiled openly, as though inviting their friendship. His accent was like Thai's, but he didn't speak English with the same ease. "We must learn to know each other better," he said and shook hands, first with Hill and then with Janowitz. Janowitz felt a lump rise in his throat. You sentimental schmuck, he chided himself.

"We'd better move this thing," he said, nodding toward the chopper, and they all turned, prisoners and rescuers alike, and started to push the big bird into the cover that had been prepared for it.

When they headed for the village, Thai and Tack led the way and Thai's father walked between Janowitz and Hill. He evidently wanted to talk but seemed to feel that his English was too rusty, so he kept nodding to them and they'd nod back. Once Tack turned to Janowitz and said, "Hey, buffalo, tomorrow we make big feast, okay?"

"*Okay!*" Janowitz replied easily, and Thai's father laughed. He was quick enough to understand the subtleties of that exchange, Janowitz was glad to see. Colonel Bussko? Janowitz wondered what he was like. Fuck me, it *was* a long way from Detroit—a long, long way.

The body of the guard was wedged in between the bottom of the bridge and a hunk of log that was caught by something in midstream. They almost missed him going over the bridge, but Suu spotted him and called them to a halt in a voice that was sibilant and cautionary. They were on the metal bridge and couldn't reach the body through the decorative superstructure, so Tack plunged in and dragged it to shore. Janowitz recognized him. He was one of the VC guards who'd been with them from the beginning. He'd been shot in the back, twice, just below the neck, and from his posture it looked as if he'd been running when he was hit.

"Who did it?" Thai asked, his eyes going automatically to the sky. They'd heard several jets flying close, and there was a distant rumble of them now. But it was difficult to believe one could have strafed the hamlet without Suu hearing it, and he said he'd heard nothing.

They moved cautiously toward the houses with Thai, Tack, and Evans spreading wide and making the pace. As they got closer, Janowitz was relieved to see that there'd been no bombing. A plane or a helicopter might have raked the buildings with machine-gun fire, but they hadn't torn the place to pieces—but where the hell was everybody? Where was Hieu? Perhaps they hadn't heard the helicopter land. The rain was steady and drenching—and the night black. It could be no one wanted to hang around and get wet. Then Tack stopped and held up his hand. He moved across to Thai and pointed.

Janowitz saw another body sprawled on the ground on the other bank of the river . . . about fifteen feet below the Y. Tack crouched, made for the river, keeping low as he crossed it and approached the body. Janowitz felt sure it was the other VC guard. As Tack bent over the body, a shot rang out—and Tack hit the ground. The reaction was so quick Janowitz thought Tack had been hit, but he saw him squirm around immediately, using the body for cover.

The shot had come from the headman's house—the first of the houses placed in the Y. All their party were on the ground now. Thai, Evans, and Tack carried pistols, but those were the only weapons in the group.

"Don't fire!" Pershing's voice rang out through the rain. "You'll be shooting at your own people!"

"Look!" Thai's father exclaimed, pointing toward the houses.

Shadows—people—were streaming from the headman's house, running back along the stream toward the woods.

"What's happened?" Thai asked of no one.

"It's simple, dad," Hill said quietly. "Pershing's taken over. I was awful suspicious of his going along," he said bitterly, his eyes still on the house, "right from the beginning."

Janowitz's mind flew. It was true, true. What the hell had they been thinking? Pershing was married to the Army. He was as dedicated as Thai any day—and as wily. How in God's name had he ever believed him? What had Pershing said? The words snapped into his brain as if they'd been etched there in pain: "But if you get Thai's old man out, we've got no objection to doing what we can then." And: "Don't thank me, Lieutenant. It's just one fucked-up war. I guess all any of us can do is the best we can." And the best *he* could do was to screw their mission—screw it till there was nothing left! And Miller and Russell! Jesus! How had he been so stupid?

"But what's he doing?" Evans demanded, his voice still relatively calm. He was apparently thinking, what the hell, they still had Thai's old man, and the forest was all around them.

Janowitz watched the exodus from the house. Pershing must have had the whole village in there. Somehow they'd got the guards . . . and Tick and little Toe . . . and Hieu and big tits, too. And then

432

they'd rounded up the villagers so they'd be unable to give a warning when the helicopter landed.

"Well, I would say ole daddy Pershing is planning a little party," Hill said stonily. "He's got six AK-47's for sure—maybe more. And he knows once he starts shooting them off, there's going to be a real circus around here." His eyes darted briefly toward the sky, and they came to rest on Janowitz. "And I figure he guesses we aren't about to leave him with the hostages he's got. So being the man he is, he's lettin' the villagers clear out before the action gets—"

Two shots rang out. It was Tack. He'd crawled to the river, slipped in, and gone upstream until he was even with the headman's house. Janowitz couldn't tell what he was shooting at, but he could see him crouched in midstream, his arm extended and the pistol flashing as he fired again.

Shadows were still scurrying from the house, and when the second round of shots rang out, there was sudden panic and the shadows started flying in every direction. Then a burst of heavy fire came. From two angles. The front of the house and the roof.

The tracers flashed right through Tack. His huge shoulders rose from the water, and then he slowly toppled backward pierced by a cascade of streaking fire. As his body tumbled into the stream, one rifle stopped firing, then the other. Villagers were screaming, and Janowitz could see some who had gone upstream now running back toward those left behind. A jet thundered overhead, burying all the other sounds in its echoing rumble. Before the sound had passed, an orange and red flare swung through the sky. It was falling toward the forest and cast huge, long shadows, making the rain look like driving sleet, but Janowitz could see all the hamlet, his memory filling in what the shadows obscured. The figure on the roof of the headman's house slithered around to get out of their line of fire, and instantly Janowitz recognized the silhouette on the light-brown matting as Russell's.

Thai swung around; his face was knotted in pain. There was no anger, just tragedy scored in every line. "We must go," he commanded, nodding back toward the woods. There were a few trees around them, although they were well in the clearing that defined the hamlet, but the flare was descending and the shadows growing longer: It was an even chance Pershing and the others hadn't spotted them. Suu moved first—and gave away them and his own combat inexperience. He ran at a crouch for perhaps six paces, and Thai hissed at him even as a burst of fire from the roof brought him down like a rabbit running across an open cornfield.

433

The jet swept away from them, but it banked and started to climb at the second burst of fire. In its roar Hill pulled at Janowitz's shoulder and started crawling toward a huge tree a few yards to their right. He wriggled along on the ground faster than Janowitz could and already had the tree between him and the headman's house when the second flare blazed out upstream from the houses. Janowitz heard bullets snapping around him and was stung from the hunks of earth they flung up. He scurried on to the tree, and Hill pulled him behind its cover. On their backs they could see the shadowed outlines of Thai and the others. So could Russell. Bullets flicked the ground all around the group, but Janowitz couldn't tell who might have been hit and who was playing dead.

"Jesus! That stubborn fucker!" Hill cursed. Janowitz rolled over. Hill's face was pressed against the tree as he peered round it. Janowitz put his face on the ground and inched around on the other side. Pershing was by a strut on the porch—firing into the sky. The thunder of the jet approached. Pershing's tracers followed it as the first rocket whooshed into the houses beyond.

"He's going to level this whole fucking place," Hill hissed. "We've got to make that woods and put as much space between us and this shindig as we can! Come on!" He hunched up, and Janowitz pulled him down. Hill knew what was on his mind. "Listen, dad," he shouted, "you aren't going to be any good to her dead! Keep the tree between you and the house—and follow me! He sprang forward and ran as hard as he could, moving from side to side to keep the tree as shield from the house—until he reached another tree and disappeared behind it.

Janowitz looked back at the headman's house. A house behind it was blazing, and he could see people running to the forest. No one was trying to save anyone. God, was Hieu one of them; was she still in the damn house? He looked up. The jet—no, it was another one—went right over the tree. The roar deafened him. A flare burst right above him and caught in the branches of the tree. The whole area was lit, drenched in a stark blue incandescence. He saw Thai crouched behind a small tree, aiming his pistol. He couldn't hear anything in the lingering jet rumble, but he turned to see what Thai was firing at and saw Pershing and Miller racing for the log bridge across the left arm of the Y. They both were carrying AK-47's. That bastard Pershing. He was going to cut off their retreat. It was time to follow Hill, Janowitz thought; Hieu has to be out by now. Be careful of Russell's fire from the roof, he warned himself. He hunched up and saw Thai fold and roll on the ground.

He could see everyone now. Evans was lying flat behind another small tree shooting at Pershing and Miller. One of the prisoners was dead, and three others were using his body as protection from Russell's covering fire. Another prisoner was coiled grotesquely at the base of a tree. Janowitz *longed* for a gun!

The explosion shook the whole tree. Even the flare swung and tumbled down further in the branches. Janowitz was spun right on his ass. He shook his head and looked quickly. The rocket had struck just short of the meeting of the rivers, blasting a huge crater. But it was only the beginning. At least three jets were zeroed in on them now, and Janowitz's head shook from their continuous roar. The headman's house got it even before he scurried back to the tree. A boom cracked his eardrums and rumbled into the sky, and the house burst into flames, the explosion sizzling in the rain, and then flashing again, an immense, crackling flashbulb. White phosphorus . . . Russell wouldn't be shooting anyone anymore.

Janowitz dashed for Thai. His quick glance in the white afterglow of the explosion picked out Miller sprawled on the bridge. Something had got him: Thai, Evans, one of the planes. There were other bodies —one a kid's, the others indistinguishable. But he saw no sign of Pershing. Evans and Thai's father were already tugging Thai toward the woods. The other three prisoners were running for it, one's head pouring blood. Janowitz grabbed Thai's legs. He was facedown, but Janowitz could see the blood falling, and there was a stringy bit of flesh dangling grotesquely from his head.

The sky was full of flares now. Explosives and napalm and white phosphorus were going in behind them, in front of them, to the sides. But above them the wonderful trees still gave their cover. They neared the steel bridge—keeping in the woods, clear of the river. As they came even with the bridge, Evans dived in, shouting a warning as he went down.

Pershing was standing in the water on the far side of the river. He had the AK-47 at his shoulder. The range was twenty-five yards— through the trees. Thai's father had turned at Evans' shout, and he took the first round in his chest, like a target—flush on—and the shots continued to tear into him, shattering and twisting him as he crumpled to the ground. Evans had fired his pistol twice, three times, but now he ran from tree to tree toward the river, his eyes bulging and frantic.

435

Pershing never swung his gun to him. Janowitz never knew why—perhaps the bombs distracted him, or the thundering planes, or the sudden whirling clatter of the approaching gunships. Evans was less than six feet from the river's bank when he burst wildly from the trees and fired point-blank. He held his arm stiff, and he kept pulling the trigger until the gun would fire no more, long after Pershing's body was smothered in the uncommitted water.

Janowitz could hear the gunships whirling now. Even amid the echoing explosions, their rattling clamor penetrated to him. They were almost overhead. He pulled Thai to the cover of a massive tree and, for the first time, saw Thai's wound. The shot had torn across his face, ripping an eye from its protective socket, letting it hang like some glutinous ball, and splintering his nose as it passed on to end its life on some less fragile structure. Incredibly Thai was still alive and breathing, the shattered face wet and glistening in the unyielding rain. Janowitz cradled his head in his arms. Evans returned and stared at them for a second in the echoing holocaust; then he bent slowly and took Thai's feet. As they lifted him, Janowitz heard the metallic thunder, heard the giant tree crack . . . they were the last experiences life was to give him.

ix

Hill had doubled back twice for Janowitz. Jesus, that stupid bastard. He didn't know shit about combat. You had to know when the wishing stopped and the goddamn steel and lead took over. It was like a knife fight: Split seconds counted—and knowing that dead men didn't get any wishing in at all. And when he saw the second jet squadron coming in, he knew they were done wishing in Megu. Get your ass out of there—or no more ass. Period. He only hoped the stupid get had taken some other way out. They were blood brothers now— thicker than soul brothers; that was only skin-deep. Janowitz was something else. More. If it came to it, he knew he'd die for that big Jewish bastard.

He ran until he thought his lungs would burst from the pain. Twice, right at the beginning, he was knocked flat by percussion, but he didn't let pain or fear or stumbling or anything stop him. There was one out —and that was distance. The flares kept changing the look of things, throwing shadows first this way, then that. They were lighting up every bit of jungle around Megu, but he knew that didn't mean shit. They still couldn't see anything through the leaves, and from the shelling going on behind him, he knew they'd found their target. After that little party at Pleiku, half the goddamned Air Force and ninety percent of the Air Cavalry would be swarming around the place like flies on a dung heap.

It was nearly four hours later when he was picked up. He'd stumbled into a clearing that looked like it had once been a Special Forces camp. Trees had been felled in a big, uneven rectangle. And the place had really been cleared—stumps and all. That's what made him think it must have been an American camp sometime. There was nothing now. Just mud and rain. Choppers and jets were still searching and probing the area. He knew he had to take a chance. He took off his first looey bars—he could always say the uniform was one the Commies gave him. He went right into the center of the area. Thank God for that kinky black hair. If they took a good look, they weren't likely to mistake him for a native. He'd been there for about ten minutes, watching his shadow shift from angle to angle in the streaky rain as the flares came and went in the distance. Then a flare popped from a chopper that flew almost over him. It was a good distance out but lit up the clearing like for a night football game. The chopper went on for a couple of minutes, and then somebody must have spotted him. It circled and slowly slanted in on him. If they'd fired, he'd have had it. All the nose guns were zeroed in on him, and there were probably two guys in back with machine guns on him, too.

"Goddamn, I *thought* you was a GI!" a staff sergeant drawled, holding his hand out to pull Hill aboard. "What the hell you doing down there?"

"Took my dog out for a walk and got lost," Hill answered coldly. The Southern accent irritated him suddenly. There were four guys on the crew besides the pilot and copilot. Two of them were spades. Hill nodded to them all.

"You get mixed up in this shoot-up?" the staff sergeant asked curiously as they lifted off. They could tell Hill had been through something.

Hill nodded. "They took me prisoner," he said.

"Well, we fixed their fucking water." The sergeant grinned. "If that makes you feel any better. We found those bastards in a little dump about ten miles from here, and they ain't going to shoot up anybody again real soon. We zapped them babies to kingdom come."

They all were nodding and smiling at Hill. Hill tried to work up a

437

smile, but he thought, shit, I got no need to smile for these pricks. They aren't going to vote me any PX privileges. One of the spades looked at him. "We blew the piss out of them, man. Bodies lying all over the place."

Hill managed to nod.

x

At Pleiku he was taken to Intelligence. He gave his unit and told them when he'd been captured. He left out the trip North. Just said they'd moved him around the jungle. They didn't even ask him if he knew anything about the raid. The next day they asked him if he could identify a few bodies. He was taken to a long metal-roofed building. Pershing's and Miller's bodies were lying on a table near the door. He identified them. Then they led him to another table at the other end of the room. About fifty Vietnamese were lined along the floor, and Hill and the officer moved along slowly. Some of the bodies were charred beyond recognition, but he saw the village chief and the baker; there were only three kids, he thanked God for that. Then he saw Thai and Thai's father. By some accident—maybe they'd fallen together, he didn't know—they were side by side. If he hadn't known Thai so well, he'd never have recognized him. Somebody'd really shot the shit out of him. Well, he'd got his father out anyway. Maybe that was something. Tack was lying right at the end of the line. It was hard to react as if he didn't know him. He looked fat and complacent in death—like Buddha. The old fucker. He was meant to die of gout and VD.

Janowitz's and Evans' bodies were lying on the table at the end of the room. Hill couldn't stop himself anymore; the tears just poured from his eyes, and when he tried to hide them, they came faster and faster. He buried his head in his hands and tried to control it, but his whole body convulsed. The officer with him touched his shoulder like a priest or something.

"Do you know them?" he said softly. Hill shook his head. He could never explain what Janowitz was doing in that captain's uniform— or Evans in the light colonel's. And when they checked their fingerprints, there was still no reason he should know Evans or remember some chopper pilot from the base—chopper pilots came and went . . . though the bastards were going to have to look a long way before

438

they found another chopper pilot like that one. God damn him, why didn't he run?

"No," he choked through his tears, "I don't know 'em. It's just—"

The officer patted his shoulder. "I know," he said consolingly. "But don't worry, son, we made them pay. We made them pay."

xi

Fortunately the orders clerk had been a spade. The unit was at Long Binh, about fifteen miles out of Saigon. He was supposed to report direct to them, but the guy had given him forty-eight hours to make the trip. He'd also given him the old shit about if you get in a fight in a bar in Soulsville, they'll have my ass, y'know; but Hill had promised like they all promise. Not that it meant anything. No one was going to fry an orders clerk; they had enough excuses to cover a ninety-day pass to Honolulu without anybody knowing.

He got a chopper ride right to Tan Son Nhut. A forty-minute bus ride and he was on Tu Do Street. He walked tall. Clean uniform, shave, MPC's in his pocket. The whole city buzzed. It shone and glittered. Cars and trucks everywhere. Girls looking haughty and beautiful and available. Their eyes danced with provocation and challenge. And even the American civilians looked good. White shirts, button-down collars. Polo shirts, shined shoes. Guys chewing gum and laughing on street corners. Big neon signs and buildings going up that looked thick and strong and prosperous. And he walked on to Khan Hoi, close to the river. He wasn't going to one of his spots—not yet—but he wanted a chick. And it was glorious. Ripe, young, eager thing, hanging on him in satin and spangles, and then upstairs, and he thought it would go on forever—in, out, in, out, the end of the fuckin' world.

Later he went to one of his places. Only he knew it wasn't *his* place now. There wasn't a face he recognized. But they knew *him*. The guy who'd taken over was a bull. Not more than six feet, but he must have weighed two forty, and it was all muscle. He wasn't all that good, though, Hill noted, 'cause his nose had been broken a couple of times, but he was cool. He didn't want trouble. He explained to Hill it'd all changed. More competition now. Lots of girls from the camps. You had to bring them in and put some meat on them before they were worth anything, but once they'd learned the trade, it wasn't so easy to keep 'em locked up. And the military had new rules now. It was tougher

439

all around. Most of Saigon was off limits. The pocket money for the police was getting bigger and bigger. He figured giving Hill two thousand dollars a place was doing him a favor. Hill didn't answer. The price went to two five . . . and then three. But there it stopped. Hill didn't want trouble either. And he could see there was a lot of trouble available.

"I'll take five now—as a guarantee of good faith." He smiled icily. "And I'll think it over."

"Five, no. I'm not carrying five," the guy said. He searched Hill's eyes. "Three, how about three? That's a fair hunk of bread to chew on."

"Yeah. That'll do—for now," Hill said finally. "I don't take long to think." He went downstairs. He wasn't going to hang around like he was waiting for it. Let him bring it. These little subtleties were important. The place had changed. Maybe he had enough loot. Maybe he should skip the second tour and go back to the States now. The guy came down. He gave Hill three envelopes. Nice thick ones.

"You're lucky I kept it going," the guy said challengingly. "It wasn't easy, y'know."

"You're lucky I set it up," Hill answered coldly. "It wasn't easy, y'know."

He knew he left him nervous. He could get his three thousand a place—maybe three five. But the guy would take a lot of moving. And setting up a new empire? It would all take thinking.

He walked back toward Tu Do Street. Jesus, pavement, telephone poles, even stoplights, the big TWA sign, Hertz, the goddamn babes with their high heels and swingin' tails. Three thousand bucks a place wasn't bad. Maybe it was time to take a breather.

He was just crossing the street to a big news rack with a splash spread of everything—*Life, Playboy, Esquire, True Confessions,* the whole lot—when he saw Tick crossing the street, going the other way. There were people all around. GI's in uniform and out, civilians. A few cars, a couple of pedicabs—but mostly people on foot, talking, hurrying about their business, girls mincing along, guys ogling. And Tick was talking earnestly with this guy. He looked like a Frenchman. They were twenty feet from Hill, moving kind of fast and Tick sawing the air with his hands, lecturing this guy about something. The guy was short and kind of bald in front. He had big, bushy eyebrows, and he looked anxious and concerned.

Hill stopped right in the middle of the road and watched them. They went to a little Renault 16 parked in front of the place that had a neon

440

sign reading "Carlson Bros. (Vietnam)." The guy unlocked the door for Tick and Tick got in. Then the guy went around and got in on the driver's side, and they drove off, moving slowly through the pedestrian traffic. A guy in a big old Buick honked at Hill, and Hill moved slowly back on the curb. The last thing he saw of the Renault was a doctor's insignia on the back bumper.

For a minute he didn't move. And then he felt he had to walk. It must have been that guy Janowitz had told him about. The guy with the daughter that fancied Evans. Well, she had another fancy coming.

And he walked, and walked and walked. He hated Tick. Of all the ones to survive it. But Jesus, it brought it back. And without wanting it, without willing it, he saw the city again. The Saigon he knew—the GIs, the pretty dollies, the shined shoes, the flashing cars, the shining neon, the big, solid buildings—all sort of blurred. It was like changing the focus on a camera when the foreground's clear and the background's blurred, and then you twist the knob, and it's the foreground that's blurred and the background's clear. It was the same city, the same streets, but he saw the poor kids hanging around in the doorways, the old women with rubber tires for shoes hawking beads to the dollies in their patent-leather high heels; he saw the smug, fat-gutted Vietnamese being pulled by men thinner than Thai's old man, pumping their pedicabs and sucking ass for their tips. He saw the rows and rows of crowded ramshackle streets with hundreds of people huddled together off the treelined avenues where American cars floated by with their stereo radios and air conditioning. He saw huge GI trucks rumble by the tiny, jogging women humping big loads in their straw and bamboo panniers.

He walked toward the river where there were no buildings of concrete and glass, no cars, no roads for cars. Where there were flies and stench and heat. Where people stared at him with fear and suspicion and dabbed their bony fingers into wooden bowls of rice, while overhead the rumble of the million-dollar jets shook their litter of tin and clapboard "homes." The huge freighters inched slowly past the alleyways without sewers, the faces without light.

Hill walked and walked. He was five miles along the road to Long Binh when he finally turned off the road . . . and into the underbush.